Nicholas Jennings

THE WOLVES

Eugen Eis steered Materna to a secluded spot beside the stables. 'That ought to give you something to think about,' he said, indicating the glowing embers of Materna's barn with smug satisfaction. 'This'll settle your hash.'

Materna smiled to himself. The fact was, Eis had once upon a time escorted a Pole and a Jew across the border with the help of his Brownshirts, and there was no getting away from that.

'You think you're a hell of a sly dog, don't you?' Eis suddenly burst out. 'In your eyes, the whole National Socialist Movement is a farce, the Führer's a crazy house-painter and I'm a bastard — right?'

Materna stared at him. 'That's putting it mildly,' he said.

D1585998

HANS HELLMUT KIRST

The Wolves

*Translated from the German
by J. Maxwell Brownjohn*

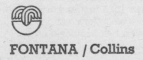

FONTANA / Collins

Originally published in Germany under the title 'Die Wolfe'
First published in Great Britain under
the title 'The Fox of Maulen' by Wm. Collins 1968
First issued in Fontana Books 1970
Second Impression March 1971
Third Impression April 1972
Fourth Impression January 1975

© 1967 by Verlag Kurt Desch GmbH, München
© 1968 in the English translation by
Wm Collins Sons & Co Ltd

Made and printed in Great Britain by
William Collins Sons & Co Ltd Glasgow

CONDITIONS OF SALE
This book is sold subject to the condition that
it shall not, by way of trade or otherwise, be lent,
re-sold, hired out or otherwise circulated without
the publisher's prior consent in any form of
binding or cover other than that in which it is
published and without a similar condition
including this condition being imposed on the
subsequent purchaser

CONTENTS

'He who howls with the pack saves his neck.'

MASURIAN PROVERB

What follows is the story of a man named Alfons Materna. It is set in one of those remote corners of the world where time seems to stand still—in Masuria, or, to be more precise, in Maulen, a village situated among the marshes, lakes and forests of East Prussia. The time-span of the story is 1932-45, thirteen years during which men devastated the world like elephants trampling a garden. Before this disaster occurred the Masurians took procreation and death as they came, like seed-time and harvest. The soil served them as bed and shroud, human passions were accepted as natural laws, and many a Masurian looked on God as a personal crony. Alfons Materna wanted to live his own life, a modest ambition which cost him dear. People died as a result, but in those days even corpses were good for a laugh in Masuria.

PART ONE

The Hour of the Wolves

1932-3

1

'That's it, then,' Alfons Materna said when he was told of his son's death. He spread his arms, half in sorrow, half in resignation, and lowered his eyes as though he wanted to prevent anyone from reading what was in them. His face remained wholly expressionless.

'It can't be helped,' he heard himself saying. 'In the midst of life . . .'

It was true. Death lay in wait from the moment of birth onwards. Babies choked, children drowned in the lake, adults were kicked to death by horses, laid low by sunstroke or snuffed out by too much hard liquor.

'I won't ask why he had to die—no one can answer that. Just tell me how it happened.'

Moritz, the bearer of evil tidings, shuffled his feet. 'I saw him lying there, that's all.'

'You know me, Moritz. Tell me the truth—I can take it.'

'They'll be bringing him along any minute,' Moritz parried. 'They're on the way already.'

Materna raised his head like an animal scenting the air. His eyes studied the man's hands as they kneaded the rim of his blue peaked cap.

'There's something else, isn't there?'

'I never said so,' Moritz replied hurriedly. He shuffled his feet. 'He's dead—that's all I know.'

The grimy grey walls of Materna's farm-house parlour hemmed them in like cliffs stained with the smoke of countless camp fires. The room resembled a cave scattered with angular, functional furniture. Even the chairs and cupboards might have been hewn in stone.

'Who sent you?'

Materna was not a tall man, but he had the gnarled strength of a tree-root. He combined the toughness and agility of a gun-dog with the cunning of a fox. Although he had not long turned forty, his grey-brown face was already covered with a mesh of fine wrinkles. He looked as if he had spent a lifetime laughing, but there was no laughter in his eyes now.

'Who sent me?' Moritz echoed. 'Johannes Eichler, I think it was.'

'That clinches it.' Materna ground his palms together and beads of sweat broke out on his forehead. 'I knew something would happen sooner or later, but I never thought they'd go this far.'

Moritz looked perturbed. 'Don't get so worked up. These things happen—God only knows why.'

'God knows plenty but men know a few things too—God sees to that. For instance, everyone has to go sometime, but some people help others on their way. That's what you call murder.'

Moritz considered himself an expert on Maulen and its inhabitants. He had felt certain that Materna's reaction to the news of his son's death would be dignified silence, averted eyes and a stiff upper lip. The man was a Masurian, after all, and in Masuria displays of emotion were confined to weaklings and old women. However, one mention of Johannes Eichler had been enough to send Materna blazing up like a bale of dry straw.

'God help them if they killed my son,' he muttered. 'If they did, I'll make them curse the day they were born.'

Materna stood at the entrance to his courtyard and watched the cart rumbling slowly towards him. The cart belonged to Johannes Eichler, he noted, and so did the two horses hitched to it. The driver, who lolled on the box as nonchalantly as if he were carting a load of flour or potatoes, was Eugen Eis, Eichler's second-in-command and in Materna's opinion, his most ruthless henchman.

Eugen Eis raised his whip in greeting. 'There he is,' he called, indicating the body at the back of the cart. 'Who'd have thought it! Here today, gone tomorrow—that's life for you.'

Materna walked up to the cart. The sight of his dead son smote him with the force of an axe wielded by a Masurian woodcutter. The summit of the tree shuddered at the first impact.

Eis nodded sagely. 'Not a pretty sight, I grant you. Those planks are a proper mess, but never mind—I'll get the blood out soon enough.'

Materna's son lay there, a twisted bundle of bone, flesh and shredded clothing. His face was a shapeless mass of gory porridge and there was a gaping hole in his chest—the sort of hole that might have been made by repeated blows with a pick-axe.

'How did it happen?'

'Plain bad luck,' Eis explained obligingly. 'He got in the line of fire.'

Materna went on staring at the tattered corpse. He had seen bodies of that sort at Verdun but never in Maulen. Death tended to do its work more neatly in Masuria.

'We were out training,' Eis continued, '—the Home Guard, that is. The training area was Maulen Moor, as usual. We were practising grenade-throwing with live ammunition. The men went forward and lobbed their grenades.' He shrugged. 'Well, that's how it happened.'

'It was murder,' Materna said dully.

'Steady on!' Eis protested. 'That's a bit steep, isn't it? Anyone'd think you had something against the Home Guard.'

'If they act like a gang of murderers yes, of course I've got something against them.'

'You're crazy.' Eis's tone implied that his patience was great but not boundless. 'Our lads chucked their grenades, that's all. How could anyone be expected to know that Alfred was lying there in the long grass, just where they were aiming? No normal youngster lies in the long grass by himself.'

Materna looked away, unable to bear the spectacle any longer. The sky overhead was like a taut steel-blue cloth. He stared up at it helplessly, but his eyes hurt and he had to shade them with his hand.

'It was an accident, take it from me,' Eis said in a warning voice. He paused. 'You'd best believe what I say. Your other son was one of the grenade-throwing party.'

'Hermann?'

'Of course. He's one of our most promising recruits. We're a broad-minded lot in the Home Guard. We don't bear malice. Anyone's welcome who cares to join."

'So you trained him to murder his own brother?'

'Call it what you like as long as you don't say it in front of witnesses. The fact is, three men were issued with live grenades. One of them was Hermann. They lobbed them. It just so happened that the things landed just where Alfred was lying. That's the way it was.'

Materna turned on his heel and strode mechanically towards the hummock where his father had planted the copper beech forty-two years before, on the day of his birth. He slumped on to the rough wooden seat beneath the tree. Before him, in a gentle fold in the ground, lay the village of Maulen, but he did not see it. His eyes were misted with tears.

'He's taking it hard,' Eugen Eis observed stolidly. 'Who'd have thought he'd make such a fuss?'

'It's a bad business,' Moritz said. 'Anything I can do?'

'Yes, help me unload.'

Before they could carry the body into the house, Margarete Materna appeared. Her face was chalky-white and her eyes wide, but she stepped up to the cart with iron composure.

'She knows how to behave,' Moritz whispered admiringly. 'More than you can say for her husband.'

'I'll never know why she picked Materna,' Eis whispered back. 'It's a mystery to me.'

'Did he suffer?' Margarete inquired.

'Couldn't have,' Eis assured her. 'He was gone in a flash.' She nodded. 'That's some comfort.'

'Where shall we put him?'

'In the parlour.' Margarete's voice sounded clear and steady. Moritz recalled that the dead youth was not her own son. Of the three Materna children, only the daughter was hers. Even so, he stared after her respectfully as she marched back into the house with head erect.

'I'll tell you something,' Eugen Eis announced as he helped Moritz to lift the body off the cart. 'Materna's an awkward customer. People are going to take sides over this, and it's high time they did—for the sake of our glorious future, and all that. At least we'll know where everyone stands.' Expertly, he rolled the body in a ground-sheet and seized one end. 'This lad took after his father—frittered away his time—dreamy, no guts or community spirit. People can't behave like that indefinitely—not in this country.'

Moritz picked up the body by its feet. 'It's a bit hard, us sweating our guts out while Materna sits there admiring the scenery. I'd like to know what he's hatching.'

Eugen Eis devoted himself to the job in hand. He deposited

the body on the parlour table and wiped his hands methodically on the ground-sheet. Finally, he said:

'They oughtn't to leave the poor bastard lying around too
long. He'll stink the place out in this weather.'

'I don't want to see or be seen by anybody,' Materna said.
He was still sitting on the bench under the copper beech.

'But you're needed back at the house, Alfons.'

Only one person in the world had called him Alfons since
the death of his parents, and that was Jacob Jablonski, his
foreman and only friend. His children—Hermann, the grenade-
thrower, Alfred, now a corpse, and Brigitte, the daughter of
his second marriage—all addressed him as 'Father'. Margarete, whom he had married after his first wife's untimely
death, called him 'Materna', much as she would have addressed
a servant.

'You can't just hide yourself away.'

'What else can I do?'

Jablonski was the one person Materna spoke freely to—
the one person who knew that even Alfons Materna could
shed tears. It had only happened twice before, once when his
mother died and the second time when the body of a girl
named Hilde was hauled out of the lake. The third time was
now.

'Don't cry, man,' Jablonski said roughly. 'Save your strength.
Your son's dead, but that's not the worst that can happen to
you—not by a long chalk.'

'Go to hell!'

'Not without you,' Jablonski retorted with a ghost of a
smile.

The two men had known each other for as long as they
could remember. They had been born in the same year,
Alfons to the mistress of the house and Jacob to a servant-
girl. It was more than probable that old Materna had fathered
them both, because they grew up together like brothers and
the older they became the more alike they seemed to themselves and their immediate circle. On the other hand, they
were far closer than most people of the same flesh and
blood.

'I feel weak, Jacob—weak as a baby.'

'You'll get over that, especially if you think Eichler's steal-
ing a march on you.'

'Eichler?' Materna demanded, sitting up. 'What about him?'
'He's on the premises at this moment.'

Materna jumped up as if he had been stung and hurried off in the direction of the farm.

'Never seen Alfons like this before,' Jacob muttered. He often spoke to himself. Every Masurian was his own best audience, or so the saying went. 'He'd better watch out, though, or Eichler'll do him down. He's had plenty of experience.'

Johannes Eichler had approached Alfons Materna's farm with a measure of caution. His beefy form seemed to waver for a moment just outside the gate. Then, catching sight of Materna seated at a reassuring distance beneath the copper beech on the hill, he strode into the house with a masterful air.

'Anyone at home?' he bellowed.

There was no immediate response, so he seized the opportunity to look around. It was years since he had been allowed to set eyes on what was reputed to be the most productive farm in Masuria. He was not unduly impressed by the interior of the farm-house itself, which was snug but unpretentious. There were easy chairs and bright gipsy rugs—even some books.

Eichler's spirits rose still further. 'Isn't there anyone I can extend my condolences to?' he called in trumpet tones.

At this, Margarete Materna appeared, looking like an allegory of sorrow. Her head was slightly bowed but her manner perfectly composed. Eichler advanced on her portentously. 'Who would have thought it possible?' he boomed.

'How good of you to come, Johannes. I appreciate your sympathy more than I can say.'

Other fine phrases followed, culminating in a reference to the inexorability of fate. They gazed into each other's eyes and clasped hands. Margarete's head, severely braided but still lustrously blonde, inclined itself towards him.

'I wish I could tell you how I really feel, Margarete.'

There was no need. Frau Materna might just as easily have been Frau Eichler. Both men had courted Margarete in the old days. Whatever the reason for her choice—youthful irresponsibility, mental confusion or abject docility—she had become Frau Materna, not Frau Eichler.

'What a deplorable thing to happen!' she said, meaning the death of her stepson.

'Ah, yes,' he replied, 'you must do your best to get over it.'

Johannes Eichler was thinking of Dog's Meadow, a parcel of land on the south side of the village. It had been part of Margarete's dowry. Without it, Materna would never have become the most successful peasant farmer in the district—Eichler felt positive of that.

'It's good of you to remember me,' Margarete breathed. She relished Eichler's presence at this juncture and made no effort to disguise the fact.

'As if I could ever forget you!' Eichler said. He contrived to look fervent and bashful at the same time. 'What about your husband? Why isn't he here by your side?'

'You know how little I mean to him,' Margarete said softly.

Her shapely breasts rose and fell. Eichler regarded them appreciatively but decided that it would be more profitable at this stage to gaze into her cornflower-blue eyes. With a protective movement of his arm he led her past the table where the body lay.

'He never did understand you,' he ventured.

Margarete discreetly acknowledged the truth of this statement with a slight inclination of the head. This gave Eichler a glimpse of the nape of her neck. He found it a pleasing and edifying sight, not unreminiscent of the upper reaches of a prize heifer's rump—and no Masurian could have devised a more flattering comparison.

'Margarete,' he said in a husky voice, 'why do we only appreciate the value of true friendship under circumstances like these?'

'You're very understanding,' she murmured.

'I've always understood you. The trouble is I've never had much opportunity to show it.'

Their idyll was rudely interrupted by the appearance of Alfons Materna. He stood in the doorway, arms akimbo, eyeing his wife and her visitor.

'Permit me,' Eichler said, striving for dignity, 'to express my heartfelt sympathy.'

'Get out,' said Materna.

'I came to express my sympathy,' Eichler insisted with a note of warning in his voice.

'To hell with your sympathy!'

Margarete glanced helplessly at Eichler, but Eichler was staring at her husband. 'Materna!' she protested. 'Remember who you're talking to.'

'I don't need any reminding.' Materna crouched like an animal about to spring. 'I'm talking to an out-and-out swine, I'm well aware of that.'

'He's not himself,' Eichler said with an effort. 'I don't blame him for losing his grip—this business has obviously been too much for him.'

Margarete, separated from the two fighting-cocks by the shrouded corpse on the oak table, ventured to intervene.

'Herr Eichler is my guest, Materna. I must ask you to respect the laws of hospitality.'

Margarete was capable of uttering such phrases with considerable conviction. She came of a genteel family—one which actually boasted a piano, so rumour had it. Moreover, she was a regular reader of the local newspaper and its serialized romantic novels, hence her frequent excursions into the non-vernacular.

'As I see it,' Materna retorted, 'Eichler is a murderer—the murderer of my son.'

'You become more uncouth every day,' Margarete declared bitterly. She glanced at Eichler as though seeking his forgiveness and stalked out of the room. Eichler sketched a sympathetic little bow in her direction and then rounded on Materna. The unction in his voice vanished abruptly.

'Now we're alone perhaps we can cut the cackle.'

'By all means,' Materna replied. He walked to the table on which his son's body lay, bent over it and turned back the ground-sheet. 'You're going to pay for this, Eichler.'

'You don't know what you're saying. I can take a joke but this is going too far—can't you understand that?'

Materna ignored the question. 'What's an appropriate price to exact for a man's life, I wonder? The death of someone else—the death of the guilty party?'

'Stop talking rubbish, Materna. If you're wise—and you're no fool—you'll take this as a final warning.'

'A warning?' Materna turned and looked Eichler full in the eye. 'It's a challenge, and I accept it.'

'Listen, Materna. I was nowhere near your son when he died, which is more than you can say for your other son. He was directly involved in Alfred's death. If you're looking for someone to pin it on, Hermann's the likeliest candidate. Think of the gossip, though—think of all the references to Cain and Abel! If you're clever you'll keep quiet and put the whole thing down to experience. You've no alternative, don't you see that?'

'As far as I'm concerned,' Materna said, 'you're a dead man.'

For the next few hours Margarete appeared to take sole charge of the Materna household. She covered all the mirrors and sprinkled white sand over the floor of the room in which the body lay. Flowers were arranged, candles distributed round the parlour, food and drink set out in the kitchen. The corpse itself was wrapped in white sheets—not new ones, admittedly, but freshly laundered.

Moritz, errand boy and spiritual comforter to the village at large, proved a great help. At his suggestion, open sandwiches were prepared, some laden with ham and others with liver-sausage and black pudding. Margarete surveyed the serried bottles and heaped plates with satisfaction.

'All who wish to extend their condolences,' she announced, 'are at liberty to come.'

They came.

One of the first and most eager to convey his heartfelt sympathy was the Reverend Dr Bachus, who quoted at length from the Scriptures and then invited all present to join in a first communal prayer round the mortal remains of the dear departed.

The Reverend Dr Bachus, who did not seem to notice the absence of Materna and Jablonski, devoted his entire stock of Christian consolation to Margarete. After that he fortified himself with bread and ham, not omitting to praise the quality of the latter—and justly so, since Alfons Materna's home-cured hams were claimed to be the finest in Masuria.

The next to appear was Klinger, the village policeman. He, too, uttered suitable words of consolation and was then persuaded to take a glass of Materna's double-distilled schnapps—clear as spring-water, keen as a razor, and reputed locally to give a man bright eyes and a warm heart,

After the third glass, Constable Klinger informed an attentive audience of the results of his inquiries—preliminary results, but nonetheless official for that. It appeared that the late lamented Alfred Materna had stumbled on an explosive charge while walking in the marshy area north of Maulen. The charge in question was presumed to be a mine left over from the 1914-18 War—to be more precise, from the Battle of the Masurian Lakes, so gloriously waged and won by Marshal Hindenburg . . .

In short, it was an accident. Alfred was a belated victim of the Great War. The mine was additionally presumed to be of Russian origin.

More local figures converged on the bereaved household. They included Ignaz Uschkurat, mayor and president of the Farmers' Union, Gottlieb Speer, building contractor, church-warden and chairman of a number of associations, Maximilian Vetter, headmaster, regional historian, organist and choir-master, and numerous other dignitaries with names like Naschinski, Porenski, Sombray, Bembenneck and Kochanowski. No villager of note or status would have dreamed of shirking his responsibilities to the bereaved family, far less of spurning Materna's schnapps.

Old Mother Mischgoreit, who put in a predictably prompt appearance, gathered up her rusty black skirts and trotted to the house of mourning. She arrived blowing hard. 'Poor innocent lamb!' she wheezed, elbowing her way forward. 'What a thing to happen!—But then, he always did look peaky, poor soul.'

One by one they filed across the white sand, stood in silence by the body, pressed Margarete Materna's hand with fervour, and then retired to the kitchen, there to be lavishly plied with food and drink by Maria, the maidservant.

Death was a festive occasion in Masuria, where God's will was accepted as a matter of course. Death simply meant that one more mortal had passed through the vale of earthly sorrow, and funerals were succeeded by cheerful dance music interspersed with military marches and communal singing.

'But where's Materna?' asked the visitors.

They could afford to utter this question loudly and without embarrassment in the maid's presence. Maria was not a local. She came from Poland and she was a deaf-mute.

'I know where Materna is,' said Constable Klinger. 'Believe it or not, he's down at the Gasthaus.'

'I hope you're not going to make trouble, Materna,' said the landlord. 'I'm ready to serve anyone, as you know, but to see you in here today of all days . . .'

'That's just it,' Materna growled. 'It's quieter here than at home.'

The landlord looked vaguely worried. 'I hope you don't think I had anything to do with your son's death.'

'Of course not. You just dished out the drink to our heroic Home Guard. It probably improved their aim.'

The Gasthaus stood in the centre of the village, opposite the church. Between them rose the war memorial, representing a dying warrior who, though in extremis, still pointed his banner skywards. It was dedicated to the fallen heroes of the parish of Maulen, vintage 1870-1871, 1914-18, and bore the inscription 'Lest we forget'. It also bore a number of names, but there was room for plenty more.

The Gasthaus had no name of its own. It was known simply as 'the Gasthaus' or 'Scharfke's'. The proprietor, Christian Scharfke, plied his trade without benefit of price-list or tariff. He seldom served anything but beer or schnapps. The latter came in three forms: clear and dry for men, sweet and sticky for women and youngsters, and brandy-style for exacting customers and special functions. Beer was served from the bottle under normal circumstances and from the cask when a festivity was in the offing. A tot of schnapps cost ten pfennigs, a glass of beer fifteen and a bottle of beer twenty. A jar of pickled gherkins stood ready for gourmets, and the hungry were regaled with tinned sardines, Bismarck herrings, cold chops and meat roll. Few people ever asked for anything more elaborate.

'A bottle of wine,' commanded Alfons Materna.

Christian Scharfke rose to the occasion. Several dozen bottles lay in the corner of his cellar, labelled *Black Cat* and *Liebfraumilch*. Anyone who chose to drink them had only himself to blame. The true Masurian regarded wine as little better than water, and water was mainly used for cattle, washing, and—not infrequently—for diluting milk.

As soon as Scharfke had vanished into the cellar Jacob

Jablonski turned to Materna. 'There he is,' he said, '—over there in the far corner.'

Ensconced at a table against the wooden partition, flanked by hat-stands and the lavatory door, sat Hermann, Materna's sole surviving son. Before him stood a tumbler and an almost empty bottle of Scharfke's 'white' schnapps, a crude but effective form of potato spirit.

Hermann's eyes were already glazed, but he recognized the approaching figure of his father and his father's faithful watchdog.

'I wouldn't blame you if you never spoke to me again, Father,' he mumbled through an alcoholic fog. 'Wouldn't blame you if you left me sitting here like a piece of furniture.'

'It'd serve you right if I did,' Materna replied grimly.

Hermann tried to sit up—more than that, he struggled to his feet. 'Spit in my face, Father—it's all I deserve. Go on, hit me!'

'Have I ever hit you?'

'No.' Hermann dropped his eyes, his manner conveying that it might have been better if Materna had done precisely that. 'I'd just like to make one thing clear. I honestly didn't know what we were doing out there—didn't have a clue. I know it doesn't alter the fact that I killed my own brother, but I wasn't to blame—really I wasn't!'

'Sit down,' Materna ordered. 'Sit down and stop blathering. It won't bring him back.'

Jablonski went up to Hermann, put one arm round his shoulders and forced him gently back in his chair. Hermann obeyed like the child he still was, for all his twenty-one years and monumental physique.

'How did you get mixed up with that bunch in the first place—the Home Guard, or whatever they call themselves?'

'You never said I wasn't to join, Father. Anyway, surely there's nothing wrong with guarding our homes?'

Materna was fully acquainted with the 'ideological' basis of the association which called itself the Home Guard. According to this, German soil was nowhere more greatly imperilled than in East Prussia. The Poles were alleged to be extending their tentacles in that direction, and, although the outcome of the great referendum of 1920 had been a clear and decisive vote in favour of German nationality, the enemy refused to accept it. Subversion and disguised immigration were the result. Polish labourers undercut the wages of East Prussian agricultural workers, propaganda leaflets fluttered through letter-boxes, atrocity stories were rife. The Masurian language, still to be heard in a few places, was described as a Polish dialect, and the international hubbub about supposedly threatened minorities persisted . . .

As a result, patriotic and nationalistically-inclined citizens created the so-called Home Guard, a network of volunteer units which found willing recruits in even the tiniest villages—home-loving civilians one and all, but led and guided by trusty veterans with combat or training experience. In Maulen, for instance, Eugen Eis—an ex-sergeant—was actively engaged in this noble work under the command of Johannes Eichler, who had held the rank of sergeant-major.

Even though the Home Guard generally possessed greater symbolic significance than fighting potential, weapons were in evidence. They came from secret arms dumps which had evaded the Allied committees of inspection. There were two such dumps in the Maulen area alone, one in the church belfry and the other in the woods, not far from the lake. They contained several dozen Model 98k rifles, sundry boxes of hand-grenades, three World War One machine-guns, and quantities of ammunition.

'Well, what did happen?' Materna demanded.

Hermann's account was comprehensible enough:' a surprise practice alert—four sections called out, i.e. platoon-strength—Eugen Eis in command—platoon moves off in direction of marshes—on arrival, stick-grenades issued to the best grenade-throwers, Hermann naturally among them—fox-holes dug —grenade-throwers briefed on their objective.

'By whom?'

'Eugen Eis—he was right behind us. He pointed out a clump of bushes fifty yards ahead—whispering, of course, because the enemy were supposed to be on top of us. We crawled another twenty yards through the tall grass, not making a sound. Really careful, we were. Out came the grenades. We pulled the pins, jumped up, lobbed and took cover. Then came the bangs. Somebody screamed. Short and sharp, it was, like a rabbit.'

'All right, that's enough.'

Materna stared at the floor. The musty smell of the bar

seemed to be giving him a violent headache. He got up, pushed open the door of the lavatory, stumbled inside and leant heavily against the whitewashed wall.

'Is he feeling ill?' Hermann inquired anxiously. He was fond of his father. It was a son's duty to be fond of his father, and Hermann was a dutiful son—at least, he did his best to be. 'Father can take plenty as a rule.'

Jacob Jablonski laid his hand on the young man's massive shoulder. 'He's taken more than enough today one way and another.'

'Is he mad at me?'

'Forget about it, lad. Go home now and sleep it off. Everything'll sort itself out—trust your father to see to that.'

'Get out, the lot of you,' Materna said from beside the body of his son. 'I want to be alone with him.'

His wife frowned. 'You don't mean me, do you?'

'I mean everyone, and that includes you.'

Margarete bowed her head in sorrowful submission and withdrew. Hermann, a solemn and dutiful figure, followed her out. The last to go was Brigitte, Materna's daughter. She glanced at her father inquiringly but without reproach. Materna gave her a brief nod.

Candlelight played over the sheet-swathed body, and a heavy, sweetish smell seemed to pervade the room. Materna opened the windows wide.

Jacob Jablonski poked his head round the door. 'Anything I can do?'

'Yes, bring me a jug of the best schnapps and two glasses.'

Jacob silently deposited the jug and glasses on the table where the body lay. Then he drew the curtains again and retired to the kitchen. None of the assembled company spared him a glance as he sat down in one corner. Munching and sipping, they all stared—wordlessly but not in silence—at the lace-draped glass door which separated the kitchen from the parlour. Through it, sharp as a knife, could be seen the silhouette of the master of the house.

Materna raised his glass, evidently to the corpse. It was hard to make out what he was saying at first. Then his voice rose.

'An eye for an eye!'—The fact that he uttered these words was later corroborated by several witnesses, since the kitchen was still crowded with sympathizers. Not only did they find it impossible to tear themselves away from Materna's schnapps, but they were hopeful that their host, who was noted for his unpredictable behaviour, would provide them with a source of gossip for months to come.

'He can be a hard man,' one of the mourners said thoughtfully,

Old Mother Mischgoreit, who had lent colour to many a wake and funeral in her time, declared that she had seen it all coming. The Topich, or Masurian water-goblin, had revealed itself to her 'He stretched out his hands and called: "Your loss my gain!"'

'Please, please!' sighed the Reverend Dr Bachus. 'The Topich is a pagan myth—a figment of the imagination.'

'I saw him,' Old Mother Mischgoreit said firmly, 'and whenever he appears someone always dies. He has to have his victims.'

The Topich or Dobnik, a small red-garbed goblin of enormous antiquity, dwelt in the glassy depths of the Masurian Lakes. He apparently got bored from time to time, because he recruited company from the upper world or captured the souls of his chosen companions by depriving their bodies of life.

'It was him who took Alfred,' the old woman insisted. 'He likes young blood.'

The Reverend Dr Bachus restrained himself with an effort. He was exasperated, and not for the first time, by the approving nods of some of those present. It was vitally necessary to speak out against superstition of this kind—necessary but risky. The inhabitants of Masuria were anything but enlightened, and it was his pastoral duty to dispel their spiritual darkness.

As it happened, the pangs of doubt which constantly beset him in his capacity as parish priest of Maulen were dispelled in the nick of time by a new arrival on the scene, namely, Siegfried Grienspan.

Grienspan, a small saturnine man, walked into the kitchen and removed his hat with a graceful gesture. 'Well,' he said in a bright, businesslike voice, 'where's this cow of yours?'

'What cow?'

'The one that just died. They 'phoned me about it—told me the carcase had to be disposed of today without fail.'

The occupants of the kitchen stared at him in consternation. Hermann looked as if he were ready to kill for the second time that day. Margarete sobbed aloud and Brigitte put down the newspaper she had been reading.

At that moment, Alfons Materna started singing in the next room. It was an old peasant song about the flowers of the field and how they were all destined to wither and die.

Grienspan became painfully aware that something out of the ordinary must have occurred. This was apparent not only from the solemn faces around him but also from the wave of righteous indignation that rose to meet him.

'I really did get a call—from Herr Jablonski, it was.'

'From me?' Jablonski shook his head. 'Impossible. I've never made a telephone call in my life.'

'In that case . . .' Grienspan lapsed into bemused silence. It dawned on him that someone had played a dirty trick—and not on him alone. He stared into the tense and expectant faces around him. They hung in the smoky room like a chain of warning beacons.

Alfons Materna went on singing.

Siegfried Grienspan was universally known in the neighbourhood. His cattle-dealing business was based in the local market town, but he spent a lot of time pedalling round the villages on a decrepit bicycle. Although true-blue Germans regarded him with a touch of suspicion, he always found plenty of buyers and sellers. 'He knows his business,' was the general verdict, '—but then, he's a Jew.' Alfons Materna seemed to get on with him splendidly, a fact which many people in Maulen found characteristic.

Jablonski took Grienspan aside and told him what had happened. Grienspan listened attentively. His head drooped lower and lower and his slight frame seemed to shrivel, but his transparent, ivory-coloured features did not change expression.

'I'll tell Alfons you're here,' Jablonski said, disappearing into the parlour. A moment later Materna appeared.

'Come in, Grienspan,' he said, waving his glass invitingly at the cattle-dealer, 'come in and welcome. Seems some devil 'phoned you on behalf of the Almighty.'

'I'm very sorry,' Grienspan said quietly. 'I know how it is. Death does more than put paid to one life—it affects others as well. You were very attached to your son, weren't you?'

'One gets attached to a lot of things in life,' Materna said. 'At the age of three I was crazy about a wooden horse. Then someone threw it in the fire. At eight I was infatuated with a dog. Later, there were various women. I married two of them. One gave me a pair of sons and died, the other gave me a daughter and slowly killed my affection for her. Something dies in us or around us almost every day. We ought to be used to it by now.'

'Your son was like you, wasn't he?'

'It's possible. Perhaps I saw him as a reflection of myself when young. Perhaps I recognized my own failings in him, my own secret longings and ambitions—all the gilded stupidity of youth. As I grew older, I wanted him to enjoy all the things I'd been incapable of enjoying myself at his age. Well, now he's dead.'

Materna pulled up two chairs and motioned to Grienspan to sit down. He carefully closed the windows and bolted the door. Then he picked up the jug, filled both glasses and held one out. The two men drank to each other.

'What a terrible accident,' Grienspan said.

'It was no accident, Grienspan. Alfred was deliberately murdered. The murderer used Hermann as a tool but I'm the one he was after. I'm unpopular in certain circles. They hate me because I tread on their corns.'

Grienspan drained his glass. His furrowed features registered concern and his frail body seemed to quiver with apprehension. He raised one hand and laid it soothingly on Materna's arm.

'I'm a Jew,' he said softly.

'No need to brag,' growled Materna.

'When I say I'm a Jew,' Grienspan persisted, 'what I mean is, I belong to one of the oldest races in the world. I don't imagine there's a single form of suffering we haven't experienced in our time. That's why I'm qualified to offer you some advice, Materna. Take things as they come—accept them patiently and rise above them. In future, steer clear of your enemies. Go on living your own life, as before. What could be better than that?'

'You've always been keen to buy my pair of greys, Grienspan. They're yours for two thousand marks.'

'I won't take them,' Grienspan said indignantly. '—not at

that price. They're worth at least two thousand five hundred.'

'Two thousand will be enough. I need cash, quickly.'

'I'll advance you two thousand as an interest-free loan, with obligation. Anyway, why do you need the money so quickly?'

'I want to buy some goodwill.'

'Can't you get it any cheaper?'

'You mean goodwill in Maulen isn't worth that much? Maybe not, but even a drop of water can be worth its weight in gold—in a desert, say.'

Grienspan shook his head. His eyes looked weary. 'I don't understand you, Materna. Revenge is a pointless thing. Everyone gets hurt in the end, especially the innocent.'

Materna smiled. 'Don't you remember the story of the dog who was left to die in the forest? His only hope was to howl with the wolves—he had to howl if he wanted to survive. Well, he howled so horribly that the wolves turned tail and fled. The consequence was, he not only survived but had the forest to himself.'

'What are you driving at?'

'Nothing much. Our local wolves make plenty of noise, but there's no reason why we shouldn't howl them down. That is, unless you can think of a better way of shutting them up.'

2

Alfred Materna's funeral promised to be an occasion of special note. Interested parties in the immediate and less immediate vicinity of Maulen showed signs of wanting to attend, but Alfons Materna had let it be known that further expressions of sympathy would be unwelcome.

To underline this, he personally nailed a board bearing the legend 'Beware of the Dog' to his farm gate and unleashed his Alsatian, an alert animal named Tyras. Tyras vanished into the barn and lay down in the straw, but one whistle from Materna or Jablonski was enough to transform the dog into a bloodhound.

As an added deterrent, Jablonski armed himself with an oak cudgel. He took his duties as gate-keeper so seriously that he refused to lay it aside, even at meals. The cudgel lay across the table, ready to hand, and the key of the gate-chain hung on a string round his neck. If anyone dared to ring the bell Jablonski let him wait for a while, then shouldered his bludgeon and marched out to the gate. His standard greeting was: 'Push off! We're in mourning!'

He even used this salutation on the Reverend Dr Bachus. However, when the latter frowned at him with cautious disapproval, Jablonski muttered something which might have been construed as an apology and substituted the formula 'No visitors allowed' for 'Push off!'

The parish priest was a peaceable man. In his view, every villager was welcome to find salvation in his own way provided he obeyed the basic rules of his, Bachus's, church—and this, he felt, ought not to be too difficult in view of the fact that his was the only church in the district.

'We're not seeing anyone,' Jablonski amplified. 'We've asked people not to pay any more calls.'

Nothing could shake Bachus's composure. 'I should be extremely grateful, my dear Herr Jablonski, if you would have the kindness to inform Herr Materna of my wish for a few words with him. You might mention that I am anxious to discuss one or two unavoidable administrative details in regard to the forthcoming interment.'

Jablonski gave an admiring nod. The parson's eloquence had always impressed him. He made a peaceful withdrawal, even omitting to shoulder his cudgel.

Materna, who appeared almost at once, called Tyras and chained him to his post. The dog lay down and opened its jaws in a mighty yawn.

'God be with you,' called Bachus.

Materna smiled grimly. 'I need all the help I can get.'

He led the way into the parlour, where Alfred still lay wrapped in his white sheets. Bachus offered up a brief and silent prayer. Then, without more ado, he said: 'I could find Alfred a particularly handsome plot in our churchyard, if you're interested.

'A handsome plot means an expensive plot—right?'

Bachus looked vaguely indignant. 'Nothing could be too good for your beloved son, surely? In any case, the sum involved really wouldn't be exorbitant. A plot in the front row near the main entrance—with extra width and double length to allow for the subsequent installation of a headstone and marble surround—would run to about a hundred and twenty marks.'

It was customary to haggle in Masuria, so Materna refrained from agreeing at once. Instead, he said cautiously: 'I'm a modest man, Vicar. Also, I'm not what you'd call a faithful son of the Church.'

'I know, I know.' Bachus magnanimously waved this objection aside. 'I have often noticed your absence at our services—almost always, in fact—but everyone comes to God sooner or later. It could be your turn, Herr Materna.'

'It could be,' Materna agreed.

The priest's eye softened slightly, but before he could embark on a warm-up for his funeral oration, Materna insisted on negotiating a form of contract. The terms were as follows:

First, the grave to be situated in a preferential position, as suggested. For this, the sum previously mentioned plus a donation of thirty marks;

Second, the body to lie in state in the church for twenty-four hours before the funeral. The church to be kept locked, i.e. no unauthorized person to be admitted. Materna himself to decide who was to be regarded as 'authorized'. For this, another hundred marks;

Third and last, the burial to take place with due ceremony at the agreed spot. Invited mourners only to attend. Once again, Materna to decide who would be welcome and who not. For this, a further hundred marks.

An additional fifty marks would be paid if his, Materna's, wishes were observed in every respect, making a total of four hundred marks—cash on the barrel, immediately after the service. Yet another hundred-mark note—intended for charitable purposes—might conceivably change hands if all went well.

'Very good, very good,' Bachus rubbed his hands approvingly. 'I would draw your attention to one thing, though. Public sympathy is very strong, you know. A large number of our fellow-citizens will wish to pay their last respects to the dear departed. Ought we really to deprive them of that opportunity?'

'Four hundred marks,' Materna said firmly. 'Four hundred marks if everything goes the way I want it—possibly five hundred. Those are my terms, and I want them followed to the letter.'

'I'm sure it can be arranged,' Bachus replied. 'Alfred will be laid to rest in a most fitting manner, I feel confident of that.'

'He was one of us,' declared Johannes Eichler. 'We must bring that home to everyone—it's the least we can do.'

'Inquiries have been coming in from all over the place,' Eugen Eis reported. 'All the boys plan to turn up. They want to show their solidarity, and we can't offend them.'

Eichler frowned. 'Nobody wants to offend anyone except Materna.'

'He's a real problem,' sighed Ignaz Uschkurat, mayor and president of the Farmers' Union. 'He's always been a problem as far back as I can remember.'

Gottlieb Speer, builder and churchwarden, cleared his throat. 'I suppose he ought to have some say in the matter. After all, he's paying out good money, and the church needs a new roof badly.'

'A roof which you hope to supply, I suppose,' sneered Eis.

'Someone has to,' Speer protested. 'I happen to be a building contractor. Roofs are my business. I don't see why I should be blamed for doing my job.'

'You mean you're prepared to take money from a man like Materna?' Eis demanded belligerently, strong in the knowledge that Eichler had given him express permission to take this line. When danger threatened the community, the men of Maulen always loaded with live ammunition and kept their fingers on the trigger. 'That's what I call betraying the cause.'

'I resent that,' Speer shouted angrily. He could tolerate the reproach that he was taking money from Materna, however indirectly, but to cast doubt on his esprit de corps was going decidedly too far. 'If I do lay that roof it'll be for the church, not Materna. What's more, I'll do the job at a reduced rate.'

'I vote we stop flinging accusations around,' Uschkurat interposed.

'Nobody's accusing anyone of anything,' Eichler said in soothing tones. Amiably, he patted Speer and Uschkurat on the arm. Both men were visibly agitated, which meant that

Eugen and Eis had achieved the desired effect. 'We all know you can be relied on to the full, my dear friends.'

Eichler was sitting with Eis and his 'dear friends' in what he chose to call his office. This was situated in an annexe belonging to Eichler's mill. Adjoining it were private quarters, including a kitchen and cellar, which made it an ideal venue for private conferences. Eichler's housekeeper kept the glasses filled like a drover watering cattle.

'We all have certain responsibilities,' Eichler pursued, 'responsibilities which we can't evade, responsibilities to the public, to the community—to the fatherland.'

Johannes Eichler was the most active figure in Maulen and had been so ever since the untimely death of his wife. The late Frau Eichler had died under circumstances which could only be termed tragic, having drowned in a milk-vat in the dairy which had been part of her dowry.

After a limited period of mourning, Johannes Eichler plunged wholeheartedly into patriotic activities and very soon emerged as Maulen's leading repository of regional and national sentiment. He also won a reputation for open-handedness. He not only arranged and provided loans, credits and mortgages but helped to found the veterans' association and other bodies. The impressive and artistically meritorious monument to the fallen sons of Maulen was yet another of his projects.

Ignaz Uschkurat, a square-headed man with the lugubrious face of a St Bernard and a body like a boulder, said: 'I'm no friend of Materna. He's too much of an individualist for my liking. He doesn't stick to the rules—manures his fields when he feels like it, switches his crops for no good reason that anyone can see, flies in the face of experience when harvest-time comes. All the same, he's the best farmer for miles around.'

'I respect that fact,' Eichler said magnanimously. 'Materna knows his business. He gets top prices for his grain and his cattle breed like rabbits. I admit all that, but I often wonder whether efficiency is the only mark of a true German.' He glanced at his trusty lieutenant, Eugen Eis.

Eis interpreted the look correctly. 'Alfons Materna is always setting himself apart from the community. He doesn't belong to any of our associations and he cocks a snook at our patriotic activities. Why?'

'Just a touch more community spirit,' Eichler said sadly. 'Is that really too much to ask?'

None of those present felt called upon to reply. They stared out of the window. Summer was on the way, rich and full-bodied. A broad field of grain shimmered in the golden light, but the men round the table were too familiar with the view to appreciate it. The sight of a schnapps bottle seemed far more alluring at present.

Eugen Eis said: 'Alfred died in peace-time but he died a hero's death. He laid down his life for Germany. It doesn't matter whether he realized it or not. We must show our appreciation—publicly.'

Ignaz Uschkurat announced an urgent call of nature and Eichler accompanied him outside. The two men stood shoulder to shoulder, harmoniously relieving themselves against the rear wall of the building. As they did so, Eichler touched casually on the subject of Uschkurat's outstanding debt to him. Among other things, he owed him miller's fees for the past four months.

'I'll settle with you after the harvest, as usual,' Uschkurat promised.

'I'm not putting pressure on you, of course—just jogging your memory. If I meant anything at all by my remark, it was this: we must stand firm and close our ranks. We're all in the same boat, and the sooner people realize it the better.'

After further intensive discussion, the conference adjourned. Its outcome could be summed up as follows: Eugen Eis was to continue his efforts to inspire his fellow-citizens with popular, national and patriotic fervour; Gottlieb Speer agreed, under pressure, to approach the Reverend Dr Bachus with the same end in view; and Ignaz Uschkurat finally declared himself ready to call on Materna in person and appeal to his conscience—always provided that Materna possessed such a thing.

'The reputation of the village is at stake,' was Eichler's parting shot. 'Not even a man like Alfons Materna can be allowed to thwart our legitimate demands.'

On the same day, Materna's farm received a visit from two boys who were universally known as the Terrible Twins, not only in Maulen but also for miles around. Their real names were Konrad Klinger and Peter Bachus, and they were the sons of the policeman and the parish priest.

'We want to see the corpse,' said Peter Bachus.

'And we want to hear what Herr Materna has to say about it,' supplemented Konrad Klinger.

Peter and Konrad were the only two boys from Maulen to attend the grammar school in Allenstein, where they were jointly renowned for their intelligence and idleness. They delighted some of their teachers and drove others to despair. Their scholastic achievements were alarmingly erratic, but their behaviour at home in the village was no less alarming.

'People usually die in bed round here,' Peter Bachus said.

'Poor old Alfred bought it in the middle of a field,' put in Konrad Klinger, 'under peculiar circumstances. We're interested in things like that.'

Jacob Jablonski leant on the gate and regarded them quizzically. 'You're a fine pair, I must say. I bet you'd put the fear of God into Old Nick himself.'

The Terrible Twins preserved a complacent silence. They were proud of their appalling reputation and seized every opportunity to build on it, both at school and at home. The holidays had just begun, so they could devote four whole weeks to trouble-making if they felt so inclined—which they did.

Alfons Materna admitted the Terrible Twins without demur. Their first stop was the kitchen, where they fortified themselves with cold beef and sausages before viewing Alfred's body. The few years' difference in age between them and the dead youth had been a barrier, but not such a barrier as to preclude friendly relations.

'Why did he have to go like that?' demanded Peter Bachus.

'We all have to go sometime,' Materna said, '—sooner or later.'

'Up till now I'd always thought of it as later,' Konrad Klinger mused. 'After all, there isn't a war on.'

'Perhaps we're always at war, only we don't realize it,' Materna said.

The two boys bent over the body, Materna watched them keenly.

'It's strange,' said Peter Bachus. 'One minute you're alive, lying in the grass, thinking of nothing, and the next—bingo! —you've had it.'

'I'll tell you something even stranger,' Konrad Klinger said thoughtfully, 'and that's the way some people crawl round the countryside chucking hand-grenades. I wonder if they know what it feels like to have a hand-grenade go off under your nose?'

Peter Bachus winked at his partner in crime. 'That's quite a thought. Maybe we ought to enlighten them.'

'You're an imaginative pair,' Materna said pensively. 'Just remember, though. Too much imagination can be dangerous.'

'Do you know the mound on the north side of the moor,' asked Peter Bachus, 'the place they call Hindenburg Hill?'

Materna nodded. 'You can see most of the moor from there.'

'You can indeed,' Peter Bachus confirmed. 'That's why Johannes Eichler could see everything yesterday. He was standing there with his eyes skinned when the grenades went off. We watched him.'

'Is that plain enough for you?' asked Konrad Klinger.

'Too plain,' said Materna.

The sky above Masuria was radiantly blue and the warm earth smelt like a plump baby fresh from its bath. Maulen seemed devoid of life.

Ignaz Uschkurat mopped his brow and groaned at the heat. On days like this the inhabitants of the village usually sprawled exhausted in the shade or lounged around in the Gasthaus. Unlike them, Uschkurat reflected, he was going to have to trudge through the village on a lonely and ultra-delicate mission. He decided to break his journey at the Gasthaus. Gottlieb Speer, his companion in misfortune, was already there, fortifying himself for an equally delicate mission.

The two men exchanged sympathetic nods and ordered schnapps with beer chasers. Neither of them felt particularly comfortable and each longed for the next hour to be over.

'I'm in the picture,' the landlord said, joining them at their table. 'They tell me you're off to beard the lions in their den.'

Christian Scharfke was always well informed, and the whole village knew why. Eugen Eis, Eichler's stalwart lieutenant, was a regular visitor to the Gasthaus and, more specifically, to Christine Scharfke, daughter of Christian. There was even talk of marriage. Not only was Christine what the locals called a strapping wench, but she would ultimately inherit the Gasthaus. Eis courted her father's favour by supplying him with confidential reports on village arcana, and his confidences often paid off.

'No one's ever tried to bar the public from a funeral in this village,' said Scharfke. 'The bigger the attendance, the greater the mark of respect to the late lamented and his grieving family.'

The landlord's underlying concern was clear. Funerals might be a pleasure to other people, but to him they were good business as well, especially when the chief mourner's name was Materna. A man like Materna could afford a lavish funeral feast complete with brass band, mountains of food, and rivers of schnapps. Custom demanded a celebration, and custom demanded that it be held in the Gasthaus.

Scharfke winked encouragingly at Speer and Uschkurat, who went on brooding in silence. 'You'll manage it. Don't be put off by a lot of stupid talk.'

'What talk?'

'Nothing important,' Scharfke said evasively, refilling their glasses. 'I pay no attention to that sort of remark.'

'What sort of remark?'

'That you're a couple of gutless wonders.'

Uschkurat and Speer looked dumbfounded, then enraged. They insisted on knowing names, but Scharfke declared that he was not the man to betray a confidence. Nothing that was told him under pledge of secrecy ever passed his lips.

'He's just trying to put a squib under us,' Uschkurat said, when he and Speer were alone again.

Or set us against someone, but who? Did Eichler put him up to it, and if so why? My God, man, what have we got ourselves into? If we do pull the chestnuts out of the fire, who'll benefit and what'll it cost us?'

They stared at one another in dismay, got up without emptying their glasses, and walked thoughtfully to the door.

One of them said, 'We can thank Materna for this.'

Old Mother Mischgoreit flitted through the village, spreading alarm among the womenfolk. Her wizened face shone with excitement.

'Why did he have to die, poor lad?' she intoned. 'Why did he have to die, poor innocent creature?' Mother Mischgoreit had plenty of spare time and a talent for using it to her own advantage.

'The old crow wants a cut in her rent, that's all,' said Johannes Eichler, when he was told. 'We'll give her what she wants. Then perhaps she'll keep her trap shut.'

The terms of this generous offer were not conveyed to the old woman immediately because Eugen Eis was unwise enough to underestimate her importance. Meanwhile her evangelistic campaign had assumed unforeseen proportions. She was persuading the womenfolk that God had laid his hand on Maulen. 'But why?' she demanded. 'That boy's death is an omen!'

The women of Maulen listened reluctantly but with mounting attention. Their total subservience to the male did not prevent them from mistrusting their menfolk in certain respects. 'Men!' sneered Old Mother Mischgoreit. 'They're incapable of seeing to the heart of things. All they want to do is cram their bellies, get drunk and flatten the bed-springs. They don't know anything about the Topich.'

The old woman continued to flit from house to house. 'The Topich has been sighted!' she announced. 'He only appears when there are terrible times ahead.'

The Topich was powerfully symbolic of the imminence of death. To propitiate him, women cast secret offerings upon the waters of the lake—rose-garlands and fresh-baked loaves, or, under certain circumstances, soiled underwear. Men made sacrifice to him too, still more secretly. Unbroached bottles of schnapps and joints of meat were committed to the deep, but nobody admitted it.

When Eugen Eis finally ran Mother Mischgoreit to earth and announced Eichler's terms, the old woman simply snorted contemptuously and demanded complete exemption from rent.

'He'll come to fetch you all unless you show him some respect. Turn over a new leaf or you'll come to a bad end —all of you!'

'She can live rent-free from now on,' Johannes Eichler decided, taking the long view. 'If that doesn't bring her to her senses we'll have to shut her mouth permanently.'

Whereupon Old Mother Mischgoreit kept quiet for a spell.

Gottlieb Speer, churchwarden, was accorded a friendly

reception by the Reverend Dr Bachus. 'What can I do for you?' Bachus inquired in his best pastoral manner.

'It's an awkward business, Vicar—awkward but unavoidable.'

'You can speak freely, Herr Speer. My years in Maulen have made me a sympathetic listener.'

Gottlieb Speer saw that there was no need to beat about the bush. With relief, he expressed his desire—his friends' desire—for a worthy and well-attended funeral. 'We don't want it said that we let our dead go to the graves unmourned.'

'I, too, would appreciate a good attendance,' Bachus assured him. 'Thus, I thoroughly approve of your request —the request of your friends and associates.'

'Everything's all right, then,' Speer said blithely. 'That's all we're asking.'

'On the other hand,' Bachus went on, 'I have never yet disregarded the personal wishes of the next of kin—they have a right to be heard. Where Herr Materna is concerned, he sets the greatest store by an exclusive private funeral.'

'Then talk him out of it,' Speer said firmly.

'I might manage to do just that,' Bachus replied. 'However, I am responsible for the upkeep of the church as well as the spiritual welfare of my flock, and you, my dear friend, are a churchwarden. Funerals cost money, as you know, and Materna is prepared to pay a high price for privacy. The man has obviously calculated the cost of this funeral down to the last pfennig. Who will foot the bill if it develops into a public function?'

'We all have to make sacrifices, Vicar,' Speer said. 'Wouldn't you agree?'

The Reverend Dr Bachus, Gothic of build and Baroque of mind, paused before replying.

'I have been making sacrifices for years, Herr Speer. I accept the need for them, though I must confess that I find it difficult on occasions—now, for instance. The church badly needs a new roof. Materna's contribution would have paid for it, and you, my friend, would have built it. Still, if you really insist that short-term considerations must take precedence over a church roof which will endure for years to come . . . Well, I've always bowed to the recommendations of the parish council.'

Speer wriggled on the horns of his private dilemma. 'You

don't see any alternative—an appeal to Materna's better nature, say?'

Bachus promptly dismissed this suggestion. 'Materna knows the score,' he said with a hint of respect. 'That man can be as unyielding as a brick wall sometimes, and I've no wish to collide with him.'

Alfons Materna gave Uschkurat no time to ask questions. Instead, he seized the initiative himself.

'I don't suppose you've come here to discuss the weather.'

'Hardly,' said Uschkurat.

'You want my advice?'

'Not exactly.'

'A loan, then? I'm amenable, provided you put up the usual security.'

'Not this time, thanks.'

'Well then, since you obviously don't want anything from me,' Materna said amiably, 'I can only inform you that I don't want anything from you. In that case there's nothing left to discuss. Enjoy your walk home—I've got some funeral arrangements to attend to.'

'Wait a minute, Materna. I'd like a word with you, man to man—farmer to farmer, if you'd prefer.'

'I'm ready to listen to you in any capacity except one. If you're here as Johannes Eichler's errand boy you can save your breath. Are you, Uschkurat?'

'There's no reason why I shouldn't talk to him. It doesn't make me his errand boy. I'm friendly with him too, after all.'

'Eichler's friends are no friends of mine.' Materna spoke quietly, almost wearily. 'If you're acting as his messenger, I'm sorry for you. We go different ways from now on.'

'Is that your last word, Materna?'

'No. Here's some good advice: you'd do better to concentrate on your wheat. It's choked with weeds.' With that, Materna turned on his heel and walked off.

Uschkurat stared glumly after him. It was borne in on him, not for the first time, that Materna was as stubborn as an ox. But Uschkurat had a hard Masurian head—hard enough to crack nuts, as the local saying went. He wondered what would happen if two such heads collided.

Barely an hour later, Uschkurat and Speer were back in the

Gasthaus. They nodded and sat down in pregnant silence. Then they ordered their customary beer and schnapps.

Christian Scharfke served them with alacrity. Grinning companionably, he flopped into a chair beside them.

'Well, how did it go?'

Uschkurat frowned. 'One does what one can.'

'No one can do more than his best,' said Speer.

That told Scharfke all he needed to know. He raised his glass to the frustrated village diplomats with something akin to compassion. Then he excused himself and went upstairs to his private quarters. Reaching the landing, he went straight to his daughter's room and knocked discreetly. Eugen Eis opened the door, clad only in his vest and pants. Scharfke seemed to take this spectacle as a matter of course.

'They didn't make it,' he announced.

'Useless bastards, both of them.' Eis wagged his head contemptuously. 'No wonder this country needs a shake-up!' He pulled on his clothes in readiness for a visit to Eichler. Christine Scharfke squealed with delight as he playfully slapped her meaty buttocks in token of farewell. Then he was gone.

He made for Eichler's mill. Eichler, veiled in soft white dust, seemed to be contemplating the rivulets of flour with reverence. Pure, healthy, concentrated cleanliness, and all produced by him . . . He felt strengthened and reassured by the sight.

Eugen Eis announced the abject failure of the Speer-Uschkurat mission.

Johannes Eichler heard his faithful henchman out, still watching the flour as it trickled over his outstretched hand. He raised some to his nose and sniffed. 'Top quality flour, that,' he said.

Eis nodded in agreement. Flour and milk were vital foodstuffs. Johannes Eichler produced the one and converted the other into butter, cream and cheese. He had no rivals in this field either, and the welfare of many people in the neighbourhood depended on him.

'I never expect gratitude,' Eichler said. 'The most I hope for is an occasional glimmer of common sense. Our fellow-villagers are pretty shrewd when there's a profit to be made, but they're not prepared to take risks. That's why some of them have to be forced to do the right thing.'

'Materna, you mean?'

'I've got a lot of faith in you, Eis, but Materna's a tough nut. You really think you can talk some sense into him?'

'I'll teach him that we act German and think German round here.'

'I'm sure I can rely on you.' Eichler's gaze returned to the flour which was trickling from the pipes into the tubs beneath. 'Only the best is good enough for us.'

'I'll make that clear to him,' declared Eis. 'If he doesn't see sense, he'd better start learning the harp.'

Eugen Eis tramped through Maulen on that hot summer day like a general inspecting the ramparts of a fortress. He arrived at the chained and padlocked gate to Materna's farm thirsting for action.

Jacob Jablonski was standing there with his oak cudgel. He grinned amiably. 'That's far enough, Eugen.'

Eis snorted. 'I could snap your miserable chain just like that!'

'Maybe. What then?'

'You tell me.'

'Our Tyras. That dog's sharp as a razor.'

'He's all wind and piss!' scoffed Eis. 'That's why he suits your lousy farm.'

'In your opinion, maybe. Anyway, you're not wanted here. We're sick of the sight of your stupid face, so get lost!'

Jablonski turned on his heel and walked back to the house. It was clear that he was highly amused.

Eis felt unendurably provoked. Taking a short run, he hurled himself at the gate. The chain snapped and the two halves swung apart.

At that moment a shrill whistle rent the air and Tyras shot out of the barn. He sprang at Eugen Eis, was beaten back by a hefty kick, adopted a new offensive position, and leapt forward once more. This time the dog circled his adversary and took him from behind.

Eis gave a yell which Tyras construed as a sign of encouragement. Joyously, he ripped the man's trouser's off. Eis's posterior shone like a full moon, but Tyras appeared to mistake it for fresh ham. He drove his teeth into it with a look of ecstasy in his yellow eyes.

Eugen Eis took to his heels, bellowing wildly.

That evening the members of the Home Guard assembled in the back room of the Gasthaus. They looked grim and determined without knowing what they had to be determined about. Johannes Eichler presided.

'Men,' he said gravely, 'I am deputizing for your unit commander, Eugen Eis, who is unfortunately not in a position to take the chair.'

Eugen Eis was not in a position to take any chair. The village Home Guard leader was lying in his girl-friend's bed, alone and on his stomach. His bottom, substantial like everything else about him and recently subjected to the attention of Dr Gensfleisch, exhibited a heavy bandage decoratively stained with ointment and iodine.

'Our respected comrade,' Johannes Eichler explained, 'has sustained an injury. In the doctor's opinion it will be some days before he is fully restored to us.'

The bulk of Eichler's listeners were young. Their faces gleamed in the lamplight like turnip-ghosts. Their eyes, pale blue for the most part, shone with devotion. Being docile and reliable youngsters, they were always prepared to believe anyone who spoke with sufficient conviction.

'I know I can be frank with you,' Eichler boomed, 'so I'll tell you in confidence what really happened. Someone turned a dog loose on Eugen Eis today—on your Home Guard commander.'

A few of those present cried 'Shame!' This was one of the two commonest words in their vocabulary. Its commendatory counterpart was 'Bravo!' The Home Guard could subsist on these two exclamations for hours on end.

'Someone has dared to attack a member of our organization,' Eichler pursued. He looked outraged, if not horrified. 'I'm worried, my friends. This is the thin end of the wedge. Before we know where we are we'll be picked off one by one. I ask you, are we going to take this lying down?'

No, no men worthy of the name could take such a thing lying down. By savaging Eugen Eis, Tyras had bitten the entire Home Guard in its collective backside.

Johannes Eichler ordered a round of beer and schnapps, then requested his esteemed and trusty comrades to sing

his favourite song, *I hunt the stag in leafy glade*. They not
only sang it, but sang it with the requisite fervour and volume.

Eichler regarded the singers with some satisfaction, simultaneously keeping an ex-sergeant-major's watchful eye on
Scharfke, who always served his customers short measure when
conviviality reached its height.

The defenders of hearth and home continued to bellow
about the noble art of venery. They were all proud huntsmen
at this uplifting moment, though they only functioned as
beaters when the hunting season actually opened in late
autumn. Shooting stag was reserved for the local gentry. While
the song lasted, however, the world—and the forests of
Masuria in particular—belonged to them.

The Home Guard brought their performance to an emotional conclusion, stretching the last note like a rubber band.
Eichler rose to his feet. 'Friends and comrades,' he began,
and the more sensitive individuals seemed to hear their hearts
—their warm German hearts—beat higher.

What they actually heard was the tinkling of glass. A win-
dowpane broke, and in flew a longish cylindrical object. It
slithered along the table, sending glasses flying, then came
to rest. A second object of identical shape came hurtling
through the window after it.

The assembled company stared at the two missiles. They
were roughly the size and shape of a medium-sized coffee-pot,
and equipped with a stout handle about a foot long. Each
of them emitted a plume of thick, oily, dark blue smoke and
a sharp hissing sound.

'Grenades!' someone screamed.

They flung themselves to the ground, dived into corners,
leapt for the door and windows. They jostled each other with
pale and contorted faces, trampling each other in their quest
for safety. They lashed out with their fists and tried to shield
themselves with their neighbours' bodies. Brimming glasses
overturned, and their contents cascaded on to the bleeding,
sweating, writhing bodies on the floor. There was a sudden
stench like a burst sewer outlet.

The grenades gave a dull phut and lay there, silent and
harmless. They had not gone off—nor could they have,
because the charges had been removed. There was a final
hiss like that of a cigar-butt dropping into a puddle, followed
by a brooding silence.

One or two figures stirred. Gingerly, warily, they shuffled forward on their knees. Amazement dawned on their pale faces, then relief. Finally, there was a burst of convulsive laughter. The first to react was one of Uschkurat's sons, who earned a reputation for initiative and presence of mind by calling for volunteers.

'After them!' he yelled in trumpet-like tones, and charged out of the room. Several Home Guardsmen followed him, eager to find the man or men who had made them wallow in the filth on the Gasthaus floor, but it was a vain hope. After pausing for a moment to savour the spectacle they had engineered, the practical jokers had high-tailed it for safety.

Johannes Eichler had by now succeeded in extricating himself from a pile of fellow-victims. 'Who did it?' he croaked. Not pausing for breath, he supplied a momentous answer to his own question. 'I can well imagine who did it, but he won't get away with it—not with us. This settles it. There'll be no half-measures from now on. Half-measures would be plain suicide. As of now, I go into action personally!'

On the evening of the same day Alfons Materna left his farm on what he described as urgent business.

He strolled down Horse Hill and across Dog's Meadow, making for the village. The night sky glittered with stars and the moon sailed ponderously between scudding shreds of cloud. The trees seemed to caress the sky with gentle fingers.

Materna entered Constable Klinger's house at almost the same moment as the Home Guard were routed by two dud hand-grenades in the back room of the Gasthaus. Materna said: 'Sorry to bother you at this hour. My watch says twelve minutes past nine. Is that right?'

The policeman glanced at the clock on his mantelpiece and nodded. 'Don't worry, I'm never off duty.' Klinger was a man of modest intellect, but there was no doubting his dogged integrity. He was a born custodian of law and order.

'Have you completed your report on my son's death?'

'Of course. It's all straightforward.'

Materna felt a momentary touch of pity for Klinger. The worthy constable was not a native of Maulen, and he was quite unequal to the special demands of the district. His eyes were as blue as open sky and his green tunic was worn but scrupulously clean.

'Can you tell me the result of your inquiries?'

Klinger cleared his throat. 'Identical statements made by a number of independent witnesses confirm that the sequence of events was as follows: while out walking on Maulen Moor, your son Alfred Materna trod on a mine or unexploded shell dating from the last war. He was killed by the ensuing detonation.'

'You seriously believe that?'

'Herr Materna,' said Klinger, 'what I believe, assume or consider possible is quite beside the point. I am governed by the results of my inquiries, by witnesses' statements given under oath.'

'What if I prove you wrong?'

Klinger became restive and started to pace up and down his office. Three maps adorned the walls, one of Prussia, one of East Prussia, and the third of Maulen and its environs.

'Herr Materna,' he said at length, 'why are you making these insinuations? What do you want, exactly?'

'The last thing I want is to see you lose your job. You're a man with a sense of fair play. I rather doubt if your successor would have such a large ration of the same thing.'

Klinger began to breathe heavily like a man in the teeth of a gale. He said: 'There's absolutely nothing wrong with my final report.'

'Except that it's incorrect. I can prove, if I choose to, that my son was fatally wounded during an illegal Home Guard training exercise—by three hand-grenades, to be precise. I can produce a statement by one of the three men involved —again, if I choose to. I'm referring to my son Hermann. He was there.'

'Not your son!' Klinger exclaimed. 'But that's terrible!'

'Terrible? For whom? For you, for me, for the members of that patriotic kindergarten, for the accuracy of your final report?'

'If your story can really be proved,' Klinger said, 'I'm in the cart.'

'You're right.'

Klinger looked bewildered. 'What do you want me to do?'

'Think it over carefully. Take your time. I'll expect you

up at the farm tomorrow afternoon, either to take a statement or for a drink and a quiet chat between friends, if you like.'

'Just cover me, men, that's all,' Johannes Eichler commanded. 'Two of you outside on the road within call, two guarding the gate and two more patrolling the outskirts of the farm—but don't do anything without a direct order from me. I want to make that quite clear. Don't be provoked into doing anything rash.'

With that, Eichler patted the service automatic in his pocket and stepped through the gate into Materna's farmyard. No one tried to stop him. Tyras only went into action at the sound of a whistle, and Jacob Jablonski was devoting himself to a jug of schnapps at Materna's suggestion.

Eichler stumped into the house. 'Materna!' he called challengingly.

'He's not here,' replied a soft voice.

The voice belonged to Frau Margarete. Eichler's expression changed to one of rapture as he strode masterfully towards her.

'We hardly saw each other for years,' he cried, 'and now, in the last two days . . .'

'It's an ill wind,' Margarete said hesitantly. 'Seeing you means a great deal to me.'

'No more than it does to me,' Eichler assured her, squeezing the hand which reposed so trustingly in his. 'Looking at you, I realize how much I've missed in life.'

Fifteen years earlier, when Margarete gave her vote to Alfons Materna, she had accepted his two motherless children and his already noticeable eccentricities in the belief that Materna and Masuria were one. But Alfons had failed in her eyes. He devoted himself to superficial pleasures and spurned local society. Johannes Eichler was steadily overhauling him, both socially and materially.

'Are you alone?' Eichler asked.

'Brigitte and Hermann have both gone to bed. The maid seems to have disappeared, and Jablonski is probably drinking himself into a stupor in some corner or other. You can't imagine what I have to put up with, Johannes.'

'And your husband?'

'Prowling around the village. He didn't tell me where he was going, but then he never does.'

Eichler pricked up his ears. 'Can you tell me when he left the house? It could be important.'

'Just before nine.'

'Interesting,' mused Eichler. 'All the same, I can't believe he'd be as careless as that.'

'What's happened?'

'An extremely unpleasant business—fortunately without serious consequences. It isn't absolutely certain that Materna was involved, but there are certain pointers in that direction.'

'Johannes,' she said softly, 'why did everything turn out the way it did? I've thought about it so often, but I can't find the answer.'

'It's been the same with me,' Eichler said. Though limited, his imagination was adequate by Maulen standards. To him, Margarete was still the young girl of yore, radiantly blonde and touchingly trustful. Her ample charms were not of the usual rustic kind. In Eichler's eyes she was a lady of breeding whom anyone but Alfons Materna would have looked up to and respected.

'I don't suppose anyone could guess what I've been through,' Margarete murmured. 'A weaker woman would have cracked under the strain.'

Johannes Eichler reached across the table and took her hand. 'Margarete,' he said gravely, 'you couldn't have loved Alfred more if he'd been your own. In my opinion he deserves a proper funeral, and I'm prepared to give him one. I'm sure it's what you would want. You must help me.'

'You can rely on me, Johannes. I know I can rely on you.'

Alfons Materna walked back to his farm. He had started to lay his traps, but it might be a long time before they caught any wolves. He inhaled the warm and agreeable night-scent that rose from the rich earth, a scent reminiscent of fresh-baked bread. The grain was ripe for harvesting. He glanced up at the sky.

Jacob Jablonski hurried out to meet him, swaying slightly.

'Eichler's inside,' he announced in a subdued voice. 'He's holding your wife's hand and whispering in her ear. Surely you're not going to stand for that?'

'Let's have some details,' Materna replied. He took Jablonski's arm and steered him towards Horse Hill, where the copper beech stood sharply silhouetted against the midnight-blue sky.

'Eichler arrived when there was no one watching the house,' Jablonski explained. 'Tyras was asleep and I was pouring schnapps down my throat, but I heard him. I climbed through the window into the garden, doubled round the house and peered into the kitchen. There they were, the two of them, cooing like turtle-doves.'

'What were they talking about?'

'You, of course. It wasn't flattering, either.'

'Interesting,' said Materna, '—made to order, in fact. Is that all?'

'Isn't it enough?'

'Not quite.' Materna stared pensively at the moon, breathing deeply. He seemed to relish the heavy perfume of the night.

'She was squirming like a bitch on heat,' Jablonski said scornfully. 'Aren't you annoyed?'

'On the contrary,' Materna replied, 'I'm delighted.'

Jablonski laid a hand on his friend and employer's arm. 'It's all been too much for you, Alfons. You've been through a lot in the last couple of days, but don't worry, it'll pass.'

'It could be a new beginning,' Materna said. 'I haven't worked out all the angles yet, but I know one thing: whoever comes unstuck, it won't be me.'

3

The day of Alfred Materna's funeral dawned. Pale as buttermilk, the sun quickly threw off its heavy mantle of moisture and burned with greedy savagery, enveloping the countryside in arid heat. The soil was like brick-dust.

The sexton made an early start on the grave. Fat-bellied home-made wreaths stood ready to hand. Alfred's stepmother, brother, and sister had kept vigil over his coffin inside the church. Outside the door, sentries posted by the Home Guard relieved each other at two-hourly intervals.

Alfons Materna was still asleep.

Christian Scharfke could not sleep, partly because of the

noises coming from his daughter's room. Eugen Eis was grunting loudly, in this instance because of his lacerated behind. However, what disturbed the landlord more than anything else was that Materna had failed to give orders for a post-funerary celebration at the Gasthaus.

Johannes Eichler, too, spurned sleep. He had gone to bed late but was on his feet again at an early hour. Thanks to Eis's honourable wounds, the whole burden of responsibility lay on his shoulders.

Eichler had organized the Home Guard death-watch roster, conducted telephone conversations with units and associations in neighbouring villages, conferred with the major, harangued the parish council, bullied the parson. 'Alfred was one of us,' he adjured them. 'We can't let him down.'

Nobody wanted to do that, but the decision rested with his father alone, and his father was incommunicado.

While Alfons Materna was still asleep, Jacob Jablonski went into action on his behalf. He called on Constable Klinger and laid information which was to add considerably to the complexities of an already complex situation.

According to the entry in the policeman's daily record book, timed 8.20 a.m., Jablonski's story ran as follows: Tyras, Materna's watchdog, was dead, presumed poisoned. The culprit was unknown, but Johannes Eichler had been in the area of Materna's farm the night before, accompanied by at least four men.

Having taken note of this report, the policeman visited the scene of the alleged crime. On-the-spot findings: the dog Tyras was indubitably dead, though whether his death had resulted from foul play or natural causes was not immediately apparent. A thorough investigation was guaranteed.

In pursuance of his inquiries, Constable Klinger thereupon —at 9.10 a.m., according to his notebook—called on Johannes Eichler. Eichler not only dismissed any suspicions in regard to himself and his men but laid a complaint of his own, at this stage against a person or persons unknown. On his submission, two stick-grenades had been hurled through a closed window into the middle of an unsuspecting circle of beer-drinkers.

'I hope you've carefully considered the implications of your complaint,' Klinger said guardedly.

'You'd do better to ask Materna that question,' Eichler

retorted. 'He's the one who started this—and all because of a dead dog. I'm only acting in self-protection. You're not suggesting I withdraw my complaint, are you?'

'Far from it. I'm just asking you to think it over carefully.'

'I'm not a mealy-mouthed pacifist, Herr Klinger—you ought to know that by now. If anyone provokes me I hit back.'

With a shrug, the policeman unscrewed his fountain pen and flipped open his notebook. 'Where's it all leading to?' he muttered as he began to write.

'You ought to be ashamed of yourself, Materna,' Margarete snapped.

Alfons Materna yawned amiably. 'Good morning, my dear. What have I got to be ashamed of? I haven't killed anyone —yet.'

'You ought to be ashamed of yourself,' she repeated. 'It's disgraceful, the way you behave!'

'You're chirpy this morning.' Materna yawned again. 'Breakfast won't be long, I take it.'

'I've been up all night, unlike you.'

'I slept all night,' he conceded. 'There's nothing like a quart of schnapps to give a man a good night's sleep and a hearty appetite. That's why I'd like a good breakfast—six eggs, say, and a couple of slices of raw ham half an inch thick.'

'Materna,' Margarete said sternly, 'I insist on our son having a decent funeral.'

'So do I. The only trouble is, we may not be talking about the same thing.'

'People want to pay their respects,' Margarete said. 'The whole village wants to be there, so I've heard, and a large number of local associations are planning to turn up.'

'They can go to hell for all I care.'

'What if I begged you to change your mind?'

'Begged? That's a new one, coming from you. All right, if it means so much to you, I might reconsider my decision if you meet certain conditions.'

'What do you want?'

'First, some breakfast. Second, Dog's Meadow. You brought the land with you when you married me, but I've never been able to touch it without your say-so. I've never liked that, as you know.'

'So you want a free hand. Is that a condition?'

'No, just a suggestion. You've made a special request, so I don't see why I shouldn't do the same.'

Dog's Meadow covered an area of almost nine acres. Its main value lay in its proximity to the centre of Maulen. Only separated from the heart of the village by the schoolhouse, it was a little-used stretch of open ground which cried out for development. Beyond it lay various small-holdings and beyond them the commanding bulk of the Materna estate, whose boundaries extended as far as the next village, traversing the forest and the southern part of Maulen Moor and running down to the lake.

'I'm willing to give you full powers over Dog's Meadow, Materna, but on one condition: you mustn't sell it or add it to your personal holding in the land register.'

'I agree,' Materna said.

'And Alfred gets a proper funeral?'

'He does. I suppose you're prepared to confirm our agreement in writing?'

'I am.'

'Don't. I'll make sure the lawyer pays us a call this morning—well before the funeral.'

Materna was still breakfasting when the Terrible Twins arrived. They sidled into the kitchen and stationed themselves in front of him, grinning expectantly.

'Well,' Peter Bachus demanded, 'what do you say now?'

'I'm having my breakfast,' Materna replied.

Konrad Klinger lowered his voice confidentially. 'Heard what happened at the Gasthaus last night?'

'Of course.' Materna dissected his last slice of ham with care. 'These things get around.'

'Well?' The Terrible Twins bent forward avidly, like two question-marks.

'I don't like awarding prizes for that sort of caper,' Materna said slowly, 'but if you really want to know what I think—well, it was a bit crude.'

'Effective, though.' Konrad Klinger clearly expected his words to fall on understanding ears. 'You should have seen them! They stampeded like cattle in a thunderstorm. Heroic, they were. I bet some of them browned their pants.'

Materna looked grave. 'I must congratulate you on your

powers of imagination. I'm assuming, of course, that you weren't there at the time. That would have been dangerous.'

'For whom?' asked Peter Bachus.

'Why, for you, if you'd been responsible.' Materna pushed his empty plate away with an abrupt gesture. 'You don't imagine our heroic Home Guardsmen enjoy being turned into panic-stricken cattle?'

'You disappoint us, Herr Materna,' Konrad Klinger said sorrowfully. 'We expected better things of you.'

Materna wagged his head. 'How gloriously young you are!'

'It was fun—that's for certain.'

'I believe you. However, you seem to have overlooked one small but important point: nothing in life is free. What if they try to pay me back for something you did?'

'We didn't mean to make trouble for you, Herr Materna,' Konrad Klinger said fervently. 'I think we'd better be going now,' Peter Bachus added.

'Why only two grenades?' Materna asked abruptly. 'It took three to kill Alfred.'

The boys halted in their tracks as if they had been brought up short by a brick wall. 'That's simple,' Konrad Klinger said. 'We couldn't get hold of more than two.'

'Did you leave any clues behind?'

'What, us?' Peter Bachus smiled. 'Of course not.'

'I wouldn't be too sure. Eichler has already lodged a complaint—against a person or persons unknown, for the time being. He's gunning for me, presumably, but he may try and get at me through you.'

'So what?' Konrad Klinger said belligerently. 'If he does, we'll hit back.'

'I know where we can lay our hands on three land-mines,' Peter Bachus put in. He sounded eager for the fray. 'We could blow up the whole Gasthaus—and the parish hall as well, if we wanted to.'

'Forget it,' Materna said firmly. 'Go home and stay there for the time being. Meanwhile, I'll try to keep you out of gaol, which is where you belong, if only for being so foolish. The very thought of it! Blowing up buildings without knowing the first thing about explosives!'

'We're always grateful for expert advice,' Konrad Klinger assured him.

Materna burst out laughing. 'Get lost, the pair of you. That's my first piece of advice. You won't get a second instalment unless you do as I say.'

'From now on,' Johannes Eichler said resolutely, 'we go over to the attack.'

'You mean there's no turning back?' Eugen Eis was sprawled sideways in his arm-chair by the window, but he had temporarily forgotten about the late Tyras's tooth-marks. 'You really think Materna will give way? What about Jablonski? They can be violent, those two—I'm the living proof of that. I wouldn't put it past them to clear the churchyard by force.'

Eichler had set up his headquarters in the Gasthaus, partly so that his immobilized lieutenant could share in the councils of war. The first-floor room that had been set aside for this purpose afforded a good view of the village square.

'Materna in sight!' Eis called from his post beside the window. 'Yes, there he is, the swine. I'd give a lot to know what he's up to.'

Alfons Materna was crossing the village square in his normal working clothes. Every eye followed his progress as he clumped along in his heavy boots, grinning at the black-garbed people who had arrived early for the funeral.

'He's gone into Klinger's house,' Eis reported. 'Maybe he wants to hold the funeral under police protection. Materna's quite capable of making a monkey out of Klinger.'

Johannes Eichler did not speak for some minutes. Eis secretly enjoyed seeing his employer labouring under difficulties. The first waves of noise from would-be funeral guests assembled in the bar-room of the Gasthaus drifted up through the floor.

Eichler started to tick off his assets. 'I already have the approval of the parish council. I can count on the support of a large number of our friends in the organization. The parson won't interfere, nor will Klinger once I've had a word with him. As for Materna, he might take on twenty men but he won't mix it with two hundred.'

Scharfke appeared. 'I'm fed up,' he announced. 'The mourners don't know what to do with themselves. The only one who's drinking is Uschkurat. He's putting it away like water, but he's paying for it himself. You ought to hear the things he's saying.'

'What sort of things?'

'You'd be surprised.' The atmosphere was getting Sharfke down—too few happy faces, too many dry throats. 'He was babbling about you a few minutes back. I didn't like his tone, either.'

Eichler decided to act. 'A beer and a schnapps all round,' he ordered. 'Chalk it up to me.'

'Materna and Klinger are crossing the square,' Eis reported from the window. 'Now they've separated. Materna's making for the vicarage. Klinger's heading straight this way.'

'A large beer and a double schnapps,' amended Eichler. Scharfke's face broke into a grin and Eis sat up on his cushions with an air of expectancy. 'A few more minutes, and we'll know where we stand.'

Eichler fixed Klinger with a half-winning, half-warning gaze. 'My dear constable, I know what I saw—to wit, two hand-grenades.'

'They weren't primed.'

'No, but they might have been. Do you expect me to wait until I'm dead before I lodge a complaint?'

The policeman was sweating copiously in his thick tunic. Eichler sensed that the man was in need of help, and he thought he knew why. Klinger's own son had probably been involved in the grenade-throwing incident, in which case he had him in his pocket. Eichler was not mean-minded in such matters. He would treat the policeman with kid-gloves provided he was ready to co-operate, and this meant, in effect, that Eichler would determine the nature of the harmony that reigned between them from now on.

'Unfortunately,' Klinger said, 'I haven't yet managed to establish the identity of the guilty party or parties.'

'Really?' Eichler smiled disarmingly. 'You may not have far to seek. Haven't you had an occasional gleam of suspicion?'

'Suspicion isn't enough. I need evidence, and to get evidence I have to proceed methodically. In practice, this means that I must establish the source of the hand-grenades before I can identify the person or persons who threw them.'

Eichler's eyebrows rose. 'How do you make that out?'

'The instrument used in a crime usually provides the surest lead to the criminal himself,' Klinger explained. 'That being so, I have to ask myself the following questions: where did these hand-grenades come from? What were they doing in this district in the first place? How did they come into the possession of the guilty party or parties?'

There was a pause. Then Eichler said in a flat voice: 'You didn't think all that up by yourself, I'll be bound.'

The policeman contrived to be aware of certain facts without taking official cognizance of them. He knew about the arms dumps but had always studiously ignored their existence.

'The possession and storing of arms and ammunition is an indictable offence,' he said stoutly.

'No,' Eichler snapped, 'you couldn't have thought it out alone. Someone must have helped you, and I can imagine who—Materna, of course.'

The policeman neither confirmed nor denied this. He simply said, stubborn as a Masurian mule: 'Either I do a thing properly or not at all—that's the way I work.'

Johannes Eichler spent the next hour trying to change the policeman's mind. Having appealed to his patriotism, he resorted to veiled threats. He couldn't believe, he said, that Klinger, an ex-soldier with a fine record, was prepared to oppose the patriotic aspirations of the community.

The policeman perspired but refused to budge. 'I'm only doing my duty,' he said. 'I won't bend the law for anyone, myself included.'

At that moment the Reverend Dr Bachus appeared. Bursting almost boyishly into the room, he announced that he had good news.

Eichler subjected him to a suspicious stare. 'Has Materna been working on you too?'

'I suppose you could call it that,' the parson replied. His trousers were tucked into calf-length boots caked with mud. To Bachus, pastoral activities were only slightly more important than the tending of his cabbage-patch, the products of which carried greater weight with most of his flock than any exposition of the Holy Writ.

'Well,' said Eichler, 'don't tell me Materna's seen the light at last.'

Bachus folded his hands, which were shovel-sized and not unduly clean. 'I'm almost tempted to describe what has happened as an example of divine intervention.'

'It happens, so they say,' Klinger ventured in a benevolently neutral tone.

'To be explicit,' Bachus continued, with dignity, 'Alfons Materna has consented to the full-scale, public interment of his son Alfred. He will welcome anyone who wishes to attend —anyone at all. He made that quite clear.'

Klinger gave a muffled exclamation of relief, but Eichler continued to look suspicious. He knew Materna too well to feel reassured.

'He gave me his hand on it,' the parson went on eagerly. 'All he wants is a worthy funeral for his beloved son. Surely we can't deny him that?'

'On the contrary,' Eichler said promptly. 'But God help him if he's trying to set a trap for us. If he is, there'll be a double funeral.'

An hour before the last rites were due to take place Siegfried Grienspan turned up, perched on his bicycle like a gaunt black crow. Jacob Jablonski opened the gate for him.

Alfons Materna emerged from the house. 'Good to see you, Grienspan,' he called. 'I didn't know you were keen on funerals.'

The cattle-dealer smiled faintly. 'I just happened to be passing.'

'And you just happened to be wearing a dark suit. I hope the cattle appreciate your elegant appearance.'

Materna put an arm round Grienspan's shoulders and drew him into the house. When they were alone in the kitchen, he said: 'Thank you.'

Grienspan dropped wearily into a chair. Cycling through the glaring heat of high summer seemed to have taxed his strength. He produced a handkerchief and mopped his brow.

'At least you look calm and collected,' he said. 'I'm glad.'

'Take a closer look and you'll see that I'm positively cheerful.'

'So you should be,' Grienspan said. 'After all, death is only a stepping-stone to another world—a better one, presumably.'

'You mean the people who helped Alfred to get there did him a good turn?'

Grienspan rose and began to pace the room restlessly, kneading his hands together. Suddenly he came to a halt.

'I had a brother once. You never knew him. I don't suppose you even knew he existed. People used to say he was different from me, and they meant it as a compliment. He got himself killed in Berlin in the riots of spring 1919—killed for what he called his convictions. Do you understand? He just stood there and let them shoot him down.'

'Some people are made like that, Grienspan. It's an honourable thing to do, even if it isn't always the best solution.'

'You say that, Materna, but what are you doing? Almost the same as my brother.'

Materna smiled. 'I've seen three things today, three things and three people that moved me. The three things were the rose outside my window, the crystal-clear water flowing into the trough for my cows, and a tree standing out against the sky. The first of the people was Jacob Jablonski, who has the same sort of blood in his veins as I do. Then there was Maria, my deaf-mute maidservant, who can embrace the whole world in a single gesture—who makes me more and more conscious of being alive with every passing day. Finally, Grienspan, there was you. Seeing you proved to me that there is such a thing as friendship after all.'

'What an obstinate man you are,' Grienspan sighed. 'You're always indulging in pipe-dreams—always trying to move mountains and change the course of rivers.'

'Things can be changed.'

'Possibly, but what about people?'

'People too. One can but try—one must try, in fact.'

Siegfried Grienspan shook his head. 'Aren't you afraid of over-reaching yourself?' he said slowly. 'But perhaps I haven't quite understood you.'

'Nobody understands anybody.' Materna seemed amused, but there was a hint of sadness in his grey eyes. 'It's one of the facts of life.'

'Perhaps I ought to go and leave you to yourself.'

'And miss all the fun?' Materna gave an almost soundless chuckle. 'I shall be very hurt if you do.'

'You're a prize joker, Materna!'

'Save your congratulations for later. I don't know if my calculations are correct, but I'm pretty sure they are. Human folly runs strictly to form.'

The rites attending the burial of Alfred Materna began at the appointed time. Punctuality was one of the most inbred virtues of Maulen's inhabitants, always provided they were sober. The death-knell rang out like the chimes of an ancient but reliable clock.

'Duty calls,' said the Reverend Dr Bachus, slipping into his surplice.

The coffin, its lid now firmly closed, stood in the open space in front of the altar. It was heaped with flowers, principally roses, which grew luxuriantly at this time of year. Flanking it were candelabra and potted laurels, and in front of it lay a strip of dark blue carpet adorned in yellow—ostensibly gold—with symbolic crosses, fishes, and crowns.

Old Mother Mischgoreit, now living rent-free, elbowed her way resolutely to the fore. 'The poor, brave, boy,' she crooned. 'How he must have smiled when Our Heavenly Father gathered him to His bosom!'

'Hogwash!' growled Jacob Jablonski. 'How could he smile with a face like a lump of porridge?'

'God have mercy on his soul!' Uschkurat said in a penetrating voice. All true Masurians were supposed to be capable of overcoming three hangovers in one day, and the mayor had just weathered his first. With a groan, he wiped his streaming brow.

Gottlieb Speer, who was standing close by, said solemnly: 'The boy died like a hero.'

'It was fate, that's what it was!' hissed Old Mother Mischgoreit.

'Quiet, please!' came the subdued but penetrating voice of the verger. 'Only the vicar talks in church. Everyone else prays or sings when instructed.'

The mourners bowed their heads. Uschkurat slumped into a pew, anxiously supported by Speer. Old Mother Mischgoreit knelt in the centre of the aisle.

The next of kin were grouped round the coffin. Margarete Materna, a black silk veil floating about her pale face, had stationed herself at its foot. Immediately behind her stood her daughter and step-son. Hermann, the grenade-thrower, stood at attention and stared solemnly into space. Brigitte sobbed into a handkerchief from time to time. Peering over the top of it, she noted that the eyes of many male mourners rested on her with appreciation.

Alfons Materna did not appear until the last minute. With an expressionless face he took up his post to one side and stood there like a stone.

'Let us pray!' intoned the Reverend Dr Bachus.

The third and fourth rows were composed of farm employees. Maria, the maidservant, stared at the floor. Jacob Jablonski had closed his eyes apparently lost in thought. Behind them stood the motionless figures of Materna's cow-man, stable-hands and tenants.

'Let us bow our heads in humble silence before the majesty of death,' said the Reverend Dr Bachus.

The congregation complied with this suggestion, though few of them felt easy in their minds. Johannes Eichler had not arrived yet, and everyone was wondering what would happen when he did. Be that as it might, the funeral had already earned a unique place in the annals of Maulen. The church was full to overflowing and the nave was thronged from door to chancel with mourners of both sexes and every age.

Clubs, associations and para-military organizations from Maulen and miles around had all sent strong representative contingents. Among them was the Gross-Grieben Veterans' Association, whose illustrious and historic banner had once been adorned with a red-white-and-black ribbon by the very hands of Field Marshal Hindenburg. This bright banner now pointed in the direction of the coffin.

Also present was the mixed-voice choir from Siegwalde, famed throughout Masuria and twice victorious at the regional choir festival. Its banner bore the edifying motto 'Through Melody to Liberty!' Next to the choir stood a detachment from the Seebergen Rifle Club, whose summer festivals enjoyed wide popularity. The Rifle Club's motto was 'Aim True for the Fatherland!'

Delegations from veterans' associations, fire brigades, sports clubs and savings groups were also in attendance, packed shoulder to shoulder. School classes had been marched into church en bloc to receive practical instruction in regional customs and patriotic ceremonial.

The local Home Guard unit had requested permission to carry the coffin containing their comrade's dead brother from the church to the grave-yard, there to deposit it in its last resting-place. Materna had not actually rejected this polite request, and his silence had been construed as approval. The only question was, who would head the Home Guard in Eugen Eis's absence?

The question was soon answered. Johannes Eichler had assumed personal command. He marched into church at the head of a picked detachment dressed in field-grey wind-cheaters. Booted feet rang on the flagstones, resolutely and in unison, making for the altar, the coffin, and Alfons Materna.

At that moment the introductory hymn came to an end. The organ gave a final groan and relapsed into silence. A deathly hush fell.

Pale and rigid, Eichler marched up the aisle with the in-exorability of a Juggernaut. Three paces from the coffin he halted abruptly. Keeping his eyes fixed on Materna, he put one arm behind him to receive the wreath of oak-leaves which a minion placed in his hand. The red-white-and-black ribbon carried the legend: 'To Alfred Materna from his Loyal Comrades.'

Alfons Materna turned and looked back down the aisle to where Siegfried Grienspan stood in the lee of a pillar. He was smiling for all to see, but some of those who noted his expression said later that it sent a shiver down their spine.

And then the impossible happened. It happened just as the Reverend Dr Bachus was adjuring the congregation to pray for the soul of the dear departed.

Alfons Materna began to move—slowly, mechanically, not unlike a puppet on strings. He took three or four seemingly interminable steps in Johannes Eichler's direction and then halted, staring at him.

The seconds dragged painfully by. Then Materna extended his arm towards Eichler. It was his right arm, and the hand that went with it was open, not clenched. In a voice which could be heard by all, he said: 'Good of you to come.'

'It was my duty to,' Eichler replied with an effort. He felt like a man who hears the gentle patter of summer rain instead of the hailstorm he had been expecting.

'I shan't forget this in a hurry,' Materna said, and his words were audible in every corner of the church. 'I can assure you of that.'

'Thank you,' Eichler said solemnly. He grasped the proffered hand—he had no choice, with several hundred eyes watching him—and bowed stiffly from the waist, possibly to hide his confusion.

'Just like Hindenburg and the Kaiser!' wheezed old Mother Mischgoreit. 'Just like the photograph above my late husband's bed!'

But the Reverend Dr Bachus cried: 'Let us give thanks! God moves in a mysterious way His wonders to perform!'

Everyone agreed that the Reverend Dr Bachus excelled himself on the day of Alfred Materna's funeral. His voice competed successfully with the organ and his outspread arms sought to fold the whole of Maulen—Materna and Eichler included —to his fatherly bosom.

'I can only describe what has just occurred here as uplifting—an example to us all!' he exclaimed. 'It is a divine dispensation.'

Old Mother Mischgoreit sobbed with delight. Uschkurat clapped a hand to his mouth and tottered out with Speer hurrying solicitously at his heels. Materna and Eichler continued to stand side by side in the first row of mourners like oven-fresh buns on a tray. The arch-enemies seemed to be enveloped in a thick, gelatinous film of unanimity. The organist pulled out all his stops.

'What an edifying sight,' mused Konrad Klinger. 'Two men standing in front of Alfred's coffin—one brought him into the world and the other showed him out.'

Peter Bachus snorted. 'Nothing but clots wherever you look, and Materna's the worst of the lot.'

'Is he?' asked Konrad Klinger. The question was addressed not to his friend Peter but to the man who stood near by, leaning disconsolately against a pillar.

Siegfried Grienspan did not reply. He pulled out a handkerchief and blew his nose.

All that the inhabitants of Maulen registered was that the reconciliation between the two village bell-wethers seemed to be complete. When the men of the Home Guard lifted the coffin on to their stalwart shoulders the first to follow them out were Eichler and Materna. Then came Margarete and the other chief mourners. The whole of Maulen and district streamed after them, thronging the churchyard.

A second milestone in this momentous day had been reached. This consisted of funeral oration, indulgently referred to by the Reverend Dr Bachus as 'lay sermons'.

The first address was delivered by a member of the Home Guard. 'We shall never forget you, Alfred!' he declared with simple brevity, and dumped his wreath beside the grave.

Other equally laconic speakers followed his example. The Masurians were not a race of orators, being more given to deeds than words. 'Farewell, Alfred!' one of the Home Guard representatives called in a voice choked with emotion. 'God rest his soul,' cried another, and a third: 'He died for his comrades and his country!' The renowned choir from Siegwalde proceeded to sing the song which had won it the regional championship. This ran:

> Through valleys green once more I'll roam,
> Where German sky-lark ever sang.
> Once more I'll tread the fields of home
> And praise the soil from whence I sprang.

As soon as the tide of universal emotion had ebbed a little Johannes Eichler stepped up to the open grave to deliver what he imagined would be the final address, not omitting to consult Materna first. 'You don't mind?' he asked in tones of comradely correctitude. 'Not at all,' Materna replied, and everyone in the vicinity noted the exchange with satisfaction.

Eichler stared down into the grave for several moments, seemingly a prey to strong emotions. Then he raised his head. His mouth opened and remained open as though words had failed him. Materna glanced at him solicitously, but he need not have worried.

'Esteemed Alfons Materna and family, dear friends, comrades! We are gathered here to bury one of our own—one of the best. We shall always honour his memory.

'Alfred saw the shape of things to come. Young as he was, he had the sort of community spirit we all strive for. He knew what love of country means—not sentimental claptrap, but something which a man must be ready to lay down his life for. That is precisely what he did.

'If we were all like him the future of our nation would be bright indeed. He is a warning and example to us all, and it should be our proud aim to emulate him. With heavy but uplifted hearts we take leave of you, Comrade Alfred. As one man, we bid you rest in peace.'

Silence fell. Eichler went over to Materna and extended his hand. Materna shook it. Old Mother Mischgoreit tottered with emotion but was propped up by Jacob Jablonski.

Grienspan shot a worried glance at the Terrible Twins, who were retiring from the churchyard at high speed. One of them emitted a loud farting noise as he went.

The bandmaster of Maulen's Volunteer Fire Brigade raised his baton and eighteen gleaming brass instruments launched into *Now thank we all our God*. Further rhetoric was temporarily drowned by the blare of trombones.

As soon as the prodigious clangour had died away the Reverend Dr Bachus stepped forward to pronounce the concluding prayer, but Materna held him back. Stationing himself at the graveside, he surveyed the faces around him with something akin to curiosity.

'We didn't allow for this,' Eichler whispered to the parson. 'It could mean trouble.'

Bachus merely shrugged. 'If he insists . . .' he sighed. 'After all, we can hardly stop him.'

A gentle breeze sprang up. It stirred the tree-tops and caressed the ribbons hanging from the wreaths. Margarete's veil billowed out, almost hiding Eichler's impassive face from view.

'What is a human life?' Alfons Materna asked. 'Every living creature has to die. People are dying all over the world, in the Far East, in Africa, America—here in Maulen, too. Chinese and Africans can die in droves without affecting us. We only think twice about death when we're directly involved—and then, perhaps, only during the few minutes it takes to bury our dead. Everyone has to make sacrifices —that's the conventional phrase, isn't it?

'And yet we ought to ask ourselves why such sacrifices have to be made. We are told that we live in an orderly world in which everything has a purpose. In that case, every sacrifice must have a purpose too.

'I am a father who has lost his son. That isn't very remark-

able in itself. The death of a human being can be entirely
commonplace. It needn't necessarily be associated with
questions of law and justice, but if it is—what then?

'There is only one conclusion to be drawn, and I shall not
try to escape it. I promise my dead son, here and now, that
he will rest in peace. I shall make it my business to see that
he does.'

'My God,' muttered Grienspan, who was standing in the
background, 'I hope nobody understands him.'

His fears were groundless. People appeared to have heard
what they wanted to hear. Perceptibly relieved, Johannes
Eichler extended his hand once more and Materna grasped it
for the second time. The bystanders almost broke into
applause.

The Reverend Dr Bachus intoned a final blessing and the
brass band struck up *Old Comrades*. The mourners formed
up to the sound of this stirring march and proceeded in
close order to the Gasthaus, where cool drinks awaited them by
the bucketful.

A few minutes later Alfred Materna's grave was just one
lonely mound among a hundred others. Maulen's churchyard had space for many more.

4

'Men are creatures of habit,' Johannes Eichler declared, pregnant with thought, 'but they can't be allowed to stay that way
or their lives lack purpose. They have to set their sights on
higher things.'

The words were addressed to Eugen Eis. Eis was listening
with outward reverence, though in his view Eichler had been
giving vent to rather too many grandiose ideas of late. They
didn't amount to much in practice. Action was called for if
Maulen was to flourish.

'To my mind there's only one thing that matters,' Eis said.
'It's time to settle Materna's hash once and for all.'

'No need to worry about him,' Eichler scoffed, lolling back
in his office chair. His belly swelled like a captive balloon
under slow inflation. 'Materna's a dead duck. I've got more

important things to worry about—moral values and finer feelings, if you like. They present special problems of their own.'

'Had a row with your housekeeper?' Eis inquired with a wink. 'One of the maids been giving trouble?'

'Nobody gives me trouble more than once.' Eichler glowered for a moment, then quickly reassumed a man-to-man smile. 'I'm inwardly dissatisfied, if you know what I mean. I suppose it's because I'm a perfectionist.'

'It's the same with me,' said Eis. 'Take Christine Scharfke, for instance. She does her level best, poor girl, but no one could call her perfect.'

'That's not what I meant, Eugen,' Eichler said sternly.

'Of course not,' Eis replied, once more the loyal devotee, 'you're thinking of higher things.'

'Precisely.' Eichler spoke with unalloyed gravity. He had been increasingly subject to these fits of meditation in recent weeks, even during convivial evenings in the Gasthaus. 'It's a German characteristic to strive for higher things, Eugen.'

'Of course,' Eis agreed, 'but what more do you want? They all eat out of your hand here these days—you've been winning all down the line.'

'I don't let it go to my head.' Eichler's self-congratulatory smile contained a hint of melancholy which suggested that his happiness was incomplete. He rose. 'I think I'll stretch my legs.'

'Feel like company?'

Eichler politely declined the offer. 'Thanks all the same. I'd sooner commune with nature by myself just at present.'

'They say Materna's got himself two new watchdogs,' Eis ventured. 'Jablonski was seen sharpening a knife earlier on, and don't forget what Fritz Fischer reported—two rifles and some ammunition were stolen from our dump in the last couple of days.'

Eichler permitted himself a superior smile. 'If Materna sets eyes on me he'll either raise his hat or go a mile out of his way to avoid me.'

'Are you scared of him?' Jablonski asked.

Materna raised his head. 'Does it look like it?'

'It does to me.'

'Good,' said Materna, 'I'm happy, but I'd be even happier

if you'd stop worrying about me and spend more time on those two new Alsatians.'

Jablonski used his cupped palm as a handkerchief, peasant-fashion and wiped the result on the seat of his pants. 'Maybe I ought to teach them to sit up and beg as soon as they hear Eichler's name,' he said scathingly.

'Like their master?' Materna smiled, screwed up his eyes as though aiming at a distant target. 'We all get the friends we deserve, Jacob. Aren't you my friend any longer?'

'I'm off to see about those dogs,' Jablonski said irritably. 'I don't answer stupid questions, especially when they come from you. Carry on like this and I'll be calling you by your surname before you know it.'

He left Materna sitting on the bench in front of the house, staring into the gathering dusk. The sky turned pink, the sun dipped behind the horizon like a coin dropping into a slot, and bluish shadows crept through the trees. One more day in Materna's life started to die. He shut his eyes.

When he opened them again he saw Maria standing beside him. Her face conveyed a question—the question it seemed to convey whenever she looked at him. 'What can I do?' it asked.

He nodded at her and began to pull off his boots. They were heavy with caked earth. Maria knelt down and helped him. There was an assurance and grace about her movements. She moved like a dancer even when she was binding sheaves or spreading dung—Materna had often watched her at her work with secret pleasure.

'Do you think I'm begging like a dog?' he asked.

Maria shook her head. Long strands of shining hair fell across her face. As always, she seemed to understand every word, even though she was a deaf-mute.

'I'm not an animal and I'll never behave like one, whatever happens—you believe that, don't you?'

She nodded. Her face beamed. It was a smooth, oval, almost childish face, but sweetly mature in outline. The graceful arc of her neck led downwards to a softly curving bosom which not even the folds of her coarse linen dress could hide.

She turned her head, as if by instinct. 'Maria,' came a loud voice from the door. 'Into the house with you this instant!'

The voice belonged to Margarete. Maria seemed to under-

stand her too, because she hurried into the house with
Materna's boots clasped to her breast.

'You ought to be gentler with her,' Materna said in a
mild voice. 'She deserves better treatment.'

'She'll have to go,' Margarete snapped. 'Things can't go
on like this.'

'She stays,' Materna said quietly. He looked up at his wife
as she stood there, breathing fast. Making demands was in
her nature, just as it was one of his main functions to
reject them. 'I still own this house, in case you'd forgotten.'

'But she's in love with you!' Margarete protested. 'Anyone with half an eye can see that.'

'I'm flattered.' Materna gave a slight groan as he bent
down to straighten his socks. 'It's a rare thing for someone
to love someone else—really love them without making any
demands on them. I certainly wouldn't call that grounds for
dismissal.'

Margarete shook her head sadly. 'How little I mean to you!
I've never been so shamefully aware of it as I have in the
last few months.'

Locals who thought they knew Alfons Materna used to
say that he had never been easy to understand. He had always
cherished a liking for dubious company. Various stories were
told of him as a boy—that he used to converse with animals
as if they were human beings, that he had fed and nursed a
sick tramp in a barn, even though the man was wanted by
the police, that he had stolen schnapps for a drink-sodden
old woman just before her death. During the war he had been
punished for fraternizing with P.O.W.s in spite of repeated
warnings, and never rose beyond the rank of private.

Added to this, Materna had always defended Jablonski
against outsiders. He had ostentatiously shared his lunch
with him at school, helped him with household chores and
accepted numerous thrashings on his behalf—and all, it was
alleged, with a view to turning Jablonski into his devoted
slave and acolyte.

What people found even more suspicious was the appearance in Maulen of Maria, the Polish deaf-mute. It was
thought to be 'indicative' that Grienspan, the Jewish cattle-
dealer, should have had a hand in this. Materna and Grienspan had set off for Poland on a goose-buying expedition one
summer day in 1922. They returned with Maria, then ten

w.   c

years old and allegedly an orphan. Materna became her father, mother, brother and who knew what else besides. At all events, no one could have been more devoted to him—some said submissive—than the silent foreigner.

'Speaking for myself,' Margarete said, 'I refuse to go on like this!'

Materna regarded her quizzically, 'You think I'm finished, don't you? I've had all the stuffing knocked out of me—that's what you think, isn't it?'

'I've simply made up my mind not to tolerate certain things any longer.'

'Now listen,' he said. 'If Maria loves me, that's her affair. If it worries you, that's your affair. If I choose to fall in love with Maria, that's my affair.'

'But you're married to me!'

'I've never forgotten that, Margarete, and I tell you quite frankly, it hasn't always been easy.'

Jablonski hurried up with his hands raised like a man warding off a blow. 'Eichler's coming up the hill,' he announced.

Materna rose to his feet. 'I'm going for a stroll and I may be some time. I'm sure my dear wife will make our honoured guest at home.'

'What do you mean by that?' Margarete demanded nervously.

'I always mean well, Margarete—didn't you know?' Materna walked briskly to the wooden gate at the back of the yard, but before he opened it he turned and faced his wife, who was staring after him fixedly. 'You've no idea how much I'm relying on you,' he called. 'I only hope you don't disappoint me.'

'What a pleasant surprise to find you here!' Eichler exclaimed. 'I really wanted a word with your husband.'

'Materna is temporarily detained,' Margarete said. 'You'll have to put up with me for the moment.'

'I can't think of anything I'd rather do.' Eichler smiled winningly and seized her hand. It was clean and smooth, and the light pressure of its fingers conveyed emotional warmth —towards him. 'You're a unique person,' he said.

Margarete dimpled with pleasure. 'Not everyone thinks so.'

Eichler was about to develop this theme when Jablonski

entered the room, grinning. He surveyed Margarete and her guest with undisguised curiosity. His grin broadened.

'Where's Materna?' Eichler demanded.

'In the woods, I should imagine,' Jablonski replied. 'He went in the direction of the lake.'

'I'll go and look for him, then.'

'He took his rifle with him,' Jablonski said casually.

'It takes more than a rifle to scare me,' Eichler sneered. He glanced at Margarete, determined to cut a good figure. 'Well, I'm off.'

'I'll come with you if you like,' Margarete said. 'A walk will do me good. I don't often get out of the house these days.'

'I'd take care, all the same,' Jablonski put in. 'Materna has been doing a lot of target practice with dummy figures. He must have at least a dozen scattered round these woods. Make sure you don't get in his line of fire.'

Eichler emitted a virile laugh. His sense of superiority soared like a kite in a gale. He strode manfully to the door and held it open for Margarete.

Leaving the farm, they traversed the fields where Materna's wheat was ripening—the heaviest, fattest ears for miles around, standing shoulder to shoulder like an army arrayed against the forces of hunger. This year as for years past, Materna would harvest a better crop than any other farmer in Masuria, Eichler noted with a touch of envy. However, Margarete's presence proved a pleasant distraction.

'Do you remember?' he asked, as they neared the trees.

Margarete nodded. She knew what he meant. They had walked through these woods together once before, long ago in the remote but unforgettable past. Reaching a clearing in the dense fir-trees, he had groped for her hand. Now, arriving at the same spot, he did likewise.

'Margarete,' he said.

'Johannes,' she replied.

Little remained to be said, though much remained to be done. Now, as then, the trees seemed to resemble a roof and the ground a bed.

'Let's sit down,' Eichler suggested.

On that far-off day, at that crucial moment, Alfons Materna had emerged from a neighbouring thicket. He greeted the recumbent couple warmly and sat down beside them without a flicker of embarrassment. Johannes Eichler, more sensitive then than now, had retired in haste. Materna had shamelessly exploited his opportunity to the full, and what had happened then had determined the course of Margarete's life —until now.

Now, as then, Alfons Materna was close by, standing in the lee of the alder-thicket with his rifle slung. Near him, armed with an oak cudgel, lurked Jacob Jablonski. Both men watched the scene that unfolded before them, Jablonski with fierce indignation, Materna with smiling composure.

Materna's smile froze abruptly as he caught sight of two more figures picking their way silently across the mossy ground. The Terrible Twins were clearly bent on pleasure.

'That's all I needed,' Materna whispered anxiously. 'They'll frighten the game away.'

Johannes Eichler bent over Margarete's supine form, pleasurably inhaling the scent of her body. What a woman she was, even now, and how undeniably worthy of him!

It was not Materna's voice that broke the spell this time, but it was as clear and youthful as his had been.

'Take care!' it called. 'There are ants round here. They crawl into everything, and it's a hell of a job to get rid of them.'

The Terrible Twins stood beside Margarete and Eichler, observing their idyll with little outward interest. Their boyish smiles could not have been more disarming.

'Can we help you in any way?' inquired Konrad Klinger.

Johannes Eichler heaved himself to his feet. 'What the hell do you want?' he roared. 'What are you doing here, anyway?'

'Just enjoying the air,' Peter Bachus replied pacifically. 'You can't expect us to walk around with our eyes shut.'

'I've had enough of you two!' Eichler bellowed. 'You're always making trouble in the village—always disturbing people.'

'Disturbing people?' queried Konrad Klinger. 'You mean —like now?'

'That explains everything,' Eichler said with menace. 'I can guess who put you up to this, and I know what to do about it!'

'You're poaching on my preserves,' Materna told the Terrible Twins. 'I don't like it.'

'We only wanted to help,' Konrad Klinger said politely. 'We were acting as beaters.'

Materna's face registered a mixture of irritation and indulgence. 'Every hunt has to be organized, and the more thoroughly the better.'

'I think I understand,' Peter Bachus replied. 'We're always open to suggestions, Herr Materna. Just tell us if there's anything you particularly want us to do.'

'Only one thing,' Materna said. 'Keep out of my private affairs.'

Konrad Klinger shook his head. 'It isn't as easy as that. We happen to dislike the same faces as you do. Anyway, what did you think of our gala performance just now?'

'Call it what you like,' Materna said. 'It could have some highly unpleasant consequences where you're concerned. Eichler doesn't appreciate comedy turns at his expense. Your only hope is to convince him that it was all a big misunderstanding. You weren't spying on him. You meant well but your motives were—as usual—misunderstood. That's what you must try and impress on everybody.'

'We'll do that!' Konrad said excitedly, realizing that a very special ball had just bounced into his court. 'We'll tell the truth. No one can have any objection to that, surely?'

The boys left Materna's wood and returned to the village, where they squatted on the steps of the cenotaph and held a council of war.

Next, Peter Bachus went in search of his father. He found him in the vestry conferring with Gottlieb Speer, church-warden, and Maximilian Vetter, headmaster of the village school and church organist. The best possible use had to be made of Materna's generous contribution to church funds, and the choice seemed to lie between re-roofing the nave and redecorating the choir and interior walls.

'Can I butt in for a moment, Father?' asked Peter.

'Very well,' Bachus said graciously. 'What is it?'

Peter launched into his story with relish. The three guardians of local Protestantism listened with scant interest at first. The whole thing sounded entirely innocuous. Peter had gone for a walk with his friend in the direction of Lake Maulen, ostensibly with the intention of listing the various species of lichen that grew in the neighbourhood.

'Very creditable,' Bachus commented with a touch of impatience. 'You won't find a wider range of mosses anywhere in Germany. But get to the point.'

'I'm just coming to it,' Peter said. 'You know those big alder-trees? Well, that's where we saw them lying.'

'Who?' Uschkurat demanded in an amused tone. 'Who would be lying there in broad daylight?'

The headmaster shook his head reprovingly. 'Maulen people don't lie around in the day-time—they work.'

'It doesn't necessarily mean anything if two people lie in the grass together, does it?' Peter produced this question with studied naïvety. Uschkurat gave a coarse laugh, and the Reverend Dr Bachus, who knew the ways of the world, folded his hands with an air of resignation.

'Well?' said Uschkurat. 'Who was it?'

'Frau Materna and Herr Eichler.'

The effect of this revelation was considerable. The schoolmaster's head stopped wagging abruptly and his mouth dropped open. Uschkurat's smile faded. As for the parson, he raised his folded hands in horror.

'Shame on you, Peter!' he said. 'It can't be true—I can't imagine such a thing.'

Almost the same words were being uttered at precisely the same moment by Constable Klinger, though his language was a trifle less refined. His son and heir had run him to earth in the bar of the Gasthaus, where he was drinking a modest beer. Beside him, also drinking beer, sat Scharfke, Fritz Fischer, and two peasants. Here, too, everyone was inclined to make fun of the story until the names of Margarete Materna and Johannes Eichler were uttered.

'Nonsense!' Klinger said firmly. He drained his beer and ordered another accompanied by a schnapps of Masurian dimensions—in other words, a treble. 'You must have made a mistake,' he declared.

'I doubt it,' Konrad insisted amiably. 'My friend Peter saw them too.'

'Then you both made a mistake,' said the policeman. 'Anyway, the whole thing may have been quite innocent.'

'Of course.' Konrad stressed the words, feeling satisfied that no one could possibly believe in the innocence of the whole thing. 'They were only lying on the ground together. Everyone does that sometimes, don't they? It's natural.'

'Of course it didn't mean anything,' growled the policeman.

'Of course not,' echoed the others.

'The only thing I don't understand,' Konrad said, 'is why Herr Eichler got so upset when we wandered past. He swore at us and ordered us out of the woods, which don't belong to him anyway. Why was that?'

'Another round!' called the policeman. 'You're far too young to understand these things,' he told his son reprovingly. 'You can safely leave them to us.'

'Things can't go on like this,' Eichler said belligerently. 'I want to know exactly where I stand with Materna.'

'You know where you stand with his wife,' Eis remarked. 'Isn't that good enough for you?'

Eichler ignored the question. He paced up and down his office like a caged lion, majestic but uneasy, before coming to a halt in front of his second-in-command.

'If that man still hasn't had enough—if he tries to bury his head in the sand—he must be treated accordingly.'

Eugen Eis nodded. He was comfortably seated in an armchair, though his wounded posterior had already healed. 'We must root him out. The question is, how?'

True to form, Johannes Eichler had a plan. His aim was to test Materna's willingness to participate in the life of the community. If he refused he would be branded as an outsider, if not actually unpatriotic. 'Then we'll expose him publicly,' Eichler concluded.

'Leave it to me,' Eis assured him, stuffing an automatic in his pocket.

Arriving at the Materna farm, Eis drummed on the gate and the new watchdogs appeared like magic. He reached for his gun, but two shrill whistles from Jacob Jablonski sent the dogs scampering back to the barn.

'They're not quite up to scratch yet, but they're coming along,' Jablonski said. 'They can tear a sack to shreds in five seconds—like to see?'

'I want a word with Materna.'

'By all means.' Jablonski opened the gate wide. 'Come right in.'

Eis wavered, scenting a trap. He couldn't see anything suspicious, but he hesitated just the same. His hand tightened on the automatic in his pocket.

'Not scared, are you?' Jablonski inquired. 'Don't worry, no

one's going to do anything to you—not today. You'll find Materna in the orchard, lying under the big pear-tree.'

He was speaking the truth. Materna was lying back with his head pillowed on his hands, squinting through the leaves and branches at the sun-drenched sky above him. Without turning his head, he said: 'To what do I owe the pleasure?'

Eis planted his legs apart and glared down at the man in the grass. 'I've got a message for you.'

'I could have told you that. You wouldn't be here otherwise.' Materna chuckled. 'Well, what does our mutual friend Eichler want this time?'

'There's a Remembrance Day service at the war memorial, eleven a.m. Sunday,' Eis said, faintly irritated by Materna's amusement. 'Anyone with an ounce of patriotism in his bones will be there.'

'And quite right too,' Materna said. 'I couldn't possibly decline such a charmingly worded invitation.'

'Secondly,' Eis recited, 'there's the anniversary of the founding of the Volunteer Fire Brigade, also on Sunday. We're planning to raise money for new fire-fighting equipment. You don't want to be left out, I suppose?'

'On the contrary, you have my fullest support. I'll contribute a hundred feet of hose and a double coupling.'

'Thirdly,' Eis continued, 'the Home Guard needs a bigger training area. We don't get enough room to manœuvre in, always cooped up on the north side of the moor.'

Materna smiled with maddening sweetness. 'What do you fancy? My wood, or Dog's Meadow?'

'We were thinking of the wood,' Eis said incredulously.

'Why stick at the wood? Don't be so modest. An important organization like the Home Guard needs plenty of elbow-room. Of course you can have Dog's Meadow—and my stretch of land beside the lake too. Is that all?'

Eis stammered that it was.

'Fine,' said Materna. 'In that case you can relieve me of your presence.'

Eugen Eis withdrew, visibly dashed by Materna's provocative acquiescence. He made a brief stop at the Gasthaus before venturing into his master's lair.

'I dealt with him,' he told Eichler. 'He agreed to everything without a murmur—crawled like a worm, in fact.'

'Typical of him,' Eichler said scornfully. 'That poor unfortunate wife of his is the one I'm sorry for—she deserves a proper man, not a wet fish like that.'

'A glass of water,' Grienspan said, slumping into the chair near the door. His face was chalky white.

Materna tossed aside his newspaper and walked over with a worried frown. 'What's up—had a couple too many?'

Grienspan pulled his cap off and a scarlet thread of blood trickled from his forehead to the corner of his mouth.

It was Friday evening, two days before the scheduled anniversary celebrations of the Volunteer Fire Brigade, the Remembrance Day service, the presentation of new equipment, and a social evening in the banqueting-room and garden of the Gasthaus. A sense of pleasurable anticipation had reigned in Maulen for some days, and the more robust members of the community were already in training for a memorable day's drinking. Occasional punch-ups were an integral part of the preparations. They seldom amounted to anything.

Grienspan made a laborious attempt at jocularity. 'Someone lashed out and I got in the way,' he said. 'These things happen.'

'In what capacity did you get in the way, Grienspan—as a customer, a cattle-dealer, or a Jew?' Materna bent over him and deftly examined the wound. 'Good God, man, you must have a tough skull. That knock would have floored most people.'

Materna fetched a basin of tepid water and some towels. Maria offered to help, but he waved her away. There was no need to dismiss his wife. Margarete was out and so was Jacob Jablonski—presumably tailing her.

'It doesn't hurt,' Grienspan said. 'It's a nuisance, that's all. Sorry to inflict myself on you like this.'

'Stop talking nonsense. You're probably suffering from concussion.' Materna carefully bathed the cattle-dealer's bleeding scalp. The wound was a couple of inches long but fortunately not deep. 'Looks like a beer-bottle to me. Who did it?'

'Someone—I don't know.'

'Hit you from behind, did he?'

'Does it matter?' Grienspan did his best to quell Materna's

mounting interest. 'Who cares who it was? Perhaps I provoked him in some way. Maybe it was my presence that did it—or maybe it was because I refused to order any schnapps. Scharfke's liquor isn't everyone's taste. Besides, I mentioned something about pig prices falling.'

'Is that any reason to hit someone over the head?'

'Ah, but I also said that if prices fell it wouldn't be by accident. I blamed it on the government's short-sighted agricultural policy and suggested that the peasant farmers and their associations were partly responsible.'

'You deserved to be hit over the head for blurting out the truth like that.'

Grienspan essayed a smile. It obviously hurt him, but he smiled all the same. Materna led him over to the sofa.

A bugle blared in the distance. Its tortured notes rang through Maulen and drifted agonizingly across the fields.

'The Fire Brigade bugle,' Materna said. 'Probably a practice alert.'

'Shouldn't you turn out?'

'I'll close the window. Besides, my ears function very badly when I want them to. As long as there's nothing genuinely on fire the others are welcome to mill around like madmen and demonstrate their team-spirit.'

The Fire Brigade bugle was first heard on the east side of the village, near the Gasthaus but beyond it. This should have been enough to arouse suspicion in itself, because it was normally blown in the centre of the village, beside the war memorial. After an unbroken silence of five minutes' duration it rang out again in the south, between the dairy and Dog's Meadow.

No deviation from normal alarm procedure could prevent the men of Maulen from doing their duty. Those who were in the Gasthaus paused only to empty the glasses in front of them. Children, too, flocked to the fire-station because they were anxious not to miss the sight of their two teachers garbed as volunteer fire-fighters. In field and farm-yard, many a peasant left wife or cow and hurried off to the village.

'Fire!' people called to each other. 'Fire!'

They uttered the cry with relative calm. Seeing no fire, they concluded that this must be a practice alert, presumably a

sort of prelude to the anniversary celebrations. Alerts of
this nature usually ended with free beer in the Gasthaus, the
cost being debited to the Brigade under the heading of
'Fire-Fighting Materials'.

The alarm bugle was now tooting south-west of the village,
somewhere behind the church and the graveyard. Its notes,
obviously the product of great exertion, offended one or two
sensitive ears.

'I've never heard Wilhelm make such a hideous din before,'
the headmaster said judicially.

Wilhelm was the verger. He was also the sexton and first
bugler in the Volunteer Fire Brigade band. No normal alarm
could be sounded without him, yet he now stood bugleless
in the middle of the village square, just behind the schoolmaster.

'I'm not blowing!' he announced with resentment.

'Who is, then?' Vetter demanded excitedly. Wilhelm protested his ignorance. His bugle was at home in his bedroom,
hanging above the marital couch—he had seen it there only
two hours before.

The men of Maulen crowded round the fire-station, shuffling
their feet and staring expectantly at the closed doors. It
dawned on them that the doors should have been opened long
ago. Ten or fifteen minutes had elapsed since the alarm first
sounded, minutes which might have proved vital in a real
emergency, but the bugle was still blaring away horribly.
The sound had changed direction again and now seemed to
come from behind Eichler's mill in the north of the village.

The murmur of male voices took on a hostile note. 'Lousy
organization!' someone shouted.

'There's something fishy going on,' Maximilian Vetter declared. 'Where's the chief?'

The current Fire Chief and president of the Volunteer
Fire Brigade was Gottlieb Speer. He hurried up, panting hard
and trying to button his tunic as he ran. His helmet, which
he always kept carefully polished, gleamed in the soft moonlight but kept slipping sideways. His crumpled, baggy trousers
cascaded over the tops of his boots. Veteran members of the
Brigade noted his sloppy turn-out with disfavour.

'What's the matter?' Speer gasped. 'What's going on round
here?'

'What the hell do you think?' someone called. 'It's an alarm.'

The Fire Chief stared helplessly at the figures crowding round him. 'What do you mean, an alarm? I never gave one.'

'Who did, then?' Vetter demanded in an inquisitorial tone. 'You're the Fire Chief, after all.'

'But not the Senior Fire Officer,' Speer retorted plaintively. He realized that he was not cutting a good figure. A number of people thought him ripe for retirement and there were plenty of would-be successors available. His rage mounted.

'It's a dirty trick, sounding the alarm without consulting me,' he protested, then added soothingly: '—it's not normal procedure, I mean.'

'What the hell!' shouted one of the men, a product of Home Guard training and thus bursting with guts and initiative. 'Get hold of the key to the fire-station—that's the main thing. Where the hell is it, anyway?'

'I haven't got it,' Speer admitted. 'I saw it earlier today, but I can't find it anywhere.'

'Bash the door down!' yelled a few resolute voices. 'An alarm's an alarm.'

Gottlieb Speer straightened his gleaming helmet with trembling hands and stationed himself protectively in front of the fire-station. The massive doors were his own handiwork, lovingly constructed and supplied at cost price. With a shudder, he saw that some men had already drawn their axes and others were advancing with a make-shift battering-ram.

'Stand back!' they shouted. 'We're coming!'

'Charge!' the children chorused in delight.

As local representative of the educated intelligentsia, Maximilian Vetter decided to step into the breach. Convinced that one of his great hours had struck, he interposed himself between the lone defender of the gates and his advancing foes.

'Men!' he called, raising his arms. 'Let's be logical about this.'

He climbed on to the refuse-bin that stood outside the fire-station and raised the practised, schoolmasterly voice that had brought so many rioting adolescents to their senses. In his experience, grown men were infinitely more amenable to discipline. The crowd promptly fell silent.

Vetter began by asking who was qualified to order a fire

practice. He answered the question himself: either the Fire Chief, in other words, Speer, or the Senior Fire Officer and Honorary Fire Chief, namely Eichler. Since Speer had not issued the order it could only—Q.E.D.—have come from Eichler.

'Does anyone here choose to disobey the Senior Fire Officer's instructions?' he concluded. 'Very well. We'll wait until Eichler comes and see what happens then.'

They did not have long to wait. Johannes Eichler had been in the woods, and not by himself. The soil of Masuria was warm and the moon a smiling disc of silver. The alarm signal had interrupted him at a delicate moment.

Furiously, he forged a path through the excited throng and marched up to Speer.

'What's the big idea?' he demanded. 'Are you crazy, or something?'

'Me?' the Fire Chief countered defiantly. 'Why pick on me? I didn't give the alarm.'

The two men faced each other like fighting-cocks, chests heaving. The by-standers scented a new scandal. One false move and the whole of the Volunteer Fire Brigade would go up in flames.

Johannes Eichler realized in the nick of time that something had gone badly wrong. Breathlessly, he said: 'You really didn't give the alarm? Neither did I. In that case, who did?'

The alerted members of the Brigade, burning to prove their mettle, felt that they had been subjected to insult and provocation. Their well-developed sense of manly dignity rebelled at the thought of falling prey to a practical joke. The collective soul of Maulen began to seethe.

'God damn it!' they bellowed. 'No one can treat us like this!'

'Steady, men!' Eichler entreated. 'I know it's a disgrace, but take it easy.'

'The way they blew that bugle!' said Wilhelm, the bugler. 'That was disgraceful for a start.'

'Don't worry,' Eichler assured him, 'we'll get whoever was responsible.'

'You won't have far to look,' said one of the crowd. The man was standing in the shadows beside the fire-station, where the moon did not illuminate his face. 'I'll lay odds it was Materna.'

'What about that Jew?' called another voice, hoarse with rage.

'It could have been the two of them together!'

'Let's not jump to conclusions,' Eichler said. 'We want justice, not revenge. All we can say at present is that whoever did it will suffer the consequences. I suggest we all adjourn to the Gasthaus and talk it over. The drinks are on me.'

'May we come in?' asked Peter Bachus.

Jacob Jablonski led the two boys into the big farm kitchen. Their heads were tousled and their shoes more scuffed and dirty than usual. All in all, they looked rather the worse for wear.

'We just wanted to say good evening,' Konrad Klinger said. 'It has been a good evening, you see.'

'A successful evening,' amended Peter Bachus.

Jablonski eyed them with amusement. 'You look as if you've been out on a cross-country run. Haven't been practising the bugle as well, I suppose?'

Alfons Materna glanced at Siegfried Grienspan. 'You know our two fox-cubs, don't you? Remarkable specimens, both of them.' He nodded to Jablonski, who retired to the yard and whistled up the dogs. Taking advantage of the brilliant moonlight, he put them through their emergency drill. The enemy was represented by a sandbag suspended in the yard entrance. The dogs tore at it savagely as it swung to and fro.

Back in the house, Materna sat his youthful visitors down and put two tumblers and two jugs in front of them. One of the jugs contained milk, the other raspberry juice. 'Well,' he said, 'why did you come?'

'We like it here,' Konrad Klinger explained. 'I don't know why, but the time always seems to fly when we're with you.'

'You can say that again,' Peter Bachus chimed in. 'It's ten o'clock already, and it was just after eight when we got here.'

Materna pricked up his ears. 'Was it?'

'Ask Herr Jablonski,' Konrad Klinger suggested. 'I'm sure he'll remember.'

Materna deemed it advisable to call Jablonski back. The dogs howled outside the door.

Jablonski listened to Materna's questions in silence. 'Eight o'clock?' he said with a grin. 'Certainly, and I'd swear to it if necessary. I'm almost positive that I spent two hours talking to these lads outside in the yard.'

Materna nodded. 'That's it, then.'

'You see?' Grienspan said. 'People have friends whether they like it or not.'

'All right,' Materna told the boys. 'We spent the whole evening together.'

Grienspan folded his hands thoughtfully. His dark eyes glowed with pleasure. 'I wish I could take things as light-heartedly as your two young friends here.'

'Light-hearted is the word,' Materna replied. 'Their contact with the world of reality is minimal.'

'I wouldn't say that,' Konrad said. 'We keep our eyes open. For instance, we saw two people cuddling on the edge of the wood this evening.'

Peter nodded. 'If you need any witnesses, Herr Materna . . .'

'That's the last thing I need.'

'But that wasn't the only reason why we turned out the Fire Brigade,' Konrad said. 'We'd been planning this for some time. We knew where the key to the fire-station was kept and where the alarm bugle was hanging. We just waited for the right moment.'

'That's enough!' Materna exclaimed. 'None of us has the least wish to get involved in your little games. We spent the whole evening together, that's all—talking about hunting, let's say.'

'Hunting and love,' Konrad suggested. 'That's what the Masurians like best, after all.'

'You don't talk about love,' Materna said, 'you make it.'

'Even with another man's wife?'

Materna's smile was serene. 'You must think I'm very dumb. Do I look it?'

'I'm sorry,' Konrad said, 'but it doesn't seem—well, very moral somehow.'

'Not moral, perhaps, but expedient,' Materna replied cheerfully. 'Every woman deserves her due.'

Hermann, sole surviving son of the house of Materna, flung

open the kitchen door. 'Some unauthorized person called out the Volunteer Fire Brigade,' he announced. 'There's a rumour that someone also stole the alarm bugle and the key to the fire-station—a complaint has already been laid. Klinger's going to have his hands full.'

It was late. The two boys had gone, and Materna and Grienspan were sitting beneath the oil-lamp, bent over a chess-board.

Hermann took no notice of Grienspan. Without sparing him a look or a handshake, he sat down on the other side of the room and said: 'I can't help it, but there's a smell of garlic in here.'

Materna glanced at his son in surprise. 'What was that?' he demanded.

'I said the room smells of garlic.'

This was something new, Materna reflected—new in his house at least. Clearly, Hermann was absorbing what his friends told him, and their words seemed to be taking effect.

Siegfried Grienspan's face had gone pale, but his hands lay motionless on the table. He felt the cool, firm pressure of Materna's fingers on his.

Materna said: 'The boy's trying to be funny.'

'No, I'm not,' Hermann said doggedly. 'I mean it.'

Materna knew, just as Grienspan did, what Hermann's crass allusion to garlic meant in practice. Jews, as every good Masurian was aware, were flat-footed, hook-nosed, and over-fond of garlic. Anyone who possessed a sensitive, i.e. Aryan, nose could smell them a mile off.

'Remarkable,' commented Materna. 'I'll give you some good advice,' he continued in a surprisingly mild tone. 'If you can't stand the air in here you'd better go up to your room.'

'Certainly,' Hermann said. He gave his father a semi-military salute and strode out with head erect, not deigning to look at Grienspan.

Materna winked at the little cattle-dealer. 'Human folly takes a multitude of forms,' he said, almost gaily. 'Some of them are dangerous, I know, but I can't help deriving a certain amount of amusement from them.'

'I'm afraid,' Grienspan replied quietly, '—afraid for you too, Materna. I can't help wondering what you're letting yourself in for. Where will it end?'

'I know,' Materna said. 'These people mean trouble, but

I've no wish to act like a coward or a fool. I couldn't live with myself if I did, and I must admit I enjoy life.'

The anniversary celebrations of the Volunteer Fire Brigade, customarily held on the first Sunday in August, brought the villagers of Maulen out in force. Their beaming faces betrayed a universal determination to enjoy themselves, preferably at someone else's expense.

Johannes Eichler, already clad in a dark formal suit, summoned his loyal lieutenant Eugen Eis for a final briefing. Having established how much free beer the Fire Brigade funds would run to, they discussed the formation of a 'flying squad'.

'No need,' Eis declared. 'If anyone opens his mouth too wide I'll shut it for him personally. It'll be a pleasure.'

'We'll have to keep a special eye on Materna, of course—if he comes at all, which I doubt. After all, he's in mourning.'

'Maybe he'll bring that daughter of his.' Eis rubbed his hands. 'Brigitte's come on quite nicely in the last couple of years.'

Eichler made a sweeping gesture, as though to convey that he bestowed her on him. 'Have fun, by all means, but make sure Materna doesn't hog too much limelight.'

'Everything'll go off all right,' Eis assured him. 'I give you my personal guarantee.'

The two most harassed fathers in the district, the policeman and the parson, were meanwhile endeavouring to curb their sons' spirit of enterprise. Preventive measures had been discussed immediately after morning service, and general agreement prevailed.

'Those lads have got to be kept on a tight rein,' Constable Klinger said firmly.

The Reverend Dr Bachus nodded. 'I'm not normally in favour of drastic action, but in this case I agree with you. It would be irresponsible for us to lead them into temptation.'

'The best plan would be to lock them up.'

'I think it will be enough if we clip their wings.'

The boys' wings had been duly clipped, or so it appeared. Their pocket-money was limited to one mark only. Half that sum would be needed for the entrance fee, and they could hardly go far on the rest.

Konrad and Peter accepted their one-mark pieces without protest and made their way to the Gasthaus. Once there, they climbed through a back window into the cloak-room and slipped into the saloon without difficulty. They headed for the bar and smacked their coins on the counter.

'Set 'em up,' said Konrad Klinger.

'That's right,' said Peter Bachus. 'We need a livener if we're going to wake this place up.'

Each of them downed ten schnapps within a quarter of an hour. Flushed and slightly unsteady on their feet, they marched into the banqueting-room with the light of adventure shining in their eyes.

Their preparations were already made.

Alfons Materna was addressing the members of his household. 'I wouldn't dream of forcing anyone to accompany me to the Fire Brigade festivities,' he told them cheerfully. 'On the other hand, I feel we ought to go. It promises to be enjoyable.'

'Count me in,' Jablonski grunted.

Margarete looked stern. 'I thought we were in mourning.'

'We're always in mourning,' Materna said with a shrug. 'What do you think, Hermann?'

Hermann felt flattered. It was the first time his father had ever consulted his opinion, so he smiled happily and gave a vigorous nod. 'I'd enjoy being with the boys on a day like this.'

'There's a practical reason too,' Materna said. 'Stay away and we risk being slandered. Go, and we boost the family reputation.'

Brigitte's face—well-rounded and petal-pink—shone with anticipation. She had had few chances of mixing with village society so far, and she yearned to spread her wings. 'Please take me too, Father.'

Materna regarded his daughter with a touch of suspicion, but he smiled at her nonetheless. Slowly, his eyes turned to Margarete. 'Well, are you going to let us go on our own?'

Margarete stared past him. 'I suppose not, if only for the children's sake.'

'Splendid,' he said. 'I took the liberty of booking us a table in advance—right up front and next to Eichler's.'

Jablonski gave an exclamation of delight. 'I can't wait to see his face when we walk in!'

Almost ceremonially, they set off. Materna headed the procession and Jablonski brought up the rear with Maria, the Polish girl, walking beside him as though sheltering beneath a tree.

'Put on a good show,' called Materna. 'Make the village think it's William Tell and his family. Hermann, try and look as if you'd let me shoot an apple off the top of your head.'

'I don't follow your meaning, Father,' Hermann said trustfully, 'but you can always rely on me.'

'I know,' Materna replied with a thin smile. 'I'm banking on that.'

The celebration was an unparalleled success—by midday, everyone felt convinced of that. As Old Mother Mischgoreit announced to anyone who failed to get out of her way in time, Old Man Mischgoreit would have swallowed his false teeth with joy if he could only have lived to see the day.

No one in Maulen had opted out of the grand communal festivities. Radiant faces met the eye at every turn and the air was filled with the sound of jovial volunteer firemen's voices and shrill feminine laughter. A general cheer went up when Alfons Materna and his family appeared.

'Glad you've come,' the Terrible Twins told him. 'You'd have missed something if you hadn't.'

Johannes Eichler quickly overcame his surprise and described a courtly bow in the direction of Margarete. Materna aroused public sympathy by waving back.

The brass band's efforts won great acclaim, with the result that popular marches such as *Old Comrades* had to be repeated several times. A fraternal atmosphere reigned throughout the hall and outside in the garden. No one could complain of Scharfke's liquor, at least at this stage. Forgive and forget seemed to be the order of the day. Materna raised his glass to Eichler and Eichler returned the compliment, an unexpected demonstration of friendship which was loudly applauded by those in the immediate vicinity.

Finally, to the strains of *The Blue Danube*, Eichler rose and invited Margarete to dance. Eugen Eis whirled Brigitte round the floor while Hermann, surrounded by friends at the bar, guilelessly sang his father's praises.

Alfons Materna really did seem to be observing local conventions for once. He presented the band with free beer, exchanged cheerful banter with the assembled firemen, and bought a number of rounds. He also patronized the small-bore rifle range in the garden and carried off first prize by scoring fifty-eight points out of a possible sixty.

Meanwhile, twilight had fallen and the more experienced drinkers of beer and schnapps began to cram their bellies with liver-sausage, slices of lemon, coffee grounds and mustard—traditional aids to the assimilation of alcohol already consumed and the future consumption of greater quantities still.

'What a bore,' grumbled Peter Bachus. 'Nothing's gone wrong so far.'

Konrad Klinger patted him consolingly on the back. 'Don't worry, our time will come.'

The boys' time seemed to have come when the band emitted a loud fanfare. The platform swayed perceptibly for a moment but held.

Peter Bachus looked disappointed. 'Maybe we got our calculations wrong.'

'You're too impatient,' Konrad told him. 'Give it a few more minutes and things will really go with a bang.'

The platform was now ascended by Maximilian Vetter, whose headmastership of the village school gave him responsibility for all species and subspecies of cultural activity. These embraced what were referred to as 'cultural diversions'. Tombola came under this heading, since the prizes to be won included a book entitled *Heroes of the High Seas*.

There was another mighty fanfare—the platform remained standing—and Vetter called: 'We now come to the Grand Draw.'

Four stalwarts in firemen's uniform solemnly carried a loaded table on to the platform. The prizes consisted of glasses, vases, shirts, ashtrays, soap, a kitchen alarm-clock, notepaper, a blanket, ornamental figures, a cigarette-case, and, last but not least, the book.

Vetter was joined on the platform by Gottlieb Speer's little girl, a tiny velvet-eyed creature dressed in apple-blossom white and wearing a bow in her hair. As daughter of the president and current chief of the Volunteer Fire Brigade, she had been selected to act as Goddess of Fortune—in other words, to make the draw.

'First number!' Vetter called in a sonorous voice.

An assistant held up the prize—the kitchen alarm-clock—and Speer's daughter drew one of the slips. Curtsying, she handed it to Vetter, who read out—nay, proclaimed—the number inscribed on it.

'Twenty-three!'

Two people stood up simultaneously, the postman's wife and a farmer. Both stepped forward and presented their tickets. Both tickets bore the number twenty-three.

The gracious smile froze on Vetter's lips. He inspected the tickets with furrowed brow, then said hurriedly: 'There must be some mistake, I'm afraid. We can't have two tickets with the same number, of course, but that can be settled later. Let's go on with the rest of the draw.'

Konrad and Peter surveyed the restive gathering with interest. Materna glanced at the boys, barely able to contain his mirth.

Vetter called out the next number. Another two winners reported to the platform. Two more winners claimed the prize after that, and the fourth draw yielded a bumper crop of no less than three winners.

Someone shouted 'It's a swindle!' in a clear, youthful voice.

'A swindle!' echoed several others. Like wildfire, the cry ran through the hall, across the garden and into the village square. The infuriated mob, or as many as had bought lottery tickets, converged on the platform, which again started to sway.

Vetter waved his arms energetically but failed to restore order. He tried valiantly to make himself heard above the tumult, but only isolated phrases penetrated the deafening hubbub of righteous indignation: '. . . an oversight . . . will be investigated fully . . . most regrettable . . .'

The bandsmen alone proved equal to the occasion. At a signal, they rose smartly to their feet. A second signal, and they came to attention. A third, and they applied themselves to their instruments with a will. That was when the platform collapsed.

'At last!' cried Peter Bachus.

A cloud of dust went up accompanied by a collective yell.

The yell turned to laughter, hysterical at first, then hearty and full-throated.

The bandsmen came crawling out of the dust-cloud. They were all unhurt, since the platform had only been three feet high, but the tuba was a mass of crumpled metal and two men were trying to extricate themselves from the rim of the big drum into which they had fallen.

This put paid to the lottery. The band struck up again, agreeably muted since its most effective noise-makers were out of action. Order had just been restored when the lights failed, plunging the hall into Stygian gloom.

A clear, youthful voice made itself heard once more. 'Don't let anyone pinch the prizes!' it called commandingly.

A woman gave an outraged yelp. 'Ugh! Take your filthy hands off me, you beast!'

'What's that?' demanded a robust male voice. 'Sorry, I thought it was your daughter.'

'Keep calm!' yelled Scharfke, justifiably apprehensive about his liquor stocks. 'The fault in the circuit will be repaired as quickly as possible. In the meantime, please adjourn to the garden, where drinks will be served by lamplight.'

The Gasthaus garden was not particularly spacious, but its few tables were rapidly cleared of their existing occupants for the benefit of local dignitaries. Scharfke lit three magic lanterns in addition to the five already hanging there. With a little of the goodwill which was always so conspicuously present in Maulen, the surroundings might almost have been described as romantic.

'Let's spend the next hour watching how they pair off,' Konrad Klinger said. 'It should be interesting—fun, too.'

Conditions were ideal. Consumption of alcohol had intensified the yearning for other forms of pleasure, and the inadequate lighting only furthered their attainment. Besides, the prevailing chaos made careful supervision impossible. From the Gasthaus garden into the alluring darkness was a mere step, and a step which was often taken. The midsummer night steamed like a Turkish bath.

Suitable places were well known to the initiated. Those who were in particular haste went no further than the back of the Gasthaus barn, where sundry piles of hay were to be found at this time of year. Also popular were the church-

yard and the grass verges of the war memorial. Few people
bothered to make long and tedious journeys—northwards
to the moor or southwards into the wood, for instance—
because their amatory activities were generally of a between-
dances nature.

Jablonski disapproved of the detailed instructions given him
by Materna but agreed to follow them out.

His orders that night were to act as Eichler's shadow.
He stood there, leaning against a tree and listening to the
exchanges between Eichler and Margarete. What he heard
aroused his disgust and anger, but he stood there without
moving until conversation yielded to pregnant silence.

Only then did he step forward. With a suggestion of a
bow, he said affably: 'Herr Materna presents his compliments
and trusts that you won't let the thought of him put you
off. On the contrary, he hopes you'll enjoy yourselves.'

Not having been instructed to wait for an answer,
Jablonski turned and walked off into the darkness. On his
way back to the Gasthaus he bumped into the Terrible Twins.
Their curiosity was as boundless as ever.

'You won't get anything out of me,' Jablonski told them
with a grin. 'I don't crack so easy—not like that platform.
You're handy with a saw, I must say.'

'A saw?' Peter Bachus said indignantly. 'Give us credit
for a bit more ingenuity than that. We just removed a few
nails, loosened a board or two and shifted a couple of
joists.'

Konrad Klinger appeared to have other worries. 'You've
got to have a word with Herr Materna straight away. Tell him
to go to the school playground. You know the bench by the
hedge? Well, Eugen Eis and Brigitte are sitting there necking.'

Jablonski trotted off. He found Materna waiting for him
outside the Gasthaus. Breathlessly he made his report.

'Splendid!' Materna said, when he heard about Eichler and
Margarete. His reaction to the news of Eis and Brigitte was
equally favourable but more positive. Nimble as a stoat, he
darted across the village square, skirted the fire-station and
made for the school. He found Eis and Brigitte at the de-
signated spot. They were still on the bench and still—as luck
would have it—in a sitting position.

'Well,' he said cheerfully, 'are you having fun?'

They untwined themselves. Brigitte subsided with apparent shame and embarrassment, but Eugen Eis rose to his full height and glared down at Materna. 'We were having a quiet chat, if you want to know. No harm in that, is there?'

'On the contrary,' Materna assured him. 'There's nothing like a quiet chat for getting results. We ought to have one ourselves sometimes, Eis. What about tomorrow afternoon, over a glass of schnapps?'

'You've got more sense than I thought,' Eis said. 'Maybe we ought to have a quiet word together, at that. It might pay.'

'It might pay both of us.' Materna agreed. 'There's more than one way of getting places, and the roundabout way sometimes gets you there quicker.'

'I think we ought to have this out, man to man.'

Johannes Eichler faced Materna outside the Gasthaus door. The damaged circuit had been repaired, so the light above the entrance was burning again. Margarete stood at Eichler's elbow.

'What a harmonious picture,' Materna said. He spoke without a trace of sarcasm. 'There's no denying it, Margarete suits you far better than me. You're more in scale, for a start.'

'Materna,' said Margarete, 'you're to blame for anything that has happened, and it's time you realized it.'

'You may be right,' Materna conceded readily. 'I only hope Eichler's the gentleman he purports to be.'

'Who says I don't act like a gentleman?' Eichler demanded.

'Be careful, Johannes,' Margarete pleaded. 'I know him —he'll talk you into something you'll regret. No one can beat him when it comes to words.'

Materna grinned. 'Words! Acts are more in your line, and I've got at least three witnesses who'll bear me out.'

Eichler advanced a step as though anxious to impress Margarete. 'Listen, Materna,' he said grimly, 'I won't have you stirring up gossip. If you expose me to the village you'll regret it.'

'Why get so hot under the collar? I've made a lot of mistakes myself and I'm ready to take the consequences. I'm not reproaching you—I don't feel entitled to.'

'Don't trust him!' Margarete cried anxiously.

Eichler fidgeted for a moment. 'Where's the catch, Materna? Come on, out with it. What are you trying to put over on us?'

'Nothing. I give up, that's all,' Materna closed his eyes. 'I'm bowing to the inevitable.'

'You really mean that?'

'I won't say it hasn't been a struggle,' Materna said. 'However, I've finally come to the conclusion that I may not be worthy of a wife like Margarete. You deserve her far more, so be happy together. You can count on my blessing.'

'Ladies and gentlemen,' called Gottlieb Speer, president and chief of the Volunteer Fire Brigade, 'we now come to the distribution of prizes.'

Normal conditions had returned to Maulen and its Fire Brigade festival. The lights were burning and the platform had undergone running repairs, so the proceedings could continue inside the hall.

The three prizes for the small-bore shooting competition were carried in: a silver-plated cup, a bronze bowl, and a pewter mug. All three articles bore the edifying motto 'Heart and Hand for Fatherland!', details of place and date and two crossed axes, symbolic of radical fire-fighting measures.

'I now yield the chair to our honorary president,' announced Speer. 'Herr Eichler!'

This announcement was not made with the usual comradely warmth, presumably because of the unpleasantness over the false alarm. It was obvious that Speer still felt affronted, and those in the know considered it petty of him to show it.

Johannes Eichler, too, lacked the fire appropriate to the occasion. He seemed preoccupied with weighty matters, but there was a hint of good-humoured irony in his voice as he presented the first prize with the words: 'The name of today's winner is Alfons Materna!'

Materna stepped forward to receive the victor's cup and brandished it above his head to loud applause.

Then something wholly unexpected happened: before anyone could stop him, Materna embarked on a speech. His tone was warm, his manner modest and his smile positively self-effacing.

'Fellow-citizens of Maulen,' he said. 'I'm not a golden-tongued orator like Johannes Eichler, who has left his mark on so many aspects of community life. I'm just a plain farmer, like most of us here. We tend our fields, we grow cabbages,

potatoes or wheat, and we leave the leadership of the
community to those who feel called upon to assume it—men
like our universally respected fellow-citizen Johannes Eichler.'

'Watch him,' Margarete warned in a low voice.

'Let him bark,' Eichler whispered back. 'He's past biting.'
He felt satisfied that Materna really had reached the end of the
line at last. The man had lost not only his son but his wife
and the valuable expanse of Dog's Meadow that went with
her. To present him with a silver cup in return added spice
to the situation.

'On the other hand,' Materna was saying, 'I share Johannes
Eichler's enthusiasm for constructive activity. That is why
I feel we have all done far too little for the valiant men
who stand ready at all times, hose in hand, to protect our
lives and property.'

'Hear, hear!' called Gottlieb Speer. These were words after
his own heart. Someone had at least taken it upon himself to
do what Eichler had omitted to do, namely, pay tribute to
his beloved organization.

'Speeches there must be,' Materna continued, his eyes
sparkling with bonhomie, 'but actions speak louder than
words. That is why, to begin with, I propose to dedicate this
cup to the younger members of the Volunteer Fire Brigade,
and hope that they will compete for it in future years.'

Universal jubilation ensued. The cup was not worth more
than twenty-five marks, true, but it symbolized victory, and
victory was a pearl beyond price. The younger fire-fighters
felt uncommonly flattered.

'As you may already know,' Materna told his enthusiastic
but unwitting audience, 'I have presented our Volunteer Fire
Brigade with a hundred feet of hose, but that is a flea-bite
compared with the enormous importance and undeniable
achievements of that organization. I am therefore donating,
in addition, a brand-new, modern fire appliance.'

'Hurrah!' chorused the crowd. 'Good old Materna!'

'And this fire appliance,' Materna pursued, 'will, if you
are agreeable, bear the name of my son Alfred. I should like
it to be a permanent memorial to him. I have always believed
that certain things should never be forgotten.'

5

'You can't help feeling sorry for him,' said the people of Maulen, meaning Alfons Materna.

They also said: 'He's in luck,' meaning Johannes Eichler. 'But then, you've got to make your own luck in this world, and nobody works harder at it than he does.'

It had been borne in on the village of Maulen that Margarete Materna wanted a divorce. Nobody had got divorced in the neighbourhood since time immemorial, but Alfons Materna had repeatedly and publicly disclaimed any intention of putting difficulties in his wife's way.

'It's very decent of him, in a way,' said the wife of Maximilian Vetter.

'Decent perhaps,' replied the headmaster, 'but hardly the done thing.'

The done thing locally was to put an erring wife across one's knee and thrash her silly with a bull's pizzle. The idea of divorce never entered a true Masurian's head.

'You see,' said Fritz Fischer, the local fisherman, '—everyone gets his just deserts in the end. There is such a thing as justice after all.'

Fischer was Materna's avowed enemy. Materna owned a sizeable stretch of lakeside land, and he had persistently refused Fischer permission to use it for fishing purposes—out of sheer malice, so Fischer believed.

'You've got to hand it to him,' said Constable Klinger. 'He's keeping a stiff upper lip.'

'But he's suffering deeply,' said the Reverend Dr Bachus, '—even if he does give an irritatingly self-satisfied impression.'

Johannes Eichler's conduct enjoyed wide approbation. 'That man knows what he wants,' was the general verdict. 'He's always hankered after her—they were childhood sweethearts, after all. Well, now he's got her. And her land.'

'Congratulations,' said Eugen Eis. 'When's the wedding to be?'

Eichler laid his hands on his paunch. 'We've got to get the divorce first, but that shouldn't present any difficulty. As to the wedding, they'll still be talking about it when your grandchildren are grown up, I guarantee you that.'

Over a schnapps—100 per cent proof, laced with red pepper and dispensed from a fat-bellied medicine bottle—Eugen Eis was apprised of further details. Margarete had gone to her sister's place at Lötzen to 'recuperate'. By all accounts, the future Frau Eichler was awaiting her finest hour with barely restrained eagerness.

'Materna simply wants to save his own skin, from the look of it,' Eichler concluded.

'Are we going to let him?' asked Eis.

Eichler raised his glass with an air of easy complacency. 'Plucked chickens don't lay eggs,' he said cheerfully. 'Dog's Meadow will drop into my lap like a ripe plum.'

A cunning light dawned in Eis's eyes. 'Have you got that in writing?'

'It's all signed and sealed. Materna has temporary control of Dog's Meadow but he can't sell it or incorporate it in his own estate. Anyway, my bride-to-be has already asked me to look after her property for her.'

'In that case, cheers!' Eis said admiringly. 'Watch out, though. Materna's a wily old fox, not a goose that goes around laying golden eggs for other people.'

'I'm telling you here and now,' Grienspan said, 'I won't do business with you any more.'

Materna grinned. 'Is that a roundabout way of saying that you're cutting your prices?'

Grienspan threw up his arms in protest. 'I just can't watch you ruining yourself like this. Only the other day you sold me two of your best cows to help finance a fire-pump which the village doesn't need. What is it this time?'

'Which do you rate higher?' Materna asked. 'A cow or a human life?'

He took Grienspan's arm and strolled through the stables. They housed thirty-six cows, four bulls, twelve horses and seventy-odd pigs, all in peak condition. The warm, powerful smell of cattle mingled with the scent of liquid manure, fresh milk and bitter-sweet pigs' dung.

'Take a look, Grienspan. I made this farm what it is. I started in a small way, but that doesn't mean I have to end up in a big way. There's a nice lot of business here for you. As a cattle-dealer, you ought to be glad.'

Grienspan shook his head sadly. 'Of course I like doing business, but not this kind. Do you really mean to break up your herd because of a woman—that woman?'

'My dear friend,' Materna said with a smile, 'I married my first wife because I was young and impressionable. My second marriage had a touch of calculation about it. Margarete was reputed to be the best match for miles around, and I was madly ambitious in those days. Well, I've paid the price.'

'And now you're ready to sell off your best breeding stock, dirt cheap, just to rectify one error of judgment?'

'Don't talk nonsense,' Materna said. 'Lame horses, dry cows and elderly pigs—that's all I'm offering you. Make me an offer.'

Grienspan did not speak for some time. He seemed to be marshalling his thoughts. Finally, he said: 'If you're up to what I think you're up to, I'll take all your surplus stock and guarantee you top prices.'

'Fellow committee members,' said Gottlieb Speer, 'I called this special meeting because I have a pleasant announcement to make in connection with the new fire-pump. It's ours!'

'And you dragged us here just to tell us that?' Fritz Fischer gave him an accusing glare. 'Materna promised to pay for the damned pump in front of the whole village. Of course he's got to fork out.'

'He's quite prepared to do that,' Speer said soothingly. 'I showed him a catalogue. He could have chosen a small pump if he'd wanted to, but he didn't.'

'Because he wants his son's name engraved on it in letters the size of a house, that's why,' retorted Fischer. 'I wouldn't shake that man's hand if you paid me.'

The official members of the committee preserved a thoughtful silence. Some of them stared out of the window. On a bench just beneath it sat two unofficial observers, listening intently. The Terrible Twins were back at school now that the summer holidays were over, but they descended on Maulen each week-end.

'Looks as if Fischer's got it in for Materna,' whispered Konrad Klinger. 'He's dangerous, only no one round here seems to realize it.'

'Fellow committee members,' Speer entreated, 'personal considerations have to take second place when important issues are at stake.'

Fischer drew himself up. 'I call the state of this country more important than a measly fire appliance.'

'So do I,' Speer hastened to agree, '—no one here would dispute that. On the other hand, the fire appliance is the only item on this evening's agenda. We can't very well refuse to show our appreciation of Materna's gift.'

'You'll be making him an honorary member next,' growled Fischer.

'An excellent idea,' Speer said promptly. 'I second that proposal.'

'It's a lousy idea,' Fischer retorted. 'Eichler'll have your guts for garters when he hears.'

Speer bridled. 'We shall, of course, be happy to take note of Johannes Eichler's views—if and when he conveys them to us, which he hasn't done so far. As far as the Volunteer Fire Brigade is concerned, Materna is our main concern for the moment. We must express our thanks and appreciation of his services in a fitting manner.'

'What's the game?' Fischer sneered. 'I suppose this is your way of getting even with Eichler because he tore you off a strip in front of everyone after that false alarm—because he didn't give you a pat on the back at the anniversary celebrations.'

'If you're after my job you can have it,' Speer snapped.

Fischer grinned. 'Not yet, thanks.'

'All right,' Speer said vengefully, 'we'll do without the pump. Materna would have paid for the presentation celebrations too, but we'll do without those as well. I'll pass your decision on to the other members of the Brigade.'

This drew a belated protest from Uschkurat, who declined to share responsibility for such a step. With certain reservations and many misgivings, he supported Speer's proposal that Materna should receive official recognition.

'And I'm dead against it,' Fischer declared. 'There'll have to be a lot of changes before I vote for a man like Materna. I don't trust him, but I'm quite prepared to give him a chance. You can tell him that, and you can tell him something else: I've got my pride. He can run me off his land, but he'll never get me out of my cottage.'

Outside the window, the Terrible Twins winked at each other. They rose without a word and vanished into the darkness, bound for the lake. Their imagination had just received a powerful fillip.

The first thing that happened when Fritz Fischer made his way home some considerable time later was that he tripped over a rope stretched across the path. He swore frightfully. Reaching his cottage, he cannoned into a long dark object. One of his fishing boats had been dragged across the entrance and the door itself was nailed shut. As a result, he had to climb in through the window, breaking a pane in the process. the room was full of hatchery boxes and his bed thickly draped with fishing-nets.

Fritz Fischer was consumed with rage. 'Shit and damnation!' he bellowed. 'What's the meaning of this?'

The answer came floating through the broken window in a spine-chilling banshee wail: 'This is your first warning . . .'

The autumn of 1932 was intoxicatingly beautiful. The sun lavished the last of its summer strength on Masuria, bathing the countryside in a golden glow.

Alfons Materna was pacing the now bare fields with Hermann at his side.

'Tell me, Hermann,' he said, 'what do you think of when you see these empty fields?'

Hermann looked slightly at a loss. 'Well, they remind me of a lot of things—hare shooting, for instance, or autumn manoeuvres.'

'I only shoot carrion and predators, Hermann. It's a principle of mine.'

This was a simple statement, but Hermann took it as a rebuke. He plodded across the potato-field in ponderous silence.

The land stretched away in front of them in a series of gentle undulations, seemingly infinite. The horizon melted into the pale blue sky.

'I make this walk across my fields every autumn,' Materna said, '—always did, even as a child. Your grandfather used to take me with him. The thought uppermost in my mind has always been: how will these fields look next year?'

Hermann's broad and ingenuous countenance reddened slightly. At length, he said: 'I suppose I'm not a farmer by nature. Soldiering's more in my line.'

'It takes all sorts to make a world, Hermann, soldiers included.' Materna's tone was unruffled. He sat down on a rock the size of a potato-sack and gestured to Hermann to join him. 'I've devoted a lot of thought to your future recently, my boy. In other words, I'd like to know what you would prefer to do most.'

Hermann hesitated briefly. He reached for the hip-flask which his father handed him and took a fortifying swig. Then he said: 'You and your men manage the farm perfectly well without me. It'll be at least thirty years before I take over, with you in your present form.'

'Possibly,' Materna replied, studying his hands. They were almost as small as a woman's, but hard and sinewy. He could crush a potato to pulp with them if he wanted. 'What do you propose to do in the meantime?'

'Well—an organizing job, let's say. I've got a gift for organization.'

'How would cattle-dealing appeal to you? Grienspan would probably take you into the business if I asked him.'

'I'm sure I'd make a go of it,' Hermann said with conviction. 'All the same, Grienspan is . . .'

'A Jew,' Materna amplified, 'and you find that off-putting.'

'I've got my principles, Father,' Hermann said solemnly. 'I'm a patriotic sort of person, and I . . .'

Materna cut him short. 'All right. If I follow your drift, you'd like to play a greater part in the life of the community.'

'You've hit the nail on the head. I'd like to be mayor some day—or at least fire chief or something similar. I've got pals in the village, and I feel at home with them.'

'Very well,' Materna said gently. 'If that's your idea of heaven on earth—I've no objections.'

'Not even though my pals look up to Johannes Eichler?'

'No, my boy.'

'That's damned decent of you.' Hermann was moved. He had obviously misunderstood his father until now. Materna not only knew a bit about farming—he could read his son's innermost thoughts, and his broadmindedness was positively Germanic. 'I'll never forget this, Father.'

'I hope not.' Alfons Materna rose with an air of decision which betokened that he had worked out his tillage plans for the coming year. The new crop took shape in his mind's eye as he walked on ahead, covering the ground with long strides.

They met at the pool in the woods on one of the last radiant autumn days of the year. Easily accessible from the Gross-Grieben road, it was a gleaming expanse of midnight-blue water the size of a circus arena, bordered by a strip of mossy ground and fringed with dark fir-trees.

'It's great to see you,' said Eugen Eis.

'I'll have to go almost at once,' Brigitte told him. 'I only came to tell you I can't stay.'

'I know, I know,' Eis smiled confidently. He was a man of the world, in so far as Maulen constituted the world. He took Brigitte's hand and pulled her towards him.

The pool in the woods was a rendezvous much favoured by lovers from Maulen and the surrounding district. Not only could it be approached by a variety of paths, most of them tortuous in the extreme, but its seclusion made it ideal for certain purposes. There were no houses near by and the trees formed a silent, protective screen. It was generally and plausibly alleged that a substantial section of the population had been begotten here.

'Scared?' asked Eis.

'What of?' Although Brigitte tried to give the impression that she was in command of the situation, her voice shook slightly. She had no experience of such trysts but did her best not to reveal her embarrassing lack of savoir faire. She knew from hearsay that Eugen Eis was the most desirable man in the district, and she did not want him to think her a prude.

'Can I trust you, Eugen?'

'Like a brother. Just try me and see.' Eis pulled off his jacket, spread it on the grass and lay down. He invited Brigitte to join him, but she hesitated.

Eugen Eis chuckled. He knew how to treat people, especially girls. You only had to cast doubt on their courage and they broke out in a rash of irresponsibility.

'You are scared, aren't you? Is it your father?'

'Why should I be scared of my father? He knows exactly where I am and who I'm with.'

W.   D

Eis sat up with a start. He looked round suspiciously but could only see water, grass, trees and Brigitte. She was a tempting objective, but not wholly devoid of danger.

'He knows? What did he say?'

'Have fun but not too much fun—that's what he said. He also said that a lot of girls only have fun once.'

'That sounds like him.' Eis relaxed and lay back in the grass. If Materna wasn't making vigorous efforts to restrain his daughter it was as good as a parental blessing. 'He's right, of course.'

Stiffly Brigitte lay down beside him.

'Comfortable?' he asked, putting his arm round her with possessive self-assurance.

She didn't know how to answer that, not having any idea whether what she was doing was comfortable or not. She scarcely felt his hand as it rested on her shoulders, then slid downwards to her breast. Her blood seemed to roar in her ears like a waterfall.

The next thing she heard was the sound of hoarse, furious barking. Eis froze, then rolled sideways and snatched his hand away.

Two dogs burst out of the dense fir-trees, closely followed by Jacob Jablonski. The animals continued to bark wildly at the end of their long double-leash. Jablonski grinned. 'Don't be scared,' he called. 'I'm only putting the brutes through their paces, but they're a job to hold.'

'Blast you!' Eis said angrily. 'Why do you have to train them here?'

'I've got to train them somewhere,' Jablonski replied without malice. He had shortened the leash now, and was standing close beside Eis and Brigitte.

Eis said: 'Materna sent you.'

'I don't need sending anywhere. I go where I like and I stay as long as it suits me.'

Jablonski sat down beside the pool some way away. He appeared to be engrossed in his dogs, who were now wagging their tails cheerfully. Before long, the man and the two animals seemed to have become part of the scenery.

It dawned on Eis that he could go where he liked with Materna's daughter—Jablonski and the dogs would always follow him.

On the other hand, he had obviously been advised against direct intervention, and this implied, once again, that Materna was not fundamentally opposed to the match.

Eis reached for Brigitte's hand. 'I think we make a handsome couple,' he said in a low voice. 'What do you think?'

Brigitte bridled and detached her hand from his. Then she made the remark she had been rehearsing for days past: 'Don't try to fool me, Eugen. You've got girls all over the place. I'm just the latest on the list.'

Eis produced a bitter smile which conveyed that he was more sinned against than sinning—that it was the girls who were after him, not the converse.

'I'm sick of the whole business.'

'But you carry on just the same.'

'Maybe I'm desperate, maybe I'm just bored,' he said. 'Maybe I haven't found a woman who really understands me.' He could marry into the Gasthaus if he wanted, he told her. Christine Scharfke was crazy about him, but she wasn't the marrying kind. Besides, was he supposed to spend the rest of his life pouring beer and schnapps and wiping up other people's slops? No, he deserved better than that.

'It's funny,' he said, fondling her vigorously, 'I've developed quite a liking for your father since I realized what a peach of a daughter he has.'

Brigitte thought for a moment. Why shouldn't she be the woman who finally provided Eugen with the steadying influence he yearned for so deeply? She felt strong enough to undertake the task. 'Do you really mean it?' she asked.

'Cross my heart,' Eis replied without hesitation. He breathed jerkily, suggestively, and his hand started to caress her thigh.

At that moment a shot rang out not far away, followed immediately by another. Jablonski's dogs jumped up and pricked their ears. Brigitte smoothed her skirt down and Eis removed his hand.

Jablonski said expertly: 'That was a carbine, not a rifle. About two hundred yards away, somewhere near the lake. Someone else is putting in a bit of practice, I should imagine.'

Cries rang out, coming progressively closer. It sounded as if a stag was crashing through the undergrowth, but the hunted beast proved to be Fritz Fischer. He burst from the trees like a champagne cork.

'Someone shot at me!' he yelled.

Eis had leapt to his feet and was regarding the noisy intruder with disfavour. Jablonski and the dogs approached, looking interested.

'You mean to say someone fired at you and missed?'

'There I was,' panted Fischer, 'sitting in a dinghy near the bank, mending nets, when suddenly someone fired at me. The first shot landed to the left of me—I ducked. The second shot went to the right—I ducked again, but that time I lost my balance and fell in.'

Jablonski grinned. 'Nice day for a bathe.'

'It was attempted murder!' Fischer yelled. 'There's only one man who'd try a thing like that, and that's Materna.'

'I wouldn't open your mouth so wide,' Jablonski advised. 'Your tonsils'll catch cold. Besides, you'll make the dogs mad.'

'I'll take that man to court!' Fischer roared.

'You're crazy,' Jablonski retorted. 'It can't have been Alfons. He never misses.'

'Who was it, then?'

'I can't believe it was Father,' Brigitte said.

Eis gave her a soothing nod. Looking down at Fischer, he said amiably: 'Don't jump to conclusions, Fritz. Judging by what you just said, you can't have seen who was shooting at you. Ever heard of a ricochet?'

'What's that!' Fischer hissed furiously. 'Who the hell do you think you are, taking Materna's side just because you and his daughter . . .'

'Cut that out!' snapped Eis.

Fischer looked bemused. 'Well, this beats everything! Johannes Eichler won't believe me when I tell him.'

'And you can cut that out too!' Eis bellowed. He was conscious of Brigitte's admiring gaze and it spurred him on. 'Just because you wet your pants it doesn't mean I have to lose my head. Do you know what we do with people who shit themselves whenever they hear a shot? We write them off. Is that what you want?'

Johannes Eichler's reaction to the above events was airily offhand. Now that he thought he had the situation in Maulen under complete control, his method of dealing with anything that displeased him was simply to order its elimination.

The recipient of his instructions in this case was Ignaz Uschkurat, acting in his capacity as mayor, not president of the Farmers' Union.

'My dear Uschkurat,' Eichler said casually, 'I hear that someone shot at our friend and associate Fritz Fischer. I don't like that.'

'Neither do I, Eichler—if it's true, of course.'

'Why shouldn't it be?' Eichler smiled sagely. 'The shots were fired in the wood. The wood belongs to Materna, and Fischer's no friend of his. That's something to be going on with. I'd gladly deal with the matter myself, but I've got more important things to attend to at present. I'm sure you'll handle it for me.'

A frown settled on Uschkurat's flat, swarthy, peasant features. 'Must it be me?' he asked, almost beseechingly.

Eichler registered surprise. 'I know at least three people who would gladly relieve you of your mayoral duties.'

'Very well.' Uschkurat rose, hitched his trousers up and withdrew. He walked as if he were carrying a hundredweight of potatoes on his back.

Eichler sat on, staring into space and thinking, not of his forthcoming marriage—that was approaching rapidly enough —but of certain developments in the outside world.

Eichler not only ministered to the men in his immediate sphere of command but kept in touch with old war-time comrades. One of them lived in Osterode, another in Allenstein, and a third in Lötzen, and all had come to the simultaneous and timely conclusion that great changes lay ahead. There were portents of a new and prodigious age to come.

Eichler had duly decided to reconnoitre the position. In the process he discovered that war-time friends and likeminded individuals in Osterode, Allenstein and Lötzen had undertaken the establishment of local branches of the National Socialist Party, together with the storm-troop detachments that went with them, commonly called S.A. units. He had recently been studying pamphlets and newspapers, among them the *Völkischer Beobachter*, *Stürmer* and *Angriff*. He even went to the lengths of ordering a book entitled *Mein Kampf*, not that he read it. Possession of it was quite enough for him.

Having studied the signs of the times with due care, Eichler familiarized his most intimate adherents in Maulen with the new epoch-making ideology. 'It can't hurt to take an interest in the movement,' was his cautious introduction to the subject. 'Maulen might even benefit from it, under certain circumstances, always provided the right ideas get into the right hands.'

Ignaz Uschkurat laboured hard under the trust reposed in him. It was days before he could summon up the courage to call on Materna, by which time the first frost of the year had arrived.

Uschkurat had to absorb a substantial dose of Dutch courage before he set off. Surprised to find Materna in a welcoming mood, he opened the conversation with a gleam of hope in his eyes.

'I hope you don't think I've got anything against you personally.'

'Why should you have?' Expectantly, Materna lit a cheroot. 'After all, I'm an easy-going creditor. I've never pressed you for repayment—not yet, anyway. You're not planning to put pressure on me, are you?'

Uschkurat threw up his hands, which resembled the scoops of an excavator. 'You can't expect me to sacrifice myself for your sake,' he said cryptically.

'I think I follow you.' Materna seemed to have a pretty fair idea of where the shoe pinched. 'You'd like to stay mayor, wouldn't you? Well, I'm prepared to help you. The only question is, what's the most effective way of going about it?'

'Anyone who wants to keep my job has to show results.' Uschkurat kneaded his hands together. 'I'm responsible for peace and good order in the village. I can't allow my fellow-citizens to go in fear of their lives.'

'That's a new one on me.' Materna said bitterly. 'I know of one case where an inhabitant of this village was blown to shreds. But let's leave that for the moment. You're here to put the screws on me but your sensitive nature recoils at the thought. You'd be glad of any way out.'

Uschkurat nodded. 'Precisely.'

Materna rose and paced the room. 'I may be able to offer you just what you need. What would you say if I made you the most successful mayor in the history of Maulen?'

'How do you propose to do that?' Uschkurat asked eagerly.

'By presenting the parish of Maulen with a unique addition to its common land. I mean Dog's Meadow.'

Uschkurat flushed. Everyone in the village knew what Dog's Meadow signified: first-class soil, ideal building land, and the finest place for communal festivities in the entire district—in short, a pearl of a property.

'Are you serious?' he gasped. 'Could you do it? Will you do it? What's in it for you?'

'Friendship, pure and simple,' Materna said with gentle irony. 'But don't let that worry you. All you need take note of officially is that I'm prepared to make over this land to the community, without financial consideration, reciprocal action or legal conditions. It would be a gift—that's the official term, I believe. Well?'

'Good God, man, they'll eat out of my hand if I pull this off.'

'And I'll be happy to tell everyone that you squeezed it out of me. The man talked me into it—that's what I'll say. It'll be all your own work. Agreed?'

'Thanks,' Uschkurat said, greatly moved. 'I'll never forget this—never! You're a good chap, Materna. I won't hear a word against you after this.' He already saw himself going down in the annals of Maulen as the man who had doubled, if not trebled, the land owned by the community. 'You can count on me from now on.'

'I hope so. That's to say, I have a temporary use for your support.' Materna folded his hands like a man at prayer. 'However, this is just between us for the moment. We'll tie the whole thing up legally in the meantime, but I decide when to break the news to our friends—all right?'

'I've noted the particulars down,' Constable Klinger said in an official tone.

Fritz Fischer looked outraged. 'Is that all you're going to do?'

The first snow had already fallen and the frost was beginning to bite into the ground. Masuria's long winter sleep was drawing near, and Fischer's charge of attempted murder seemed to be sinking into oblivion too.

'I don't need you to remind me of my duty,' the policeman said coldly. 'You'd do better to watch your own behaviour.'

'My behaviour?' Fischer demanded in a rage. 'First I'm barricaded out of my own home, then someone takes pot shots at me, and this evening my big fish-tank was rifled—there must have been half a hundredweight of eels in it.'

'Was it locked up?'

'What do you mean, locked up? Stop quibbling, Klinger. The lid was on—that's good enough. If they aren't there someone must have pinched them.'

'That's conjecture, not evidence.'

'Why the hell don't you clear this up once and for all? Give that bastard Materna a going over!'

'It's inadvisable to mention names when there's no evidence and no strong lead to go on,' Klinger said reprovingly.

Fritz Fischer felt grossly betrayed. He didn't know what Maulen was coming to these days. Klinger had been spinning him along for weeks and nobody seemed prepared to offer any active support. Staunch cronies of long standing had let him down flat, and even the policeman did nothing but make difficulties.

'So you're not interested in finding the guilty party?'

'I have my rules of procedure and I stick to them,' Klinger replied.

Fischer swore under his breath. Turning on his heel, he swept out of the policeman's house and made for his bicycle, which was leaning against the churchyard wall. Beside it stood Siegfried Grienspan.

'You seem to have a puncture,' he said amiably. 'I was just passing, so I . . .'

'Jesus Christ Almighty!' Fischer roared, his nerves at breaking-point. One glance had told him what was wrong with his bicycle. There was no air in either of the tyres. 'Have you been mucking around with it?' he demanded menacingly.

Grienspan looked shocked. 'Why on earth should I? I only wanted to help.'

'Help? Did you want to help your bosom pal Materna by letting the air out of my tyres? You'd like to finish me, the pair of you, but I'll show you. I'm up to your filthy Jewish tricks!'

'Shame on you!' Grienspan said bravely—sadly, too, because he was ashamed for him. 'How could you say such a thing!' He walked off, a stooped but curiously dignified figure, shaking his head ruefully.

Fritz Fischer glared after him in triumph. At least there was one person in Maulen he could put in his place. He did not notice the Terrible Twins crouching behind the church-yard wall a bare twenty yards away, motionless as two stone statues. The only sign of life about them was the gleam in their eyes.

Having fortified himself at length in the Gasthaus, Fischer set out for home, wheeling his bicycle and cursing. He could scarcely believe his eyes when he neared his cottage by the lake. The walls had been garishly daubed with paint. The place looked like a zebra, except that there were red stripes as well as black and white.

'God Almighty!' Fischer exclaimed, beside himself with rage.

He stood rooted to the spot for some moments, then hur-ried towards the cottage. A bewildering sight met his eyes as he stared through the open door. The living-room was completely empty save for a rotting fish in the middle of the floor.

It was some minutes before the mist lifted from Fischer's eyes. When it did, he noticed two long shadows stretching from the open door to the putrid fish. He looked round and saw Konrad Klinger and Peter Bachus watching him with close attention.

Fischer's head drooped wearily. At a loss how to react, he said nothing.

'Nice place you have here,' Konrad Klinger said brightly. 'Reminds me of one of those abstract paintings. Didn't know you were keen on modern art.'

'Congratulations,' Peter Bachus said, just as brightly. 'It's a cute idea, painting your cottage red-white-and-black. No one in the district will dare to copy you.'

'Go to hell,' Fischer said weakly. His voice rose to a bellow as he added: 'What in God's name did I ever do to you?'

'It's all quite simple, really,' Konrad explained. 'If you want to live in peace you've got to let your neighbours live in peace too. All that's needed is a little goodwill on both sides.'

Peter Bachus proceeded to expatiate on the chemical pro-

perties of certain substances, with particular reference to the
contamination of water. This could be brought about by
effluent from factories and tanneries, also by the addition
of chemicals.

'They say one drop of acid can poison two thousand gallons
of water. A couple of bottles would be enough for Lake
Maulen, and they wouldn't cost much more than half a
hundredweight of eels. You might like to think that over.
Take your time, but don't take too long.'

Winter descended on Masuria like an eagle swooping on a
rabbit. Snow swathed the countryside, and Lake Maulen was
frozen over by the beginning of December. The villagers
retired indoors and stoked their stoves.

Old Mother Mischgoreit pulled on her thick sheepskin coat
and hobbled busily from house to house.

'It's uncanny, this weather,' she announced. 'You can
hardly wee-wee without freezing up. There hasn't been anything like it for fifty years. It must mean something!'

'Someone ought to silence that old bitch once and for all,'
Eugen Eis declared. 'She's always upsetting the village. Even
the men get jumpy when she's around.'

Johannes Eichler simply laughed and applied himself to his
grog like every other winter-bound Masurian. Brewed according to a time-honoured formula, this beverage consisted of
rum (indispensable), sugar (optional), and water (inessential).
The Masurians' other traditional winter occupation was sitting
and thinking, and when they ran out of food for thought they
just sat.

The Christmas holiday was festive but uneventful. Johannes
Eichler went to stay in Lötzen with his future bride. Eugen
Eis got drunk and remained so for three days. The Reverend
Dr Bachus, temporary ruler of Maulen, celebrated Christ's
birth with a will. Even standing room was limited in church.

On New Year's Eve and New Year's Day Christian Scharfke
chalked up his biggest turnover in years. The bar was thick
with smoke and good-fellowship. Two peasants spent the
night in the snow without suffering any ill effects, and their
reappearance next morning was greeted with roars of laughter.

On January 5th, in twenty-two degrees of frost, it seemed
that an unusual experience was in store for the inhabitants
of Maulen. There was a report from Johannisberg that a

wolf had infiltrated the district, probably from Poland, and was lurking somewhere in the Grieben-Siegwalde-Maulen area. The beast had apparently broken into hen-houses, savaged red deer, attacked dogs and threatened human beings.

'This menace must be dealt with as quickly as possible.' The decree travelled from the chairman of the rural district council, via the local administrator and Mayor Uschkurat, to Johannes Eichler, who raised the alarm. Here, at last, was a chance to show what he and his men were made of. A project of this kind required organization, but organization was Eichler's forte. He got Eis to muster all the leading villagers, and they turned out to a man, aglow with enthusiasm and eager for the chase.

Eichler's plan of campaign quickly assumed vast proportions. Determined to involve the whole area in his wolf-hunt, he sent the chairman of the rural district council a message to the effect that 'all aspects of the operation' were under his control. The chairman's reply was: 'Good hunting!'— a signal mark of confidence.

Where feats of strategy were concerned, Eichler rivalled Marshal Hindenburg at the Battle of Tannenberg—or so it was generally alleged. He divided the surrounding countryside into operational sectors and assigned a column of beaters to each with orders to converge on Maulen. Eichler himself was to lead the guns.

'It'll be a picnic,' he declared confidently.

The preparations took up an entire day and half a night. Headquarters were established in the Gasthaus, where grog was brewed in a wash-bucket.

The great drive was to be launched from five points simultaneously at five o'clock sharp next morning. Before this came the distribution of alcoholic refreshments. Sector commanders were issued with full canteens and there was a special allocation of piping hot sausages—half a pound to each active participant—the cost being borne by one of the Home Guard's special funds.

The atmosphere was that of a public holiday, happy and expectant. Soft leather boots padded silently across the snow and cheerful conversation filled the frosty morning air. Wilhelm, verger, sexton and senior bugler of the Volunteer Fire Brigade band, stood ready to sound a huntsmanlike call on his instrument.

Johannes Eichler, who turned up swathed in furs, aroused universal admiration by wearing a grass-green huntsman's hat. Eugen Eis acted as his gun-bearer.

The sector commanders reported their groups present and correct, the riflemen saluted, and Eichler acknowledged their salutes with a confident air. Glancing at his watch, he saw that there was a few minutes left before the start of the grand drive. He decided to put them to good use.

'Form a half-circle round me, men!' he commanded.

While his followers were clustering round him there came a distant jingling of sleigh-bells. Having expressly forbidden all unnecessary noise until the drive began, Eichler treated Eis to a reproving glare.

'Must be that Materna again,' Eis observed.

The jingling sleigh hove in sight. It was drawn by two of Materna's best horses, to be sure, but the lone figure on the box was that of Jacob Jablonski. Grinning like a nutcracker, he brought his team to a halt in the middle of the assembled huntsmen.

Eichler's face darkened. 'What's the meaning of this idiocy?'

'Just what I was going to ask you,' Jablonski said gleefully. Reaching behind him, he lugged the carcase of a large grey animal off the sleigh and flung it to the ground. It landed just in front of Eichler's fur-lined boots.

Alfons Materna had shot the wolf during the night. He fired once, felling the beast cleanly and deeply wounding Johannes Eichler at the same time.

Fritz Fischer did not make his way home from the abortive wolf-hunt until nearly midday. He was full of grog and deep in thought. Not even the most lavish distribution of free drink could efface the impression that Eichler had sustained a defeat, and Eichler's taciturn manner tended to confirm this. He informed the chairman of the rural district council that the wolf had been duly dispatched and received a message of thanks and appreciation, but it did little to raise his spirits.

Like a number of others, Fischer began to ponder critically on the Eichler era. He continued to do so until the moment when he thought he saw his cottage burning. It was wreathed in dense clouds of smoke.

Horrified, he rushed towards it, only to discover with relief that the chimney was blocked. A fir-tree protruded from it, and hanging from the fir-tree was a placard which read: 'Stolen from Materna's wood—witnesses available.' A bundle of oily rags was burning in the stove and the cottage stank like a sewer.

On Fischer's table lay a sheet of paper bearing the following message in block capitals: 'The time for reflection is past. This is your final warning.'

Fischer stood there for several minutes, limp as a tree in a cloud-burst. Then, steeling himself for what he had to do, he set off briskly for the village.

First, he went to see Constable Klinger and told him that if he had ever laid charges, whether against an unknown party or against Materna personally, he hereby withdrew them. Klinger not only accepted this decision but commented on its wisdom.

Next, Fischer called on Speer and Uschkurat. He assured both men that he was now in full agreement with them on all outstanding points, not excluding the proposal to bestow honorary membership of the Volunteer Fire Brigade on Alfons Materna. He was congratulated on his excellent judgement.

Finally, Fischer hurried to Materna's farm.

'I've come here for a frank talk,' he said simply.

'I'm listening,' Materna replied. He gestured towards Siegfried Grienspan, who was standing beside the window. 'But perhaps you owe someone an apology first.'

'That isn't necessary,' Grienspan said, looking embarrassed and uneasy. 'I don't want any apologies.'

Fischer did not hesitate. 'I beg your pardon. I made a mistake and I'm sorry. Do you accept my apology?'

'But of course,' Grienspan said promptly, 'I don't bear grudges.'

Fischer thereupon launched into a lengthy statement, the gist of which was that men were fallible creatures and easily prone to misunderstanding. 'We're neighbours,' he concluded. 'In my opinion, we ought to behave as such.'

'Your moderation astounds me,' Materna said drily.

Fischer's carp-like face looked positively transfigured, almost as if it had been basted with butter. 'You have your farm and I have my fishery. There's no reason why we should tread on each other's corns.'

'I know what you'd like. You'd like to extend your fishing rights to my stretch of lake-shore. Well, I might agree to that on certain conditions.'

'Name them.'

'If you really behave like a good neighbour from now on, you can fish from my land.'

'I'm your man, Materna,' Fischer assured him. 'I'd do anything for my fishery. We'll get on like a house on fire from now on, you see if we don't.'

'Stranger things have happened,' Materna said. 'Let's hope for the best, shall we?'

Johannes Eichler deemed it advisable, in view of recent developments, to summon his paladins for a pep-talk. Accordingly, he invited them to a 'confidential discussion' in the back room of the Gasthaus Scharfke.

Eugen Eis was first into the arena, as instructed. It was his duty to make the usual preparations: room temperature warm, beer cool, schnapps cold, a large arm-chair for Eichler, a lower one for Eis, folding chairs for the others.

Hermann Materna, the promising recruit, marched in full of fire and determination—not that he knew what was required of him. He grasped Eis's hand and shook it vigorously.

'What's on the agenda today?' he asked. 'Do you know, Eis?'

'Of course I know.' Eis didn't know, but no born leader makes such an admission to a subordinate. 'I was told in confidence, though.'

Christian Scharfke sidled up to Eis and drew him aside. 'I'm afraid there may be trouble,' he whispered.

'It's your job to see there isn't any. Everything has to go off smoothly today. Eichler's got a bee in his bonnet about something.'

'Maybe,' Scharfke said, 'but women's emotions are beyond my control. Christine refuses to do any serving, and all because of you, Eugen. She says you've been running after Brigitte Materna, and she won't put a glass on any table you're sitting at.'

'She's talking bullshit,' Eis exclaimed angrily. 'If you want to know, I've been acting on secret instructions.'

'I believe you,' Scharfke said. 'All the same, just try explaining that to my daughter.'

'I haven't the time now—you do it for me. Make sure she serves the drinks and keeps her trap shut. I'll give her a personal explanation when the party's over.'

Meanwhile, other invitees had arrived. Uschkurat, Speer and Fischer turned up in a threesome, which was not their normal custom. They entered with heavy tread, looking as if they had come to bury someone.

Johannes Eichler, who reached the place of assembly immediately after them, seemed to be in excellent form. His opening words were: 'There are great times ahead, my friends. All I can tell you at the moment is, you're in for a big surprise!'

They drank in silence, observing a time-honoured custom that mental exertion should be preceded by alcoholic stimulation.

'Our young friend Hermann will stand guard against unwelcome intruders and eavesdroppers,' Eichler announced in friendly tones.

'Yes, sir!' Hermann said promptly.

The order did not come as a surprise. Just as Eugen Eis acted as Eichler's chief of staff in Maulen, so Hermann had recently been fulfilling the functions of an aide-de-camp. Eagle-eyed, he took up his post outside the door.

'Gentlemen,' Eichler said, as soon as Hermann had withdrawn, 'let's get down to business straight away.'

Eichler's faithful henchmen nodded gravely, but they avoided their leader's eye and their leader did not fail to register the fact.

'We all know where the main source of trouble in our village lies,' Eichler pursued, undeterred. 'We also know that it would be a stain on our good name to tolerate the situation any longer. I take it we're all agreed on this point?'

His confidence did not seem wholly justified, to judge by the half-hearted nods of those present. For the first time, Eichler became fully aware of their mulish indifference, and it filled him with mounting uneasiness. Almost impatiently, he said: 'Well, *aren't* we all agreed? If not, we'll be playing into our enemies' hands. No one wants to do that, surely?'

Eichler's question was greeted with ominous silence. Noting

it with some alarm, he resorted to a method which almost always paid off—the direct appeal.

'What do you think, Fischer?'

Fischer wriggled like an eel, but a moment later he seemed to be swimming in Eichler's wake again. 'Materna's been on at me. He tried to put the screws on me, but I wasn't having any. I don't trust him.'

'Good,' said Eichler. 'That's something at least. What about you, Speer?'

'Well, he did foot the bill for the church repairs—and offer to buy a new fire appliance. I think that puts us under a certain obligation.'

'A certain obligation, of course.' Eichler soared grandly above considerations of this kind. If that was the only stumbling-block, he wasn't worried. 'A few pots of paint and a new fire-pump are no substitute for community spirit. What's your view, Uschkurat?'

'Well,' Uschkurat said, 'even Materna can show community spirit sometimes.'

'How do you mean?' Eichler asked. His sarcasm was studiously mild.

'He's made the parish a present of Dog's Meadow—given it away just like that!'

'No!' yelped Eichler. 'He can't have—I don't believe you.'

'It's a fact,' Uschkurat replied simply. 'I've got it in writing. It's all legal and above board.'

Eichler shook with rage. 'That's the meanest trick anyone's ever played on me! He won't get away with it, though. There are going to be some changes round here, you mark my words!'

Towards the end of January, Old Mother Mischgoreit started to haunt the village again.

'I saw the Topich as I was crossing the lake,' she proclaimed in oracular tones. 'He popped out of a hole in the ice, right in front of me. He was wearing his red cap and staring at me.'

'Have you taken to the bottle?' inquired the Reverend Dr Bachus, wrinkling his brow.

Old Mother Mischgoreit snarled at him. 'I'm only a poor old woman,' she said with a baneful smile. 'Some people have cellars full of consecrated wine, but not the likes of us.'

The parson withdrew in confusion and notified Klinger. The policeman said: 'We might get her for disturbing the peace, but I doubt it.'

In school, Maximilian Vetter tried to convince his pupils that there were no such things as water-goblins, but had to admit that he made little impression on them. He appealed to Eugen Eis for help.

Eis ran Old Mother Mischgoreit to earth and told her that if she didn't stop her nonsense she'd have to pay rent for her cottage again.

'No one'll be paying rent soon,' she retorted boldly. 'The world's falling apart at the seams.'

The old crone became more obsessed and vehement with every passing day. Scurrying through the village with matted hair and clothes awry, she forced her way into the Gasthaus and harangued everyone in the bar.

'You'll all die like dogs!' she declared. 'It won't be long now.'

'Who told you that?' someone demanded. 'Your water-goblin?'

Old Mother Mischgoreit glared at the company. 'Drink first, then drown—that's what the Topich said. It'll rain blood, he said. Remember that, you dogs!' So saying, she shuffled off into the snow and disappeared.

They did not find her until three days later, on January 29th. She was floating in the ice-hole in the lake, apparently drowned. Her hands were clamped to her left breast in the putative region of her heart.

Quite a few people in Maulen whispered secretly that the Topich had come to fetch her. 'There are dark days ahead when the water-goblin appears,' they added. 'He's never satisfied with a single victim.'

'What does a dog do when someone lashes out at it?' Materna asked. 'Tries to get out of the way, of course. Well, that's what I'm doing.'

'Forgive me, but I can't help doubting that after all that has happened in recent weeks.' Siegfried Grienspan studied his glass. His face was impassive but his eyes shone alertly. 'Don't you think a little toleration is called for?'

'Dead men are the most tolerant of the lot,' Materna said grimly. 'They have one great advantage over the living —they can't die any more.'

It was late at night. Candlelight danced over their faces and red wine glowed in the glasses on the table. Jacob Jablonski was sitting in the shadows in the far corner of the kitchen with the dogs stretched out at his feet. Materna fell silent.

Grienspan said: 'You're a brave man, Materna.'

Materna smiled. 'You're wrong there. Mean, cunning and vindictive would be nearer the mark. I just can't bring myself to make way for a man like Eichler—not without a fight.'

'You're deliberately punishing him.'

'I've run out of punishments, Grienspan,' Materna leant back in his chair. 'I can't think of a worse one than letting him have Margarete.'

'That's unfair and ungrateful, Materna.' Grienspan spoke with evident reluctance. 'It isn't beyond the bounds of possibility that Eichler and your wife have a genuine regard for one another. They may even be in love.'

'We'll soon see.'

'That Dog's Meadow business,' Grienspan said reprovingly. 'You oughtn't to have done it, you know. Eichler will never forgive you.'

'So what? He'll have to marry her now if he doesn't want the whole village to call him a fortune-hunter. In short, I've got him hooked.'

'How did it happen?' Eichler demanded. 'How could it have happened without our finding out in time?'

'It's typical of those weak-kneed bastards,' Eis said. 'They always lick the boots of the highest bidder.'

'What about you, Eugen? Have you been making up to Materna like the rest?'

'Only his daughter. There's a big difference.'

Eichler groaned. 'God, what lousy material I have to work with!' He glanced at Eis sharply. 'Did you know about Dog's Meadow?'

'No, really I didn't—I swear it. I was getting places with the Materna girl, too. She was ready to eat out of my hand, and she knew as little about the Dog's Meadow scheme as I did. Materna dreamed it up all by himself.'

Eichler was shaken to the core. He clutched his chest as though to convey that he had cherished a viper in his bosom, but his words were less emotional.

'What can we do?'

Eis shrugged. A battle had been lost. To a born fighter, the only course was to rally the surviving troops and regain their allegiance.

'I hesitate to mention it at this particular time,' Eis said, 'but what about your dairy? I've been running it for years now. What I mean is, I've never let you down, have I? I don't expect you to sign it over to me straight away, but I'd welcome a guaranteed share of the profits—say thirty per cent.'

Eichler's fortunes were at a low ebb, and he knew it. Righteousness had once more fallen prey to the forces of evil. Tormentedly, he asked himself what he, of all people, had done to deserve such a fate.

6

The word Maulen did not, as some malicious people alleged, derive from *Maul*, meaning 'trap', as in 'shut your trap', but from *Mühle*, or 'mill'. There were three villages by that name in Masuria, to wit: Gross-Maulen, Klein-Maulen, and Maulen proper.

By the beginning of the nineteenth century Maulen's name had already figured twice in local records. The first entry concerned a miller named Leberecht who murdered his wife, her lover, and her mother, who had acted as go-between. He was acquitted. On the second occasion, a band of South German mercenaries in the service of France were waylaid and robbed in the vicinity of Maulen during the Napoleonic Wars. Thus, two of the most salient characteristics of Maulen's inhabitants declared themselves even in its historical beginnings: a sense of honour and a spirit of aggression.

The middle of the nineteenth century—spring 1852, to be precise—saw the discovery on Maulen Moor, near what was known as Hindenburg Hill, of the grave of Friedrich der Schwarze, a knight who got his name from the black armour encasing his bones. This proved that the soil of Maulen had been enriched by Germanic blood as early as 1410, when the Teutonic Knights were battling against the heathen Pole.

In 1888 Maulen became the scene of large-scale military manœuvres in which live ammunition was used. General Dennwitz-Pleiderer and his staff officers spent the night at the Gasthaus Scharfke and an entire battalion was billeted in the village. Next year the population of Maulen shot up by fifteen per cent, a phenomenon which earned it the not unmerited sobriquet of 'Soldiers' Rest'.

In 1904 Maulen lost the services of three policemen in quick succession. A poacher named Uschkurat—no relation of the subsequent mayor—gunned them down in the woods. In 1914 Marshal Hindenburg passed through the village by night, and an extensive Russian burial-ground beside the road to Siegwalde testified to his ensuing victories. Eighteen of Maulen's fathers, sons and brothers left their bones in France during the war to end all wars.

At the great plebiscite of July 1920 the Masurians voted overwhelmingly in favour of Germany. There were only seventeen exceptions in Maulen, and these were quickly given an opportunity to leave the land which they were reluctant to see under German sovereignty. This marked the beginning of operations by the Home Guard, founded by Johannes Eichler, who embarked on his public career in 1923. In 1927, after organizing the Fire Brigade, Sports Club and male voice choir, he established the local branch of the Stahlhelm, or League of Combat Veterans.

The villagers were almost exclusively Protestant, patriotic and proud of their local traditions. By 1930 almost ninety per cent of the population voted German Nationalist.

The Social Democrats commanded only thirty electoral votes, the Communists one. Zealous attempts were made to establish the identity of this blot on Maulen's escutcheon, but in vain.

After 1930 the picture changed. The National Socialists appeared on the scene, winning more and more votes at each election. By 1932 they claimed thirty-one per cent of the poll. Johannes Eichler tolerated the new movement at first, then quietly contacted his war-time friends in Allenstein, Lötzen and Osterode, who had founded local branches of the National Socialist Party.

The Nazis' assumption of power marked the beginning

of a new age in Maulen, and the general representative of
that new age, both in Maulen and its environs, was none
other than Johannes Eichler.

The news that a certain Adolf Hitler had acceded to the
Chancellorship seemed to rouse Eichler from a dark and
dismal dream. He realized at once that it was time to unfurl
the only true banner. A new dawn was breaking, a dawn
whose like Germany had never witnessed before.

'We must hold a torch-light procession,' Eichler declared.

'But there aren't any torches,' replied Eis, who had still
to perceive the signs of the times with sufficient clarity.
'Anyway, even if we had some, who would carry them?'

'Every right-minded German in Maulen!'

Eis could hardly dissociate himself from sentiments of this
kind. He, too, had heard the announcement on the radio.
'Assumption of power' had a magic ring to it, and he didn't
want to be left out. 'Tell you what, we'll organize a sort of
National Day, with a remembrance service at the war
memorial.'

This was not enough for Eichler. If he could not have a
torch-light procession, he wanted a bonfire at the very least.
'A pile of logs in front of the war memorial, a can of petrol,
and away we go!'

Eis concurred. For an hour he listened to Eichler con-
versing by telephone with his fellow-ideologists in Osterode,
Lötzen and Allenstein, loudly and with mounting optimism.

'We've called out the whole population,' Eichler said at
last, '—everyone who feels a duty towards this great country
of ours, that is.'

While Eichler and Eis were thinking German thoughts,
Maximilian Vetter greeted the clarion call with a touch of uneasiness. Having heard tidings of the formation of a 'cabinet
of national concentration', Hindenburg's down-to-earth appeal
for careful deliberation, and Johannes Eichler's announcement
of a German National Remembrance Day, complete with
bonfire celebration, the headmaster decided that it was time
to test the direction of the wind.

His first call was on the Reverend Dr Bachus whom he found
digging up a clamp of potatoes. The parson was sweating profusely.

'Well, Vicar,' he said, 'what do you think of the latest political developments?'

Bachus drove his fork into the ground and leant on it. 'Why ask me? I'm not a politician.'

'You're not worried?'

'Only about my potatoes. The frost seems to have got at them. As for the other thing, I've never been an opponent of nationalism—never voted Social Democrat, either, unlike some people I know.'

Vetter retired in confusion. He was a nationalist too, and had always been. If he had ever voted Socialist—which could not be proved beyond doubt—he had done so in good faith. There was no disputing his loyalty and patriotism. Hurriedly, he made for Klinger's house.

'Have you heard?' he asked. 'Hitler is the new Chancellor.'

Klinger shrugged. 'Someone has to be.'

'But aren't you worried that it's Hitler, of all people?'

'Nothing worries me,' the policeman said. 'I'm a public servant like you, and as public servants we have our duty to do. I come under the Ministry of Justice, you come under the Ministry of Education. We just do our job.'

Vetter hurried out, jumped on to his bicycle, and pedalled the three miles to Gross-Görchen. On arrival he asked to speak to Herr von Schwernitz-Weibel, a retired army officer and local land-owner.

'Major,' Vetter began respectfully, 'I've come about the present political situation.'

'Balls to the present political situation,' said von Schwernitz-Weibel, who was a gentleman of bucolic demeanour. He was reputed to have relieved himself into a bush during one of the Kaiser's hunting parties, remarking to the royal princess who happened to be present: 'Your Royal Highness must take life as it comes.'

In short, von Schwernitz-Weibel was an original of a type rarely found in Masuria.

'My dear headmaster,' he pursued loudly, 'give those brown-shirted buggers a couple of weeks and they'll dish themselves.'

'Perhaps you underestimate them, Major,' Vetter ventured.

'All right, a couple of months—a year at the most. Till then, we grit our teeth and keep our powder dry. I've had to wait days before getting a shot at a prime stag, but it was worth it in the end.'

Vetter left the autocratic old gentleman feeling unreassured. Von Schwernitz-Weibel probably thought he was a secret Red too. He pedalled back to Maulen meditating on those two eternal inseparables, Goethe and Germany. Such was the basis on which the future must be built. Back in the village, he paraded the pupils in his first and second classes.

'Boys and girls,' he announced, 'there is to be a remembrance service at the war memorial this evening. I propose that we gladden the hearts of those present with a song, the one that starts: "Homeland, thou that gently in my heart reposest."' He took them through it fifteen times until even he was stirred by its beauty.

Those who attended the evening remembrance service at the war memorial seemed equally stirred. The school choir had seldom sung with such fervour, volume, or inaccuracy.

'Youth!' Johannes Eichler exclaimed appreciatively between verses. 'Youth is the corner-stone of the future!'

He was not alone in appreciating the solemnity of this momentous occasion. Bright moonlight and freshly fallen snow combined to bathe the scene in magical radiance. Everything seemed to glow mysteriously, from the stark and simple outlines of the village to the stark and simple faces of its inhabitants.

Almost the entire population had obeyed the summons. Few had dared to stay away, and even Alfons Materna had turned up with his entourage.

Studying the earnest faces of the school-children, Materna whispered to Jablonski: 'They're bellowing their hearts out, poor kids. They'll get pneumonia if they're not careful.'

Thirty mouths continued to open and shut in unison under Vetter's spirited direction. The hymn seemed to have a dozen verses or more. The villagers started to fidget. It was cold on that historic evening—cold as charity.

Johannes Eichler, himself a living block of ice, realized that the shrill piping of the school choir was in danger of ruining the atmosphere. Maulen's inhabitants had begun to warm their frozen feet by stamping in time to the music, and childish voices were plaintively demanding to see the bonfire.

Eichler reacted as a man of action should. Almost before Vetter's charges had finished their song, he stepped forward.

'Today marks the beginning of a new era in Germany,' he said hurriedly. 'We shall be able to say of ourselves that we were privileged to witness a day which will brand itself on the minds of our children and our children's children.'

'He may well be right,' Materna remarked to his immediate neighbours, but Eichler, who was as conscious of his compatriots' warm hearts as of their freezing feet, called out: 'Light the bonfire!'

Fire meant warmth, and warmth was the prime requirement. Eugen Eis lit a bundle of kindling which protruded from the side of the bonfire, and tongues of flame licked their way along the twigs towards the heart of the wood-pile.

Eis had supervised the building of the bonfire late that afternoon. It was constructed with great skill. First came brushwood, then dry pine-wood, then copper-beech logs, and, finally, oak-branches. The flames ought to have shot sky-high, but they didn't. Instead, they progressed slowly, sending out a noxious yellow cloud of smoke as thick as cotton wool.

'What a stink!' exclaimed Konrad Klinger, who had wormed his way to the front of the crowd with Peter Bachus at his side. The boys were now standing next to Alfons Materna, their eyes gleaming triumphantly.

'How did you manage it?' asked Materna.

'Rags,' whispered Konrad. 'We shoved wet rags between the logs and poured a couple of buckets of liquid manure over the top. That did the trick.'

He was right. Fanned by a light breeze, the dense fumes assaulted the noses of the bystanders, who reeled back, coughing, retching and gasping for air.

'Lousy inefficiency!' Eichler muttered, glaring resentfully at Eis. The National Remembrance Day celebrations had smoked and spluttered their way to a standstill, and Eichler knew it. One woman had to be carried away, close to asphyxia, and Vetter shooed his pupils to safety.

'It reeks!' Peter Bachus exclaimed with ill-concealed delight. 'It reeks to high heaven!'

'To the Gasthaus!' Eichler called in ringing tones, eager to save the situation. 'A glass of beer will do us good, my friends. The first round is on me.'

Materna rose to the occasion. 'And I'll stand every loyal German here three tots of Scharfke's best schnapps. Every lady of the same calibre gets at least one glass of the sweet stuff. Further rounds on request.'

That evening, the evening of 30th January 1933, Johannes Eichler made what was probably the most momentous announcement he would ever make. He certainly believed as much when he signalled to Eugen Eis to call the crowded bar of the Gasthaus to order.

Mounting a chair, he said: 'This day decides the destiny of our beloved Fatherland. Adolf Hitler, our Leader, has assumed power with the blessing of the venerable old Field Marshal and President.'

'Bravo!'

'With effect from today, a local branch of the National Socialist German Workers' Party exists in Maulen. I am the Local Group Leader.'

'Hurrah!'

The beer-taps hissed loud and long.

'Blessed are they that toil,' Materna told his fellow-workers with a wink. 'The harder you work the more profit I make.'

For all his pleasantries, Materna never hesitated to lend a hand himself, especially when a job was more than usually arduous or unpleasant. This applied to the annual round of manuring and muck-spreading, which on his farm took place in mid-February—earlier than normal.

The peasant farmers of Maulen called him crazy, but their scorn was mingled with respect. Materna always produced the finest harvests, even if he did manure his fields in the middle of winter.

He organized the dirtiest job of the year on methodical lines. Maria and Jablonski took care of the dung while Brigitte and Hermann drew the liquid manure from the pit. Materna, who knew every patch of ground which needed manure or could do without it, scattered and sprayed his fields in person.

'I need a breather,' Hermann said, wrinkling his nose. Although dominated by the conviction that work of this kind was beneath his dignity, he was impelled to do it by a sense of filial duty. Besides, his father's good example could hardly be ignored. The old man did almost as much work as the rest of them put together.

Materna decided to take a friendly interest in Brigitte, who was ladling liquid manure into the barrel-wagon.

'Well, my girl, how goes the romance?'

'If you mean Eugen Eis, Father, there isn't a man round here to touch him—I'm positive of that.'

'You could be right.'

'And just in case you're interested—nothing definite has happened yet.'

Materna restrained his mirth with difficulty. 'I should hope not, in this weather. What happens when spring comes?'

'I'm your daughter,' Brigitte replied simply.

'That's just what I'm afraid of. On the other hand, I sympathize with your wishes. I can't think of anyone who'd suit you better. You need a husband like Eis.'

'Eugen's wishes are what matters. He needs a woman who'll make it her job in life to love him wholeheartedly.'

Materna was so surprised that he dropped the big scoop and splashed his face with manure. Brigitte continued to toil away doggedly until the barrel-wagon was full.

Hermann reappeared shortly afterwards, looking refreshed. He set the horses in motion and drove the dung-cart out into the fields, accompanied by his father.

Materna watched Hermann as he drove the horses with rough and vigorous movements. He handled the beasts as if they were machines.

'Not really your kind of job, is it, my boy?' Materna said, with every appearance of sympathy. 'If I know you, you'd rather be with your pals, especially now that so much is happening.'

'I'm afraid you're right, Father.'

Materna waited until the barrel-wagon was empty before he continued. 'You know, Hermann, it hurts me to see you doing such an uncongenial job. You're a Materna, and we Maternas like to put our heart and soul into everything we do.'

'Hundred-per-centers, Father, that's us.'

'Why not let yourself go, then? From now on I want you to be Party loyalty personified. If you need a uniform you can have one. If you want to dress up a whole detachment of Brownshirts—all right, I'll be glad to foot the bill. Follow me?'

'All the way,' Hermann replied unsuspectingly.

Materna rubbed his hands. 'Get on with it, then.'

'I was the one who founded the Maulen branch of the National Socialist Party,' declared Eichler. 'That makes me the senior local representative of the Reich. The next step is to decide on my immediate subordinates.'

The villagers round him nodded, indulging in their favourite occupation: they not only respected authority but accepted it with a faith which they sincerely felt to be creditable.

'From now on,' Eichler continued, 'the Party will govern all forms of life and activity in our village, just as it does throughout Germany. All who are co-operative will be welcomed with open arms. Similarly, each and every one of Germany's enemies will be overthrown and destroyed.'

This historic conference, which took place in the Gasthaus on 12th February, 1933, discussed preliminary measures to be taken against 'malcontents, subversives, and anti-social parasites'. Having resolutely declared war on all such, Eichler asked for active support and got it without delay.

All those present applied to join the Party. It turned out that some—Eis, Fischer and Vetter, for instance—had already made moves in that direction. They had contributed to Party funds, procured pamphlets, and taken out subscriptions to National Socialist newspapers. Hermann Materna was already a 'founder member of the S.S.', though no one in his circle realized that he had become so on his father's advice.

'I'm delighted,' Eichler told him. 'That's what I call initiative —and we'll be attaching a lot of importance to initiative from now on.'

Everyone nodded. Whether Royalists, Nationalists or National Socialists, they all felt their hearts beat higher whenever Germany, Masuria and the village were involved. It was a point of pride to do as the others did.

Johannes Eichler proved to be a born leader of men. He not only rallied aspiring Party members to his banner but arbitrarily dissolved any narrow-minded and potentially obstructive organization which refused to accept the idea of National Socialism without question. One of these was the

Stahlhelm, or League of Combat Veterans. Eichler was the ideal man to dissolve the Maulen branch, since it was he who had founded it.

His next move was the so-called 'integration' of the Home Guard, though the initiative came officially from Eugen Eis. Eis requested that the 'loyal and devoted men of the Home Guard' be received into the bosom of the Movement. Eichler replied that the function of the Home Guard was to guard the home. This, however, was also the function of S.A. Consequently, the Home Guardsmen would become storm-troopers forthwith.

Eichler now introduced the concrete proposals which everyone had been waiting for. They concerned the allocation of official posts in the Party's local branch. Maximilian Vetter was invited to take charge of organization and propaganda, with special responsibility for youth, public education and the arts. Ignaz Uschkurat was nominated National Socialist Farmers' Leader and head of the agriculture and forestry section. Gottlieb Speer was to wield influence over local trade and handicrafts, with additional responsibility for welfare and social security. Roads and fisheries went to Fritz Fischer, and Christian Scharfke's experience as an innkeeper qualified him for the post of Party treasurer.

These well-considered proposals were keenly debated by the assembly, but not for long. All present declared, with an extraordinary degree of unanimity, that it was their bounden duty to accept.

Only one post—possibly the most important of all—remained to be filled, and this was the leadership of the S.A. Nobody realized at the time that Eichler was destined to commit his most unforgivable blunder in this respect, but then, neither he nor his associates had the gift of clairvoyance.

'I don't want to push my claims, of course,' Eis murmured confidentially to Eichler, 'but I wouldn't mind heading the S.A.'

'I can't imagine anyone more suitable,' Eichler assured him. 'All the same, we mustn't rush things.'

A little later Eichler drew Hermann Materna into a corner. 'I can't tell you how happy I am to have you with us,' he said, laying a hand on the young man's arm. 'Tell me quite frankly, do you have anything special in mind for yourself?'

Hermann had, thanks to his father's far-sighted promptings. 'Just to be here is enough for me, but I'd regard it as a great honour to command the S.A.'

'I'm sure you would,' Eichler said quickly. 'You're excellently qualified for the job, my dear Hermann, and you can count on my backing. All the same, we mustn't rush things.'

Next, Eichler retired into a window alcove with Eugen Eis. It was just before midnight, and the air was thick with smoke and roseate dreams of the future. An atmosphere of noisy good-fellowship prevailed.

Eichler told Eis that he had no intention of ordering, requesting or demanding—he simply hoped for understanding. The position was as follows: Hermann Materna had tendered his claims to the leadership of the S.A. He, Eichler, would naturally have preferred Eugen Eis, but it might be wise and advantageous to cut the ground away from under certain people's feet. 'Quite apart from that, the Party mustn't punish a son for his father's sins—that's to say, it mustn't be seen to do so.'

After a brief mental struggle, Eis agreed, gambling on the possibility that Hermann might become his brother-in-law. There would be no harm, from a long-term point of view, in putting him under an obligation.

Eichler was now able to make the following announcement: 'I am entrusting the command of our storm-troop detachment to our respected young friend and Party member, Hermann Materna. I feel sure that he will prove worthy of his appointment. As for my old and trusted comrade-in-arms, Eugen Eis, I hereby appoint him my second-in-command, that is to say, Deputy Local Group Leader.'

There was an enthusiastic 'Hurrah!' from all present, but they quickly recognized their mistake and corrected it. Expressions of enthusiasm had to take a different form these days. At once, a triple 'Sieg Heil!' thundered through the Gasthaus.

Scharfke's cat leapt off the counter in terror, knocking several glasses to the floor. An unsuspecting peasant in the public bar choked on his beer, and Christine Scharfke declared that it went through her head 'like a knife'.

'From now on,' Eichler said with deep satisfaction, 'the

enemies of our beloved Germany had better beware. I'll tell you this much, my friends: we're in for some historic times!'

'God willing,' Speer chimed in, then corrected himself quickly. 'Under the Führer's leadership, I mean.'

The founding of the Maulen branch of the National Socialist Party was swiftly succeeded by the wedding of Johannes Eichler and Margarete, née Majewski, formerly Materna. It took place on 5th March 1933, and was scheduled to be the biggest, grandest and most elaborate wedding Maulen had ever witnessed.

It began with a church ceremony. Eichler did not dispense with this ritual, even though certain tensions had recently grown up between Party and Church. No such tension prevailed in Maulen. The Reverend Dr Bachus seemed quite willing to tender unto the spirit of the times what belonged to it by right.

The parson had readily discussed the theme of his sermon with Johannes Eichler in advance. True, he did not actually represent Jesus as a National Socialist reformer who had been murdered by the Jews, as some of his fellow-divines were already doing, but he was quite prepared to incorporate a benevolent reference to the Führer and Chancellor in his closing prayer.

The Terrible Twins were among those who attended the wedding, there being no immediate reason to exclude them. Since one father was officiating and the other an invited guest, Eichler had to put up with the presence of their offspring.

The scene in church was not only pleasing to the eye but, by Maulen standards, novel. This was principally due to the rich velvety brown which encased the bridegroom's sturdy limbs. Eichler was wearing the Führer's uniform, and his bride's soft and silky snow-white gown formed an effective contrast to it.

Alfons Materna was one of the few locals who had not been invited. Jacob Jablonski stayed away too, unlike Hermann and Brigitte. They had not only received invitations but been pressed to accept them by their father.

Not the least of Hermann's motives for attending was a wish to command the guard of honour provided by the S.A. —his S.A.! Some of them had already acquired uniforms and a few boasted gleaming belts and cross-straps. In Hermann's case, everything gleamed, from his honey-brown boots to the silver-plated eagle on his cap. Alfons Materna had kitted his son out regardless of expense.

'Please leave the church two by two, as detailed!' Vetter called briskly when the service was over. As Party Organizer, he had been placed in over-all charge of arrangements. 'Hurry, please. Pairing off must take place immediately!'

Peter Bachus raised his eyebrows: 'What, in church?'

He got no response, not even a withering glare, for the local Brownshirts' first hour of glory had struck. Hermann bellowed an order and twenty-four right hands shot up to form a sort of tunnel. Passing along it with the woman who was now his wife, Johannes Eichler felt a thrill of patriotic pride.

The large and orderly wedding procession left the church, crossed the village square, and veered left in the direction of Eichler's mill. All work had ceased on this festive day, and long trestle tables had been set up in the spacious main hall, together with some rough but reliable benches borrowed from the school and Gasthaus. A four-piece band consisting of violin, clarinet, double bass and drums launched into a dis-enchanted rendering of Wagner's *Entry of the Guests*.

Johannes Eichler held his bride's foliage-bedecked chair for her, every inch the country cavalier, and Margarete, now Frau Margarete Eichler, sank into it with a grateful upward smile at her imposing husband.

Vetter's arrangements shunned outworn conventions. In-stead of seating married couples together, he put the parson's wife next to the policeman and assigned the policeman's wife to Fritz Fischer. Fischer's sister, who occasionally cleaned his cottage for him, went to Uschkurat, Frau Uschkurat to Gott-lieb Speer, Frau Speer to the parson. Eugen Eis was seated next to Brigitte Materna, and Hermann found himself beside Christine Scharfke.

'Delighted,' said Hermann, with a semblance of a bow. Now that he had assumed command of the Maulen S.A., he re-garded himself as a member of the officer corps.

'Goodness, Hermann,' Christine said happily, 'you look like a cockerel today. I wonder if you perform like one.'

Chief organizer Vetter busily straightened benches, bullied the band, summoned supplies of beer and schnapps, poked his nose into the kitchen, and directed fidgety children to the communal lavatories. Looking around nervously for the Terrible Twins, he was relieved to see that they had modestly taken their places at the foot of the table nearest the door.

Fräulein Audehm, the midwife, had been recruited to pre- pare the grand wedding feast which everyone was so eagerly awaiting. There could have been no better choice, for Fräu- lein Audehm was conversant with all the mysteries of Masur- ian cuisine. She had asked for five sucking-pigs, seven geese, nine ducks and twelve chickens, not to mention the raw material for ten bowls of brawn, twenty of eels, and thirty of grilled herring. Drink stood ready by the barrelful.

'My dear friends,' Eichler called. 'I suggest we cut out the speeches and get down to business straight away. Let's all enjoy ourselves!'

This proposal commended itself to everyone. Eugen Eis demonstrated his knowledge of music by calling on the band to play *Old Comrades*.

Thanks to Konrad and Peter, who had not been idle in the meantime, the band failed to comply with this suggestion. The boys had made the musicians their first concern. They were drinking beer whose potency had been cunningly augmented with pure alcohol and wine which consisted of slightly diluted brandy.

Shortly before the meal began the drummer swayed and collapsed into his big drum. The clarinettist, who was crawling about on all fours looking for a lost reed, upset the violinist, who sat down drunkenly on his fiddle. The bass- player maintained a rock-like stance, but he was hardly able to provide much musical entertainment on his own.

'I'll put those drunken sots under the pump until their balls drop off,' said Eugen Eis. 'They'll be making music again inside the hour.'

Meanwhile, spirits were rising despite the absence of music. A seductive scent of roast sucking-pig filled the room as the platters were carried in. The Reverend Dr Bachus rose to his feet, and, as a self-styled friend of the family, em- barked on a lengthy speech. Taking advantage of the fact that even Bachus had to draw breath occasionally, Eichler intervened with great presence of mind and wished his guests a hearty appetite. 'Dig in, folks!' were his precise words.

This was easier said than done. The steaming dishes stood

ready on the table and the guests' one desire was to cram themselves with sucking-pig, goose, duck, chicken, and whatever else they might be offered. There was, however, a practical difficulty, to wit: no eating irons.

Fräulein Audehm appeared in the doorway. 'Someone's pinched the cutlery!' she screeched angrily.

Director of Organization Vetter, who was fluttering around behind her like a nervous bat, said: 'The cutlery was in a box, but it seems to have disappeared.'

Johannes Eichler turned pale. 'This,' he said, 'is rank sabotage.'

At that moment the lights went out, plunging the mill in gloom. There was an embarrassed silence, broken only by the delighted but inopportune scream of a female guest. It was still far too early for such diversions.

Eichler's commanding voice cut through the darkness. 'Eugen!'

'I'll fix it,' Eis called back.

The ovens began to smoke horribly. Acrid smoke engulfed the festive gathering, easily swamping the fragrance of roast sucking-pig. Fräulein Audehm gave a shrill scream and threatened to faint.

'Ugh!' ejaculated one of the male guests with passionate indignation. 'I just downed my schnapps, and what was it? Water, plain water!'

'I can't find any spare fuses!' Eis called from the door. 'They must have been pinched too, damn and blast it!'

Eichler's voice was low and menacing but very distinct. 'This is the bloody limit. No one's going to louse up my wedding-day and get away with it. I'll show no mercy from now on.'

'You stand to lose far more than your money, Materna. You could lose your children too. Doesn't that worry you?'

Siegfried Grienspan had called in, ostensibly because he happened to be passing by. He was now sitting with Materna, Maria and Jablonski, drinking mulled wine beside the stove in the big farmhouse kitchen. The men were smoking Dutch cigars. Grienspan, who received regular consignments of these from a cousin in Holland, doubled the pleasure they gave him by sharing them with Materna.

'What a split personality you are, Grienspan! First you

W.   E

make me a present of these exquisite cigars, and then you start trampling around on my conscience.'

Grienspan smiled. 'I know, I know, but then I'm only an old Yid.'

'You're the son of your father, like everyone else.'

'Not where courage is concerned, I'm afraid. He had the Iron Cross First Class.'

'That's rich! Your father fought for a country which disowns his son.'

'Grienspan has a point,' Jablonski said, looking thoughtful. 'Better watch out, or you can say goodbye to Hermann and Brigitte.'

Materna shrugged. 'The father and child relationship doesn't always mean much. I've known plenty of sterling characters whose children aren't worth a damn. As for me, all I've managed to produce is a fighter, not a farmer. It makes me laugh.'

'You'll never change him,' Jablonski told Grienspan. 'He takes the long-term view.'

'Of course I do,' Materna said promptly. 'It's part of the old peasant tradition, when you come down to it. You always plan for the next harvest. When you raise cattle you think years ahead—a generation ahead, if you're planting a forest. It hardly matters if Hermann wants to play the hero, and if Brigitte feels like a bitch on heat—well, why shouldn't I let her off the lead?'

'I wish I had your light-hearted approach,' Grienspan said.

Materna drained his glass and flung it at the stove with an exuberant gesture, but there was sadness in his eyes.

Maria was kneeling on the floor by the stove. He drew her gently towards him, almost as if he needed someone or something to hold on to.

'Did you ever hear how my father died?' he asked Grienspan.

'No, but I suppose you're going to tell me.'

'They say he laughed himself to death.' Materna seemed to brighten at the thought. 'It was during the Battle of the Masurian Lakes. We had three generals lodging here at the farm. One of them looked down the barrel of a sentry's gun. The gun went off, and there was one general less. The second tripped over a wine-bottle on the cellar steps and broke his neck, and the third fell into the manure-pit, caught pneumonia, and died. That was why we won the Battle of the Masurian Lakes, or so the story goes. Anyway, my father was so amused by it all that he went into a paroxysm of laughter and his heart simply packed up.'

'I suppose that's how you'd like to go,' Jablonski said wryly. 'You won't, though—not with Eugen Eis as a son-in-law.'

'We're all condemned to make our own mistakes. Besides, Brigitte isn't a naïve little girl. She's a hot-blooded creature. I was the same, except that I had more self-control.'

'Eis ought to congratulate himself, then.' Jablonski did not try to conceal his indignation. 'He not only makes a first-class match but gets a good lay into the bargain.'

Materna remained wholly unimpressed. 'No bear gets honey out of an empty pot.'

'Ah, so that's it!' Jablonski said with a grin. 'Brigitte can have her fun, but Eis doesn't get a penny of your money.'

'That's it more or less,' Materna agreed cheerfully. 'After all, I'm not an old man and I wasn't the guilty party in the divorce. Why shouldn't I get married again? Who knows, I might even father some more heirs.'

Materna took his hand from Maria's shoulder and held it in front of her. Maria, who seemed to have heard and understood everything, grasped it with a smile, then tenderly rested her head against his knee.

'So that's the answer!' Jablonski exclaimed. 'Trust you to think of a solution like that.'

'Today,' Materna said, 'people in the village are telling each other that this is the day of the big wedding. It's true, except that they haven't seen anything yet.'

7

The swastika banner floated above Maulen, and beneath it stood Johannes Eichler, flanked by his henchmen. They stood there, stiff and motionless, apparently gazing far into the future. They were being immortalized on film.

The occasion for this group photograph was the laying of the foundation-stone of Maulen's Party Headquarters. Eichler had provided the necessary land free of charge, but no one seemed to have noticed that the new building would form an extension of his own house.

Enthusiasm was universal during these early months of 1933. Even the lesser lights of the village—the Naschinskis, Poeskis, Sombrays and Kochanowskis—had applied for Party membership. Constable Klinger was reputed to have sung the *Horst Wessel Song*, loud and clear, and when the Reverend Dr Bachus crossed himself it was almost as if he were making the sign of the swastika.

Uschkurat had mounted an eagle over the door of his mayoral residence, and a portrait of Hitler hung on his office wall. Speer saw to it that the Volunteer Fire Brigade joined the S.A. almost to a man. Maximilian Vetter rejoiced the villagers by adorning his school with flags and enlisted Fischer's help in organizing all that was susceptible of organization. Eugen Eis, who never doffed his uniform except when going to bed, was only surpassed in zeal by Hermann Materna.

Eichler not only gave orders but extended help to all in need.

He visited the poorest of the poor and backed his words of comfort with material assistance. Karl Sämigkeit, a disabled ex-serviceman, got a new artificial limb, and Frau Quäslau, a widow and mother of numerous war heroes, was plied with flowers and coffee. Even before it had started to react to Hitler's name, the organized youth of the village received a new punch-ball and two pennants.

One case of special note—though it later proved to be a regrettable blunder—concerned Ludwig Grabowski, who was released from gaol as a result of the first amnesty, mainly at Eichler's insistence. Grabowski was serving a sentence for arson, but his crime was said to have had political undertones. He had apparently set fire to his barn in protest against the corrupt Weimar Republic—not, as some alleged, in order to claim the insurance money. Released shortly after the National Socialists came to power, he unfortunately turned out to be anything but the symbol of a resurgent Germany which Eichler had hoped he would become.

For all the dazzling successes of those early months, some setbacks were inevitable. The first of them occurred at the Grand Freedom Rally of March 1933, though its implications went largely unheeded.

It was privately assumed that Materna had engineered the whole thing. People were unanimous that a man like Materna could hardly succeed in stemming the tide of history. Be that as it may, he tried.

The general theme of the Grand Freedom Rally—officially organized by the Maulen branch of the National Socialist Party—could be summed up as: We are German to the core and no one can stop us being so. Principal speaker of the evening: Johannes Eichler.

As local director of organization and propaganda, Vetter assumed responsibility for the introductory singing, the readings from *Mein Kampf*, and the 'German Prayer' which was to conclude the proceedings. He did his level best to make them a success, and justifiably so, in view of his fiasco at Eichler's wedding.

Vetter paid particular attention to the problem of spontaneous patriotic interjection. Like everything else, these were to be organized with traditional German thoroughness. To this end, Vetter recruited three helpers: Kern the butcher and Baumann the postman, both of them avowed Party loyalists, and Grabowski, the honourably discharged convict, from whom it seemed reasonable to expect a more than average readiness to help.

'You,' Vetter told the postman, 'will shout "Shame!"—nothing else, just "Shame!"'

'Fair enough,' Baumann said promptly. 'When?'

'When the time comes.'

'Ah!' The goodwill on Baumann's loyal but sheep-like countenance was unmistakable.

'And you,' Vetter said, turning to the butcher, 'will simply shout "Justice!" Can you do that?'

Kern radiated keenness and enthusiasm. 'Can I!' he replied. 'I'm very hot on justice, especially when it comes to meat prices.'

Vetter went into greater detail. Whenever the speaker showed signs of outrage, the cry 'Shame!' must ring out promptly. If he seemed concerned, especially about the future of Germany or Maulen, that was the moment for a cry of 'Justice!' Vetter would make the appropriate signals, namely: right hand raised to chest-height: Shame!—left hand laid on chest in region of heart: Justice!

'And me?' Grabowski demanded impatiently. 'What do I do?'

'I have a very special assignment for you,' Vetter told him. 'You only go into action when I clasp my head.' He smiled complacently. The point he intended to make was one of his own devising, and of which Eichler had signified his complete approval. The basic principle was: know thine enemy!

This presented difficulties, Maulen being a place where avowed enemies of the people were at a premium. Siegfried Grienspan was the only Jew for miles around, so other threats to Germany's existence had to be found. Fortunately, Vetter had already solved this vital problem. His contention was that the real enemy lurked just across the border, only a few miles from Maulen itself, waiting for signs of weakness, itching to attack, filled with a deep detestation of all that was truly German—in other words, the Poles.

Vetter had unearthed some peculiar documentary evidence of Polish perfidy in the shape of memoirs written by Coigny, a former member of Napoleon's Imperial Guard—and a more ingenuous witness could scarcely have been found. Eichler was going to quote Coigny's verdict on the Poles in the course of his speech: 'They are a race devoid of humanity, capable of allowing a soldier to die on their doorstep without raising a finger to help him. There is nothing praiseworthy about them. They always abandoned their houses. The Germans never did so. They were humanity personified.'

'Your slogan, Grabowski, will be "Out with the Poles!"'

'Out with the Poles!' Grabowski echoed the words gravely as if repeating an oath. 'It sounds good, but what do I get out of it? My throat's so dry these days I can hardly speak.'

Grabowski had been drinking like a fish recently, as Vetter well knew. Grabowski's wife and a farm-hand looked after the farm and the farm-hand slept in Grabowski's bed —allegedly as a space-saving measure. Whether for this reason or another, Grabowski relied on the charity of friends to assuage his unlimited thirst.

'We all have a job to do,' Vetter said. He made a brief calculation and decided that his special fund could run to a bottle of schnapps. 'My own slogan will be: "Let us march to the East!"'

Baumann looked perplexed. 'March where?'

'To the East.'

'Why not?' Grabowski said, his eyes avid for schnapps. 'I'm ready to march anywhere as long as there's something in my hip-flask.'

'There's going to be a Grand Freedom Rally in the village,' Hermann informed his father. 'Everyone's invited, and I'm guarding the hall with my Brownshirts. Coming?'

Alfons Materna leant back in his arm-chair. His son had been providing him with some moments of pure delight recently. Hermann strutted around like a cock on a dung-heap. 'I can't wait to see you in action,' he said.

'You'll come, then? Good!' Hermann extended a hand as though welcoming his father to the ranks of the S.A. 'I've really licked the lads into shape—you'll be amazed.'

Materna took the hand that had been so cordially proffered and examined it. 'You ought to keep your nails cleaner, my boy, now that you're always shaking hands with people.'

Hermann laughed. That was typical of the old man—prickly as a hedgehog sometimes, but a good sort at heart. Not only had he fitted out almost the whole of the local S.A. detachment, but he unaccountably refused to take credit for the fact. 'This is just between us for the time being,' Materna had said. 'There's no need for anyone to know who's gilding the grave-diggers' spades.'

Hermann, already clad in full-dress S.A. uniform, produced a Hitler salute, confident that it would gladden his father's heart. Nothing in Materna's expression betrayed how much it amused him. As soon as he had been deprived of Hermann's majestic presence, he called Jablonski.

'We're going to mingle with the people again today,' he announced.

'If you say so,' Jablonski replied. 'Shall I take a gun along?'

'No, not even a pocket-knife.'

'What's the matter, feeling suicidal?'

'Just curious, that's all. You know it's my worst vice.'

'They're longing to make mincemeat of you, Alfons.'

'Don't worry, I won't give them the chance. I don't care if they think I'm yellow. Besides, we'll take Maria and Brigitte along too.'

'Are they supposed to keep you out of temptation, just by being there?'

'Did you ever hear about the time my father went to the

circus in Allenstein when he was a boy? A lion escaped from
its cage. Everyone screamed and ran except Father. He
just climbed into the empty cage and bolted the door because
it was the safest place he could think of. Well, I take after
him.'

The Grand Freedom Rally got off to an extraordinarily
promising start. The population of Maulen streamed into the
Gasthaus, practically filling the assembly-hall a quarter of an
hour before the official opening and giving the S.A. plenty to
do.

'Everything's going like clockwork,' Vetter said happily.

Constable Klinger was controlling the approaches to the
hall while the Brownshirts, under Hermann Materna, ensured that the people inside took their seats in an orderly manner. Even the Reverend Dr Bachus had put in an appearance.
He was sitting in the front row, in company with other
village dignitaries.

'All the most reliable people have turned up,' Eis announced
with satisfaction.

Another source of satisfaction was that the Terrible Twins
were away at school in Allenstein, so no malicious interruptions
were to be feared from that quarter.

Vetter hurried up to Eichler and Eis. 'A triumph of
organization!' he reported. 'No one has stayed away, not even
Materna. He's next door in the bar.'

'What are we going to do now?' demanded Eis. 'Shall we
stop him entering the hall, show him into a front row seat,
or just ignore him?'

Eichler peered round the door into the Gasthaus bar.
Materna and his party were sitting at a table near the counter.

'Maybe Scharfke will deal with him for us,' Eis said.

Materna was not ordering beer or schnapps, but wine—
several bottles of it. This was a shrewd move because it put
Scharfke in temptation's way. Never averse to making a profit,
the innkeeper was not only tolerating Materna's presence but
waiting on him politely.

'Well,' said Eis, 'he's here to stay now, whether we like it
or not.' He noted, almost with glee, that Eichler had begun to
perspire slightly. 'Just look at the man smile—behaving like
a lamb, he is.'

'Yes, but for how long?' muttered Eichler.

As a prelude to the Grand Freedom Rally, Eugen Eis walked up to the speaker's lectern and called for silence.

'Quiet!' he roared, then added: 'The Rally is officially opened!'

The expectant, cathedral-like hush that ensued was shattered by the combined efforts of choir and brass band.

'Magnificent,' commented Alfons Materna in the bar next door. He raised his glass. 'I wouldn't have thought anyone could produce so much noise—Maulen's making tremendous strides in that respect. Let's drink to the fact that we're not forced to listen at close quarters.'

Jablonski grinned like a chopping-block, as the Masurian expression had it. Brigitte kept watch for Eugen Eis while Maria stared into her glass. Wherever she looked, she always saw Alfons Materna.

'How's the wine?' Scharfke inquired solicitously. 'It's the best I've got.'

'It tastes all right, even so,' Materna replied.

Eis walked into the bar. Although he did not shake hands, he greeted Materna and his daughter and even nodded benevolently in the direction of Jablonski and Maria.

'Aren't you needed in the arena?' Materna asked, indicating the door of the assembly-room.

Eis sat down. 'Things are going smoothly.'

'What's it all about?'

'The usual—I'll get you a copy of Eichler's speech if you're interested.'

Materna got up and walked to the door of the hall with Jablonski following at his heels like a shadow. A tide of verbiage surged to meet them. Eichler was speaking, but it was impossible to distinguish his exact words.

Before opening the door, Materna turned to Brigitte. 'You wait here for us—and you make sure she does,' he added to Maria, who nodded.

'I'm going to enjoy this,' he went on. 'Stop looking so grim, Jacob. I feel like a bit of harmless fun, that's all.'

Eichler's speech was highly effective, not least because he had rehearsed the crucial passages several times in front of a mirror. The only trouble was, the organized interruptions were not functioning as they should.

The root of the matter was that Vetter had stationed himself directly opposite his band of hecklers instead of alongside them. In consequence, they mistook his right hand for his left. Thus, when Eichler spoke of justice and Germany's rights, Baumann yelled 'Shame!' Similarly, when he demanded the extermination of subhuman elements, Kern raised a bellow of 'Justice!'

However, the moment of real disaster did not arrive until, as though drawn by magic, Alfons Materna elbowed his way towards the speaker's lectern. Jablonski caught him by the sleeve, but he freed himself almost angrily.

'Germany,' Eichler was proclaiming, 'must be prepared to fight for its present and future existence.' He breathed heavily like a runner breasting the tape as he neared the climax of his peroration. 'Freedom demands a high price, my friends.'

Quite a number of the audience were listening with rapt attention—indeed, some of them seemed positively overwhelmed. Materna took advantage of their preoccupation to move even closer.

'Our struggle is ennobled by the justice of our cause,' Eichler boomed. 'Our enemies must be made to realize this. Anyone who attacks us will find that he has bitten off more than he can chew.'

'Out with the Poles!' Grabowski bellowed hoarsely.

Vetter was clasping his head, and that was Grabowski's signal. Noting that Vetter continued to clasp his head, Grabowski repeated his clarion call: 'Out with the Poles!'

This interjection provided Eichler with a welcome breathing-space. He looked up from his notes and reached for the glass of water in front of him. While he was drinking, Materna's voice came to his ears.

'May I be allowed to raise one small point?' the voice said, gently but distinctly. 'The cry "Out with the Poles" is based on an obvious misapprehension.'

A graveyard hush fell over the room, broken only by Eichler's stertorous breathing. Every head swivelled in Materna's direction. 'To shout "Out with the Poles!" implies that the Poles must be in,' Materna pursued with an amiable smile. 'I don't see any Poles here, do you?'

'You're splitting hairs,' Eichler growled.

'No,' Materna replied, amiable as ever, 'just applying the basic rules of the German language.'

'All right, all right,' snapped Eichler. Feeling parched, he reached for his glass again but found that it was empty.

To the mounting amazement of all present, Materna joined Eichler on the platform. 'If we're going to speak German,' he said in tones of apparent concern, 'we ought to speak it properly, otherwise we're open to misunderstanding. Take the colour of the Movement's uniform, for instance. It's known as khaki-brown, yet some ignorant people think khaki-brown is the same as cack-brown—in other words, shit-coloured.'

'Ushers!' Eichler roared.

Hermann Materna raced up, accompanied by two S.A. men, but his father was undeterred. 'Take a look at these splendid uniforms,' he said, indicating the three Brownshirts. 'Would you call them shit-coloured? Well, would you?'

'Of course not,' replied an S.A. man who felt that the question was directed at him personally.

Materna sounded as if he were defending an inalienable human right. 'That brown is nothing like the colour of shit, whatever some people say. Don't be misled, my friends. Shit looks quite different, believe me!'

Universal tumult broke out. Eichler ordered the intruder to be ejected from the hall, but it was far too late. Mindful that Materna had generously financed their uniforms and that his son Hermann was their commander, the Brownshirts wavered. What was equally surprising, Constable Klinger made no move to intervene.

Meanwhile, Materna explained loudly that his intentions had been of the best. He could not stand idly by and hear the S.A. uniforms—which he had paid for—compared with human ordure. He reiterated the word again and again, and for several minutes the hall seemed to reverberate with nothing else.

Maximilian Vetter sat slumped in a corner, convicted of inefficiency and muddled thinking. The village notables roosted on their chairs like chickens on a perch. Constable Klinger decided that no crime had been committed and interposed himself between Materna and the S.A.

Finally, at the end of his tether, Eichler called: 'Order, my friends! Let's get back to the point!'

However there was no restoring the exuberant, freedom-loving atmosphere of the rally. Some of the audience were still giggling stupidly to themselves.

Materna brazenly insinuated himself into the front row, but he did not stay there long. In response to a whispered message from Jablonski that Brigitte and Maria had disappeared, he rose hurriedly and went to find Scharfke.

'Well, where are they?' he demanded.

The innkeeper shrugged. 'I'm only interested in customers when they order drinks and pay for them,' he replied sullenly. 'What else they do is no concern of mine.'

Materna nodded at Jablonski, who ducked under the counter and pinned Scharfke against the wall. 'Sharfke,' he said kindly, 'you're a fat pig. Would you like me to tell Klinger who shot that deer in Materna's wood last week?'

'It wasn't me!' Sharfke protested. 'I'm no poacher.'

'Of course not, you leave the dirty work to other people.' Jablonski did not have a jot of evidence to support his allegation. 'You just sell stolen meat at outrageous prices.'

This seemed to refresh Scharfke's memory considerably. He looked round, leant forward with a confidential air. 'I didn't breathe a word, mind.'

Materna realized that something had happened. 'Tell us all you know,' he said harshly, 'and don't beat about the bush.'

According to the innkeeper, Brigitte, Maria and Eugen Eis had remained seated at the table after Materna and Jablonski left the room. They drank some more wine—with obvious enjoyment, Sharfke added.

'Get to the point,' growled Jablonski.

'Brigitte and Eugen whispered together for a while,' Scharfke resumed hurriedly. 'Then they got up to leave. Maria tried to stop them. She caught Brigitte by the arm, but Eugen wasn't having any.'

Materna flushed. 'You mean he hit her?'

Scharfke hastened to deny this. 'Brigitte and Eugen went out. Maria tried to follow them at first. Then she ran into the hall.'

'I didn't see her.'

'She didn't get far. She bumped into two Brownshirts, right by the door. Someone yelled "Out with the Poles!" just at that moment, so they promptly carried her out of the Gasthaus.'

Materna and Jablonski hurried off to find Maria. They found her where they expected to find her—on a bench in the angle formed by the church and the churchyard wall. This was where she usually waited for Materna after morning service.

'Come here,' Materna said, 'come here to me.'

Maria got up. She came towards Materna and Jablonski with small weary steps. Her head drooped and her arms hung limply at her sides.

Materna went to meet her with his hands outstretched, and she fell into his arms as though her strength had failed her. He lifted her head to look into her face. Her eyes shone with tenderness, but blood was trickling from the corner of her smiling mouth.

'Don't fret,' Materna said gently. 'Don't fret any more.'

She nodded, but he could feel her trembling. He waited patiently until the trembling had stopped, then turned to Jablonski.

'Take Maria home, Jacob. I'll catch you up. I've got a couple of things to do here in the village first.'

Materna hurried to the dairy. The big windows above the loading-ramp were in darkness, but a thin sliver of light came from the office behind. He ran up the short flight of wooden steps on tiptoe, opened the outer door, and made his way across a small landing to the office. He crouched slightly and then, without taking a run, hurled himself at the door.

It burst open, leaving him standing in the middle of the room. Eis and Brigitte stared up at him from an improvised couch of butter cartons draped with blankets.

Materna did not appear to notice their disarray. Blinking in the dim light coming from the paraffin lamp in one corner, he said: 'Sorry to break up the party.'

Eugen Eis swiftly hoisted his trousers and buckled his belt. Brigitte pulled her skirt down over her thighs but continued to lie there stiffly.

Eis did his best to save the situation. He drew himself up, discreetly buttoning his flies as he did so, and said: 'You have to take things as you find them, Materna. Your daughter and I are in love.'

'It's true,' Brigitte confirmed eagerly.

Materna regarded Eis with suspicious affability. 'Ju because two people copulate it doesn't mean they have to spend the rest of their lives together. If it did, you'd be married a dozen times over by now.'

'I'm serious this time,' Eis declared.

'It's all arranged,' Brigitte chimed in.

Materna rounded on her. 'Shut up! You're in Maulen, and women aren't consulted in Maulen. Either you get married or you don't. We'll soon see.'

'What's that supposed to mean?' Eis asked darkly.

'I own one of the most profitable farms in the district. I don't have a wife but I've got two children, that girl lying there and a son who likes playing soldiers. As things stand, they'll both inherit—one more and the other less. It all depends.'

'I couldn't care less!' sneered Eis.

Materna laughed silently, studying Eis through narrowed eyes. 'Hermann isn't the ideal farmer's heir—I suppose that's what they're saying in the village. That being so, my only course is to look around for a fine upstanding son-in-law. What do you think, Eis?'

'You're wrong!' Brigitte said fiercely. 'Eugen loves me for myself!'

'I'm glad to hear that. It's a comfort to know that my daughter's in good hands. You see, I'm thinking of marrying again.'

Eugen Eis knew at once what that meant. He had gone as pale as a lump of cottage cheese. 'If that's the case,' he stammered, 'I have to admit . . .'

'Eugen!' shrieked Brigitte, outraged. She jumped up, heedless of her skirt and blouse. She looked like a carelessly wrapped pat of butter.

'Don't get me wrong, Brigitte,' Eis protested. 'Nothing can change my feelings towards you, but I didn't reckon on your father playing such a dirty trick.'

Materna turned to face Brigitte. All the life had gone out of his movements. 'Come home, girl,' he said.

'No!' she cried. Her face was flushed and her eyes glinted with Materna obstinacy. 'It's all settled. There's no going back now. I'm going to have a child.'

People were not prudish in Maulen. They quietly tolerated what the wives of Kern the butcher or Baumann the postman did, nor were those ladies alone in their goings-on. They did not take it too seriously either, if girls made an occasional slip. Many a girl added to her dowry by so doing—indeed, Johannes Eichler's long-time housekeeper was ruined so often that she eventually made an excellent match.

Everyone acknowledged the seductive potency of spring and high summer in Masuria. Spring and summer past, the pleasures of bed and the flesh were mightily stimulated by the snows of winter—that, too, had to be acknowledged. And if the odd child arrived too early people simply shrugged and said: 'These things happen.'

It was different with Materna. The villagers were puzzled by him, as usual. 'Why Maria?' they asked each other. Everyone in Maulen knew that the girl worshipped Materna and no one begrudged either of them the pleasures that might accrue from their association. What mystified people was that Materna should want to *marry* the creature.

The news caused a mixture of amusement and lively indignation, both inside the village and far beyond its borders. It was not that she was a Pole, and the fact she was deaf and dumb was regarded as a very minor impediment. Many married men in Maulen would have swapped their wives for a deaf-mute any day of the week.

No, what really shocked people was that Maria was a humble employee and almost twenty years younger than Materna. If he intended to marry her despite that, it could only be as a way of cheating Brigitte and Hermann out of their inheritance.

'That man is capable of anything,' muttered the villagers. 'Where will it all end?'

'He'd never do such a thing!' Brigitte said.

'I wouldn't advise him to,' Eis said menacingly.

'I get the feeling he's just playing with us. He's very generous at heart. He's trying to test us—you mark my words.' She nestled against Eis's encircling arm. 'Perhaps he just wants to annoy Mother. I've always got on very well with her.'

'It might pay to keep in with her,' Eis said, pondering on the present Frau Eichler.

'Father's very eccentric, anyway—you'll have to get used to that.'

'He strikes me as quite normal sometimes.' Eis continued

to ponder. 'Still, even eccentricity can have its advantages if you handle it the right way. They say he's worth half a million marks.'

'Love me?' Brigitte asked, looking radiant.

'Of course I do,' he replied. 'Your father must give us his blessing, though—properly, too. Love isn't everything.'

8

'Not again!' exclaimed Johannes Eichler. 'Human weakness is one thing, but rank failure I won't stand for.'

Standing stiffly in front of him like a row of milestones were three leading members of the local Party: Eugen Eis, Hermann Materna, and Maximilian Vetter. None of them looked particularly at ease.

'I don't ask much.' Eichler thrust his hand into the breast of his tunic like an over-sized Napoleon. 'All I ask is that everyone in Maulen does his duty. As Maulen's senior Party official, I won't have the Movement held up to ridicule—and that applies to me as well.'

Hermann did not move a muscle, staunchly determined to take whatever was meted out and take it without flinching. Eugen Eis breathed a sigh of relief because he realized that Eichler's real target was Vetter. Vetter, who seemed to sense that he was to be the scapegoat, ventured to explain.

'As far as the slogan "Out with the Poles!" is concerned,' he said, 'the idea really came from Eis.'

The idea really had come from Eis, who had got it from Eichler himself, but this did not prevent Eis from donning an air of injured innocence. 'I like that!' he protested. 'Fancy trying to put the blame on me!'

Eichler bludgeoned the schoolmaster with sheer vocal power. 'You ought to be ashamed of yourself!' he blared. 'Only weaklings try to shirk their responsibilities.'

Hermann nodded approvingly. He too found Vetter's conduct shameful. The man had no dignity—and to think he used to put the fear of God into him at school!

Eichler moved in for the kill. 'You are relieved of your post as director of organization and propaganda forthwith. Steps have already been taken to dismiss you from the Party, and the education authorities have been requested to transfer you as soon as possible. We have no use for failures like you in Maulen. Now get out!'

Vetter wept.

'An unavoidable necessity,' Eichler observed, almost mildly. He had just delivered an effective object lesson which would soon be bruited about and bear fruit accordingly. 'By the way, please accept my deepest sympathy. Materna's decision to marry that maidservant of his affects you both, I imagine. He's obviously trying to cut you out of his estate.'

'It's the principle that matters,' Hermann said.

Eis frowned. 'A lot can happen in the meantime.'

'Let's hope you're right,' said Eichler, pouring schnapps for himself and his visitors. They drank to the continuance of their work in the common cause and then parted with a Hitler salute.

Eugen Eis and Hermann Materna strolled harmoniously across the village square towards the Gasthaus, Hermann drawn by the pneumatic charms of Christine Scharfke, Eis by the prospect of a cold and soothing beer.

'Eichler really wiped the floor with Vetter,' Hermann remarked with a touch of admiration.

'Yes, but who'll be next on the list? One of us?'

'Why us?' Hermann said staunchly. 'What can go wrong as long as we keep our noses clean?'

'We can keep them as clean as we like—Eichler's the one who decides whether we're in or out.' Eis shrugged moodily. 'He keeps us hopping about like a bunch of trained fleas, and I don't like that.'

'But he's the boss around here.'

Eis's eyes narrowed. 'That needn't be a permanent state of affairs, either.'

Hermann did not follow the drift of his companion's remark. 'No point in worrying about something that may never happen. I prefer to concentrate on the present.' He was obviously thinking of Christine Scharfke.

'I know this much,' Eis said. 'Whoever gets the boot next time it won't be me—not me. I've got a black-list of my own.'

'You ought to see Eis and that son of yours,' Jablonski said. 'Pals through politics, that's them. They've got drunk together several times. Another few days and they'll be strolling down the village street arm in arm.'

Alfons Materna was in the stable with Grienspan, inspecting a mare which was due to foal. Neither man showed any interest in Jablonski's remarks.

'It's going to be a difficult birth,' Grienspan said. He ran his hands deftly over the mare's twitching belly. 'I've heard of a new method, though. You can speed up tricky deliveries with special massage. The mare can still die, but there's a fair chance of saving the foal.'

Jablonski moved closed. 'They're a proper team, the pair of them—like two cheeks on the same arse, and what Eichler says comes out of the middle.' He grinned.

Materna gave an indulgent smile. 'Hermann's having the time of his life. He likes organizing people. Giving orders and obeying them is his idea of heaven.' He took the mare's head in his hands and pulled it against his chest. The animal not only suffered his embrace but nuzzled his cheek.

'All the same,' Jablonski said, 'this Brigitte-Eis business is a disgrace.'

Materna shook his head. 'Women are unpredictable creatures. If Brigitte insists on having the fellow—all right, she can have him.'

'Well, I think you're mad to allow it,' Jablonski said angrily.

'You're entitled to your opinion.'

Jablonski stalked out. Materna lifted the mare's head and looked into its eyes. 'He's right, of course—decent people always are. The only trouble is, you're not alone in this world. We're like strands in an enormous carpet, tightly interwoven with a thousand other strands.'

'Listen, Alfons,' Grienspan said quietly. He was the only living soul apart from Jablonski who called Materna by his Christian name. Maria would have done the same if she could speak. 'I've saved a fair sum. We could use it to set up shop somewhere else—Poland, for instance. I've been offered a small farm south of Cracow.'

'The land south of Cracow is good,' Materna said, '—almost as good as ours, I'm told. Rich grain-land, and the conditions for pig- and poultry-rearing are said to be ideal. All the same, I'm not interested.'

'Think it over, Alfons. Take your time.'

'My father and grandfather lived on this farm. If I wanted to be melodramatic I'd say I was born here and I mean to die here, but that would be a load of rubbish.'

'Then what keeps you here?'

'You're embarrassing me, Siegfried.' Materna gave the cattle-dealer a look of entreaty, but Grienspan refused to let him off the hook. 'My motives are almost identical with the ones our brown-shirted friends always make a song and dance about. I love this country.'

'I know,' Grienspan said softly. 'I'd find it a wrench to leave here too.'

Jablonski reappeared. 'I've been doing some hard thinking.'

'That's bad,' Materna said.

'I've been thinking,' Jablonski insisted, 'and I've come to the following conclusion. It isn't unusual for children to desert their father, but nothing's final in this world except death, so why shouldn't they return to the fold—with a little help, of course?'

Grienspan gave a warning frown. 'I should leave well alone if I were you.'

'No, no, this is interesting,' Materna said. 'If Jacob thinks he can show Hermann that his self-styled friend would do him in the eye as soon as look at him, who am I to stop him?'

'There shouldn't be any difficulty,' Jablonski said confidently. 'One woman can throw any number of strong men off balance.'

In Maulen, where the shrinking violet was an almost unknown species, love was a straightforward business. Hermann Materna differed from the rest of the village, however. In love as in politics, he was an avowed idealist. Everything had to be as pure and spotless as his new uniform. He might be in love with Christine Scharfke, but he respected her nonetheless.

'You're so gallant,' Christine said, sighing.

'Who could be anything else, with you?' he asked gravely.

It had all started when she was his table-companion at Eichler's wedding feast. A tremor ran through his frame and his eyes went glazed. Since this could not be attributed to excessive eating and drinking, it had to be love.

'We can't talk properly here,' she said from the other side of the bar. 'What about nipping up to my room?'

Hermann frowned. 'I don't think we ought to do that. I wouldn't like to harm your reputation.'

That was Hermann all over—a pure youth who laughed at dirty jokes but only out of camaraderie. He never understood them. He saw Christine as he wanted to see her: a devoted German wife and the future mother of German children. He held her hand and his fingers occasionally strayed into the neighbourhood of her breast, trembling with suppressed desire, but nothing more happened.

'I'm not getting anywhere with him,' Christine told her father.

'He's Materna's son,' Scharfke pointed out, 'and Materna has a fat bank balance. He could buy up half Maulen if he wanted to. Bear that in mind, girl.'

Christine Scharfke, warm-blooded by nature, was rather like a saucepan of cream simmering over an eternal flame. Many men had enjoyed her favours, but in Hermann's case she felt neglected and unappreciated, if not spurned.

Grabowski, the drunkard, sat in the Gasthaus bar for hours on end these days. Jablonski was financing his drinks, and he repaid Jablonski by bombarding Christine almost continuously with suggestive remarks. 'You don't have to turn into a virgin just because you're in love' was one of his favourites.

Needless to say, Christine had no intention of doing any such thing, and it irked her when Grabowski further suggested that the reason why the worthy Hermann didn't was that he couldn't. This, she felt, was a direct aspersion on her charms.

For days she wavered between duty and inclination. Grabowski continued to blather drunkenly at her, and even the Terrible Twins seemed to regard her with covert amusement. Slowly but surely, the ingredients of a distressing and momentous incident came to the boil.

Grabowski, happily imbibing pint after pint of alcohol, said: 'Some get itchy throats like me. Others get the itch somewhere else. People are like that.'

Eugen Eis leant across the bar: 'What a life, Christine, what a life!' He loved making profound observations about life, especially when he was drunk.

'You're all right,' Christine said tartly. 'You're engaged.'

'So are you.' Eis buried his head in his hands to show that he was a prey to mental anguish. 'What does it mean, though —engaged?'

The word meant little enough in Maulen, particularly when the sap was rising and opportunity knocked. Hermann was far away and Christine's room was tantalizingly close at hand. Eis reached for the glass which Christine pushed towards him.

'I'm not happy, I'll say that much.'

'But your fiancée's expecting.'

'It was fate,' Eis said darkly.

'It wouldn't have happened with me,' Christine spoke with a touch of pride. 'I'm clued up.'

'I know, but you're one in a million. I can vouch for that.'

Christine, polishing glasses, glanced into the public bar. It was empty except for Grabowski, who sat at one of the tables grinning stupidly to himself. The bottle in front of him was almost full.

'A man can't help his nature,' Eis said. 'What about going upstairs?'

'You're a devil.' Christine's voice was low and throaty. She dried her hands and refilled his glass unasked. 'I'll go on ahead. Don't keep me waiting too long.'

Hermann Materna was in the fire-station, instructing the subordinate commanders of his S.A. detachment. The subject: field training by sections.

'The main thing is a clear word of command,' Hermann said. 'Orders must always be given in a loud, distinct, authoritative tone.'

The S.A. section-commanders, three in number, nodded. They all possessed powerful lungs, this being one of their chief claims to promotion.

'Hermann Materna?' called a youthful voice from the door. It belonged to Peter Bachus.

'Here!' Hermann said promptly.

'Telephone for you, over at the vicarage.'

Hermann told his section-commanders to take a break and hurried across to the vicarage. Picking up the receiver, he said: 'Hermann Materna here.'

He was sure it was Johannes Eichler's voice—in fact he was prepared to swear to it afterwards. Distorted by the old-fashioned telephone, the hoarse but imperious voice said:

'Confidential briefing session immediately. In the Gasthaus, Room No. 3.'

'Yes, sir!' Hermann barked obediently. He replaced the receiver and marched off to the Gasthaus, where he mounted the stairs, knocked at the door of the room in question, and sang out: 'Hermann Materna reporting as instructed!'

There was no reply. All unwitting, Hermann knocked again. The lack of response annoyed him. He had been ordered to report there, and an order was an order, so he tried to effect an entry by force. The voice of his beloved was raised in a request for peace and quiet.

Suspicion dawned in Hermann's mind. He stood there and pondered the situation perplexedly. Finally, he drummed on the door like an African tribesman sounding the alarm. One or two interested spectators sidled up the stairs.

The inevitable happened. Hermann Materna caught his friend and Party comrade, Eugen Eis, with his fiancée. If he had been carrying a gun he would have drawn it. As it was, he refrained from soiling his hands by resorting to fisticuffs.

Maulen's S.A. Commander and Deputy Local Group Leader stood face to face, glaring at each other. The Party threatened to disintegrate.

Triumphing over his initial speechlessness, Hermann called Eis a dirty rat, filthy swine and a rotten bastard. Christine, who was characterized as a tart, whore and trollop, got off comparatively lightly.

This exhausted Hermann's vocabulary. Fuming, he elbowed his way past the gaping onlookers and out into the street. Then, a proud but solitary figure, he strode across Dog's Meadow and up Horse Hill.

His father was standing there with Jablonski, almost as though he had been expecting him. The two men regarded him amiably.

'It's Christine, Father,' Hermann said. 'I caught her with Eugen Eis. What ought I to do?'

'You must know that without being told,' Materna said quietly.

'I want to do the right thing, of course, but what is it?'

Materna's tone was candid. 'To be honest, Hermann, I ought to rub my hands and say it's an ill wind that blows no one any good. You're shot of that girl and it won't be long before your sister finds out what sort of man she's got herself mixed up with. Eugen Eis has killed two birds with one stone, in a manner of speaking.'

'I'll break every bone in his body!' Hermann roared with sudden fury. 'I'll take him apart, the filthy goat!'

Jablonski grinned at Materna. 'They're hot on threats, these lads. Lucky they don't always carry them out, isn't it?'

Eugen Eis was equally prepared to do the right thing—he had no alternative. First, he got fully dressed. Then he went straight to Johannes Eichler.

He found the acknowledged boss of Maulen in his mill, checking the flow of flour. Eichler found the process both topical and symbolic. Countless little grains, wizened and insignificant-looking, were being transformed into snow-white purity by the methodical application of enormous pressure. It was a metamorphosis of values, a refining process which provided nourishment for humanity—German humanity.

'I can't help being moved,' Eichler said gravely. 'Flour is bread, and bread means life.'

Eugen Eis might have added something to this, 'life' being one of his favourite catchwords, but he dared not delay. It was time to take firm action.

'Ah, life!' he said, congratulating himself on having devised an excellent transitional phrase. He went on to speak of an 'unfortunate series of coincidences'—not an unskilful turn of phrase either, or so he thought, but all Eichler said was:

'Come on, out with it! What's the trouble this time?'

On Eis's submission, he had been seduced. Christine had 'lured him into a trap'. Resignedly, he concluded: 'And before I knew where I was, I was on her bed.'

Eichler's eyebrows rose. 'You weren't caught in the act?'

'More or less.'

'Who by? Not Hermann Materna?'

'I'm afraid so,' Eis admitted with downcast eyes. 'Somebody must have put him up to it. He acted like a maddened bull. I didn't get a chance to explain that I'd been tricked into the whole thing.'

'Blast!' Eichler said furiously.

He proceeded systematically, making inquiries, interrogating witnesses in person and appealing to their solidarity. 'I can't have the Party jeopardized by every chit of a girl who likes opening her legs,' he told them, tempering severity with humour.

These preparations made, Eichler convened a 'secret Party tribunal' for the same evening. It was one of his principles never to let the grass grow under his feet.

The atmosphere was icy at first. Hermann did not deign to look at Eis, but he had come, and that was half the battle. He sat there with adamantine composure, dutifully obeying the summons of his Local Group Leader.

Eichler opened the proceedings with an assurance that he was not prejudiced for or against anyone present. Truth was his sole concern. 'Nothing can be more dangerous or unworthy than mistrust between comrades,' he declared. 'This is just what our enemies are waiting for.'

This Eichlerian dictum appeared to make some impression on Hermann Materna. Hopefully, Eichler bent his gaze on the S.A. commander. 'If Eugen Eis is found guilty, his days in Maulen are numbered—I should like to make that quite clear.'

Eugen Eis grew restive. He shot Eichler a glance of warning and entreaty combined, but Eichler was devoting his full attention to Hermann. Hermann, who had faith in his Local Group Leader, began to bask in the glow of official favour.

'If what I hear is really true,' Eichler pursued inexorably, 'nothing will deter me from taking the sternest measures, but is it really true? Well, Eis?'

'Of course not,' Eis said hastily. Realizing that he had been thrown a lifebelt, he clutched it at once. 'It isn't true because it can't be true.'

Hermann drew himself up. 'I know what I saw,' he growled.

Eichler gave an approving nod. 'Of course, but appearances can be deceptive. It wouldn't be the first time.' He planted his arms flat on the table in his favourite Lion of Maulen attitude. 'Let's talk man to man—Party member to Party member. I call upon Eugen Eis to tell us if he feels he has anything to confess.'

'Nothing,' Eis replied promptly.

'But I caught him in Christine's room!' Hermann protested. 'I've got witnesses to prove it, too.'

Eichler leant forward. 'Couldn't he just have been having a chat with her?'

'With his shirt off?'

'Eugen Eis,' Eichler demanded sternly, 'kindly explain that.'

Eis, who had pondered the question, did so. 'I'm more or less the same build as Hermann, as you see, and Christine was making some night-shirts for him as a surprise. She was taking my measurements, that's all.'

'I accept your explanation,' Eichler said solemnly. 'I took the precaution of questioning Christine Scharfke separately, and her story tallies. I'm afraid you've done her a cruel injustice, Hermann.'

The meeting dragged on for a considerable time, but it was eventually crowned with success. Eugen Eis offered his apologies for what he still considered to be a harmless indiscretion. Hermann Materna, displaying the magnanimity demanded of him, declared that, although outward appearances suggested a different explanation, the solemn assurance of a Party member must be accepted.

The two young men shook hands. Certain scars remained, but the main thing was that Eichler had preserved Party unity and village solidarity. This was essential in view of what lay ahead, notably the forthcoming elections.

Maulen was bathed in sunlight on election day and the sky looked like a canopy of softly gleaming silk. Morning service and Holy Communion, vote-casting and free beer, public festivities and a social evening—all seemed assured of ideal conditions.

'A God-given day,' observed the Reverend Dr Bachus, blinking contentedly in the morning light after a restful night's sleep.

'A thirsty day,' said certain other inhabitants of Maulen.

'A memorable day,' said Alfons Materna, '—or it will be if things go the way I forecast.'

The bells rang out, Christian Scharfke tapped his first barrel, and the Brownshirts mustered at the fire-station.

Johannes Eichler summoned the local Party dignitaries for an early-morning briefing. 'Let's fortify ourselves first,' he suggested.

No one declined the invitation. Margarete's touch was apparent in the dishes of food laid out in the gleaming white, newly painted office. There were two hams, one boiled and the other raw, plump sausages of divers kinds, jars of smoked and pickled herring, and a chunk of Tilsit cheese the size of a breeze-block. The drink was brandy.

'We've a hard day ahead of us,' Eichler said, 'a hard but glorious day.'

No one ventured to dispute this. They hacked off chunks of food with the knives provided, stuffed them into their mouths, and flushed them down with alcohol. The general mood was was one of exultation.

Meanwhile, the Reverend Dr Bachus distributed consecrated bread and wine to the faithful. They accepted it with more than usual alacrity because there was an official ban on the sale of refreshments throughout the hours of polling.

Nothing seemed to have been overlooked. Eichler's Party machine was functioning in top gear, as it had been for weeks. Flamboyant posters, printed appeals, personal visits, verbal persuasion—all had been used to the full.

'Victory will and must be ours!' was Eichler's official forecast. His unofficial forecast, to Eis, was: 'We'll get a hundred-per-cent vote out of these weak-kneed swine. It'll be a walk-over.'

The crucial question on the ballot-paper was: 'Do you support Adolf Hitler's Party? Yes or No?' Two circles were provided, a large one for 'Yes' and a smaller one for 'No'. No true German could be in any doubt about the correct answer.

'Even Materna won't be able to louse that up,' Eichler said confidently. 'He'll have to toe the line if he doesn't want trouble.'

The Party's arrangements embraced the whole village, from Eichler's tenants in the north to the fishing-grounds in the south, from Uschkurat's farmers in the west to the small-holders who scratched a wretched living from the stony land in the east. The organization spared no one, not even children and dotards.

The lazy and undecided were winkled out of their nooks and crannies by drummer-boys selected and trained by Kniese, the schoolmaster who hoped to step into Vetter's shoes. Legs planted firmly apart, Kniese's Hitler Youth Wolf Cubs be-laboured their calf-hide drums with fervour and chanted an election ditty composed by Kniese himself. The opening words were:

> Turn out and vote now, one and all,
> The Führer and the Party call . . .

These strains were borne to Alfons Materna's ears. The road to Gross-Grieben passed close to his farm, and tall hedges availed little against the shrill incantations of Kniese's young devotees.

Materna was sitting on the bench in front of the house, digesting a midday meal of goose stuffed with apples and six different kinds of herbs. Maria had once more proved herself an outstanding cook—one of the thousand attributes which gladdened his heart every day. He smiled to himself, and the smile did not fade even when Hermann strutted up looking like a peacock in courtship plumage.

'I've come to fetch you,' he announced.

'You sound like Death in the school play—or is that the Party speaking?'

'I came to ask you to vote, Father. Everyone ought to turn out.'

'I've seen a lot of elections, my boy, but it's been years since I tasted such a magnificent goose. My digestion means more to me than any election.'

'But the fate of Germany's at stake, Father. I'm asking you to register your vote, not as an S.A. commander, but as your son.'

'For Germany's sake?'

'Of course.'

'All right, if it means so much to you.' Materna rose. 'I'm as anxious to do my bit for Germany as anyone else.'

The end of the polling was officially scheduled for five o'clock that afternoon, but Johannes Eichler and Eugen Eis were already running through the electoral register three hours before the booth closed.

The register indicated who had still to vote. There were very few gaps in the line of crosses, but the names of reluctant voters were jotted down on slips of paper and handed to the S.A.

Promptly, the Party's storm-troopers spread their net. Their catch included a toothless, gibbering old age pensioner who had not left his garret in the old folks' home for months, two gnarled and feeble-minded peasant-women, a young couple of voting age who had been disporting themselves in the bushes near the village pond, and an old and ailing farmer. He was borne into the polling-booth in triumph and died soon afterwards, secure in the knowledge that he had obeyed the call of duty.

The drummer-boys continued to bang and squeak like clockwork toys. Mouths agape, they sang:

> *Adolph Hitler's cause is just.*
> *Let all his foes be ground to dust,*
> *Every true-born German must*
> *Vote for Adolf Hitler!*

Barely an hour later only three crosses were missing from the list. The names in question were those of Materna, Jablonski and Grabowski.

'Get them!' Eichler commanded.

Grabowski, village toper and much-lamented victim of the Weimar Republic, was the easiest to find. He was lolling in his favourite spot by the cemetery wall, drinking. His private reserves had enabled him to beat the ban on liquor sales during polling hours. Cheerfully drunk, he staggered to the polling-station.

'Not too late, am I?' he inquired, giggling.

Eugen Eis, who was waiting for him outside, said: 'About time too, you drunken sot. Get in there and do your stuff.'

'I'd have come sooner,' Grabowski hiccupped, 'only I had to fortify myself first. There are big things at stake, aren't there?'

'Of course, man, of course! Your life'll be at stake if you don't get inside that booth in double quick time.'

'Yes, sir!' Grabowski cried in semi-military tones. He even tried to click his heels. 'I'm a voter, I am. I'm going to do my electoral duty. No one'll be able to say I let the Führer down. Long live the Führer!'

'Cut the cackle and get in there,' Eis said. The man was beginning to fray his nerves and attract unwelcome attention. 'Get in there and make your cross.'

'A cross?' Grabowski's watery eyes registered blank amazement. 'Me make a cross, like in church? Is that really what the Führer would want?'

'Are you trying to make a fool of me?' Eis demanded, uneasily aware that this garrulous drunkard was doing just that. One or two bystanders were already grinning suspiciously. 'Just get in there and put a cross inside the right circle.'

'Ah!' Grabowski glanced around, clearly savouring the interest he had aroused. 'I'm to put a cross inside the circle, am I? A church cross or a swastika?'

It finally dawned on Eis that there was an underlying reason for Grabowski's protracted tomfoolery. 'All right,' he whispered, 'I'll stand you a half-bottle.'

'A half-bottle for a whole cross?'

'A whole bottle, then. Now get cracking.'

'Long live the Führer!' cried Grabowski. 'I've got something to thank him for now.'

Alfons Materna and Jacob Jablonski rolled up shortly afterwards, complete with S.A. escort. Two men preceded them and two brought up the rear. The people who had collected outside the polling-station made way for the procession in awed silence.

'Anything for Germany's sake,' Materna said gaily.

Johannes Eichler, who had been warned of his adversary's approach in advance, emerged from the polling-station and advanced a few steps to meet him. 'I'm happy to see,' he said loudly, 'that even you have come to do your duty.'

'It's a pleasure,' replied Materna.

'Eichler eyed him sternly. 'You wouldn't oppose the Führer, I feel sure.' He uttered these words in a clear and audible voice, then added in a warning undertone: 'Far be it from me to count on your sense of decency, Materna. I'm simply assuming that you're not an idiot.'

'Even if I were, it could hardly detract from my admiration for our beloved leader.'

'Well said,' Eichler replied, feeling easier in his mind.

The belated votes of Materna and Jablonski filled the last gaps on the electoral roll, thereby bringing polling to an end in Maulen more than an hour before the hour officially laid down. It was a triumph of organization and a personal triumph for Eichler.

With simple pride, the Local Group Leader sent the following wire to District Headquarters: *Maulen solidly behind Führer and Party. Heil Hitler! Signed: Eichler.*

Meanwhile, Constable Klinger was making an announcement in front of the polling-station: 'Listen a minute, folks!

Polling is completed and the votes are already being counted.
A result is expected shortly.'

This was momentous news because it automatically implied
that drink could flow freely. Scharfke at once began to issue
free beer from an improvised stall in front of the polling-
station.

Those of the villagers who had not already assembled flocked
to the scene. Brownshirts supervised the queue in front of
the hissing beer-taps and the Fire Brigade band formed up,
ready to greet the election results with a rousing march.

For the last time that day, the drummer-boys went into
action. Their childish voices, already cruelly overtaxed, broke
into another of Kniese's bits of doggerel:

> *Hail to the Führer's victory,*
> *For victory it has to be.*
> *Anything else would be a sin,*
> *That's why the Führer's bound to win.*

Alfons Materna turned to Constable Klinger, who was
standing beside him. 'The voice of the people, I presume,' he
remarked with glee.

'Election slogans, more like,' Klinger said cautiously. 'Election slogans are allowed.'

'But I distinctly hear the words "Führer" and "sin" in close
conjunction. Does it mean anything?'

'Search me,' replied the policeman. 'I leave little refinements like that to the Party.'

Counting took little more than half an hour, at the end of
which time the doors of the polling-station were thrown wide.
Eugen Eis emerged and raised one hand. The drummers be-
laboured their skins and the brass band blew a triple fanfare.

Johannes Eichler appeared. His voice cut the expectant
hush like a knife. 'Party members, friends and comrades-in-
arms, respected fellow-citizens! I shall now announce the
result of the election.'

Here he inserted a judicious pause, savouring the moment
which he rightly felt to be the most important in his political
career.

'The electoral roll comprised the names of two hundred
and eighteen persons,' he proclaimed. 'Of these, two hundred

and seventeen registered their votes. This means that nobody
failed to do so, since the missing vote was that of Anton
Leipski, who died in the early hours of the morning.'

Eichler paused again. 'Two hundred and seventeen votes
were registered by the two hundred and seventeen persons
who turned up at the polling-station. All ballot-papers were
valid, making two hundred and seventeen valid votes cast.
Of these two hundred and seventeen votes, two hundred and
seventeen were cast for the Party. Votes against: nil. In
other words, a hundred-per-cent turn-out and a hundred-
per-cent vote in favour of the Party.' Spontaneously, he added:
'This is the happiest day of my life.'

'Three cheers for our beloved Führer!' called Eis.

But before the requisite Sieg Heils could ring out, before
the drummer-boys could torment their drums and the willing
bandsmen spit into their mouth-pieces, a quiet, firm, clearly
audible voice made itself heard—Materna's voice. It said:

'There must be some mistake.'

'What's that!' Eichler demanded in boundless amazement.
'At a solemn moment like this, when the German people have
come forward as one man . . .'

'You may well be right about that,' Materna said. 'The one
thing you're certainly not right about is that election result.'

'It's official—a clear-cut manifestation of the popular will.'

'Possibly, Eichler, except for one small detail. Your figures
don't tally.'

Eichler marched across to Materna, leonine and menacing.
Surrounded by the listening, watching, pleasurably gawping
inhabitants of Maulen, he said: 'Take my advice, Materna.
Think carefully before you speak—in your own interests.'

'There's nothing to think over,' Materna replied firmly.
'At least one "No" vote was cast—I know that perfectly well.'

'Two "No" votes,' said Jablonski, ranging himself alongside Materna.

Hermann gave a yelp of horror. 'It can't be true, Father!'

'It's a malicious lie!' yelled Fritz Fischer. 'The S.A. must
step in—the police, too. Don't just stand there, Klinger, do
something!'

'I'll take action as soon as I know who I've got to take
action against,' Klinger said. 'If the returns have been falsi-
fied, there's a case for criminal proceedings.'

Johannes Eichler's fleshy face had gone red as a beetroot.

'Any opponent of the Führer is an opponent of the nation. That puts him beyond the pale and makes him an enemy of the people. Are you against our Führer, Materna?'

'What a question!'

'Then you voted Yes?'

'No.'

Eichler had apparently reached the end of his tether. Almost beseechingly, he glanced at Eugen Eis, but Eis was contemplating his finger-nails with rapt attention. Other usually reliable Party members were staring at the ground. Hermann's Brownshirts were standing stiffly to attention and the villagers of Maulen preserved an air of remorseless stupidity.

Materna said: 'It isn't enough to make a cross beside the word. Yes. Things aren't as simple as that.'

'All right, all right—in that case you're for the Führer.'

'I revere him,' Materna declared. 'But these ballot-papers only asked us to support a party, just as if it were an ordinary party—like the Communists, say. Only a mutton-headed bureaucrat could think up a thing like that. Our Führer isn't to be bartered like a piece of merchandise. That's why I put a cross against "No".'

'Same here,' Jablonski said.

'Three "No" votes!' croaked Grabowski, who had been promised another bottle, this time by Materna. 'With me it was just a slip of the pen. My hand was unsteady because I hadn't had enough to drink.'

'It's a foul conspiracy,' was all Eichler could think of to say.

'This is a matter for official investigation,' Klinger announced firmly. 'I hereby declare all voting records confiscated.'

Meanwhile, another four citizens had come forward, among them Maximilian Vetter, who had been relieved of his Party post. They, too, announced that they had voted No for the same reason as Alfons Materna. They, too, alleged that they revered the Führer but had been unable to stand by and see him degraded by such a bureaucratic and un-German form of words.

'This is the end,' groaned Eichler.

Eugen Eis eyed him without compassion. 'Who for?'

9

Events associated with the Maulen elections became the subject of numerous conflicting allegations. Some dismissed the whole thing as a regrettable error and others called it a malicious fabrication, but a few people whispered the word 'fraud' and three went so far as to utter it aloud.

Eichler's premature announcement was not only broadcast several times by the provincial radio station at Königsberg but relayed by the national network. Before the day was out, the Maulen branch of the National Socialist Party received a number of congratulatory telegrams from highly placed and influential Party members.

Meanwhile, Constable Klinger was doggedly doing his duty as he saw it. Everyone he encountered in the process claimed to be entirely innocent and sought refuge in the authoritarian principle. In other words, everyone had simply carried out Eichler's orders in good faith.

The national authorities requested clarification from the province of East Prussia. The provincial authorities put pressure on the regional authorities, and the regional authorities assailed branch headquarters at Maulen with demands for a scapegoat.

'I must speak to you urgently,' Eis said.

Materna was standing at the farm gate with his thumbs hooked in his braces. He wore a slightly grim expression. 'I suppose you'd like me to settle Eichler for good.'

Eis denied this, but he could not conceal his surprise at this evidence of Materna's intuition.

'Eichler wants you to talk me into quashing the fraud allegations, is that it?'

'Can we talk frankly?'

'I thought we were doing that already.'

Eis peered round cautiously. 'Look,' he said, 'we're sort of related—at least, that's the plan.'

'Not my plan,' said Materna.

'It's a foregone conclusion. Your daughter's child needs a

W.   F father, and that's where I come in. I think it would be better if we worked together in future.'

'Better for whom? All I know is, Eichler's in it up to his neck, and he's got no one to blame but himself. I could let him off the hook by perjuring myself, but that would stick in your craw, wouldn't it? You're number two in the Party stakes. If Eichler goes to gaol, you step into his shoes.'

'Wouldn't that suit your book?'

'Like hell it would! Johannes Eichler is a lion—or a wolf, whichever way you look at it—but you're just a jackal. You make me puke.'

'Steady on, Materna.' Eis could be thick-skinned when the occasion warranted it. 'You ought to think of your daughter's happiness. Think of your future grandchild.'

'Jacob!' Materna called across the yard. 'The dogs!'

Eugen Eis beat a retreat and hurried back to Eichler.

'I tried every last thing,' he reported. 'I appealed to his better nature and made all kinds of offers, but he wouldn't budge.'

'Typical of him,' Eichler said morosely. He was labouring hard under his recent disappointments. There was the possibility of a Party inquiry—perhaps, even, of criminal proceedings. The consequences might be catastrophic and would certainly lead to his dismissal from the post of Local Group Leader. 'And all because he's dying to get even,' he added.

'He had the cheek to call us jackals.'

Eichler shook his head sorrowfully. 'I'm sickened by the whole business.'

'I suppose I ought to have some sort of family feeling for him,' Eis pursued, 'but after this—well, I just can't raise a flicker. I'm going to put that bastard where he belongs.'

Eis helped himself to Eichler's schnapps without waiting for an invitation, boldly selecting the best bottle in sight—a potent grain spirit blended with liquid honey and known in East Prussia as 'Bear-Trap'. He drained two brimming glasses before continuing.

'We're playing for keeps now,' he said. 'From now on, everything must go like clockwork or we'll really come unstuck.'

Eichler realized that his position was more than awkward, but the thought of surrender did not enter his head. To show

that the Lion of Maulen could still roar, he relieved Hermann
Materna of his post as commander of the S.A.

The worthy young man suffered visibly. His first step was
to drink himself into a stupor, but not before giving vent to
some injudicious remarks about the local Party and its leaders.
Shortly afterwards he left Maulen for Lötzen, where he joined
Siegfried Grienspan's business. Having started as a sort of
unpaid assistant, he very soon, with financial aid from his
father, became a partner in the concern. He proceeded to
organize the cattle-dealing business as he had once organized
his squad of Brownshirts, and—lo!—business boomed.

Eugen Eis was appointed chief of the local S.A. This post,
coupled with that of Deputy Local Group Leader, lent him
special weight, and it was this weight which he threw into
the scales at the crucial moment.

'Materna has finally been unmasked as an enemy of the
people,' he declared. For the last time, he sought Eichler's
approval of any action he might take. 'Can I have a completely
free hand?'

'What must be,' Eichler replied, 'must be.'

The same evening, Eis met Brigitte by the lake. The meeting
was arranged by Fritz Fischer, who had been appointed deputy
commander of the S.A. His willingness to act as a go-between
was dictated by political foresight.

'Don't believe what people are saying,' Eis murmured,
nuzzling Brigitte's right ear. 'Just believe me.'

'I came, didn't I?' she replied with convincing simplicity.

They climbed into a boat and sat there in the gathering
twilight. The woods seemed to be sinking into the depths of
the lake and the dark waters were engulfing the sky.

'Your father may not realize it, but I've got a soft spot
for him.' Eis grasped her hand and pulled her towards him.
Obediently, she snuggled against his chest and slid to the
bottom of the boat.

'Your father's only human, after all. Even he must have
his weaknesses.'

'Let's not talk about him,' she said, breathing hard.

They did not talk about him—in fact they did not talk at
all for the next fifteen minutes. They lay together on the
duck-boards in an atmosphere redolent of pitch, stagnant

lake-water, and luke-warm sweat. The boat rocked violently. Then they fell apart, panting, and lay there inert.

'He was young once,' Eis ventured. 'There must have been times in his life when . . .'

And so it went on—veiled allusions, leading questions, tender avowals. Eis tried to sneak up on his objective. He listened to Brigitte's replies with fond attention, cajoled her, petted her, and perseveringly steered her back to his chosen theme: even a man like Materna must have a skeleton in the cupboard . . .

Eventually, Brigitte remembered a name—a name which her mother had mentioned when the subject of divorce was being discussed. 'You can't treat me the way you treated that Amrein woman,' Margarete had said.

Eis's hand slid upwards in the direction of Brigitte's thighs. She lay back once more, and the tempo of her breathing increased. Through layers of pink cotton wool, she heard him say: 'What was the name again?'

'Amrein,' she panted ardently, 'Amalia Amrein.'

'You gave me your son to look after,' Grienspan said with a smile. 'I never knew friendship could be such hard work.'

Alfons Materna found it amusing to reflect that Hermann, of all people, should have joined Grienspan's business. 'The poor boy needed some form of distraction. He took his dismissal like an honest whore fired from a brothel for slacking. It hurt his pride.'

'Well, I've been trying to impress on him that even cattle-dealers have their pride. Hermann thought that applied to Aryan cattle-dealers only.'

'Chuck him out if he gives you too much trouble, Siegfried.'

'I can't do that, I'm afraid. He already chucked me out.'

Materna laughed till the tears came. The world was getting funnier every day. 'He chucks you out of your own business and you take it just like that?'

'I had no alternative. He refused to work with me, so I had to let him work for me on his own.'

'And what are you doing meanwhile?'

'Celebrating with my friends.' Grienspan raised his glass to Materna, Jablonski and Maria, also to Peter Bachus and Konrad Klinger, who were listening with rapt attention.

Materna laid his hand on Maria's shoulder. 'I'll break out the champagne when we get married. You're all invited—just you, nobody else. We'll make it a day to remember.'

They beamed at Materna delightedly, and Materna smiled at Maria, but Maria jumped to her feet, staring anxiously at the window. At the same instant it shattered and a stone the size of a man's fist sailed in accompanied by a shower of glass. A second or two later, in a hoarse, malevolent chorus, there came a crudely rhythmical cry of: 'Jews out! Jews out! Jews out!'

Jablonski reached the door first, closely followed by Materna and the two boys. Grienspan walked over to Maria and motioned her back into her chair. He sat down beside her and nodded reassuringly.

Outside, the chase began. The intruders had already vanished into the darkness, but their pounding footsteps were clearly audible. They were making straight for the main road and Maulen. The two boys ran like tigers, swiftly but without stamina. In the end it was Jablonski's dogs which made the running and headed one of the fugitives off, a white-faced gibbering youth who trembled and gasped for breath.

Jablonski sniffed the air briefly. 'He's done it in his pants, but that often happens when people open their mouths too wide. One thing seems to lead to the other.'

Materna shone his torch on the youth's face. It was coarse and flabby, and it belonged to one of Ignaz Uschkurat's sons.

'What'll we do with him?' asked Jablonski.

'Tan his hide,' chorused the boys.

Materna shook his head. 'Not good enough. He deserves something far worse. We'll treat him decently.'

Uschkurat's son was escorted into the front parlour of the farmhouse, where Materna pulled up a chair for him.

'Perhaps he could do with a drink,' Materna said to Grienspan. 'There's nothing like shouting for giving one a thirst.'

After a moment's hesitation, Grienspan poured out a glass of Franconian wine and set it in front of the budding anti-Semite, who stared foolishly at his dusty boots. He seemed highly put out by the turn of events.

'Your very good health,' Materna said cordially.

Meanwhile, the two boys had hurried off to the village. Konrad sought out his father while Peter went in search of Uschkurat. Both men were invited to the farm for a glass of wine and a chat about a matter which might prove to be of some importance. Neither hesitated to obey the summons.

Uschkurat started when he saw his son sitting in Materna's front parlour.

'What's he doing here?'

'He's my guest,' Materna explained.

Constable Klinger, inured to the world's surprises, behaved as if he were paying a social call. He ignored the broken window and the huddled figure of Uschkurat's son and devoted himself to his wine. Pleasurably, he sniffed the glass that had been set before him.

After they had all drunk, Materna said: 'May I pick your brains, Herr Klinger?'

The policeman nodded affably. 'By all means.'

'Let's take a hypothetical case. I'm sitting here with my friends when suddenly a stone the size of a man's fist comes sailing through the window. Then I hear voices shouting: "Jews out!" How would you define that in legal terms?'

'Well,' Klinger replied, 'in the first place, it would mean that someone had trespassed on your premises. Then there's the stone. That would constitute wilful destruction of private property. Finally, there's the cry of "Jews out!", which might amount to a breach of the peace. All in all, given a magistrate with a sense of fair play, I'd say the culprit would get several months in gaol.'

Materna raised his glass and drained it with a grateful glance at the policeman. Then he looked at Uschkurat, who had turned puce with rage.

'If I preferred charges on the basis of what I have just told you,' Materna said, 'what then?'

'I would take note of the particulars, pursue my inquiries, and let the law take its course.'

Materna made no comment. Uschkurat rose with a grunt and walked over to his son. Grabbing him by the lapels, he pulled him slowly to his feet, like a crane. Then he slapped his face hard, first with the back of his hand, then the palm. Having repeated this process in reverse, he dropped the boy like a hot potato.

'No charges,' said Materna. 'The matter has resolved itself.'

'Bloody fools!' Eis roared, eyeing the remains of his raiding party with contempt. 'Fancy getting caught like that!'

The survivors stood there, conscious of having failed but equally conscious that they had only tried to carry out an order. Or had it only been a suggestion? They couldn't remember any more.

'This sort of thing brings the whole Movement into disrepute,' the S.A. commander continued. 'I can only describe it as anti-Party behaviour.'

Eis conveyed the unpleasant news to Eichler, who realized that this abysmal failure on the part of his subordinates would only undermine his position still further. He racked his brains for a fitting solution.

It took him some hours of intensive thought to find one —solitary thought, too, since Eis merely eyed him with covert glee and declared himself bereft of ideas.

'The S.A. has no use for failures,' Eichler announced at length. 'Young Uschkurat is hereby discharged with ignominy. As of now, he ceases to be a member of the Party and its ancillary organizations. That effectively severs his connection with us.'

Eis felt an involuntary twinge of admiration. Eichler was an apt teacher. His decision relieved the Party and his own Brownshirts of all responsibility. Any charges which might be preferred would be laid against a private individual, and that was no skin off anyone's nose.

'The fight goes on, then,' Eis said. 'It's war to the knife now. The first thing is to air Materna's dirty linen in public, and I'm the man to do it.'

Going in search of Amalia Amrein, Eis found her in Siegwalde, the village north of Maulen. She was living on her brother's farm, tending his poultry and vegetable-garden and nursing the conviction that she had been cheated out of the best years of her life.

'Do you know Alfons Materna?' Eis asked her.

'That swine?' she hissed. 'Who doesn't?'

These words came as balm to Eis's soul. He regarded the

woman in front of him with mounting favour. For all her acid-drop eyes, pug nose and repellent breath, she had the clear, pure voice of a canary.

'I happen to share your opinion of him,' Eis said. 'It could be to your advantage.'

Amalia Amrein pricked up her ears. There was a hint of madness in her eyes. All she wanted was justice—justice for all the terrible things she imagined she had suffered at Materna's hands. 'He ruined my life, the bastard.'

'I'm sure he did, but that sort of statement won't get us very far. We need evidence, facts, eye-witness accounts.'

'You can have any amount of them. I'd do anything to get even with him.'

Eis learned that Amalia Amrein had entered Materna's service as a housekeeper some years previously.

'I always did my duty. No one can say I'm anything but clean, honest and hard-working.'

'Of course not,' Eis said soothingly. 'I suppose he paid you a pittance and exploited you shamefully. That's him all over, but it isn't good enough for our purposes.'

Amalia Amrein started to disgorge. Apparently, no woman was safe from Materna. Once or twice—twice at least—he had actually smacked her backside.

'I can't make much out of that,' Eis remarked. In Masuria, an occasional smack on the rump was more a mark of homage than a moral lapse.

'He was carrying on with Frau Kern, the butcher's wife —and Frau Baumann, the wife of the postman. I can swear to that.'

A lot of other people had sampled the charms of these two well-known village sirens, Eis reflected. Far heavier guns would be needed to bring down a man like Materna.

'Why didn't he make a pass at you, Frau Amrein?'

'He wanted to all right, but I wasn't having any. Besides, he likes young meat—children, for preference.'

Eis swooped on his prey like a buzzard. 'Did you say children?'

'I certainly did. He climbed up the stairs after Maria when she was still a kid.'

'How old was she, exactly?'

'Just on fifteen, the little slut, but she hung round him the whole time like a bitch on heat.'

Eis tried to tie Amalia Amrein down on this point. It was not easy at first, but her memory began to function in the required fashion as soon as he promised her an ex gratia payment in the event of a successful prosecution. A hundred marks could always be withdrawn from Party funds for interrogation purposes.

Amalia Amrein finally declared herself ready to attest the following facts on oath:

(1) She had several times seen Alfons Materna put his arm round Maria, thereby bringing his hand into contact with her breast.

(2) She had repeatedly intercepted glances between Maria and Alfons Materna which clearly indicated an intimate relationship. Maria's eyes were often dark-rimmed and her sheets rumpled.

(3) She had surprised Alfons Materna emerging from Maria's bedroom at night. He looked utterly exhausted, and alleged that Maria was running a temperature.

'That'll have to do,' Eis said. 'We'll get him for corruption of a minor, misconduct with a ward, and who knows what else besides. Are you ready to swear to all this?'

'Every last word of it.' Amalia Amrein gave a lethal scowl. 'Anything, just as long as that bastard gets what's coming to him.'

The Maulen detachment of the S.A. went resolutely into action in the weeks that followed, fortified by intensive sessions of evening training. Maulen seemed to be emerging from its millennial sleep, or so Eugen Eis evidently believed, because his favourite phrase was: 'The place is waking up at last!'

The Brownshirts roamed the neighbourhood in small operational groups, only to meet with insidious resistance on the part of hostile but unidentifiable elements. Sand was systematically inserted between the links of the S.A.'s chain of command. Numerous false alarms were raised as a result of telephone calls purporting to come from Johannes Eichler or Eugen Eis. The genuineness of the voices, which sounded characteristically curt, crisp and imperative was never doubted.

On receipt of such calls, the Brownshirts would congregate at the fire-station, war memorial or community centre. Dirk in belt and pistol in pocket, they stood there thirsting for action, but nobody took any notice of them. This caused considerable ill-feeling.

'We must keep Materna under surveillance from now on,' Eis ordered, '—day and night, if necessary.'

'But he doesn't have a telephone.'

'Then he gets his hangers-on to telephone for him. I want them.'

The telephone commands which had caused so much confusion ceased abruptly. Instead, the village broke out in a rash of painted slogans. If the S.A. daubed 'Jews out!' on the churchyard wall, the following day would see the appearance of more lettering in the same size and style. 'Jews out!' was supplemented by the words 'Nazis too!' or 'Hitler first!'

Incidents of this kind not only exasperated the S.A. but made the villagers laugh, which was far worse. When the Brownshirts put up a streamer between two oak-trees outside the school, it was quickly joined by another. The first read: 'Germany Awake!', the second: 'Hitler's a Nightmare!'

'Something's got to be done,' Eis exclaimed furiously to Constable Klinger. 'You'd better catch the people responsible if you want to keep your job.'

'The people responsible for what?' asked Klinger.

'For daubing slogans on walls, of course.'

'You mean the S.A.?' The policeman stood his ground like a runic stone on a lonely heath.

Eis's eyebrows contracted. 'You'll regret that,' he said menacingly. To him, Constable Klinger was a latent enemy of the people. Mayor Uschkurat's sense of patriotism was equally suspect. Having delayed Materna's marriage to Maria for months, he now declined to raise any more official objections. Even the parson was showing scant appreciation of national and village interests, because he stubbornly refused to use the pulpit as a rostrum from which to denounce the scandalous activities of unpatriotic paintbrush-wielders.

'What's got into this lousy village?' Eis growled. He sent for the men who had been spying on Materna and asked them what he was up to.

'He lies around in his garden, mostly,' they reported, '—just lies there on his back and does nothing.'

'He's public enemy number one, I tell you!'

'Could be,' the Brownshirts agreed. 'How do we go about proving it, though?'

'Step up the pressure, and that's an order!'

The S.A. needed no second bidding. Working in pairs, Party activists called on the baker, the butcher, the grocer, the shoemaker, smith and carpenter. Having harangued them, they distributed hand-printed posters bearing the legend:

This is a German and Aryan concern.
No Jews, Poles or moral reprobates served here.

'Hang them up where everyone can see them,' commanded the Brownshirts.

The placards were duly exhibited, but by next day they had all acquired an additional strip of paper. This read:

Boot-lickers and time-servers welcome.

Eugen Eis quaked with fury at these new developments and the S.A. worked overtime. One call to arms followed hard on the heels of another. Every gambit used by the elusive foe was to be met by a counter-move. From now on, every poster, streamer and painted slogan was guarded by a sentry.

Unfortunately, the sentries did not always escape unharmed. One of them had a sack thrown over his head, whereupon his hindquarters were stripped and daubed with paint of an appropriately yellow-brown shade. Two other sentries suffered a similar fate shortly afterwards. The lavish use of paint suggested that someone of financial standing was involved, and Materna had recently sold Grienspan another three pigs.

'This has got to stop!' Eis fumed. After pondering the situation carefully, he compiled a list of potential suspects. Alfons Materna headed the list as a matter of course, but his son Hermann might well be aflame with thoughts of revenge. Besides, he was working for Grienspan now, so he must have access to money. Then there was Christian Scharfke. Public disorder always boosted his turnover. What was more, his daughter had some reason to feel jilted, and women in that condition were capable of any infamy. Finally, Eis bethought himself of the Terrible Twins, who were once again on holiday.

Promptly, he sent for the parson and the policeman. 'If

either of you is involved in these outrages, whether directly or indirectly, you'll regret it.'

'You must be out of your mind,' said Klinger.

The Reverend Dr Bachus frowned. 'With the best will in the world, I feel bound to protest against such an insinuation.'

'Don't quibble!' snarled Eis. 'I'm simply holding you responsible for what your sons have been up to.'

'Our sons?' Bachus looked genuinely astonished. 'They spend their whole time poring over books. They're reading Hitler's *Mein Kampf* at the moment, and I've even seen them dipping into the *Völkischer Beobachter*. I don't remember a time when they've put their holidays to better use, and as a parent I can only rejoice in the fact.'

Klinger had also noted the boys' new-found enthusiasm with satisfaction. 'As far as the so-called signs of the times are concerned, they've recognized them—I'd take my oath on that.'

Peter and Konrad had indeed recognized the signs of the times. Their minds were alert, their hearts beat high, and they managed to achieve a maximum of effect with a minimum of effort. There was an ample demonstration of this at the grand S.A. rally on the following Thursday. Two smoke-bombs and a canister of tear-gas purloined from the still substantial stocks of the illegal Home Guard organization proved more than enough to rout the Brownshirts. In place of the missing items, the boys left a receipt inscribed in block capitals with the words: 'For our beloved S.A.'

The Brownshirts coughed, spluttered and wept. Eyes streaming, they stumbled to the exit, and for a few brief moments the Maulen detachment of the S.A. disintegrated.

The same evening some storm-troopers waylaid Jacob Jablonski, who happened to be strolling through the village, and beat him up. He lay in the gutter like a felled tree.

Also that evening, two tipsy members of the S.A. chased Maria. They tried to throw her to the ground and drag her into a ditch, but she lashed out with her hands and feet, spitting, scratching and biting. She eventually escaped with nothing worse than a torn blouse and skirt.

Also that evening, half a brick smashed one of the church windows and another landed on Constable Klinger's desk. Maximilian Vetter fled into Materna's wood, hotly pursued by a band of storm-troopers. Ignaz Uschkurat woke up to find his barn afire.

'Now we're getting somewhere!' roared Eugen Eis. In his view, there was an element of compensatory justice in these incidents, since the S.A. had suffered every conceivable form of provocation. A few of his men were currently undergoing medical treatment for injuries inflicted by Jablonski. As for Maria, she had flaunted herself in a highly provocative manner, thereby inviting compliments of a tactile nature.

It was untrue that the church window had been smashed. It had simply cracked, presumably as a result of climatic conditions. The half-brick on Klinger's desk was readily explained by the fact that he always used stones as paper-weights. As for Uschkurat's barn, it was insured, and over-insured at that. The mayor had obviously made a good thing out of it.

Johannes Eichler, who seemed to have taken refuge in the joys of marital life at this crucial juncture, was sought out by a delegation of leading citizens headed by Ignaz Uschkurat.

'A lot of things have been happening lately,' Uschkurat said. 'Are we really to take it that they were done with your approval?'

Eichler stood there like an oak-tree on a summer morning, robust and leafy, but he could already feel the axe biting into his trunk. 'No,' he replied, 'not with my approval.'

'But they were done in your name.'

It was an inauspicious time. The night sky burned pale above Maulen and the houses lay silent like slumbering beasts. The Topich might easily be lurking by the lake-shore. Women tossed restlessly in their beds, waiting for their menfolk and knowing that they waited in vain.

'Some definite action must be taken,' Uschkurat said firmly.

Eichler brooded for a while. The members of the delegation watched him in awestruck silence, convinced that he was planning great things. Eventually, he said: 'There's nothing for it, I suppose. I shall have to take the bull by the horns. In other words, gentlemen, I must pay a call on Alfons Materna.'

'Materna,' Eichler began, portentously but with a hint of

entreaty, 'I've come here to appeal to your better nature.'

'I don't have one,' Materna replied, '—at least, not the sort you can work on.'

It was long past midnight. The two men stood confronting each other in the big farm kitchen, Eichler in Party uniform, Materna in a nightshirt.

'You think I'm a bastard, don't you?' Eichler said.

'Yes,' Materna replied simply. 'A patriotic bastard, if that's any comfort.'

Eichler cleared his throat. 'I came to ask you something. I don't find this easy, believe me, but what about burying the hatchet? Call it an armistice, if you prefer.'

The faint smile died on Materna's lips and his face lost all expression. 'What's the matter, Eichler, reached the end of your tether at last? You have, haven't you? You know who's really digging your grave, don't you? Surely you can sense that he wants everything you've got as well as everything I've got? I'm talking about Eugen Eis.'

'Don't, Materna! It isn't true.'

'A few days ago Eis stood just where you're standing now and suggested that we join forces against you. He wants to finish you.'

'You're a cunning devil, Materna, but are you a liar? Somehow I don't think you are.'

'You think right,' Materna replied, almost sadly.

This clinched matters. Eichler galloped back to the village like a maddened bull, seeing red and bellowing for Eugen Eis.

'You're a bastard,' Eichler roared, 'a dirty, rotten, miserable, low-down bastard!'

Eis stared back at him levelly. 'That's a nice thing to say to a friend.'

'I'll strip you of every job you hold.'

'You won't, you know. You couldn't afford to, not after all I've done for you.'

'You've stabbed me in the back,' groaned Eichler.

'Cut out the sob-stuff. We both know the score.' Eis sat down in Eichler's arm-chair and stretched his legs. 'I've learnt a lot from you, one way and another.'

'You deserve to be shot!'

'And you've got a bloody bad memory.' Eis noted Eichler's

every movement with slightly narrowed eyes. 'What about that first wife of yours? I drowned her in a milk-vat just the way you wanted it. And what about Materna's son? Those hand-grenades were just what the doctor ordered from your point of view.'

Eichler roared like a wounded beast and his face became a waxen mask mottled with hectic red patches. He leant forward, gripping the edge of the desk.

'I'm past caring about anything except my position here in Maulen. Say what you like about me, Eis, but try to prove one word of it and you're a dead man. You know me. I stop at nothing when I'm roused. As senior Party official and Local Group Leader of Maulen, I'm relieving you of all your duties as of now.'

'No you don't!' The muscles twitched in Eis's cheeks and he bent forward menacingly. His hand crept to the pistol in his hip pocket. 'You wouldn't dare.'

'I would—I've no choice. I'm dismissing you from the S.A., depriving you of Party membership and sacking you from the dairy. You'll leave Maulen within forty-eight hours. I'm kicking you out, Eis, and good riddance to you!'

At that moment, a few loyal Party henchmen happened to be relieving themselves in the road outside Eichler's house. They shuffled their feet and stared up at the lighted windows. The other windows, which gave on to the mill yard, were out of sight.

As these men later testified, they saw the shadows of Eichler and Eis clearly silhouetted against the drawn blind. From their animated gestures, they appeared to be arguing.

One of the witnesses was Grabowski. Listening intently as the voices rose in volume, he made out a few words. Eichler was heard to say 'You bastard!', or it could have been 'You lousy bastard!' 'Stab in the back' was another phrase heard by witnesses.

Then several shots rang out in quick succession. There was a tinkling of glass, a cry, and the sound of something heavy hitting the floor. No one could say exactly how many shots were fired, but estimates ranged between six and a dozen.

The witnesses rushed into the house. There they were confronted by a shocking spectacle. Eichler lay sprawled across

his desk, riddled with bullets. Eugen Eis stood in the middle
of the room as though turned to stone. Blood was seeping
from his forehead.

'Some bastard fired at us,' he muttered, pointing to the
broken window overlooking the yard. He shuddered 'The
dirty murderer!' he roared suddenly. 'Whoever did it was
after us both, and I can guess who it was!'

Late that night Constable Klinger appeared at Materna's
farm.

Materna yawned. 'I need my eight hours. Can't you leave
a man to sleep in peace?'

'Not tonight.'

'You look tired,' Materna said. 'I'm not surprised—it's
nearly dawn.'

'Dawn or not, I'm on duty,' Klinger replied. He dropped
into a chair and asked for a glass of water, then revealed that
he wanted to speak to Jablonski as well.

'What were you doing earlier on?' he asked, when Jablonski
had joined them.

'Sleeping,' said Materna.

'Sleeping,' Jablonski echoed. 'I was beaten up yesterday
evening. At least five men set on me, and that was two too
many. Three I can handle.'

'Feel like getting your own back?' inquired the policeman.

Jablonski grinned through bruised lips. 'I'll slaughter them
the next chance I get.'

'Something out of the ordinary must have happened, Herr
Klinger,' Materna said. He was as restless as a watchdog
scenting a fox. 'You wouldn't be here otherwise, not at this
hour.'

'So you were asleep,' Klinger mused.

'What's the trouble?'

'Johannes Eichler was shot dead during the night.'

Klinger reached for the glass of water in front of him and
sipped it, watching Materna and Jablonski as he did so. He
saw surprise—consternation even, but nothing positively incriminating. Putting his glass down, the policeman noticed that
they exchanged a look of discreet inquiry. Their eyes seemed
to glow with secret understanding.

'Great minds think alike, eh?' drawled Klinger. 'Each of you thinks the other might have done it, but which one was it?'

'Why not me?' Jablonski asked brightly. 'I was beaten to a pulp. Isn't that a good enough motive for shooting the man who started it all?'

'My motives were just as strong,' said Materna. 'Eichler's men tried to rape the girl I intend to marry.'

'I might easily have whipped out my revolver,' Jablonski put in.

'Or was it a rifle?' asked Materna, who seemed ready to supply any evidence that might be required.

Jablonski gave an obliging grin. 'I take care of the dirty work round here. Want to arrest me, Klinger?'

The policeman brushed this suggestion aside. 'You'd just love that wouldn't you!'

'Don't you think we're capable of murder?'

'Of course, you and a number of other people in the village, but there's one thing that puzzles me. If it had to happen, why was Eichler the only one to bite the dust? Why not Eis too?'

'Congratulations,' Materna said. 'You've put your finger on the salient point. Still, if it's any comfort to you, I'm quite sure Eis's turn will come sooner or later.'

'That's a reassuring thought. I'm only sorry I shan't be here to see it at first hand.'

'Why? You're not leaving us, are you?'

'I have to. I've had a notification of transfer in my pocket since yesterday. They're kicking me upstairs to Allenstein. I'll be doing a desk-job from now on.'

'We'll miss you.' Glancing out of the window, Materna saw that the pale morning sun was edging above the horizon.

'Damn it!' Klinger exclaimed suddenly. 'This is a pretty bleak corner of the world but I've been happy here sometimes —happier than I've ever been anywhere else. Before I leave Maulen I'll make it my last official job to save your neck, Materna. I imagine you've still got some use for it.'

Outside, the dawn sky burst into flames.

Johannes Eichler's death shook the whole of Maulen and its environs. Eugen Eis took it particularly hard. At the very grave-side—and the funeral was one of the grandest the

village had ever witnessed—he promised to avenge his friend
and patron, political leader and trusted comrade-in-arms.
He would seek out his murderers and bring them to justice
—he swore it by all that was holy.

However, inquiries dragged on and came to nothing. Two
C.I.D. men were called in, one from Allenstein and another
from Königsberg itself, but neither came to any definite conclusion. This was wholly attributable to Constable Klinger,
whose diligent but disjointed preliminary investigations proved
to be a stumbling-block. They not only put a brake on further
progress but steered inquiries in an extremely perilous direction. In short, Klinger managed to cast suspicion on the S.A.
He ultimately succeeeded in finding two Party members who
could not produce a firm alibi for the time in question. Worse
still, he hinted that Eis might have shot Eichler himself.

The C.I.D. men assigned to the case wriggled like worms
on a hook. They conceded that Klinger's arguments were
sound in themselves but pointed out that it was not their job
to stir up a hornet's nest.

'This is a question of law and justice,' Klinger told them
firmly, 'not politics.'

The detectives, who were now avowed National Socialists
but fully alive to the interests of the State which paid them,
brushed this aside and begged Klinger not to raise political
issues. The policeman retorted that the results of his investigations were beyond dispute.

The shadow of suspicion dispelled none of Eis's vigour and
determination. Having loudly proclaimed that he was going
to maintain and develop the traditions established by his
late lamented leader, he soon found an opportunity to do
just that.

His chance came on the day when he was summoned, as
senior Party official and Local Group Leader of Maulen, to
assist the district authorities at Lötzen in their inquiries. A
Jew was to be taken into protective custody.

This subhuman creature had allegedly aroused the ire of
honest citizens on numerous occasions, sometimes by maintaining a pregnant silence or suggestively clearing his throat,
sometimes by wearing a complacent smile. The last straw came
when he refused to contribute to one of the Party's voluntary
fund-raising schemes and took to his heels.

The Jew's name was Siegfried Grienspan.

Grienspan dried his hands on a towel and straightened up. 'That calf still won't come,' he said.

'We can't wait for it,' Materna told him impatiently. 'You mustn't hang around any longer. Your rucksack is packed and ready.'

'First things first,' replied Grienspan.

Materna's sense of uneasiness mounted. 'Raising cattle isn't my only function in life.'

They sat down on a bale of straw. Materna pulled out his hip-flask and offered it to Grienspan, who shook his head. Materna was feeling apprehensive, both about Grienspan and the cow. The cattle-dealer ought to have been over the frontier long ago and the cow ought to have calved hours before.

'What will they do with you if they catch you?' he asked.

'How should I know?' Grienspan smiled gently to himself. 'Perhaps they just want to interview me—in their own inimitable way, of course.'

'You know,' Materna said thoughtfully, 'everything's so well organized these days I think we ought to set up an organization of our own—a sort of courier service.'

'Not a bad idea. If you need money for anything like that, Hermann has instructions to milk my business of any given amount and put it at your disposal—any amount, and no questions asked.'

'Done,' said Materna. 'From now on we're in the freight business and you're our first consignment—to a better world, let's hope.'

They knelt in front of Emmy, the cow which still refused to calve. The suffering beast stared up at the two men with tormented, doleful eyes, and Grienspan massaged her trembling flanks with deft and supple hands.

'An animal like that has a relatively simple life,' Materna said. 'Eat, digest, give milk, make dung, sleep, bear a few more calves, then die—that's all there is to it.'

'The same goes for a lot of human beings,' replied Grienspan. 'They're satisfied with their miserable lot. Even when they're persuaded to kill it doesn't mean much more to them than dropping dung.'

Materna took another pull at his hip-flask. 'It doesn't take much to kill someone,' he said pensively.

'Especially not when the killer thinks he's doing a good deed—serving the ends of justice, for instance, or defending his country. It's shocking the number of perfectly sound reasons there are for committing the foulest crimes.'

'The night Eichler was killed, Klinger thought either of us might have done it—Jacob or me. And you know what? Each of us thought the other was a potential murderer. I find that a disturbing thought.'

Grienspan shook his head. 'There are times when murder flourishes like a weed, but anyone who can recognize a weed knows what flowers are like too.'

'You're a poet, Siegfried,' Materna said. 'It's high time you made tracks.'

Outside, Jablonski's dogs began to bark. Materna listened for a moment and then glanced at Grienspan. The little man had bowed his head and was massaging the recumbent animal in front of him. Materna took the cap off his hip-flask and looked towards the door.

Jablonski was standing there, pale-faced. He said: 'The Brownshirts are here—at least thirty of them, with Eugen Eis in command. They've got the place surrounded.'

'I'll go quietly,' Grienspan said.

'There's no question of that.' Materna squared his shoulders. 'You're needed here. Get that cow to calve and leave the rest to me.'

'Shall I set the dogs on Eis?' asked Jablonski.

'Not at all. Tell him I'll see him.'

The tall and menacing figure of Eugene Eis loomed over Materna like a cat confronting a mouse.

'It's no use trying to fool me,' he said. 'You're sheltering that Jew, aren't you?'

Materna grinned. 'You really think I'd do a thing like that? Just to prove how ideologically sound I am, I might point out that I named my prize bull Hermann after the great Hermann Goering, not after my son.

'Cut out the cheap humour,' Eis said loftily. 'I've got you at last.'

'You must think I'm a complete fool.' Materna smiled with

every sign of amusement. 'I'm the goose who can lay golden eggs, remember? Or doesn't Brigitte's dowry mean a thing to you now? I could turn her into a prime catch if I wanted to.'

Eis pricked up his ears. This was an entirely new tack. 'What do you mean, if you wanted to?'

'Precisely what you think I mean.'

'It isn't as easy as that,' Eis said. 'There's that Polish creature, Maria. She'll have to go, for a start.'

'I agree.'

'Does that mean you're prepared to make Brigitte a principal beneficiary? Would our son inherit too?'

Materna nodded. 'We can put that in writing and have it legally attested. Brigitte will inherit half my estate, and I'm willing to make certain financial dispositions in advance.'

'You're talking sense at last.' Eis looked highly satisfied. 'We can get hitched tomorrow as far as I'm concerned.'

'I hope you don't think I'm making all these concessions out of pure kindness of heart.'

Eis dismissed the idea with a lordly gesture. 'Of course not. I know you don't think much of me.'

'That's an understatement,' Materna replied amicably. 'You make me want to throw up.'

'Never mind, I'm not petty-minded. You'll be left in peace from now on, I guarantee that.'

Materna rubbed his hands. 'I hope you're not planning to put me out of my misery. I'm not Eichler—I'm quicker on the draw and I never miss.'

'I won't give you a chance to prove it.'

'Let's wait and see, shall we?' Materna said drily. 'First, I'd like to make it clear that you're not getting something for nothing. Brigitte's dowry is a high price to pay, and I naturally expect a quid pro quo. In the first place, you must help me to get Maria safely across the Polish frontier.'

'Why not? I don't care what happens to her as long as she goes.'

'That's settled, then. Maria will be escorted to the frontier by you and your men. It's only a few miles, after all.'

'What? You actually expect me to . . .'

'You in person. I shall hold you responsible for seeing that she reaches Poland without incident. If I know you, you won't find it hard to convince your men that they're doing work of national importance—deportation of alien and subversive elements, let's say.'

Eis struggled for words. At length he said: 'I might be able to arrange it. When is the operation supposed to take place?'

'Tonight.'

Eis's misgivings evaporated at the thought of the benefits he would reap. 'All right,' he replied.

'Of course, you can't expect me to hand Maria over just like that. She must have an escort I can trust.'

'No!' Eis at once realized what this meant—nothing more nor less than an additional safe-conduct for Siegfried Grienspan. 'You can't expect the S.A. to escort a Jew across the border.'

'Those are my conditions. I told you I wasn't giving anything away free.'

'All right,' Eis said angrily, 'I'll do it! The girl and her companion will be across the frontier inside three hours. Then I collect.'

'The calf's arrived,' Grienspan said. 'It's a sturdy little creature—full of bounce already.' He walked over to the water-tub and sluiced his hands and arms. 'The cow's doing pretty well, too, all things considered.'

'Thanks, Siegfried.'

'It's I who have to thank you, Alfons—I overheard most of your conversation with Eis. Don't you think you're paying too high a price?'

'Human life is an expensive commodity. Besides, I'm not paying out. I'm just investing in our freight business. Are you ready to leave?'

'What will Maria say?'

'Nothing,' Materna replied gravely. 'She can't speak, but I know she'll understand.' He turned to the girl. 'It's time, Maria,' he said indicating her suitcase, which had been packed and ready for days.

She nodded. Her eyes were as dark as the pool in the woods beyond the farm, but she smiled as if to give him strength.

He took her hands in his and they gazed at each other, picturing the moment of their first meeting, he a happy man and she a timid child whose wide eyes shone with fear until she recognized him for what he was: a human being who loved his fellow-men. From that moment onwards, she had begun to live. She had known a great deal of happiness in the years since then, and her first smile each morning had lasted the whole day through.

'I want to thank you,' Materna said gently.

She understood every syllable formed by his lips, interpreted the expression in his eyes and the least movement of his mouth. She had done so the first time he put his arm round her in the orchard. It was a midsummer evening and the night promised to be stiflingly hot, but several years were to pass before he made love to her in earnest.

'Go back to Poland,' Materna said tenderly. 'Stay there for a while. You know I'll never forget you. I may join you or come to fetch you before long. We belong together, you and I.'

She rested her forehead against his for a moment, nothing more, but she understood.

'It's time to say goodbye,' Grienspan said, picking up his rucksack.

Materna filled three glasses. 'I may follow you sometime. It doesn't matter if it's weeks, months or years—people who have formed our sort of ties never say goodbye for good.'

Jablonski came in to announce that the Brownshirts were waiting.

Materna nodded. 'It won't hurt them to wait a few minutes longer.'

Going out into the yard again, Jablonski held an inspection of the truck and escort. He checked the vehicle's lights and insisted on examining Eis's papers. Eis swore under his breath but complied.

Meanwhile, Materna picked up two of the brimming glasses and handed them to Maria and Grienspan. Raising his own, he wished the travellers bon voyage.

'Why don't you come with us?' Grienspan asked for the umpteenth time.

'And miss all the fun?' Materna replied, making a vain attempt to look cheerful.

Grienspan emptied his glass. 'In that case, I'll set up our next staging-post on the other side of the frontier. How are you going to deal with Eis and his cronies?'

'Oh, them!' Materna grinned. 'They're in for a rude shock, only they don't know it yet. Once they've escorted you to the frontier they'll really be in trouble.'

The truck got under way. Eugen Eis sat beside the driver, staring fixedly ahead, and another two Brownshirts gazed with equal grimness and determination over the tail-board. Between them, pale against the gloom, something white fluttered in the breeze like the wings of a moth. Materna knew that it was Maria's headscarf.

'I don't know whether to pity them or envy them,' said Jablonski, who was standing beside him at the gate. They watched the truck until its tail-lights vanished into the darkness like glow-worms on a summer night. The dogs lay at their feet, relaxed but alert.

'I don't suppose it'll be long before the next consignment leaves for Poland—if you're scared, that is.'

'I may be a village mongrel, but I can howl like a whole pack of wolves when I want to.'

'There aren't enough wolves in the world to drown all the voices crying out for freedom.'

Jablonski grinned sympathetically. He bent down and fondled the dogs' ears. 'You really believe that?'

'I have to,' Materna replied. 'I won't give up hope, not for all the money in the world.'

PART TWO

The Wolves' Banquet

1938-9

1

Alfons Materna was sitting in the farm-house kitchen reading a newspaper with apparent enjoyment when Jablonski burst in. His attentions seemed to be focused on the *Völkischer Beobachter*, irreverently known in the Materna household as 'the Comic'.

'The barn's on fire!'

Materna barely looked up. All he said was: 'Why do you have to yell the whole time? You're not in the S.A.'

Jablonski wagged his square head resentfully. 'You must have misheard me, Alfons. I said, the barn's on fire.'

Materna smiled at him over the top of his newspaper. 'I know,' he replied.

'You know?' Jablonski perched gingerly on the edge of a chair, looking mystified. He reached for the schnapps bottle which Materna pushed across to him and took a long, fierce pull. 'You must be out of your mind, Alfons.'

'Don't worry, I know what I'm doing.' Materna glanced towards the window, where the darkness was already lit by flickering flames.

Jablonski had been the first to see them, or so he thought, as he returned from a visit to the village police station. Klinger's successor had summoned him to appear there on the trivial pretext that his bicycle lacked a rear light. Well, it lacked one no longer. Jablonski had removed the constable's and mounted it on his own machine.

Practical jokes of this kind had become a favourite Maulen pastime in recent years, and Jablonski had been itching to tell Materna about his latest piece of ingenuity. Then, as he neared the farm, he realized that there was something strange about the familiar scene. The main barn was shrouded in a sort of mist.

Pedalling closer, he realized that it was not mist but smoke —clouds of it. Materna was probably burning old clothes, out-of-date identity cards or potentially dangerous documents, a frequent practice now that his human freight business was doing such a brisk trade.

The clouds of smoke became tinged with orange and flames licked through the roof of the barn.

'What about our visitors?' Jablonski asked, fortifying himself with another swig of schnapps. 'Are they safe?'

'They're in Emergency Centre No. 1,' Materna replied, 'in the dug-out beside the fir-trees.'

'Thank God for that, anyway.' Jablonski looked relieved. 'That's one problem solved. What about the fire?'

Materna shrugged equably. 'I could do with a new barn.'

Jablonski stared at his friend and employer in surprise. Materna's face, lit by the flames from the window, wore a cunning smile. 'Man,' Jablonski said at length, 'I envy your nerve.'

'We can't put the fire out. The barn will be gutted, but there's no need to worry about the other buildings. They're too far away, and there's no wind.'

'I wouldn't be so calm in your place, Alfons. I know you're well insured, but that could be the whole trouble.'

'You mean people will say I set fire to my own barn for the sake of the insurance money?

'They'll poke around in the ashes and dig up something nasty, you can bet on that.'

'There's no need to worry.'

'What makes you so sure?'

'I just know, that's all.' Materna laid his newspaper aside and got up. Outside the window, the sky was mottled with scarlet.

'All I know is, you didn't fire the barn yourself.'

'Don't you think I'm capable of arson?'

'Yes, but you'd never have left me out. Besides, whoever did it made a lousy job of it. We would have turned it into a proper firework display.'

'You're too sharp by half, Jacob. However, our fire-loving friends have done me a favour. They'll help my reconstruction work and burn their grubby fingers at the same time.'

Jablonski cocked his head. 'There goes the fire alarm. Our volunteer fire-fighters will be on the doorstep in another ten minutes.'

'In that case we must present them with the spectacle they're expecting. It would break my heart to disappoint them.'

Maulen's Volunteer Fire Brigade did not turn up until

Materna's barn was almost burnt to the ground. If the gallant members of the brigade showed no particular haste, it was not because they lacked a sense of responsibility. Experience had taught them that little could be done about burning barns, especially in high summer.

'You're just in time!' Materna called. 'If you can't save the barn you can always quench your thirst.'

'We do our best,' said the current fire chief, one of Uschkurat's six sons. The worthy Gottlieb Speer, who was serving in the infantry, had already attained senior non-commissioned rank and was soon to become an officer in the army reserve. Maulen could readily dispense with his presence for a while longer.

Uschkurat's son performed his duties stolidly. He ordered hoses to be run out and the fire-pump manhandled into position. Then he commanded: 'Water on!'

A modest jet of water arced towards the tottering heap of incandescent timber. The pump squeaked and the fire-fighters gazed expectantly at Jablonski, who was approaching with tumblers and bottles of schnapps.

'Water off!' ordered young Uschkurat, with rare intuition. He walked over to Materna, who was watching attentively. 'Nothing more to be done, I'm afraid. As soon as I heard it was only your barn on fire . . .'

'Who told you that?'

'Someone shouted: "Materna's barn's on fire!" '

'Who exactly? How could he have known it was only the barn?'

Young Uschkurat pondered deeply, little knowing that he had just helped to lay a trap. 'That is a bit strange, I must say.'

'He must have second sight,' Materna said. 'Either that, or he was there when the barn was set on fire.'

Uschkurat junior scented complications. 'Water on!' he called promptly, taking refuge in violent activity.

Materna surveyed the crowd that had gathered round the blazing barn: interested spectators, would-be helpers, children who had sneaked from their homes—the usual throng of gaping bystanders. He looked around for Eugen Eis but he was not among them.

Bruno Buttgereit, who had succeeded Old Mother Misch-goreit as the village oracle, elbowed his way to the fore.

'Yet another sign from God, who hath created heaven and earth!' he announced. 'For it is written: the Lord shall send down fire upon the sinful sons of men to destroy them!'

Once a respectable cobbler, Bruno Buttgereit had sat in his workshop thirty years, working hard and keeping himself to himself. Then, a few months previously, enlightenment had dawned, and from that day forward he fervently proclaimed the end of the world—and this at a time when the Thousand Year Reich was still in its infancy.

'Flee from the wrath to come!' he cried. 'It will be terrible indeed!'

One of the firemen guffawed, unaware that he had just heard a subversive remark, but Uschkurat junior was not so amused.

'You're obstructing the Fire Brigade in the execution of its duty,' he said sternly. 'That's a serious offence.'

'Get him inside the house,' Materna told Jablonski. 'If he insists on talking himself into a hangman's noose, I'd prefer him not to do it on my premises.'

Having once more urged the crowd to flee from the wrath to come, Buttgereit allowed himself to be led away. Jablonski had promised him some fresh liver-sausage, and in Masuria even a prophet appreciated such things.

The throng of sensation-seeking onlookers parted as a horse trotted leisurely into their midst. This animal, a grey, was a familiar sight in Maulen and the surrounding district. It was named Adolf II, allegedly after its sire, a stallion from Burgundy, and its owner was Baron Alarich von der Brocken, ex-cavalry officer and lord of the manor.

'Well,' the Baron inquired brightly, 'who's burnt his fingers this time?'

'That remains to be seen,' replied Materna.

Still mounted on his lofty charger, the Baron stretched out his hands as if to warm them in the flames. Adolf II snorted indignantly and Alarich von der Brocken patted his neck. 'It stinks round here,' he observed.

'Keep at it, men!' shouted Uschkurat junior, determined to show who was in charge. Although entitled to respect, the Baron was not a leading light in Party and local government circles.

Alarich von der Brocken bent down so that his mouth

was close to Materna's ear. 'You're fully insured, I take it?'

'To the limit,' Materna replied.

A faint flush suffused the Baron's long horsey face, but it might have been the reflection of the dying flames. Adolf II happily pawed the ground as though eager to help put out the fire.

'You intrigue me, Herr Materna,' said the Baron. 'I've heard one or two things about you, but I'd like to know more. Do me the pleasure of calling on me at Gross-Siegwalde in the next few days.'

A man appeared on the extreme edge of the crowd. Slowly, like a heavy tank, he forged his way to the front. It was Eugen Eis.

'Heil!' called the Baron, giving Adolf II a touch of the spurs. The grey reared angrily and pranced off.

Baron Alarich von der Brocken, master of Gross- and Klein-Siegwalde, was what is commonly called a Junker and, consequently, an antedeluvian phenomenon. History had passed him by, so people said, yet he managed to live and live well. Indeed, after confining himself for years to the administration of his sizeable estate and still substantial fortune, he had begun to exploit his strangely assorted connections in an ostentatious way.

Not only was he on intimate terms with Colonel von Hindenburg, the late President's son, but Hermann Goering was alleged to have shot many a royal stag on his estate. Then, again, there were casual references to 'my old friend the War Minister' or to 'Rudi'—Rudi being Rudolf Hess.

No one would have minded this name-dropping if the Baron had not taken to meddling in local affairs, concentrating primarily on Maulen. This may have been a matter of pure convenience, since his main estate, Gross-Siegwalde, lay little more than two miles away and was thus within ten minutes' gallop. Unwelcome though his appearances were, they could not be ignored, so people accepted them like sporadic thunderstorms.

Materna watched him ride off with a vaguely pleasurable sense of anticipation. 'Perhaps we've been wrong to dismiss the Baron,' he said to Jablonski. 'I've a horrible feeling he's one of us.'

'Could be,' Jablonski replied. 'All the same, you'd better take care of your son-in-law first. He's on the war-path.'

Eugen Eis steered Materna to a secluded spot beside the stables. 'That ought to give you something to think about,' he said, indicating the glowing embers of the barn with smug satisfaction. 'It's fate, that's what it is.'

'Don't worry,' Materna retorted, 'I knew what I thought of you long before this bonfire started.'

'Perhaps it'll teach you that you can't make a fool of me and get away with it for ever.'

This kind of plain speaking had been customary between the two men for years now, ever since Brigitte had married Eis and acquired a half-share in her father's estate. Eis was no Eichler—he spurned honeyed words.

'It's time you came to a decision,' he snapped.

'I'm still alive,' Materna replied cheerfully, 'and as long as I'm alive, nobody inherits.'

Eis gestured at the remains of the fire. 'This'll settle your hash.'

Materna smiled to himself. The fact was, Eis had once upon a time escorted a Pole and a Jew across the border with the help of his Brownshirts. There was no getting away from that. What was more, Brigitte had not been pregnant. She had merely pretended to be.

'You think you're a hell of a sly dog, don't you?' Eis said. 'In your eyes, the whole National Socialist Movement is a farce, the Führer's a crazy house-painter, and I'm a bastard —right?'

'That's putting it mildly.'

'If there's one filthy unpatriotic swine in this district, Materna, it's you.' Eis rubbed his hands. 'Never mind, everyone meets his match some day, and you've met yours. People will take it for granted that you started this fire yourself.'

Materna sighed. 'I never thought I'd yearn for the good old days when Eichler ruled the roost here. He was a beast of prey, but you behave like a wild boar—no, that's not fair —like an ordinary pig run wild—and I say that even though I like roast pork.'

'Save your breath Materna. All I'm saying is, this fire will finish you. You'll get five years.'

'You've got an alibi, of course.'

'I was sitting in the Gasthaus, and I've got at least a dozen witnesses who'll swear to it.'

Materna nodded. 'What if I can prove who the fire-raisers really were?'

Eis gave a confident laugh. 'If you can do that, I'm a rabbi.'

'Seven men were involved,' Materna said calmly. 'Two of them acted as look-out, two carried the petrol, two set fire to the place, and one was in command. Anton Dermat and Felix Kusche, known as Bubi, touched the petrol off. Fritz Fischer was in charge.'

Eis gulped. 'How the hell do you know that?' he asked hoarsely.

'I just know.' Materna eyed Maulen's pocket-Napoleon with a touch of curiosity. The man was visibly disconcerted. 'Well, do you still think I'm for the high-jump?'

Eugen Eis retreated to his headquarters, the offices of the local branch of the National Socialist Party. Housed in what was, by local standards, an impressive new building, these comprised administrative offices, a conference-room, lecture-rooms, the records' office and People's Library, and finally, separated from the rest of the block by an ante-room, the real nerve-centre; Eis's private sanctum.

Fritz Fischer, who now commanded the S.A., lounged in the most comfortable chair, swigging schnapps and regarding his Local Group Leader with a complacent expression.

'Well, how did we do?' he demanded. 'I reckon we made a good job of it. The whole thing went like clockwork.'

Eis slumped into the chair behind his desk. An oil-painting of the Führer hung on the wall above him, gazing triumphantly eastwards. Eis snatched the bottle from Fischer and took a pull himself.

'Tell me,' he said accusingly, 'did you introduce yourselves to Materna one by one before you went to work? He can identify all seven of you.'

Fritz Fischer looked bewildered. 'But he was alone all the time. My scouts reported that everyone else was out. Materna was sitting by himself in the kitchen from start to finish. The window was open and the lights burning, so we could watch him the whole time. He was reading a newspaper. He can't have seen a thing—we had him under constant observation.'

w.   G

'I don't care. He knows every last detail. There's been a monumental balls-up, I tell you.'

Eis stared blankly round the room, clearly labouring under the strain of intense thought. At length, not having reached any satisfactory conclusion, he said: 'That man could put half the S.A. in the dock if he chose to.'

'What can we do to stop him?'

'We'll have to find someone to pull the chestnuts out of the fire for us, and quickly. I think I know who.'

'So do I,' Fischer said. 'Sacrifices have to be made when the Party's prestige is at stake, and I can think of one person round here who's redundant.'

Eis nodded. 'But how the hell did Materna find out?' he brooded. 'I'd feel a whole lot happier if I knew.'

The answer was simple. The entire operation had been observed by Materna's current crop of 'visitors'. This consisted of a former member of the Reichstag, a small, silent, morose-looking Communist who had latterly been employed by a haulage firm in Königsberg; a lay preacher belonging to an obscure Nonconformist sect, mild-mannered and good-natured but eager to remain at liberty; and finally, Councillor Erich Wollnau, member of the German Socialist Party, former trade union leader, and ex-head of various Socialist welfare organizations, unvaryingly cheerful, lively and optimistic.

The three men were awaiting reshipment to Poland. The next consignment bore the number 48 and was scheduled to leave in the next few days. Refugees, who arrived at Materna's staging-post by night and departed the same way, spent most of the day in darkness.

Assembly Point No. 1 was a subterranean chamber beneath Materna's barn. It contained straw, a heap of blankets, and a shelf stacked with canned food. There were two entrances but no lights, and a permanent watch was kept.

Thus it was that, when the fire-raisers approached, Councillor Wollnau saw them coming. He was used to the darkness and had an acute sense of hearing which enabled him to tell whether a rustle in the straw was caused by a mouse or a rat. Cautiously, he alerted his companions in misfortune. Then, ducking low, he ran to the kitchen and informed Materna of developments in a practised whisper quite unlike the sonorous voice on which ministers had complimented him in the old days. Materna listened without turning his head.

'Don't try and stop them,' he decreed at length. 'Keep watch and report to me later.'

The lay preacher, adept in committing large chunks of the Bible to memory, made a mental note of every word that reached his ear. The ex-member of parliament used his gift for organization to register every detail of the proceedings. Meanwhile, Erich Wollnau co-ordinated his companions' reports and conveyed them to Materna.

Sitting under the lamp, apparently reading, Materna learned that there were seven men in the party. One was watching him, two were standing guard, two toting cans of petrol, and two busying themselves with matches. Of the latter, one answered to the name 'Anton' and the other to 'Bubi'. The leader was addressed either as 'Sturmführer' or 'Fritz'.

This told Materna all he needed to know.

'Congratulations, my friends,' Materna said to his visitors, now gathered round him in Emergency Centre No. 1, a camouflaged dug-out hidden among the trees. You behaved magnificently.

'Do you dish out medals as well?' drawled the Communist ex-member of parliament.

The lay preacher cleared his throat. 'God has yet again stretched forth his hand to save us.'

'Strange,' said the Communist, 'I didn't see it.'

'Steady, gentlemen!' pleaded Councillor Wollnau. 'We can't afford statements of principle in our position.'

Materna chuckled. 'You must get on each other's nerves, cooped up together like this.'

'You're wrong.' The Communist took Materna's torch and shone it on his companions. 'We're agreed about the one point that matters most.'

Utterly dissimilar though they were, the three men exchanged a smile of sympathetic understanding, but Materna did not pause to savour the little interlude.

'I'm speeding up your departure,' he said. 'Tonight seems to be a favourable time. The Gasthaus will be packed after the fire, and schnapps always makes them sleep like logs. Jablonski is ready to leave—he'll guide you to the frontier. You'll be in Poland by daybreak.'

'May I stay behind?' asked Wollnau.

Once a highly respected senior civil servant, Wollnau was attired in the sort of clothes customarily worn by a Masurian farm-worker in the fields: shapeless boots with knot-infested laces, baggy blue denim trousers, and a coat resembling an ill-converted strait-jacket. Beneath it was an incongruously white shirt of Materna's.

'You want to stay?' Materna said. 'You like it so much here you can't tear yourself away?'

'You may think my request for further hospitality absurd, Herr Materna.' Wollnau's voice was gently persuasive—the voice of a committee chairman. 'On the other hand circumstances could arise in which my presence might be of use.'

Materna raised his eyebrows. 'As a witness or an adviser?'

The Communist ex-member of parliament grew restive. 'We can't stand here chatting for ever,' he said, shouldering his rucksack. The lay preacher picked up his suitcase, but the beam of light from Materna's torch lingered on Wollnau's face.

Blinking in the glare, Wollnau said: 'Think what you like, but I can't leave Germany just like that—not yet, anyway.'

'Very well,' Materna replied after a longish pause. 'In that case, be my guest for a bit longer, but only on one condition: you do nothing without consulting me in advance.'

'That I promise you,' Wollnau said gratefully. 'I give you my word.'

'Let's hope I never have to remind you of your promise.' Materna did not sound entirely happy. 'But now to business, gentlemen. May I ask those who are understandably eager to leave us to follow me?'

At noon next day a small girl appeared at Materna's farm. Her name was Sabine Gäbler, and she was the daughter of Maulen's present village policeman.

'Visitor for you, Jacob!' called Materna, who was sitting on the bench beside the front door with a sketch-pad on his knee. The top sheet was covered with rectangular shapes. Sabine sidled up, looking interested. She was as inquisitive as a whole litter of puppies.

'What's that supposed to be?' she demanded, studying Materna's rough sketch with bright, observant eyes.

'My old barn was burnt down. I expect you heard about it.'

'Last night, you mean? I know, I was there, but I didn't

like to bother you and Jacob. You had plenty to do, what with the fire—and your visitors, of course.'

Materna gave a slight start. This snub-nosed little girl with the pony-tail managed to be everywhere at once. She climbed trees, peered through windows and lurked in dark corners. Clearly, nothing escaped her.

'You know a lot, don't you?'

'Nearly everything,' Sabine replied. 'I still don't know what you're drawing, though.'

'I'm making a preliminary sketch for my new barn.' Materna always addressed Sabine as if she were a grown-up—she appreciated it. 'It's going to have a threshing-floor, store-rooms, grain-bins, cellars—all the frills.'

'The fire was a good thing for you, then?' Sabine craned over Materna's shoulder for a better look. 'That's what my father says, and so does Eugen Eis. Herr Eis nattered to my father for over an hour. Herr Fischer was there too—you know, the man with a face like a carp.'

Materna refrained from questioning her on the subject. With relief he saw Jablonski approaching.

'There you are, my little darling!' Jablonski exclaimed, flinging his brawny arms wide. Sabine ran to meet him. She cannoned against his massive chest, threw her arms round his neck, and pulled herself up. Jablonski swept her high into the air to the accompaniment of squeals of delight.

Materna watched the scene benevolently. Sabine had been an enthusiastic ally of theirs ever since her father, a widower, had been sent to Maulen to replace Constable Klinger. The alliance dated from her first encounter with Jablonski.

The little girl had been sitting, sad and forlorn, on the bottom step of the war memorial, clutching a doll which had been decapitated by an S.A. truck. Jablonski, on his way to the Gasthaus, not only offered to repair the doll but did so quickly and with formidable success. From then on, he was an object of feminine adoration.

'Let's have a look at you,' Jablonski said, holding Sabine at arm's length. 'Did you comb your hair carefully?'

'I always do, before I come to see you.'

'What about your teeth?'

'I brush them every night, the way I ought to.'

'Not in the mornings?'

'Must I? All right, if you really think I ought to.'

Ritual greetings of this kind could go on indefinitely, as Materna well knew. Jablonski's repressed paternal instincts had at last found an outlet: from now on, he wanted his small protégée to be prettier, cleaner and more lovable than any other child in the world.

'Your girl-friend has sharp eyes,' Materna ventured. 'She even knows we had visitors recently.'

'Three or four visitors,' Sabine supplemented, clinging to Jablonski like a vine. 'I didn't tell anyone, though.'

Jablonski smiled at his employer with covert pride, but Materna's worried face did not brighten.

'Sabine has ears like a lynx,' Jablonski said. 'She can tell the difference between nearly all the bird-calls.'

'Maybe she can tell us what went on in her father's office when Eis and Fischer called on him.'

'You should have heard them!' A feline glint came into Sabine's eyes. 'They were dying to find someone to blame the fire on. They found someone, too.'

'No need to tell us,' Jablonski said quickly. He turned to Materna. 'I don't want her involved.'

'Of course not, but if she insists on telling us, by all means let her do so. Personally, I'd be very interested to know who it is.'

'Grabowski, of course!' said Sabine. 'Who else?'

It was a positive stroke of genius to cast suspicion on Grabowski. Since there was clearly no prospect of pinning the fire on Materna and no question of implicating the S.A., Grabowski was the obvious choice.

'It must have been him,' Eis declared.

Fischer nodded and Constable Gäbler looked impressed. 'It wouldn't be his first offence.'

'Grabowski's done time,' Fischer chimed in. 'Everything goes up in flames when he's around. It may have been all right under the Weimar Republic, but times have changed since then.'

Lavishly provided with leads, the policeman embarked on his inquiries. He elicited the fact that Grabowski had no alibi for the time of the fire. He claimed to have been lying around dead drunk, somewhere between the churchyard wall and the war memorial.

'Any witnesses?' demanded Gäbler.

'Can anyone prove different?' retorted Grabowski.

The policeman went in quest of the truth he wanted to find. At Fritz Fischer's suggestion, he had jotted down the names of two Brownshirts in his notebook. These potential witnesses were Anton Dermat and Felix Kusche, nicknamed 'Bubi', both tried and trusty men and both marked out for rapid promotion.

Dermat and Kusche presented themselves for interrogation with alacrity. 'Well, Constable,' they said, 'what do you want to hear?' Then, in complete unanimity, they revealed that they could swear to having seen Grabowski at the time in question—ten or twenty minutes past nine.

'Ah!' said the policeman. 'And what direction was he proceeding in? Not in the direction of Materna's farm, by any chance?'

'Precisely.'

'Was he carrying anything? Any inflammable-looking material—a can of petrol, say?'

'How did you guess?'

This solved the case to Gäbler's satisfaction. Having expressed his grateful thanks, he predicted the imminent arrest of Grabowski and set off to look for him.

Grabowski, the village drunkard, lay snoring in the tall grass in Dog's Meadow. Sabine, who ran him to earth there, had been sent with a message to the effect that Materna was waiting for him with a jug of schnapps.

Looking at his inert form, she quickly came to the conclusion that she would never be able to cope with him on her own. Sabine had some experience of these matters. The environs of the Gasthaus were her favourite haunts, so she was familiar with drunks of every description. She hurried back to the farm.

'He's lying there like a capsized chopping-block,' she announced. 'I can't move him by myself, but you could, Jacob.'

Jablonski picked up a bucket and set off across the fields with Sabine skipping along at his side. 'You're bright as a button, my little grasshopper,' he said admiringly.

Grabowski was lying under a bush. His tortured, stertorous snores, which could be heard a hundred yards away, indicated a prodigious intake of alcohol.

Sabine filled the bucket at a nearby stream and lugged it over to Jablonski, who knelt down beside the sleeping man.

'Grabowski,' he said, 'You've got to get up.'

Grabowski's only response was to draw up his legs like a hibernating animal and roll sideways, so Jablonski tipped the contents of the bucket into his face.

'Ugh!' spluttered Grabowski, who was allergic to the taste of water. Painfully, he propped himself on one elbow and stared round, bleary-eyed.

'Materna wants you,' Jablonski told him. 'He's got a jug of schnapps for you.'

'Schnapps?' croaked Grabowski. 'You just said my favourite word.' He tried to stagger to his feet, only to collapse in a heap. Jablonski bent down and levered him into a sitting position. Then, throwing the human wreck across his shoulders, he trudged off. Sabine trotted after him.

'Goodness!' she exclaimed with glee. 'I don't know how you manage it.'

Spurred on by Sabine's admiring glances, Jablonski carried the drunk back to the farm and dumped him on the kitchen table. It took nearly an hour's concentrated work by Materna and Jablonski to render Maulen's most fanatical drinker semi-capable of interrogation.

'Did you know,' Materna said briskly, 'that they want to arrest you for arson?'

'That's ridiculous!' Grabowski protested, still speaking with difficulty.

'What if they produce witnesses?'

'Bungling idiots! Nobody can tell me how to start a fire. Your barn was burnt down by amateurs, so it can't have been me.'

'You're in Maulen, Grabowski, remember? They're looking for a scapegoat.'

'And it's my turn this time?' Grabowski asked, almost soberly.

'Looks like it.'

'Have I got Eis to thank for this?'

'Maybe.' Materna noted Grabowski's agitation with a touch of misgiving. 'I advise you not to do anything stupid, though.'

'I'll wring the bastard's neck, so help me!'

'First things first,' Materna said firmly. 'For a start, you'd better let us hide you.'

'I won't have my professional reputation ruined by anyone, let alone a swine like Eis!'

'Get him out of here,' ordered Materna.

Jablonski seized the still mouthing Grabowski and hustled him off to Emergency Centre No. 1, where Councillor Erich Wollnau was waiting to instruct him along lines laid down by Materna in advance.

The following night saw a second outbreak of fire in Maulen, this time at Eugen Eis's dairy. Very little survived, despite the manful endeavours of the Volunteer Brigade.

The conflagration, a highly professional piece of work, was started in two places at once by someone who shrewdly took the direction of the wind into account. Dry timber, worm-eaten beams, cartons of butter and greaseproof paper went up with a roar.

Unhappily, Eugen Eis was not insured.

Alfons Materna made his way through the dense fir trees and climbed down into the dug-out, having first given the pre-arranged signal. The only occupant of Emergency Centre No. 1 was Erich Wollnau. He looked tired and gloomy.

'My God,' he said, 'you really gave me a job this time, Herr Materna.'

'Has Grabowski gone?'

Wollnau bowed his head. He had tried to talk some sense into Grabowski, but in vain. The man was fated.

Grabowski had preserved a sullen and suspicious silence to begin with. Almost an hour passed before he opened his mouth. Then he said: 'Let me wet my whistle. I might be able to think straight if you do.' Obediently, Wollnau handed him the schnapps jug.

'He picked it up and drained it like a glass of water. Then he made for the steps as though all the hounds in hell were after him.'

Materna shook his head sadly. 'Poor fellow.'

'I tried to restrain him but he shook me off and I hit the back of my head on a plank. When I came to he was gone.'

'I'm not blaming you,' Materna said dully.

'But I can't help feeling that I've failed you.'

'Not for the last time, I hope, Councillor. Failure is all the rage these days. As for Grabowski, he was done for in any case, one way or another.'

'May the Lord have mercy on his soul,' said the Reverend Dr Bachus when he heard that Grabowski had leapt into the inferno which he had so expertly kindled himself.

The spectators had already started to drift away from the scene of the fire. The flames had subsided, and Grabowski, who had only just evaded capture by Constable Gäbler, was a charred corpse. There was little more to be seen.

'We're in the clear,' Fritz Fischer whispered triumphantly to Eugen Eis, who looked less sanguine. They not only had a scapegoat, but a dead scapegoat. It was the neatest possible solution to all their troubles.

Eis merely growled in reply. He walked over to Grabowski's corpse and flipped back a corner of the blanket that covered it with the toe of his boot. 'Human garbage!' he said contemptuously.

'His brain must have been like a sponge,' Fischer remarked. 'No wonder he was wide open to criminal temptation.'

At that moment, Alarich von der Brocken put in a belated appearance on his grey stallion.

'Your fires burn faster than I can ride,' he said. 'I must try and adapt myself to the pace you set.'

Eugen Eis, the injured party, greeted the Baron with a touch of deference—there being few spectators present. He informed him that a sort of fire-fiend had been at work, a madman egged on by the forces of evil.

'Sounds most dramatic,' commented the Baron. He eyed the scene sardonically from the back of his tall charger, shook his head once or twice, and then rode off. Eis kept watch for Materna, and it was not long before he appeared.

'Well,' Materna inquired, 'who's winning—in your opinion, that is?'

'I'd call it a draw for the moment, but it won't be for much longer. Another few minutes and you'll have a brand new grandson to inherit all that lovely money of yours. The midwife's already doing her stuff.'

'It hadn't escaped me that my daughter was having a child at last. The question is, who's the father?'

'What the hell do you mean? I am, of course.'

'What makes you so sure? After all Brigitte's recent goings-on, surely I'm entitled to a few doubts on that score.'

'You mean sod!' Eis hissed. 'You're trying to diddle me out of my child's inheritance!'

'I told you I wasn't going to do you any favours,' Materna retorted. 'Try and get used to the idea.'

2

Eugen Eis stood looking down at his wife's new-born baby. It was late on the night of the fire.

'He's got my eyes,' he observed.

'He's got your voice too,' the midwife assured him. 'He makes enough noise for three.'

Eis took this as a compliment. He scrutinized the infant keenly. At length he said: 'I don't like his nose.'

The boy's nose bore no resemblance to his own, nor to Brigitte's. The lower lip and chin were equally displeasing in their lack of Eis-like vigour and robust Materna-like determination. He wondered who the brat would take after.

'I don't fancy him,' Eis said at last. He stomped into Brigitte's room and stationed himself beside the bed. 'What sort of a child is that?' he demanded in a harsh voice, ignoring her pallor and exhaustion.

'It's mine,' Brigitte replied weakly. 'At least there's no doubt about that.'

Eis narrowly restrained a bellow of rage and humiliation. This, he felt, was the last straw. First the dairy, and now this abortion of a baby. Was his life's work to be destroyed in the space of a single night, inheritance included?

'Everyone has to pay sometime,' Brigitte's voice sounded faint, but there was an edge to it.

Eis was seized with another impulse to cry out, to punch the woman in the face, to tell her that she was a dirty whore —that is, if she had really been unfaithful to him, which he could well believe. He did not bellow with rage because Fräulein Audehm, the midwife, was almost certainly eaves-dropping on the other side of the door, and Fräulein Audehm had sharp ears and a quick tongue.

Bending over Brigitte, he asked in a subdued, menacing undertone: 'Who's the father?'

Brigitte felt tempted to smile. The sight of Eugen Eis trembling with rage and uncertainty was as good as a tonic.

'Maybe you're incapable of fathering a child,' she said with provocative sweetness. 'I know I'm capable of becoming a mother—I've proved it.'

Eis made a titanic effort to control himself. Speaking with difficulty, he said: 'If my wife has a child, I take it for granted I'm the father.'

'But you're not sure, are you?'

'We'll talk about it another time,' he parried. 'I'm all in. Everything's been happening at once.'

When Baron Alarich von der Brocken rode into Materna's courtyard on his snorting steed, Adolf II, he was greeted by Hannelore Welser. She stood on the doorstep watching the feudal spectacle with an amused smile. With his rust-red breeches, snow-white waistcoat and jet-black jacket, the Baron looked like a cutting from a huntin' and shootin' magazine.

'Good day to you, my dear lady!' he called, gallantly but over-loud.

'You must have come to the wrong place,' Hannelore replied gaily. 'This is Materna's farm, not Buckingham Palace.'

The Baron gave a gratified smile. 'If you're talking about my new riding outfit, lovely child, I put it on especially for your benefit.' He swept off his leather cap with a flourish.

Hannelore Welser was twenty years old, small and dainty but full-bosomed and darkly pretty. Smooth silky hair fell to her shoulders, enclosing her delicate face like a tawny golden frame. Materna had introduced her into his household nearly a year before. Nobody knew where she came from with the exception of Jablonski and Materna himself, but she was reputed to be a distant relation of the master of the house and was treated as such. Materna called her by her Christian name and she addressed him as 'uncle'.

For all her dainty appearance, Hannelore could fight like a tiger. She needed to, in view of the admiration she aroused in some of the village menfolk.

'Seeing you makes my old heart beat like a drum,' the Baron boomed. Adolf II nodded emphatically and pawed the ground. 'I was hoping to catch a glimpse of you at the fire the other night, but I probably got there too late.'

'I was away visiting relations. Nothing would have induced me to miss you otherwise.'

'We ought to get to know one another better, you delightful creature. My door is open to you day and night—you know that.'

'What are you trying to do, alienate her affections?' Materna called smilingly from the door. 'That's a punishable offence, you know.'

The Baron made a sweeping gesture. 'I plead guilty,' he said. 'And please don't tell me there are enough women in my establishment already, Materna. That would be true but tactless. The house lacks a mistress, and I'm still a bachelor.'

'Is that a proposal?' Hannelore asked brightly. 'Perhaps you'd better fortify yourself before you launch another attack.'

Having dismounted and passed the reins to Jablonski who stood grinning in the background, the Baron kissed Hannelore's hand with elaborate courtesy. She was not only gay and charming but a born lady—Alarich von der Brocken was an expert judge of womanhood.

'What is a delicious little thing like that doing in this God-forsaken neck of the woods?' he asked Materna when the two men were installed in the front parlour, one tall, broad-shouldered and majestic, the other small and gnarled like a tree-root.

'She has to live somewhere,' Materna replied.

'Are her parents alive?'

'Only her father, but nobody knows exactly where he is at the moment—gaoled or in a concentration camp, most probably.'

'Incredible!' exclaimed the Baron. 'It nearly gives me apoplexy when I hear things like that.' He mopped his brow. 'I wouldn't refuse a glass of your famous schnapps.'

He got what he wanted, sniffed appreciatively, drank, and gave a rapturous smile. 'I must come here more often,' he said. 'Apart from anything else, I've been sleeping badly.'

Materna smiled back at him. 'For the pleasantest of reasons, I trust.'

The Baron was clearly flattered by Materna's allusion to his picked band of female attendants. He maintained six of these, one for every day of the week bar Sunday, when he slept alone. 'Do you disapprove of my hobbies?' he asked.

'On the contrary. Your way of life seems to offer a host of agreeable possibilities—in theory, at least. How it works out in practice I wouldn't presume to judge.'

'Why don't you study the subject more closely at my place? I came here to invite you, as a matter of fact.'

Materna raised his eyebrows. 'You wouldn't be trying to distract me, would you, Baron?'

'Call it that if you like.' Alarich von der Brocken refilled his glass. 'Anyone who can produce a schnapps of this quality must have good taste, and anyone who can make a unique creature like Fräulein Welser so obviously happy must have a good aura. Why bother with Maulen and its miserable inhabitants? You'd do far better to get drunk with me.'

'I'd be glad to occasionally, but there are other pleasures in life.'

'What if I felt an itch to share them?' The Baron leant forward eagerly. 'You may think I have enough distractions as it is, Materna, but do you know what occurred to me the other night, while I was watching that fire? I suddenly realized how isolated I am. I seem to have missed a devil of a lot these past few years.'

Alarich von der Brocken had transformed his estate into an ivory castle. He had tried to live his own life, shunned politics, and avoided the villagers. And then, at long last, he had come up against Alfons Materna.

'I'd give anything to join you,' he said.

Materna stroked his chin for a moment. 'Everyone has something to lose, Baron, but you have a great deal. Why not hang on to what you've got?'

'Does that mean you're turning me down?' the Baron demanded indignantly.

'I'm simply advising you to steer clear. This is a dangerous business, not one of your feudal hunting parties.'

The Baron swore, more in sorrow than in anger. 'God Almighty, man, what the devil do you take me for?' He stood up and prepared to leave.

Eugen Eis cowered behind his imposing desk like a worm in an apple core. The heavy, sweetish smell of the burning dairy still lingered in his nostrils.

In front of him, restless but watchful, stood Fritz Fischer. His hands twitched nervously. 'What's the matter, Eugen?' he inquired. 'Run out of ideas?'

'Me? Never!' Eis's tone was unconvincing. 'All the same, I've half a mind to throw the whole thing up. I slave my guts out and nearly ruin myself, and what thanks do I get?'

'I appreciate what you've done for this place,' Fischer assured him gravely.

'Would you like to take over my job, Fritz? You can—right now, for all I care. Just say the word.'

Fischer wisely refrained from doing any such thing. He hesitated for a moment, gulped, and then said: 'We're a team, Eugen.'

'Nobody's indispensable,' muttered Eis, '—except the Führer, of course.'

'But we're in the same boat. If one of us goes we both go—and then some wet fish like Amadeus Neuber will take over.' Neuber was the current director of organization. 'You wouldn't like to see that happen, would you?'

'What! Is Neuber planning to step into my shoes?'

Fritz Fischer neatly ducked the question. 'Who cares what that parasite thinks? We're the ones who count. Your problems are mine. For instance, I know you weren't insured. That's your biggest worry at the moment, but it can be put right.'

Eis looked bewildered. 'How do you mean?'

'It's quite simple. I'll get you a back-dated policy for any sum you care to mention.'

'You do that, Fritz, and you can name your own price.'

'Just appoint me your deputy—Deputy Local Group Leader and head of Party associations. That's all I ask.'

'Why not, when I'm on a sure thing?'

'What am I going to do with you?' Materna asked Erich Wollnau, his sole visitor for the time being. 'Where do we go from here?'

'Just say the word and I'll vanish, Herr Materna.'

'Where to, if I may ask? Across the frontier?'

'I don't know. It's all very difficult.' Wollnau spoke quietly, almost as if he were ashamed. 'I feel like a soldier on the run.'

'And you think it's more praiseworthy to be dead than a deserter?'

They were strolling cautiously through the fir-trees while Jablonski kept watch for intruders.

'Even a person like me still has a few friends. Would it be difficult to get a message to them?'

'Difficult but not impossible. I have an efficient accommodation address in Lötzen, where my son Hermann works as a cattle-dealer and adviser to the district authorities. By all means write your letters, but what do you propose to do in the meantime?'

Wollnau dropped his eyes for a moment. 'I suggest that I leave you for a fortnight or so. Then I'll come back again. Don't worry, I'll manage all right.'

Masuria was still the most sparsely populated part of Germany, a land of lonely lakes enclosed by dense masses of forest and interspersed with farms. Living rough was no great problem now that harvest-time was approaching. Wheat-ears were ripening in the fields, turnips and cabbages sprouting in vegetable-gardens. Fish were so abundant that a man could catch them by hand with a modicum of practice. The nights were still warm and there were plenty of new haystacks to sleep in.

'Anyone would think I was dying to get rid of you,' Materna said bitterly. 'What do you take me for?'

A deep flush suffused Erich Wollnau's normally pallid face. 'There isn't one man in a hundred thousand who'd dare do what you've done for me and those like me,' he replied vehemently. 'I can't thank you enough, but it would be irresponsible of me to burden you with my presence any longer. I don't want to put you in jeopardy.'

'You underestimate me,' Materna said, '—or, rather you underestimate my self-interest. I've been giving you a lot of thought lately. Am I right in assuming that you know a good deal about the law?'

Wollnau raised his eyebrows. 'Certainly. I was attached to the Prussian Ministry of the Interior for some time.'

'Splendid. In that case, I'll get you all the law-books, commentaries and specialized literature you need. Your first job will be to draft an indictment for arson. I want it sewn up so tight that nothing can slip through it. Are you prepared to help?'

'I'm already working on it,' Wollnau replied eagerly.

Ignaz Uschkurat, as yet mayor and president of the Farmers' League, was approaching his darkest hour, the hour when he ceased to be a not unauthoritative member of the Maulen community and lapsed into insignificance like a stone dropped into a bog.

For the moment, however, he greeted Eis and Fischer with unwitting friendliness. Observing their approach from a distance, he sensed that they had problems and felt flattered that they had brought them to him.

'Sorry about the fire,' he said. 'A most unfortunate business altogether.'

Eis shrugged. 'It could be worse. After all, the dairy can always be rebuilt.'

'Of course,' said Uschkurat, 'always assuming that you can raise sufficient funds.'

'He can,' Fischer interposed, ranging himself alongside Eis.

'Really? I didn't know Eugen was insured.' Uschkurat, who felt pretty sure of his ground, looked faintly surprised. He was not only president of the National Socialist Farmers' League and mayor, but also, thanks to the contacts afforded him by those jobs, the local representative or agent of the East Prussian Assurance Company, whose specialized fields of insurance were farming, market gardening, and forestry.

Fischer's eyes twinkled. 'You're wrong about Eugen not being insured. He is.'

'You don't say?' Uschkurat's uncertainty dwindled. 'Well, well, I'm glad to hear it.'

'So you ought to be.'

'I'm sorry he isn't insured with me. I'd have been drawing a nice fat commission cheque all these years if he had been.'

'Wrong again, Ignaz.' Fischer glanced at Eis and chuckled silently. 'He's insured with you and your company, and so am I.'

'Surely not?' Alarm flickered in Uschkurat's eyes. 'I don't know anything about that.'

'You've got a memory like a sieve,' growled Fischer. 'Almost exactly a week ago—last Friday, it was, just before supper— we were sitting at this very table having a drink to celebrate the policies we'd just taken out with you—comprehensive fire insurance, to be precise. We paid our first premiums on the spot. Don't you remember?'

Ignaz Uschkurat pulled out a blue handkerchief of Masurian proportions—it would comfortably have covered a tea-table—and mopped his brow. Sweat oozed from every pore of his body.

'I can swear to it, anyway,' Fischer pursued inexorably.

'Anything Fritz can swear to, I can too.' Eis delivered himself of this statement as though announcing a government decree. 'We both signed the contracts in your presence and handed over our first premiums. That gave us immediate cover.'

'You're not disputing the facts, are you?' Fischer demanded. 'Maybe you simply mislaid our completed forms or forgot to send them off straight away,' he added kindly. 'You were behind with your correspondence—overworked. Well, don't worry, you won't lose by it.'

Ignaz Uschkurat, normally a man of giant stature, seemed to have shrunk several sizes. 'What am I to do?' he muttered, slumping back in his chair.

'Be sensible,' recommended Fischer.

'Think of your commission!' Eis laughed heartily. The game was as good as won. 'You always get commission on new insurance, and you're welcome to it in this case.'

Eis counted out ten hundred-mark notes on the table, one by one. 'You'll take these, Uschkurat, unless you're a complete fool. Cash on the barrel and our grateful thanks—doesn't that appeal to you?'

Uschkurat drew a deep breath. 'What if I refuse to play?'

'This is an emergency,' Eis replied. 'We must stand shoulder to shoulder if we want to survive—the Führer says so.'

'And anyone who opposes the Führer deserves to be eliminated,' Fischer cut in, sharp as a razor. 'Is that plain enough for you?'

'All right,' Uschkurat said querulously. 'If that's the way it has to be, I'll do it.'

This effectively signed, sealed and delivered him into Eis's hands, and Uschkurat knew it. He accepted his fate passively rather than humbly, bowing his head like a man on the scaffold.

'That's that, then.' Eugen Eis breathed a sigh of relief, satisfied that the rough spade-work had been completed. The rest could be entrusted to a good lawyer and the due process of Greater German law.

'That's that, then,' Fritz Fischer echoed. He had at last succeeded in putting the great Eugen Eis in his pocket. He now knew far more about the local Party boss than was good for the local Party boss. 'The rest is pure routine,' he thought to himself, but he did not say so aloud.

Maulen was still visited at week-ends, though not as regularly as of yore, by the Terrible Twins. Both were now studying in Königsberg, where they shared lodgings. Peter Bachus was reading medicine and Konrad Klinger law. The five intervening years had wrought little change in their temperament.

They put up at the vicarage with Peter's father but never lingered there long because they preferred to spend their time at Materna's farm. Hannelore Welser was a powerful attraction from this point of view, and they paid strenuous court to her, keeping an eagle eye on her and one another. Materna noted their endeavours with benevolent interest.

'Anything special happen last week?' asked Peter.

Hannelore shrugged. 'Two fires.'

'Nothing special, then,' Konrad observed. 'Arson has always been a favourite Masurian sport.'

Peter edged forward, pushing his friend slightly to one side. 'Anything else, Hannelore?'

'Yes,' she replied with a smile. 'Someone proposed to me.'

'Who?' they asked simultaneously.

'The Baron.'

'Ridiculous!' Peter said.

'Disgusting!' Konrad chimed in.

The two friends looked at each other with a trace of anxiety, provoked by the sparkle in her eyes. Not for the first time, they withdrew for purposes of joint consultation.

'I'll castrate the old goat, you see if I don't,' Peter whispered. 'I'm not studying medicine for nothing.'

'Wait until I've qualified,' Konrad advised him. 'I'll defend you free of charge.'

Laughing, they quickly decided that the whole thing had been a joke, though in rather poor taste. Hannelore greeted their return with an amused smile.

'We've come to an arrangement,' Konrad announced. 'You'll certainly marry sometime, but it'll be one of us two—

everyone else is barred. There's no hurry, though. We can wait.'

Hannelore led her two boy-friends off to see Materna and explained the situation. 'They're tossing up for me,' she protested.

'It's a contract,' Konrad amplified.

'In her best interest,' said Peter.

Materna, who was playing cards with Jablonski, nodded and chuckled, but Jablonski eyed the two young men with a touch of disapproval.

The days when Peter and Konrad had revelled in local skirmishes were past. Their efforts had borne no fruit whatsoever. Maulen grew more Nazified with every passing day, and East Prussia and Germany with it. Fathers joined in, mothers raised no objection, and children proudly climbed into uniform. Peter and Konrad felt that their fellow-countrymen had turned into one vast herd of cattle.

The two boys' attitude towards their fathers had lately become tinged with pity. The Reverend Dr Bachus, having flirted with Nazism for some time, was now rediscovering Christianity—though generally in his cellar, where he kept the Communion wine. Klinger senior was still stationed at Allenstein, where he co-ordinated the activities of other custodians of the law from behind a desk. He seemed to find the job arduous, because he slept a great deal, spoke little, and took care not to say what he thought.

Watchful observers of the Maulen scene surmised that Hannelore Welser was a sort of bait deliberately dangled by Materna so as to keep the two keenest, brightest and most active young men in the district within his orbit. Apart from this, Materna was an excellent host, and Hannelore prepared his meals according to traditional recipes handed down by her family. She knew how to season the stodgy food of Masuria in the Polish manner and endow it with French refinement. The result was mute and ecstatic greed.

It was after one such banquet that Materna asked his youthful friends to do him a favour. Konrad, the legal brain, was requested to study an indictment for arson, and Peter, the medical student, to take a scientific interest in the workings of a field gun. Jablonski had all the relevant details.

Konrad Klinger took the brief which Councillor Wollnau

had drafted for Materna and Peter Bachus duly went into conclave with Jablonski.

Peter learned that Amadeus Neuber, the ever-industrious village schoolmaster, had secured a former Russian field gun from some regional museum or other. This was to be solemnly installed in front of the school-house at a ceremony which might, Jablonski hinted, give scope for ingenuity.

Konrad's verdict on the indictment was enthusiastic in the extreme.

'Would it hold water?' Materna asked.

'It's a magnificent piece of work. Who drafted it? There's something almost classical about its style.'

Peter Bachus, equally enraptured, said: 'Just imagine, a field gun in the middle of the village! My fingers are itching to set it off.'

'We must make sure it's pointing in the right direction,' Materna told him. 'It's no use going off at half-cock.'

Amadeus Neuber, Maulen's present headmaster and director of organization, had not only secured an influential position in the community but was determined to maintain and extend it. To this end, he single-mindedly devoted himself to that section of the population which was currently said to be Germany's guarantee of the future, to wit, the younger generation.

A substantial proportion of Maulen's youth came under his direct influence, since those who attended school belonged either to the Hitler Youth or to the *Jungvolk*, its junior equivalent.

'To whom are we true?' Neuber demanded.

'The Führer!' came the ritual response.

'And who are our enemies?'

'The Führer's enemies!'

The better-disciplined children yearned to demonstrate their loyalty, but Sabine Gäbler, the village policeman's daughter, had a question.

'How long is this class going on for?'

'Until we're all agreed on the things that matter.'

'We always are.'

'Well said, my child.' Neuber's pale eyes rested on Sabine with benign interest. Sabine was precocious, and not merely in mind. Her lips had an alluring curve, her breasts were small but perceptible, and her bottom already showed marked promise. Neuber approached her with a frank and friendly air.

'Sabine,' he said, taking her affectionately by the chin, 'just suppose, for argument's sake, that your father made a critical remark about the Führer. What would you do?'

'Daddy would never say a thing like that, and if he did I wouldn't listen.'

Neuber moved closer and laid his hands on her shoulders. Gripping them gently, he discovered that she aroused his well-developed aesthetic sense, which was founded on the classical ideals of beauty. Greek and Nordic, Hellas and Hitlerism—the gap had to be bridged, even here in Masuria.

'World history is being illumined by the radiance of German greatness,' he proclaimed. 'The East would have sunk into the gloom of oblivion if we had not preserved it.'

There followed the inevitable story of the bombardment of the Refectory, the Teutonic Knights' main assembly-hall in the Marienburg. Mention of the Teutonic Knights introduced the question: 'What were they fighting for?'—and this elicited the well-rehearsed collective response: 'For the German race!' A further interpolation—'Who were they fighting against?'—produced the answer: 'Against the Slavs!', meaning the Poles. The Refectory in the Marienburg possessed a central supporting column whose destruction would have brought about the collapse of the whole building. Thanks to a miserable traitor within the fortress, a red cap—'a *red* cap, boys and girls!'—was hung from a window to provide the Poles with a mark to aim at. They fired, but failed to hit the target because of their inadequate skill at gunnery.

'And this is the light in which you should regard the field gun which it has been my good fortune to secure for our beloved village, and which will shortly, and with due ceremony, be installed in our midst.'

Having given his charges one more lesson in the rudiments of nationhood, Amadeus Neuber turned his attention to another guarantee of Germany's future, the adult females who had been recruited into the so-called National Socialist Women's League—christened the 'Hitler hens' by Jacob Jablonski. Their leader was the widow of the unforgettable and unforgotten Johannes Eichler, Frau Margarete, who had become a National Socialist institution in the village.

Margarete administered her late husband's substantial estate, politically as well as financially. She had become a National Socialist Hero's Widow, a role which suited her as much as it appealed to her. Everyone in Maulen paid deference to her, but Neuber outdid them all. 'A woman like you ought to wield far more influence than you do,' he told her, adding, to all and sundry: 'Our beloved German women deserve a hearing.'

The members of the Women's League clustered round Neuber like hens round a cockerel. 'In my opinion,' he crowed, 'no decision ought to be taken by the local branch of the Party without the prior agreement of our womenfolk— or, rather, note should be taken of their views.'

'An excellent idea,' Margarete declared firmly, and her fellow-hens nodded in concert as though pecking up Neuber's words one by one.

'I am at your service night and day,' Neuber assured his audience. 'When real values are at stake, who should feel responsible for them, if not us?'

On his arrival at Gross-Siegwalde, Alfons Materna was greeted by the Baroness. Although nearing forty, Elisabeth von der Brocken was still unmarried. Tall, slim, and uncommonly graceful, she resembled a young poplar bending in a spring breeze.

'Welcome, Herr Materna,' she said, regarding him with a hint of friendly curiosity. Little more than two miles separated Siegwalde from Maulen, yet the two places were worlds apart. Elisabeth never left the manor or its grounds except to visit Berlin, Marienbad or Nice.

'The Baron wanted to see me.'

'My brother is busy for the moment, don't ask me what with. But if you'd care for a cup of tea . . .'

'By all means, especially if there's a drop of rum to go with it.'

Elisabeth's face relaxed into a smile. 'To be honest, I didn't quite know what to offer you.'

'Really?' Materna sat down unceremoniously in a pale blue rococo chair. 'Visitors of my kind must be pretty rare in this house. I suppose you were wondering how to treat me.'

'You're right,' she admitted. 'To be frank, I was also wondering what my brother could want with you. It worries me a little.'

Materna surveyed the slightly dog-eared splendour around him with a touch of uneasiness—fine woods peppered with worm-holes, tapestries depicting faded armies of horsemen, curtains which looked stylish but a trifle tattered.

'If it's any comfort, I can assure you that I don't want anything from your brother—nothing whatsoever. I'm a farmer, not an aristocrat.'

Elisabeth inclined her head slightly to one side, disclosing her profile. Materna studied it admiringly. Egg-shell china could not have made a more fragile impression, but he was given no time to enjoy the spectacle. Alarich von der Brocken appeared in a dressing-gown of gold brocade, a Jovian, operatic figure straight out of an eighteenth-century conversation piece. His voice blared like a trombone.

'I hope you haven't put the wind up our guest, Elisabeth. I need his co-operation.'

He met his sister's look of reproach with a bland smile and led Materna into the next room, which was a sort of library. Books on the art of venery were bound in green, history in blue, philosophy in black, erotica in red. Red and green were the predominant colours.

Alarich von der Brocken did not linger long in the library, but steered his visitor down a passage into the so-called 'audience-chamber', a large room whose focal point was a spacious chaise-longue. The walls were lined with double arm-chairs and surmounted by naked cherubs.

The Baron subsided on to the chaise-longue and gestured towards an arm-chair resembling a hip-bath. Materna sank into it, his eyes alight with curiosity.

'First,' the Baron said, 'I'd like to prove to you that my bad reputation—of which I'm inordinately proud—is founded on fact. If I know you, you won't refuse an offer to inspect what the villagers call my harem. You needn't be shy.'

He clapped his hands in positively oriental style, and the portière curtain was drawn back to reveal a young woman with bovine but warmly sensual features and a curvaceous body.

'The entire contingent, please, as arranged.'

At once, six prize specimens of femininity paraded under Materna's wondering gaze. They resembled a human landscape—softly undulating hills which invited the traveller to tarry a while, delightful valleys, eyes like pools of peace and contentment.

'An excellent turn-out,' commented the lord of the manor, noting Materna's admiration with some pride. He proceeded to introduce the joys of his full existence. Materna learned that their names corresponded to the initial letter of the days of the week, from Margot (Monday) to Felicitas and Susanne (Friday and Saturday).

'My charming companions are normally employed in the house and garden. They're well paid and lovingly treated. Also, the job carries a pension.' The Baron made a regal gesture of dismissal. 'Thank you, my dears,' he called, and the six Graces disappeared.

'What more could a man want?' Materna asked drily.

Alarich von der Brocken frowned. 'I do have certain pleasures in life,' he said, 'but they won't last for ever, I fear. A man who begins to lose his touch with women is readily attracted by the thought of manipulating men.'

'I hope you're not planning to manipulate me.'

'No, I'm thinking in terms of a joint venture. For instance, what about organizing a small but efficient private army—financed by me, recruited by you and operated by us both? How does that appeal to you?'

Materna thought for a moment. 'It could be damned risky.'

'But that's the whole attraction!'

'It's an intriguing idea, certainly, but you might be risking your neck, you know.'

'If I can't live the way I want I'd sooner die.'

'You may get your wish,' Materna replied. 'Very well, I'll consider your suggestion.'

Eugen Eis was determined to celebrate the birth of his son in a manner befitting the putative heir to the Materna estate, but he had failed to foresee a number of not inconsiderable complications.

The first opposition came from his wife Brigitte. 'Eugen,' she said, clasping the baby tightly to her breast, 'this child is mine and mine alone.'

'Of course,' he replied. 'You're its mother. On the other hand, I'm your husband, and that makes me its father.'

'What if I dispute that?'

'I shouldn't if I were you,' he said softly. 'I'm a man of the highest integrity—everyone knows that. If you destroy my reputation the results could be disastrous. A frail little creature like that child might come to harm. Take that any way you want.'

Brigitte turned away, cradling the baby protectively in her arms, and made for the door, but Eis barred her path.

'My son deserves nothing but the best, just because he is my son. We're going to celebrate his arrival properly—I owe it to my good name.'

The next complication, which was utterly unforeseen, came from Amadeus Neuber. Eel-like, Neuber slithered into Eis's office and conveyed his cordial thanks for the invitation.

'I take it for granted, of course, that you will make a point of dissociating yourself publicly from the practice of Christian baptism, which is all too common, even now. A National Socialist name-giving ceremony is the only conceivable thing.'

'Naturally,' Eis lied. 'I'd thought of that, of course, but . . .'

'Let me handle it,' Neuber insisted. 'I'll organize the whole thing on the latest official lines.'

Alerted by Brigitte, the Reverend Dr Bachus hurried from his wine-cellar to Party Headquarters and presented himself in the Local Group Leader's office, swaying gently.

'What do you want?' Eis demanded.

'Is it really true that you intend to deny your son the benefits of Christian baptism?'

'I'm a National Socialist,' Eis replied stolidly.

Bachus quoted national tradition and drew attention to the patriotic sentiments and wholly German national awareness of substantial sections of the clergy. Being an understanding man, he did not insist on baptism alone. On the other hand, he protested strongly against the plan to hold a name-giving ceremony only. In the latter instance, he would have to draw certain regrettable conclusions.

'I have my obligations.'

'What about your duty to the Church—and your wife?'

'I can't cut myself in half, blast it!'

Eventually, after a protracted verbal wrestling-match, they

devised the following plan: Eis's son would be christened for
his mother's sake, but only in the presence of the immediate
family. The public name-giving ceremony could take place
as soon as the christening was over. Eis agreed, confident
that he had hit upon a shrewd compromise.

However, more storm-clouds blew up on the horizon.
Materna appeared and insisted on speaking to his daughter in
private. Without waiting for Eis's permission, he went straight
to Brigitte's room. He emerged after about fifteen minutes,
grinning to himself.

'A splendid child,' was all he said.

'So it should be,' Eis retorted. 'It's mine.'

'If you say so, Eis. Time will tell.'

'And your promise about the inheritance?'

'I shall keep it, of course—always provided you really
are the father.'

'I shall make that quite clear to everyone.'

Eis dealt swiftly with his next problem, which seemed
trivial enough. Bruno Buttgereit, the village Jeremiah, ventured into his presence and appealed to him to mend his ways.
Eis referred him to Fritz Fischer, who was in the next office
working on his pet project. This envisaged the bringing of every
club and association within the Party fold, and, thus, within
his personal sphere of control.

Fischer was predictably annoyed by the appearance of 'the
poor man's Jesus', as he insisted on calling Buttgereit. He
ordered two Brownshirts to escort him to the top of the steps
and then, taking a short run, kicked him hard in the rump as
an object lesson. Buttgereit staggered and fell into the dust
without a word. It was some time before he picked himself
up, bruised and bleeding.

'Praise the Lord!' Fischer bellowed after him. 'His will be
done in all things!'

All Eugen Eis's hopes seemed to be taking shape. The name-
giving ceremony was assuming the proportions of a Party
rally. The whole of Maulen, with the usual Materna exceptions, was on its feet bright and early.

The festivities took place on two planes, as it were. The
masses were entertained in the Gasthaus from an early hour.
Meanwhile, their leaders assembled at Party Headquarters for
the ceremony which Amadeus Neuber had arranged with

great care on the principle that certain standards must be set.

Most of the assembly-room was occupied by contingents of the Hitler Youth and National Socialist Women's League, whose contribution to the proceedings consisted of songs and recitations performed singly and in groups. Also in evidence was a recorder quartet much dreaded for the sopor-ific quality of its thin and querulous tone.

Sabine Gäbler had been selected by Neuber to recite a particularly impressive poem composed by the Reich Youth Leader, but Sabine was missing. She claimed to be suffering from an indisposition of an intimate nature—so intimate that Neuber could not very well check on its authenticity.

The centre of the stage was occupied by the father, i.e. Eugen Eis, resplendent in his golden-brown S.A. uniform. He was holding the child in his arms—a point on which he had been most insistent.

Brigitte, hovering near him, had eyes only for her baby. She did not seem to notice the clusters of candles burning on the swastika-bedecked table nor the oil-painting of the Führer which surveyed the gathering with lofty complacency from its vantage-point on the wall.

At a signal from Neuber, the proceedings opened with a song—none of your antiquated and sentimental religious mumbo-jumbo, to quote Neuber, but the triumphant clarion call of Greater German national awareness. 'As Germans heed our call today,' sang the choir, 'so heeds the world tomorrow.'

The second item was listed as 'Recitation No. 1'. A chorus of mixed voices, conducted by Neuber, broke into a sort of incantation which ran:

> To create life is to preserve it.
> There can be no parents without children.
> Those who yearn for the future must love the present,
> And the name of the present is Hitler.

Five more verses of a like nature followed, some for solo voices and others for the choir. Amadeus Neuber took evident pleasure in the performance, unlike the congregation, which perspired glumly. The room was small and packed with people. Every member of Maulen's élite dozed in dignified silence except Fritz Fischer, who had been banished to a corner. Fischer resented Neuber's presumption. Not content with having organized the ceremony and conducting the choir, the schoolmaster was actually preparing to deliver a speech.

'Jumped-up pipsqueak!' Fischer whispered to his fellow-Brownshirts who stood beside him. 'He'll shit himself with self-importance if he's not careful.'

Neuber began his address with an account of ancient Germanic customs. The heroic race which had so consistently defeated the decadent world power of the day, Rome, had also maintained the highest ethical and moral standards—and that without benefit of Church or Christianity.

By the time Neuber reached Hölderlin and Schiller the eyes of the congregation had glazed over. The baby was remarkably quiet, thanks to the schnapps which Eis had taken the precaution of pouring down it while Brigitte's back was turned. Still penned in his corner, Fritz Fischer cleared his throat in an indignant fashion and glanced ostentatiously at his watch.

Neuber took the hint. Concealing his own resentment with an effort, he swiftly moved on to Adolf Hitler but did not dwell on him for long. Slightly out of breath, he called: 'Let us now proceed to the name-giving ceremony!'

'I name this child Adolf Eugen Friedrich Alfons Eis,' announced the father.

The general consensus was that Eis had shown great ingenuity. The first name symbolized dedication to the Führer, the second belonged, conventionally enough, to the father, the third paid homage to the great Prussian king, and the fourth was a direct allusion to the Materna inheritance. Murmurs of approval were heard.

The recorder quartet gave a lamentable rendering of a Third Reich air while the appropriate entry was made in the 'genealogical register'—by Neuber, needless to say. Neuber then conducted the choir in another spoken chorus:

He who now in cradle lies
Will march tomorrow 'gainst the foe.

Neuber was also responsible for the ritual presentations that followed: a documentary record of the ceremony, the genealogical register, and a copy of that unrivalled best seller, *Mein Kampf*. The *Horst Wessel Song* brought the proceedings to an ear-splitting conclusion.

'That concludes the ceremony,' Neuber announced proudly.

'And about time too.' Fritz Fischer advanced on the Party organizer, flashing his wrist-watch. 'You've overrun your time by a good half-hour.'

Neuber looked profoundly hurt. He had been expecting words of commendation, not a headlong assault by the village bull. He sprang to his own defence.

'The special solemnity of the occasion . . .'

'Doesn't preclude careful organization!' snapped Fischer. 'I couldn't care less, personally, but I can't expect my men to feel the same. They're used to absolute punctuality.'

Eugen Eis, who had handed the baby back to his wife without sparing it or her another glance, stepped between the two men. Throwing his arms wide, he clasped Fischer and Neuber to his breast and cried: 'What about a drink, my friends? It cools the blood.'

Sabine Gäbler reached Materna's farm at almost the same time. The locked gate presented no obstacle to her. She clambered over it, dropped to the ground, and patted the dogs as they jostled her, sniffing and wagging their tails.

The front door was bolted from the inside, but Sabine picked up one of the wooden clogs arrayed against the wall and beat a rhythmical tattoo on the panels. The call-sign was three short raps and one long, repeated twice.

Jablonski opened the door at once. Seeing who it was, he opened his arms and Sabine leapt at him like a playful puppy craving affection.

'We weren't expecting you,' he said. 'You're always welcome, though.'

'I know,' she replied gravely.

Jablonski led her into the farm kitchen, where Materna was seated at the table with a man she had seen once before. The man looked at her with faint mistrust but did his best to smile. Jablonski introduced Sabine by name, referring to her as 'my little friend'.

'And what's your name?' asked the child.

'Wollnau,' said the stranger, in response to a nod from Materna.

Sabine wiped her hand carefully on her rough blue cotton dress and extended it. 'How do you do?' she said, then added brightly: 'You must like this better than that hole in the woods.'

'Sabine, my love,' Jablonski said gently, 'sometimes people see things which aren't there—you do understand that, don't you?' Sabine nodded vigorously. 'That's why there's only the three of us here—you, me, and Alfons, nobody else.'

'Of course,' she said, sitting down close beside him. 'You can't tell everyone everything you know, I've learnt that much. It's different with you, though. I tell you everything.'

Materna leaned forward intently. 'And you've got something to tell us now, haven't you?'

'How did you guess?'

'It's written all over your face.'

Sabine pondered for a moment. 'How long does a candle take to burn?'

A gleam came into Materna's eyes and Wollnau regarded the little girl with astonishment, but Jablonski raised a hand as if to insist that his protégée be treated with discretion.

'It depends on the type of candle,' Materna said, '—on its length and thickness.'

'I'm thinking of an ordinary wax candle about six inches long.'

'In that case,' Materna replied, 'the burning time would be about three-and-a-half hours.'

Sabine knit her brow. 'It was lit this afternoon, just before four o'clock. That means it would burn out at about half past seven. Is it half past seven yet?'

'Where did you see this candle?'

'At Fritz Fischer's place.'

It seemed that Sabine had been shadowing Fischer at Jablonski's suggestion. She had seen him heaping dry straw together in the stable adjoining his cottage. Having soaked this with paraffin, he propped a lighted candle in the middle of it and went back to the christening celebrations in the village.

'But that's criminal!' exclaimed Wollnau.

'It's a crude but effective method,' Materna observed calmly, '—almost foolproof, too. It isn't the first time it's been tried in Masuria.'

Jablonski looked grim. 'If the swine wants to singe his backside, why should we stop him?'

'Even if we wanted to,' Materna said, glancing at his watch, 'it's too late now.'

Meanwhile, back in the Gasthaus, one climax was succeeding another. Dancing was in full swing and the first couples had begun to sneak off into the gloaming. Boisterous groups thronged the bar, and the success of the evening could be gauged from the fact that several of the revellers had already drunk themselves into a stupor.

One of the more amusing refinements of this unique celebration was known as 'corpse-toting'. This consisted in loading drunks on to a table-leaf and transporting them outside to the accompaniment of scatological songs. The ceremony was conducted by Fritz Fischer.

'Lift!' came the command, and six Brownshirts hoisted the table-leaf and its inanimate occupant on to their shoulders. At the command 'Unload!' the victim slid, in the manner of a burial at sea, on to the dung-heap. Roars of delighted laughter greeted every such interment.

'That makes seven!' Fischer announced with pride.

In the banqueting-hall the first rowdy communal dances were getting into their stride. Everybody formed up in a long line, men and women alternately, so that all each dancer saw was the posterior of the person immediately in front. The big drum supplied the beat while the other instruments ground out a monotonous tune. The floor-boards thudded dully and clouds of dust rose from the cracks.

'Reverse!' shouted Neuber, who was acting as caller.

The dancers turned about with tipsy, bear-like clumsiness. Outstretched hands gripped hot and sweaty hips and women squealed aloud, mouths agape in glistening wet faces.

'Reverse!'

One couple collapsed and lay there. Two more stumbled over them, and before long the floor was heaped with bodies. Legs protruded from the heap and so did hands, but the latter were swiftly withdrawn. The squeals turned into screams of sensual pleasure. One man triumphantly held a pair of women's knickers aloft and waved them like a banner.

'Victory on all fronts!' Fritz Fischer exclaimed delightedly.

Glancing lake-wards through one of the open windows he thought he saw a promising red glow in the sky.

Eugen Eis eyed the scene with a certain detachment, his manner proclaiming that he was above such things—that the baser pleasures indulged in by his fellow-villagers now left him cold. He was not too old, merely too wise in the ways of the world. His wife had deceived him and would pay the penalty one day. Christine Scharfke, who had given him some unforgettable moments, had moved to the regional capital. Other women sought his favour but he never gave something for nothing. Even his amours had to pay. He relished his burgeoning sense of superiority.

'Friends, Party members, comrades!' he called. 'We have always stood shoulder to shoulder through thick and thin . . .'

At that moment a shrill voice cried: 'Fire!'

Eis halted in mid-sentence. 'Where?'

'Down by the lake.'

Fritz Fischer did his best to look perturbed. 'Not near my place, surely?'

'Looks like it.'

Eugen Eis slowly removed his arms from the shoulders of his two vassals, Fischer and Neuber. He stared suspiciously at Fischer, who opened his mouth once or twice, apparently struggling for the right words. It was a well-rehearsed re-action.

The cry of fire was taken up by a number of voices. Glasses were rapidly emptied, couples disentangled themselves, men swore, and the music died away.

The cry changed to: 'Fire at Fischer's place!'

Eis grabbed Fischer and drew him into the nearest available corner. 'If you've dared to take advantage of my recent difficulties . . .' he began, but Fischer jerked his arm away.

'Why jump to conclusions, just because I took out some insurance lately with your help? You don't really think I'd . . .'

'Certainly I do!'

'Well, even if I did—even if I did make the most of a good thing, you ought to be the first to understand.'

'You're a bastard,' Eis said, but without much heat.

3

Only a few days after these events, Maulen received a visit from a man by the unremarkable name of Willi Meier. He was of medium height, sinuous as an eel, and smooth-faced as a baby. Just to complete this strange amalgam, he moved like a jockey out of the saddle and spoke like a barber soaping a customer's chin.

His outward appearance was deceptive, however. To those who were acquainted with him or had the misfortune to cross his path, he was known—not inaptly—as 'Killer' Meier. As one of the most successful Gestapo men in the country, he made a speciality of investigating awkward and unpleasant matters which were better concealed from the public eye.

Willi Meier arrived in a funereal black Mercedes accompanied by two bulky men who flanked him like oaken chests on either side of a walking-stick. They had no need to talk or think—their chief did that for them. In return, they did the rough work, relieving Meier of the necessity to soil his hands. All in all, they made a perfect team.

Eis greeted Meier with studied negligence. The man might look like a travelling salesman but he did come from Königsberg, and that was a circumstance which could not be overlooked.

'Anything I can do for you?' Eis asked in a semi-cordial tone.

'Possibly.' Meier gave a boyish smile. 'I'm here on instructions from the Gauleiter.' He whipped out a sheet of paper with the speed and dexterity of a conjurer. 'My credentials.'

Eis scrutinized the document suspiciously. The signature —'Erich Koch, Gauleiter'—was familiar to him. He inquired the purpose of Meier's visit.

'I'm here to investigate certain incidents,' Meier replied amiably.

Eis found Meier's manner engaging and his smooth rosy face entirely ingenuous. He decided that the authorities had sent along a sort of overgrown errand-boy. 'In that case, make yourself at home. Anybody acting for the Gauleiter can rely on my whole-hearted support.'

'Splendid,' said Meier. 'I shall be glad to enlist your co-operation if circumstances require it. First, however, there's the question of accommodation. Two single rooms in the Gasthaus will do for my men, but I should prefer something quieter and more intimate.'

Eis took the hint. Meier evidently liked comfortable quarters, efficient service and preferential treatment. If that was what he wanted, he should have it.

'There's always my place.'

'Perfect,' Meier said at once, studying his finger-nails with deep concentration. 'I'm sure you can guess why I'm here,' he went on. 'I've no doubt your conscience is clear, but what about this man Materna? I'd like your opinion of him.'

'He's a cunning swine,' Eis said venomously.

'Because he managed to become your father-in-law?'

Eis looked suspicious, then came to the conclusion that Meier was only joking. 'What has he been up to this time?'

'He filed charges,' Meier replied, '—charges which caused quite a stir in the Gauleiter's legal department.'

Eis had some difficulty in grasping what was going on. 'Materna is a scheming bastard—he wants to diddle me out of my wife's inheritance.'

'That is beside the point,' Meier said with exasperating affability. 'All that matters is that Materna sent the public prosecutor a document which knocked him sideways. He picked himself up and limped off to see his boss, and his boss limped off to see *his* boss, and so on until the whole heap of dynamite landed in my lap. That's why I'm here.'

'Is it because of the fires?' Eis saw his smooth-faced visitor nod. 'If so, I can supply you with any number of explanations.'

'Later, perhaps. No need to rush things.'

'I understand.' Eis breathed a sigh of relief. It seemed clear that the gentleman with the unctuous smile intended to take it easy before getting down to work. 'Follow me, please.'

Meier inspected Eis's guest-room with an expert eye. The house had been enlarged and refurnished at Party expense. It was a village show-piece in the fashionable peasant style, and its varnished wood and white walls spoke of cleanliness and solid comfort.

'I hope you'll feel at home,' Eis said. 'Quite a few district officials have enjoyed staying here.'

Willi Meier looked reasonably satisfied, though he had known more luxurious quarters before now—the Park Hotel in Königsberg, for instance, where he had stayed while investigating the activities of the regional commissioner for industry and commerce. His inquiries had been successful: the regional commissioner had officially committed suicide after signing a full confession.

'Is the pillow to your liking?' asked a voice from the door— a voice which Meier at once classified as 'promising'. 'The texture of a pillow can be very important. Do you like firm mattresses? They're supposed to bring you sweet dreams.'

'My wife,' said Eis, introducing Brigitte. 'She will be attending to your needs, if you've no objection.'

'How could I possibly object!' 'Killer' Meier threw up his hands in mock protest. They were pale and thin—almost transparent—with joints like knots.

'We want you to feel at home here.'

'In every way,' added Brigitte.

'Your hospitality will make my task considerably easier,' Meier assured them. He sounded pleased.

Fritz Fischer had been keeping his ear close to the ground recently. His Brownshirts, now trained as 'observers', were in duty bound to report any incident of note, so it was not long before he learnt that Maulen had received a visit from some top brass.

He jumped on to his motor-cycle—a steel-blue 500 cc. B.M.W. with official number-plates—and roared to Party Headquarters trailing a decorative plume of dust behind him. On arrival he went straight to the Local Group Leader's office and inquired if Eis had any jobs for him.

Eis greeted him warmly. 'You've come at the ideal moment. One of the Gauleiter's men has just arrived.'

'What the hell does he want?'

'He's here to investigate those fires.'

Fischer sat down abruptly. 'Fair enough, let him. He can ask all the questions he likes so long as he gets the right answers.'

'Are you sure everything's buttoned up?'

'The simplest thing would be to bust Materna's head in. That would solve our problems once and for all.'

'Of course it would,' Eis conceded, anxious to please his lieutenant. Fischer needed some encouragement in view of the task that lay ahead of him. 'Putting a permanent stop to Materna's activities would certainly be the best solution. On the other hand, there are one or two other factors to be considered.'

One of the factors was that Materna had yet to make a will. The man was taboo and would remain so until he tied everything up legally. By all means put the screws on him, by all means make trouble for him, but only a legal signature on his last will and testament could provide the happy ending which Eis so fervently desired.

'In the meantime, we'd better take a few precautions,' he said. 'I'll try to keep the Gauleiter's man at bay while you talk some sense into our feather-brained friends.'

Faced with the prospect of a task after his own heart, Fritz Fischer swung into action. He decided on a method which the unforgettable Eichler had used to great effect: the art of direct persuasion.

He issued the S.A. with a general alert, and the entire contingent—forty men from Maulen and the surrounding district—flocked into the Gasthaus assembly-room. Here they paraded for inspection.

After striding along their ranks, gazing into forty vacuous but resolute faces, Fischer addressed them. His opening words—'Fellow-comrades of the S.A.!'—said almost all there was to say.

'I'm noted for my sense of humour,' he proclaimed, 'but even I fail to see the joke when some swine dares to suggest that the S.A.—and that means us—is a sort of fire-raisers' club. What do you think of that, comrades?'

Forty faces froze in disbelief and a harsh buzzing sound arose, expressive of profound contempt.

Although Fischer had expected this reaction, he looked round carefully for someone who did not appear outraged enough. He found a suitable subject in the person of Emil Kopetzki. Emil had never carried any weight in Maulen and never would, but at this particular moment he was making village history by grinning quietly to himself.

'What's so bloody funny?' Fischer snapped.

'It just tickles me, the whole thing.' Emil Kopetzki surveyed the frozen faces round him with childish amusement. 'When you come down to it, what does it matter if someone does set fire to his house? It's a local tradition.'

Fischer's voice rose to a commanding bellow. 'That,' he roared, 'is a piece of downright insolence!'

Kopetzki was duly beaten up. The S.A. chief's most reliable cronies went into action first and their example was obediently followed by others. There came into being what the *Völkischer Beobachter* would have referred to as 'a mood of popular indignation'. This expressed itself in a rain of kicks and punches. One man spat.

'Enough!' called Fischer. He gazed darkly at the inert body of Emil Kopetzki. 'That's what happens to anyone who has the cheek to besmirch our good name.'

The village rang with youthful laughter. Innocent and trusting little creatures of school age clustered round their teacher, Amadeus Neuber. In their midst, like a steel monster, stood the field gun.

'This gun belonged to the Russians who were routed by our great Marshal Hindenburg,' announced the schoolmaster, '—the man who entrusted Germany to our beloved Leader, Adolf Hitler.'

For once, the children did not react to the sound of that magic name. Instead, they stared in awe at the steel colossus which was henceforth to adorn their school, fingering the convex metal of the barrel, the massive base on which the gun-carriage rested, the man-sized wheels—bigger than those of any haywain they had ever seen.

'This gun, which has been given into our safekeeping,' Neuber went on, 'used to fire a 105 mm. shell.'

'Could it still fire?' Sabine inquired, edging forward.

'Of course, my child.' Amadeus Neuber drew her to his side. As though by chance, he rested his hand on the nape of her neck. They made a pretty picture, the tireless pedagogue and the child thirsting for knowledge quite Pestalozzi-like, thought Neuber. 'The gun could certainly be fired if the right ammunition were available.'

'And is it?'

'A few rounds, but they are intended for the inaugural

ceremony. However, they aren't what we call live ammunition, merely blanks of the sort used for firing salutes.'

'Where are they kept?'

'In a box under my bed. Would you care to see them?'

Sabine pondered this proposal, but being blessed with a healthy distrust of human nature, decided to consult Jacob Jablonski first. She withdrew discreetly.

Meanwhile, Neuber was savouring the lively enthusiasm of Maulen's younger generation. He swung a small girl high into the air and set her down on the thick barrel with a flourish. Her little skirt fluttered deliciously and there were shouts of merriment from the other children.

Neuber worked the breech-block back and forth. The mechanism was well oiled and in excellent condition. 'First class precision workmanship,' he announced. 'Captured from the Russians but manufactured in Germany by the famous firm of Krupp. Just one more example of our contribution to world progress.'

The children's wonderment heightened, if anything, by the arrival of Alarich von der Brocken and Adolf II. Reining his horse in, the Baron studied the martial monster with a certain nostalgic interest. He asked where it was to be mounted.

'Here in front of the school,' Neuber informed him, '—as a memorial and an object lesson. It's primary function will be symbolic.'

'Guns should always point in the direction of the enemy,' observed the Baron. 'How are you going to manage that? Our hereditary foes are in the east, but that's where the school stands. The Gasthaus is in the west, the north is neutral, and we're allied with our friends in the south.'

Having posed this thorny problem, the Baron regarded Neuber with a quizzical smile. The schoolchildren also eyed their mentor inquiringly, impressed by the notion that a gun should for ever point at the foe. Neuber looked more than a little disconcerted.

'Perhaps you would consider the church a suitable target,' ventured the Baron.

'An excellent suggestion,' Neuber said promptly.

Now it was the Baron's turn to look disconcerted. Had he really been outwitted by a simple village schoolmaster? His displeasure communicated itself to Adolf II, and the stallion snorted fiercely, 'Who said anything about a suggestion?' he demanded.

'It's a capital idea in any case, Baron. We'll put it into effect straight away.'

Neuber threw himself into the role of gun-layer. Cranking with a will, he made vertical and horizontal adjustments to the gun's aim. Alarich and Adolf II departed with a series of ostentatious snorting noises.

Standing at the door of his church, the Reverend Dr Bachus saw the menacing barrel of the gun begin to move, tentatively at first, then steadily in his direction. He seemed to be staring straight down the muzzle. A shell fired at that moment would have passed straight through his chest and shattered the door.

'My God,' he muttered to himself, 'I wouldn't put anything past these people!'

The grim finger of steel rose until it pointed at the window above the main door. Neuber was aiming at the central column which supported the church roof. If a shell were fired now the building would collapse like a pack of cards.

Bachus fled to his cellar and opened a bottle of Communion wine with trembling hands. 'Things can't go on like this,' he groaned as he drew the cork, '—not like this!'

Willi Meier eyed Brigitte appreciatively as she brought in his breakfast. 'This is the life!' he exclaimed. 'I like it here.' He inhaled the scent of bread which had come from the oven only a few minutes before. The soft creamy butter was yellow as egg-yolk and the honey redolent of lime blossom.

Meier's gaze became appraising. He noted Brigitte's dreamy expression and the fleshy shoulders barely concealed by her peasant blouse. 'You're spoiling me,' he said. 'Anyone would think you were trying to lead me astray. Are you?'

Brigitte returned his smile. 'You're not here for fun— you have a job to do.'

'It can wait. In my experience, a little time-wasting works wonders. Let people stew in their own juice for a while and they soon soften up.' He took her hand and laid it against his chest as though to let her feel his heart. It was beating steadily enough. 'Well, you gorgeous creature, what are you after?'

Brigitte drew herself up, bosom heaving. 'A woman can do these things without any ulterior motive.'

'So I've been told, but I'm a practical man. To my way of thinking, one good turn deserves another. I fancy you and I imagine you fancy me. Why be bashful? You only have to state your requirements and I'll do my best to fulfil them. Who is it—your husband or your father?'

Brigitte stared at his legs. They were like the legs of an adolescent boy, thin, stringy and undeveloped. His feet, by contrast, were fully developed and a jack-boot shape.

'They aren't very nice, all these ideas you have about me,' she said. 'What's more, you don't seem to know much about women in general. Perhaps I'm simply yearning for a little tenderness—even if it's only for a few minutes.'

He put his arms round her. 'You may be a cunning bitch or you may be telling the truth. Either way, I've got a soft spot for you, and my soft spots last quite a while if they're properly nursed. You look as if you know the right treatment.'

Carefully planned in advance by Fritz Fischer, the 'spontaneous punishment of a malicious slanderer by outraged members of the S.A.' seemed to be bearing the requisite fruit. Nobody felt inclined to undergo the same fate.

The object of chastisement soon turned out to be a man of honour after all. Having bled like a stuck pig and been cooled off under the pump by several fellow-Brownshirts, Kopetzki voluntarily proclaimed to the entire S.A. that he was ashamed of himself. He apologized for his un-German behaviour and begged their forgiveness.

Fischer nodded magnanimously and the zealous victim beamed as if he had received a Christmas present. 'If anyone else comes along and calls our S.A. an arsonist's club,' he continued, 'I'll bust him on the nose myself.'

'Quite right,' said Fischer. 'Truth will out. It needs a helping hand sometimes, that's all.'

The S.A. commander did not waste a moment. Taking advantage of a brief pause for refreshment in the Gasthaus, he went to work on Scharfke.

'What do you know about these fires?'

'Nothing. They just burned.'

'How did they start, Scharfke?'

'How should I know?' the innkeeper knew perfectly well what Fischer wanted to hear. 'Natural causes, I suppose. You don't think anyone in Maulen will say different, do you?'

Fischer left Scharfke and headed for the second man on his list, Ignaz Uschkurat. Uschkurat, whose sole remaining ambition was to be left in peace, signed the prepared document which Fischer put in front of him without a murmur.

The Reverend Dr Bachus was next in line. Fischer found the parson in his garden, removing weeds from his rose-beds.

'Right, Herr Bachus,' said Fischer. 'From now on, you're going to talk some sense into the misguided outcasts of Greater German society who still sneak off to church. Pump a bit of patriotism into them—you know the sort of thing. Nobody who doesn't pray for the Führer has the right to call on God, and more in the same vein. Also, anybody who credits the S.A. with arson is guilty of un-Christian thinking. Got it? Right, put that in your next sermon.'

'Good God, sir!' the parson exclaimed in a sudden access of rage. 'What the devil do you take me for?'

'A sensible man.' Fritz Fischer produced a snappy Hitler salute, about-faced, and marched off.

He also tried to speak to Neuber, but Neuber was evasive.

'I know where my duty lies—I consider myself directly responsible to the Führer.'

'You mean you're going to make trouble?'

Neuber vigorously denied this, but he left Fischer in no doubt that he was above such mundane considerations. People often misunderstood those who aspired to higher things, but nothing could be more worthwhile or important than to . . .

'Wind-bag,' muttered Fischer. Neuber's days in Maulen were numbered, he felt sure of that. In the case of Materna, whom he intended to tackle next, he felt even more confident. No one could spurn public opinion for ever and get away with it—not in Maulen.

He ran into Materna in the middle of the village. Without preamble, Materna said: 'If you don't call off your witch-hunt straight away I'll turn you into dog-food.'

'Threats don't frighten me,' retorted Fischer, '—even when they come from you. Push off or I'll whistle up my Brown-shirts.'

'If you knew what I know about you,' Materna said stolidly, 'you'd be squirming like an eel.

Fischer wavered. Not that he liked to admit it to himself, but Materna's grin made him feel uneasy. 'All right,' he said, 'spit it out.'

Materna recounted what had happened on the day of the Eis christening. At 3.10 p.m. precisely Fischer had gone to his kitchen and removed a wax candle from a cupboard. He had then, at 3.15 p.m., gone to the barn, where he soaked a heap of straw with paraffin from a ten litre can and put the candle in the middle of it . . .

'You're making it up!' Fischer snapped.

'I can produce a witness.'

Fischer's self-confidence evaporated. Details of this kind could only be known to someone who had been observing him closely, and this meant that Materna had him over a barrel.

'That's settled, then,' Materna said. 'Either you stop behaving like an animal or I put you behind bars.'

Alone again, Fischer leant wearily against the nearest wall. Things can't go on like this,' he muttered, grinding his teeth in impotent fury. 'I've got to get hold of that witness and work on his conscience.'

'We've a hard job ahead of us,' Fischer confided to the five faithful Brownshirts who had gathered round him, a select band of hard-muscled, heroic-eyed men, all thirsting for action.

'There's a subversive in our midst,' he announced.

'Let's dig him out!' one of the five suggested eagerly.

'Don't worry, we'll get the bastard if we have to turn this village upside down,' Fischer assured him. 'Someone's been spying on us behind our backs.'

'It must be Bruno Buttgereit,' declared Bubi Kusche, who was one of Fischer's most loyal satellites. 'He's always snooping around. You can't even have a quiet beer without him turning up and blathering about the end of the world.'

The other Brownshirts nodded in confirmation. 'He even sticks his head through bedroom windows,' reported one. 'Besides, he spends a lot of time at Materna's place, stuffing his guts and shooting his mouth off. We won't be able to unbutton our flies soon without Materna hearing about it,'

'Fetch him,' Fischer ordered triumphantly.

Bruno Buttgereit, the village prophet, was dragged into Fischer's presence. He stared past the S.A. commander and his men with a strangely serene expression, and for a brief moment they all fell silent.

'Heil Hitler!' Fischer called in a challenging voice, and his five paladins grinned with delight. 'Did you hear me, Buttgereit? I just said Heil Hitler.'

'God be with you,' Buttgereit replied.

This provoked a neigh of laughter. Fischer and the others threw back their heads and slapped their thighs. One Brownshirt expressed his uncontrollable mirth by holding his stomach.

'Tell me, Buttgereit,' pursued Fischer, 'why do you hate us so?'

'I don't hate you,' Buttgereit replied. 'My religion tells me to love all men, even you, but I find I can't love everyone to the same extent. That's a sin in itself.'

Though totally incomprehensible to the five Brownshirts his words were construed by Fischer as hostile religious propaganda. 'Would you say I was capable of arson?' he demanded in a brusque voice.

'Yes,' Buttgereit replied quietly, 'but God will forgive even you, for his goodness and mercy are infinite.'

Silence fell, abruptly quenching the flow of artificial merriment. Fischer nodded portentously at his men. His voice sounded almost sorrowful now, but his eyes shone with a mad light. 'So you think we're a bunch of bastards, do you?'

'I didn't say so.'

'No, but you think so, and that's worse. It just goes to show what an artful swine you are. Well, we don't stand for that sort of thing. Anyone who insults us insults the Führer because we and the Führer are one—he said so himself. You're an enemy of the people, Buttgereit.'

'We're wasting time!' shouted one of the five.

Fischer shook with suppressed excitement. 'Bruno Buttgereit,' he said gravely, as though administering an oath, 'if you value your miserable life, you'll repeat the following after me: I shit on my Jewish God and acknowledge that my only duty is to the Führer.'

'I shit on your Führer,' Bruno Buttgereit replied harshly, 'and I put my faith in God, our one true Lord.'

At this, they fell on him and beat him to death.

'Serves him right,' said one Brownshirt in an uncertain voice. He and his companions stared down at the battered corpse with revulsion.

Fritz Fischer said: 'We didn't want it this way but we hadn't any choice. It was an act of moral self-defence.'

'Besides,' put in Bubi Kusche, well-trained and indisputably ripe for promotion, 'the man had a weaker constitution than people thought. A few kicks can't have done him any harm. He probably died of a heart attack.'

Fischer felt satisfied that the witness of his fire-raising activities had ceased to exist. 'His God didn't stop us doing a good job, anyway. Another of the Führer's enemies bites the dust.'

Alfons Materna was in his barn, changing the blades on a chaff-cutter, when he heard the news of Bruno Buttgereit's sudden death.

'Heart attack?' he inquired after a few moments' reflection.

Jablonski nodded. 'While being interviewed by the S.A.'

Materna had known Buttgereit only slightly. He had been impressed by the man's courage and sincerity but understood nothing of his religious views. All he knew was that anything which brought a person happiness or serenity was entitled to respect, always provided that he did not force others to seek salvation in his own way.

'Have they reached any official conclusion?'

'Oh, yes, they're all quite happy—the policeman with his inquiries, the doctor with his post mortem and the Local Group Leader with the official verdict. Death was due to heart failure, so they say.'

'And you don't believe them?'

'I wouldn't put anything past those jackals.'

Materna ran his thumb over one of the blades. It was blunt. 'Perhaps you ought to have a word with your little friend Sabine.'

'You think she knows what's going on?'

'She will if anyone does,' Materna said confidently.

Buttgereit's death did not cause much of a stir in Maulen.

The parish clerk's comment was that he had been not only a nuisance but 'abnormal'. Uschkurat merely shrugged, and the Reverend Dr Bachus declared that he would pray for Buttgereit even though he had turned his back on the Church.

Eugen Eis, who seemed quite unimpressed by the whole affair, had other problems on his mind. Willi Meier, the snooper from the Gauleiter's office, had spent the last two days in the regional capital with Brigitte, ostensibly checking files. Eis didn't know whether to threaten his wife with a thrashing or praise her initiative.

Sabine Gäbler turned out to be as well informed as Materna had expected. She had not only eavesdropped on the proceedings in her father's office but taken a peek at his papers, and her memory was excellent.

'Good heavens, girl!' Materna exclaimed admiringly. 'You're more reliable than a dictating-machine.'

This commendation flattered Jablonski and delighted Sabine. Her father was a dry-as-dust bureaucrat, and her aunt, who had taken the place of her dead mother, never lifted a finger unless she absolutely had to. It was Jablonski who had taught her to fish, prune roses, groom horses, tell the difference between various plants. He was her whole world, and she told him everything she knew.

As usual, this was a fair amount. Materna learned that Fischer and five of his men were responsible for the wretched Buttgereit's death. Sabine named them all.

'So it was murder,' Materna said, pale with fury, '—not for the first time, either. Buttgereit believed in his own god, and that can be fatal in this day and age. Remember that. When the right opportunity comes along we'll raise the matter again.'

'And is that all we're going to do for the time being?'

Materna silently began to sharpen his cutter-blades.

Eugen Eis spent several hours of the following day with Maulen's first lady and wealthiest widow, Margarete Eichler.

'Nice of you to bother about an old woman like me, Eugen.'

Eis protested quite as ardently as she had expected, if not more so. 'Don't say that! There isn't a woman in Masuria to touch you.'

Margarete sighed. 'Ah, Eugen, you're always so gallant.' She daintily proffered a glass and he took it. It was filled with a sticky liqueur which would have been enough to induce nausea in any self-respecting Masurian male, but Eis sniffed the sweetish liquid manfully and managed to conceal his disgust.

He realized that he could have Margarete any time he wanted—her willingness was quite unmistakable. This was the main reason why he visited her in broad daylight, at least for the moment. He had yet to decide between Materna's estate and Margarete's potential dowry, but this merely underlined his local supremacy. He was in a position to choose. Sooner or later, one way or another, Maulen would belong to him.

'Are you happy with Brigitte?' Margarete asked.

Eis made a dismissive gesture which denied the validity of such a question. 'I know Brigitte is your daughter,' he replied, 'but she's Materna's daughter too. I venture to doubt if she could ever rival a woman of your calibre.'

Having laid his egg, he bade her a chivalrous farewell and hurried home on winged feet. Clearly, he had chosen his moment well. Willi Meier's black Mercedes was standing outside the door, but neither he nor Brigitte could be seen. Eis regarded this as an auspicious sign.

Closing the front door carefully behind him, he took off his shoes in the hall and crept upstairs to the guest-room in his yellow-brown socks. There, as expected, he heard his wife's voice. Brigitte was giggling shrilly, but not shrilly enough. He knew every phase of her laughter. She would not give tongue properly until things had reached a crucial stage, and they had not reached that stage yet.

Eis was neither jealous nor angry. From a personal point of view, what went on behind the door left him virtually cold. He was interested only in its political implications.

'We go well together, don't we?' came Meier's complacent voice. 'We were made for each other.'

Eis felt a twinge of admiration. Brigitte knew her stuff, though she had been dead to him as a wife for some time now. While he was toiling for the Party, she had gone her own sweet way.

He heard her laugh again, more shrilly this time. He had not been mistaken. After a brief pause her ecstatic giggles turned into moans and the bed began to creak in a rhythmical way.

Eis waited sixty or seventy well-gauged seconds before making a move. Then he turned the door-handle, noting as he did so that Brigitte had not deemed it necessary to lock herself in, as she usually did.

He opened the door, saw what he had expected to see, said simply: 'So sorry!', and shut the door again like a hotel guest who has mistaken the number of his room.

That was all. Visibly satisfied, he descended the stairs feeling confident that he had just won a major victory.

4

'I've been considering your scheme,' said Wollnau. 'If you really want to set up a small but efficient private company, I don't see any legal objection.'

Materna, who was sitting in the far corner of the front parlour, shook his head. A book lay open on his knee but he was not reading. He was not talking either. Words failed him whenever he thought about Buttgereit's death, and his mind returned to it constantly.

'I found the idea ridiculous at first,' Wollnau pursued in an encouraging tone. 'However, it gradually dawned on me that it was a brainwave.'

'It was idiotic,' Materna burst out, '—idiotic, like everything else round here. We're dealing with psychopaths, not honest-to-God criminals.'

Wollnau glanced up from the ledgers he was working on. 'You mustn't reproach yourself,' he said gently.

Materna gave an exclamation of impatience. 'The fact remains that Buttgereit would still be alive if I hadn't made that remark to Fischer.'

Wollnau compared two sets of figures. He was in the process of saving Materna a tax bill of several hundred marks. 'What's the matter with you? Tired, or looking for an excuse to back out?'

'Good God, man, you sound just like Jablonski. Why don't you concentrate on my accounts and leave it at that?'

'I'm not worried about your accounts,' Wollnau said politely. 'All that worries me is your state of mind since Buttgereit's death. Besides, I'm afraid it's a nuisance for you, my being here. I'd quite understand if you wanted to get rid of me.'

'You're staying,' Materna said, '—at least until you've finished my books. Apart from anything else, you'll be getting some company the day after tomorrow or two nights from now at latest.'

'So you're not giving up,' Wollnau said with quiet satisfaction. 'You don't mean . . .'

'Why not? The freight business is my favourite hobby.' Materna shuffled around in his chair, adjusted the cushions and settled his legs more comfortably before continuing. 'Well, what about the legal position? What have you cooked up for me?'

'The marshy ground between your wood and Lake Maulen belongs to your estate, doesn't it?'

'Only part. A third of it belongs to Gross-Siegwalde—i.e. to the Baron.'

Wollnau nodded. Producing a sketch-map which he had prepared with Jablonski's help, he spread it out on the table and pushed it across to Materna. 'You ought to drain it.'

'It would cost a fortune. We'd need a large labour force, too.'

'Precisely.'

Materna fell silent. At length, after studying the sketch with parted lips, he said softly: 'You really think it would work?'

'It's just a question of making the right approaches. I handled a similar scheme myself some years ago, when I was still in harness.'

'What are you waiting for, then?' Pent-up energy burst from Materna like water from a breached dam. 'Of course, it's the perfect answer. Wait till the Baron hears about this! We must get down to work right away.'

Willi Meier lay beside Brigitte, weary but far from relaxed. 'The man just said sorry,' he brooded. 'That was all he said —sorry. What did he mean? Does he always react that way?'

'No.'

'How does he usually react?'

Brigitte sat bolt upright. 'I hope you don't think this sort of thing happens all the time.'

Meier evaded the implied question. 'Does he want some-

thing out of me?' he demanded. 'You can be quite frank. I'm
very accommodating in these matters.'

'Who cares what he wants,' she said, tossing her head
petulantly.

Willi Meier was not without a certain knowledge of the
law. First, he had been caught in flagrante, and, secondly,
depending on the construction one chose to put upon it,
there was a possible charge of malfeasance to be reckoned
with. On the other hand, Meier could hardly imagine that
a man like Eis would try to put a spoke in his wheel.

'You'd better watch Eugen,' Brigitte said, almost inaudibly,
with her lips close to his chest. 'He's hated me like poison
ever since I refused to let him make love to me any more.'

'Is that so?' Two vertical furrows etched themselves into
Meier's normally unwrinkled brow. 'What about you?'

'I despise him.'

'I see.' Meier wondered what he had got himself into.
Everything had seemed too pleasant and uncomplicated at
first. 'Do you think your husband will try something on?'

'If I know you, Willi, you'd get the better of him even if he
had a dozen witnesses—which he always has. He isn't in your
class.'

Meier pushed her away and got up hurriedly. It was
high time to do something positive. 'I'll sound him out,' he
said, pulling on his trousers.

'That's right, Willi,' Brigitte said encouragingly, 'you deal
with him.'

The Terrible Twins arrived in Maulen for the week-end
earlier than usual. It was late on Friday afternoon when they
dumped their small mock-leather suitcases at the vicarage
and set off for Materna's farm, bent on dazzling Hannelore
Welser with some brilliant small-talk.

They were stopped in the village square by a small figure
with long wispy hair, bright eyes and a snub nose. 'You're
always in such a hurry,' Sabine said. 'Have you seen what
we've just got?' She indicated the field gun in front of the
school-house.

'Useless old wreck,' observed Peter Bachus. 'Still, it'll make
a nice change for the dogs when they get sick of cocking
their legs against a tree.'

'I don't suppose it would fire,' Konrad Klinger said judicially.

'Yes it would!' Sabine assured him. 'There's even some ammunition.'

Peter gave a pitying smile. 'What would a little shrimp like you know about such things?'

'I'm not a little shrimp!' Sabine retorted angrily. 'I'm almost as grown up as you are. I know more, too.'

'Really?' Konrad edged Peter slightly to one side. 'Tell me, where's this ammunition?'

'At Neuber's—in a box under his bed,' she reported eagerly, addressing herself to Konrad alone. 'It's only what they call blank ammunition, though. You couldn't do anything exciting with it unless you doctored it first.'

'The child has some pretty nutty ideas for her age,' Peter said. His tone was entirely benign. 'She's holding us up, though—we've got better things to do than hang around here all day.' He nudged Konrad in the ribs.

Sabine pouted. 'And they say you used to be ready for anything!'

'Maybe,' Konrad replied. 'All the same, we've never been experts on live ammunition.'

'Spoilsports, that's what you are!' she shouted after them across the village square. 'I bet you still wee-wee the bed at night!'

'She gets it from Jacob Jablonski,' Peter said as they hurried off.

Konrad nodded. 'You could be right. We learnt plenty from him ourselves.'

They were greeted at the farm by the sight of Hannelore standing in the doorway.

'I've been expecting you,' she said.

'Good,' they replied in unison.

'Yes, you can help me peel some potatoes.'

A summons of this kind was nothing out of the ordinary. It gave them a chance to flirt with her, though always as a threesome. Neither of the boys left the other alone with Hannelore for an instant. They did their best to be as fair as possible, true, but this did not preclude competition. Indeed, they toiled like galley-slaves to win her favour.

'You've got beautiful hands,' Peter said.

'You're clever with them, too,' supplemented Konrad.

'I've never seen such hands.'

'Of course not. They're unique.'

Hannelore smiled at Jablonski, who was lounging at the kitchen table. 'Seeing you like this,' Jablonski said, 'I could almost mistake you for useful members of the National Socialist community. You certainly look stupid enough, sometimes.'

Peter and Konrad tried to outdo each other in potato-peeling as in everything else. 'Stop distracting us with your subversive remarks, Jacob,' said Peter. 'Worry about your little friend Sabine instead. She's talking a lot of rubbish these days.'

'Rubbish?' barked Jablonski. 'The girl never talks anything but good sense.'

'Including the stuff about field gun ammunition?'

'Sabine has some bright ideas,' Jablonski declared with pride. 'She can even teach me a thing or two.'

'If you say so,' Konrad replied thoughtfully. 'All the same, she's letting her imagination run away with her where that gun's concerned. It would take an expert to get it to fire properly.'

'An explosives expert?' Jablonski said slowly. 'I may be able to help you there.'

'What do you know about explosives?'

'Practically nothing, but I've got contacts I could get in touch with. Anything to give Sabine a treat.'

On the morning of the following day, a Saturday, Alfons Materna rode off to Gross-Siegwalde on a bicycle which had once belonged to his friend Siegfried Grienspan.

Elisabeth, the Baron's sister, greeted him as if she had been expecting him.

'You're always welcome,' she assured him with a warm smile.

'Don't speak too soon,' he replied.

'Is it something important?'

He nodded, and they strolled down the passage to the drawing-room in evident harmony.

'In that case,' she said, laying her hand on his arm in a way which invited trust. 'I'd like to be there when you talk it over.'

Materna sat down on a full-bellied sofa upholstered in patterned silk—a riot of brick-red and egg-yellow roses. Elisabeth sat down beside him and they drank coffee and chatted as though they had chatted together a hundred times before.

Alarich von der Brocken appeared in the doorway. 'Well, well,' he said raising his eyebrows, 'did you come to see me or keep a date with my sister?'

'I've just been trying to explain to Herr Materna that you're a little difficult to deal with,' Elisabeth said sweetly. 'I told him you're not the sort of man to take an unnecessary risk.'

'Stuff and nonsense!' the Baron said promptly, feeling slighted. 'I'll grab any nettle I'm offered—as long as I'm wearing gloves, of course.' He sat down four-square, radiating determination. 'Fire away, my friend.'

Materna proceeded to outline the scheme devised by himself and elaborated by Wollnau. This envisaged:

First, the draining of the marshy ground south of Maulen, two-thirds of which belonged to Materna and one-third to the Baron. All expenses to be shared on a pro rata basis;

Secondly, the securing of land development permission from the competent authorities. An application had already been drafted and would be lodged by the Baron with the help of his personal connections;

Thirdly, the recruitment of a labour force, to be carried out by Materna in Poland. The procuring of the requisite labour permits was another matter which would entail wire-pulling, and this belonged to the Baron's sphere of operations;

Fourthly, the construction of a barrack-room to house the workers, this to be built on Materna's land. The said workers to be supervised by Jacob Jablonski, who spoke Polish. Any substitutions or replacements in the labour force to be arranged by Materna;

Fifthly, the workers—twelve or fifteen to begin with—to be available to either partner, on request, for special projects of a short-term nature.

'Impossible!' Elisabeth exclaimed, giving her brother some wholly superfluous encouragement. 'Alarich would never lend himself to such an idea.'

'On the contrary, my dear. Kindly stay out of this—you don't understand these things.' Eagerly, the Baron seized the papers which Materna had produced from his briefcase.

Elisabeth's face wore a mischievous smile as she left the room, but her brother was too engrossed in Materna's plans to notice. His eyes grew wider and wider.

'Magnificent!' he cried after a pause. 'Superb spade-work, that. The authorities will lap up the idea—they can't fail to, what with all this stuff about Lebensraum, land reclamation, private initiative, foreign labour, and so on. You'll get a decoration before you're through.'

'Your general agreement will be enough for the time being. 'You've got it.'

'No questions asked—no strings of any kind?'

'As far as I'm concerned,' the Baron said, 'we're proposing to drain a marsh and that's all. If it so happens that we acquire the services of a dozen stout fellows in the process —with official permission—that will be purely coincidental. And if a gang of thugs—far be it from me to mention the S.A. by name—happens to cross swords with our chaps, that will be equally coincidental. Am I right?'

Materna nodded. 'More or less.'

They shook hands like cattle-dealers sealing a bargain and the Baron sent for an inaugural bottle of champagne, which was served by the Tuesday and Thursday girls.

After they had drunk to one another, Alarich von der Brocken leant forward with a positively imploring air.

'One thing, though,' he said gravely. 'Don't go playing private armies without me. It was my idea, and I insist on joining in.'

'Well, and what can I do for you?' Eugen Eis inquired with extreme affability. 'Sit down, Herr Meier—make yourself at home. We pride ourselves on our hospitality in this part of the world, as you know.'

The Gestapo man sat down in silence. The silence lengthened, but Eis waited with smiling composure. At length, grown wary, Meier asked: 'Do you know why I was sent here?'

'Whatever the reason, I imagine your trip has turned out to be unnecessary. I only hope you enjoyed your stay.'

Willi Meier's eyes narrowed. He was immeasurably annoyed by Eis's attempt to discard him like a load of rotten turnips. 'There's something fishy going on here—you know that perfectly well.'

'That's life. There's always something fishy going on some-where.'

'More than one person is mixed up in these fires—a child could see that. You're involved yourself, but the main offender is your S.A. commander, Fischer. You wouldn't deny that, would you?'

'Why should I, when you're so sure of your ground? All the same, you'd have to live in Maulen to get any idea of the real circumstances. Take me, for instance. I don't just head the Party here. I'm a magistrate, land-owner, dairy pro-prietor, flour-miller, and a mass of other things besides. The other senior Party members also lead full lives for the good of the community, but you can't do that sort of thing in Maulen and keep your hands lily-white. Maulen isn't Königsberg, and Masuria isn't Prussia. All that matters is to keep the Party flag flying, and that's what we're doing. In my opinion, you ought to do the same.'

'You seriously expect me to declare the case closed?'

'Of course, that's exactly what I do expect.' Eis laughed raucously. 'After all, the interests of the community come first. You aren't here just to enjoy yourself—let alone under-mine the local branch of the Party.'

No one had ever tried such rough and ready methods on Willi Meier before. He felt a violent impulse to whistle up his bloodhounds, throw Eis into a cell, and work him over until he could do no more than gasp an affirmative to any question he was asked.

Eis restrained the impulse for him. 'Everything comes second to the Party with me,' he declared, '—everything and everyone, including my wife. You might bear that in mind.'

Meier's lips became a thin line and blotches appeared on his deceptively boyish face. He sat forward in his chair as though about to pounce, but he remained seated.

'You see, Herr Meier,' Eis went on, 'we simple country-folk know what loyalty means. My men would go through fire for me, but don't take that too literally. I'm only telling you because I hope you're a man of honour as well as a Party member—for my wife's sake, apart from anything else.'

'That's enough!' Meier hissed angrily.

'You're going, then?'

'As soon as possible.' Meier jumped up. 'I'll leave one of my men behind to tie up any loose ends, Party-fashion. As for me, I need a change of air badly.'

Only three or four people were aware of Josef Leitgeber's presence in Maulen. He was a young man of medium height, with a face like a hamster and a marked abhorrence of long words.

'Yes,' he said, when Jablonski asked him if he knew how to handle ammunition and explosives.

Leitgeber had been consigned to the care of Materna's freight business in company with a Catholic priest. Both men had travelled from Königsberg via Lötzen concealed in a cartful of pigs destined for slaughter. Like the majority of Materna's visitors, they were quiet and unassuming people.

'Suppose you've got a 105 millimetre gun and a number of rounds consisting of a shell-case filled with cordite only—in other words, blanks. Could you turn them into live ammunition?'

'I could,' Leitgeber said tersely.

Once a lumberjack from the Bavarian forests, Leitgeber had started by helping to paste up anti-Nazi posters, initially as a favour to some school-friends. Then, when the Gestapo turned up at his parents' house, he went to ground in Augsburg, where he worked in a machine-shop by day and converted ordinary radio sets into short-wave transmitters by night. Later, he manufactured bombs out of explosives. The only photograph that had ever been taken of him now adorned a police poster above the caption: 'Wanted for subversive activities . . .'

'What would be needed to turn these blanks into live rounds, Herr Leitgeber?'

It seemed that the prime requirement was a projectile of some kind. This could be improvised either out of a lump of metal or a stone of suitable size. Leitgeber could not, of course, guarantee much penetrative power, but the fragmentation effect would be considerable.

Jablonski got in touch with Sabine, who duly trotted over from the village with a blank round purloined from Neuber's bedroom.

'Good,' said Leitgeber. Sniffing like a truffle-hound, he combed Materna's barn for materials. He found several large stones, a lump of iron for whetting scythes, and a thick metal tube. Collecting his finds and a number of tools, he retired to the dug-out in the woods where he turned up the paraffin-lamp to its fullest extent and set to work. His fellow-traveller, the priest, murmured prayers in an undertone without casting a glance at his dog-eared breviary. His eyes were fixed on the embryonic shell.

After two hours of hammering and filing, Leitgeber silently handed the finished shell to Jablonski, who clasped it to his broad chest and hurried back to the farm.

'Look what I've got!' he called to Peter and Konrad, cradling the shell in his arms. 'Well, what do you think of that?'

'Not bad,' Peter commented. 'Looks almost like the real thing.'

Konrad examined the unusual object gingerly. 'You've really got something there,' he said. 'Where did it come from?'

'Never you mind. Care to take it off my hands?'

'Give it here,' Konrad said joyfully. 'It's about time we had a bit of action round here. Even if it doesn't bring Germany to its senses, it may make Maulen sit up and rub its bleary eyes.'

Maulen's leading citizens were once more seeking agreement and failing to find it. It was already Friday, but no one had yet decided who was to deliver the speech at the field gun ceremony to be held that week-end. As a result, feelings were running high.

The entire Party élite had assembled in the back room of the Gasthaus. Each man present was a 'leader' of some sort. One headed the S.A., another the Hitler Youth, a third the Farmers' League, a fourth the agricultural labourers, and a fifth those who engaged in trade and commerce. They all helped to organize and raise money for the Party, all contributed to what was known as popular enlightenment, all belonged to the vanguard of the unique and irresistible Movement.

'We must pull together,' someone said. All eyes turned to Eugen Eis. 'The time has come.'

'To have a drink, you mean?'

Eis's little joke was greeted with roars of laughter but did little to mitigate the tension. He could simply have announced that he would deliver the inaugural address himself or ordered someone else to deliver it, but that was precisely what he did not do. He feigned neutrality and watched the outbreak of hostilities between his two lieutenants, Fischer and Neuber, with apparent unconcern.

'I would again point out,' Neuber said, 'that the gun was acquired on my initiative. Moreover, since its presence is primarily of symbolic importance, the whole matter comes under the heading of public education, for which I am responsible.'

'You're wrong there,' amended Fritz Fischer. 'Guns are aids to military training, and military training is the S.A.'s pigeon.'

Controversy might have raged along these lines for hours to come. Eis welcomed the rivalry between Fischer and Neuber because it curbed Fischer's increasing arrogance and Neuber's burgeoning ambition. Playing one off against the other was a staple ingredient of village diplomacy.

Very deliberately, he said: 'The gun is due to be inaugurated on Sunday morning. Tomorrow there will be a ceremony to mark the outbreak of war, and tomorrow night a dance. That means three speeches at least.'

'Leave them all to me,' Neuber said, unabashed. 'It's my responsibility as Director of Education.'

Fischer started to reply, but at that moment a cacophonous din broke out close by. Maulen's brass band, now known as 'the United and Augmented', had gone into action in the assembly-room of the Gasthaus.

'Is this one of your diversionary tactics?' Neuber shouted at Fischer.

'As far as I'm aware,' Fischer shouted back, 'noise-making is one of your specialities.'

At a nod from Eugen Eis, Fischer sent one of his men to investigate. He trotted back with the news that the music had been specially commissioned by the Baron, who was in one of his mellow moods.

Alarich von der Brocken had recently shown himself a music-lover, and there was little anyone could do about it. He not only bought instruments and sheet music but kept the bandsmen lavishly supplied with drink.

As on other occasions, the Baron had alerted his musicians in advance. Mounted on Adolf II, he rode straight into the assembly-room from the garden to the strains of the *Hohen-friedberger March*, the band's customary form of greeting. He then dismounted, pulled up a chair, and produced a hundred-mark note from his wallet. Placing this on the floor, he called out: 'Do your stuff, men! Bring tears to my eyes!' There followed a succession of sentimental tunes whose titles spoke of unrequited love, the billows of the Baltic, and birches bending in the summer breeze.

'Why now?' Fischer demanded belligerently in the back room. 'I can hardly hear myself speak.'

'A blessing in disguise!' shouted Neuber.

Eis's commanding voice cut across the hubbub. 'I propose we take a vote between Fischer and Neuber, secretly and in writing.'

This suggestion was received with universal relief. The Party dignitaries proceeded to vote without delay, and within five minutes the following result emerged: seven votes for Fischer and the same number for Neuber.

Eis, who abstained, could scarcely conceal his satisfaction. 'Let's adjourn for a pee,' he ordained loudly. 'Drinks and smokes are on the house.'

The next few minutes were devoted to what might charitably have been described as lobbying. Neuber drew the Hitler Youth leader into a corner while the ever practical Fischer called Bubi Kusche to his side. Kusche reacted with Pavlovian predictability. 'I follow,' he said. 'Anyone who doesn't toe the line gets done.'

Back in the assembly-room, Alarich von der Brocken had attained a sufficiently mellow mood. He raised his hand and the sentimental folk-tunes died away. Pulling out another hundred-mark note, he placed it beside the first and called on the band for something which would put some fire in his belly.

At once, marches rang out: first—as usual—*I Hunt the Stag in Forest Wild*, then *Through Night to Light*, and, finally, *The Great Elector's Cavalry March*. At this, Adolf II neighed joyfully and pranced across the assembly-room, mangling the parquet with his hoofs.

'Carry on!' cried the Baron.

Bubi Kusche had meanwhile gone to work on the Hitler Youth leader. A short verbal exchange was followed by more cogent forms of persuasion. Kusche's fist thudded into the man's solar plexus and he doubled up like a jack-knife.

The result of the second ballot was as follows: eight votes for Fischer, six for Neuber.

'Why didn't you say so straight away?' Fischer demanded, surveying the voters with a complacent air. Eis permitted himself an enigmatic smile.

'We'll see who has the last laugh,' Neuber muttered balefully.

Konrad Klinger and Peter Bachus approached the village square with caution. A blare of martial music was coming from the Gasthaus and dogs were howling at the moon as it sailed through the pale night-sky.

'Almost like the old days, eh?' whispered Peter.

'Thank God for the Baron's taste in music,' Konrad replied. 'We could make enough row to raise the dead and no one would notice.'

This was true, but it did not prevent them from setting about their nocturnal task with extreme care. Leaning against the fire-station, they surveyed the village square. The church looked dark and cavernous, the war memorial stood there in the dim moonlight like the sole surviving column of some historic ruin, and the schoolhouse resembled a barn with windows. The gun in front of it, coated with a generous film of oil, gleamed magically.

'All right,' Peter said, 'let's go.'

But neither of them moved. Borne to them above the strains of the band came a metallic sound. Straining their ears, they heard it again—a noise like the clink of stone on metal.

'There's something funny going on,' Peter hissed. 'Don't tell me someone's beaten us to it!'

They left their bulging briefcase propped against the fire-station wall and worked their way round the village square. Having negotiated the dark pool of shadow cast by the church, they reached the side of the school and edged towards the field gun. There, illuminated by the moon, which emerged abruptly from behind a cloud at that moment, they saw a small and nimble figure hard at work on the breech mechanism.

Konrad abandoned his crouching stance and walked over to

the gun. 'Are you crazy, Sabine?' he said. 'What the devil are you up to?'

'Doing your job for you,' Sabine retorted.

'A child of your age ought to be in bed at this hour,' Peter said indignantly. He bent over the gun and examined it. 'She's been trying to damage the thing,' he reported in tones of alarm. 'She's gone and shoved a lot of stones up the spout.' He turned to Sabine. 'I ought to tan your hide.'

'Either it shoots properly or not at all,' she replied petulantly.

'Better take her to Jacob,' Konrad suggested.

'Yes,' Peter said. 'Come along, shrimp.'

'You lay a finger on me and I'll kick your shins till they're black and blue!' threatened Sabine.

Peter stepped back hastily. 'She'd do it, too.'

'Listen, Sabine,' Konrad said, 'you're making a big mistake, you know. Ask Jacob Jablonski.'

'It's no use asking Jacob. He doesn't know anything about this.'

'Why don't you ask him all the same?' Konrad took her arm gently. 'We're acting on his behalf—cross my heart.'

'If you say so it must be true,' she replied gravely. 'All right, I'll go, but I'll never forgive you if you're fibbing.'

As soon as she had scampered off, Konrad and Peter set to work. They felt around in the breech and removed the stones. The breech-block had sustained a few minor scratches, but it slid back and forth without difficulty.

'German craftsmanship,' Konrad observed with a grin.

Peter fetched the briefcase and removed Leitgeber's home-made shell. Gingerly, he slid it into the breech. It fitted. He closed the breech-block, and it clicked home like the door of a safe.

'That ought to do the trick,' he said.

The following day—Saturday—opened on an unusually cheerful note.

The sound of singing issued from the school-house, where the children were rehearsing their contribution to the evening's festivities. Although Neuber's mind was not on his work he did his duty just the same. Indeed, he even derived a measure of relaxation from instructing some of the girls in breath-control, gently pressing their diaphragms in the process.

Constable Gäbler was cleaning his boots outside his front door, indefatigably and with military precision. The Reverend Dr Bachus gazed heavenwards, but only for meteorological reasons. His vegetable-garden would have benefited from a short sharp shower of rain.

'*The fire that burns in German hearts . . .*' sang the children.

Numerous helpers from the Hitler Youth and German Girls' League were already decorating the assembly-room under Bubi Kusche's supervision. The streamers all bore legends referring to the great day when the captured field gun would be inaugurated. Above the speaker's rostrum, for instance, hung a white banner edged with scarlet and adorned with the following words in bold black characters:.

> *No foes survive our German soil to stain.*
> *They in Masuria's marshes all lie slain.*

'We must aim at the word "foes",' said Konrad Klinger, who was strolling casually past the open windows of the hall with Peter Bachus.

Peter nodded. 'If we hit the cross-beam we'll bring half the roof down.'

Feeling cheered, they left the village and headed for Materna's farm, where they were met by Jacob Jablonski.

'The house is off limits for the moment,' Jablonski announced. 'Alfons is working on something.'

'Let him. We've come to see Hannelore.'

Jablonski jerked a thumb over his shoulder. 'She's in the vegetable-garden. I'd take a couple of hoes along if I were you—it'll save you a trip.'

They took his advice—wisely, as it turned out, because Hannelore's friendly greeting was coupled with an injunction to weed the paths between the beds. This kept them fully occupied until lunch-time.

Meanwhile, Materna and Wollnau were working on the last of the documents relating to their drainage scheme, an application addressed to the regional authorities in Allenstein.

'They won't dare say no,' Wollnau declared, '—not unless

they're prepared to risk being suspected of sabotaging the creation of Lebensraum.'

'The Baron has fixed an appointment with them for Monday morning. His connections ought to do the trick, so it only remains for me to thank you from the bottom of my heart, Herr Wollnau, and bid you goodbye.'

'But this is just the start.'

'For me, perhaps, but not for you. The next consignment leaves for Poland tonight, during the celebrations. They'll all be trying to drink each other under the table.'

'The ideal moment, Herr Materna, but not for me. I can't desert you at this stage. Even if the scheme is approved promptly, there'll still be plenty of problems to sort out.'

'You want to stay on, then?'

'For the moment, yes.'

'Are you prepared to spend most of the next few weeks in the dug-out?'

'If I must, but there is an alternative. I speak fluent Polish. What about passing me off as your Polish foreman?'

Materna wagged his head admiringly. 'You've got guts, I'll give you that. All right, I won't say yes or no right away. We'll wait and see how things shape.'

A cheerful sense of anticipation continued to pervade the village. The school choir was now rehearsing a delightful song which ran:

> Let us wander, hand in hand,
> Through the Führer's promised land.

Eugen Eis escorted Margarete Eichler to the assembly-room under the watchful gaze of the villagers and showed her the preparations for the evening's festivities.

'Just as dear Johannes would have wished it,' Margarete said approvingly.

Eis flashed her a smile of gratitude. 'Maulen still remembers how much it owes to him.'

At that moment, Brigitte was sitting perched on her husband's desk. Behind it, leering at her and breathing heavily, sat the man who had been entrusted with mopping-up operations by 'Killer' Meier, a beefy-looking individual named Friedrich Wilhelm Pampusch.

'I can't alter any of this,' Pampusch said hoarsely, gesturing at the papers in front of him without taking his eyes off Brigitte's fleshy thighs. 'My job is to close the inquiry into these fires—wrap it up neatly and file it.'

'But you needn't be too quick about it. You could always spin things out a bit.'

'Why, dear lady?'

'Can't you guess?'

Of course he could. Brigitte clearly valued his companionship. 'Very well,' he said flattered. 'After all, Meier told me to close the case but he didn't say how quickly.'

Brigitte looked pleased. 'Just act as if everything is still in the air—one or two people in Maulen won't like that.'

'Anything for you,' he declared, squeezing her hand. 'You must explain your ideas in greater detail, though. I'm staying at the Gasthaus—Room No. 3.'

'I'll call in about eight, then. That's when the celebrations start.'

Much as he had welcomed his brilliant electoral triumph over Neuber, Fritz Fischer was beginning to feel apprehensive about the evening's festivities because his speech was still unfinished. He read some of the completed passages aloud to the ever-faithful Bubi Kusche but derived little comfort from his prompt and vociferous cries of approval, e.g. 'Bravo!' and 'You can say that again!' It was obvious, even to Fischer, that Kusche was a poor judge of public speaking.

Fischer would have liked to seek Eugen Eis's comradely advice, but Eis was busy with Margarete Eichler. Constable Gäbler, right-minded German though he was, could only draft police reports. Neuber was best qualified to help, but it was out of the question to concede defeat by soliciting aid from him. At last, after much heart-searching, Fischer was compelled to fall back on the Reverend Dr Bachus.

Bachus, who was probing his compost-heap with a pitchfork, had just come to the conclusion that it needed more liquid manure. Chastened by previous encounters with the S.A. commander, he eyed his visitor with some misgiving.

However, Fischer displayed an almost Christian spirit of reconciliation. His grin was carefully designed to convey the maximum warmth, and his opening remarks concerned the vicar's personal well-being, the state of his compost-heap and the weather outlook, in that order. Finally, to Bachus's astonishment, Fischer steered conversation to the subject of sermons and the undoubted skill which went into their composition. Bachus modestly demurred, but Fischer was having none of it.

'Nonsense, you're my man!' he said abruptly, looking as if he were about to give the parson a jovial slap on the back. 'As you may have heard, I'm supposed to be giving the main speech this evening.' Quick as a flash, he whipped the draft from his breast pocket. 'Would you care to run your eye over this? It could do with a bit of polishing, and I'd appreciate your expert opinion.'

Rightly construing this as a command rather than an invitation, Bachus surrendered with a sigh. Fischer followed the parson into his study and refused to leave until he had devised some suitably fiery and patriotic phrases for insertion in his speech. Although he insisted on the retention of several passages which earned Bachus's disapproval, the final draft was larded with references to 'providence', 'divine dispensations', and 'the hand of God'—but then the Führer himself had never balked at such turns of phrase when occasion demanded.

'That's it, then,' Fischer concluded. He omitted to thank the parson—not, as it turned out, that he had any great reason to do so. 'Roll on eight o'clock,' he said. 'This ought to make a few people sit up and take notice, I'll bet.'

'You may be right,' Bachus agreed.

Eugen Eis stood in the middle of the living-room attired in his underpants, waiting for a shirt which Brigitte had forgotten to press. Things had been going from bad to worse now that she no longer hero-worshipped him.

'How much longer have I got to wait?' he shouted.

'Till I'm finished!' she shouted back.

Eis walked over to the full-length mirror and inspected his reflection. He made a majestic picture, even—or especially —in his underpants, as many a female admirer had confirmed. It surpassed his comprehension that the wife of such a man should be indulging in extramural activities.

Outside in the kitchen, Brigitte was ironing his shirt with lethargic indifference. Unlike him, she was already dressed. Her snug-fitting flowered silk dress cunningly incorporated the

w.   I

colours of Masuria, which were the subject of an impudent rhyme now frowned on by all true patriots:

> *Liquor turns our noses red,*
> *Brawling gives us bruises blue,*
> *White hair comes from too much bed,*
> *Hence Masuria's colours true.*

In a laundry-basket beside the ironing table lay the child whose paternity had been so triumphantly claimed by Eugen Eis as a form of lien on the Materna estate. The baby, which should have been asleep hours ago, was whimpering to itself. Brigitte regarded it with a touch of anxiety, reluctant to leave the house while it was still awake and restless.

Abruptly reaching a decision, she resorted to a traditional Masurian recipe for inducing deep and lasting repose in fractious children: she reached for the schnapps bottle in the kitchen cupboard, filled a medium-sized wine glass, and poured it down the baby's throat. The baby sucked greedily at the liquor and closed its eyes, dribbling contentedly. This done, Brigitte picked up the ill-ironed shirt and carried it into the living-room, where she threw it carelessly over a chair.

'And about time!' Eis said indignantly.

'I'm going out too.'

'What do you mean?' he bellowed. 'I thought I'd made it clear that I wanted to go to this thing alone.'

'You can, for all I care. I've got something quite different in mind. Guess what?'

'You're to stay here and mind that brat of yours—my son, I mean.' Fräulein Audehm usually baby-sat for them when they went out, but Eis had given her permission to attend the festivities in the assembly-room. Chaining Brigitte to the house had been intended as a form of salutary punishment. 'Take that dress off at once!'

'No, not now. Maybe later.'

With that, Brigitte presented her backside in a provocative manner and flounced out of the room. For a moment, Eis stared after her in disbelief. Then he hurried after her, out of the living-room, down the passage, through the kitchen, and into the open air.

'Come back at once, you filthy little tart!' he yelled.

'Get back inside, you pig!' she retorted. 'Your cock's hanging out!'

It dawned on Eis that he was still in his underpants. He clapped a hand over his crutch and retired in haste, swearing horribly and praying that none of his henchmen had witnessed his embarrassing predicament.

He donned the carelessly ironed shirt and buttoned his golden-brown Party tunic over it, uttering a steady stream of oaths. One of his shirt-buttons was missing, the uniform jacket had beer-stains on it, and his boots could have done with a polish. The only redeeming feature was his cap with its impressive golden eagle. He clapped it on his head, brooding on his wife's iniquity. There was no question of his not attending the ceremony or the ensuing festivities—his presence was indispensable to their success—but would it be wise to leave the baby on its own?

He peered into the laundry-basket. The child seemed to be fast asleep, but Eis knew from bitter experience that this might be an illusion. Eugen junior could lie there like a picture-book angel one minute and roar like a wounded beast the next.

'Some mother you've got,' Eis observed bitterly.

His despairing gaze lighted on the kitchen cupboard. With a sigh of relief, he walked across to it and took out the schnapps bottle. Filling a medium-sized wine glass to the brim, he went over to the baby, shook it gingerly into a state of wakefulness, raised its head, and poured the liquor down its throat. The tiny creature gulped and whimpered exhaustedly, then relapsed into total silence.

'You can't beat the old-fashioned methods,' Eis said happily. He covered the child up and left the house. The ceremony was due to start in a few minutes.

'The Local Group Leader's on his way!'

The cry was transmitted by the sentries in the village street to those who were guarding the main entrance, and from them to the crowded assembly-room. Fritz Fischer, every inch the S.A. commander, raised an imperious hand.

The United and Augmented Band blew into its brass instruments and belaboured its drums, producing a monstrous din which an acute ear might have recognized as the *Baden-*

weiler March. This was acknowledged to be a favourite of the Führer, and, consequently, of Eugen Eis.

Eis expressed his thanks in a dignified manner and made for the seat of honour. Here, in full view of the gaping multitude, he saluted Margarete Eichler, whose status as Maulen's first lady entitled her to the chair on his right. He sat down with a flourish and nodded at Fischer and Neuber so skilfully that each thought the nod was directed at himself alone.

Amadeus Neuber reacted swiftly. With positive bravura, he assumed control of the proceedings. The only introductory item on the official programme was a sort of anthem entitled *He who Loves the Führer Knows the True Meaning of Devotion,* but Neuber had boldly extended the scope of the programme. Hardly had the anthem died away when a spoken chorus rang out, followed by a recitation, another song, another spoken chorus, and another recitation.

> *When deepest darkness o'er our country lay*
> *And loyal Germans started to despair,*
> *True freedom's flame flared up as bright as day*
> *And lo!—the German Eagle took the air.*

These words were by Willibald Adolf Glauke, who was a regular contributor to the *Preussische Zeitung* and one of the Third Reich poets who had correctly and opportunely gauged the political temperature. No school library was complete without a copy of his collected poems, entitled *Marching and Praying.*

Fritz Fischer, clearly unable to appreciate epic verse to the full under present circumstances, fidgeted restlessly in his chair. Neuber's brazen bid for the limelight only confirmed what he knew already: the man was his enemy in thought, word, and deed.

'*The light that comes from on high, where true greatness sits enthroned . . .*' recited a junior member of the Hitler Youth in a shrill, piping voice. Then his memory failed him and he came to an abrupt halt. No one ever learned who the personification of true greatness was, but Adolf Hitler was the only possible candidate.

Fritz Fischer rose to his feet. It was time for his speech,

and nothing was going to stand in his way. Ignoring Neuber's frantic signals, he strode up to the rostrum.

'Esteemed Local Group Leader,' he began in a clarion voice. Silence fell—deep, devout, and mindless. The S.A. commander hurled his next words straight at Neuber like a series of missiles. 'Comrades, valued Party members, men and women of Germany!'

Having thus uncoiled the mystic rope which bound the members of his audience together, Fischer warmed to the task of tying them up in neat parcels. His voice rang with self-assurance.

'Providence is with us,' he brayed. 'The history of our nation clearly demonstrates this. Hard as our enemies have tried to stab us in the back—and in the last war we were set upon by almost the entire world—we have always felt the guiding hand of God above us, through all our ordeals, retained the blessing of the Almighty.'

'Anyone would think we were in church,' Neuber muttered in a penetrating undertone which could be heard yards away. A certain restlessness made itself felt in the ranks of the National Socialist élite.

'Our unique nation,' Fischer boomed, '—a nation whose privilege it once was to break the world supremacy of the Roman Legions, a nation which has not only endured for thousands of years but outlived all its enemies—must have been destined by Almighty God to inscribe its name in the book of history, indelibly and in letters of flame!'

Above Fischer's head, suspended from the large central beam which supported the ceiling, hung the appropriately red-white-and-black streamer alluding to the enemies of the Reich. The rostrum beneath it was wreathed in a thick garland of oak-leaves woven by members of the German Girls' League.

'Our Greater German heritage, which revealed itself with such clarity in the battles of the Great War, that uniquely uplifting moment in our history; the workings of Providence, before which we stand with heads bowed in humility but conscious of our national vigour and strong in the knowledge that the blessing of the Almighty is omnipotent . . .'

There was a mighty crack like the sound of a giant slap in the face, followed by a brief but violent hiss and a dull thud. Wood splintered, and the ceiling seemed to dissolve into a thousand fragments.

The oak-leaf border round the patriotic streamer fell heavily on Fritz Fischer, wreathing his neck and shoulders. On his head, hanging down over his ears, sat a bird's nest of splinters and jagged greyish-white fragments of plaster from the ceiling. He stared stupidly into space, then swayed and grabbed the lectern in a state of collapse.

The occupants of the hall leapt from their seats and stood there with their mouths gaping like barn doors. There was a single shrill scream, then silence.

At this point, Eugen Eis was seized by a paroxysm of uncontrollable mirth. The laughter swelled, jerking Fischer out of his trance. He rushed at Neuber, bellowing: 'That was your bloody gun!'

'It's a put-up job!' Neuber shouted back. 'You fixed it as an excuse to get rid of me!'

Eis, by now on the verge of asphyxia, laughed until the tears streamed down his face.

Elsewhere, Brigitte tried unsuccessfully to evade the octopus embrace of Pampusch, who was beside himself with delight and kept shouting: 'Let's live a little!'

Elsewhere, Alfons Materna put his signature to a document headed 'Application for permission to drain the marshes south of Maulen', and Wollnau said: 'This marks a new chapter in the history of Maulen.'

Elsewhere, Brigitte's baby was lying back on its pillows, puce in the face. Its little fingers twitched convulsively. A brief but violent tremor ran through its limbs. Then it died.

Eugen Eis continued to roar with laughter, clutching his sides and fighting for breath. It was a long time before he recovered himself.

5

'I can't tell you how sorry I am,' Fritz Fischer said.

'Thanks,' Eis replied absently. He was standing in his dairy, gazing into the electric churn as it tirelessly dissected the butter, kneading it together, tore it apart again, and remoulded it into thick lumps.

'I hear the poor little chap choked to death.'

Eis nodded. 'A tragic accident.'

'Was it?' Fischer said, narrowing his eyes.

'Death was due to asphyxia—the doctor says so. He says it's quite common with babies. You wouldn't dispute that, would you?'

'I'd take good care not to—I mean, it sounds quite plausible. What if someone comes up with a different theory, though?'

'Who?' Eis asked sharply.

'I was just asking.'

'If anyone tries to pin anything on me, I'll kill the bastard.' Eis clenched his fists, breathing hard and baring his teeth like a mad dog. 'I'll show no mercy—you can tell that to anyone who needs telling.'

'Don't worry,' Fischer replied, 'everyone'll toe the line —even Neuber, though nothing's sacred to that man.'

Eis transferred his gaze to the tiled floor. 'I'm really cut up about this, believe me. It takes a lot to shake me, but this has bowled me right over. The fact is, I'm far more sensitive than most people imagine.'

'What about your wife?'

'She's taking it badly too.'

It was true. Eis and Brigitte had stood over the child's body in silence, each consumed with guilt because each felt uniquely to blame for its death. Their actions had been well-meant but lamentably irresponsible.

'Why did you leave him?' Eis demanded.

'Why didn't you stay with him?' she retorted.

Dr Gensfleisch, who had been summoned in haste, carefully examined the dead baby and announced that the cause of death was asphyxia. Then, as though speaking to himself, he added: 'Some of the local milk seems to have a high alcoholic content—but then, nothing is impossible in Masuria.'

Eugen Eis started at this discreet dig, noting at the same time that it elicited a similar response from Brigitte. However, he merely registered her reaction without interpreting it.

'It was an act of God,' he ventured, and Brigitte nodded humbly. He felt a twinge of satisfaction. His wife, who had lately been leading such a tempestuous life, seemed to have rediscovered the hub of her existence—in other words, himself.

'It's funny how death brings out the best in people,' Eis

remarked thoughtfully to Fischer. 'She acted as gentle as a lamb—sort of purified. I couldn't help feeling comforted.'

Fischer agreed with alacrity. 'Of course not. I know what it's like to look death in the face. They loosed off that gun at me, remember?'

'The shell missed you by a mile, Fischer.'

'Only because they botched it. What do you expect from a miserable worm like Neuber? We'll have to act fast if we don't want to be picked off one by one.'

Eis shrugged. 'I haven't caught anyone shooting at me yet. Besides, who says they were aiming at you? They didn't hit you, after all.'

'You mean you're not going to make Neuber pay for this?'

'Bring me some evidence I can use and I'll hang him. I've got enough on my plate already without worrying about your vague suspicions.'

Fischer's tone became menacing. 'So you're leaving me in the lurch.'

'I'm in mourning, blast you! If you choose to fling mud at Neuber that's your business. Get your facts sorted out and we'll have another talk.'

Organ music drifted across the village square as the Reverend Dr Bachus stealthily approached his church. He opened the west door with care and peered inside. At the organ, playing with all the stops out, sat Amadeus Neuber.

Bachus tiptoed closer. Having mounted the wooden steps to the organ loft, he received another shock. The bellows-boy turned out to be none other than Friedrich Wilhelm Pampusch of the Gestapo. Pampusch was listening with dewy-eyed rapture. Indeed, to judge by appearances, he was on the verge of shedding tears of emotion.

'Bach!' he shouted, catching sight of the parson. 'Great stuff, what?'

Bachus overcame his surprise sufficiently to nod. He walked up to the organ. Amadeus Neuber stopped playing and looked round, but Pampusch took some time to emerge from his trance.

'Bach really slays me,' he announced, '—makes me feel quite different inside.' He walked off down the aisle with his head held high and spiritual contentment written all over his beefy face. Music touched a chord even in his adamantine breast—music and women, of course. He, too, was only human.

'What do you want?' asked the bewildered parson.

Neuber smiled suavely. 'I've got a proposition for you. We might even come to some form of agreement.'

Bachus stared round as though seeking assistance, but the church was empty. The air felt cool and dank.

Neuber's smile persisted. He said: 'I'm going to lay my cards on the table. I was wrong to regard you and your Church as enemies of the Movement. I frankly admit that.'

'What changed your mind?'

'Fritz Fischer.'

'He told you so?'

'Not in so many words. I gathered it from his speech. Only you could have drafted a speech like that, Herr Bachus.'

'You sound very certain.'

'I'm positive. You either wrote it or helped to write it. I'm not reproaching you—quite the reverse, in fact. I very much hope that we shall be able to work together harmoniously from now on. Call it a sort of pact between the intellectuals of the village, if you like.'

Bachus looked dumbfounded. 'You intend to play me off against Fischer?'

'Not necessarily. Not if I'm satisfied that you won't allow yourself to be played off against me—by Fischer, for instance. I should find that very disagreeable, very disagreeable indeed. The effect on your position here could be equally disagreeable. Do I make myself clear?'

'Abundantly clear.'

'I'm glad.' Neuber raised his hand and ran it delicately over the polished surface of the organ-bench. 'I look forward to establishing a pleasant working relationship with you, Vicar. For a start, you might tell me—in confidence, of course —how much of Fischer's speech you concocted for him.'

But Bachus shook his head. 'No,' he replied, to Neuber's astonishment. His voice was hoarse but steady. 'No, Herr Neuber.'

A few days later, two government cars drove into Maulen and halted in the village street. The films of dust on their glossy black paintwork did little to mar their solemn and commanding appearance.

Only one occupant got out, a plump but dignified gentleman with a stiff gait and an irritatingly disdainful air. Having inquired the whereabouts of the mayor's office from an inquisitive child who was loitering near by—Sabine, needless to say—he set off for Uschkurat's house.

Once in Uschkurat's office, the visitor introduced himself as Senior Administrative Inspector Schielke, acting on behalf of the regional authorities at Allenstein. He asked for a large-scale map of Maulen and the land register.

'What for?' Uschkurat inquired.

'Government commission,' was the Senior Inspector's portentous reply. He extended an authoritative hand, got what he wanted, and stalked out.

'Drive on to Gross-Siegwalde!' he called to the chauffeur of the first car.

Uschkurat telephoned Eis. 'There's a government commission in the offing,' he reported.

'More snoopers!' groaned Eis. 'What the hell do they want?'

'Search me,' said Uschkurat, and hung up.

'Government commission!' reported Fritz Fischer's look-out man in the Gasthaus.

Fischer demanded further details—exact time of arrival, size of party, nature of transport, probable objective. The answers he received were sketchy in the extreme and far from satisfactory.

'Bungling idiot!' he yelled down the 'phone, which vibrated madly. Fischer relished the sound because it reminded him of radio broadcasts by the Führer. 'Our intelligence network still isn't up to scratch yet, but it will be by the time I've finished with you.'

Fischer's look-out felt personally affronted. His first move on putting down the 'phone was to say 'Shit!' His second move—undertaken on the spur of the moment, as he later confessed—was to ring Amadeus Neuber and inform him 'for information only' of the presence of the government commission.

'Thank you,' Neuber said warmly. 'Good of you to tell me. I appreciate it. What was your name again? Schlaguweit, Ernst Schlaguweit—not an easy name to forget. Can I rely on you to keep me informed of further developments, Herr Schlaguweit?'

Neuber scented problems ahead, and other people's problems were not unwelcome to him. He set his pupils an essay on 'What I owe the Führer' and stationed himself at a window overlooking the village square.

He saw Eugen Eis arrive and vanish into the mayor's office. Shortly afterwards Fritz Fischer roared up to the house on his B.M.W. 500, leapt off and ran inside. Neuber rejoiced at the sight, but he would have given a lot to know what was going on.

The only man in Maulen who was entitled to feel really well informed was Alfons Materna. He owed his information to Sabine, the one person who had heard the magic words 'government commission' *and* the order to the chauffeur to drive on to Gross-Siegwalde.

'You're a marvel,' Materna told her. 'You deserve a little present.'

Sabine asked for some binoculars 'so as to be able to see more' and was duly presented with a pair from Materna's personal supply depot. Materna's next step was to alert the Baron.

'Things are under way,' he announced.

Alarich von der Brocken sounded surprised. 'So soon?'

'Are you ready for them? That's the main thing.'

'Any time. I'll have some champagne put on ice straight away.'

Before making for the marsh, Materna went to the dug-out to have a word with Erich Wollnau, who handed him a sheaf of notes. 'Just the sort of points a civil servant would be likely to raise,' Wollnau told him with a smile. 'I ought to know —I used to be one myself.'

Jablonski met Materna at a prearranged spot overlooking the marsh. He was carrying a large board to which was pinned a large-scale map headed 'Proposed Plan of Operations'. Appended to it were detailed schedules, financial estimates, and plans for labour utilization.

'Let's hope the Baron behaves like a semi-normal human being,' Jablonski said gloomily.

'Why?' asked Materna, surveying the marsh. 'Are you worried that he won't?'

'Worried isn't the word for it. He acts like a complete buffoon sometimes.'

The two official cars nosed their way carefully across the

field and drew up a few yards from Materna. The Baron, who was the first to get out, was attired in a worn and shabby outfit of unfashionable cut. He looked as if he had borrowed it from his head forester, and his manner matched his dress. He behaved like a character out of a novel about rural life—a respectable, quietly self-assured nobleman from the backwoods, aristocratic but earthy.

'He ought to have gone on the stage,' Jablonski muttered admiringly.

'I've no doubt there are some flaws in our joint scheme,' the Baron announced with becoming modesty. 'On the other hand, it irks us to see so much land lying fallow. Many tons of grain could be grown here annually if our idea goes through. However, that's what you are here to decide, gentlemen.'

The gentlemen nodded. Not only did the decision rest with them, which went without saying, but nobody was trying to put pressure on them. They were pleased and impressed by this singular fact.

At a signal from the Senior Administrative Inspector, an expert applied himself to the operational plan. 'Good groundwork,' he announced after ten minutes. He then asked a number of questions, all of which Materna answered satisfactorily.

After another half-hour the expert started to rub his hands. Two minutes later he looked at the Senior Administrative Inspector and nodded. The die was cast, not that anyone actually said as much.

The Senior Administrative Inspector began to hum and ha like the true guardian of national interests that he was. 'Even if we were to approve your scheme,' he said grudgingly, 'I very much doubt if government funds could be made available.'

Materna glanced briefly at Wollnau's notes. 'Pursuant to a directive issued by the Ministry of the Interior in August '33, 7c funds may be applied to 9b projects provided that they appear to guarantee an increment in national income.'

The Senior Administrative Inspector looked at the Junior Administrative Inspector and the Junior Administrative Inspector looked at the expert on land development, who promptly delved around in his briefcase. When he had found what he was looking for, he passed it to the Senior Administrative Inspector. The latter read the document with care. At length he said:

'I can see you've done your homework thoroughly, gentlemen. It strengthens my confidence in you and your project, I must confess.'

'May I suggest that we all adjourn to my place for a modest snack?' said the Baron.

'I see no reason why we shouldn't accept your kind offer.' The members of the Senior Administrative Inspector's entourage registered enthusiastic approval. Now that the commission had virtually completed its work, any loose ends could be left to the land development expert and Jacob Jablonski.

'These bureaucrats!' the Baron hissed to Materna. 'They won't forget this day in a hurry.'

'Maybe not,' Materna replied. 'I doubt if any government has ever subsidized this sort of scheme before.'

Constable Gäbler sat hunched over his desk. In front of him lay a number of files, each more perplexing than the next. His daughter Sabine was squatting beside the bookcase in the corner of the office, reading the latest 'Wanted' list.

'Can't you play somewhere else?' he asked.

'Why, am I disturbing you?'

She wasn't disturbing him, of course—certainly not when she was behaving with her present quietness and decorum. Gäbler couldn't even hear her breathe, yet he felt an urge to be alone—if only so that he could put his head in his hands and think. Problems were piling up thick and fast.

First, there was Fritz Fischer's allegation that someone had attempted to murder him with a field gun. Next came a complaint from Amadeus Neuber: housebreaking and theft of ammunition from a locked receptacle. Felix Kusche, commonly called Bubi, had complained that law-abiding citizens, himself included, were being subjected to threats of physical violence. Finally, Uschkurat was insisting that steps be taken against public disorders of a subversive nature. It all amounted to a heap of trouble.

'What am I to do?' Gäbler groaned, teetering on the brink of despair.

'Chuck it in the wastepaper basket,' Sabine said sweetly.

The same idea had already occurred to the policeman, but he was shocked to hear such worldly wisdom issuing from the lips of a guileless innocent like his daughter. He assumed a stern but kindly air.

'Now, now, my girl, that's no way to talk. What has it got to do with you, anyway?'

'Nothing,' replied Sabine, gazing up at him with wide-eyed innocence. 'I don't suppose it's anybody's business but the Party's.'

The policeman opened his mouth, let it hang open for a considerable time, and then shut it again. Sabine's remark might have been childishly naïve but it had a germ of truth. After a brief pause for reflection he hurried off to the Gasthaus and mounted the stairs to the first floor, where he knocked on the door of Room No. 3. Friedrich Wilhelm Pampusch's powerful voice invited him to come in.

Pampusch was lying on the bed with his boots on and a copy of the *Völkischer Beobachter* athwart his belly. The strains of a tango were oozing from the radio on the bedside table.

'Listen to that!' the Gestapo man cried rapturously. 'Bach, male voice choirs and marches—they knock me flat. So do tangos. Tangos get me in the pit of the stomach. Do you tango? Last year in Königsberg I won first prize at the Tiergarten Café—me and a snappy little blonde. I bet that surprises you, doesn't it?'

Gäbler looked duly surprised. He had to hear the tango through, down to the last treacly note. However, the ensuing foxtrot dispelled Pampusch's interest in the radio from one moment to the next. He growled something about 'nigger music', switched off, and asked abruptly: 'Well, what's on your mind?'

'That explosion last Saturday night, during the speeches.'

'Don't talk about it,' Pampusch said grimly. 'I was on the job when it happened, but I said to myself: what's it got to do with us? If the local bigwigs want to bombard each other, steer clear. —And that's the advice I can give you, my friend.'

Constable Gäbler withdrew. Ever mindful of the axiom 'Whatever serves the national interest is right', he bethought himself that Maulen's personification of the national interest was Eugen Eis. What could be more logical than to leave the decision to him?

Carrying his files gingerly, like a time-bomb, the policeman paid a call on the Local Group Leader.

'Unless I'm much mistaken,' he said, 'these are Party matters. I leave them in your good hands.'

'Well, there they are,' Eis said, gloomily contemplating the sheaf of paper. 'And now where are they?' His hands moved sideways and downwards. The files slid, gathering speed, into the waste-paper basket.

'You here?' Brigitte said. 'I was just coming to see you.'

Her father was standing in the kitchen doorway, regarding her with a faintly worried smile. 'It always amazes me how often we have the same idea.'

They rarely met these days, and their exchanges were usually limited to a few words or a single glance, yet there was a tacit understanding between them.

'Are you very disappointed with me?' she asked.

Materna sat down beside her. 'You chose your own way of life.'

'Without your consent, Father—against your wishes.'

'You underestimate me,' Materna said quietly. 'If I'd really dug my toes in I could have stopped you from marrying him, but that was the last thing I wanted to do—at the time.'

Brigitte rose uneasily to her feet. 'You've no idea what sort of person I've turned into.'

The kitchen chair creaked as Materna sat back. 'You always were impulsive and hot-blooded, even as a girl, and girls have a habit of turning into women.'

'You don't despise me?'

'Why should I?' Materna sounded more amused than contemptuous. 'When you said you wanted to marry Eis I gave the matter a great deal of thought. To my surprise, I found there were a number of arguments in your favour, one of them being that marriage to him might do you some good. That being so, I had no right to get upset when things didn't go according to plan.'

'That's putting it mildly.'

'You're a Materna. You never do things by halves.'

'No, and now my baby's dead.'

Her father did not reply. 'He died here in this room,' she went on fiercely. 'There was nobody here. He died all on his own.'

Materna leant forward with an expression of brooding melancholy. 'What's the matter, Brigitte?' he asked. 'Do you believe you're to blame for your child's death?'

She went to the cupboard and took out a bottle. 'Schnapps, that's what did it. I gave him a glass—a medium-sized wine glass. I didn't fill it right up, just poured about half an inch out of the bottle—down to the upper edge of the label. I didn't think it would do him any harm.'

She put the bottle down on the table, but he pushed it aside. 'Nearly everyone round here does it occasionally,' he said.

'But my baby choked to death.'

Materna transferred his gaze to the bottle. The label read: 'Pure Distilled Danish Grain Spirit, 40 per cent'.

'So you poured him a glass—about half an inch out of the bottle.' Brigitte nodded dumbly. 'And then you took a swig yourself, presumably to set yourself up for the evening.'

'No, I didn't. I hardly ever drink.'

'Why keep schnapps in the kitchen cupboard, then?'

'I use it for cooking.'

'Does Eis ever touch it?'

'He doesn't need to. He keeps bottles of his own all over the place—even under the bed. I only get his leavings for the kitchen.'

'That explains everything,' Materna said. 'Come here, girl. You see? The level is well below the top of the label.'

Brigitte's eyes widened. 'What do you mean?'

'Do I have to spell it out for you?' Materna replaced the bottle carefully on the table. 'Eis probably gave the baby another dose after you'd gone.'

'It must have been him!' Brigitte said excitedly. 'It couldn't have been anyone else.' Almost inaudibly, she added: 'I'll kill that man . . .'

'An understandable impulse,' observed Materna, who was already half-way out of the door. 'However, I'd prefer it if you didn't—in fact I forbid you to. I'm still your father.'

On hearing from the Baron that the drainage scheme had received official sanction, Materna disappeared from Maulen for three days. He climbed into his dog-cart and headed eastwards in the direction of the Polish border which was only a few miles away.

'Good luck!' Jablonski called after him.

Materna cracked his whip. 'I hope I don't miss anything while I'm gone.'

Jablonski grinned as though to convey that nothing could possibly happen while Materna was away, but he was wrong. Materna's absence was precisely what lent such mystery to the incident which occurred the same evening.

Everything seemed peaceful enough to begin with. The Reverend Dr Bachus meditated in his garden, Fritz Fischer fished and Eugen Eis mourned the death of his son. For once, no sound of singing came from the school-house. Amadeus Neuber strolled down the village street, keeping a weather eye open for his little guarantees of Germany's future—Sabine not least among them. Catching sight of her, he beckoned her over with a fatherly smile. His outstretched hand patted her head and slid gently downwards until it rested on the nape of her neck.

'Hello, my dear, and what are you doing here?'

'Just standing around, Herr Neuber.'

'Just drinking in the joys of existence, eh? Well, that shows a classical—indeed, a Greek—attitude to life.'

'But not a Germanic one?'

Neuber laughed heartily. He always found Sabine's remarks so refreshing. 'The main ingredient of our national culture is Germanic, of course,' he said, putting his arm round her. 'However, we must never forget the related culture of Greece, which flourished in warmer climes than our own. It produced some superb vases adorned with magnificent paintings of the human body. I have a very wonderful book about them.'

'At school or in your bedroom?'

'In my bedroom, Sabine.' Neuber's hand slid to her waist. 'Would it interest you to look at it?'

'Very much,' Sabine assured him. To her, Neuber's bedroom was the room where the box containing the rest of the field gun ammunition still stood, and it exerted a magical attraction on her. Remembering herself just in time, she added regretfully: 'Well, maybe tomorrow.'

'Whenever you like.' Neuber strove hard to conceal his disappointment. He would have to possess his soul in patience for a while longer. His roseate dreams of a pure and un-defiled world were slow of fulfilment.

Sabine left the village and headed west. Turning off the main road, she sauntered down a country lane for a couple of miles until she reached Geierwiese. A hundred yards short of the small railway station she sat down on a heap of stones and waited.

The evening train from Lötzen was due in a few minutes. It was a crawler which transported farm produce, livestock and passengers from village to village at a snail's pace, but it also connected with the express from Königsberg, and that was the train customarily taken by Konrad Klinger and Peter Bachus.

Sabine's sharp eyes caught sight of them as soon as the train drew in. They got out and made for the heap of stones.

'Hello!' Peter called. 'Planning to startle us?'

Sabine tossed her head. 'Don't be silly.'

'Maybe she wanted to give us a nice surprise,' suggested Konrad.

'I'm not Hannelore.'

They set off for Maulen with Sabine between them, chuckling as they went.

'I don't see anything to laugh at,' Sabine said.

'Why, what's happened?'

'Nothing much, worse luck, except that you won't get any fun and games at the farm this week-end. Alfons is in Poland and Hannelore's gone to visit some relations.'

Konrad smiled. 'You'll have to stand in for her, then.'

'All you can think about is girls!' Sabine said fiercely.

'What makes you think that?'

'You never keep your mind on the job. Why did you leave it at Fischer—why not Neuber too? What's good for one . . .'

They sat down beside the road on one of the numerous heaps of road-mender's stones. Sabine swung her legs.

The evening sun sank behind the horizon as though lowered on wires. The sky became bathed in vivid red light, flared up like a gigantic fire, then faded quickly. Purple shadows fell, but the heat of the day lingered, seeping out of the stones and sandy soil and creeping up the gnarled trunks of trees parched by the summer sun. The sky began to gleam like molten silver.

Sabine chattered away ceaselessly. She reported on her father's inquiries into the field gun incident, which was officially attributed to spontaneous combustion. She also told of Fischer's allegations concerning Neuber and Neuber's counter-measures against Fischer. Finally, she mentioned Neuber's open invitation to inspect his book of Greek vase-paintings.

'I'm sure I could get my hands on that ammunition box. I could send him out of the room for something.'

'Not a bad idea,' commented Peter.

'Too risky,' Konrad said firmly. 'Besides, if Jablonski found out what we were up to he'd take us apart.'

'We needn't tell him,' said Sabine.

By this time, Peter had also realized that the plan was not without its dangers. 'No,' he said, 'you're far too young to get involved in that sort of thing. It's too tricky.'

'Cowards!' Sabine exclaimed angrily.

'Don't say that,' Peter told her. 'Just think what your be-loved Jacob would say. He wouldn't be exactly overjoyed, would he?'

Sabine shrugged. She trotted home in silence, flanked by the two boys, but before disappearing into her father's house she turned and hissed: 'Lame ducks, that's what you are: And to think I was pinning all my hopes on you . . .'

The moon sailed sedately over Maulen, gilding the roof-tops. Cows, sheep and pigs were all asleep, but a few dogs still kept vigil.

Trade still flourished in the Gasthaus. The bar was almost full. In the assembly-room, augmented by the S.A. choir and a women's League quartet, the Glee Club was rehearsing a patriotic song under Fritz Fischer's direction. Singing was a thirsty business as Fischer knew. A keg of beer—debited to Party funds under the heading of 'Aids to Popular Enlightenment'—stood ready to hand.

Constable Gäbler was leafing through his files and pondering on the difference between law and justice. He wondered gloomily how to reconcile the two.

The Reverend Dr Bachus was sitting huddled in his cellar, trying to drown his worries and disappointments in wine, but it was no good. The more he drank the more he could take. The oblivion he sought was becoming an expensive commodity. Without moving, he squinted at the cellar steps.

His son Peter was standing there, and behind him, like a shadow, lurking the inevitable Konrad.

'How are you, Father?'

'Well,' Bachus replied, 'very well indeed. I'm thinking.'

'Anything we can do for you?'

The parson laughed harshly. He was holding a bottle of Communion wine by the neck. 'Life's immensely funny, Peter, did you know that? The Good Lord must be a practical joker—there's no other explanation for what happens to us here day after day.'

'Why don't you do something about it?' demanded Konrad.

Bachus looked up. There was an agonized smile on his lips. 'I used to pray for God's blessing on this age of ours,' he said, '—honestly and sincerely. It isn't so easy for a man of my cloth to switch from benedictions to curses.'

The two boys left the vicarage and perched on the churchyard wall, as they used to do in the old days. They sat there, unspeaking, staring out over the village square. The moonlight did not reach them but the choral cacophony from the Gasthaus did.

> *The grey geese to the east have flown.*
> *My heart in wild abandon yearned*
> *Until the sun of freedom shone*
> *And all our foes to ashes burned.'*

'It's sheer provocation, that row,' Peter said.

Konrad nodded. 'You're right. We ought to follow Sabine's suggestion.'

The sound of fervent singing came to the ears of Amadeus Neuber, who was lying fully dressed on his bed. The lamp beside him shone on his book of vase-paintings, illuminating muscle-packed masculinity, dainty maidenhood, goatish revelry, bloated lust, yielding nymphs . . .

Neuber stirred restlessly and sat up. The book slipped from his hands and fell to the floor near the ammunition box, but he paid no heed. Hurrying to the door, he opened it and peered intently into the night.

'Who's there?' he called hoarsely. After a moment or two, he whispered: 'Is that you, Sabine?'

There was no reply. He crouched there motionless for

some seconds, but in vain. With a sigh, he switched off the
light and closed the door behind him. He strolled off into
the darkness, aimlessly at first, past the field gun and across
the village square. Finally, he made for Constable Gäbler's
house, where Sabine was doubtless tucked up in bed and
asleep. He stared up at the darkened windows for some
time.

Neuber sighed again. He circled the house, smoked a
cigarette, and strolled on in a kind of dream.

Soon afterwards a muffled explosion shattered the nocturnal hush. It reverberated through the village, rattling
window-panes and causing the contents of glasses in the
Gasthaus to vibrate in sympathy.

Amadeus Neuber's bedroom was a smoking shambles.

Eugen Eis was in his living-room when the explosion occurred.
His baby son's body reposed in a silver-mounted casket in
the centre of the room, not that this marred his concentration.
He was drafting operational plans for the funeral on numerous
sheets of expensive hand-made paper adorned with the eagle-
and-swastika. 'Private Reception', he wrote, 'Seating of Principal Guests, Wreaths and Floral Tributes, Funeral Addresses,
Order of March . . .'

Eis shook his head resentfully when he heard the explosion.
Without realizing the highly unusual nature of the sound, he
felt distracted.

Brigitte appeared in a billowing night-dress. 'I need some
peace and quiet,' he said, indicating his notes.

'You must be deaf,' she retorted. 'I almost fell out of bed
just now.'

Eis laughed coarsely to demonstrate his superiority. 'You've
fallen into plenty of beds in your time—why not out of one for
a change? Anyway, I'm busy with these funeral arrangements.
We're in mourning, in case you'd forgotten.'

'You're not in mourning. Even that coffin is just an excuse
for another of your stupid speeches.'

Eis drew a deep breath. 'Why, you . . .'

Brigitte was spared the inevitable tirade because at that
moment Fritz Fischer burst in, fuming, snarling, and clearly
determined to brook no opposition. She withdrew hastily.

Fischer sounded like a locomotive letting off steam.
'Neuber's going to try and pin this on me,' he hissed. 'Some-

body blew his place up, but it wasn't me—honestly it wasn't. I give you my word of honour.'

Eis was tempted to make some sarcastic observation about Fischer's word of honour, but before he could do so Neuber appeared. He looked agitated and his pallid face glistened with sweat.

'I have to report a vile and calculated act of vengeance!' he croaked.

'Committed by you,' Fischer said promptly. 'You reduced your house to rubble just to get back at me.'

Neuber fought for breath. 'First you try to hang the field gun business on me and then you blow my bedroom sky-high. My house is an official residence, I'd remind you. That means you've destroyed government property.'

Being more than a match for Neuber physically, Fischer lunged at him but was brought up short by the baby's coffin. 'If I'd really wanted to blow you up,' he shouted, 'they'd be scraping you off the walls by now!'

'You tried to murder me!' Neuber shouted back. 'It was sheer luck that I escaped.'

'Shut up!' roared Eis. 'You're in the presence of the dead, damn your eyes!'

Silence fell. Eis straightened his son's coffin, growling at the intruders like a bulldog. There was bitter disillusionment in his voice when he next spoke.

'What are you trying to do, comrades—stab me in the back?'

'What do you mean?' Neuber protested. 'Can I help it if my house gets blown up?'

'Don't take that accusing tone with me!' Fischer snapped in a renewed access of fury. 'This sort of thing shouldn't be allowed to happen.'

'I'll tell you something else that shouldn't happen,' Eis said. 'I don't like to see senior Party officials brawling in public. We wash our dirty linen in private.'

'In private?' exclaimed Neuber. 'That bang woke up every dog for miles around.'

'You always do things by halves,' Eis said disgustedly. 'If you two really want to eliminate each other, be quick about it—silent, too, if possible—but don't involve the Party.'

'Come outside, Neuber,' called Fischer. 'I'm going to part your hair with an axe.'

'I favour different methods,' Neuber replied stiffly. 'I carry a good deal of weight in the Party, and I regard it as a duty to use my influence to the full.'

Eis snorted. 'I'm still the Party round here, and I'm in mourning—kindly remember that.' He drummed his knuckles on the coffin. 'Let's get our priorities straight. First the funeral. After that, we'll see.'

Eugen Eis stood on the doorstep of his house to greet the principal mourners, namely: Ignaz Uschkurat and his wife, a bird-like woman who nodded the whole time but seldom spoke; Constable Gäbler and his corpulent sister, who could hold enough drink to fill a barrel; Margarete Eichler, escorted with polished gallantry by Amadeus Neuber, director of organization and propaganda; and Fritz Fischer, who had to content himself with the local chieftainess of the German Girls' League, Fräulein Fröhlich, joyful by name and joyful by disposition. She laughed often and boisterously, baring her equine teeth and unconsciously pawing her escort with strong masculine hands.

As a prelude to the small and intimate gathering which customarily preceded a funeral and the public jollifications attendant on it, everyone was offered a welcoming glass of schnapps—medium-strength liquor from which no immediate effect was to be expected.

'Don't stand on ceremony!' Eis called cheerfully, indicating the table just inside the door, where bottles were massed like a Prussian guard of honour. There was Masurian-style coffee, laced with liquor and known as 'Tin-Opener', for the ladies; for the men, 'Bear-Trap' schnapps of guaranteed potency and reliable grain alcohol in litre bottles.

Large numbers of candles shed a soft radiance on the coffin, which stood in the centre of the room with refreshments disposed round it in a sort of horseshoe.

'Sincere condolences!' chorused the mourners, raising their brimming glasses.

'Many thanks,' Eis replied.

Everyone gave a vociferous welcome to Herr Naschinski, the local bank manager, from whom Eis was planning to borrow money. Frau Naschinski purred with pleasure as the bereaved father amorously patted her skinny shoulders. An equally warm reception awaited Herr and Frau Poreski: he a war veteran whose commercial interest in milk and edible fats rendered him not unimportant to Eis's dairy; she an honoured member of the National Socialist Women's League and president of the Daughters of the German Hearth.

Eis had just adjured his guests to make themselves at home when Friedrich Wilhelm Pampusch put in a farewell appearance. He was clearly happy to be leaving Maulen unscathed. Attired in S.S. uniform, he advanced on the coffin bearing a wreath of white roses, but before he relinquished them he broke one off and presented it to Brigitte with the words: 'A modest token of my grateful and enduring appreciation.'

The mourners took their seats, concentrating happily on the plates of food in front of them. Nobody spared the coffin a glance.

After the cold dishes came the greasy entrées, and after them the roasts. These were followed by sweet dishes and, later, by 'fillers'—small sausages, slices of brawn, cheese, cakes, and marzipan. Every course was washed down with digestive draughts of schnapps. The fist-sized glasses used earlier on had now been replaced by vase-like receptacles of much greater capacity.

Bubi Kusche was helping to wait on the guests, but he preferred to spend most of the time in the kitchen with Fräulein Audehm, whose talents were not confined to midwifery and regional cooking alone. She possessed other attributes, as many a male villager could confirm.

'It's going to be quite a party,' Bubi said, staring at Fräulein Audehm's posterior. 'I can feel it in my bones.'

'Really?' She glanced towards the kitchen door, from behind which came sounds of muffled revelry. 'Don't tell me you're all worked up again.'

'Any objections?' Bubi asked boldly, reaching for her.

'Not on the kitchen table, surely!' she protested, but Bubi felt that the moment was opportune.

'Nobody'll disturb us,' he assured her. 'They've got more than enough drink in there to keep them busy.'

Inside, Eis was purposefully going the rounds. Each man had a full bottle in front of him and was in honour bound to empty it as quickly as possible. Constable Gäbler issued everyone with repeated, solemn and unsolicited assurances that, as local custodian of the laws currently in force, he could be relied on to the hilt. Herr Naschinski declared his readiness to advance Eis all the credit he needed, and Herr Poreski, Deputy Farmers' Leader and Uschkurat's probable successor as mayor, announced his intention of drafting a report to the effect that Eis's dairy was the best in the neighbourhood.

Eis then devoted himself briefly to the fair sex. Having clinked glasses with Constable Gäbler's porcine sister, who was shovelling food and drink down her throat with a series of animated grunts, he put his arm round Frau Naschinski, who uttered a predictable coo of delight. This done, he took Fräulein Fröhlich into a corner and squeezed her jutting, uniformed breast with perfunctory swiftness. Promptly, her hands groped their way down his front.

Evading this tribute to his masculinity, Eis paid a visit to the kitchen and was hugely entertained by the spectacle that met his eye. 'Carry on!' he called jovially. The fact that he had caught Bubi and his companion unawares gave him a hold over them, and every little hold helped.

Back in the living-room, spirits had risen still higher. Friedrich Wilhelm Pampusch was winding up the gramophone which stood ready in the far corner of the room. There could be little doubt about his choice of record—a tango, naturally. Uschkurat clapped his approval and one or two of the ladies hummed the tune.

Stationing himself between Fischer and Neuber, Eis clasped them to his breast with affectionate vigour. 'We're a team,' he said earnestly. 'You wouldn't want to let the side down, would you?'

There was only one answer to this appeal. The two men bowed their heads in silence and avoided one another's eye. The expectant hush that followed made it even easier to hear the cloying strains of the tango and the voice of Friedrich Wilhelm Pampusch.

'What a dance!' he sighed. 'In the foxtrot you just skitter around like a poodle that wants to lift its leg and isn't allowed to. Waltzes are just a substitute for schnapps—you spin round and round until you get dizzy. But a tango . . . Ah, what perfection, what elegance!'

'Give us a demonstration!' Eis called encouragingly.

'Yes,' said the others, 'show us how!'

Pampusch coyly demurred—'like a bashful virgin', as the chieftainess of the German Girls' League observed in a penetrating undertone—on the grounds that his kind of tango required a lot of floor space.

'No problem there,' Eis told him. 'We'll clear the tables away.'

The Reverend Dr Bachus protested in a quivering but indignant voice. 'You can't do that!'

'Yes we can,' Eis retorted. 'We'll put the coffin in a corner.'

The mourners carted away chairs and stacked the tables two deep against the wall. Space was found for glasses and schnapps bottles on the window-sills.

Pampusch paced out the dance floor with long predatory steps. 'Sorry,' he said at length, 'it still isn't good enough.'

'Get those tables outside!' shouted Eis.

'What about the coffin?'

'Stick it up on end.'

A pall of tobacco-smoke and schnapps fumes enveloped the mourners, and their concerted voices roared like a waterfall.

'My God!' Bachus groaned. He swayed and grabbed at Fräulein Fröhlich for support. The leader of the German Girls' League docilely suffered his embrace while Eis fetched a chair. The parson half-collapsed on to it, muttering: 'There's a limit to everything . . .'

'Not in this house there isn't,' Eis retorted gaily. Assisted by Fischer, Neuber and Kusche, he removed the coffin and left it outside the front door.

'Now for the tango!' cried Friedrich Wilhelm Pampusch. He put another record on—a current favourite entitled *Oh, Donna Clara*—and strutted over to Brigitte like a cockerel.

'I don't tango,' she said.

'Lady volunteers forward!' bellowed Eis.

To the amazement of all, Constable Gäbler's sister heaved her two hundredweight into a standing position. Fervent applause greeted this initiative, followed by murmurs of admiration. Everyone gazed open-mouthed at the devoutly dancing pair as they swept the floor with long pantherish strides, leg 'twixt leg, pivoted abruptly as though planning to subside on to a sofa, or bent at the waist like hinges, the female partner leaning backwards with the male bestriding her. They were an expert couple, if a trifle on the bulky side.

Fritz Fischer swore appreciatively and tried to put his hand on the knee of the woman next to him, then swore again when he found that Neuber had got there first.

'It's too bright in here!' called Herr Naschinski, and Kusche obediently switched off the centre light. Only the mellow and congenial glow of a standard lamp remained to illuminate the entwined and swaying figures of Eis's guests.

Eis himself had taken a seat beside Margarete Eichler. 'Revolting display, isn't it?' he whispered. 'I have to put up with these things, but they hurt me deep down inside.'

'Never mind, you're in command of the situation,' she said admiringly.

'I learnt a lot from Johannes. He was a great example to me.'

'You have a lot of qualities in common, too.'

Eis felt cheered by the evident success of his soirée and started to enjoy himself. However, he was not allowed to do so for long.

'The coffin's gone,' Bubi Kusche announced in an agitated voice.

Eis uttered a bellow of rage and detached himself from Margarete. 'Lights!' he called.

The centre light came on again, much to everyone's fury. Expanses of bare flesh were hastily covered and tangoing couples collapsed on the dance-floor. The Reverend Dr Bachus, who appeared to have recovered his senses, stared round incredulously. Fräulein Fröhlich of the German Girls' League gave a screech of disappointment and Constable Gäbler looked official.

After a general hue and cry, the coffin was eventually discovered on the steps of the Gasthaus. Attached to it with a drawing-pin was a 'For Sale' sign.

'Who'd have the gall to do such a thing?' demanded Eis.

Fischer snorted like a maddened bull. 'Need you ask? Materna, of course.'

'Maybe,' said Uschkurat. 'He's away, though.'

'It could have been one of his side-kicks.'

'I wouldn't have said it was in his line.'

'Who the hell cares?' Eis cut in. 'Some bugger carted the coffin away, and I regard it as a personal insult. Somebody's going to pay for this, you mark my words!'

Brigitte gave a contemptuous shrug. 'You're a great one for words. Hot air—that's all they ever amount to.'

6

'It's all fixed,' Materna said. He handed the reins to Jablonski, who had come out to greet him on his return, grinning all over his face. 'Things can start moving now.'

He got Hannelore to bring him a hearty peasant breakfast —three raw potatoes sliced thinly and fried in fresh butter, two half-inch slices of raw ham cut into cubes, and four eggs beaten up with cream—and downed it with appetite.

'I shall want to see Wollnau in about an hour's time,' he announced, wiping his plate. 'First, I must have a word with the Baron.'

'He's in a hurry,' Hannelore said as she watched him mount his bicycle and pedal off in the direction of Gross-Siegwalde.

Jablonski nodded happily. 'Nice to see him back on form —reminds me of the old days.'

Materna was greeted at Gross-Siegwalde like visiting royalty. As he drove into the grounds, the gardener on duty near the gate saluted him and rang a bell. Two of the Baron's six concubines appeared at the head of the drive, smiling and waving, and at the top of the steps stood Elisabeth von der Brocken. She was blushing faintly, and her figure was 'subtly enhanced', as a Paris fashion magazine had prophesied, by an olive-green gown.

'There you are at last,' she said, extending her hand.

Materna gave an embarrassed grin. 'Don't say you were expecting me.'

'Not only expecting you, Herr Materna—we were worried about you.'

Materna suspected that this was a slight exaggeration but he felt flattered just the same. The Baron appeared, wearing an exotic smoking-jacket of red-and-green-striped brocade. He took charge of Materna and led him into the library.

'Well?' he asked. 'Did you have a successful trip?'

'Whether it was successful remains to be seen, but this particular part of my mission is completed. I've recruited fifteen Polish labourers and another fifteen are available whenever we care to send for them. Built like prize-fighters, the lot of them, but their minds operate on the same frequency as ours. My friend in Poland selected them personally.'

'Congratulations, my dear chap.' With a touch of pride, the Baron added: 'I haven't exactly been twiddling my thumbs during your absence.'

Materna learnt that the Baron had managed to secure definite official sanction for the scheme and that a substantial government grant was already in the pipe-line. An Allenstein firm with special experience of Labour Corps contracts was to start work on the labourers' barrack-room the following morning.

'What do you say to that?' the Baron concluded.

Materna said nothing at first. Alarich von der Brocken's sudden rash of activity had its suspicious side.

'I hope you intend to stick to the terms of our agreement, Baron.'

'To the letter. That goes without saying.'

'I decide how the Poles are to be used, right?'

'Right! Except in an emergency, of course.'

'But I decide what an emergency is.'

The Baron chuckled. 'Of course, my dear fellow. There won't be any arguments, I can assure you. After all, we're in this thing together, so we might as well enjoy ourselves.'

'For as long as we can.'

'For as long as humanly possible.' The Baron, who clearly saw no point in prolonging the conversation, rose to his feet. 'But I mustn't deprive my sister of your company any longer —she values it immensely. I wonder why.'

'Because of her brother's curiosity, I suspect.' Materna grinned. 'He seems to think that what he doesn't worm out of me, she will.'

'Heaven forbid!' exclaimed the Baron. 'You're barking up the wrong tree there, my friend. Speaking as one partner to another, I advise you not to mistake Elisabeth's motives. You're dealing with a woman. The fact that she's my sister is purely coincidental, so be warned.'

Early next morning, three lorries rolled up from the west laden with timber for the labourers' barrack-room. Almost simultaneously, another truck appeared from the east and deposited fifteen Polish workmen on the edge of the marsh south of Maulen.

'Right, lads. Let's get to work!' called Jablonski, brandish-

ing Wollnau's plans like a field marshal's baton. His summons
was uttered first in German and then in Polish, of which he
knew enough for everyday use. Materna's Polish sufficed to
order a drink or issue simple instructions, but neither he
nor Jablonski could rival the linguistic expertise of the man
who now approached the building site from the direction
of the woods. It was Erich Wollnau, a pale-faced, stoop-
shouldered figure dressed in a clean but threadbare suit.

Mingling with the Polish labourers as if he were one of their
number, Wollnau proceeded to act as interpreter for the
German building contractor and the Poles, who set to with a
will.

Jablonski hurried off to warn Materna of Wollnau's un-
scheduled appearance. Materna, who had just sat down to
his second breakfast of the day, left his plate untouched and
hastened to the building site, where he found Wollnau in the
thick of things.

'He really looks as if he belongs,' Jablonski said, wagging
his head ruefully.

'Get him over here,' Materna ordered. This was easier
said than done because Wollnau was busily engaged in
sorting out prefabricated sections of weather-boarding, but
Jablonski finally dragged him away.

'With the best will in the world, Herr Wollnau,' Materna
said, trying to sound severe, 'it just won't do.'

'On the contrary,' retorted the former civil servant, 'it's
the only way. You need someone here with a fluent command
of both languages.'

At that moment the Polish foreman came up and said something to Wollnau, who returned to the fray. Nothing could
have seemed more natural.

The barrack-room's raised wooden foundations were laid
with a speed which said much for Wollnau's efficient supervision. The side-walls were up by mid-morning, and Wollnau
even found time to arrange for the construction of a wooden
swastika which would later adorn the entrance to the hut.

'Herr Wollnau,' Materna said during the lunch-break, 'I
hope you realize the implications of your public appearance
here today.'

Wollnau nodded. 'Either I disappear promptly or I stay
on for an indefinite period. Well, I'm needed here. Besides, I
was thinking that next time someone crosses the border it

might be one of our Polish labourers. That would automatically create a vacancy here—for me.'

Materna pondered the suggestion. 'Its a tempting idea,' he said at length.

'That's settled, then,' Wollnau said cheerfully. 'From now on, I shall call myself Wollnowski.'

With that, Erich Wollnau, former legal adviser to the Prussian Minister of the Interior, became Erik Wollnowski, one of the Polish workmen who had officially been recruited to drain the marsh south of Maulen. He moved into the barrack-room and received a warm welcome from the Poles, who had been warned to take any surprise developments in their stride.

'Obstinate cuss, isn't he?' Jablonski observed thoughtfully.

'You never realize your mistakes until it's too late,' Materna said. 'Still, we may as well be hanged for a sheep. Apart from the fact that our necks aren't worth much, we've risked them often enough already.'

Eugen Eis, who had noted the developments in the marsh with some uneasiness, found the whole thing slightly sinister. He even sent for Ignaz Uschkurat, whose views went largely unheeded these days, and asked him for his expert opinion on the project.

'Well,' the mayor said thoughtfully, 'a scheme of that size doesn't cost nothing. They must be spending several hundred thousand marks on it, but I suppose Materna knows what he's doing.'

Eis was so alarmed by the mention of such a sum that he tackled his wife.

'Your father's behaving like a madman again. He ought to be locked up.'

Brigitte smiled. 'Is he still giving you trouble?'

'Trouble I can handle. No, it's worse than that—he's chucking your money down the drain.'

'You can't stop him doing that and neither can I.'

'Really?' he drawled. 'Listen, Brigitte, I know we haven't been hitting it off too well recently, but we're still man and wife. We're a partnership, so to speak.'

'Oh, is that what we are?'

'Yes, if I say so. There's no reason why things shouldn't be the way they were before, but I'd have to insist on one or two

conditions first. For instance, we both bear a certain responsibility for your father's behaviour. Something will have
to be done about him sooner or later.'

'What, for instance?'

'Well, you're his daughter. If you're doubtful about his
sanity you have the right to apply for power of attorney.'

'On whose behalf?'

'You're still married to me, Brigitte,' Eis said with menace.
'It's about time you realized where your duty lies.'

So saying, he left the house. He could easily have sought
consolation from Fräulein Fröhlich of the German Girls'
League, but he decided to put his time and energies to better
use.

Margarete Eichler gave him a cordial welcome. He feasted
his eyes resolutely on her as he followed her into the house
—the pure Aryan profile, the radiant blue eyes, the romantic
but ultra-German hair-style, the swan-neck and milky skin,
the intellectual brow, bovine figure and straight gaze . . .

'You attract me,' he confessed.

'I think of you a great deal, too.'

He grasped her hand. 'There's a sort of bond between us,
isn't there? I feel it more and more strongly every day.'

The marsh south of Maulen resembled a shallow bowl. Sur-
veyors' reports had indicated that the ground fell away towards
the lake, so the initial plan was to cut two drainage channels
through the sandy lip of the bowl. Time allowed: two weeks.

They were a comparatively peaceful two weeks for Maulen.
Spies posted by Fritz Fischer in consultation with Eugen
Eis could only report that the workmen were working. They
got generous breaks, true, but they toiled hard for eight
hours a day.

'Nothing else to report?' Fischer demanded suspiciously.

'Jablonski holds a sort of muster parade every morning
and evening.'

'What does he say to them?'

'Who knows? They all jabber away in Polish.'

Fischer's spirit of vigilance would not let him rest, but
it was some days before he visited the site in person. Leaving
his motor-cycle in the woods, he worked his way forward in
approved training-manual fashion, using every scrap of available cover.

Inevitably, he was spotted. The first sight that met his eyes as he rounded a hummock was two pairs of razor-toothed dogs' jaws, and above them Jablonski's grinning face. Jablonski gave an exclamation of delight.

'Hello! What have we got here?'

'I was just . . .'

'Paying us a visit? Don't give me that, Fischer. We can do without visits from the likes of you.'

'I go where I please.'

'That's a new one,' Jablonski retorted cheerfully. 'This is private property. Anyone who wants to set foot on it has to ask our permission, and we're choosy about our visitors.'

'Do you know who you're talking to?' roared Fischer.

'Do I!' Jablonski was clearly enjoying the situation. 'Get lost, Fischer. If you'd like the dogs to engrave a monogram on your arse, I can arrange it.'

The words 'engrave' and 'monogram' smacked of Materna and were obviously a reference to higher authority. 'Arse' was pure Jablonski—Materna would have said 'backside' —but Fischer thought it advisable to retire in any case.

'I won't stand for this sort of treatment. I'll be back.'

He returned the same day, this time accompanied by Constable Gäbler, who claimed that he had come to inspect the personnel list. He was fully entitled to do so—indeed, it might have been described as his duty. Thanks to Sabine, everyone knew of his impending arrival well in advance.

Gäbler assumed his most correct and courteous tone. 'I'd just like to make the usual check, with your permission.'

The Baron's eyes twinkled. 'I see you've brought a special constable along to help you.'

'Herr Fischer is accompanying me in his official Party capacity.'

'Which one, if I may inquire?'

Fischer stepped forward. 'The Local Group has a department responsible for public works, organization and co-ordination of the same. That's one of my jobs.'

'Really?' Materna observed sarcastically. 'When did you take it on—an hour ago?'

'That's beside the point,' snapped Fischer. He would not have dreamed of admitting that this marsh-draining subversive had hit the nail on the head. Public works, hitherto an unimportant and unwanted post, had been one of Uschkurat's

w.   K responsibilities until half an hour before. Fischer had not found it difficult to place the department under 'provisional S.A. command' for vague but cogently stated reasons which were of interest to no one.

'Shall I tell you what the Party can do?' the Baron inquired pleasantly. He feasted his eyes briefly on Fischer's outraged face but intercepted a warning glance from Materna just in time. 'It can prove to me, once and for all, that it appreciates true pioneering spirit, as exemplified by this scheme of ours.'

There was a general sigh of relief. Materna smiled and Constable Gäbler resumed his benevolently official expression. Fischer tried to make up his mind whether the Baron's little jest was good-natured, malicious, or no jest at all, but failed to reach any firm conclusion.

Gäbler proceeded to check the Polish labourers against his list. He called out the names in alphabetical order and was rewarded by a series of unintelligible barks from the assembled Poles.

'Everything seems to be in order,' the policeman said eventually. He folded the list and replaced it in his pocket. 'We may as well go now, I suppose.'

Fritz Fischer laid a hand on Gäbler's arm. 'Not yet,' he said. 'I want to say a few words to these people first.'

The Baron was on the point of protesting, but Materna quelled him with a single glance.

Fischer's speech ran as follows: 'Men, you have come to Germany to work. We welcome this, and are happy to have you here. You are taking part in the immense task of reconstructing the Greater German Reich. We appreciate your help, which is why we offer you the protection of the Party and its various agencies. Each of you can have complete confidence in the Party. If any problems arise, don't hesitate to consult me.'

To anyone with even a rudimentary knowledge of Polish, Wollnau's translation of the above was a delight.

'That man speaks first-class German,' Fischer said. 'Where did he learn it?'

'At school,' replied Erich Wollnau, alias Erik Wollnowski.

'You don't sound like a labourer.'

'I was a senior civil servant.'

Fischer gaped and Materna frowned, but the Baron looked

highly amused. 'Did you say: senior civil servant?' Fischer demanded incredulously.

'Yes.'

At this point, Fischer displayed the fruits of efficient ideological instruction. Following a propaganda-inspired train of thought, he said loftily: 'You belong to a political minority, I take it?'

'In a manner of speaking.'

'Persecuted by hate-ridden nationalists, eh?'

'You could call it that.'

Fischer could see it all now. 'Evil swine!' he said, meaning the Poles. 'To think that the most valuable members of the community should be forced into menial jobs just to keep body and soul together! If that doesn't cry out for action . . .' He offered the persecuted senior civil servant his hand. 'I hope you find the working conditions here to your satisfaction.'

Wollnau-Wollnowski politely expressed a similar hope. Then he placed himself at the head of his Poles and led them off in the direction of the marsh.

'Your scheme deserves the support of the local Party authorities,' Fischer said curtly, more to the Baron than Materna. He turned on his heel and strode off with Constable Gäbler in tow. Both men felt satisfied that they had done their duty.

Materna stared after them. 'Thank God their intelligence doesn't match their arrogance, otherwise we'd be in real trouble.'

The Baron fished out a handkerchief and wiped the tears from his eyes. 'That Wollnowski fellow is a joker of the first order. Fancy claiming to be a grade-one civil servant!'

'That's just what he is—German, too, not Polish. He's enjoying a spot of leave at the moment—at least, that's what he calls it. He insists on staying in Germany at all costs.'

Alarich von der Brocken stood lost in thought for a considerable time. At last he said: 'A man of his intelligence is bound to play a decent game of chess. Send him over to my place the next chance you get. I'd like to take him on.'

A file lay open on Amadeus Neuber's desk. Inscribed in bold black letters on the cover, which was a cautionary shade of crimson, were the words: *Specimens of Subversive Pro-*

*paganda Material—for Confidential Party Use Only. To be
kept under Lock and Key.*

The file contained, *inter alia*, a slim volume entitled *Voices
of the Church*, and one of the articles in the latter was
headed: *Questions addressed by a sincere Christian to the
legally constituted authorities.* In the official view, these questions represented an insidious attack on the current political
system. An accompanying memorandum drew particular attention to the sixth of these ten questions, which read as follows:

*'If our Leader believes that he has been chosen by divine
providence—and no one would venture to dispute this—we are
surely justified in assuming that he feels an absolute and
unconditional obligation towards God. It cannot therefore
be doubted that a God-given leader is himself subject to
divine leadership. However, since the Christian Church is
alone empowered to act in God's name . . .'*

'What impertinence!' exclaimed Neuber. Carefully, he removed *Voices of the Church* from his file of subversive propaganda. Bachus had repeatedly avoided him of late, but he
had made up his mind to nail the parson once and for all. To
this end, he summoned Ernst Schlaguweit.

'I much appreciate the way you've been keeping me informed,' Neuber said cordially. 'It's high time your constructive attitude was rewarded.'

Schlaguweit gave a little bow of gratitude. 'The S.A. is ripe
for reorganization.'

'Reorganized it shall be,' Neuber assured him. 'I look upon
you, not Kusche, as the future commander of the S.A., but
there are one or two hurdles to be cleared first. We must
proceed methodically.'

'I'm a methodical man,' Schlaguweit declared. 'Where do
we start?'

'With Bachus.'

Schlaguweit obediently took the subversive document which
Neuber handed him. Fifteen minutes later he slapped it
down on the parson's desk, together with some more conventional Party literature.

'Something for your next sermon, Vicar!'

'Very well,' Bachus said resignedly. 'It wouldn't benefit anyone if people thought I was a subversive.'

'That's the spirit!' Ernst Schlaguweit rubbed his hands,
happy in the knowledge that he could now report the total

success of his mission. 'I'll look forward to hearing you next Sunday, then.'

'Oh, my God!' Bachus groaned when the Brownshirt had gone. 'The things they expect me to do . . .' Gloomily, he started to look through the literature which Schlaguweit had left behind. There was a tract entitled *Why the True German must be an Aryan*, an anthology called *Eastwards We Ride —Five Centuries of German Song*, a pamphlet on *The Jew and his Crime against the German People*, and a historical survey ranging from Arminius, the Cheruscan prince, to Hitler, Leader and Unifier of the Greater German Reich.

The Reverend Dr Bachus groaned again. Then came a moment when the darkness seemed to lift a trifle. Nestling among the official literature in his slightly tremulous hands lay *Voices of the Church*. His eyes lighted on Question No. 6 and were promptly held by the red underlines.

'That's a glimmer of light at least,' he muttered. He forced himself to concentrate on the question, reading it through several times and making notes. The consumption of a bottle of Franconian wine—a Würzburger Stein 1933—aided his thought processes considerably. Before long, he was possessed by a kind of euphoria.

This euphoria lasted until his sermon on the following Sunday. It ended precisely twenty-five minutes thereafter.

Bachus opened with the grand old words 'Beloved brothers in Christ'. They were addressed to all who gazed up at him from the pews below, sinners in spirit and, more particularly, body, incorrigible planters of weeds in the garden of God, sheep with matted wool—in short, the whole of Maulen. It was not long before Bachus came to the subject of God and the Führer:

'We are all guided by our Leader, but he, as he has so often stated, is guided by divine providence—in other words, by God in his infinite and unfathomable goodness. If God grants His favour to our Leader, our Leader must feel gratitude towards God. Since God is all-powerful, our Leader's power can only derive from Him.'

Bachus really went to town on Question No. 6. He reverted to it again and again, firing verbal salvoes over the heads of his dozing congregation. Finally, with parched throat but immense conviction, he cried: 'We give thanks for our Leader, but it was God who sent him to us!'

The last hymn rang out lustily, wresting those who were still asleep from their slumbers. Every eye was focused on the altar, beyond which, out of sight but not out of mind, lay the Gasthaus.

Bachus found Neuber and Schlaguweit waiting for him in the vestry after service. 'Well,' he asked, 'how was it?'

'Good enough,' Neuber replied coldly. 'That sermon of yours might have been written by a self-confessed traitor to the regime.'

'But I based it entirely on the material I was given.'

'Material? What material?' Neuber knit his brow. 'I wouldn't know anything about that. All I know is, some of your ideas came straight out of *Voices of the Church*, which has officially been declared a subversive publication.'

'One moment!' protested Bachus. 'The periodical you mention was officially handed to me by Herr Schlaguweit on your behalf.'

Neuber stared at Schlaguweit with elaborate surprise, and Schlaguweit responded with an equally elaborate shrug.

'I don't remember giving Herr Bachus a subversive periodical,' he said. 'A church magazine, did you say? Where would I have got such a thing? Really, Vicar, you must be joking!'

'Be that as it may,' Neuber said deliberately, 'the fact remains that treasonable and subversive ideas have been disseminated from the pulpit of this church. The consequences could be most unpleasant.'

No one realized this more clearly than the Reverend Dr Bachus, many of whose fellow-clerics had been convicted for similar offences. His legs turned to jelly and he sank on to a chair, watched in silence by his tormentors.

There was a long pause. Then, without raising his eyes, Bachus said: 'My motives were of the best.'

'But of course,' Neuber agreed, all sweetness and light. 'It must have been an oversight on your part.'

'You're right,' Bachus replied weakly. 'It was an oversight.'

'Spoken like a man!' Neuber said. 'I take it you're ready to co-operate with me against Fischer—at long last. You'd better tell the whole truth if you want to stay out of prison. Well, did you help to write that speech of Fischer's?'

'Yes,' Bachus murmured almost inaudibly.

'Are you ready to swear to that?'

Bachus hesitated, then nodded.

Fischer's goose was cooked, Neuber told himself—the parson's too, not that he minded. The innocent always had to suffer with the guilty.

'Right, Vicar, we'll get that down in writing straight away. The rest will take care of itself.'

Alfons Materna headed for the village churchyard. It was early afternoon in the middle of the week, an unusual time for such a visit but one which would ensure that there were no unwelcome observers.

Margarete, formerly Frau Materna and now the widowed Frau Eichler, was waiting for him beside her late husband's grave. She was kneeling, but not in prayer. Her fingers were busily removing weeds.

Materna came up and stood behind her. 'You'll get your hands dirty.'

Margarete looked round. She had changed little in the past few years. No woman would have been prematurely aged by the even tenor of her existence.

'I have to speak to you,' she announced.

Materna sat down on a bench near Eichler's grave. 'I'm listening.'

'I've been worried,' she went on, loosening the earth round some velvety blue pansies.

'Not about me, surely?'

'Yes, in a way. You can't sever all your ties with the past. For instance, I worry about Brigitte. She's my daughter too, after all.'

'What worries you about her? Her share in my will, her husband, or what? Whatever you're worried about, it certainly isn't me.'

Margarete bent low over the grave. Her hands kneaded the soil with mechanical vigour. 'I'm only a woman,' she said in a muffled voice.

'And what conclusion do you draw from that?'

'I feel I'm being forced into a decision.'

'By Eis?'

'What if the answer were yes?'

Materna laughed silently to himself. 'Congratulations! He obviously appreciates you for what you're worth—in other words, half Maulen.'

He stared up into the branches of a neighbouring pine-tree.

They were deeply etched by the passage of the years—stark, gnarled branches which had thrust their way into the world under the impulse of life-giving sap, produced needles in abundance, seeped resin, turned barren as bone, and burst once more into fecund, juicy cones.

Still smiling, Materna said: 'I suppose you just want my advice so you can go and do the opposite. All right, here's my advice: snap him up.'

'You misunderstand me. I wouldn't go so far as to say that your interests coincide with mine, but a little co-operation would benefit us both. You see, much as I respect and admire Eugen, my sights are set on higher things.'

Materna's amusement increased. Margarete had evidently tasted blood. Did she want to become queen of Maulen?

'To be absolutely candid,' she went on, 'Eugen has his good points but he's nowhere near as shrewd or able as Johannes was. He doesn't assert his authority properly, and he certainly wouldn't be able to if you and I joined forces. We control almost the whole of Maulen between us. What do you say?'

'It's worth considering,' Materna replied with a grin. 'Needs a lot of thought, though.'

'And in the meantime?'

'We play a waiting game.' Materna got up and pointed to Eichler's grave. 'Your late lamented husband may well be getting some company before long. Things can change over-night in Maulen.'

'This is nineteen thirty-nine,' Amadeus Neuber said to Eugen Eis. 'May I take the liberty of pointing out that we shall soon be in a position to celebrate the twenty-fifth anniversary of the Battle of Tannenberg and the Masurian Marshes?'

'Fine,' replied Eis. 'Let's celebrate. Celebrations never do any harm—they take people's minds off things.'

'I'll set up an organizing committee,' Neuber suggested. 'Thank you for entrusting the preparations to me.'

Eis's eyebrows met in a suspicious line. 'Not so fast, Neuber. You aren't trying to short-circuit our mutual friend Fischer again, are you?'

'Not at all,' Neuber replied righteously. 'Fischer will be a member of my committee—that goes without saying.'

Shortly afterwards, 'in consultation with the Local Group

Leader', Neuber announced the formation of his committee, a triumvirate consisting of himself, Fischer and Uschkurat, representing the Party, the S.A., aud the population at large. Neuber considered the inclusion of Uschkurat a brilliant stroke. Uschkurat seldom offered an opinion of his own these days, so he could be relied on to support the chairman of the committee, in other words, Neuber himself.

Uschkurat duly said nothing, unlike Fritz Fischer, who quickly made it clear that his presence did not imply a readiness to accept orders because nobody on the committee was competent to give him any.

'This is only a sort of preliminary discussion,' Neuber hastened to assure him.

'Who's in the chair, then? You? I oppose that.'

Neuber, who was prepared for outbursts from Fischer, preserved his equanimity. Soothingly, he stressed that the purpose of the meeting was to discuss one or two preliminary points 'on a basis of complete equality'.

'I oppose that,' Fischer repeated. 'No equality exists between subordinate Party organizations and the S.A. I won't stand for any form of discrimination.'

'Nobody's trying to discriminate against you,' Neuber replied with enormous forbearance. 'This is the anniversary of one of the greatest and most glorious battles in world history. We must celebrate it with fitting dignity and turn it into a unique occasion in the life of our community. The climax of the whole affair will be a pageant.'

'A what?'

'A pageant based on the history of the region,' Neuber explained. 'As far as possible, it will be a patriotic counterblast to the notorious Christian-Jewish Passion plays—the one at Oberammergau, for instance.'

'Ridiculous!' barked Fischer. 'I won't have my men mixed up in that sort of thing.'

Neuber drew himself up and threw out his rather narrow chest. 'May I request Party member Uschkurat to leave us? It shouldn't take more than a few minutes to clear the air.'

Uschkurat left the conference chamber with extreme alacrity and sought refuge in the ante-room, where the secretry of the Local Group regaled him with schnapps. 'That's the stuff,' he sighed contentedly after the first glass, but before he could accept another Fritz Fischer cantered past, snorting like a bull. He charged across the village square to the vicarage.

'What's eating him?' Uschkurat asked.

'I expect Herr Neuber waved a piece of paper under his nose,' replied the secretary, '—a piece of paper with the parson's signature on it.'

The ensuing train of events lasted little more than three minutes. There were several witnesses: Uschkurat, who had trotted after Fischer out of curiosity; the baker; the verger; a woman who had come to arrange for her baby to be christened; and Sabine.

Sabine was at her favourite post beside the war memorial. When Fischer stormed past she followed him, with the result that Materna received a fairly accurate account of what happened.

Fischer barged into the vicarage and bellowed for Bachus. He eventually ran him to earth between the stables and the vegetable garden.

'You bastard!' he hissed, breathing hard.

Bachus bridled. 'My good man,' he began in a placatory tone, but Fischer cut him short.

'Who the hell do you think you are?' the S.A. chief demanded. His voice had the cutting edge of a circular saw. 'What's the idea of making me out to be a priest's lackey? Trying to dish me, are you?'

'Herr Fischer,' Bachus said stiffly, 'I'm not used to being addressed in this fashion.'

'You hypocritical lump of horse-shit!' Fischer screamed. His face went tomato-red and chalky-white by turns. His right hand twitched convulsively and his left clutched his chest in the cardiac region.

'What's the matter?' Bachus asked with genuine concern. 'Is your heart giving you trouble?'

'Don't change the subject. You signed a piece of bumf to the effect that I was an arse-licking priest-lover. Well, you can take it all back, and quickly at that.'

'You're wrong, Herr Fischer. I signed nothing which I couldn't reconcile with my own conscience.'

'Your conscience? Don't make me laugh? We're going to make a clean sweep in this village, Bachus. Types like you aren't wanted here.'

'Please restrain yourself, Herr Fischer,' the parson said,
trembling, but Fischer was beyond restraint. The sight of
Bachus quaking only spurred him on, and the presence of
spectators did not displease him.

'Pin back your ears and listen, Bachus. Unless you're
completely out of your mind you'll say that your signature got
on to that piece of paper by mistake. You were the victim of
malicious provocation, and you apologize.'

'What if I refuse to make such a statement?'

'If you refuse I'll finish you, even if it means levelling
your prayer-palace to the ground. Today's Friday. I'll give
you twenty-four hours to put matters right. Otherwise, you'll
preach your last sermon on Sunday morning—I guarantee
you that.'

The following day dawned fair. Normal temperatures and
an almost cloudless sky augured well for work in progress
in the fields.

Saturday afternoon was devoted to inspecting livestock,
repairing machinery, pacing farm-yards, cleaning house, doing
neglected chores. More and more minds turned to the Gasthaus as the day wore on.

'How peaceful it all looks,' the Reverend Dr Bachus said
bitterly. He wavered between church and wine-cellar— then,
with a sigh, decided in favour of the latter.

The Baron, who had sent for the village band, was sitting
in a cane chair on his terrace, listening to an alternation
of folk-songs and marches, but none of them brought him
complete contentment.

Elisabeth von der Brocken, the Baron's sister, had invited
Materna over, ostensibly to discuss the welfare of the Polish
workmen. She laid her hand on his arm as they strolled
through the grounds, ostensibly to emphasize a point.

Eugen Eis was paying court to Margarete Eichler, but
with little success. Margarete effectively nipped romance in
the bud by demanding details of his dairy and other commercial interests.

By arrangement with the leaders of the Hitler Youth and
German Girls' League, Amadeus Neuber had called a special
parade for the late afternoon on the pretext that he intended
to carry out some pre-military training. Nobody could possibly

object, least of all the parents, who welcomed the knowledge that their turbulent offspring would be safely occupied for a couple of hours.

Neuber's voice rang out over the school yard. 'Fall in! Left, right, left, right, left . . .'

The youngsters hurriedly formed up, girls and boys in separate contingents. Neuber strode down the girls' ranks with an expression compounded of martial severity and paternal benevolence. He found one or two faults—heads inadequately combed and backs insufficiently straight.

'And where is Sabine?' he inquired.

'She's off sick.'

Neuber's eye lost its martial fire. The absence of Sabine put a blight on the proceedings, so he decided to devote himself to the boys—the Brownshirts of tomorrow. An hour's drill would do them no harm.

Neuber's activities were reported to Fritz Fischer, who laughed disdainfully. A short while later he was standing in the village square with the S.A.—the Brownshirts of today —drawn up in front of him.

'Men,' he proclaimed, 'we never go about things in an underhand way—not us! We shoot straight and pull no punches.'

The Brownshirts bore out this statement by marching to the fire station and fetching the drums of paint that stood ready inside—one drum each of black, white, red, and brown.

Constable Gäbler stood at his office window and peered round the curtains. Acting on the principle that discretion was the better part of valour, he left the house by the back door, climbed over two garden walls, and paid a surprise call on Eugen Eis. The Party boss was not at home, but Brigitte announced that she would be glad to keep Gäbler company until his return.

Meanwhile, Fritz Fischer was following the progress of his painting party with eyes aglitter. As soon as an expanse the width of a barn door had been satisfactorily primed, he issued more detailed instructions.

'A swastika on either side,' he commanded. 'The slogan in the middle will be: "Germany awake—Down with Yids and Priests!".'

A Brownshirt named Sombray had been selected for this operation. Sombray's father had a monopoly of all the decorator's work in the neighbourhood, and his promising

son shared the Führer's erstwhile ambition to become an artist.
His brownshirted comrades looked on in awe as he gave
a convincing demonstration of his talents. Sombray's swastikas
seemed to glow and the word 'Germany' presented an almost
three-dimensional impression, whereas 'Yids' and 'Priests'
looked as if they had been daubed on the wall in human
excrement.

'Good work!' Fischer called approvingly. 'A few patriotic
choruses, and we can all go and have a quiet drink.'

At Materna's farm, Hannelore Welser had turned on the
radio. Königsberg was broadcasting *From the Mountains to
the Sea*, an hour-long medley of popular music, but Hannelore
was not listening. Impatiently, she turned to Jacob Jablonski,
who was playing with the dogs, and asked: 'What can be
keeping Peter and Konrad all this time?'

What had kept them was Sabine's account of the S.A.'s
operations. As they listened to her, the mawkish strains of a
tango drifted across from Eis's house.

'You ought to take a look in there too,' Sabine said.

Squinting through a crack in the carelessly drawn curtains,
Konrad and Peter were presented with the spectacle of Constable Gäbler receiving a tango lesson from Brigitte. He was
sweating profusely and hopping around the room like a tipsy
kangaroo.

Konrad blocked Sabine's view. 'There's nothing for you
to see, my girl.'

'Oh, go on! I know all about life and that sort of thing.
Besides, my father can't dance the tango and play cops at
the same time.'

The next sound that came to their ears reduced even them
to silence. The thirty Brownshirts in the village square had
burst into song.

> '*We'll sink our knives in churchmen's flesh
> And watch the red blood spurt . . .*'

Such were the two recurring lines of the song which Fritz
Fischer and his men bellowed in the direction of the vicarage.
Fischer had taken a trifling liberty with the original text, which
spoke of knives being sunk in Jewish flesh, but his poetic
licence was justified. It was an age since any Jew had defiled
the soil of Maulen. The only one known to the S.A. was a

certain Siegfried Grienspan, but he had escaped their clutches years before.

'Well done, lads!' called Fischer. 'Once more from the beginning.'

Down in his cellar, the Reverend Dr Bachus trembled.

That evening, the S.A. gathered at Scharfke's to celebrate their victory over the forces of 'reaction, obscurantism and clericalism'. The brass band had left the Baron in peace and transferred their attentions to the Gasthaus.

To judge by his heavy breathing, sweaty face and feverish eyes, Fritz Fischer was determined to make a night of it. His hand went to his chest every now and then, as though to convey that his heart belonged to his men and the Movement.

At one stage in the evening, Uschkurat found the S.A. commander at his elbow as he was relieving himself in traditional fashion against the back wall of the Gasthaus. 'You really shouldn't have done that to the parson,' he ventured cautiously. 'Bachus isn't a bad chap at heart.'

Fischer was outraged. 'Anyone who says that is a subversive himself, and if there's one thing I won't stand for it's subversives.'

Shortly afterwards, Ignaz Uschkurat was invited outside by two Brownshirts and shown the error of his ways. Having been hit over the head several times and kicked in the pants, he was barred from the Gasthaus until further notice.

Back in the bar, Fritz Fischer demanded menacingly if anyone had any objections. Nobody had except Franz Nickels, an insignificant peasant farmer from north of Maulen, who never opened his mouth except to order a beer. In this instance, Nickels was unwise enough to grumble: 'Let's have a bit of peace and quiet!' He too was hustled outside, hit over the head and kicked in the pants.

The schnapps flowed even more abundantly after this, and ordinary customers in the bar were privileged to join the warriors of the S.A. in song. *Germany, Thou art our Pride* was quickly followed by a rendering of *Eastwards We Ride*.

The singers mimed the words of the song with great realism. Mounting chairs, they clasped the backs as if they were horses' necks and shuffled madly round the bar. Finally, six Brownshirts enthroned Fischer on a table-top and galloped in a circle, faster and faster. It was not long before the first piece of furniture smashed and two full bottles of schnapps exploded against the wall. The postman sustained three broken ribs. All in all, the atmosphere was sublime.

'Now the *Horst Wessel Song*!' panted Fischer.

Some said later that these were his last words—his political testament in a manner of speaking.

Staggering slightly but still on his feet, Fritz Fischer was escorted outside by Bubi Kusche. Here the S.A. commander attempted to get his motor-cycle going, but without success. The B.M.W. spluttered briefly, back-fired, spat, and then relapsed into silence.

'Shit!' exclaimed Fischer, and dealt the machine a savage but ineffectual kick. 'It's enough to make a man spew!'

Another set of last words, though Bubi Kusche tactfully suppressed them. He could only report that Fischer had set off in a southerly direction, bound for his cottage.

Fischer tottered slowly through the night. The ground seemed to undulate beneath his feet and the air flowed over him like tepid soup. On the outskirts of the village he vomited with beneficial violence, uttering a series of leonine roars as he did so. Then he marched on, filled with a mounting sense of triumph.

It had been his day! He had shown them! He was going to exterminate those rats—smash, drown or strangle them until there was none left! He unbuttoned his flies and spread his legs to give the water free passage. Laughter bubbled up inside him. He had already reached the small birch-wood. He always stopped for a pee here, like a dog visiting its favourite tree. He chortled foolishly to himself at the thought.

Then his laughter died. A flour-sack was thrown over his head with lightning-speed and deftly pulled down to his knees.

'Got him!' said a cheerful voice.

'Lash him to the tree,' said another.

Fischer overcame his initial shock sufficiently to attempt to struggle, but he felt as if he were caught in a vice. His captors picked him up, pinned him against a tree-trunk, and proceeded to truss him like a bale of straw.

'What do we do with him now?' someone asked.

'Treat him the way he treated Buttgereit.'

Fischer gave a stifled groan inside his sack. He had fallen into the hands of his enemies. Whoever they were—Materna's men, Neuber's hangers-on, Jews, Communists—there must be at least half a dozen of them. It never dawned on him that his assailants were two in number and half his age.

The voices sounded menacingly muffled, as though their owners were wearing cloths over mouths that slavered with the lust to maim and kill. Fischer gasped for air and wondered with horror what they would do with him.

'He's done it in his pants,' announced one of the voices, sounding positively concerned. 'Fancy shitting himself when we haven't even started yet!'

Trembling, Fischer listened to the argument that followed. One of his tormentors was all for giving him short shrift, another for prolonging the agony.

'Mercy,' he whimpered, 'have mercy on me, I beg you!'

'What a vocabulary the man's got! He actually knows the word mercy. I bet he doesn't know what it means.'

'What do you want me to do?' wailed Fischer. 'You only have to say.'

'Well, you might say "I shit on the Führer". How about that?'

Fischer did not reply for a moment. Then he shouted wildly: 'I shit on the Führer, I shit on him, I shit . . .' His voice died away to a gurgle.

Someone said: 'Pity his friends in the S.A. couldn't have heard that. It's just the sort of lesson they need.'

'I think he deserves a reward for being so co-operative,' said the other voice. 'As a token of our appreciation, we'll let him go this time—with a painted arse, of course.'

'Of course. I vote we give him a swastika on each cheek. There ought to be plenty of room for a couple of big ones.'

Fischer did not stir. He seemed to be in a state of collapse.

'Hello,' said Peter Bachus, 'don't tell me he's fainted.'

Konrad Klinger stepped forward quickly and began to untie the ropes that held the limp body to the tree. The two boys laid Fischer on the ground and removed the sack.

'You're the medical expert,' Konrad said impassively. 'What do you make of him?'

Kneeling beside Konrad, Peter felt Fischer's pulse and laid his head against the motionless chest.

'He's gone,' he said quietly.

The silence seemed to roar in their ears. Interminable seconds dragged by.

'How did it happen?' Konrad asked in a shocked voice.

'Heart attack, I reckon.'

Konrad whistled. 'Just like poor old Buttgereit!'

'Yes, except that we hardly laid a finger on him. He must have had a weak heart—we weren't to know.'

'Are you sure a post mortem will bear your theory out?'

'Pretty sure.'

'In that case, let's cover our tracks and get out of here. Materna can advise us what to do if anyone can.'

7

Fischer's disappearance passed unnoticed until Monday, when his body was discovered by some children playing in the woods. Sabine, who was one of them, held the others back. As a policeman's daughter, she knew that the proper course was to inform the competent authorities, to wit, her father. Having instructed the other children to form a sort of cordon round the scene of the discovery, she notified her father and then trotted off to Materna and Jablonski.

'Poor kid,' Jablonski said. 'Sorry you had to be the one to find him.'

'It wasn't all that bad,' Sabine told him stoutly. 'I've seen plenty worse things in those crime reports they send Daddy.'

Materna coughed. 'We won't keep Sabine. I'm sure she doesn't want to miss the rest of the fun.'

'I'll keep in touch,' Sabine said, and hurried off.

Constable Gäbler had meanwhile taken the steps appropriate in such cases. After summoning Dr Gensfleisch, who acted as Maulen's police surgeon, he informed the senior Party and local government representatives, namely, Eis and Uschkurat. Eis telephoned Neuber and Neuber telephoned his contact man in the S.A., Ernst Schlaguweit. Uschkurat, mindful of his Saturday night beating-up, informed Bubi Kusche.

Before long, the birch-wood was swarming with people.

Eis's non-committal comment on the tragedy—'Most regrettable'—was widely copied. Much use was also made of the word 'fate', and many qualified it thus: 'sad fate'.

Then Bubi Kusche appeared. He marched solemnly up to the uncovered body and greeted it with a Hitler salute.

'Your death will be avenged, Fritz!' he announced.

Constable Gäbler coughed discreetly. 'With all due deference to your feelings, nothing so far indicates that Herr Fischer died a violent death.'

'He had enemies!' trumpeted Kusche. 'A man of his sort would never have died from natural causes. He sacrificed his life for the Movement, I tell you!'

Eugen Eis, who liked everything in the local Party organization to run along lines of his own choosing, had no wish to see Fischer turned into a martyr. He wanted no sensations, no premature heroes' deaths in Maulen.

'In my view,' he said, 'we ought to wait for the official medical report.'

Dr Gensfleisch completed his examination of the body and said tersely: 'Heart failure.'

Bubi Kusche shook his shaven head in mulish disbelief. 'The whole thing stinks to high heaven.'

'Hardly surprising,' retorted the doctor. 'The man fouled his pants.'

'How dare you talk about our S.A. commander like that!'

'I'm talking about a body which I've just examined in my capacity as a medical practitioner. A dead man's status has no bearing on my examination or the wording on his death certificate.'

Bubi Kusche refused to be pacified. The reputation of the S.A. rested on his shoulders now, or so he believed. 'I'm going to prefer charges!' he shouted vaguely, but Eis laid a restraining hand on his arm.

'What do you hope to achieve, Felix?'

Kusche had a pretty fair idea. The leadership of the S.A. was at stake. 'Justice must be done. Fritz was the victim of his enemies.'

'Nonsense,' snapped Eis. 'This is an absolutely straightforward case—aren't I right, Doctor?'

Gensfleisch nodded. 'No marks of bruising, no abrasions, no contusions, no signs of strangulation. All we do know for certain is that he was drunk.'

'That concludes the first part of the official inquiry,' Gäbler announced promptly, in response to a nod from Eis.

Eis said: 'May I invite you all to a modest snack at the Gasthaus?' This suggestion met with a ready response, as he had known it would. Sagely, he added: 'Felix Kusche will join us, of course.'

Over the first glass of beer, Eis expressed his thanks to Gensfleisch and Gäbler. Then he turned to Kusche.

'I appreciate your loyalty to our late lamented friend and comrade,' he said. 'On the other hand, you surely don't want him to become the subject of unworthy rumours.'

'I intended the exact opposite, Local Group Leader.'

'We're agreed in principle, then. We both want to avoid involving the Party and the S.A. in any scandal. Fischer is dead—nothing can alter that.'

'But his reputation. . . .'

'His reputation will be safeguarded as a matter of course. However, there's more than one way of doing that.'

'All I meant was, he can't have died for nothing.'

'Of course not. He died of a heart attack. That could be interpreted as a sign of overwork.'

'He sacrificed himself for the Movement.'

'He devoted every last ounce of energy to the Party—yes, you could say that.'

Kusche chewed on this and liked the taste. Reaching for the schnapps bottle, he took up the Fischer legend and proceeded to embroider it. A veritable symbol of Greater German manhood, Fritz Fischer had been nearing the climax of his brilliant National Socialist career, sustained by the love and affection of his S.A. comrades and fellow-members of the Party, when his overtaxed heart, which had beaten so steadfastly in the service of the community, failed, and he sank lifeless upon the soil of his beloved homeland.

'Very nice,' Eis commented, restraining his mirth with difficulty. 'Carry on.'

'And his last words, as any number of people can confirm, were: "Sing me the *Horst Wessel Song* once more before I go, comrades." '

Amadeus Neuber was inculcating some important historical truths into the children of Maulen.

'Charlemagne's extermination of the Saxons, which was

undertaken for reasons of political necessity, makes him a forerunner of Adolf Hitler, our Leader.' He got no further, because at that moment Ernst Schlaguweit appeared and asked to speak to him urgently in his capacity as director of organization and propaganda. —

Neuber nodded. He set the children an essay on 'Why we have to make sacrifices for the Fatherland' and instructed Sabine to take charge while he was gone. Sabine stepped forward obediently.

'Keep order during my absence,' he said, taking her chin playfully between thumb and forefinger. 'I know you won't let me down.'

Once in his house, Neuber set a bottle of schnapps on the table and asked: 'Well, how do things stand?'

'The doctor says it was heart failure and Gäbler agrees,' Schlaguweit replied. 'Bubi Kusche tried to kick up a stink but Eis slapped him down. We don't want any scandals in Maulen, he said—meaning he doesn't, of course.'

Neuber smiled thinly and leant back in his chair. One thing was clear: with Fischer out of the way, he was Maulen's undisputed second-in-command. One more step, and he would be top dog.

'So it was just a heart attack . . . Does everyone in the village believe that?'

Schlaguweit hesitated. 'There are one or two rumours going around. After all, Fischer did have enemies.'

'I wasn't one of them,' Neuber said promptly. 'I never hated the man—just pitied him occasionally. He didn't measure up to his job—that's no secret—but who am I to pass judgement on him now he's dead? Besides, everybody in the village knows I'm not a violent man.'

Schlaguweit hastened to agree. 'Of course not, everybody knows that. I can only tell you this much: if anyone as much as hints the opposite, he'll have me to reckon with.'

'That's nice to know.' Neuber stretched his legs luxuriously. 'Party Member Fischer's death is a matter of some concern to me. I wonder who could have been responsible.'

This meant 'Who can we pin the blame on?', as Schlaguweit realized only too clearly. He racked his brains for a suitable candidate. 'Well, there was that argument with Bachus . . .'

'The parson? Surely not! The man's a weak-kneed fool.'

'How about Uschkurat? He was thrown out of the Gast-haus on Fischer's orders. They beat him up.'

'Uschkurat? He's quite incapable of decisive action of any kind. No, other forces were at work here, take it from me.'

Schlaguweit's puzzled stare persisted, so Neuber had to make his meaning even plainer.

'What disturbs me is your friends in the S.A. Their com-mander is done to death, but they make no concerted move to avenge him or restore their tarnished reputation. I ask you, Schlaguweit, are you going to take this lying down like the rest of them?'

Schlaguweit registered a mixture of agitation and be-wilderment. 'Fischer made Kusche his second-in-command. Some of us regretted the fact, but we had to accept it.'

'Fischer is dead, and dead men don't have deputies. You're next on the seniority list.'

Schlaguweit swallowed hard. 'Well, I've always been funda-mentally opposed to Fischer and Kusche—especially Kusche, in fact. He doesn't represent the proper S.A. spirit, to my way of thinking.'

'Ernst Schlaguweit,' Neuber said solemnly, 'the time has come for you to show your true colours. You can count on my fullest support.'

'But what ought I to do?'

'Have the moral courage to take the only proper step—with my help, of course. Kusche wanted to get his grubby hands on the S.A. and he balked at nothing in the process—not even Fischer's death. Prove that, Schlaguweit! Make it abundantly clear to everyone, and don't stop to count the cost. Your hour has struck!'

'I understand,' Schlaguweit said with sudden decision. 'When higher things are at stake, no price is too high to pay.'

Fritz Fischer's funeral was neither specially grand nor speci-ally uplifting. Disharmony quickly manifested itself during the preliminary conference whose purpose was to decide where the coffin should lie in state.

'In front of the war memorial,' suggested Kusche. 'Not in church—dear old Fritz never pandered to religion.'

Neuber, speaking as director of organization, said: 'We

shouldn't entirely ignore popular tradition, for all that.' He shot an imperious glance at Schlaguwcit, who reacted like litmus paper.

'You're right,' he said. 'I spit on the Church, but not on the people. We've got to take public opinion into account.'

Problems of this kind had to be discussed without reference to Eugen Eis, who was comfortably incommunicado. The more his subordinates wrangled the easier they were to control.

'I'm speaking on behalf of the S.A.,' Kusche announced in a challenging voice.

Schlaguweit received another encouraging glance from Neuber. 'I question that,' he retorted. 'I very much doubt if you, of all people, have any right to speak for the S.A.'

The two men rounded on each other, bristling. Each of them had publicly stated his claim to leadership of the entire S.A. contingent. They were within an ace of hurling themselves at one another.

Neuber watched the scene with covert satisfaction. Loftily, he said: 'Whoever assumes command must be capable of welding all schools of thought into a unified whole.'

'Just what I'm trying to do,' said Kusche.

'Like hell you are!' said Schlaguweit.

In the end, both men reported to Eugen Eis.

'As senior Party representative,' Eis proclaimed, 'I alone wield effective control over the S.A. You, Kusche, will assume provisional command, and you, Schlaguweit, will lend Kusche your fullest support. I shall announce my final decision in due course.'

The two men clicked their heels and saluted. From now on they watched each other like hawks, leaving Neuber free to organize things as he pleased.

Fritz Fischer had been laid out in his coffin since the early hours of the morning, thanks to the efficiency of Anton Germanski, the master carpenter, and his two apprentices. The catafalque was draped with black bunting furnished by the Party from its extensive stocks. In place of candles, a quartet of Brownshirts held flaring torches in their hot and heavy hands.

There was little activity in the village square until noon. The members of the death-watch spent most of the time staring into space, watched only by a handful of inquisitive children. Sabine, who was one of them, suddenly called out: 'Look, one of them's got his fly-buttons undone.'

All four sentinels promptly clapped a hand over the same place. The torches swayed and the children tittered delightedly. Each sentinel was reassured to find, contrary to expectation, that his flies were securely buttoned, and each reflected smugly that one of the others had made an exhibition of himself.

At three o'clock, almost to the minute, the drummers and trumpeters of the Hitler Youth came to life with horrendous effect. Calf-hide boomed and brass blared in the opening bars of *The Great Elector's Cavalry March*.

Meanwhile, Bubi Kusche had stationed himself on the verge of the war memorial and was watching the mourners assemble. He noted with satisfaction that nobody had dared to absent himself.

Ernst Schlaguweit joined Kusche on the steps of the war memorial. They tried briefly to dislodge each other, but the cement oak-wreath surrounding the base provided too firm a foothold and the spectacle that met their gaze proved a welcome distraction. Thronging the village square were schoolchildren solemnly attired in black and grey or grey and white. On the left stood the mixed voice choir, basic colour-scheme blue and red, on the right the male voice choir in hunting green. The Rifle Club, whose members favoured field-grey, filed out of the Gasthaus followed by bemedalled and ramrod-backed veterans, mostly bearded. Finally, like some brown bird of paradise, Eugen Eis appeared with the Widow Eichler at his side.

The Führer's youthful devotees continued to bang and blow, effortlessly drowning any murmur from the crowd. It was less a question of mourning Fischer's demise than of celebrating his departure.

Even Alfons Materna put in an appearance, escorted by Jacob Jablonski minus dogs. He flourished his top-hat in all directions, rather like a head of State. Eugen Eis acknowledged his provocatively loud greeting with a casual wave of the glove, but his face preserved its adamantine immobility. He did not react to provocation, merely made a mental note of it.

The last rites at the war memorial began. The S.A., substantially reinforced by detachments from elsewhere, enclosed the coffin like a living, breathing wall of esprit de corps. The usual preliminaries—fanfares, recitations and chorus singing—were followed by commemorative addresses.

Local Group Leader Eugen Eis: 'His boots are tramping down the last long road . . . always a shining example . . . call upon the younger generation to emulate him . . .'

Mayor Ignaz Uschkurat: 'He was capable of anything—I mean, a highly capable man. Much as we shall miss him, who of us here would begrudge him his well-earned repose?'

Acting S.A. Commander Felix Kusche: 'We shall never forget you, Fritz, we promise you that. "Felix," you said to me shortly before your death, "Felix, you know what really matters to me, you know my plans for the future. . . ." '

Almost everyone realized what Kusche was driving at, and some of those present, notably Eis and Materna, found it hard to conceal amusement. Then Neuber pushed Ernst Schlaguweit forward.

Though not a scheduled speaker, Schlaguweit burned to outshine Bubi Kusche. 'Fritz Fischer was a great man,' he proclaimed. 'The piece of paper in my hand represents his last written communication. It is a sheet from a message-pad, and it is addressed to me. It reads: "Get on with the job!" '

The full text actually read: 'Get on with the job or I'll have your guts for garters!' and it referred to Fischer's anticlerical operation, but that was of secondary importance.

Last of all came director of organization Amadeus Neuber: 'All things considered, Fritz Fischer was a man of our age, a symbol of the Third Reich . . .'

'Hear, hear!' said Materna, who was enjoying himself hugely.

'They're getting nuttier every day,' Jablonski muttered in his ear. 'Talk about a Thousand Year Reich! If they carry on like this, the country'll be full of morons long before then.'

At a signal from Eis, the performers transferred themselves from the village square to the churchyard. The Reverend Dr Bachus hurried on ahead, the Brownshirts shouldered the coffin, and the villagers brought up the rear. The proceedings moved inexorably towards yet another climax.

Bachus began to speak. He seemed entirely oblivious of

what Fischer had done to him a few days earlier, but the villagers' memory was green in this respect. Most of them knew as little about Christian charity and forgiveness as they did about the spirit of reconciliation which death ought, so Bachus assured them, to bring in its train.

Bubi Kusche's voice made itself heard, not loudly, but with defiant clarity: 'It's a disgrace, the way that priest takes poor old Fritz's name in vain . . .'

Then he slipped. He later claimed that he had been deliberately pushed, but the allegation could not be proved. His only piece of circumstantial evidence was that Ernst Schlaguweit had been standing immediately behind him.

At all events, he slipped, stumbled, and fell headlong into the grave. The spectators surged forwards, craning their necks and chattering like a band of inquisitive monkeys. Straining bodies swayed to and fro, villagers gravewards and Brownshirts outwards, but the latter were in a clear minority. At least five of them toppled into the grave to join their acting chief, Schlaguweit, in the lead.

They lay there in a jumbled heap, hiding the two would-be S.A. commanders beneath a flurry of clawing hands, flailing legs and writhing bodies. Bachus lapsed into bemused silence while they extricated themselves from the pit, which took them some time.

Baron Alarich von der Brocken chose this moment to enter the churchyard mounted on Adolf II. 'Damnation!' he exclaimed as he trotted straight into the crowd. 'I apologize for my horse—the brute's completely out of control. Am I in time? I'd hate to think I missed seeing Fritz Fischer laid beneath the sod.'

'Get it over with as quickly as you can,' Eis hissed fiercely to Kusche and Schlaguweit, who now stood beside him, red-faced and plastered with earth.

His order was obeyed with alacrity. The coffin thudded into the grave accompanied by a hasty prayer and a few handfuls of soil. Shovels went into action, a mound took shape, and wreaths were laid on top—wreaths with black-white-and-red ribbons dominated by swastikas and inscribed with messages such as 'In Undying Memory', 'True to the Last', 'For Maulen and Masuria', 'For People and State', 'For People and Fatherland', 'All for Germany', 'For Fatherland and Führer'. Alfons Materna's wreath bore the blue-white-and-red ribbon of Masuria and the stirring inscription: 'Lest We Forget'.

The tempo increased steadily as Kusche and Schlaguweit competed for Eis's approval. The two aspiring Brownshirts chivvied the mourners to and fro, collected the flowers together and threw them on the mound, stacked the wreaths and arranged the ribbons so that they showed.

'Well, that's that,' said Eis. 'About time, too—another couple of minutes and there'd have been a riot.' He raised his voice and addressed the crowd: 'And now, my friends, to the Gasthaus!'

Eugen Eis was extremely dissatisfied. While the villagers drank their fill at government expense and indulged in malicious gossip, he was holding a post mortem on the funeral.

'I didn't like it,' he grumbled, 'I didn't like it at all.'

Amadeus Neuber was the sort of man who had an answer for everything. He had one now: according to his theory, Fischer's lack of close relatives had robbed the funeral of a focal point.

'Nothing goes down quite so well as a grief-stricken widow,' he said, and went on to imply that Fischer's lack of popularity and less agreeable characteristics had also contributed to the unpleasant atmosphere. 'These things leave a nasty taste,' he concluded.

'That's a dirty lie!' cried Bubi Kusche.

'It's the unvarnished truth,' declared Ernst Schlaguweit.

Eis gave a disdainful shrug. 'Who cares? The fact remains that the funeral was a complete flop—in fact you could almost call it sabotage.'

Eis had been humiliated when Margarete Eichler declined his arm after the burial with the words: 'This would never have happened in Johannes's day!' The implied criticism bored into his mind like a woodworm in soft timber. Then there had been his wife's scornful laughter, the smirking faces of the villagers, the Baron's unbridled amusement, and—worst of all, perhaps—an indulgent and almost pitying glance from Materna.

Amadeus Neuber quoted further reasons for the fiasco, e.g. the weather (unseasonably warm) and the timing (an hour too early—farmers, labourers and tradesmen had been obliged to leave work prematurely). 'Besides,' he said, 'I wasn't over-impressed by the S.A.'s performance.'

'Lack of unified command!' snapped Kusche.

Neuber turned on him. 'Are you implying a lack of decision on the part of the local Party leadership?' he demanded, but Eis's indignant frown told him that he had overstepped the mark.

'The S.A. will make amends,' Schlaguweit said eagerly, '—I can vouch for that.'

'And I vouch for the S.A.'s unswerving loyalty to the Local Group Leader,' declared Kusche. 'His wish is my command. What counts is esprit de corps, not sectional interests.'

This clinched matters. In Eis's view, neither man was an ideal S.A. commander, but it would be wiser to choose the one who toadied to him alone and owed Neuber nothing.

It was long past midnight before he got a chance to speak to Kusche in private. 'Bubi,' he said, as they stood side by side in the lavatory, 'I'm looking for a man who'll back me to the hilt.'

'Me, you mean.'

'Are you really with me?'

'All the way.'

The two men shook hands. Kusche beamed with delight and returned to the bar, where he poured schnapps after schnapps down his throat as though bent on drowning. He savoured his victory to the full. Schlaguweit was the first to learn the great news.

'Report to me at ten sharp tomorrow morning,' Kusche told him.

'To you?'

'Yes, to your commanding officer. And now drink my health before I use you as a punch-bag.'

Shortly afterwards Kusche slumped to the floor and rolled under the table, singing a tuneless paean of triumph. Fritz Fischer had found a worthy successor.

The Gasthaus remained packed until the small hours, and Scharfke notched up a record turn-over. The more racially privileged members of the drinking population bayed, bawled and babbled at each other for many a convivial hour.

'Get me out of here!' Kusche commanded in a muffled but imperious voice.

'Certainly, Sturmführer,' Ernst Schlaguweit replied, clicking his heels. He hauled Kusche outside and propped him against the dung-heap, which felt agreeably warm and yielding.

'Thanks, friend,' Kusche muttered.

'The pleasure's all mine.' Schlaguweit waited doggedly until Kusche had fallen asleep on his feet. As soon as he started snoring, he rolled him into the liquid manure pit.

Konrad Klinger and Peter Bachus called at Materna's farm the day after the funeral. Materna offered them coffee, but they asked for schnapps out of the blue jug—his own special distillate.

'We're old enough for it now,' Peter said.

'I know,' Materna replied with a smile, and poured them each a glass. 'It's a local custom to gauge a man's virility by his consumption of liquor.'

'Don't be too hard on us,' Konrad pleaded. 'We've had a lot on our minds lately.'

'Whose fault is that?'

'My father's.' Peter hesitated, and Konrad went on: 'The Vicar is a good chap, but his performance at Fischer's funeral was the end. He knuckles under too easily.'

Materna looked reprovingly. 'If the Vicar spoke out he would be finished. Do you honestly expect him to court martyrdom, here in Maulen of all places? Besides, even if Fischer did treat him like a dog, that oughtn't to affect the way he conducts a funeral.'

'Father was different in the old days,' Peter Bachus said bitterly, '—quite different.'

'We were all different in the old days,' growled Materna. 'I used to play the fool. Now I lie low and say nothing. Konrad's father always believed in the rule of law, even after the Nazis came to power. Now he uses his job as a policeman to pervert the course of justice and save human lives in the process. As for your father, Peter, he used to have a sincere belief in what he preached. Then his faith failed him for a while. That's why he's in such a wretched state of mind.'

The two boys stared at the floor. 'All right,' Peter said, 'I take your point, but it's a pity when someone with the ability to do something does nothing.'

A note of warning came into Materna's voice. 'I know you

do your bit, the two of you, but you're appallingly careless. Everybody's luck has to run out sometime.'

'We can afford to take a few chances in Maulen.'

'Don't be too sure. One false move and we'll have the whole pack baying at our heels. It could happen any day of the week. I've tried to prepare for the worst, but what about you? What happens if the Brownshirts decide to take a closer interest in your activities?'

Peter smiled. 'We've taken a few precautions too, you know.'

Materna learned that they had both joined the National Socialist Students' League. Peter was deputy treasurer of the Königsberg branch and Konrad, incredibly enough, director of ideological training. One of their friends was the illegitimate son of a Gauleiter, another the son of a colonel in the S.S., and a third as good as engaged to the daughter of a senior government official.

'You see?' Konrad said with a grin. 'In our own humble way, we belong to the intellectual élite of the nation—useful connections all over the place, strings ready for pulling, contacts ripe for tapping. We had a good teacher.'

'I don't know whether to feel flattered or ashamed,' Materna said ruefully, but he poured them another schnapps all the same.

Felix 'Bubi' Kusche had barely arisen from the manure pit when he gave proof of unsuspected initiative and efficiency. One of his schemes was an intensified search for 'enemies of the people'.

His first step was to form a special squad of experienced and reliable Brownshirts and place them under the command of Ernst Schlaguweit. Schlaguweit ground his teeth in fury but accepted the assignment, coupled with an injunction from Kusche to 'show me what you can do'.

Strutting complacently across the village square to the Gasthaus, Kusche began to meditate on his new status. He had done it! Eis trusted him and the villagers already greeted him with the deference due to his rank.

Scharfke's manner was wary rather than deferential. Kusche chose a seat by the window and continued to meditate between swigs of beer. A list of local 'enemies of the people' took shape in his mind.

The first name on the list was, of course, Materna's, but Kusche mentally consigned him to the tender mercies of Eugen Eis. Then came Amadeus Neuber, not an enemy of the people in the conventional sense but an avowed opponent of the late lamented Fritz Fischer. However; Neuber was not an easy nut to crack. His time would come, but not yet. That left Bachus, the parson, a defenceless and therefore ideally suitable target for attack. It was high time to settle his hash.

'Special Squad Commander, to me!' Kusche called through the open window of the Gasthaus, and Ernst Schlaguweit doubled across the square.

His conference with Sturmführer Kusche was of short duration. Within an hour, the churchyard wall was again daubed with swastikas, and beside the west door hung a garishly hand-painted poster bearing the following inscription:

> *The Jews crucified God.*
> *The Führer condemns the Jews.*
> *Therefore, the Führer is on God's side.*
> *Where does the Church stand?*

'We're prettying the place up,' was Schlaguweit's facetious explanation to passers-by. He stopped a party of children and asked them where they were going.

'To see the vicar,' they replied, '—Confirmation class.'

'Cancelled,' he said curtly, '—church closed for repairs.'

In the end the Reverend Dr Bachus appeared in person. He froze at the sight of the Brownshirts' handiwork, and it was some time before he found his tongue.

'What is the meaning of this?'

'Sanitary precautions,' Schlaguweit told him. 'Outside first, then inside. This building stinks.'

A look of consternation came over the parson's face. 'What do you mean?'

'There are germs inside. No admittance without adequate disinfection. The S.A. is acting on behalf of the public health authorities.'

'But this is absurd!' Bachus exclaimed angrily.

Schlaguweit assumed a menacing tone. 'I would remind you that you're addressing the commander of an S.A. unit engaged in carrying out a specific order, Vicar. Your church is crawling with bugs and lice—we have sworn statements to that effect. Your best plan would be to shut up shop until further notice.'

'I protest!'

'Protest all you like—you're a Protestant by trade. The fact remains that we're going to clean this place up once and for all. This is only a modest beginning.'

The parson was temporarily spared further argument by a summons to a dying parishioner. He went his way in silence.

Eis bumped into Materna outside the door of the hut which housed the Polish drainage workers. His father-in-law greeted him with suspicious affability.

'Cut out the small-talk, Materna,' Eis said brusquely. 'I'm here on official business.'

'Party or local government? I'd like to know, so I can address you in the correct manner.'

'You find my presence unwelcome, I suppose.'

'On the contrary, I've been expecting you. Why didn't you come before—nervous?'

Eis snorted contemptuously. He felt a momentary urge to brush the impudent little man aside but suppressed it in the nick of time. Not only was Materna noted for his exceptional physical strength, but he could call on the services of sixteen Poles, four dogs, and Jacob Jablonski. These factors had to be taken into account.

Materna chuckled as if he had made an innocent little joke. 'Very well. If I may be permitted to say such a thing to a leader of men like yourself, follow me.'

He opened the barrack-room door invitingly and Eis peered inside. The interior of the hut was Prussian in its stark and orderly simplicity: pinewood furniture aligned with mathematical precision, beds draped with crisp coverlets of brightly checked material, chairs and lockers drawn up like a regiment on parade, and, on the walls, neatly stencilled on wooden plaques or squares of cloth, patriotic slogans such as 'Work Ennobles!', 'All for Germany!', and even 'The Führer Knows Best!'

'I imagine you'll appreciate all this for what it's worth.' Materna said with a grin. 'Since we're alone, I may as well tell you that the Poles can't read German.'

'I wouldn't put it past you to supply them with inaccurate translations, either,' Eis retorted.

'Who knows, Eugen? But please state your requirements. Shall I tell the Baron you're here, or would you like me to line up the Poles for your inspection? It would mean a loss of man-hours, but I could always send in a bill to the regional treasurer's office.'

'I'd like to see your workers' papers.'

Nothing in Materna's expression revealed how unwelcome he found this particular request. It implied that his son-in-law's visit had an underlying purpose.

Eis's manner seemed to confirm this. Having studied the personnel list, he examined the individual work permits with a slowness which might or might not have denoted extreme concentration. Eventually he extracted one of the permits and laid it on top of the pile. It belonged to the man known as Erik Wollnowski.

'Wolnowski is the German-speaker, isn't he?' Eis said. 'He intrigues me, I'd like to meet him next time I come. He smiled, then added casually: 'Oh yes, I shall be coming again, but not alone.'

He was scarcely out of sight before Materna picked up the 'phone and called the Baron.

'Eis is getting warm,' he said. 'Try and stall him any way you can.'

All this—the S.A.'s latest operation against the Church and Eis's meeting with Materna—took place on a Friday. By Saturday morning, Eugen Eis had received an invitation to join Alarich von der Brocken and a few close friends for a post-prandial get-together.

There could have been no higher honour, for no common-or-garden villager had ever been privileged to attend such a function. Eis temporarily forgot all about Wollnowski, his wife, and the S.A. Arriving at Gross-Siegwalde punctually, he was gratified to find the Baron waiting on the terrace to greet him.

'Welcome to my humble abode!' boomed Alarich von der Brocken.

'I'm much obliged for the invitation,' replied Eis, a little stiff at first.

'Well, we keep on running across each other but we've never been properly introduced. I thought it was about time we got to know each other better. Don't you agree?'

Eis glowed. 'I couldn't agree more.'

The Baron smote his guest vigorously on the back. 'After all we aren't just a bunch of clod-hopping country squires and you aren't a narrow-minded fanatic. Background doesn't matter a bugger when the future of Germany is in the balance, what?' He put his arm round Eis's shoulders and steered him into the house. 'My friends are itching to make your acquaintance,' he assured him, indicating several seated figures engaged in decorous conversation. 'Gentlemen, our Local Group Leader!'

Conversation ceased, but the gentlemen made no immediate move to rise. Horse-faced, bone-headed, well wined and dined, they continued to survey Eis negligently from the depths of their leather arm-chairs.

Eis recognized them all. Any child in the neighbourhood would have recognized them, but no one from the village had ever seen them all together in a bunch. Eis's heart beat higher at the sight. It was a great moment—the Party's chief representative welcomed into the bosom of East Prussia's venerable landed aristocracy!—and the credit was his alone. The first hands were being extended in his direction.

'You seem a pretty normal, human sort of type at first glance. Where did you serve?' This courteous inquiry from Herr von Knobelsdorf-Vierkirchen, formerly one of the Kaiser's aides-de-camp and now, as for almost eighteen years past, engaged on a volume of memoirs entitled *I Watched Him Reign*.

Beside von Knobelsdorf-Vierkirchen sat von Waldenburg-Danuschow, the man who had once volunteered to close down the 'hot air factory', or Reichstag, with a lieutenant and ten picked men. This project had since been completed by an ex-corporal, though with rather more than ten men.

Next came a von Kleist—one of the many. This particular bearer of the name had won fame as a horseman in his day, not least because of his dictum: 'Thigh-pressure is the secret of success, and not only with horses.'

'Keen on riding?' he demanded sternly.

'In a manner of speaking,' Eis replied, shaking the hand

W.   L

whose touch so many ladies of high degree were said to remember with a thrill of pleasure.

Eis's next introduction was to Count Kalkreith-Schlaven-
Schlarbach, the hero of Liége, La Croix and Lilienberg.
A general but never a field marshal, he had been robbed of
the recognition he so richly deserved by political intrigue—
in his view, one of the fundamental causes of Germany's
defeat in 1918.

Beside him, again, sat Baron Schlachtwitz, ill-favoured
scion of a great house. He had only attained the rank of lieutenant, being slightly deformed, but his family estate teemed
with some of the finest stags in Masuria.

A little apart from the rest stood a man who bore the undis-
tinguished name of Schulz. Having married the elderly
Countess Sanden and inherited her fortune, he had gone on
to achieve fame as a breeder of bloodstock.

'I want you to feel thoroughly at home with us,' Alarich
von der Brocken announced.

'But of course, Baron.' Eugen Eis proudly took his seat
in the midst of this exalted company. He, too, spread his legs
and tried to look bored.

A butler circulated among the guests with glasses of white
rum, amber brandy and ruby-red Burgundy—a concoction
known to initiates as a 'Stained Glass Window' and served
at a temperature of 57 degrees Centigrade precisely. The
Baron's special refinement was to add a dash of Polish vodka.

'Glad to welcome you to our little circle, Eis,' Alarich von
der Brocken said, raising his glass. 'Meritorious service creates
its own aristocracy. Old Schultz has been one of our number
for some time now.'

Schulz, long inured to condescension of this kind, smilingly
drank a toast to Eis, who downed the whole of his Stained
Glass Window at a single gulp. His beaker was promptly
refilled, the Baron's staff having been instructed to pay particular attention to the newcomer's requirements.

Eis beamed with delight as the landed gentry drew him
into conversation. The frustrated general treated him to a
special account of his strategic dispositions prior to the
battle of Lilienberg, evoking unabashed yawns from those who
had heard the story several dozen times before. Herr von
Kleist, the noted horseman, produced some intimate reminis-
cences of Princess Cilly-Agathe. Affectionate laughter greeted

these anecdotes, although they, too, were hoary with age. Finally, Herr Schulz buttonholed Eis and suggested the formation of an S.A. cavalry troop, for which he could, needless to say, supply any number of mounts.

Eis listened happily, asked the right questions and gave the right answers. He felt that he had been accepted, and it gave him a warm glow inside. The Baron drew him aside.

'Enjoying yourself?'

'Immensely.'

'I'm glad. To be honest, I've been anxious for a quiet chat with you. It's about the drainage scheme. As you know, I've got myself involved with that chap Alfons Materna. He talked me into it, and now I can't shake off the feeling that he's a slippery customer.'

'You're dead right,' Eis assured him. He had switched to a mixture of beer and champagne now, and was relishing every drop. 'Materna's as artful as a wagonload of monkeys.'

'My impression exactly! Instinct tells me that he makes a habit of pulling the wool over people's eyes, which is one of the reasons why I value our acquaintanceship. I trust your experience.'

'I've had plenty of that, especially where Materna's concerned.'

'Can I rely on you to notify me in advance if something blows up? May I assume that you won't hesitate to warn me if the man gets mixed up in anything shady?'

'You may, Baron. I give you my word.'

Hand clasped hand, eye met eye, glasses clinked. The Baron beamed and Eis felt that he had at last joined the ranks of the elect. The butler poured him a large café cognac. Joyfully, he gazed round at his new friends among the old aristocracy.

'Real community spirit,' he sighed. 'That's Germany for you!'

The Reverend Dr Bachus sat beside his dying parishioner, an elderly man who lived on the outskirts of Maulen. He had once belonged to the Community of Seekers after God, one of Masuria's numerous sects, but he now besought the blessing of the True Church before embarking on his last long journey.

'I'm a sinner, Vicar,' he whispered again and again.

'So are we all,' the parson would reply.

The old man lingered on, but Bachus persevered in prayer. At intervals he fell asleep from exhaustion and snored gently, but as soon as the figure on the bed began to speak again he woke with a start and leant forward to catch the muttered words.

Although the parson's fundamental reluctance to go home may have contributed to his perseverance, it did not detract from his endeavours. For half a day and an entire night, he remained beside the death-bed of an old and friendless man.

Before the old man closed his eyes for the last time, he cried out: 'The Church is dead! It died before me, but my God is the only God. I am going to Him!'

Bachus bowed his head and prayed. It was late in the afternoon when he shuffled slowly back to the church. His limbs were leaden with fatigue and his back drooped under an invisible burden. His smarting eyes saw no one, but he did notice that the church door was wide open. After a moment's hesitation, he entered.

Solemn but consoling silence enveloped him. The scent of burnt-out candles, mouldering beams and cool flagstones flowed over him. He felt a sudden and overpowering urge to kneel before the altar. First a prayer, he told himself numbly, then—God forgive him!—a bottle of wine, and, finally, sleep. A dreamless sleep prefaced by the feeling that he need never wake again.

'My God,' he murmured to himself, 'forsake me not!'

The dying rays of the sun slanted down through the tall stained glass windows, bathing the floor of the nave in brilliant pools of light—wine-red, silver-blue, amber-yellow. It was as if the church had been daubed with paint by the fingers of some gigantic hand.

Behind Bachus stood a child. It was Sabine, not that he saw her.

What he did see was a dark brown patch at the top of the chancel step, immediately facing the altar. Screwing up his eyes, he identified it as a heap of ordure—human ordure.

'The S.A.,' Sabine said. 'Bubi Kusche left his card behind.'

'This is the end,' the vicar said in a flat voice. Quietly, as though drawing on his last reserves of strength, he added: 'Even my time had to come.'

He did not go to the wine cellar. Instead, he sat down at

his desk and, weary as he was, composed the sermon which
he intended to deliver the following day. He started to tremble
as the impotence of his words dawned on him, but he continued to write steadily.

That Sunday, the Reverend Dr Bachus adopted the unusual
course of reading his sermon verbatim from a prepared draft.
This meant, to quote official sources, that the original text
existed 'in manuscript form'.

The opening words were simple and unemotional. 'All
men are God's creatures without exception,' Bachus read.
'The Lord holds us all in the palm of His hand. Mysterious
though His ways may appear—and what He suffers to be
done here on earth at the present time is beyond human
comprehension—they are never without a purpose. Some day,
whether in this world or the next, that purpose will be revealed.'

Bubi Kusche, dressed in civilian clothes but on duty, did
not know what to make of these remarks. He gazed up at
the pulpit uncertainly. Was the statement that all men are
God's creatures an insidious and subversive allusion to the
Jews, or was it a standard formula of the routine type?
Whatever it was, some members of the congregation began
to whisper excitedly.

'God is goodness,' Bachus went on. 'The Disciples were
enjoined to charity. Understanding and forgiveness are Christian commandments.'

Kusche turned to his escort of Brownshirts and gave a
derisive grin, but the citizens of Maulen relapsed into their
usual torpor. Jaws sagged and heads sank wearily on to
chests.

And then it came, issuing from the pulpit like a clap of
thunder: 'Yet there came a day when Our Lord drove the
merchants, money-changers, hypocrites, liars and charlatans
from the Temple, rebuking, punishing and chastising them.
And his wrath was exceeding great!'

The sleepers awoke with a start, and even the most obtuse
members of the congregation realized that Bachus had
changed into top gear. His sermon promised to be what it had
always been in the old days, a robust piece of Sunday entertainment.

'Forgiveness does not imply silence, nor does it mean

turning a blind eye. In certain cases, it entails penitence on the part of the sinner. A man who uses a church as a cess-pit is guilty of bestial behaviour. Indeed, he is lower than the beasts!

'God is never offended, not even when animals in human shape foul his place of worship, but the man who dares to do such a thing will pay the penalty for his sacrilege. The Lord will punish him and all his kind.

'He who does not know what man is or what he can become—how can he know the meaning of true patriotism, which is the awareness of belonging to a community of equals, for all are equal in the sight of God? No uniform can bestow special rights or privileges of any kind.'

Finally: 'It is written that we should render unto Caesar the things which are Caesar's, but it is also written: render unto God the things that are God's. Here lies the great divide. God rejects wanton hordes of uniformed savages, and so does the Church.'

'That's enough, Herr Bachus!'

Felix Kusche was standing in the aisle. Behind and on either side of him, his men had also risen to their feet in a solid phalanx sixteen strong.

Bachus glared down from the pulpit, white-faced but undeterred. 'You dare to interrupt my sermon?'

'You've preached enough high treason here for one day. I arrest you in the name of the Führer. Follow me at once!'

The congregation stirred excitedly. A fierce buzz of protest broke out, but it exceeded the bounds of discretion only for a few seconds and only in isolated cases. The few people who had stationed themselves at the pulpit steps melted away before the S.A.'s resolute advance.

Kusche reached the pulpit at the head of a wedge-shaped formation of Brownshirts, but before he could storm the steps Bachus came down of his own accord, pale, silent, and clearly resigned to his fate. The storm-troopers quickly surrounded him.

'Quick march!' ordered Kusche. He was trembling with satisfaction. Maulen would at last have to recognize him for what he was: power incarnate. With supreme self-assurance, he turned and faced the congregation.

'Here endeth the lesson!' he crowed. 'This shop is closed until further notice.'

8

The arrest of the vicar in mid-sermon quickly blossomed into a public sensation of the first magnitude. It caused a tremendous stir, but as the dust settled so the inhabitants of Maulen began to tell themselves—with relief, in many instances—that Kusche had been blessed with more luck than judgement.

His first stroke of luck was that the vicar had consented to accompany him without so much as a word of protest. Bachus had been locked up in the fire station under guard. Four storm-troopers were deemed sufficient to restrain him.

The second fortunate coincidence was that Eis happened to be temporarily out of the way. He was at Gross-Siegwalde, drinking a mixture of Burgundy and champagne known as Turk's Blood, recounting details of his bucolic love-life, and refusing to accept any telephone calls.

'Herr Eis wishes to remain undisturbed,' Alarich von der Brocken told his butler, but hurried to the telephone at once when informed in a whisper that Herr Materna wanted to speak to him personally. Materna's account of what had just happened in church seemed to rob him of speech for several seconds. Then he said: 'What do you think we ought to do?'

'Put a squib under Eis. He must get Bachus released at once—without a moment's delay!'

'Steady, my dear chap,' replied the Baron, who had recovered his composure by now and sounded brim-full of optimism. 'After all, what can happen to the gallant parson? It won't hurt him to cool his heels in the fire station for a couple of hours—in fact it'll make him even madder at Kusche, and that suits our book. An alliance with the Church, what? Besides, Eis may go sour on me if I start pestering him so soon.'

The moment Materna was dreading seemed to have arrived. Alarich von der Brocken had started to take a hand in Maulen's affairs without an adequate knowledge of the local rules. Once Bachus was securely under lock and key it would be exceedingly difficult to obtain his release.

Meanwhile the village postmistress had her hands full—so much so that she barely had time to eavesdrop. Constable Gäbler telephoned his superiors, Kusche conferred with an S.A. major, and Neuber spoke to the Regional Director of Organization.

The Regional Director of Organization went to the Regional Director proper, only to discover that he had already been informed of developments by the S.A. 'Things are really humming in Maulen!' was the Regional Director's cheerful verdict, and the Regional Director of Organization, who had been planning to pass on sundry misgivings planted in his mind by Neuber, hastily expressed approval instead.

Thus originated Kusche's third and most important stroke of luck. A telegram arrived. It was addressed to the Local Group Leader, but many of the villagers were already acquainted with its contents by the time it reached Eis's desk, where it lay unopened. As the postmistress joyfully revealed to her friends in the Party, the telegram read as follows:

'CONGRATULATIONS ON YOUR BOLD INITIATIVE STOP AM SENDING FAVOURABLE REPORT TO GAULEITER STOP CONTINUE RUTHLESS AND DETERMINED SUPPRESSION OF SUBVERSIVE ELEMENTS WHENEVER NECESSARY AND KEEP ME INFORMED STOP LONG LIVE THE FUHRER STOP SIGNED LEBERECHT REGIONAL DIRECTOR NATIONAL SOCIALIST PARTY'

Eugen Eis had only just returned from visiting Gross-Siegwalde when Bubi Kusche burst into his office and reported total victory.

'Pleased, Local Group Leader?'

Eis's limbs felt like lead, his forehead was streaming with sweat and a brass band seemed to be playing inside his skull. The Baron had got him so fuddled that he found it almost impossible to collect his thoughts.

'Congratulations,' he mumbled, slurring the word. 'Carry on like this and you could go far. Personally, I'm going to have a kip.'

The next telegram from Regional Headquarters requested Bachus's transfer to Allenstein gaol.

'Can I speak to you?' Sabine asked sweetly.

Her question was addressed to Felix Kusche, who was sitting in the Gasthaus surrounded by fellow-Brownshirts and a litter of schnapps- and beer-bottles. The sound of raucous and triumphant voices filled the bar.

'Shut up!' ordered Kusche. 'I can't hear what this little sparrow's on about.' He turned to Sabine. 'Well, what do you want?'

'I want to tell you something—in private.'

'Hark at her!' guffawed Ivar Mielke, a Brownshirt noted for his exquisite sense of humour. 'A bit young for that sort of thing, isn't she?'

There was a roar of boisterous male laughter, but Kusche said: 'Spit it out, girl. We don't have any secrets in our mob.'

'All right, if you say so,' Sabine replied. 'You're wanted outside. There's somebody waiting for you on the bench beside the school playground.'

Kusche's cronies grinned—they knew that well-worn trysting-place. 'Who is it?' they chorused. 'Come on, Sabine, tell us her name!'

'I can't. It isn't anybody's business but Bubi's.'

Kusche felt flattered. It was only natural, now that he occupied one of the leading posts in Maulen, that the women-folk should begin to vie for his favours. 'All right,' he said, 'it can't hurt to take a look.'

He left the Gasthaus and crossed the now deserted village square, heading for the spot in question. The bench stood against a thick hedge between two chestnut-trees, but it, too, was deserted.

'Anyone there?' he called in an undertone.

'No need to whisper,' a voice replied pleasantly. 'There's no one else around, so we've got the place to ourselves.'

A shadowy figure, bulky but of medium height, emerged from the shadow of the farther chestnut-tree. It stepped into the moonlight, and Kusche found himself face to face with Jacob Jablonski.

'What do you want?' he asked, as peremptorily as he could manage.

'For the moment, Bubi, a quiet chat.'

'Herr Kusche, if you don't mind!' the S.A. commander said haughtily. 'I don't bandy nicknames with the likes of you.'

'And I've never yet called a pig by its surname.'

'I've a good mind to call out the S.A.'

'You won't, though, Bubi. I'm very sensitive to noise. One peep out of you and I'll shove my fist down your throat.'

'You wouldn't dare assault a man in my position.'

'Wouldn't I? If I did, I'd be assaulting plain Bubi Kusche, not the commander of the S.A.'

Kusche quickly computed the odds. Flight was inadvisable, especially as Jablonski's dogs were bound to be lurking somewhere in the bushes. On the other hand, a trial of strength would be downright lunacy. The man was as strong as an ox—everyone in the village knew that. All in all, his safest bet was to behave with the dignity proper to his rank.

'All right, what was it you wanted to talk about?' Kusche had moderated his tone now. He sounded composed and a trifle condescending.

'About you and the vicar.'

'State your views. I'll take note of them.'

'Like hell you will! They really are my views, by the way, not Materna's—I'd like to make that quite clear. What they amount to is this: it's high time someone took you down a peg. What with your feeble-minded and swinish attempt to turn the church into a shit-house and your glorious victory over a poor, brave, defenceless parson, you've just about hit rock bottom, even for Maulen.'

'We can talk it over quietly tomorrow, if you insist,' Kusche said desperately.

'Why put off till tomorrow what we can do today?' Jablonski came a step nearer. 'What you need is a short sharp dose of your own medicine, and I'm going to see you get it.'

So saying, he grabbed Kusche and proceeded to work him over. The hors d'oeuvre consisted of two mighty slaps in the face, one with the palm and the other with the back of the hand.

Kusche struggled fiercely, but Jablonski clasped him to his coffer-like chest in a suffocating embrace and then smote him several times on the back of the neck with his open palm. Kusche went down on all fours, whereupon Jablonski belaboured his jutting posterior like a football. No damage was inflicted on any more vital portion of his anatomy.

'Right,' said Jablonski, who showed little sign of exertion. He heaved Kusche to his feet one-handed. 'Now get out of here, you bastard. Go tell your brownshirted pals all about your latest victory—they'll be lost in admiration.'

The inhabitants of Maulen were intrigued to note that Eugen Eis paid three visits to the regional capital within the space of a few days.

'The regional capital means Regional Party Headquarters,' they told each other. 'Where else would he have gone?'

One of Mayor Uschkurat's would-be successors, of whom there were now three, was heard to declare before numerous witnesses in the Gasthaus that Maulen was due for some sweeping changes—'And about time too!'

'This could be the turning-point,' Schlaguweit commented hopefully.

The remark was reported to Kusche, who greeted it with some misgiving. The knowledge that people were whispering behind his back made him feel nervous. The wildest rumours circulated. It was said that Eis was planning a complete re-organization of the Party's local branch, that the S.A. was to be remodelled, that all Party posts were to be re-allocated. Eis himself smiled silently and with devastating effect. All he would say was: 'Wait and see!'—which many construed as a threat.

The only thing that marred Eis's satisfaction was Brigitte's total lack of curiosity. Whenever he told her that he had to pay yet another visit to the regional capital, her only response was: 'Don't mind me. Go as often as you like.'

'If you really want to know,' he confided finally, 'I'm having a top-quality sporting outfit made by a first-class tailor. The Baron has invited me to go shooting with him. What do you think of that?'

'At least it'll give the hares something to laugh at before someone else shoots them.'

Eis shrugged his broad shoulders and stalked out. Nobody in the village understood him—but then, he had risen above his fellows. Alarich von der Brocken sought his company and men of birth and breeding treated him with respect. He was someone at last!

Sure enough, he returned from his fourth trip with a magnificent hunting outfit. 'Don't tell me he's throwing in his lot with that toffee-nosed crew!' said one S.A. man in the

Gasthaus, but another opined that it was merely camouflage and a third that 'good old Eugen' could twist anyone round his little finger.

Eis was the cynosure of every eye when the Baron's car came to collect him on the day of the shoot. He climbed in with panache, attired in hunting green. His elbows, knees and seat were adorned with doeskin and his legs encased in boots that shone like fresh varnish. A pair of binoculars dangled from his neck. Ernst Schlaguweit, who had tendered his services for the occasion, handed him two guns: a sort of blunderbuss the size of an elephant-gun and a double barrelled shot-gun for small game.

The Baron enthused over his appearance. 'Splendid, splendid!' he exclaimed. 'Just like a cutting from the latest issue of *Field and Forest*. You're going to lend tone to our little party, I can see.'

Eis gave a complacent smile. 'I try to model myself on you, Baron. Take that riding outfit of yours for a start . . .'

'You've got natural breeding, Eis. I'm sure you'll bag many a royal stag before you're through.'

It was a superb night, the night of the shoot. The air was as clear as crystal. Buildings emerged in sharp outline, stars shone, and trees looked as if they had been drawn on the sky with a fine brush.

The same night, Kusche knocked on Neuber's door. He was still feeling apprehensive. Stiff and cautious at first, the two men exchanged resounding platitudes on the subject of community life, individual responsibility, their current concern for the welfare of Maulen . . .

'Quite so,' said Neuber. 'For instance, the present relationship of the S.A. to the Party, in particular to the department for organization and propaganda, that is to say, to me . . .'

'It can be improved,' Kusche assured him. 'That's one of the main reasons why I'm here.'

Carefully disguising his satisfaction, Neuber proceeded to exploit the opportunity that had presented itself. 'Unfortunately, people only seem to pull together when things go wrong.'

'Wrong?' Kusche's tone was guileless in the extreme. 'Has something gone wrong? I didn't know.'

'No?' Neuber's tone was equally ingenuous. 'Weren't you beaten up by Jablonski the other night?'

Kusche exploded like a geyser. 'Who had the cheek to tell you that?'

'The whole village is talking about it,' Neuber said blandly.

'The bastards! How the hell can they say that? There wasn't anybody around, bugger it!'

Neuber permitted himself a condescending smile. Kusche was a stupid yapping mongrel, not an opponent to be taken seriously. It shouldn't be too difficult to deal with him now.

'I'm always in favour of worthwhile co-operation,' he said. 'However, there are one or two blemishes to be eliminated first. I'm thinking mainly of the S.A.'s prestige. It doesn't matter whether or not you really were beaten up. What matters is whether or not people believe the story. You know what the locals are.'

Kusche nodded bitterly. 'You mean we ought to do something positive—about Jablonski?'

Neuber folded his arms and looked smug. The seed had been sown. 'If you deal with Jablonski successfully, the S.A. will be masters of Maulen once more.'

'Leave it to me,' Kusche said darkly. 'We'll fix him so his own mother wouldn't know him—he's been asking for it.'

There followed a series of preparatory moves which led eventually to an incident that passed into village history as 'the Battle of Maulen Moor'. The S.A. set to work with grim determination under Kusche's leadership, but their opponents were not idle either.

True to form, Bubi Kusche favoured drastic action. 'I say we march straight up there, grab Jablonski, haul him back here, and beat the daylights out of him.'

Spontaneous assent! March up there and grab him, period —it was a plan worthy of the Brownshirt mentality.

Then a dissenting voice made itself heard. 'Did I hear you correctly?' inquired Ernst Schlaguweit. 'We simply go and fetch him from Materna's farm?'

'Of course. What's the matter, wetting your pants already?'

Schlaguweit, who had been carefully primed by Amadeus Neuber, knew precisely which line to take. 'It's just that I'm all for careful tactical planning. I think we ought to avoid Materna's home ground.'

'What do you mean, man? Are you suggesting we sen
Jablonski a polite invitation to come and call on us?'

General laughter greeted this sally, but Schlaguweit wa
undeterred. 'Jacob Jablonski could take on three men single
handed. So could Materna, probably, and he owns a lot o
firearms as well. Then there are the dogs. Last but not least
there are fifteen Poles almost on the doorstep. With the bes
will in the world, I don't think we could pull it off.'

The laughter died, and one or two Brownshirts knit their
brows in unaccustomed thought. Kusche chewed his lower lip
nervously.

'I'm against unnecessary bloodshed,' one of the S.A. men
said abruptly, stressing the word 'unnecessary'.

Eventually, even Kusche agreed that a certain measure of
caution was indicated. The S.A.'s council of war lasted
well into the night and disposed of nearly a dozen cases of
bottled beer. The final consensus was that Jablonski must be
apprehended in the middle of the village. The only question
was, how?

Another hour was devoted to this thorny problem. Then
Kusche found the solution. 'He will be invited—or summoned,
whichever—but not by the S.A. direct. We'll get a third party
to send for him—the mayor, say. That oughtn't to arouse his
suspicions.'

Schlaguweit claimed the floor again. 'He might come at
that, but he's bound to bring his dogs with him. They'll leave
their mark on a few of us, take it from me.'

The Brownshirts fell silent again. They were always ready
for a fight, but pointless self-sacrifice was another matter.

'What if there was an outbreak of rabies? Even a rabies
scare might do the trick.' This suggestion, which emanated
from Storm-trooper Mielke, virtually assured his promotion
to section-leader. Kusche fell on the idea eagerly.

'Good thinking, Mielke. The sooner we get started the
better.'

'We'll need Constable Gäbler's help.'

'That's no problem.' Kusche gazed round triumphantly.
'He'll play—it's just a question of handling him right.'

The plan, as reformulated, now went as follows: at the
proper time, a solid and respectable citizen would inform
Gäbler that he had every reason to suspect a case of rabies
in Maulen. The regulation procedure in such cases was, first,

to place the suspected dog in quarantine, and, secondly, to order that all other dogs should be either chained up or kept in a confined space. This would shorten the odds considerably and facilitate Jablonski's capture.

'I'll tip Gäbler the wink tomorrow morning,' Kusche announced. 'Once I've done that, we're in business.'

He overlooked one thing, however. Enlisting the policeman's aid meant alerting his daughter, and that was tantamount to warning Jablonski and Materna in advance.

'Operation Jablonski' had to be postponed for a few days because several members of the S.A., led by their commander, were urgently required elsewhere. The Reverend Dr Bachus was due to be tried at Allenstein.

The Brownshirts piled into a truck and roared off, singing obscene songs. On arrival at the court-house they formed up and marched resolutely into court, where they appropriated the front two rows of seats reserved for the public.

The only other representative from Maulen was Alfons Materna, who had turned up uninvited but was determined to be present. Apart from anything else, he was financing the parson's defence.

'Look at it this way,' he told Bachus. 'We've as much chance of winning as if we'd bought a lottery ticket. If we do win, it'll be a miracle.'

Dr Rogatzki, Bachus's defence counsel, was privately reputed to be one of the last decent men left in his profession. On the other hand, he could no longer afford to bring off any brilliant court-room coups without risking his own neck. 'Judges who preside over special tribunals aren't noted for their humane attitude,' he told Materna with a wry smile. 'This one operates like a well-oiled machine—you'll find that out soon enough.'

In fact, what with his smooth and rosy face, silky voice and benevolently watchful eyes, Judge Krüger made a rather favourable impression at first sight. The first words he uttered after declaring the court in session were:

'This seems to be a pretty cut-and-dried case. I don't think we need waste too much time on it.' He stared intently at the spectators' seats. 'My normal practice on such occasions is to exclude the public. However, I take it that the spectators are an organized body of men undergoing instruction in

constitutional procedure. This being so, I shall permit them
to remain on the understanding that their behaviour accords
with the dignity of this court.'

Then, and only then, did Krüger allow his gaze to rest
on the accused. The Reverend Dr Bachus was seated between
two policemen who flanked him like massive pillars. His head
drooped and he looked ill.

'Flabby old wind-bag,' Kusche remarked judicially to his
cronies. 'To think people used to look up to him!'

Having subjected Bachus to the usual preliminary questions, Krüger leafed casually through his papers. He seemed
sure of his ground—in fact he had probably agreed on the
sentence to be imposed with his superior, or so the public
prosecutor surmised.

'Prisoner at the bar,' Krüger said mildly, 'the court is in
possession of a draft sermon. Is it yours?'

'Yes.'

'Did you deliver that sermon?'

'Yes.'

Defence counsel had some difficulty in catching the judge's
eye, but he finally obtained permission to speak.

'I should like to draw the court's attention to two points:
first, my client has never denied his intention of delivering the
sermon as drafted; but, secondly, he was never able to complete his sermon. It follows from that . . .'

'Nothing follows from that, Dr Rogatzki—that is to say,
nothing of any import.' Krüger smiled apologetically. 'The fact
remains that this address was drafted and delivered, whether
wholly or in part is immaterial. It would be equally immaterial
were the accused to attempt to persuade us that he was unaware of the significance of his remarks.'

'I can produce witnesses who will testify that the tone
of the sermon was wholly innocuous.'

The public prosecutor leapt to his feet. 'The prosecution
can also produce witnesses—in large numbers, what is more.
They will testify the exact opposite.'

Judge Krüger amiably brushed this aside. 'What need for
witnesses when we already have material evidence of the
most incontestable kind? I call upon the public prosecutor
to read the document in question.'

The public prosecutor did so in a harsh monotone. From
time to time, and whenever he came to a particularly suspect

passage, his voice took on a stridently emphatic note. These punch-lines were prefaced by a hissing intake of breath.

Dr Rogatzki said doggedly: 'May it please the court . . .'

'That will not be necessary.' Judge Krüger's tone was gently sympathetic rather than aggressive. 'I can well imagine the sort of arguments you propose to submit—tone of voice, and so on—but what is the point? The sermon exists in writing, its authenticity is beyond dispute, and most if not all of it was actually delivered to a congregation of at least two hundred persons. This proves beyond a shadow of a doubt that an attempt was made to influence a large section of the public.'

'But not all who heard the sermon took it to mean what it might appear to mean here in court, under prevailing conditions.'

'Not all, certainly, but a large proportion. Nothing else could account for the spontaneous manner in which the accused was arrested.'

'Well said!' Kusche's enthusiastic bellow prompted his brownshirted comrades to other manifestations of approval, but Judge Krüger raised his hand.

'Come, come!' he chided paternally. He smiled into the sudden hush. 'Very well, Dr Rogatzki, let me put it this way: even if statements of this kind existed only in letter form, and even if that letter had never reached its destination, they would be quite sufficient to warrant a conviction.'

This seemed to sum up all that there was to be said. Defence counsel made a few more submissions, but he might have been whistling into the wind for all the effect he had. No more questions were addressed to Bachus, who sat there with his hands folded, grey-faced and unseeing.

The judge's concluding words were uttered in a gracious, sympathetic, almost slumbrous singsong. With rosy face tilted to one side and hands slightly raised as though in benediction, he said: 'Ten years' penal servitude.'

The day got off to a comparatively peaceful start. Storm-trooper Mielke, the Brownshirts' court jester, called on Constable Gäbler and asked to speak to him 'as a farmer and private citizen'. He made a special point of this.

Gäbler was standing in his back yard, stripped to the waist. The air was pleasantly warm, and, being a stickler for cleanliness, he enjoyed nothing better than sluicing himself under the pump. 'Well,' he inquired jocularly, 'want me to arrest someone for you?'

Mielke grinned back at him. 'It's only about a dog this time—my dog. I had to shoot him, I'm afraid.'

'Getting past it, was he?'

'No, he went for me—had his tail clamped between his legs and foam on his muzzle.'

The policeman dried himself hastily. 'Sounds like rabies.'

'I know,' Mielke said. 'That's why I came.'

'We'd better do something about it straight away.'

Gäbler pondered briefly on the proper course of action. First, he climbed into his uniform. Next, he viewed the body and ascertained that a quantity of foam still adhered to the animal's jaws. Finally, he rang the regional veterinary officer. The vet heard him out in silence. Then, with an audible yawn, he said.

'Do I suspect rabies? Well, yes, I suppose so. I'll probably drop by during the day—or tomorrow, maybe. Till then, quarantine all dogs and put up warning notices. I rely on you to do the right thing.'

His faith was justified. Having notified the mayor, Gäbler put up four notices, one facing each of the cardinal points. The inscription read:

> SUSPECTED RABIES!
> ALL DOGS TO BE KEPT CHAINED UP
> STRAYS WILL BE SHOT
>
> *By Order*

News of this development soon reached Materna's farm by way of Sabine, who was rewarded with a second hearty breakfast. Between mouthfuls, she recounted all she knew.

'It was Mielke's dog. The poor thing could hardly move anyway. I suppose it was time someone put it out of its misery.'

Jablonski looked worried. 'Rabies is no joke. I'd better lock our dogs up at once.'

'It's odd, though,' mused Materna. 'I know Mielke's dog. It really was pretty decrepit, and old dogs don't normally catch rabies. What's more, we've never had anything like that in the village—except among the human population, of course.'

'Mielke's funny,' said Sabine, licking a spoonful of honey. 'He was playing barbers with his dead dog—all by himself.'

Materna leant forward. 'Tell me more.'

'Well,' she said, 'just as I was on my way to school I heard a shot. I scooted there as fast as I could, keeping under cover, and there was Mielke with a shaving-brush in his hand, bending over the poor old thing. Just imagine, he was lathering its face.'

'You must be joking!' exclaimed Jablonski.

Sabine gazed up at him, wide-eyed. 'Don't you believe me, then?'

'Of course I do,' Jablonski said hastily.

'Why shouldn't he?' Materna chimed in. 'Fact is stranger than fiction, especially in Maulen.'

At that moment the parish factotum appeared, a wizened little man in a coarse blue serge suit. He was a disabled ex-serviceman and old age pensioner, but still gamely determined to do his bit.

'The mayor sends his compliments,' he announced. 'Herr Jablonski is requested to call on him between four and five o'clock this afternoon for the purpose of checking personnel lists.' Having received the customary schnapps from Materna, he shuffled off.

Materna grinned. 'A strange coincidence, wouldn't you say?'

Jablonski sent Sabine off to give the remains of her breakfast to the dogs, who barked joyously. 'I'm beginning to understand,' he said. 'Without my dogs I'm only half a man. So they're out for my blood, are they? All right, if they want a fight they can have it.'

'Don't leave me out, Jacob. This could be the chance we've been waiting for, but we must make the most of it.'

What followed was an exercise in small-scale strategy undertaken by all interested parties.

Prospects looked good. Eugen Eis was at the Baron's house, where amateurs of the noble art of venery were gathered for yet another drinking session.

At the same time, Alfons Materna was reported to have been strolling in the grounds with Elisabeth von der Brocken, the Baron's sister. He was wearing his Sunday best and she, so it was alleged, was holding his hand—in broad daylight, too.

Amadeus Neuber could, in case of need, have produced a witness to testify that he was working on his pageant, *Heroes under Hindenburg*, subtitle: *Masuria's Finest Hour*. Sabine Gäbler had chosen this day of all days, when the Muse's breath was hot in his ear, to call on him and ask to see his reproductions of Greek vase-paintings. He handed her the book almost abstractedly.

Constable Gäbler was three miles from Maulen in the farthest corner of his official domain. Ernst Schlaguweit had gone to earth with Fräulein Audehm, the midwife, who never said no to anything in trousers. The peasants were mostly at work in their fields and the other citizens kept out of the way. The S.A. had taken over the village.

Under the tried and tested leadership of Felix Kusche, the Brownshirts took up their positions in a semicircle round the mayor's office. One squad of reserves lurked in the Gasthaus, and another, destined for the main assault, in the fire station. Picked hand-to-hand fighters distributed themselves systematically round the village square, behind trees, in doorways, beside the church, on the war memorial steps and in the lee of the school-house.

The plan of battle was classic in its simplicity. It ran: 'When Jablonski goes into the mayor's office, close in. When he comes out, nab him and haul him into the fire-station in double quick time.'

Everything seemed to be going according to plan. Jablonski was extraordinarily punctual. Kusche clocked his arrival in the village at 1600 hours precisely.

'We've got him!' he said in a delighted whisper. The sight of Jablonski padding through the village without his dogs reassured Kusche and his companions in no small measure. Their morale rose by leaps and bounds.

Jablonski duly entered the mayor's office but did not linger more than a couple of seconds. Instead, he dashed through the building, opened a rear window, and jumped out. The sentry posted there recoiled in terror but raised the alarm vociferously as soon as Jablonski was at a safe distance.

Kusche reacted with great presence of mind. He emerged from his hiding-place behind the war memorial like a cork from a bottle, crying: 'After him, men!' and dashed across the square with exemplary speed. 'Tell the reserves to follow at once,' he instructed his runner. 'Forward, men—at the double!'

Jablonski vaulted two garden fences and trotted southwards across Dog's Meadow. He seemed to be tiring, despite his comparative lack of haste, because he halted from time to time and listened to the blundering footsteps of his pursuers.

'Cut him off!' Kusche yelled. 'Assault party left wheel, reserves to the right. Pincer movement, objective: birch-wood. Unarmed combat specialists, follow me!'

These commands bore witness to Kusche's qualities of leadership. They were, from a military aspect, clear, concise and logical. What Kusche did not know and was incapable of guessing was that Alfons Materna, for his part, had not only foreseen what would go on in Kusche's head but had laid his plans accordingly.

Jablonski trotted into the birch-wood, which formed part of the Materna estate, and the Brownshirts plunged in after him, scenting victory. Egged on by Kusche, they converged from three sides like hounds closing in for the kill.

'Now we've got him!' bellowed Kusche. 'Grab him and let's get out of here!'

His voice rang with triumph. Jablonski stood at bay in the middle of the wood, hemmed in by Brownshirts.

And then, from bushes and burrows all round the Brownshirts, there arose a score of stalwart figures supported by dogs and led by Alfons Materna, who was brandishing an oak cudgel.

'I'll teach you to trespass on my land!' Materna shouted, preparing to strike the first blow. 'Charge!'

Back in Maulen, everything looked normal. The villagers, who were determined not to get involved, went grimly about their daily work. Mayor Uschkurat washed his hands of the whole affair, and he was not alone. Armadeus Neuber, who had just completed Scene 13 of his historical drama, could not resist reading it aloud to Sabine:

'Hindenburg in conversation with Ludendorff, both bending over a map-table. Hindenburg: "He who carries the Fatherland in his heart cannot but proclaim the truth. His feats of arms will become milestones in human history!"'

Sabine listened patiently and then slunk off before Neuber could treat her to any more excerpts.

In the Baron's drawing-room, Eugen Eis was playing the dashing horseman. He demonstrated how he used to leap into the saddle while serving with a cavalry regiment in the First World War, the saddle being represented by the back of a massive arm-chair. Amid cries of encouragement from his new-found friends, Eis took a run and hurled himself through the air. He landed so infelicitously that he broke a leg.

Alfons Materna stood on the battlefield surrounded by his men. He took stock of the situation. The Brownshirts had been routed after suffering numerous casualties, among them Kusche, whom he had dealt with personally.

'They won't come back in a hurry,' Jablonski said, fondly patting his dogs, which had done yeoman service.

Materna surveyed his fellow-warriors. None of them was seriously hurt, though a few displayed grazes, cuts and bruises. Erich Wollnau had a decorative smudge of blood on his high-domed forehead and seemed touchingly proud of it.

'If I may offer one or two bits of advice from the legal point of view . . .' he began, but Materna cut him short.

'Thanks, I don't think that will be necessary.' He grinned. 'No German worthy of the name concedes defeat, and Kusche's boys are no exception. As long as we play the whole thing down and don't rub their noses in it, we can take it for granted that the Brownshirts will grit their teeth and say nothing. I reckon it'll be quite a while before they indulge in any more heroics.'

9

The Brownshirts sat around looking slightly dazed. Prominent among the wounded was Bubi Kusche, who lay on a stretcher in their midst. Large numbers of first-aid dressings had been applied by a storm-trooper with army medical corps experience, but Dr Gensfleisch had been summoned and was due at any moment.

'We won!' Kusche cried. 'More or less,' he added, in a failing voice.

The fact that total victory had eluded the S.A. was ascribed to a number of factors. For one thing, they had been dazzled by the sun. For another, their boots had slipped on the mossy ground. Then again, a ceremonial dirk wasn't much of a weapon—truncheons would have stood them in much better stead. Finally, there were the dogs. Love of animals had dissuaded them from tackling the enemy as ruthlessly as circumstances demanded.

'What about planning?' said Schlaguweit, who had ostensibly been prevented from taking part by the grave illness of a close relative. 'Our planning must have been pretty sketchy.'

Kusche groaned in agony and closed his eyes, but he was spared further humiliation by the arrival of the doctor.

'Well, well,' Gensfleisch said briskly. 'Looks as if you've had quite a party.' A brief examination of the wounded produced the following tally: one suspected fracture of the skull, two cases of concussion, three broken ribs, four severe contusions, five extensive abrasions, and a multitude of lesser injuries. Kusche was one of the five sufferers consigned to hospital.

'Is it serious?' asked Schlaguweit, whose interest in the latter case was of the liveliest.

'A matter of weeks,' replied the doctor, '—maybe longer.'

'Do your best for him,' Schlaguweit said exultantly.

Gensfleisch got the five men to hospital and then drove to Gross-Siegwalde in response to an urgent call from the Baron, who had reported 'a sort of riding accident'. He found Eugen Eis lying on a sofa surrounded by six noblemen and Schulz the horse-breeder. Eis made a valiant attempt to smile and pointed to his leg.

'We've already administered a mild anaesthetic,' said the Baron, indicating a row of bottles.

Dr Gensfleisch inspected the bottles closely, then picked out one containing raspberry spirit from the Black Forest. The Baron gave an approving nod and the doctor poured himself a glass. Having sipped it slowly, he turned his attention to his patient.

'Nothing serious,' he announced at length. 'Just a broken leg. A few weeks in plaster should do the trick.'

Eis sat up with a start. 'A few weeks!'

'Months, if you aren't sensible.'

'Do your best for him.' It was the Baron's turn to say this, and he said it with equal exultation. He put his arm round the doctor's shoulders with a flourish and drew him aside. 'Be thorough, my dear fellow. Take your time and don't rush things. Nothing is more important than a man's health.'

'What's been going on round here?' Gensfleisch asked in an undertone. 'Half the village seems to be in hospital.'

'The right half, I trust.'

'That would depend on your point of view,' the doctor said cautiously. 'Personally, I'm prepared to make any sacrifice in the interests of public health.'

The Baron guffawed. 'You seem to have got the right idea, Doctor. Give my regards to Herr Materna and put him in the picture about my esteemed guest's riding accident. He'll be interested.'

Dr Gensfleisch climbed into his diminutive rattletrap and drove up to the farm, where he was intercepted by Jablonski.

'I gather you may be in need of my services,' he said casually.

'Who gave you that idea?' Jablonski demanded with a suspicious frown. 'We don't need a doctor.'

'What about a friend, then?'

'Friends are at a premium these days.' Jablonski submitted Gensfleisch to a searching stare. 'All right, I'll tell Alfons you're here.'

Materna appeared at once. Having led the doctor into his den, he asked: 'What made you think someone here might be in need of medical attention?' He listened intently while Gensfleisch gave full particulars of his S.A. patients.

'It takes two to make a quarrel,' Gensfleisch concluded. 'Cracked skulls tend to come in pairs, if you know what I mean.'

'It depends how thick they are,' Materna replied, smiling to himself. 'Anyway, what's a punch-up in Masuria? It's a form of popular entertainment.'

'To you, maybe. Your lads made a real mess of those Brownshirts.'

'Have they talked?' Materna asked keenly.

'They'd never talk about a thing like that.'

Materna went to the cupboard and took out a bottle and two glasses. 'I'd like you to try my red-currant wine, Doctor. I can recommend it.' Gensfleisch nodded. 'So you've treated a number of injured men. A few of them were Brown-

shirts, but that may be pure coincidence. Minor injuries sustained while undergoing instruction in unarmed combat,
perhaps—that version might commend itself to certain people.'

'I'll be glad to spread it around, Herr Materna.'

'You're being very obliging, Doctor. Why, exactly?'

'Because I'm impressed by what you're doing here.'

Materna shot Gensfleisch a warning glance. 'I don't know
what you mean. I haven't done anything worth mentioning.'

'Don't you trust me?' Dr Gensfleisch rose uneasily to his
feet. His eyes looked tired and his hands fidgeted nervously.
'Of course you're entitled to distrust me—who wouldn't,
after all the bogus death certificates I've signed for the sake
of peace and quiet?'

'You have your problems, I realize that. Why should you
want to add to them?'

'Because I'd like the right to smile again, if only in private
—surely you understand? Besides, you may be in for some
damned difficult times. You've been trying to insure against
them, I know, but are you going about it the right way?'

'You have a suggestion, from the sound of it.'

'Yes, I think you ought to provide the S.A. with a sop of
some kind—something to soothe their injured pride. I propose
we invent a few casualties in your camp.'

'Very well,' Materna replied, sitting back in his arm-chair.
'If you really want to join in, go the whole hog. What about
one of your bogus death certificates?'

A look of surprise and incredulity flitted across the doctor's
face. Then he brought out his wallet and removed several
sheets of paper. 'I always carry the necessary forms around
with me, complete with official stamps. Well?'

'Put them away, Doctor. I wouldn't want you to regret
your offer later on.'

But Gensfleisch was already filling out one of the forms.
'What name shall I put?'

'Wollnowski—Erik Wollnowski.'

'Cause of death?'

'Anything you like.'

'All right. In view of the circumstances, let's make it
cerebral haemorrhage resulting from a multiple fracture
of the skull—that sounds plausible enough. It'll not only
save the Brownshirts' reputation but give them something
to worry about. After all, what are a few broken bones

compared with a nice juicy corpse?' Casually, he passed the form to Materna, who weighed it in his hands.

'This could cost you a lot more than your job, Doctor. You're risking your neck.'

'I've been doing that for years, not that anybody realized it, thank God. Anything else?'

'Would you like to know what I plan to do with this death certificate?'

'Not necessarily. Maybe later, when everything's settled. 'In that case, is there anything I can do for you, Doctor?'

'Yes, give me a bottle of your delicious red-currant wine —make it three bottles, if you like.'

'Only three for the time being,' Materna said. 'Just to make sure you come back again.'

When Amadeus Neuber heard that Local Group Leader Eugen Eis had been incapacitated until further notice by an accident sustained in the course of sporting activities, he bowed his head and gave thanks to a gracious Providence. Maulen was now at his beck and call.

His first official act on being appointed 'Deputy Senior Party Representative and Local Group Leader in charge of day to day business' was, tactfully enough, to visit his stricken leader. Eis lay on his own bed, heavily swathed in plaster, having fiercely declined to be moved to the district hospital.

'How on earth did it happen?' Neuber inquired. 'It looks pretty bad. You'll be laid up for some time, I imagine.'

'Balls!' growled Eis. 'I've got an iron constitution. You needn't stare at me like that, Neuber—there's plenty of life in me yet. What's more, I intend to keep my finger on the pulse, so don't get any wrong ideas.'

'If you're alluding to the leadership of the Local Group, I can set your mind at rest. Everything will carry on as usual, I guarantee.'

'It had better! I want to be kept informed of every last little detail.'

'But of course.' Neuber wished Eis a speedy recovery and departed in haste.

The first person to call on him at Party Headquarters was Ernst Schlaguweit, who stood smartly to attention in the doorway, raised his right arm in salute, and expressed his heartfelt congratulations. Confidentially, he added: 'So we've done it at last, eh?'

Neuber waved his minion into a chair. Anxious to create an impression of punctilious deference, the Brownshirt waited until he was addressed. He did not have to wait long.

'How are things with the S.A.?'

'The unit is ready for action again.'

'Casualties?'

'Five men unfit for duty, including Kusche.'

'Most regrettable, though I'm afraid it was largely his own fault. We must make the best of the situation.'

Schlaguweit guessed what was coming. He was placed in command of the S.A.—'Provisionally, for the time being. We shall have to get official confirmation of your appointment.'

'Thank you for putting your faith in me,' Schlaguweit's expressionless, sheep-like countenance flushed scarlet. 'I'll never forget this.'

'I sincerely hope not,' replied Neuber. 'What Maulen needs is the wholehearted and unqualified co-operation of all parties. Let's start right away. What's next on the books for the S.A.?'

'Whatever the Deputy Local Group Leader considers right.' Neuber's heart rejoiced. This answer exemplified the new spirit to which he aspired. He saw himself as the unifier of Maulen.

'Perhaps we ought to start by giving Materna a real going over,' Schlaguweit suggested.

Neuber concealed his astonishment at this proposal. 'Well,' he said indulgently, 'Materna is still at the top of our black list, of course, but he can wait. We have more important things on hand at the moment.'

'Such as?'

'My pageant, Schlaguweit—my pageant commemorating the twenty-fifth anniversary of the Battle of Tannenberg. There's nothing to stop us going ahead with it now.'

Sinister tidings reached the village from Materna's farm: there was a dead man up there, so the story ran—a victim of physical violence.

Just as Materna had foreseen, the S.A.'s reaction to the

news was one of simple pride. They regarded the fact that a fatal casualty had been inflicted on the foe as confirmation of their fighting ability.

Amadeus Neuber, who was the only person to recognize the inherent dangers of the situation, sent for Schlaguweit immediately and ordered the S.A. to take cover.

Schlaguweit looked mystified. 'But my men want to celebrate their victory—and my promotion, of course.'

'Nonsense!' snapped Neuber. 'Kindly make yourself scarce and keep quiet about the whole affair. Not a word, understand?'

'Yes, sir,' Schlaguweit replied with an effort. He kneaded his hands till the knuckles cracked.

Neuber eyed him with vague apprehension. Clearly, the man's mental processes were more complex than he had imagined. He assumed a kindlier tone.

'Wounds heal and bones mend, my dear fellow, but a dead body is a different kettle of fish altogether, especially in Materna's hands. We could be in for a nasty shock if we aren't careful.'

In fact, the first person to get a shock was the alleged corpse. To Wollnau's astonishment, Materna presented him with his own death certificate.

Meanwhile, in the barn, Jablonski and two of the Poles were knocking up a plain pinewood coffin. They painted it black, attached cast iron corner-pieces and handles, then filled it with stones and screwed the lid on.

Wollnau looked bewildered. 'What is this? Why have I been killed off?'

'Because at the moment you're more use to us dead than alive.' Wollnau shook his head, but Materna went on. 'Eis got on your track as soon as he started poking his nose into our business—you know that. The Baron managed to sidetrack him temporarily, but he has a lot of time on his hands now. Apart from that, nobody knows what schemes his deputy may dream up.'

It slowly dawned on Wollnau what was expected of him. 'My time in Germany is up, you mean?'

'I'm afraid so, Councillor. I can't guarantee your safety any longer—nor my own, as long as you're around.'

'When do I leave?'

'Tonight. I'll escort you to the frontier myself. It'll be a relief to know that you're in safe hands with my friends in Poland. Grienspan is looking forward to seeing you.'

Wollnau's face darkened. 'It's hard. I don't want to go, but I appreciate your reasons. Erich Wollnau's disappearance and Erik Wollnowski's death will put your official records straight. One minus one equals nought.'

'Exactly. What's more, the S.A. will owe me a human life. I don't know when I'll present the bill, but it could be worth something.'

'It's very strange, the whole affair,' mused Wollnau, who now seemed resigned to his fate. 'I don't suppose we'll meet again.'

'What makes you so sure? You don't imagine I'd let a valuable asset like you disappear just like that, do you? No, no, there's a nice little niche waiting for you. Our freight business can always use men of your ability.'

Wollnau brightened visibly. 'Thank you. That's what I call a real parting gift.'

'Don't thank me, I'm simply taking advantage of you. We won't find another legal adviser of your calibre so easily, nor such a talented organizer and linguist.'

Materna proceeded to initiate Wollnau into the mysteries of his freight business. It was, he told him, a sort of partnership, the two principal partners being Materna himself and Siegfried Grienspan. Working capital was pumped into the concern from both sides of the frontier. The border between East Prussia and Poland was supposed to be hermetically sealed, but Jablonski knew almost all the few loopholes that did exist. In addition, a senior customs inspector named Kortner happened to be an old war-time friend of Materna's. If there was one lesson the war had taught them, it was that human being were not cattle to be slaughtered on the altar of ambition or ideology. There were virtually no problems on the Polish side—Siegfried Grienspan saw to that.

'I can tell you one thing straight away, Alfons,' Wollnau said. 'You're going to have to increase your turnover.'

'Fair enough, Erich,' Materna replied. 'It won't be my fault if we don't. I'll deliver the goods, and one fine day I may come across myself.'

Next day, Alfons Materna appeared in the village accompanied by Jablonski, three Poles and two dogs. The procession was watched with no little concern by a wide variety of people. Its objective: the police station.

Constable Gäbler managed to escape in the nick of time by climbing over his garden wall and vanishing into the distance. This was a welcome and expected development. 'Daddy's in a blue funk,' Sabine had announced. 'He's scared stiff you're going to prefer charges because he won't know what to do.'

Materna, whose position was awkward in the extreme, did not feel entirely happy in his own mind. If he did not report Wollnowski's 'death' it might lead to unwelcome speculation; if he did, the 'corpse' would have to be produced.

Delighted by Gäbler's evasion of his responsibilities but careful not to show it, he preserved his grimly determined mien and strode into the mayor's office.

Uschkurat also made an attempt to flee, but Jablonski caught him and pinned him firmly behind his desk. The mayor sat there, trying to convey total insignificance.

'I don't know what you want, Materna, and I don't want to know.'

'One of my men was killed yesterday.'

'I had nothing to do with it—nothing whatsoever.'

'Did you or did you not lure Jablonski into the village?'

'Why on earth should I do that? I've got enough worries as it is. I can't take it any more—I'm resigning here and now.' Once a sturdy peasant—robust and imperturbable, with fists like chunks of granite—Uschkurat had come to the end of his tether. He was as softy as putty.

'I'm going to drop this killing into your lap whether you like it or not, Uschkurat. You can retire after that, for all I care. You ought to have done so years ago, incidentally. That farm of yours has gone to rack and ruin.'

Materna proceeded to off-load, well aware that he was doing so in the wrong—and, thus, the right—quarter. The mayor's office was the best possible place to dump his garbage if he wanted to raise a general stink.

'Someone helped to lure Jablonski into a trap—with your help, Uschkurat. He managed to get away by the skin of his teeth. He was then pursued on to my land. My workmen, who happened to be on the spot, were attacked. While they were defending themselves, one of them was killed. I hereby prefer charges against the men concerned.'

'But not here—please not here!' Uschkurat pleaded. 'Constable Gäbler is responsible for this sort of thing.'

'Responsible but unobtainable, which leaves you holding the baby—so do something, Uschkurat.'

'But what, in the name of God?'

'You ought to know,' Materna said kindly, and departed, accompanied by Jacob Jablonski, three Poles, and two dogs.

Alarich von der Brocken was the next to spread alarm and despondency. He rode into the village square on Adolf II, reined in beside the war memorial, and shouted for Constable Gäbler.

Sabine obligingly informed him that her Daddy was out.

'Bravo!' roared the Baron, audible within a wide radius. 'Dead bodies all over the place, and not a policeman in sight. I call that rich!'

He swung his charger round and trotted straight to Eis's house, where he dismounted and announced his intention of visiting the sick.

'And how are you, my dear fellow?' he boomed.

'Mustn't grumble,' Eis replied laconically, giving an imitation of a wounded hero.

'I'm sure you need all the rest you can get, but I owe it to you to tell you the truth. To be blunt, this village is going to the dogs.'

'I beg your pardon?'

'In your absence, I mean. You only have to be laid up for twenty-four hours and all hell breaks loose.'

'If you're talking about the death up at Materna's, Baron, what of it? People are always popping off.'

'Yes, my dear chap, but the dead man was employed on the drainage scheme, in which I have an interest. Ergo, he's one of my men—or was.'

Eis, who felt immensely indebted to the Baron for broadening his social horizons, looked dismayed. 'That changes the whole picture, of course,' he said hastily. 'Leave it to me. I'll teach those idiots to make a muck of things as soon as my back's turned.'

Alarich von der Brocken was dismayed. He had been expecting excuses and evasions. This lightning readiness to act was not at all what Alfons Materna had intended when he turned him loose on Maulen's Party boss with instructions to place a couple of squibs under his well upholstered behind.

'Please don't make a fuss,' he entreated. 'It isn't worth getting hot and bothered about.'

'All the same, Baron, now that we're fellow-sportsmen, in a manner of speaking . . .'

'Exactly, my dear Eis. That's precisely why we shouldn't allow a little thing like this to cloud our friendship. Why not avoid unnecessary fuss and settle the matter between ourselves?'

'I call that very understanding of you, Baron, I must say.'

Alarich von der Brocken breathed a sigh of relief. The risk of a tornado had receded, but Materna would no doubt welcome a local storm as long as its effects were confined to the village alone.

'That's agreed, then. You'll simply talk a bit of sense into those over-eager subordinates of yours and leave it at that. Nothing like keeping your team on a tight rein, what?'

Eis wasted no time. Not only was he indebted to the Baron, but it paid to keep his minions on their toes. He summoned Neuber, Schlaguweit and Uschkurat to his bedside without delay.

Alarich von der Brocken withdrew to a neighbouring room, where he was entertained with the utmost courtesy and attention by Brigitte. He studied her with an appreciative eye, then said gallantly: 'There's something extremely vital and spirited about the way you move, dear lady—I find it quite fascinating to watch you.'

Brigitte concealed how flattered she felt to receive such compliments from an acknowledged expert in his field. 'I'm a married woman, Baron,' she said in mock reproof. 'Also, my father is a simple farmer.'

'Marriage has never prevented me from admiring a member of the fair sex. As for your father, I like him. We get on exceedingly well together. My sister is delighted.'

'My father will be happy to hear that.'

'He knows it already. Elisabeth is quite another person when he's with her. She adapts herself to him. Why shouldn't we do the same?'

'We might discuss it,' Brigitte said warily, '—next time a favourable opportunity comes along.'

The word 'opportunity' was uttered almost simultaneously in the room next door. 'Just because I'm flat on my back,' Eis said, 'that's no reason for anyone to regard it as an opportunity to play fast and loose.'

'I would never do such a thing,' Neuber assured him promptly. 'I'm concentrating on my pageant. You've no objection to that, I take it?'

'Not as long as everything else ticks over smoothly. This dead Pole business is a real cock-up. He was the Baron's man as well as Materna's, and that alters things considerably. Didn't anyone have the sense to realize that?'

Nobody had, so Schlaguweit stepped into the breach. 'I can tell you this much: it would never have happened if I'd been in command. I warned Kusche more than once.'

'On my advice,' Neuber put in, and Uschkurat said hurriedly: 'I didn't like the plan either. It felt wrong, somehow.'

'But it happened,' snapped Eis. 'That's why I'm ordering you to get the whole thing sorted out in double quick time.'

'Gäbler won't make any trouble,' Schlaguweit reported. 'I've already softened him up.'

'You can have my job on a plate,' said Uschkurat. 'I'm prepared to take all the blame—anything, just so long as I can enjoy a bit of peace and quiet at last.'

'I know the perfect way of lowering the temperature,' Neuber said confidently, '—my pageant. Public festivities give people something else to think about. It can't fail.'

'Do what you bloody well like,' Eis growled, not displeased with the result of his pep-talk. 'I want everything to run smoothly, that's the main thing.'

This virtually eliminated Materna's problems, even if it did not solve the Party's. Erik Wollnowski's funeral could take place without fear of incident.

It was a funeral without parallel in the annals of Maulen. No bell tolled, no guard of honour turned out, and the new vicar—a skinny substitute priest with a reedy voice and big feet—did not bother to exert himself.

No festive atmosphere prevailed in the village, either, since there were to be no free drinks in the Gasthaus afterwards. The villagers shunned the proceedings, partly because the S.A. had thrown an unobtrusive cordon round the churchyard.

W.   M

The few inquisitive spectators who did peer round their curtains at the funeral procession saw, first, the cart bearing the coffin. It was drawn by a team of four Materna-bred horses—noble beasts with superb muscles rippling beneath satiny skin—and expertly driven by Jacob Jablonski. Behind the coffin walked Alfons Materna, and behind him, with ponderous tread, came fourteen hulking Poles.

The churchyard was deserted, the trees looked lifeless, and even the birds seemed to be mute.

'Everything's going according to plan,' muttered Jablonski.

'Don't tempt Providence,' Materna said cautiously, '—not while that coffin's still above ground.'

Willing hands lowered the coffin into the grave, and all that could be seen before long was a neat mound of earth. Three wreaths were deposited on the mound, one from Materna and Jablonski, one from the Poles, and a third from the Baron. The latter bore the apt inscription: *Death, where is thy sting?*

'Now the headstone,' said Materna. 'Quickly! The sooner we get out of here the better.'

The stone, designed, ordered and paid for by Materna himself, was lying ready near the grave. The crating and hessian wrapper were removed to reveal a slab of black-veined marble. On it were the words:

> *Here lies*
> *Erik Wollnowski,*
> *Civil Servant Grade One,*
> *who sought his country*
> *and failed to find it.*

Amadeus Neuber continued to work on his pageant, devoutly and with mounting optimism.

'I hope and trust that everyone will join in,' he proclaimed. 'This pageant will be a test of our spiritual unity. I call upon all constructive and progressive sections of the community to participate!'

Messages poured in from all quarters to the effect that it would be an honour to take part. No Party organization wanted to be left out, and Neuber revelled in the heady awareness that Maulen was marching in step behind him.

'This is going to be an evening to remember,' he promised.

'I still have a few scenes to polish off, but I shall have them ready in time, never fear.'

At this stage, he summoned his closest associates for a preliminary reading, to be followed by a discussion of casting possibilities. He began by quoting typical passages from three scenes, e.g.:

Scene One

'Headquarters at Tannenberg, an austere but dignified room, sparsely furnished. Hindenburg in conversation with Ludendorff.

Ludendorff: The Russians have the advantage of us.

Hindenburg: Numerically, perhaps, but our morale is unshakeable!

Scene Two

Russian Headquarters, a gorgeous mansion. Exotic and decadent atmosphere. Samsonov in conversation with Rennenkampf.

Samsonov: Who is this fellow Hindenburg? Never heard of him.

Rennenkampf: We shall destroy him, just as we destroy everything in our path, like a steam-roller. Destroy, exterminate and raze to the ground— that is our policy.

Scene Three

German soldiers billeted in a Masurian village. The prevailing atmosphere is one of simple and unaffected comradeship.

First Soldier: We drove them into the marshes and shot them down in droves. The survivors scampered off like rabbits.

Second Soldier: And we owe it all to good old Hindenburg.

First Soldier: Yes, he's a real German. When the country's existence is at stake, he shows no mercy.'

'Hot stuff!' Schlaguweit exclaimed, clapping his hands. 'Makes you realize you're on hallowed ground.'

The others applauded with equal enthusiasm. Neuber gave a modest bow.

'But how does it end?' Schlaguweit went on. 'Don't keep us in suspense, Deputy Local Group Leader.'

'Well,' Neuber replied after a moment's hesitation, 'if you

insist, I'll give you one more example from the final scene.'
He cleared his throat and resumed:

'Hindenburg Hill, radiant with the light of dawn. Hindenburg
discovered alone. Ludendorff enters and hurries towards him.
Ludendorff: Victory is ours at last!
Hindenburg: I never doubted it for a moment. I had implicit
faith in my gallant men.
Ludendorff: You are the saviour of Germany, Field Marshal.
Hindenburg: I only did my duty, though I did it with a distant
but still more glorious prospect in view. Some day, someone
will be sent to complete my work. If Providence smiles upon
me, it will be I who entrust the Fatherland into the devoted
hands of that man, whose coming we all yearn for so deeply.'

There was universal astonishment at these prophetic, if
apocryphal, words. To think that Hindenburg had actually
foreseen the coming of Hitler! Stirred by the thought
that they were indeed living in wondrous times, Neuber's
audience broke into another round of fervent applause.

'I welcome this demonstration of unanimity,' Neuber
said happily and went on to enlist the services of all present.
Everyone was assigned some task or other, from the issuing
of tickets to the unfurling of patriotic banners.

'And now, my friends, we come to the question of who is
to take part in the pageant itself.'

'The S.A. are at your disposal to a man,' Schlaguweit
announced.

'Their services will undoubtedly be required,' Neuber
replied smoothly.

He unfolded a carefully prepared cast list. According to
this, the chief character—Field Marshal Hindenburg—was to
be portrayed by none other than Ernst Schlaguweit, while
S.A. Section-Leader Mielke was to play General Ludendorff.
German women engaged in nursing and tending the troops
were to be represented by members of the National Socialist
Women's League and German Girls' League. As for the
troops themselves, who better entitled to personify them than
the gallant S.A.? Members of the Hitler Youth were also
privileged to take part, but only as soldiers of subordinate
rank.

'What about the Russians?' someone inquired. 'Who's going to play them?'

'I can hardly expect my lads to take on a job like that,' interposed the leader of the Hitler Youth.

Naschinski, an aspirant to the office of mayor, diplomatically suggested that the Russians might be portrayed by the few people in Maulen who did not belong to the Party or its ancillary organizations.

'How about Materna's Poles?' suggested Mielke. As a noted humorist, he could afford to make such a quip. However, Neuber hastily brushed the suggestion aside.

'The Russian soldiers won't present any difficulty. There is one problem though—the enemy generals. One can't deny that they were men of a certain intelligence, and they'll have to be played as such.'

Neuber glanced inquiringly at Uschkurat, but Uschkurat stubbornly refused to volunteer.

'Perhaps Peter Bachus and Konrad Klinger would fill the bill,' he suggested boldly. 'They're on holiday at the moment, aren't they?'

After a moment's hesitation, Neuber fell in with the idea. 'They're a bit young, but wigs, beards and make-up ought to put that right. See if they'll do it, Uschkurat.'

Uschkurat went in search of the boys and found them in their favourite spot. They were perched on the churchyard wall with their legs dangling.

Having communicated 'the festival committee's proposal, expressly approved by the Deputy Local Group Leader', he asked them flatly: 'Well, will you or won't you?'

Peter and Konrad eyed each other for a moment. Then Konrad said: 'If it means so much to the committee, how can we possibly refuse?'

It was summer 1939. Developments in Germany at large provided endless opportunities for grander festivals, longer speeches and more impressive demonstrations, but Maulen concentrated whole-heartedly on the preparations for its own day of public rejoicing. The first rehearsals were held, posters were designed, and the state radio station at Königsberg signified its intention of broadcasting excerpts from the festivities.

Bubi Kusche continued to pine away in hospital and Eugen Eis was still confined to bed. The Baron visited Eis from time to time and the leader of the German Girls' League called on him once at his request, but all she did was spoil the atmosphere by rhapsodizing about Neuber and his patriotic effusions.

Konrad Klinger and Peter Bachus gave Materna a hilarious account of their roles as Russian generals.

'Do you know your parts?' he asked, smiling.

'Everything's going like clockwork at the moment, but you never know what'll happen on the day. We may be so overwhelmed by the solemnity of the occasion that we wreck the whole performance.'

'Build up your strength,' Materna advised. 'Hannelore's giving us duck and red cabbage for dinner.'

The sun shone down, day after day, out of a sky like a gleaming azure dome, and the earth radiated warmth and fragrance. Far from any arterial road, miles from the nearest railway station and tucked away in the farthest corner of the Third Reich, Maulen thrilled with expectancy.

Far away on the edge of the marsh, the Poles sang:

> Tread the grass
> And it rears its head.
> Snap a twig
> And the tree still thrives.
> But break a man's heart
> And he will die.

Schlaguweit neglected hearth and home and devoted himself entirely to his theatrical responsibilities. He had even begun to walk and talk in what he fondly imagined to be a Hindenburg-like fashion.

'There's a new batch of girl pioneers in the next village,' Mielke told him. 'I'm going to give them the once-over. Coming?'

'I've got more important things on my mind,' Schlaguweit replied sternly, and stalked off.

Alarich von der Brocken invited Brigitte Eis to go for a walk. They strolled in the direction of Maulen Moor, ostensibly to inspect the progress of the drainage scheme.

'You warm my heart,' he confided.

'Only your heart?'

'I'm getting old. You may be interested to know that I'm thinking of settling down at last.'

'With whom?'

'With someone who gives satisfaction in every respect, from brewing coffee to warming my bed at night—not to mention my heart.'

Brigitte smiled and shook her head. 'I'm still married.'

'Never mind,' the Baron said encouragingly, 'there's no reason why that should be a permanent state of affairs.'

Meanwhile, Alfons Materna was at Gross-Siegwalde, taking yet another stroll through the grounds with Elizabeth. The gravel crunched beneath their feet, drowning their heartbeats.

'I ought to go,' he said.

'But it's such a lovely evening, Alfons.'

He started at the use of his Christian name. Wollnau had been the last person to claim this rare privilege just before his departure.

'From the sound of it,' he said, almost brusquely, 'even you aren't immune to the magic of a summer night.'

'It isn't just tonight, Alfons—I've been like this for weeks, and all because of you.'

'Then I suggest we go and stand in front of a mirror, the two of us.'

'Don't bother, I'm short-sighted. I rely on instinct.'

'Things tend to look different in the cold light of day, my dear.'

'But tomorrow's a long time off.'

Tomorrow was several hours away, hours during which something totally unexpected occurred: the Masurian night spawned a monster.

Ernst Schlaguweit was Maulen-born. His father, whom he had lost at an early age, was killed while felling a tree on the family smallholding. The only recorded comment of young Ernst, who had witnessed the accident, was: 'Why didn't he watch out?'

Having inherited his farm early in life, Schlaguweit took scant interest in its management, which he left to his mother and two sisters. His interests lay elsewhere, and he pursued them, as events showed, with considerable success. He regarded his career in the S.A. as a just dispensation of Providence.

Schlaguweit's impassive face betrayed little of the potent and painfully repressed emotions that stirred within him. His hands often twitched under the stress of excitement and there were moments when he found it impossible to speak. 'You're German to the marrow,' Neuber had once told him. 'Strong feelings combined with a stiff upper lip. I congratulate you on your self-discipline.'

Schlaguweit was, as he himself perceived with great clarity, a quite exceptional person. He secretly despised Neuber's literary pretensions and made little attempt to hide his abhorrence of his fellow-Brownshirts' love of boozing, brawling and whoring—they were all equally devoid of true strength and greatness. He also loathed women, just as he occasionally loathed himself for being consumed with desire for them.

'Three of those girl pioneers are still there for the asking,' Mielke reported. 'One of them's a prize specimen with real Germanic buttocks.' The S.A.'s professional comedian chortled with glee. You can have her if you like.'

'Not interested,' Schlaguweit replied. As a face-saver, he added: 'Got my own source of supply, thanks.'

Restlessly, he wandered through the darkened village. Passing the Gasthaus, he halted in the village square and stood there lost in thought for some time. Then he took a route which Eugen Eis had unwittingly shown him in the days when he was still a humble storm-trooper on look-out duty. He had several times seen his erstwhile commander disappear into the Widow Eichler's house, there to remain for a considerable period.

'Why not?' Schlaguweit asked himself. 'If a man has to, now and then, there's no reason why he shouldn't be choosy. Perhaps it takes the best to attract the best.'

The more he thought about it, the more convinced he became. Margarete Eichler was only a woman, but a woman of standing. Taking her to bed would, in a sense, be like coupling power with property—a positively organic process.

He knocked discreetly, and the door opened to reveal the object of his desires: Margarete Eichler, clad in a voluminous nightdress and carrying a candle. He interpreted her smile as a sign of encouragement.

'Dear lady,' he said gallantly, 'I was just passing, and I felt I simply had to pay my respects.'

'At this hour?' she replied, faintly surprised but not displeased. Eugen Eis's confinement to bed had recently compelled her to forgo his agreeable and beneficent attention. She missed his robust and purposeful presence—in short, his masculinity—and Schlaguweit seemed to be bent on pleasing her. It would be uncharitable to turn him away.

'I know it's late, dear lady, but not too late to lay my devotion at your feet.' This sentence was borrowed from an ultra-German historical romance in which a masterful aristocrat had wooed a high-born lady with notable success.

Flattered by so much gallantry, Margarete invited Schlaguweit to come in. The good man might be a trifle uncouth as yet, but he was a trier. She did not feel averse to accepting him as one of her pupils, especially as she was alone in the house. Expectantly, she sank on to the sofa.

Schlaguweit hurled himself at her with the pent-up force of water cascading from a broken dam. She did not even have a chance to cry out.

Her body was not discovered until next day.

While Constable Gäbler was still staring helplessly round the room, trying to decide what had happened and what ought to happen next, tidings of Margarete Eichler's mysterious death spread through the village like wildfire.

Eis turned pale on hearing the news, then collected his scattered wits and summoned Gäbler to his bedside forthwith. Gäbler obeyed the call with relief and alacrity. He carefully locked the body inside the house, posted the parish factotum outside, and hurried off to see Eis.

'Have you made sure nobody can get in?' was Eis's first question. 'What about money, valuables and papers—are they safely locked away?'

'I didn't touch anything,' Gäbler assured him, slightly mystified by his unexpected reaction.

'I'm holding you responsible for seeing that nothing is removed.'

The policeman's perplexity increased. 'I'm sorry, I don't quite see what you're driving at.'

Realizing that he had made a mistake, Eis moderated his tone considerably. 'I'm chained to this damned bed, Gäbler

—that's why I'm relying on your help. The poor woman had nobody, you see—just her daughter, and she's my wife. I shall have to take on the job of settling her affairs.'

'I quite see that, but investigations into the cause of death will have to take priority.'

'How do you mean, investigations? What is there to investigate?'

Gäbler reported that the body was lying, scantily clad in the middle of the living-room. The back of the skull was deeply depressed, possibly as a result of contact with the arm of the sofa. 'Her clothing was torn and disarranged,' he concluded.

Eis took some minutes to dispel Gäbler's suspicions, enlisting the aid of a bottle from his bedside table. 'Perhaps she was taken ill—a choking fit or something of that kind. She swayed, grabbed at thin air, slipped, and hit her head on the arm of the sofa. . . .'

'To hear you tell it, you might almost have been there,' Gäbler said admiringly. 'Yes, I suppose it could have happened like that.'

Eugen pressed home his attack. No unnecessary fuss —Maulen was a peace-loving village—incursions by outside authorities were, at best, a disruptive influence. 'Bear this in mind, too: Frau Eichler was universally admired. Everybody in Maulen regarded her as a symbol of all that is finest in German womanhood, and not only in her capacity as president of the Women's League. It would be unthinkable to associate her with a crime of violence.'

'Quite, quite,' Gäbler agreed. 'However, I shall have to ask for a medical report.'

'Of course, but Doctor Gensfleisch is a co-operative man, as we know from past experience. I'll have a word with him. After all, he's my doctor.'

Gensfleisch did not view the body until he had spoken to Alfons Materna. His examination was lengthy, exhaustive, and carried out in complete silence. Constable Gäbler watched him mutely, growing more and more uneasy as the minutes dragged by.

At last, the doctor asked for soap and towel and washed his hands in a leisurely manner. Then he said: 'What would your reaction be if I told you this was a sex-crime—rape and murder, say?'

'God forbid!' replied Gäbler. 'Anything but that!'

'So you'd prefer death by misadventure, eh?' Gensfleisch finished drying his hands. If Materna wanted a delay of twenty-four hours he should have it. 'That does seem to be the likelier alternative, as a matter of fact. However, there are certain unusual features about this case. I shall have to carry out a further examination in greater detail. Until then, these premises are to be kept locked.'

Inconclusive though this was, Gäbler felt entitled to breathe a sigh of relief. 'The doctor won't commit himself,' he told Eis. 'He wants to show how conscientious he is first, but it'll all boil down to death by misadventure in the end, you mark my words.'

That night, Materna crossed into Poland, where he conferred with Grienspan and Wollnau in a hut near the frontier. He was back in Masuria by dawn, bearing two copies of a legal document drafted by Wollnau. This document, a power of attorney, was designed to turn Maulen upside down.

Materna sent a message to Brigitte asking her to call at the farm that morning. A similar summons went to the village notary.

'Brigitte,' he said without preamble, 'the time has come for you to make a decision. Whom do you trust more, Eugen or me?'

Brigitte gave a wry smile. 'Why ask?'

'Then sign this.'

With Brigitte's signature safely appended and witnessed, the legal position was as follows: Johannes Eichler, that tragic victim of circumstances, had left his entire estate to his widow, since deceased under equally tragic circumstances. Being comparatively young, she had not made a will. Since Margarete's sister in Lötzen was also dead, her sole heir was her child by her first marriage, Brigitte Eis, née Materna. Under the terms of the present document, duly signed and witnessed, Brigitte surrendered all her rights in favour of her father, Alfons Materna. This meant, in effect, that he wielded control over eighty per cent of the village real estate, together with the mill, four leases, and eleven promissory notes.

Materna's eyes gleamed with anticipation. 'Now,' he said, 'let's see what they all make of that.'

The first person to react to the changed situation was Amadeus

Neuber, who conveyed his wish for a 'frank and open' discussion with Materna. The bearer of this message was Ernst
Schlaguweit, whose courteous and friendly manner did not
altogether offset his haggard and distraught appearance.

'Shall I boot him up the arse?' Jablonski asked eagerly.

'All in good time,' Materna replied. 'If Neuber wants to
speak to me he can come up here. I'll be in the pigsty for
the next couple of hours.'

Jablonski grinned. 'Very appropriate.'

Neuber turned up shortly afterwards. His smile was cordial
and he even extended his hand instead of raising it in the
Hitler salute.

'Can't shake hands, I'm afraid,' Materna told him. 'I've
just been feeling a pregnant sow—she must have at least
a dozen piglets up there, I reckon.'

Neuber was undeterred. 'I've always admired your skill
as a breeder.'

The two men were separated by a chest-high partition,
stoutly built and encrusted with dung which emitted a persistent bitter-sweet stench. Neuber held his breath as far as
possible, but his cordiality was unimpaired.

'I'm here on what might be described as a personal mission
—a very personal mission.'

'Why don't you come inside the sty? I've got another two
sows to check.'

Taking his courage in both hands, Neuber followed Materna
inside. One of the sows greeted him with a joyous grunt,
slobbered over his shoes and tried to devour his trousers.

'Herr Materna,' he said, cautiously pushing the importunate
animal away, 'it's quite conceivable that we may, in a certain
sense, have been adversaries until now—in the most chivalrous way, of course. However, I realized that you're not a
man to be ridden over rough-shod.'

'So you want to come to terms?'

'Yes, I should like to conclude a sort of pact based on
mutual understanding. After all, we do have a number of
aims in common.'

'One of them being the elimination of Eugen Eis?'

Neuber looked round nervously, but there was nothing to
be seen except fat and gleaming pigs, clean troughs and
thick wooden partitions. They were quite alone.

'I wouldn't put it quite as crudely as that,' he replied. 'I'm more concerned with creating a new and better spirit in this place.'

Materna leant casually against the whitewashed wall. 'This new spirit of yours—does it entail studying Greek vase-painting in the company of minors?'

Neuber's sudden pallor vied with the whitewash on the wall. 'What are you hinting at?' he stammered.

'It's more than a hint,' drawled Materna.

'It's a filthy lie!' Neuber said fiercely. 'Someone has been slandering me.'

'I don't know about that. Sabine Gäbler would be prepared to testify to some rather peculiar behaviour on your part—not to use a stronger term. As you know, it's an offence even to attempt . . .' Materna left the sentence unfinished.

Neuber neglected to push the importunate sow away. The animal nibbled at his turn-up, and undisturbed, grunted happily and dropped some acrid-smelling dung. The schoolmaster drew several deep breaths and decided that it would be better not to pursue Materna's accusations any further.

'Be that as it may,' he said with an effort, 'I've never been a personal enemy of yours.'

'I know, you've always let other people take first crack at me.' Materna was smiling indulgently now. 'You aren't a dim-witted brute, Neuber. That's why I'm banking on your common sense.'

'What do you mean, exactly?'

'In the first place, we aren't partners and never will be. Apart from anything else, you aren't in a position to make conditions unless you're prepared to risk a whole heap of trouble.'

Overcome by the stench of pig, Neuber clutched the dung-encrusted wall for support. 'What do you really want? Tell me.'

'Make sure I'm left in peace from now on. Then you can do what you like in Maulen—hold your festival and so on.'

Neuber inhaled deeply. The pig's dung seemed to have taken on the fragrance of roses. 'That's a reasonable offer,' he said briskly. 'I accept. What's more, I invite you to our gala performance—as one of the guests of honour.'

'Thanks,' replied Materna. 'I never could resist a good laugh.'

Blood-red posters the size of bath-towels adorned the immediate and less immediate environs of Maulen. Nailed to fences and stuck to walls, displayed in the school-house and posted on the church door, they proclaimed, in fat black lettering:

> GRAND FESTIVAL
> *on the occasion of the Twenty-Fifth Anniversary*
> *of the Battle of Tannenberg.*
> *Held in memory of our great war leader*
> *Field Marshal Paul von Hindenburg*
> *under the patronage of Gauleiter Erich Koch*
> *and in the presence of Regional Director Ludwig*
> *Leberecht.*
> *Organized by the Maulen branch*
> *of the National Socialist German Labour Party*

Amadeus Neuber's plans, unanimously approved by the festival committee and casually sanctioned by Eugen Eis, envisaged a series of functions covering a period of three days:

Friday—Day of the S.A.
Storm-troop contingents converge on Maulen. Display of fieldcraft, including balloon-shooting and grenade-throwing. Communal supper provided by field kitchen. Torchlight procession and memorial address. Speaker: Untersturmführer Ernst Schlaguweit. Social evening.

Saturday—Day of the Movement
Morning: fair-ground activities, including shooting competition, sack-race and tombola. Afternoon: display given by winners of S.A. fieldcraft competition, together with junior drumming and choral competition. Folk-dancing by members of the German Girls' League, gym display by the 'Faith and Beauty' ensemble, wrestling match by Hitler Youth.
Evening: Pageant, followed by Gala Ball.

Sunday—Day of the People
9 a.m. Band concert in village square.

10 a.m.: shooting competition in three groups—rifle, small-bore, and pistol—open to members of all organizations, associations and clubs taking part.

Midday: laying of wreaths at war memorial, dedication of colours, communal prayer of thanksgiving.

Afternoon: choral competition for newly presented Walther von der Vogelweide Challenge Cup. Classical and Germanic tableaux presented by local schoolchildren.

7 p.m.: closing demonstration and Grand Tattoo.

9 p.m.: open air dancing.

The festival committee had set up its headquarters in the school-house. There were the following administrative sub-divisions: Accommodation, Artistic Direction, Catering, Festival Literature, and Box Office. Tickets for the pageant were in short supply because Neuber's patriotic drama was reputed to be the *ne plus ultra* of the entire festival.

Regional Director Leberecht had already arrived with what he chose to term 'a small entourage'. So had Ottheinrich Schnirch of Radio Königsberg. Schnirch was known throughout East Prussia for his commentaries. Whenever he described the Führer arriving, departing, passing by, or making an entrance, his listeners felt that the sun had emerged in all its splendour. Women were stirred to the core and tears of loyalty stole unbidden into many a strong man's eye.

Schnirch was as eager to be entertained by Frau Eis as Regional Director Leberecht, so Brigitte had her hands full. Eis himself, hobbling gingerly around on a new stirrup-plaster, smiled notwithstanding. If only for a few brief hours, his branch of the Party seemed to have become the navel of the Greater German world.

By Friday afternoon, Maulen had transformed itself into an armed camp. All the school classrooms, the fire station, two barns, the Gasthaus outbuildings and portions of the vicarage had been requisitioned as emergency billets. The S.A. and Hitler Youth had erected a village of tents in Dog's Meadow, and almost every bed in Maulen was occupied twice over—a circumstance conducive to much harmless pleasure.

'Our broadcast today comes from the village of Maulen,' were the opening words of Schnirch's first commentary. 'Maulen is a small village inhabited by simple, upright, hard-working folk, nestling amid gently undulating hills and bordered by fields which testify to the exemplary diligence of those who till them. An idyllic place, a place in which to meditate on the joys of existence and creative endeavour, a place steeped in quiet German sincerity—thus it is year in, year out. Today, however, on this glorious afternoon, as the sun emerges from behind the clouds and shines down in all its prodigal splendour . . .'

Here Alfons Materna switched off and went to take Elisabeth for a prearranged stroll. They sauntered through Maulen, savouring the stir they caused.

'You're popular these days,' Elisabeth said.

'I'm amazed,' he replied. 'It must be because you're with me.'

They were greeted deferentially. Ordinary citizens raised their hats, Party members their arms. Mothers bent down and whispered to their children—approvingly, it seemed, since the little ones gazed at Materna and his companion with wide, awestruck eyes. Even Schlaguweit saluted, but Materna, who happened to be chatting animatedly to Elisabeth at the time, did not appear to notice.

'How far do you think my new popularity goes?' he said. 'I've a good mind to put it to the test.'

Amadeus Neuber scurried, nimble as a stoat, from one centre of activity to the next. Such were his preoccupations that he had to miss the dress rehearsal of his poetic and patriotic drama, but his two specially appointed assistant producers, Konrad Klinger and Peter Bachus, stood in for him with the greatest efficiency.

Neuber was currently engaged in the difficult task of seating the guests of honour. Party dignitaries would occupy the front row, of course, but where to put Materna? It was as essential not to offend him as it would be inadvisable to favour him too openly. . . .

While he was still brooding on this problem, Eis telephoned. 'They tell me Materna's coming,' he said indignantly. 'You don't mean to say you actually invited the fellow?'

'Kindly permit me to explain,' Neuber replied in a clipped voice. 'Your instructions were to invite Baron von der Brocken and his sister. That being so, I could hardly leave Materna out.'

'All right, all right, carry on,' Eis growled, and hung up.

Neuber's seating-plan worries proved to be superfluous, as it turned out, because Regional Director Leberecht assumed the functions of an usher when the time came. Having appropriated the centre seat as a matter of course, he waved his host's lady, Frau Brigitte, into the place on his right and invited Elisabeth von der Brocken to sit on his left. The Baron promptly seated himself next to Brigitte and Elisabeth beckoned Materna to sit beside her. Eis stood there, plaster-legged and furious, until the Baron noticed his predicament. 'Eis, my dear fellow,' he called, 'I insist that you sit next to me. Please don't deprive me of the pleasure.'

This disposed of the main seats. The fact that the rest were unreserved did not prevent them from being filled in strict order of current precedence.

'The performance can begin!' Neuber proclaimed with relief.

The curtains, specially run up for the occasion, formed a vivid expanse of black, white, and red bunting surmounted by a German eagle in gold and flanked by potted laurels. On one side sat the brass band and on the other stood the choir, which began to intone, in the manner of a Greek chorus:

> *'History has witnessed many mighty feasts,*
> *but none so mighty as that of the German nation*
> *as it faced its destiny, resolute unto death,*
> *on this our hallowed soil.'*

Here, as Neuber was delighted to note, Regional Director Leberecht nodded for the first time. Ottheinrich Schnirch was breathing heavily with his mouth open, and even Materna looked unusually attentive.

There followed a so-called prologue designed to proclaim that history always has an underlying purpose and that, in consequence, no bloodshed is ever in vain.

'Death is the seal on our pact with eternity . . .'

This prologue was spoken by Sabine, who stood there robed in a snow-white, Germanic-looking tunic, with a bronze band enclasping her long golden hair.

Regional Director Leberecht nodded twice at the sight of her, Alfons Materna smiled affectionately, and Ottheinrich Schnirch moistened his protuberant lips. A lusty voice called

'Bravo!' from the back of the hall, even before Sabine had uttered a word. The voice belonged to Jacob Jablonski.

Sabine faltered several times—a thing which she had never done at rehearsal—but the audience did not take it amiss even when, instead of 'bestial foes and loyal comrades', she declaimed: 'loyal foes and bestial comrades . . .'

'Delightful little thing,' Leberecht commented benignly.

'Fine figure for her age,' said Schnirch.

'I can't think what's got into her,' muttered Neuber. 'She was the only one who never forgot her lines—but that's stage-fright for you.'

The pageant proper now began. There was a muffled roll of drums and the curtains parted to reveal a backcloth lit by a flickering red glow. The effect unleashed the first burst of applause.

Two unmistakably German women were discovered with children clinging fearfully to their skirts. One of the women cried: 'They're coming, they're coming!' and her child screamed with terror. The other replied, with simple conviction: 'But God has never yet deserted our beloved Germany. He will surely send us a saviour in our hour of need!'

At this point, a spotlight shone full on the German eagle above the stage. Even Amadeus Neuber was surprised, but he supposed that it must have been a bright idea on the part of one of his assistant producers. Fervent applause rang out, and the Regional Director was seen to clap several times.

The arrival of Hindenburg was greeted with a thunderous ovation in which the entire hall joined. Ernst Schlaguweit had the presence of mind to ad-lib a salute from the stage and the band broke spontaneously into *Deutschland über alles*, at which everyone rose and joined in with a will.

Neuber suppressed a desire to hide his face, but the performance eventually got under way. Hindenburg delivered his first trenchant lines, e.g.: 'Anyone who fails the Fatherland is a low cur.' Applause. 'The true German does his duty and be damned to the consequences.' More applause.

'Frederick the Great plus Schiller,' the Baron observed wryly. 'How edifying!'

While the call to arms was still ringing out on stage, a low droning sound, as of heavy lorries, made itself heard in the distance. Nobody in the hall appeared to notice except

Alfons Materna, who raised his head like a dog snuffing the air.

While delivering his next equally trenchant lines, Hindenburg-Schlaguweit turned his back on the inhabitants of Maulen. This was unwise, since his field marshal's breeches were alarmingly baggy in the seat, but Schlaguweit was having trouble with his beard. Its adhesive properties had failed.

A faint titter ran through the audience, sympathetically initiated by Regional Director Leberecht. The villagers were beginning to be amused. Neuber's uneasiness increased sharply when he noticed that Materna was grinning, but his darkest hour had yet to come.

It was heralded by the appearance of the Russian generals, alias Konrad Klinger and Peter Bachus in wigs and false beards. The two youths had lavishly bedecked their uniforms with medals of every description, including some that looked as if they had come out of a cracker. Clanking and jingling like human Christmas trees, they strutted about the stage talking in a clipped officers' mess German which brought the house down.

Worse still, from Neuber's point of view, was their apparent ignorance of the text. They plied their rapturous audience with colloquial phrases which reduced Neuber's script to absolute bathos. For example, instead of exclaiming: 'What is it that bears down on us? I am filled with nameless dread,' Samsonov growled: 'What's that, for God's sake? It's enough to make a man shit his breeches!'

While Neuber, for his part, was filled with a very specific dread of impending disaster, Alarich von der Brocken's keen ears had also picked up the dull grinding noises in the distance. He cocked his head and glanced at Materna.

Hindenburg-Schlaguweit had reappeared on stage and was doggedly ploughing through his part. He seemed unmoved by the fact that the scenery swayed from time to time and displayed admirable fortitude even when a bevy of Russians, launched from the wings at the most inopportune moment, swarmed across the stage behind him. Although Schlaguweit himself stumbled over the occasional word, the people of Maulen took such minor blemishes in their stride.

Next to appear on stage were two German soldiers who,

though decoratively and mortally wounded, found time to
expatiate on patriotism, loyalty, and the virtues of a hero's
death. They lay there, gazing into the German heavens, then
leapt to their feet and raced off stage under the impetus of a
mild electric shock.

The Regional Director stopped nodding and the faces of
his entourage froze with disapproval. Eugen Eis, who felt
heartened by this evidence that nothing could function
smoothly in Maulen without his personal supervision, wore
a smug grin. Alarich von der Brocken and Alfons Materna
were listening intently to the still distant but mounting roar of
engines.

Meanwhile, chaos had broken out on stage. The audience
alternated between shocked silence and gusts of hysterical
laughter. Hindenburg-Schlaguweit lost his breeches as well
as his beard, Ludendorff-Mielke tried vainly to remove his
cap from the wall to which it had been nailed, and when
the conquering heroes started to celebrate their victory, the
scenery collapsed. To cap everything, the banner which was
unfurled just before the final curtain turned out to have no
black swastika on a white ground. It was red, flamboyantly
and unadulteratedly red!

A deathly hush fell, broken only by the persistent drone of
heavy vehicles. They were getting nearer.

'The *Horst Wessel Song*!' called Eis.

The Regional Director rewarded his presence of mind with
an approving nod and the brass band struck up without
delay. Amadeus Neuber fled from the hall. On the uncur-
tained stage, a fight seemed to have broken out between
Hindenburg, Samsonov, Ludendorff and Rennenkampf. The
soldier-actors formed a jostling ring round them but eventually
they, too, straggled off.

Conscious that the Regional Director's gaze was resting on
him at this momentous juncture, Eugen Eis made a supreme
effort to reassert his leadership. Hobbling to the front of the
hall supported by two Brownshirts, the Local Group Leader
announced: 'We now come to the really festive part of the
evening. I call upon the Regional Director to open the Ball.'

The Regional Director did not demur. Swiftly smoothing the
wrinkle from his golden-brown tunic of plain, Hitlerian
cut, he bowed gallantly to Brigitte and offered her his arm.
The band struck up a waltz, a small space was rapidly

cleared at Eis's vocal insistence, and the regional potentate and his partner began to revolve sedately. Other couples followed his inspiring example.

The music pounded away. Energetically assisted by members of the public, brownshirted ushers enlarged the scope of the dance-floor with muscular enthusiasm. To the strains of a hellish din in waltz-time, the festivities got under way at last.

Alfons Materna fought his way to the exit. Numerous well-intentioned citizens barred his path, plying him with friendly looks, meaningful handshakes and whispered words of friendship.

'Good to see you back in the saddle,' Uschkurat said, cordially confidential. 'You've no idea how glad I am. Let's hope Maulen has turned over a new leaf at last.'

'Hope springs eternal,' Materna replied, sidestepping him.

His next hurdle was Naschinski, front-running candidate for the office of mayor. 'Heartiest congratulations!' exclaimed Naschinski. 'Your return to community life has been greeted with enthusiasm by every right-minded person in Maulen.'

Mielke, the Party's court jester, elbowed his way forward wearing an expression of irritating and uncharacteristic solemnity. 'I've always been on your side,' he said, '—I hope you realize that.'

Materna extricated himself from the throng and stumbled into the open air, breathing deeply. The Baron was outside the Gasthaus, as he had hoped. He was smoking a cigar and peering along the village street with his head slightly on one side.

The muffled roar of engines crept towards them. Thin strips of light from masked headlamps danced in the darkness as the vehicles approached, shattering the star-spangled blue of the tepid Masurian night and drowning the strains of the band.

A scout car passed them first, crawling along tortoise-like in low gear. Then, clattering like volleys of rifle-fire, came motor-cycles with dark figures crouched over them; then trucks, angular boxes with sharp edges which ripped leaves from the trees; and, finally, tanks, mobile purveyors of concentrated destruction.

The earth quaked, windows rattled, and Masuria trembled. Alfons Materna bowed his head.

'No two ways about it,' Alarich von der Brocken said in a harsh voice. 'German troops on their way to the Polish frontier.'

'That means war.'

'Not necessarily, but it's probable.' The Baron might have been reading a weather forecast. 'Thanks to my friends in Berlin, I've known for quite a while that war is regarded as inevitable in certain quarters. Territorial adjustment—that's what they call it.'

Materna turned on his heel without a word, and the Baron followed him. They crossed the village square and halted in front of the war memorial. The bronze hero still pointed his banner at the dark sky.

'I can guess what you're thinking, Alfons,' the Baron said. 'You were just in the process of putting Maulen in your pocket, but a war could upset all your plans.'

'Hitler is a complete idiot. We always realized that.'

'Of course,' the Baron replied, almost gaily.

'Yes, but how much do we have to go through before everyone grasps that simple truth? There may be rivers of blood, mountains of corpses, millions of wrecked lives. . . .'

'You sound pessimistic, Alfons.'

'I am.' Materna did not speak again for some time. Then he said: 'We shall have to start all over again, probably. War gives a tremendous boost to the herd instinct. Intelligence gets completely swamped by patriotism.'

'I always thought you relished danger. Besides, we'll be able to get away with murder if there's a war on.'

'I don't expect people to understand me,' Materna said, turning away. 'There's nothing lonelier than a dog marooned in a pack of wolves. Its only ambition is survival, and the same goes for me. Survive—that's the order of the day.'

'But you'll make the most of the situation, won't you?'

'I won't give up, that's all.'

PART THREE

The Flight of the Wolves
1944-5

1

'Sign,' said Eugen Eis, negligently tapping the sheet of paper with his riding-crop.

Ignaz Uschkurat's hands trembled as he bent over it. 'Can't I at least keep my wood?' he pleaded.

'You'll sell them both—the field and the wood.' Eis looked bored. 'Either that, or your son goes in front of a special tribunal and gets the chop. Please yourself.'

'My God, Eis, you've turned into a hard-bitten bastard,' Uschkurat muttered savagely. He signed the document, then left the back room of the Gasthaus with his head hanging.

Eis took his riding-crop and pushed the deed of sale across to Scharfke, who folded it with nimble fingers and stowed it in his wallet.

'I've got to hand it to you, Eugen,' the innkeeper said admiringly. He uncorked a bottle of brandy and filled two glasses. 'Aren't you afraid he may make trouble, though?'

Eis emitted a scornful laugh and drained his glass. His eyes studied Scharfke without expression. 'Nobody puts one over on me. I've done nothing that isn't absolutely legal and above board. Law, order, and the interests of the State—that's all I'm concerned with. If anyone comes along and says I've been using the war to feather my own nest I'll stop his mouth for him. Not even Materna would dare to say that.'

'You're right, of course,' Scharfke assured him eagerly. 'Nobody can shit on your doorstep and get away with it—you've made sure of that. All these purchases have been made in my name, and I'm just a private individual. The fact that I'm your father-in-law is purely coincidental.'

Their new relationship had come into being in 1941, three years before. Eis's first marriage to Brigitte had been dissolved in 1940, under not altogether propitious circumstances. The Materna clique had succeeded in proving adultery against him in four separate cases, so he was forced to agree to a divorce rather than risk the consequences of a skilfully engineered scandal. Twelve months later, after careful consideration, he had married Christine Scharfke.

'I'm sacrificing myself for the good of the country,' Eis

declared. 'I owe it to the Führer to do that, and nobody's going to stop me.'

Eis had recently taken to making such pronouncements in a bored voice, almost as if he were reading out the latest fatstock prices. Gone were his days of fanatical enthusiasm—of that he was well aware. Gone, too, was his erstwhile mistrust of those around him. This had turned into cold disdain as soon as he realized that most people were like cattle. Higher authority was all that held them together, and Maulen knew no higher authority than Eis himself.

'What's your daughter up to?' he demanded suddenly. 'She's been displaying some peculiar tendencies lately— almost petit bourgeois, they are.'

'If Christine has been dolling herself up, it's in a good cause. She's working on the mayor at the moment.' Sharfke gave his son-in-law a meaningful wink.

Eis nodded. Mayor Naschinski was next on their list. His poultry farm would fit nicely into Sharfke's budding empire, which was systematically developing into a private venture of vital importance to the local war effort.

'If things go on at this rate, we'll soon have done what we set out to do—create a disciplined and effective counter-force to the unco-ordinated private undertakings of certain people I could mention.'

This was a reference to Alfons Materna, whose name never passed Eis's lips unless it was absolutely unavoidable. Materna's very existence was a challenge to him. Even though the man seemed to have withdrawn into his shell in recent years, Eis could never allow himself to forget Materna's baneful interference in the past. There was a score to be settled, and times were favourable to the settlement of scores.

'I had a few drinks with Sergeant-Major Fackler yesterday evening,' Eis said, outwardly casual, '—on you, by the way. You can put them down to business expenses. Fackler's worried about those French P.O.W.s of his. They're getting itchy feet, and at least two of them are potential escapees.'

'He could always unload them on to Materna.'

'You suggest it to him—I don't want anything to do with it officially. Just think, though. If Materna lets P.O.W.s escape it could have all sorts of repercussions—useful repercussions.'

Scharfke grinned. 'You're a sly one, Eugen.'

Eis studied his boots. Then he said softly: 'People who cross swords with me always regret it sooner or later. That applies to everyone—you included, just in case you ever take it into your head to forget all I've done for you. You're a rich man, Sharfke. You can't take it with you, so maybe you won't risk leaving it before your time.'

Alfons Materna inhaled the warm and humid air of late summer. 'The wild geese are growing restless,' he said. 'Normally, they don't get ready to fly south until late October, when the first mists come.'

Jacob Jablonski cocked an appraising eye at the pale milky clouds above. 'The temperature's normal enough. Must be instinct. Those birds probably sense that we're in for a busy time—and I'm not talking about the weather.'

Glancing in the direction of Horse Hill, Materna saw four figures heading for the farm. They were marching in step. Jablonski, who had caught sight of them too, identified them as Sergeant-Major Fackler, two French prisoners of war, and an armed escort.

'Looks like trouble,' Jablonski muttered.

Sergeant-Major Fackler, aged about thirty and blessed with a wound in the left buttock which mysteriously refused to heal, had a face like a pink and bloated balloon. His voice was mellifluous, partly because of the sticky liqueurs with which he lubricated it several times daily.

'You put in a request for some prisoners of war,' he purred.

'Yes, a year ago.'

'Well, you can have these two right away.' Fackler jerked a thumb over his shoulder.

There, clad in tattered uniforms stripped of insignia, stood a dark-haired youth and a grey-haired old man with a wrinkled face. They stared intently at Materna, who glanced suspiciously at Jablonski.

'The young one was a waiter in a Paris eating joint,' Fackler explained. 'He's wizard with cattle. The other's a professor—plants and that sort of thing. He knows a good bit about gardening and vegetable-growing. They both speak reasonable German.'

Materna eyed Fackler keenly. 'I can always use extra labour,' he said. 'On the other hand, why so helpful all of a sudden? You never gave me any P.O.W.s before, only foreign civilians. Besides, I thought prisoners of war were only allocated with the consent of the Local Group Leader.'

'I'm the one who decides what to do with these people,' Fackler retorted. 'The applications come to me and I either grant them or turn them down, always bearing in mind the welfare of my men. A schnapps ration never comes amiss— say a bottle per head per month. It's a sort of agency fee.'

Materna chuckled. 'That sounds normal enough. You can take the first two bottles with you when you go.'

Fackler grinned contentedly and made a curt gesture with his thumb. The prisoners of war walked over to Materna, removed their caps, and bowed. Fackler nodded his approval. He was a man of many whims, and one of these was that the prisoners of war in his charge must treat German civilians with proper respect.

'You'll get a lot of fun out of these two,' he said. 'If not, just complain to me and I'll work the bastards over.' Fackler rubbed his hands in high good humour. 'Fine, you're responsible for them from now on.'

'What does that mean in practice?'

'You fetch them every morning exactly one hour after sunrise and return them half an hour before sunset. You're entirely responsible for them during the day. That's all.'

Materna looked first at Jablonski and then at the prisoners. He scribbled a receipt and signed a form headed 'Security Regulations'. Sergeant-Major Fackler got his two bottles of schnapps plus an extra bottle and eighteen inches of smoked sausage. He saluted respectfully before taking his leave.

Materna led his new acquisitions into the farm kitchen, where Hannelore Welser fed them ham sandwiches and milk warm from the churn. They ate rapidly and in silence until they could eat no more. Then, with an apologetic glance at Jablonski, the younger of the two men asked if he might speak openly.

'I have no secrets from Jacob,' Materna replied.

The young Frenchman bowed to each of them in turn. 'My name is Ambal, Pierre Ambal. My companion is Professor Bonnard. We are happy to be here at last.'

'I don't quite understand.'

'We are exactly where we wanted to be,' Ambal said with a smile. 'On the first stage of our escape.'

Materna concealed his surprise without undue difficulty. It took a great deal to surprise him these days. 'I'm afraid you've come to the wrong place,' he said calmly.

Pierre Ambal's smile broadened. 'We came across one of Professor Bonnard's former students the other day—a Pole. It was a touching reunion. We told him of our escape plans and he mentioned your name. He told us that we would be safe with you, and that you would pass us on. Well, here we are.'

Materna leant back in his chair. 'This is either a mistake or a practical joke. Did Fackler put you up to it?'

'This Pole,' pursued Ambal, 'is called Machlowicz, Christian name Jan, twenty-seven years old, born in Cracow. The pass-word he gave me was Siegfried G.'

Jablonski beamed at him. 'You've come to the right place all right.'

'No,' Materna said firmly, glancing at Professor Bonnard. 'You're here to work on the farm. You can't disappear as long as I'm responsible for you, do you understand?'

Bonnard looked thoughtful. 'Of course, Monsieur Materna. Your meaning is quite clear. If we escape from here you will be held directly responsible, and that would never do.' He looked hard at Ambal, who evidently found it more difficult to accept the situation. 'For your part, please excuse us for having underestimated the problems of your position. What do we do now?'

'Make yourselves useful for the moment—you won't have a bad time here. We'll see how things shape. There must be some way out, but what puzzles me is why you were sent here so promptly. Coincidences do occur, but not in Maulen.'

'Mayor Naschinski indecently assaulted me,' grumbled Christine Eis, née Scharfke. 'Several times, what's more.'

'The bastard's ripe for plucking, then,' Eis said.

'Shall I tell you what happened?'

'Don't bother, I can guess the details.'

Christine had put on a bit of weight, but local taste favoured women who offered a good handhold. She also smelt strongly, but—as her husband noted with the discernment of a connoisseur—seductively. He sank deeper into the now well-worn leather arm-chair behind his official desk.

Naschinski's successor—and there were three more aspirants

to the office of mayor—would have to be selected with care. He who had most to offer stood the best chance.

'I'm sick of being mussed around,' Christine said petulantly. 'I won't stand for it much longer, Eugen—a woman needs love and affection.'

'You get plenty of that as it is,' Eis retorted. Emotional outbursts were out of tune with the times. 'Pull yourself together, Christine. We're paving the way for a great future, the two of us. You can indulge in sloppy sentimentality later, when the war is won. Until then, get on with the job.'

Eis still found it necessary to issue such reprimands from time to time. It was not sentimental attachment that had prompted him to raise her to his own level, after all, but an eye to the long term. In this respect, Christine's Gasthaus background made her a far apter pupil than Brigitte, his first wife. Christine knew how to add two and two.

As soon as she had gone, Eis prodded a bell-push with the riding-crop which he had taken to carrying everywhere in recent months. Ernst Schlaguweit, exempt from war service because of his indispensability to the home front, appeared like magic. Schlaguweit was devoted to Eis now, mainly because Eis knew too much about him.

'Get Naschinski,' commanded Eis. 'After that, Pillich, Schwiewelbein and Frontzek, in that order.'

'Right away, Local Group Leader!' Schlaguweit saluted. Summoning two minions who were permanently on call in the outer office, he instructed them to fetch the Party members concerned, which they did with dispatch. Maulen was admirably organized. People only had to see Schlaguweit and his men to know precisely what time of day it was.

The Naschinski case was disposed of in a bare fifteen minutes. Eugen Eis dispensed with any form of long-winded preamble. He simply slammed his riding-crop on the desk, barked out three or four forceful sentences, and presented his ultimatum.

'A depraved swine like you isn't fit to be mayor of this village. I've half a mind to hand you over to the police, but the community's interests come first. That poultry farm of yours must be placed in safe hands.'

The safe hands turned out to be Scharfke's. Pale as death and quaking with terror, Naschinski signed what was put in front of him. Then he retired hastily, thanking his lucky

stars that Eis had not threatened him with an immediate post-
ing to the Russian front.

'My dear friend,' Eis told each of the would-be mayors
in turn, 'present circumstances demand the mobilization of all
national resources. People are clamouring to share in this
honourable and profitable venture, but they have to offer
convincing proof of their goodwill.'

All three—Pillich, Schweiwelbein and Frontzek—were more
than willing to supply this. One offered his fish-pond, complete with carp. The second declared his readiness to sacrifice
a prize sow and a litter of ten piglets, together with a dozen
geese. The third offered a ton of seed-corn, four wagon-loads
of hay, and—by implication—his wife.

'The Party member I shall select,' announced Eis, 'will not
only be able to call himself mayor. He will also be entitled
to put up three notice-boards outside his house: Chief
Administrator, Justice of the Peace, and District Farmers'
Leader.'

They immediately raised their bids to the extent of a five-
year-old stallion, a brand-new chaff-cutter, two hundredweight
of butter, four hand-woven blankets and a dozen hens.
Scharfke busily entered these items in his books.

'I want nothing for myself,' Eis piously assured each candidate. 'My only concern is for the good of the community.'

At the week-end, Maulen received a visit from the Regional
Commissioner for Agriculture, Fisheries, and Forestry. This
was none other than Materna's son Hermann. Sweeping into
the forecourt in his requisitioned Opel Olympia, he climbed out
and raised his right hand in a conspicuous Hitler salute.

'Heil Hitler!' he shouted to Jacob Jablonski.

'Don't bust a gut,' Jablonski retorted. He pointed a thumb
in the direction of the barn. 'The boss is messing around in
there.'

Hermann nodded, took a bottle of schnapps from his car,
and made for the barn with Jablonski following at his heels.
They found Materna in a small partitioned enclosure at the
back, carefully filling rows of bottles with yellowish-brown
liquid. The place reeked of petrol.

'Heil Hitler!' Hermann called again.

Materna glanced up from his work. His face was expressionless, but his eyes glowed with pleasure when he saw his

son. He said: 'Just in case you're thinking of singing the *Horst Wessel Song*, don't bother.'

'Later, maybe.' Hermann invariably looked grave, whatever he was saying and wherever he happened to be. He shook his father's hand warmly and handed him the bottle he had brought.

Materna studied the label with approval. 'Who'd have thought it?' he said, winking at Jablonski. 'You're developing into a real connoisseur, Hermann. Where will it end, I wonder?'

A ghost of a smile flitted across Hermann's face. 'I've brought you two cans of petrol,' he said, propping his bulk against a packing-case. 'They're in the boot of my car. The greaseproof paper parcel next to them contains explosive—only ten pounds of it, I'm afraid, but I managed to get hold of a dozen grenades as well.'

Jablonski emitted a low whistle. 'I used to think you were a shit, Hermann—a prize shit, admittedly, but a shit for all that. What persuaded you to leave the herd?'

'I'm the son of my father,' Hermann answered with simple pride.

'It took you long enough to realize it, but I congratulate you on the final result.'

Hermann radiated a sort of modest integrity—a quality which had not escaped the notice of the regional authorities in recent years. His long-standing membership of the Party and proven business acumen put him among the élite, inspired confidence and merited trust. He also boasted some influential patrons, among them Baron von der Brocken, who was reputed to be an intimate friend of Reich Marshal Goering. It was only natural, therefore, that he should be entrusted with missions of importance to local government and the national war effort.

Having helped the other two to sample the contents of the bottle, Hermann said: 'I don't know if you're interested, Father, but I could get hold of an entire supply depot.'

'Arms and ammunition?' inquired Jablonski.

'No, canned food—meat, sausage, cheese. Cases of drink, too. There'd be about ten tons of the stuff to begin with— maybe fifteen.'

'Fetch it here,' Jablonski said promptly. 'I could work miracles with a couple of hundredweight. A well-lined stomach can influence a lot of things: love, patriotic sentiments, even Party policy. Isn't that right, Alfons?'

Materna relapsed into one of the silences which possessed him more and more often these days. At length he said: 'It would be an official dump, I take it?'

Hermann nodded. 'They've given me an entirely free hand. I can locate it wherever I think fit—even here at the farm.'

'No,' Materna replied, 'not here. The site of an official supply depot is bound to be recorded, which means that it's liable to inspection. I can't afford to have people snooping round here at the moment.'

'I follow you,' replied Hermann. 'You'd prefer me to off-load the stuff on the local Party bosses, is that it?'

'More or less.' Materna stared at the hard clay floor of the barn. 'Don't offer it to Eis direct, though. Speak to Scharfke.'

'That bastard?' Jablonski exclaimed angrily. 'He's got enough as it is.'

They broke off. Pierre Ambal, the younger of the two prisoners of war, appeared in the doorway with an empty crate. He eyed Hermann curiously.

'Heil Hitler,' said Hermann.

Ambal's expression changed to one of incredulity. He glanced helplessly at Materna, who passed him the bottle.

'Did my ears deceive me just now?' he asked, taking a swig.

'You'll hear stranger things than that before you're through, Pierre,' Materna told him. 'My farm may be in Germany, but it's still my farm. My son happens to be a Party bigwig of the first order, but he's still my son.'

'In that case, Heil Hitler,' said Ambal. He began to stow the bottles of petrol carefully in his crate. 'I tried one of these things out, by the way. They're completely fool-proof. Your invention, Jacob?'

'No, a traditional household remedy,' Jablonski replied modestly. 'Just Molotov Cocktails with a few improvements of my own.'

The basic principle: a bottle filled with petrol. The neck was stuffed with rag, the rag dipped in petrol and ignited, and the bottle thrown. The contents exploded as soon as the bottle burst.

The improvements: a special stopper which obviated the

W.   N risk of premature ignition; a flax wick that would burn in all weathers; and, finally, bottles of a special thin glass which smashed even on soft ground if thrown with sufficient force.

Pierre Ambal laid the bottles in neat rows and deftly packed them with wood-shavings. The other three watched him in silence as he shouldered his crate and trudged out.

'Reliable?' asked Hermann.

Receiving no answer and realizing that his question required none, he reverted to the supply depot and Scharfke.

'So why pick on him? Looking after a food and liquor store may have its liabilities, but it's got all kinds of advantages too.'

'Exactly, my boy. That's your selling-point. Scharfke has a good deal to offer in exchange—I'll tell you what to ask for in due course. As soon as he takes the bait you can make a whole series of extra conditions. One thing, though: make sure Eugen Eis is safely out of the way before you start bargaining.'

'I see. I'm supposed to get Scharfke to allow me, a regional commissioner, to take charge of goods which unofficially belong to Eis. You really think Scharfke will go along with that?'

'Provided you make the bait big enough and dangle it so that he bites quickly, yes. Why not?'

'My God,' Jablonski said, 'if Eis gets wind of it he'll kick Scharfke all round the village. It won't occur to him that it's his own arse he's kicking.'

Eugen Eis was spending that Saturday evening—officially, of course—with a sizeable party of brown-uniformed, white-bloused females, to wit, girl pioneers of the Labour Service. They belonged to a unit recently transferred to Maulen from the occupied territories in the east.

'We shall now sing a song in honour of our esteemed guest,' announced the girls' Amazonian commanding officer. 'Do you have a special request, Local Group Leader?'

The girl pioneers sweated with expectancy as they hung on his words, or so Eis fondly imagined. He was, after all, the only man in their billet.

'You've done so much for us,' continued the Amazon. 'Tell us what we can do for you—you only have to ask.'

Eis almost grinned at this, but remembered just in time that he was there in his capacity as head of local government. The girl pioneers had to be handled like Dresden china —officially, that was. Government directives were quite explicit on this point. Besides, he felt little inclination to take the Amazon up on her offer. The girls looked a pretty green bunch.

'What about *When the golden sun of evening*?' he suggested in a casual voice.

They burst into song almost instantaneously, shrilling the words loud and clear. Eis studied the bold outlines of the Amazon, who was sitting next to him. His eyes travelled down them by stages: forehead, nose, lips, chin, neck, breasts. Here they lingered, appreciatively but not for long. His patriotic gaze had rested on many a better bosom in its time.

He listened impassively as they sang, giving an occasional nod of approval. It was pure routine. As Local Group Leader, he was capable of listening to all manner of absurdities without showing boredom. Innumerable songs, speeches and slogans had flowed over him in the past few years.

'Ladies of the Labour Service,' he said, rising to his feet, 'temporary adjustments in our front line carried out in accordance with the Führer's overriding strategic considerations, whose inestimable wisdom will soon reveal itself—in short, pressure of circumstances—have brought you to this lovely village of ours. And, even though you have been here only a short time, I can truly say that we have taken you to our hearts, which beat, like yours, for the Fatherland.'

He had been invited to coffee and cakes, followed by a brief tour of inspection and 'an informal get-together'. The nurturing of such contracts was mutually beneficial: Eis supplied the ladies with extra rations and they extolled him in their reports to higher authority.

'This beautiful corner of Germany, ladies,' he continued in ringing tones, 'has always been exposed to threats from across the border. The evil Slav has tried to invade us more than once, but we are not so easily shaken. That is why we regard the creeping menace from the East with cool defiance. If the enemy insists on poking his nose into our homeland we'll bloody it for him—that is, if he still has a nose to bloody!'

He laughed scornfully, as he always did when he used this phrase. It never failed. The girl pioneers laughed too, and their commander's pale blue eyes shone with approbation

'None of us need lose any sleep,' he cried, twinkling at them now. 'We are entering the sixth and decisive year of the war with undiminished faith in final victory, unbroken and unbowed. We aren't finished yet, not by a long chalk. We still possess unlimited reserves. To quote one of my own numerous measures, I have recently extended the local poultry farm, mobilized its resources and placed them in the loyal and devoted hands of the Party. The results of this will soon become apparent. With effect from tomorrow there will be more eggs for you—almost twice as many as before. I also propose to make special allocations of milk, butter and cheese. Please do not thank me, ladies. My one concern is that you should feel at home here.'

They applauded him vigorously. He was not only a man of his word but a man, period, and able-bodied men were at a premium in Maulen and its environs.

The girls' commander thanked him, matching his apt and resounding phrases. With the official part of the proceedings over, she expressed the desire for a word in private and invited him into her office, which doubled as a bedroom.

'I can't tell you how much I appreciate your helpful attitude,' she said, pouring him a glass of wine. 'As long as there are still people like you, we can face the future with confidence.'

'To the future,' said Eis, raising his glass.

'I must tell my uncle,' she mused. 'I'm sure he'll be delighted to hear how admirably you treat German servicewomen in Masuria.'

'Your uncle? You don't mean to say . . .'

'Yes,' she replied with a faint smile. 'My name isn't Henriette Himmler for nothing. I'm related to him.'

Eugen Eis's jaw dropped. 'Just imagine!' he gasped, turning puce with excitement.

Henriette Himmler shook her head modestly. 'It isn't all that important—not to me, at least. I never expect preferential treatment or anything of that kind. On the contrary, I look on it as an added responsibility. Can you understand that?'

'Can I?' Eis replied, highly impressed. 'That's what I call

the proper German spirit—deserving of respect and admiration. I hope you'll let me express my respect and admiration for you in the most practical way possible.'

Amadeus Neuber, still headmaster and Deputy Local Group Leader, but now, in addition, head of ideological training, president of the veterans' association and Party welfare chief, had lately felt tempted to rediscover his faith in God. Seated on the bench outside the school-house, he gazed across at the church with a pensive, almost nostalgic expression. Congregations had been increasing steadily in recent months, and this—among many other things—had given Neuber food for thought.

The present vicar, who had officiated in a caretaking capacity for the past year, was a septuagenarian named Kampmann. He approached the school-house with an ingratiating air, raised his hand in the Hitler salute, and said: 'God be with you.'

'Good evening,' replied Neuber, striving to match his friendly tone. 'I really ought to have said "Heil Hitler", oughtn't I?'

'As you wish, just as you wish,' the parson said quickly. 'My greeting was merely a tribute to Our Maker. After all, Christ died for all men.'

'And the Führer lives for them.'

'Of course, if you say so.'

The Reverend Albrecht Kampmann had the admirable and, for a Masurian, extremely rare ability to avoid quarrelling with people. Nothing ever seemed to get under his skin.

'Business is brisk, I hear,' Neuber said in a mildly confidential tone. 'A dozen more in church this Sunday than last.'

'It may have had something to do with the weather,' Kampmann replied apologetically. 'On the other hand, it could be the influx of refugees.'

It was impossible to catch Kampmann out—Neuber, who had put him under surveillance, was forced to this conclusion very soon after his arrival. He stuck exclusively to the Bible and almost exclusively to the New Testament, taking scrupulous care to avoid all topical allusions. He also made a point of including the Führer and Reich in his prayers, nor did he do so with any suspicious overtones.

'A glorious evening,' said the parson, peering a trifle lugubriously at the flawless blue of the summer night. 'Tomorrow will be a fine day—one of the last, I fear.'

'What do you mean?' Neuber asked, quick as a flash.

'The hundred-year almanac forecasts a short wet autumn followed by a long cold winter.'

Neuber did not comment, and the parson continued on his way in silence.

No chink of light escaped from the houses, which were blacked out in accordance with regulations, but the village hummed with activity. Voices drifted along the main street and filtered across the square from the surrounding bushes. Shapeless figures moved through Maulen, cloaked in darkness.

Amadeus Neuber shivered and massaged his hands as though to prevent his spidery fingers from folding in prayer. Fear gripped him, a fear which formed like mist, billowed about him and then dissolved, usually with the advent of daylight.

It was impossible to supervise the village any longer, impossible to keep a check on every last detail of what went on there. The place had swollen like a festering sore. There were no more clearly defined zones of control. Materna had turned into a sort of will-o'-the-wisp and the parson mouthed eternal platitudes. Farmers and tradesmen slunk about their daily work in silence, exchanging curt nods. Baron von der Brocken had handed over his estate to a bailiff and moved to South Germany with his sister and Materna's daughter Brigitte.

Then there were the foreign bodies: the prisoners of war in the enlarged fire station, the garrison troops billeted in the Gasthaus, the hundred girl pioneers in their huts on the moorland north of Maulen, and, finally, nearly fifty refugees, old men, women and children—an idle shiftless lot, in Neuber's opinion, and just so many more mouths to feed.

He emitted a deep, sobbing sigh, like someone in the throes of a nightmare. He still performed all the most vital functions in Maulen as far as circumstances allowed—he, not Eugen Eis. Eis lorded it and exploited every opportunity to feather his own nest. He, Neuber, had forgone all public recognition and personal privileges, as God was his witness. Even so, there were a few people in Maulen who could bear witness to his integrity, decency and magnanimity, and he had already

)egun, methodical man that he was, to collect testimonials in
his favour.

A certain sense of relief pervaded him when he remembered
this, but it never lasted long—least of all during his nocturnal
vigils on the bench in front of the school, as he watched
the comings and goings in the village square and spied on the
women who hung round the fire station where the prisoners
of war were housed. Shameless, wanton, un-German hussies!
He would have liked to hurl himself on them, drag them into
the open and send them for trial—indeed, he had tried to do
so a couple of times, but without success. The bitches were
too quick for him, and the ones he did manage to catch
had bitten and scratched like wild beasts.

'Is that you, Amadeus?' inquired a woman's voice from
the hedge beside him. 'You're breathing so heavily. Have you
got someone with you, or are you feeling ill?'

'Don't come too close!' squeaked Neuber, who had recognized the voice at once. It was Christine Eis, Scharfke's
daughter. 'People might misunderstand the situation if they
saw us together at this hour.'

'You flatter yourself,' sneered Christine, moving towards
him. 'Anyway, I'm not under age.'

Neuber winced at this crude allusion to his former weakness, however aesthetic its underlying motivation. It was his
Achilles' heel, his one professional blunder—the shackle he
was destined to wear until he rid himself of Eugen Eis, who
was in possession of sworn affidavits on the subject. It was
clear that Eis had mentioned it to his wife, probably in bed.
He wondered who else knew. Even Schlaguweit had taken
it upon himself to smirk at him and make sly remarks lately.
He was at the mercy of these people—he, a cultured man of
artistic bent and profound intellect. . . .

'Did your husband send you?'

Christine gave a short, mirthless laugh. She sat down on the
bench, leant back, and indecorously spread her legs. 'You
needn't worry,' she said. 'I haven't any plans to seduce you
—I know it wouldn't work with you, and so does Eugen. I just
happened to be passing, that's all.'

'Don't tell me you mistook the school for the fire station.'

'If you're talking about the P.O.W.s you can keep your
dirty cracks to yourself. They could land you in trouble.'

'Please!' entreated Neuber. 'It was only a joke.'

'A bad joke. Make one more like that and I'll show you what I'm made of.'

Neuber was tempted to tell her that he knew precisely what she was made of but he was not feeling suicidal, just worried. 'In times like these,' he fluted in a conciliatory tone, 'we of the Party must stand by one another. We can't afford any misunderstandings, can we?'

'Your lectures are wasted on me,' she retorted, but she sounded slightly mollified. 'If you really want to know, I came because I wanted someone to talk to.'

Neuber did not believe her—she had never sought his company before. Her presence could only constitute a manœuvre, a diversion, perhaps an alibi. Who could tell, with a diabolical woman of her kind?'

'I'm glad,' he assured her. 'Is Eugen away on duty again? He'll wear himself out, poor man.'

They chatted for a while, staring into the darkness. The village was quieter now. The sounds of whispering, cooing, creaking, panting and groaning were replaced by utter silence but only momentarily. A train shrieked and rumbled in the distance.

The rumbling quickly grew in volume. There was a metallic screech and a shrill whistle, and then the sky was bathed in a fiery glow which flared up abruptly and subsided. A savage explosion rent the air, drowning every other sound. Deathly silence descended on the village.

'What was that?' Christine asked in a stupefied voice.

'An accident,' Neuber whispered. 'Either that or sabotage by those devilish partisans. What on earth is the country coming to?'

'I'm tired,' Materna said.

'No wonder,' replied Jablonski.

They had attended morning service in order to show their faces in the village. Nobody seemed to take undue notice of them, even though many church-goers paid more attention to Materna than the vicar during the sermon. Materna sat slumped in his pew like a repentant sinner, the better to sleep, and the inhabitants of Maulen exchanged whispered references to the rumour that he was drinking like a fish lately—night after night, so it was said.

Materna and Jablonski were now sitting on a garden

bench, waiting for lunch and gazing ruminatively at Horse Hill with their hands folded on their stomachs. The scent of roast sucking pig filled their nostrils.

On the grass, barely ten feet from them, lay Hermann. He was lying on his side with his clenched fists held in front of his face like a boxer on the defensive, right fist to chin, left at eye-level. His lips emitted a faint and irregular snoring sound.

Cheerful voices could be heard coming from the kitchen. These belonged to Materna's two refugees—the two, that is to say, who were officially registered as members of his household. At the present time they were larking about with Pierre Ambal, the prisoner of war. Ambal seemed to be enjoying himself thoroughly—in fact, his voice sounded rather like the cry of a peacock parading its finery.

Ambal's enthusiasm was hardly surprising, since the cheerful refugees were Hannelore Welser and Sabine Gäbler. Having spent several years in Berlin, Hannelore had gladly returned to Materna's farm at the earliest opportunity. Sabine had been sent to the Rhineland when her father was assigned to police duties in the occupied territories, but was permitted to return to Maulen after being bombed out. Jablonski, in particular, was glad to see her back—so glad that he actually showed it.

'They sound happy,' he said in a slightly disapproving voice.

'Don't begrudge them a little fun.'

'But the girls are as good as engaged.'

'That doesn't mean they have to go around with long faces. Besides, they don't really know who they're engaged to.'

This was a typical Materna brainwave. In order to heighten suspense and alleviate tension at the same time, he had invented a form of multiple engagement. Hannelore and Sabine had plighted their troth with Peter Bachus and Konrad Klinger, but jointly and without pairing off into two definite couples.

A camouflaged truck hove into view to the right of Horse Hill, on the road from Gross-Grieben to Maulen. It lumbered towards the farm, its grey-green bulk looking ponderous and slightly menacing.

'Army, probably,' said Jablonski.

'Could be S.S.'

'Jablonski leapt to his feet. 'We'd better take cover, then.'

'No,' said Materna. 'Carry out emergency procedures and wait. You know what to do.'

Jablonski shook Hermann roughly and hustled him into the house, shouting through the window: 'Girls keep calm, men into the barn and hide anything you see lying around. Then stand by for further instructions.'

The truck drew nearer. Materna had guessed right: the number-plate bore the S.S. insignia, and the uniformed figures of an officer and a driver could be seen behind the dusty windscreen.

'Open up,' called Materna.

The cumbersome vehicle halted with its bonnet almost touching the heavy iron-bound bars of the gate. After a moment's hesitation, Jablonski walked over to the gate and opened it. The truck headed straight for Materna, who was waiting by the front door, and Jablonski closed the gate behind it.

The officer jumped out. There was something pantherish about his movements, and his lean young face seemed to glow with an inner fire. He raised his hand in a casual semblance of the Hitler salute, then made a sign to the driver, who turned the truck and reversed it so that its tail-board exactly faced the front door.

The canvas flaps were thrown back and the tail-board fell with a clank of chains. Two heavily armed S.S. men climbed out stiffly and posted themselves on either side of the truck. With their assistance, a wizened little man in concentration camp uniform emerged from the interior.

The little man hurried over to Materna and flung his arms round his neck.

'Siegfried!' Materna exclaimed hoarsely. 'Siegfried Grienspan!'

Jablonski drew nearer with a look of disbelief. He saw the officer laugh and the S.S. men lay their weapons aside. Another five scarecrows in concentration camp uniform climbed out of the truck.

'My flying squad,' Grienspan explained, indicating them with a flourish. 'The Wollnau-Grienspan group's latest innovation.'

'Are we safe here?' asked the officer, looking round.

Grienspan smiled. 'Nowhere safer.'

'Where can I put the truck?' was the officer's next question. 'Which line of approach ought we to seal off?'

'Jablonski will take care of that,' Materna told him. He felt happier than he had done for years as he took Grienspan's arm and led him into the house.

'I can hardly believe it's you,' he said, when they were in his den. 'How are you?'

'Still alive,' Grienspan replied, as though reporting a miracle. 'Maria's still alive too. She's well—very well, all things considered. I get the impression that she feels happier and happier as the months go by. She senses that it won't be long before you're together again.'

'Thank God,' Materna said, and the words seemed to sum up everything there was to say.

Materna's kitchen and cellar yielded all they had to offer, which was a good deal, even at this stage of the war. Hannelore and Sabine supplemented the roast sucking pig with a score of jars, tins and bottles, and ham and sausages completed the spread on the big kitchen table.

Grienspan's friends, ceremoniously waited on by Hermann, clustered round Hannelore and Sabine. S.S. uniforms jostled the striped pyjamas of the concentration camp—a spectacle which the girls took some time to get used to. The assorted party in the kitchen dug in with a will. Meanwhile, in the den, Grienspan was acquainting his old friend with the finer points of his latest system.

The plan, which had sprung from Wollnau's fertile brain, was to set up a small team which could move freely about the German interior with as little risk and as much official assistance as possible. 'An S.S. squad armed with special permits and engaged on an important mission which people will be chary of interfering with,' Wollnau had said. 'I suggest we make them a unit specializing in the transportation of escaped concentration camp inmates—after all, that's what most of us are.'

Awestruck, Hermann inquired the source of their arms, equipment and papers. Grienspan told him that all the items they needed had been 'borrowed' from an S.S. unit serving in Poland, and were guaranteed genuine: the uniforms, the truck, the submachine-guns—even the concentration camp clothing.

'And the men?'

'They're genuine too, up to a point. Our officer really is an army lieutenant, though he's been on the run ever since the Hitler bomb plot. The three other S.S. men are or were trained soldiers, but one is technically a deserter and the other two are political refugees. They've belonged to our team for months. I and the other five are more or less what we appear to be—Resistance fighters of long standing, including one Jew, namely, me.'

'You must have been through hell, Siegfried,' Materna said.

'I'm tougher than I look. Also, I've got friends. You saved my life that time, Alfons. Some men deliberately court death more than once, but I'm not one of them, so I survive as best as I can. That means killing those who want to kill me. It's as simple as that!'

They were sitting over a bottle of Franconian wine which Jablonski had produced from Materna's carefully hoarded reserves. Looking at each other keenly, but with brotherly affection, they saw that they had aged. The network of lines in their faces had grown deeper and more pronounced. Materna eyed his friend's sparse crop of wiry grey hair with a touch of pity. Grienspan thought he detected infinite weariness in Materna's pale blue eyes.

'It won't be long now,' he said.

'No, the end is in sight.'

Grienspan held his glass up to the light. The wine gleamed like rain splashing on young birch-leaves. He said: 'I look forward to the day when we can walk through the village again, shoulder to shoulder, and revel in the glorious feeling that this is our home.'

'You're a dreamer,' Materna said quietly, and drained his glass. 'Perhaps that's why you've survived.'

'Don't tell me you've given up hope—not you of all people.'

'I've abandoned my illusions, that's all. I can't imagine myself singing and dancing in Maulen again. My imagination won't extend that far. I can't even picture the delights of a Masurian wake.'

Grienspan shook his small grizzled head. His right hand curled round the empty glass as if it were a grenade. 'What you're saying is, you can't wipe out the past. Well and good, but there is another side to the coin, and that's us.'

'But who are we, Siegfried? Men charging tanks with their bare fists, ants squashed by jackboots.'

'All right, Alfons—you've done enough, more than enough. All you need do now is wait.'

'I could always assassinate Eis.' Materna gave a short laugh. 'The trouble is, his successor is waiting to step into his

shoes, and he's a rattlesnake. Anyway, I don't have the guts
to act as judge and executioner. I'm too squeamish and not
self-righteous enough.'

'Couldn't it be just that sort of attitude which is prolonging the war?'

Materna shook his head as he refilled their glasses. 'You
still seem to think there's such a thing as justice. You believe
that crime entails punishment. Well, maybe it does, but not in
this world.'

'The guilty won't get away.'

'I'm not so sure, Siegfried. I'm afraid they're more likely
to escape than the innocent. They have a greater talent for
survival.'

'Let's forget it,' Grienspan said. 'I didn't come here to argue
with you. I'm not asking you to join us, either. All we need is
food, ammunition, and fuel.'

'I'll give you all I've got.'

'Thanks, Alfons. There's just one more thing. An ammunition train was blown up outside Greierswalde yesterday evening. I'd like to get in touch with the group that did it. With
your connections, you might be able to help. Any idea
where I can find them?'

Materna nodded. He was smiling.

'Well, who was it?'

'Us.'

2

'I've got to talk to you,' said Eugen Eis, levelling his riding-
crop at the empty chair beside his desk.

'That's lucky,' replied his father-in-law, sitting down in a
markedly leisurely fashion. 'I wanted to discuss one or two
things with you, but you were always out when I called.'

'I've been busy.' Eis frowned. Scharfke's slightly reproach-
ful tone annoyed him. If he still hadn't learnt who he was
dealing with, it was high time to teach him a sharp lesson.
'Do you dispute the fact that I've been busy the whole time?'

Sharfke gulped. 'No, of course not. All the same, I'd
welcome it if you'd co-operate with me a bit more closely
in future.'

'You've got the wrong end of the stick,' Eis said. 'It's you who co-operate with me.'

He had spent Saturday night with the girl pioneers. Sunday had seen him at the headquarters of a neighbouring branch of the Party, conferring War Service Crosses on deserving Party members. The hours thereafter had been devoted to a long overdue social evening with Sergeant-Major Fackler and his merry men, a function which had, as usual, developed into the most appalling binge.

'You're lucky, Scharfke. All you have to do is look after your Gasthaus and watch your bank balance grow—thanks to me. I've got several hundred people to worry about.'

'They're in good hands,' Scharfke observed.

Eis's seat of power groaned as he shifted his considerable bulk. Wearily, he wondered why he bothered to beat about the bush. Was it necessary? Certainly not with Scharfke. Scharfke had supplied him with Christine, and that was the extent of his usefulness. The innkeeper's value to him paled into insignificance beside his daughter's achievements, and it was time he realized it.

'Right,' Eis said, reverting to a tone of command. 'I shall be needing larger consignments of food from now on. Extra rations for the girl pioneers—eggs, mainly. You deal with it.'

'Me? Why me? I've got nothing to give away.'

'We're not giving anything away. I say this is a worthwhile investment, and what I say goes.'

'Of course,' Scharfke agreed hastily, '—under normal circumstances, yes. Unfortunately, I've already made other arrangements.'

'What's that? You mean you've done a deal without consulting me first?'

'But I couldn't get hold of you, Eugen—I told you. I had to act quickly.'

'Well, what's it all about?'

'They're installing a supply depot in Maulen—about ten tons of drinks and foodstuffs. It'll be kept directly under my—I mean, our—supervision, in one of the Gasthaus store-rooms. Top quality goods, Eugen, and there's an official wastage rate of ten per cent. How about that!'

'Who sold you the idea?'

'Hermann Materna—he's in charge of the scheme.'

'Did he make any conditions?'

'Well, you can't expect something for nothing. It's a question of you scratch my back, I'll scratch yours. In order to get the depot at all, I had to offer a few concessions.'

'For instance?'

'Nothing much—just an extra consignment of food to Hermann Materna's office, eggs included. We should be able to manage it, I reckon, now we've got Naschinski's poultry farm in our pocket. Then there's a few hundredweight of flour, potatoes and seed-corn—but what's that compared to scores of cases of canned stuff? I ask you, is that good business or isn't it?'

Eis stared ahead of him with a total lack of expression. He seemed to see straight through Scharfke, also the wall behind him and the oil-painting that hung on it, an attempt to portray the beauty of the Masurian lakes in harsh blue, fungus green and digestive brown.

'Fair enough,' he said at length. 'You can go.'

Scharfke rose. His knees were trembling and his voice croaked hoarsely as he said: 'I hope you haven't got the wrong idea.'

'I hope so too,' Eis replied.

He pressed the bell and Ernst Schlaguweit appeared like a jack-in-the-box. He halted in the doorway and saluted, panting slightly from exertion.

'Reporting for duty, as instructed.'

Eis regarded him with hooded eyes. Schlaguweit felt his palms go moist. He wondered if he had anything on his conscience but came to no firm conclusion.

'Come in,' Eis said. 'Take a pew.'

Schlaguweit breathed more easily—the use of slang was a good sign. Feeling reassured, he sat down.

'Schlaguweit, old friend,' Eis went on, putting a bottle of brandy on the desk, 'help yourself. You're a person to be relied on, aren't you?'

'All the way, Local Group Leader!'

'I appreciate that. Your kind of loyalty deserves to be rewarded.'

Schlaguweit poured himself a brandy and downed it to steady his nerves. When Eis spoke of loyalty there was usually hell to pay.

The Local Group Leader reached for the bottle himself.

'I'm a generous man, Schlaguweit,' he declared. 'I pride myself on my community spirit. Those who belong to our ranks enjoy certain well-merited privileges, but there are some who abuse them in a brazen and criminal manner.'

'Yes,' said Schlaguweit, 'swine like that do exist.'

'But they shouldn't, Ernst—not in our ranks.'

Schlaguweit scowled. 'Who is the bastard?'

'A man I trusted implicitly, a man who enjoyed privileges which ought to have gone to someone more deserving—someone of your calibre, Ernst. I've been sold down the river to Materna.'

'No!' Schlaguweit exclaimed loudly. He fortified himself from the bottle.

'It's true. A man we trusted has had the unspeakable effrontery to give Materna everything I've sweated my guts out to accumulate for us all—you included, Ernst. He mustn't be allowed to go unpunished.'

'Who is the dirty swine?'

'Christian Scharfke.' Eis studied his henchman slowly. 'Can I rely on you?'

Schlaguweit's voice was flat, almost feverish. 'To the hilt.'

S.S. Major Rattenhauer, a special emissary from Supreme Headquarters, had convened a meeting in a small conference-chamber on the first floor of Allenstein town hall.

Among those invited were the Regional Director, the chairman of the district council, a senior police officer, and two experienced detectives. Also present was a councillor named Engel, who was responsible for internal security and, thus, for the local police force.

'You're in big trouble,' were Rattenhauer's opening words. 'Incidents of the most alarming nature have occurred in the Allenstein-Lötzen area during the past two weeks.'

He nodded to his adjutant, who produced a list and proceeded to reel off the contents in a monotone. A Gestapo vehicle had been set on fire, the police station at Osterode had been broken into, two political prisoners had been sprung from Hohenstein gaol, and a policeman had been murdered in Allenstein itself.

'And now, to cap it all,' said the Major, 'this ammunition train gets blown up near Geierswalde. An unparalleled act of sabotage in the immediate vicinity of the Führer's Headquarters, gentlemen! Well, what have you got to say for yourselves?'

The chairman of the district council announced that he had ordered an immediate tightening up of security precautions. The senior police officer assured Rattenhauer that this order had been implemented without delay, but felt bound to point out that his men were pitifully thin on the ground and grossly overworked. Councillor Engel, too, was able to prove, quoting from a prepared brief, that directives calling for increased vigilance and ruthless action had been issued.

'I can only conclude that your directives were inadequate, vague and lacking in punch,' Rattenhauer said reprovingly.

The Regional Director hastened to agree and the chairman of the district council nodded. Both of them subjected Engel to a searching stare.

Engel, a rosy-cheeked jovial-looking man of about forty, realized that the hot potato had been passed to him and decided on a policy of cautious prevarication.

'In my view,' he said, 'the answer is to co-ordinate our various measures more closely.'

'That's not enough,' Major Rattenhauer said sharply. 'Don't just co-ordinate them—step them up as well. Mobilize every last man, call up your reserves.' Then, as though to clinch matters, he added: 'I'm acting on direct orders from the Führer.'

This shaft went home. After conferring for another three hours, they came to the following conclusion: Rattenhauer was to assume personal command of the whole operation. Councillor Engel would act as his principal adviser on local affairs and the senior police officer as his chief of staff. The policeman was assigned two senior assistants, one each from the Gestapo and the S.A., the latter charged with the speedy recruitment of a force of armed auxiliaries.

'May I draw your attention to the possibility that we may be able to call on the services of some ex-policemen resident in the district?' Councillor Engel produced the suggestion with due diffidence. 'Even retired policemen could be useful.'

'Good idea,' said Rattenhauer. 'Rope them in. We need everyone we can get.'

'We might also take a look at any police officers who have been seconded to other duties—in local government, say.'

Councillor Engel did not look at anyone as he spoke, but rummaged busily in his papers.

'What sort of chaps are they?'

Engel coughed. 'I imagine they've blotted their copy-book in some way—perhaps by showing an insufficient appreciation of political developments.'

Rattenhauer rose like a fish. 'So what? This is a question of home defence—war service, in other words. Anyone who refuses to toe the line one hundred per cent risks his neck. As far as I'm concerned, you can give these fellows a last chance to show what they're made of.'

'Even a man like Tantau?' Engel inquired softly.

'Tantau? Who's he?' Rattenhauer found the name vaguely familiar. He felt sure he had heard it somewhere, probably in a disagreeable context.

'One of the finest detectives the police service ever produced, or so they say.' Engel qualified every statement with extreme care because he knew he was treading on dangerous ground. 'He served with the Berlin C.I.D. for years—headed "S" Division, which deals with special cases of homicide. They say he was enormously successful, too, but then he was suddenly—well, transferred for some reason unknown to me. If we could only use him we'd be almost bound to get to the bottom of this business. He's reputed to have a sort of sixth sense.'

Major Rattenhauer took the bait. He asked where Tantau was. In Königsberg, Engel told him, working as a common-or-garden government clerk. If the Major wished, he could be in Allenstein inside three hours.

'Get him,' commanded Rattenhauer. To cover himself, he telephoned the State Security Bureau in Berlin and asked to speak to S.S. General Müller. He was informed that Müller would swallow his misgivings about the employment of Tantau provided no political considerations were involved. Of course Rattenhauer might keep a close watch on him—in fact, the greatest care was indicated. 'You see,' Müller concluded, 'once he picks up the scent, nobody who has a guilty secret ever gets away. You ought to bear that in mind, my dear Rattenhauer.'

But Rattenhauer's mind was already made up. The only people with a guilty secret were the saboteurs, criminal elements of the worst kind. What did Müller mean, political

onsiderations? Everything had a political side to it these
days. Tantau would guarantee the success of his special
mission, that was the main thing.

'I favour offensive tactics,' he told the chairman of the
istrict council later, over an extended lunch. 'A tight
ordon, plenty of beaters, a couple of first-class shots, and the
eathers soon fly!'

Rattenhauer's excellent appetite was whetted still further
when he learnt that he had been assigned three dozen auxiliary
olicemen. These, so he was informed over dessert, were
lready on their way from Lötzen. Shortly afterwards, Coun-
illor Engel announced the arrival of Tantau.

'I'll soon get him on his toes,' Rattenhauer announced
riskly. He withdrew, patting his stomach, to the conference
oom. Here he was greeted by the sight of an almost dwarfish
gure in a baggy suit. The jacket bulged at the elbows and
ne trousers resembled threadbare sacks. Protruding from this
artorial fiasco was a tortoise like head set with a pair of
rovocatively friendly eyes.

'Are you Tantau?' the S.S. major asked in surprise.

The little man smiled. 'With respect, yes,' he replied in the
oice of an obedient child, 'Christian name Heinrich.'

'Chief Superintendent Tantau?'

'So my identity card says.' Tantau fished out his papers and
roffered them to Rattenhauer. 'At present employed by
he civil service, primarily on statistical work.'

'You've been assigned to me,' said Rattenhauer.

'As a statistician?'

'As a policeman.'

'Are you sure there hasn't been some mistake, Herr
Rattenhauer?'

'Major Rattenhauer, if you don't mind,' the S.S. officer
mended in a mildly reproving tone.

'Ranks always did confuse me,' Tantau said, almost plain-
ively. 'They change too often—in fact they get on my nerves
ometimes. For instance, I don't set the slightest store by being
ddressed as Chief Superintendent.'

Rattenhauer drew a deep breath and expelled it slowly.
He fidgeted with a piece of paper for some moments, folding
nd unfolding it. Tantau watched him calmly. At last, Ratten-
auer said:

'I have a special assignment for you, one which will exercise all your powers of detection. Show me whether you really are the prodigy people say you are.'

'Ah,' replied Tantau, 'I'm afraid I must utter a word of warning—in your own interests.'

'You refuse?'

'I never refuse an assignment,' Tantau assured him. 'On the other hand, you seem to be insufficiently well informed about me. If you were, you might not want me to accept.'

Rattenhauer's eyebrows rose threateningly. 'Are you trying to be difficult?'

'On the contrary, Herr Rattenhauer, difficulties are just what I'm trying to avoid. Do you know why I was relieved of my job? No? Well, there were a number of reasons. One of them was that I was on the point of arresting the S.A. chief of staff for fraud, embezzlement and forgery. It happened almost by accident, as a sort of by-product of a murder case. A man can't change his nature—you must know that.'

Rattenhauer thrust his hands deep into his pockets and stuck out his chin. He studied Tantau with feigned amusement. 'This time,' he said, 'in the sphere of operations to which you are being assigned under my command, nothing and nobody will be taboo.'

'Are you positive?' Tantau asked doubtfully.

Rattenhauer gave vent to an exclamation of impatience. 'Our job is to hunt down a gang of disgusting criminals, creatures with blood on their hands—in other words, murderers.'

'Are you familiar with Globotnik's theory?' Tantau inquired politely. 'He lists twenty-four sets of circumstances leading to acts which are commonly called murder but need not necessarily be so in every case.'

'Stop quibbling, Tantau! We can do without that sort of theoretical twaddle. We haven't a minute to lose, so get cracking.'

Tantau rubbed his small, delicate hands. 'As you wish,' he replied.

'He's got to go!' Jablonski said furiously.

Materna was in the barn examining one of the automatic pistols stored there by Grienspan. He said: 'These gadgets look more complicated than they are.'

'Didn't you hear what I said?' demanded Jablonski.

'How could I fail to?' Materna replied imperturbably. You've been a bit too noisy altogether recently, and we can't afford to be noisy. Silence is the order of the day.'

'He's got to go, I said!'

'Sit down and take a look at this, Jacob. First-class British workmanship. The bolt action is remarkably simple, so it's easy to clear any stoppages. Very heavy on ammunition, though. One or two operations would clean us out, and we can't bank on getting any more, I'm afraid. No, we'll have to stick to our good old-fashioned methods.'

'Are you going to listen, Alfons, or aren't you?'

'Not if it's about Pierre Ambal again. It is, isn't it?'

Jablonski nodded and leant against a crate. 'He's getting cheekier every day.'

'To you?'

'Me he shows a little respect to, but not the girls. You ought to see the way he behaves in the kitchen, Alfons. It's impossible.'

Such complaints were not new to Materna, who had been deriving secret amusement from them for days. However, Jablonski's championship of womanhood was not only amusing but faintly disturbing. Father complexes of this type could lead to complications.

'Now listen to me, old friend,' Materna said, growing serious. 'The girls are both old enough to take care of themselves . . .'

'Not Sabine!' Jablonski broke in. 'She's little more than a child and I'm her guardian. I feel responsible for her. Anything wrong with that?'

'Nothing at all, except that Sabine is nineteen now, and she hasn't shown any signs of needing your protection—certainly not in that respect.'

'No? That young scoundrel had the cheek to put his arm round her and give her a squeeze. I saw him at it through the kitchen window.'

'Well? Did she fight him off or call for help?'

'She doesn't realize who she's tangling with. Besides, she's as good as engaged. Konrad and Peter may not be ideal for her, but they're the best prospects available. That Ambal fellow is completely out of the question.'

'Good God, Jacob, who's asking you? The girls know their own minds. Anyway, a hug like that may have been quite innocuous—just a spontaneous mark of affection.'

'Let's hope it was,' growled Jablonski. 'In any case, I don't intend to tolerate that sort of behaviour in future—I thought you ought to know.'

Materna wagged his head. 'I'd like your worries! You ought to spend a bit more time checking our equipment. The bicycles need new tyres, also bigger carriers. We'll be taking even more stuff with us on our nocturnal excursions in future.'

There was the sound of a rapidly approaching car. Jablonski heaved himself off the packing-case. 'That's Hermann's rattle trap.'

Hermann Materna could only spare a few minutes. He had come to deliver three cans of petrol, two rifles and a Very pistol. He also announced that he had just dumped five truck-loads of stores at the Gasthaus.

'Scharfke's face was a study,' he said. 'I unloaded fifteen tons on him, all at once. The place is piled to the ceiling.'

Materna pricked up his ears. 'He wasn't pleased?'

'Far from it. He even tried to cancel the whole thing, but it was too late for that, of course.'

'In other words, Eis is against it,' Materna said. 'That means he already suspects that the supply depot is anything but a friendly gesture. Remarkably shrewd of him—but then, Eis has all the instincts of a predator.'

'He only needed to read the official directive I brought with me.' Hermann handed his father a copy. 'As senior Party representative here, he will be held personally responsible for the depot's maintenance and supervision. We've got him over a barrel, and he knows it.'

Materna congratulated Hermann on his welcome news. Then he said: 'If I know Eis, he won't take this lying down. He'll do something about it, but what?'

'Take it out on Scharfke, probably,' replied Hermann. 'Eis never forgives anyone for stepping out of line, let alone for hanging a millstone round his neck. Somebody has to suffer.' He gave one of his rare grins. 'Eugen's been lucky with his fathers-in-law.'

Jablonski nodded. 'It could work out well. What about putting another spoke in his wheel—Ambal, for instance? He's a lady's man. Nearly every woman in the village is crazy about him, and that includes Christine Eis.'

'How do you know?' Materna asked.

'These things get around. Besides, Pierre told me himself that he's noticed her staring at him in the village. He knows what he's talking about, that boy. Couldn't we make something out of it?'

'It's a bit risky,' mused Materna, '—damned difficult to arrange, too. It would be a miracle if it came off.'

'Why not?' Jablonski said. 'You were the one who called Maulen a place of unlimited possibilities. I'm coming to believe it myself.'

It was shortly before the Sunday on which, in earlier years, the Masurians had been accustomed to celebrate their harvest festival. This had entailed rising early, downing a quick schnapps, attending church and the ensuing ceremony at the war memorial, visiting the fair in the village square, and, finally, dancing the night away in the Gasthaus. The advent of harvest-home signalled the year's greatest consumption of hard liquor.

This was still prodigious. Wine and spirits were in extremely short supply and the war-time beer looked and tasted like dishwater, but almost everyone in Maulen had a cupboard full of bottles of schnapps distilled from grain or potatoes.

Distilling was strictly prohibited and subject to severe penalties, but none of the villagers worried about that. There were one or two last, as it were, hallowed rights which even Eugen Eis respected—not least because he himself exploited this source of supply to the full.

Potato spirit was generally consumed by landless citizens, labourers, artisans, refugees, and junior officials such as the postman. The peasant farmers continued to distil their traditional grain spirit. They drank most of it themselves, too, only parting with an occasional bottle for the benefit of middle-ranking officials such as the village constable, subordinate Party leaders such as Neuber, and, more recently, Sergeant-Major Fackler, who supplied cheap labour in the form of prisoners of war.

The village élite, consisting of Eugen Eis and his closest associates, had considerable quantities of loot at their disposal, including cognac from France, fruit liqueurs from the

Balkans, and champagne from the Crimea. On the other side
of the fence, Alfons Materna was still producing the excellent
schnapps for which he had been famed when the Thousand
Year Reich was no more than a glint in Adolf Hitler's eye.

Thus, even in the dark days of 1944, the Führer's twelfth
year, Maulen was not destitute of what was locally known as
'spiritual consolation'. It helped the villagers to forget a lot
of things, at least temporarily, but they had discovered of late
that liquor was subject to the law of diminishing returns.
Euphoria was of far shorter duration than the resultant
hang-over.

'We're going to celebrate this harvest festival as pleasantly
as possible,' Materna announced. He pulled the map on the
table towards him. 'What's more, we'll bring it to a really
memorable conclusion.'

'Must we?' said Jablonski. 'Why can't you forget everything for once and take it easy?'

'Because today is the perfect day,' Materna replied, studying the map. 'Our kind of harvest needs special climatic conditions—like a fog of schnapps over everything.'

His finger tapped the village of Kurken, south of Lake
Lasker. 'Grienspan left me an accurate sketch-map of this
district.' He produced a sheet of paper. 'You see the small
rectangle on the edge of the village, between the main road and
the woods? Hermann put that in.'

'What does it represent?'

'A petrol dump, probably belonging to the command area
of the Führer's Headquarters. It's guarded by a few S.S.
men, but they'll probably be celebrating harvest-home in
their own way.'

'Couldn't we tackle it another time? After all, we've got
guests today, and there are two choice geese roasting in the
oven. They may spoil, but that petrol dump won't run away.'

'All right,' Materna decided. 'First things first.'

Hannelore Welser and Sabine Gäbler had made elaborate
preparations for the festive meal. The guests referred to by
Jablonski—Peter Bachus and Konrad Klinger—were already
sitting in the kitchen talking nineteen to the dozen.

Peter and Konrad had both graduated after a brief spell of
'home front' service. One had been assigned to Dr Gensfleisch,
who was ostensibly ill and in need of an assistant, and the

other was working in Dr Rogatzki's chambers at Allenstein. This relatively painless form of conscription was the outcome of a series of skilful but far from inexpensive manœuvres. Among those involved were Baron von der Brocken, Hermann Materna and his Regional Director, and some secret friends of Erich Wollnau who still managed to wield influence in their various fields.

'This is probably the last harvest-home of the war,' Peter said, ploughing through his roast goose with gusto.

'It could be the last one we ever celebrate on Masurian soil—who knows?' Konrad Klinger refilled the glasses. They were Materna's best, full-bellied goblets of sparkling blue-white crystal which were only brought out on special occasions.

'We're not done yet,' Materna said.

He raised his glass to the two girls, who were sitting there in silence, then to the two young men, then to Jablonski. 'Even if I knew the world was going to end tomorrow,' he said, striving to sound gay and unconcerned, 'I'd plant my little tree all the same. Wasn't it Martin Luther who said that?'

The others matched his mood. They clustered round him, temporarily oblivious of the things that were happening in the outside world, of the threats that loomed over them, of the horrors that constantly, with the brutal insistence of a whiplash, impelled their thoughts in the same direction—towards a mysterious haze of uncertainty beyond which anything might lie.

Materna kindled their memories and they warmed themselves in the glow of recollection. Events which seemed aeons away, though they were only a few years removed, became larger than life, more colourful, more alluring.

At a nod from Materna, Hannelore wound up the old gramophone and Sabine picked out a record—a Viennese waltz. She walked over to Jablonski, dropped a graceful curtsy, and smilingly asked him to dance.

Jablonski placed a rugged arm round his dream-child with a wonderfully tender gesture and waltzed her gravely round the kitchen.

And so they danced, laughed and chatted the afternoon away, until evening came and Materna pulled out his fob-watch and said: 'You must excuse Jacob and me. We have to take a short trip.'

After a moment's hesitation, Konrad and Peter rose too
and offered to escort them, but Materna was adamant.

'No, you stay here and look after the girls. Jacob and I
plan to entertain ourselves in our own way—alone, if you
don't mind.'

'It's gone ten o'clock already,' Eis said, feigning concern. 'I
find it so hard to tear myself away. There's such an aura of
integrity about you, my dear Henriette—such a German aura,
if I may so put it.'

He had not called on Himmler's niece empty-handed, but
bearing a basket of poultry—an old Masurian harvest-home
tradition, or so he assured her. In return, he had been showered
with words of gratitude.

'You're very welcome to stay,' she replied, '—if you're enjoying yourself, that is.'

Eis brazenly assured her that he was enjoying himself,
averting his gaze from the coffee in front of him and the
woman beside him. Both seemed uncommonly insipid tonight,
and he was used to more piquant offerings.

'We lead a very simple life here,' Henriette said. Whether
or not she was referring to the weak coffee, she spoke with
modest pride. 'Simple but conscientious, as befits women
engaged on work of national importance.'

'I admire you!' Eis exclaimed abruptly. Laying his hand
on her arm in an access of fervent but properly restrained enthusiasm, he felt the moist warmth of sinewy flesh creep
through her coarse linen blouse.

He hastily withdrew his hand, murmuring an apology, but
a moment later he returned to the fray. 'Yes, I admire you,
not only as a leader of women but as a woman in your own
right—please forgive my frankness. Your revered uncle
has every right to be proud of you.'

They were alone in Henriette's private quarters. One or
two senior girl pioneers were sitting in the next room, chatting
and drinking coffee secretly laced with brandy, but Eis welcomed their presence. Protected by this cordon sanitaire,
he could pursue his prey in safety.

Henriette's pale blue eyes shone with self-assurance. 'Dear
Uncle Heinrich!—I always call him Heini, by the way. Yes,
I do hope I've given him some reason to be pleased with
me.'

'Are you in constant touch with him?'

'Uncle Heini is a busy man, of course, but he got one of his aides to write to me recently—that shows how over-worked he is. He plans to pay me a visit as soon as time permits and his duties bring him to this area.'

Eugen Eis had thought himself proof against any shock, but the very possibility of greeting the Reichsführer S.S.—the mightiest of the mighty—in the middle of Maulen was so overwhelming that he snorted with emotion.

Henriette, who interpreted this as the effect of her uniquely personal aura, leant towards him, but he evaded her with some skill, converting the gesture into another glance at his watch. 'How time flies when I'm with you! It really is unforgivable of me to have taken up so much of your time.'

'No, please,' she said quickly. 'It's a pleasure to spend it in your company.'

'How charming of you,' he replied. 'In that case, I think I might take the liberty of joining you again towards midnight without making myself too conspicuous. After all, today is a day of thanksgiving.'

Ernst Schlaguweit, commander of the relics of Maulen's S.A. contingent, paraded his followers and addressed them.

'Men,' he said, 'as you know, one of our new duties is to guard the supply depot. It will mean a lot of extra work, but we mustn't let that get us down. Just to set a good example, I'm going to stand guard myself—not regularly, but from time to time. What's more, I'm going to take the middle watch tonight, from ten till two.'

And there he now stood, on the edge of the village square near the side door of the Gasthaus store-room, peering into the night. He was armed with a carbine, two stick-grenades, his S.A. dirk, and his 'comforter', a special implement consisting of a two-foot length of garden hose filled with lead.

The Gasthaus lay silent, the bar having been closed by the office of the Local Group Leader on the grounds that this was not the time for noisy celebrations, however traditional. Scharfke did not object to such closures since there was little profit to be made from selling drink these days. If things continued to deteriorate, the bar would soon be running at a loss. Consequently, the innkeeper had welcomed the Party's patriotic decision and set aside three bottles of champagne from the supply depot for his own personal consumption.

Hard drinking was being done elsewhere in Maulen that
night. Ernst Schlaguweit not only knew this but could hear
the results from his lonely post. Raucous male singing and
whinnies of feminine laughter issued from several houses. The
guardian of the supply depot sneered at the sound. Let them
soak, he told himself. He was girding his loins for action.

He walked to the only lighted window in the Gasthaus and
tapped gently on the pane. The sound of his knocking seemed
to reverberate like thunder, but no one except Scharfke heard
it.

The innkeeper opened the window and leant out. 'Who is
it?' he asked in a blurred voice. Then, recognizing Schlaguweit, he said: 'Come in, Ernst, you old sod. The champagne
corks are popping tonight. Lovely stuff from my supply
dump—a case got damaged in transit and one or two bottles
are going spare. You can have some if you like.'

'You're drunk, you pig.' Schlaguweit made the statement
with satisfaction. 'Come out here. It's time you had a pee.'

'I'll do it through the window,' threatened Scharfke.

'Don't you dare! I'm out here, and I'm on duty.'

Scharfke gave a bleating laugh. 'Don't be shy. No need
to beat about the bush if you want something out of me.
Well, what is it?'

'The key to the store-room.'

'Over my dead body!' Sharfke retorted, but without for-
feiting his alcoholic bonhomie. 'You'd like that, wouldn't
you?'

'Don't be a fool, it's only for security reasons. I heard
noises coming from inside. Sounded like someone creeping
around in there.'

'What? In my store?' Scharfke hastily retracted his head.
Rushing across the room to a cupboard, he opened it and
took out a bunch of keys. Schlaguweit, who could see him
clearly through the open window, rejoiced at the sight.

'I'll cover your rear, Christian,' he said when Scharfke
had joined him outside.

'Is that carbine loaded, Ernst? Safety catch off?'

'I've got my comforter—that's good enough.'

'If there's someone after my stores, we'll murder him. I'm
relying on you, Ernst.'

'You do that.'

'I'll cover your rear, Christian,' he said, when Scharfke bent forward, laid his ear against the planking, and listened.

'I can't hear anything,' he whispered.

'Take a look,' Schlaguweit urged him. 'You're in for a big surprise, I promise you.'

Scharfke fumbled hurriedly with his keys, opened the door, and peered into the darkness. Schlaguweit switched on his torch, and its bright circular beam danced across mountains of crates, sacks and cartons.

'You must have made a mistake.'

'I never make mistakes,' replied Schlaguweit.

So saying, he raised his length of loaded garden hose and brought it down with great force on the back of Scharfke's skull. There was a dull thud, a stifled groan, and Scharfke folded up. Schlaguweit played his torch on him. The innkeeper's legs twitched briefly like those of a sleeping dog and then lay still.

'That ought to do the trick,' Schlaguweit muttered. He dragged Scharfke to the foot of the nearest pile of crates and rolled him over on his stomach. Then he pressed a champagne bottle into his clenched hand and stepped back to admire his handiwork.

Like a stevedore, he spat on his hands and proceeded to dislodge the uppermost crates one by one. It was strenuous work, and he was panting by the time he had finished.

A final heave, and the crates at the top started to sway. With a soft slithering sound which ended in an almighty crash, they fell on top of Christian Scharfke's prone body, burying him beneath several hundredweight of assorted stores. Red wine oozed from the broken planking.

'An accident,' said Schlaguweit, recovering his breath. 'Just what the doctor ordered.'

'There isn't a proper man among you,' Christine scoffed. 'All wind and piss, the lot of you.'

These heartening words were addressed to Sergeant-Major Fackler and his two junior N.C.O.s, who were called Schlamke and Lufter. They, too, were celebrating harvest-home. The invitation had come from the Local Group Leader, but Christine was representing him in his absence—a promising sign.

Fackler, who had already met Christine on a number of occasions, knew her more than slightly.

'If we aren't good enough for you,' he said with a hint of a yawn, 'you only have to say.'

Christine Eis, née Scharfke, had abandoned all her inhibitions long ago. She could sleep where and with whomsoever she pleased. Eugen Eis approved of sex as a means to power, and so, far from hindering her activities, he positively encouraged them.

'You're like all the rest,' Christine said, leaning back on the sofa, '—like animals.'

'Steady, we're N.C.O.s, if you don't mind!'

This protest came from one of the two men who were sitting close beside her, crowding and fumbling with her— Lufter or Schlamke, it didn't matter which: they were completely interchangeable. Words of endearment were uttered in a mechanical monotone, hot hands clamped themselves on her neck, slid sideways to her shoulders, described a rapid arc, downwards and forwards, to her breasts, palpating, squeezing, massaging. . . .

'You make me sick!' Christine said fiercely. 'Everyone round here makes me sick.'

'The best way to cure that is to lie down,' Fackler said. 'Why don't you do that?' He reached for his zither.

Fackler cherished musical ambitions, though his repertoire was limited to two or three pieces. His favourite was a kind of Bavarian waltz entitled *Grilled Sausage*, but he could also play a folksy melody which sounded vaguely like *At the Fountain by the Gate* and a popular song which urgently recommended the listener never to say goodbye, only au revoir.

'When it rains Leberwurst and snows Sauerkraut,' warbled Fackler, plucking his jangling strings with panache, 'then my heart sings a happy song, tralala!'

As he sang, he took in the scene through slightly narrowed eyes which had seen much, even though much of it lacked variety. He saw a dense jungle of furniture, a thick green carpet resembling an ill-mown lawn, and a high-backed sofa the colour of clotted blood, too low to sit on comfortably and too narrow to lie on—in other words, a slipway leading straight to the carpet.

'Turn the lights down,' commanded Fackler, whereupon he

began to intone his folk-song in a plaintive, tremulous baritone. The night was still young, and Eis would not, on his own submission, be home before midnight.

'You ought to be ashamed of yourselves,' Christine told the N.C.O.s.

'Why?' asked one of them. 'Why should I be ashamed of myself when I've got a clean shirt on? Want to take a look?'

'Your men have no manners,' Christine told Fackler. 'They don't know how to treat a woman—nobody here does! They knead you like a lump of dough. You ought to take a few tips from those P.O.W.s of yours—proper men, they are.'

'Anyone special in mind?' asked Fackler, strumming his zither. 'What about Ambal, the one who turns all the women's heads? Do you mean him?'

But Christine was past replying. The two N.C.O.s, feeling that their virility had been impugned had intensified their efforts. Fackler watched the trio, plucking at his instrument as though eviscerating a chicken.

Christine slid with practised ease from the sofa to the carpet, where her clothes were ripped off her.

'Me first,' said Fackler, kneeling down. He was the ranking N.C.O., after all. It was he who had received the invitation from the master of the house, now so tactfully absent, and he who had provided the mood-music. There were certain priorities to be observed.

At that moment, Ernst Schlaguweit burst in without knocking.

'Sorry to break up the party, folks, but first things first. There's been a frightful accident. It's my old friend Christian Scharfke. Christine's father—he's dead.'

Ignaz Uschkurat, once Maulen's highly respected mayor, was weeping silently. The tears trickled down his ravaged face, one by one.

He was drunk, of course, like almost everybody in Maulen that night, but in his case drunkenness showed signs of becoming a chronic condition.

Three of Uschkurat's five sons had been killed in action. One had deserted, and the fifth still worked, sullen, idle and rebellious, on his farm. His wife had died too, of rat poison. She had drunk it mixed with rum the previous Christmas.

'I'm all alone now,' Uschkurat muttered to himself.

'Cheer up,' Amadeus Neuber said brightly. 'Don't be down-hearted, there's always me.'

'You?' Uschkurat blinked at him through a mist of tears, half hopefully, half in scorn. 'You're as big a rat as the others.'

Neuber kept his temper. 'Don't say that. I'm used to being misjudged, but it still hurts.'

'What did you do when they took all my jobs away?'

'I was against it, Ignaz.'

'But you didn't say anything, let alone do anything, not even when they squeezed my property out of me bit by bit —my cattle, my grain, my wood. They're to blame for my wife's death, too, and my sons'.'

'No one regrets these things more than I do, Ignaz, but how can I help you unless you help yourself?'

'What am I supposed to do—kill Eis and Schlaguweit and a dozen more besides, including you? There isn't any other way.'

'Well, you could always prefer charges on an official basis. I'd even help you—to draft the denunciation, I mean. Mind you, nobody must know for the moment that I'm so firmly on your side. You do understand, don't you? I'm not all-powerful here—not yet, anyway.'

'You think it would do any good, preferring charges?'

'Ask Materna, but you needn't tell him I advised you to.'

'I already asked him.'

'Well, what did he say?'

Everybody has to pay for his mistakes sometime—that was what Materna had said, among other things. He also said that anyone who gambled away his hard-earned property, denied his conscience and sold his soul was a poor slob, whichever way you looked at it.

'What did he say?' repeated Neuber.

'He didn't say anything,' Uschkurat mumbled. 'He's got worries of his own.' His eyes widened suddenly, as though enlightenment had dawned. 'I'm a low-down miserable slob,' he said, and started snivelling again.

Neuber let him get on with it. While waiting, he studied his hands, which were a constant source of pride to him. They were almost as small as those of the eleven-year-old refugee girl whom he had taken into his home—together with her mother, of course. The thought of the cuddly little creature quite warmed his heart.

'What have you got to lose, Ignaz?' he asked after a lengthy pause. 'You can't be worse off than you are already.'

'You're right!' exclaimed Uschkurat, squaring his shoulders. Then he slumped back in his chair again. 'But I may get gaol if I slander Eis—he told me so himself.'

'The court might interpret that as a threat,' Neuber said. 'Just one more crime—a serious crime, too, if only you handle it properly with my help.'

'My God,' Uschkurat said, wavering, 'this is like playing with fire. I'll have to think it over carefully.' He got up and shambled to the door. 'I'll tell you this much, though—I'm burning up inside. I want justice.'

'Quite right,' Neuber commented approvingly. 'I know a a lot of people in Maulen who'll thank you for acting like a man again. Think of the old days, Ignaz. People looked up to you then. There's a man you can trust—that's what they used to say.'

Uschkurat nodded dumbly and left the school-house feeling slightly cheered. He teetered across the village square and made for the beech-trees beside the churchyard wall. He had left his bottle of schnapps propped against one of them— he couldn't remember which.

Getting down on all fours, he circled the trees and found what he was looking for in the roots of the third. He lolled back against the trunk with his legs extended and drank deeply, gazing into the close and oppressive darkness with glazed eyes. There was a magical glow in the sky, which hung low over the village, and the branches above him seemed to rustle like silk. He tore his shirt open with both hands and groaned.

The next time he raised the bottle and, consequently, his head, there was a brief flash of summer lightning. Maulen, the village square, the beech-trees, the churchyard wall—all sprang into sharp focus. And there, leaning against the wall, Uschkurat thought he saw a man staring across at him— a small man with a pale face, unmistakable in its clarity.

'Grienspan!' shouted Uschkurat, but his cry was swallowed up in the returning darkness. He heaved himself to his feet

W.   O and staggered to the churchyard wall. 'Where are you?' he croaked, slapping and scrabbling at the stones. 'Where are you, Grienspan?'

There was no reply, no sign of anyone at all.

Uschkurat subsided against the bare wall with his hands still raised and his body shaking like that of a man in a high fever. Then he ran back to the school-house as fast as his legs would carry him. Panting, he burst into Neuber's room and shouted: 'I saw him—I saw him quite clearly! He was standing in front of me, as large as life!'

Neuber looked resentful. He had been about to look in on his little refugee girl. She was a restless sleeper, normally, and tended to kick her bedclothes off. It was his custom to cover her up again, having first adjusted her position with a deft and tender touch. He always savoured these intimate little moments.

'Who are you talking about?'

'Grienspan,' Uschkurat insisted. 'Do you remember him, or was he before your time? Siegfried Grienspan, the Jewish cattle-dealer from Allenstein. He disappeared about ten years back. I saw him just now, leaning against the churchyard wall and staring at me—his eyes went through me like a knife! Where could he have come from, and what does it mean?'

'It means you're drunk as a fiddler's bitch,' Neuber replied coldly. 'You've been seeing things.'

'I saw him, I tell you!'

'You're crazy, you poor fool.' Neuber spoke with a mixture of contempt and disillusionment. There was nothing to be done with the drunken idiot—to believe otherwise would be yet another error of judgement on his part. Rage bubbled up inside him. 'Push off and keep your mouth shut if you don't want to end up in Kortau.'

Kortau, a township near Allenstein, boasted an insane asylum. There was a saying: 'He who sticks his neck out goes to Allenstein; he who sticks his neck out too far goes to Kortau'—and everyone in the village knew it.

As soon as Ignaz Uschkurat heard the word Kortau he hung his head and slunk out.

Alfons Materna lay in the long grass, looking up at the stars. He could hear the rhythmical croaking of frogs, overlaid with a drunken babble of human voices.

Jacob Jablonski lay beside him on his stomach, peering across at the huts which stood in the field between the wood and the main road, little more than a hundred yards away. Light still streamed from several of the windows and radio music drifted into the night mingled with shouts of raucous laughter.

Every now and then, if only for a second or two, silence descended, heavy and menacing. Sometimes the tread of a sentry could be heard, or the rattle of a distant truck, but the noise from the huts soon drowned everything else.

Two explosive charges had been laid. One, pushed through the barbed wire fence on the end of a long pole, nestled against a stack of petrol drums. The other was attached to the supports of the small wooden bridge over the stream—the only means of access to the fuel dump, and, consequently, the only route out. The fuses ended in a device the size of a kitchen alarm clock which lay beside Materna. This had come from Grienspan, who had acquired it, via Polish partisans, from some British saboteurs for whom it had been dropped by parachute. Its land of origin was the United States.

'Why hang around?' grumbled Jablonski. 'What's the point?'

'It's only just gone midnight,' Materna told him. 'The sentry didn't come on duty until ten minutes ago—he won't be drowsy enough yet. It won't hurt the others to have another drink, either. The more the merrier, from our point of view.'

Their bicycles lay ready to hand and their line of retreat was carefully mapped out. If they observed all the proper precautions, it should take them about three hours to get back to Maulen.

'It doesn't matter too much,' Jablonski insisted. 'Set those charges off and let's get out of here.'

Materna stared at the sky. 'I don't want to.'

'What's that supposed to mean?'

'It's hard,' Materna said, almost inaudibly, 'it's damned hard, but what else can I do?'

Jablonski shook his head. 'What's the matter? Not scared, are you?'

'All I wanted to do was survive, and survive as pleasantly as possible. I've always wanted a quiet life for as long as

I can remember, and what's the result? Here I am, getting ready to blow up a petrol dump. Why am I lying here, Jacob?'

'Just what I was wondering. You only have to throw that switch and we can get out of here.'

Materna threw the switch and two mushrooms of flame shot skywards. The one by the bridge went up with a muffled roar and faded quickly. The other, beside the petrol drums, flared up and burst, gaining height and expanding into a billowing ball of fire tinged with furnace-red, orange-yellow, and foam-white.

'Let's go,' said Materna.

3

'You're taking your time,' Councillor Engel said reproachfully. 'Another petrol dump went up last night.'

'I know,' replied Tantau, without looking up from his papers. His tone was serene.

'Well, go on. What do you propose to do about it?'

'What do you expect me to do, cancel the explosion?' The little detective laughed impishly to himself. 'I don't know a great deal about East Prussia, Herr Engel. I was simply transferred here. However, one feature of this peculiar country struck me very quickly. People have little capacity for logical and consistent thought. The predominant characteristic is a fertile imagination, especially in Masuria, and that is hardly calculated to make my work any easier.'

'You mean you're giving up?'

Councillor Engel felt worried. Major Rattenhauer was already pressing for tangible results, and he held Engel responsible for getting them.

'From my point of view,' Tantau said, toying with a pair of compasses, 'a few more explosions and operations on this scale won't do any harm.'

'How do you mean?'

Tantau looked up with a smile. 'I'm not here to accelerate anyone's promotion or consolidate his present position— let me make that quite clear. I'm working neither for you,

Herr Engel, nor for Herr Rattenhauer. Are we agreed so far?'

'Nobody asked you to do any such thing,' Engel said, sitting down.

'Asked, no, expected, yes. That's what I'm trying to warn you about.'

Engel studied the little man's gnome-like countenance with mounting uneasiness. Tantau had been ensconced behind his desk for days now, reading reports, messages and statements, scribbling notes, drawing up lists and plans, making sketches, playing with his ruler and compasses. He merely nodded when reports were conveyed to him, and his normal response to requests for his opinion was to grin stupidly.

'I was assured that you always did a quick and thorough job,' Engel said in a dispirited voice.

'That is hardly a guarantee. Besides, I must point out that my successes are based on the use of personal methods.'

'But you've been given a completely free hand,' Engel protested. 'You're far less restricted here than you ever were in Berlin—I've made sure of that. You needn't worry about treading on people's corns.'

'I don't intend to.'

'Herr Tantau,' Engel said coaxingly, 'may I remind you of the Gerschke case—the man who used to attack and rob courting couples, and murdered five of them?'

'Seven,' amended Tantau.

'All right, seven. The C.I.D. spent months hunting for the murderer before the case was handed over to you. You got him inside a few weeks.'

'Eighteen days, to be precise.'

'It was the same with the cinema box-office robberies in Berlin, the sex murders in Düsseldorf and the Hamburg air-raid murder, when the man killed his wife and three children so that he could marry another woman. How long did you spend on those cases? A couple of weeks at most.'

'I was only in Hamburg for three days, and two of those were spent visiting a friend—an expert eel-smoker.' A gluttonous smile settled on Tantau's face. 'Do you know what his secret was? It was mainly to do with the way he prepared the eels—he used to spread them with a home-made paste of butter, oil and herbs. They tasted superb.'

'I'm sure they did,' Engel said, wondering how to stem

Tantau's epicurean revelations, but Tantau had the bit between his teeth.

'He wanted to leave me the recipe in his will, but he died a few months ago in an air-raid. He was burnt to a crisp, poor man, and he had the formula on him at the time. I doubt if I'll ever taste such superb smoked eel again.'

'Listen,' Engel cut in brusquely, 'we're wasting valuable time. I put it to you—can we afford to do that?'

'Certainly we can. I must wait for our friends to carry out another two operations—three preferably.'

'But that might take weeks!'

'Months, perhaps—who can tell? On the other hand, it might be only a matter of days if I get hold of some usable evidence—not just the remains of foreign explosives, but personal items such as an article of clothing or a bicycle.' Tantau grinned. 'The best thing, of course, would be a lost identity card.'

Engel shuffled nervously in his chair. 'I don't feel easy in my mind,' he confessed.

'Cheer up,' Tantau said. 'Remember, Herr Rattenhauer will be feeling just as uneasy, if not more so. That's a comforting thought, isn't it? You might pray for a miracle, too. Believe me, miracles do happen, even in our business.'

'But what can I tell Rattenhauer?'

'You might try the following line of argument: normally, a certain relationship exists between a criminal and his crime. In murder, as in many other acts of violence, the act itself enables one to form conclusions about the agent and the agent is reflected in his act. Whether by design or accident, whatever the nature of the case, the agent leaves a signature which reveals something of himself.'

'I follow your theory, but it doesn't apply here—not a hundred per cent. That's what you're driving at, isn't it?'

'You really have understood, I see. No, the acts of sabotage which we are dealing with here don't presuppose any criminal tendency or disposition. The people responsible may be either partisans, imported saboteurs, or locals—probably the latter, in view of their detailed local knowledge. In that case, we may be dealing with men whose motives are founded on moral, ethical considerations.'

'Never quote that theory to Rattenhauer.'

'He'll have to take it into account.' Tantau pulled his map towards him and studied its maze of lines and circles with something akin to affection. 'Even an experienced detective can be floored by the unpredictable—for instance, a man with a head stuffed with moral principles and an automatic pistol in his hand. For all 'that, acts of violence do give one something to go on, especially if they're repeated. They can be analysed. They also leave clues behind, however insignificant, and clues mount up.'

Engel gave an exclamation of delight. 'You mean you're on the track after all?'

'Possibly. Take a look at this. The red circles show where sabotage has occurred, the larger concentric circles in blue indicate the saboteurs' probable range—estimated speed, travelling cross-country by night with the aid of bicycles, between four and six miles an hour. And mark this: if my first theory is correct, the saboteurs, who are probably intelligent and determined men, will seldom if ever operate in the immediate vicinity of their base. They are far more likely to pick places within range but as far from base as possible.'

'Excellent. So your lines and circles already point to the probable location of the saboteurs?'

'According to my first theory, yes. I have at least three up my sleeve, but the first generally proves the most useful in practice. Just to reassure you still further—if you regard it as reassurance—we're looking for people of strong character and firm convictions. They shouldn't be too difficult to pick out in times like these, should they?'

Councillor Engel ignored this remark. He stared at the spot on the map where the lines and circles intersected, like rays converging on a focal point.

It was an area which encompassed the villages of Siegwalde, Gross-Grieben, and Maulen.

'I'm warning you,' Eis said to Christine. 'Don't get any stupid ideas or you'll regret it.'

Christine did not reply. She had seemed blind and deaf to him ever since she learned of her father's death.

'Still not talking to anyone?' Eis scrutinized her keenly as he climbed into his uniform trousers. 'You ought to have bought yourself a new dress, a black silk one. That's the least you could have done for your old man. I'd have paid—in kind, of course. Christian's memory is worth that much to me.'

She looked at him for the first time. Her big eyes rested on him, black-ringed and menacing. Seconds dragged by in silence.

'Well?' he demanded uneasily. 'What's on your mind? Speak up.'

She turned away with an abrupt movement and mechanically started to tidy her hair. The sight of herself in the mirror revolted her.

'All right, so don't talk. Maybe that's the best policy, anyway. You're in mourning, so shroud yourself in silence— it'll make a good impression at the funeral. Just stand there and hold my arm—I'll take care of the speechifying.'

Christine's ominous gaze sought his reflection in the mirror.

'Listen carefully,' he said, stationing himself close behind her. 'Suspect me of anything you like—tell me so to my face, if you want to, but breathe a word to anyone else and you'll soon find out that I'm capable of more than you thought.'

Eis did not wait for an answer. Struggling into his best tunic, he went on: 'I'm genuinely sorry about your father's death and I wouldn't advise anyone to question my sincerity, either. Nobody was to blame, least of all me. I was busy somewhere else at the time, and I've got witnesses to prove it. It was an accident sustained while performing duties of national importance. That's the official cause of death, understand?'

He polished his War Service Cross on his sleeve, glancing at his watch as he did so. Then he took Christine's arm and jerked her roughly to her feet. 'If you don't pull yourself together there'll be another funeral. I've taken the precaution of buying enough ground to bury the lot of us.'

Christian Scharfke's funeral was simple, as befitted the times. Eis had decreed this and Schlaguweit had made sure that the public did not attend. No death knell tolled, and the time of the funeral was communicated to invited guests only.

'Everything's going according to plan,' reported Schlaguweit, who was waiting at the churchyard gate in a dark civilian suit. 'Nobody's turned up—just the usual morbid old hags and a few bored refugees. Shall I tell them to get lost?'

Eis shook his head. 'Let's get it over.' He clamped Christine's arm against his side and marched across to the open grave.

There were more wreaths than mourners. Eis himself had ordered three: one in his capacity as Local Group Leader, one as a magistrate, and one as a relative of the deceased. All the ribbons attached were adorned with swastikas. Two more wreaths came from Schlaguweit, who was not only the commander of the S.A. but a friend and comrade. The other twenty had been paid for by various organizations, associations and clubs.

Among those detailed to attend the funeral were the director of organization, i.e. Neuber, the current mayor, the farmers' leader, two tradesmen, five Brownshirts, four of whom acted as uniformed pall-bearers, and two representatives each from the Women's League, Hitler Youth and German Girls' League.

The vicar, who was there by arrangement but only for the purpose of uttering a brief prayer, stood to one side. Behind him hovered the ten inquisitive spectators, eight of them women. Several of the latter were already sobbing to themselves in a suitably funereal manner.

'Dear fellow-mourners and Party members,' Eis began, 'men and women of Germany. We are gathered here today to bury one of our most respected citizens. Snatched from us at a grim but glorious moment in our history, he did not live to see the final victory for which he yearned so ardently. His death lays an added burden of responsibility on our shoulders. . . .'

So much for the preamble. Funeral addresses, too, had become a routine part of Eis's duties. He now touched upon the personal aspect. 'Our late lamented friend and comrade departed this life in the fulfilment of his obligations to the community. He watched faithfully over the stores entrusted to him, burned the midnight oil—even turned to and lent a hand himself. And that was how it came about.'

Eis, who had started to gallop through his speech, drew a deep breath and studied the mourners closely to see if anyone was wearing a suspicious expression. No one was, but, just to preclude any misunderstanding, he repeated in an emphatic tone: 'That was how it came about. It was a tragic accident, nothing more.'

He heard Christine sob. The sound had a salutary effect on the other mourners, who looked deeply moved. The only exception was a young man whom Eis had overlooked until now. Young Dr Bachus, Dr Gensfleisch's assistant, had insinuated himself into the gawping knot of uninvited guests. He appeared to be grinning.

Eis faltered for a moment and then brought his address to a swift conclusion. It was time for the most effective and stirring passage of all.

'These are hard times, momentous but hard. They call for stout hearts and a sense of pride. Sacrifices are unavoidable. Christian Scharfke's death comes as a deep loss to me personally. He was not only a comrade-in-arms of many years' standing but a loyal friend. My wife has lost a beloved father, and I have lost a man whom I, too, came to love like a father.'

He paused, seemingly unable to continue, and gave Christine's arm a warning squeeze. After staring at the ground as though moved beyond words, he suddenly raised his head. 'We shall never forget you, Christian Scharfke!' he cried. 'We shall always revere your memory—that I promise you!'

He nodded to Schlaguweit and Schlaguweit nodded to his Brownshirts, who deftly lowered the coffin into the grave. While the vicar was still praying, Eis passed his wife the shovel and guided her hand three times to the pile of sand, tipping the remains of the last shovelful into the grave himself.

The others followed his example, but as he was standing there in silence young Dr Bachus elbowed his way forward.

'Didn't you hear the result of my post mortem?' he inquired. 'You ought to read my report. It doubts whether the fatal injuries sustained by the victim of this alleged accident could all have been caused by the packing-cases that fell on him.'

Eugen Eis tucked his chin in and flinched like a man who had been treacherously punched below the belt. He stared at Peter Bachus as though he had only just caught sight of him. 'Don't bother me with it now, young man,' he said evenly. 'This is a funeral, can't you see?'

He turned to his wife and put his arm round her with a protective air. Peter Bachus walked off looking moderately pleased with himself.

Schlaguweit received orders to report to the Local Group Leader's office immediately after the funeral.

'Ernst,' said Eis, 'I'm thinking of appointing you manager of the Gasthaus and the property that goes with it. Do you feel up to the job?'

Schlaguweit beamed. 'I'll handle things just the way you want them—I always do.'

Eis nodded. 'Good for you. First, though, I'd like you to give young Dr Bachus the once over. He talks a load of rubbish, that boy. Get it out of his system.'

'You couldn't have come at a better time,' Materna told Peter Bachus. 'I've something important to discuss with you.'

'That's lucky. I wanted a word with you too.'

'About the girls?'

'About Eugen Eis.'

Materna wagged his head. 'That sounds ominous. I thought I told you to give him a wide berth.'

'I'm sorry, Herr Materna, but I trod on his corns—hard. I couldn't help it.'

Modes of address between Materna and the Terrible Twins, as they once were, had not changed down the years. He still treated them like children and they still treated him with respect. Indeed, they were so anxious not to forfeit their semi-filial status that they had flatly rejected his invitation to call him by his Christian name after they graduated.

'What happened?' Materna asked, when they were installed in his den over a green earthenware jug of home-made schnapps.

'Christian Scharfke was buried before I had a chance to make out a death certificate.'

'That's nothing new, not in Maulen. Ask Dr Gensfleisch.'

'I examined the body very carefully. In my opinion, death resulted from cerebral haemorrhage. The base of the skull had been struck with a blunt instrument—tubular, probably. The packing-cases that fell on him fractured a number of bones, but it's unlikely that they killed him.'

'You told Eis this?'

'In the churchyard. He was flummoxed at first, but then he set Schlaguweit on mc. I simply refused to speak to him.'

'Have you any idea of the risks you're running?'

'I've given Eis something to chew on, that's all I know. With a bit of luck he'll choke himself.'

'But have you thought it over carefully?'

'What is there to think over? I've got him where I want him at last. This is the moment I've been waiting for. It's what you want too, isn't it?'

'No.'

'Why not?'

'In the first place, I've no objection to the rats killing each other off. Secondly, you didn't say you had definite proof. It's just a theory.'

'But it's enough! I can make plenty of trouble for Eis— you know how these things are done.'

'Of course, that's why I was interested to hear how Eis reacted. He did the logical thing—he passed you on to Schlaguweit, and Schlaguweit . . .'

'. . . murdered Christian Scharfke, in my opinion.'

'Yes, and it probably wasn't his first murder, either. He's an old hand.'

'So what? I'm not scared, not if you help me. You will, won't you?'

'Not this time,' Materna replied firmly.

'Then I'll handle it on my own—I must. It's time I did something drastic about these swine.'

Materna hesitated. 'I've always tried to shield you from certain things, you and Konrad. I wanted you to enjoy life as much as possible.'

'But who can, these days? Besides, I'm not interested in an easy life. I don't care what I do.'

Materna rose and began to pace the room. 'I suppose you've wondered about me occasionally, you two—worried about me too, I hope. Are you prepared to take the same risks?'

'We are.'

'Voluntarily, Peter? Without any form of compulsion, without regard to personal considerations or feelings?'

'From personal conviction,' Peter affirmed, more earnestly than was his wont.

'All right, call it conviction. It doesn't really matter why people try to fight this cancer. They may do it out of hatred, or revenge, or a sense of fair play, or love of adventure, or moral principles. Their motives may be altruistic or selfish—it doesn't matter. The main thing is, they're against it.'

'We've been against it long enough, haven't we?'

'Yes, lad, but I insist on disciplined opposition. You can join me, but make no mistake about it: what I say goes. Understand?'

'I understand. Konrad thinks exactly the same way.'

'That's settled, then. Rule number one: no head-on collisions with Eis. Rule number two: keep any evidence against him for future use. That means you'll have to do your best to allay Schlaguweit's suspicions.'

'All right. I thought things were moving at last, that's all.'

'So they are,' Materna replied. He called Jacob Jablonski and asked him to find Sergeant-Major Fackler. 'Give him to understand that we don't need our French P.O.W.s any longer. Let him think they've been after the girls.'

'Is that true?' Peter asked with a frown.

Materna smiled. 'You've a lot to learn, lad. And now, come with me.'

He led the way up to his bedroom. A big man was lying on the feather bed. His face was waxen and his body looked stiff and lifeless, but his hands moved restlessly on the heavy coverlet as though searching for something.

'He was wounded last night,' Materna said. 'Show me what you can do. Try to patch him up, but remember: as soon as you lay a finger on him you'll be in it up to your neck and you won't get out in a hurry. It isn't too late to change your mind.'

Peter Bachus did not even answer. He was already bending over the wounded man.

'It was a false alarm,' reported Schlaguweit. 'I put the screws on our little doctor and he took it like a lamb.'

'He's no lamb,' Eis said darkly. 'Did you make it clear to him that he'd get the chop if he opened his mouth too wide?'

'Did I! He refused to speak to me at first, but I cornered him in Dog's Meadow, down by the hay-rick. I grabbed him by the collar and asked him if he had anything against us. Nothing, he said. When I brought up the question of the death certificate and asked him about his findings, he took one look at my comforter and mumbled something about it all being a joke.'

'I don't think much of his jokes,' Eis growled, slightly mollified. 'He'll supply a death certificate, then?'

'He'll cough up—he knows which side his bread is buttered.'

'I wonder if Materna had anything to do with it,' mused Eis. 'That young puppy was quite vicious in the churchyard, and now he sits up and begs. I wonder why.'

'That's quite simple. He couldn't prove anything, thanks to my expert stage management, so he tried to bluff and Materna warned him off. Materna's no fool.'

'No, and he's getting more and more careful. The cunning swine spends his whole time rooting around on his own territory. If he farts, the stink gets blamed on someone else.'

Schlaguweit nodded. 'As soon as he scents trouble he dives for cover. Heard the latest? He's asked Sergeant-Major Fackler to find other employment for those two P.O.W.s of his.'

'Why should he do that? They've never shown any inclination to run away, even though we thought they might at one time. What has he got against cheap labour?'

'They've been after the women, I shouldn't wonder.' Schlaguweit grinned with relish. 'That Ambal fellow is a sly dog. A lot of the village women are keen on him.'

'Really?' drawled Eis, pricking up his ears.

'I don't know what the bitches see in him, not when there are so many better specimens around. Besides, it's less risky with us. Intercourse with prisoners of war carries a term of five or six years' imprisonment, as far as I can remember.'

'Really?' Eis repeated, even more alertly. He folded his hands and screwed up his eyes in a simulacrum of thought. 'You're right, my friend—sexual intercourse is no laughing matter. It isn't just a question of racial purity. There are other issues at stake, issues affecting the war-effort. It's possible that we haven't paid sufficient attention to them until now. Wouldn't you agree?'

Schlaguweit eyed him doubtfully but responded with an unqualified affirmative.

'In the old peacetime days,' Eis went on, 'these things regulated themselves almost automatically, by a process of natural selection. Wartime is an exceptional time, though. We have to adapt ourselves to it in every possible way. People's needs must be met.'

Schlaguweit's expression had changed to one of admiration. Eis's schemes always gave him an expectant thrill. 'If there's anything I can do,' he said, leering.

Eis leered back. 'I need somebody with a flair for organization, not a sex maniac. We've got to think of the community, Ernst. Take Fackler's men—they need individual care and attention and they're not getting it. The girl pioneers are in a similar position. See what I'm driving at? Again, what about youngsters home on leave who want to visit their girl-friends? Where can they take them?'

'Into the woods, as usual.'

'In warm weather, yes, but we've got to think further than that. It'll be winter before long.'

'I know it isn't quite so simple in snow, but it can be done. It's a damned short-lived pleasure, though, I must admit.'

'Ernst Schlaguweit,' Eis said solemnly, 'Maulen leads the field in a lot of respects, so why not in this one too? Allenstein has already built three houses for recreational purposes, one of them for officers and senior Party members. We needn't go to those lengths straight away, but we must do our best to make life pleasant for those who are serving their country. It's our bounden duty.'

'Yes, sir,' said Schlaguweit. 'I follow you, but how do we go about it?'

Eis issued a brisk series of directives. Scharfke's Gasthaus, now under Schlaguweit's management, was to make its premises freely available to visitors, that is to say, without maintaining a register or other inconvenient form of control. The bar-rooms were to be given over to systematically organized social gatherings, including regular get-togethers for those home on leave.

'It's a brilliant idea!' exclaimed Schlaguweit.

Eis expatiated on his scheme for some time longer, confident that it would not only spread joy but, in so far as this was possible, enhance his prestige still further. At last, casually flicking through his desk diary, he said: 'By the way, Fackler can take those two prisoners of war off Materna's hands.'

'I'll see to it.'

'You can have one of them for your brother. Tell Fackler to reserve the other for me—Ambal, that is. He can make himself useful around the house. My wife has been feeling pretty low recently, and no wonder. She badly needs a little relaxation.'

'I'd like to take a look around,' Tantau announced.

Councillor Engel looked delighted. 'So things are moving at last. Do you know where to head for?'

'I know virtually nothing—just a few small points which may be important and could prove vital under certain circumstances. One never knows until the last minute.'

'Just as you say,' replied Engel. He had given up pressing Tantau for exact details. 'I'll inform Major Rattenhauer immediately that you're going into action.'

'You misunderstand me,' Tantau amended. 'In order to go into action, as you put it, I shall need certain technical aids.'

'An official car is at your disposal, Herr Tantau. You only have to apply.'

'Putting in applications is too laborious. It's a nuisance to have a different car and driver each time. It doesn't suit my methods.'

'Very well, I'll put it to Major Rattenhauer as a special request. He won't be particularly pleased, though.'

'That's his affair,' Tantau said quietly. 'Just to kill two birds with one stone, Herr Engel, you might inform Herr Rattenhauer of my other requirements at the same time.'

'Isn't a car of your own enough? What else do you want?'

'For one thing, a driver of my own choosing, like the car. Then I shall need some means of radio communication—three sets will be enough for a start. Further, I would appreciate an escort, also of my own choosing. And, finally, I want to be assigned the C.I.D. man from Passenheim who investigated the recent incidents—Budzuhn, I think his name is.'

'Budzuhn? But he's a fifth-rater—he can hardly string two words together properly. Why pick on a brainless flat-foot like that?'

'Because I can read. Even if you're right about his lack of brains there's no doubt that he has a nose like a blood-hound—his reports prove that. He also knows the area pretty well, and I need a guide.'

Engel retired before Tantau could come up with any more

equests. Ten minutes later he was back again, fluttering in
Rattenhauer's slipstream. The S.S. major stationed himself
in front of Tantau and glared at him silently for some seconds
without producing the slightest effect. The little detective responded with an expectant smile.

'Who the devil do you think you are?' Rattenhauer demanded furiously. 'What makes you think you can waltz in
here with a list of demands?'

'I'm planning to work, not waltz,' Tantau replied in a mild
voice. 'For my work, I need men and equipment which
fulfil my requirements.' ——

'Anything else you'd like?' sneered Rattenhauer.

'Yes, just one more thing.' Tantau looked like a boy
confiding his heart's desire. 'I'd like a special warrant which
will give me temporary authority over all police and administrative departments in the district, including those of the
Party and its affiliated organizations.'

'You're off your rocker!' snapped Rattenhauer. Councillor Engel edged behind him and made warning faces over his
shoulder. 'I've a bloody good mind to send you back where
you came from.'

'As you wish,' Tantau replied amiably. 'I'm quite amenable.'

The S.S. major swept out with Engel in tow, leaving Tantau
bent over his work as if nothing untoward had occurred.
A quarter of an hour later Engel reappeared, red-faced and
sweating but looking somehow refreshed.

'You've done it,' he announced. 'I talked him round. He
granted all your requests.'

'Including the warrant?'

'That too, though he jibbed a bit. He expects you to report
immediately every time you make use of it—in fact he'd
prefer you to get his approval in advance whenever possible,
but I don't imagine you'll always be in a position to do that
in practice, will you?'

'Hardly ever.'

'All right, carry on, and don't hesitate to contact me if
you need anything else.'

'Good. In that case, kindly supply me with full details of
all doctors and veterinary surgeons resident in the area
between Lakes Lasker, Spirding and Maulen. The same goes
for nurses, midwives and medical orderlies, also hospitals,
both civilian and military.'

'How do you suggest I proceed?'

'That's your problem.'

'But what do you hope to achieve?'

'Traces of blood have been found,' Tantau replied, his tone conveying that this fully explained the situation. Bending over his desk, he added: 'Please see that Inspector Budzuhn of Passenheim reports to me as soon as possible.'

Inspector Budzuhn reported barely two hours later, a big heavy, rotund man with a pig-pink, ivory-smooth face, the eyes of a faithful hound and ears like saucers. His voice was as high-pitched as a eunuch's, but strong and flexible.

Tantau invited him to sit down. Budzuhn might be a clumsy-looking baby elephant—a figure of fun who doubtless provoked mirth at beer-drinking sessions and could not expect promotion while current standards of selection prevailed—but he was a man after his own heart.

For his part, Budzuhn sensed that he was welcome. The diminutive chief superintendent bore a name which was known and uttered with reverence by every novice in the force, but the inspector greeted him as he would have greeted a fellow-wayfarer on a lonely road. Tantau gave him a wonderful sense of security.

'Two nights ago,' Tantau recapitulated, 'shots were exchanged between an army patrol consisting of two men and a party of three or four, presumably civilians. One member of the patrol was killed and the other wounded. The opposition got away on bicycles.'

Budzuhn nodded. He ringed the site of the nocturnal skirmish on the map and drew a plan of it with a few deft pencilstrokes.

'Strange people,' he said. 'They made a run for it as soon as they were challenged by the patrol. Then, when they were fired on, they fired back. They only loosed off a few shots, though—four or five at most, and three of them were hits. Remarkable that. They must have been experienced shots. I found four empty cartridge cases—98k carbine. Obviously ammunition that had been stored for a long time.'

'And the blood?'

'I found that when it got light.' Budzuhn tapped a path on his sketch-map. 'One of the civilians was wounded—seriously, to judge by the amount of blood he lost. The cycle tracks tell the same story. Two were normal, the third was made by an unladen bicycle, and the fourth machine was overloaded. That's how they transported the wounded man.'

Tantau nodded approvingly. 'Go on.'

'I said to myself, a man who is bleeding profusely and has to be carted off on a bicycle will probably go on losing blood. They wouldn't have been able to bandage him up on the spot, so they probably did a makeshift job on him later. Well, I went on looking and I found four more patches of blood on two roads covering a total distance of nine miles. Then I lost the trail.'

Tantau pictured Budzuhn trotting along the country lanes, head down. He saw the mountain of flesh kneeling, scratching, feeling, sniffing like some gargantuan bloodhound. 'Please mark the exact location of the blood on my map,' he said, '—in red pencil, so that it looks pretty.'

Deliberately, with slightly parted lips and protruding tongue, the inspector pencilled in his crosses, one for each patch of blood, at steadily increasing intervals.

When he had finished, Tantau pulled the map across and studied it for a considerable time. 'It checks,' he said at length.

'What checks?'

'My original calculation,' Tantau pointed to the centre of his circles, squares and lines. 'This is the area I'd like to familiarize myself with. You, my dear Inspector, have just substantiated my theory.'

'How, exactly?'

Tantau did not lose patience. It was too much to expect a first-class bloodhound to be a brilliant logician as well. 'Let us assume, Budzuhn, that you had taken part in an operation of this type and that one of your men had been seriously wounded. What would you have done? You'd have got him to safety, wouldn't you?'

'Perhaps to a doctor, if I knew one I could trust.'

'Quite right. We must bear that in mind. First, however, we must assume that the wounded man was brought to safety as quickly as possible, i.e. by the most direct route. And now, line up the ruler with your crosses. Now extend the line, working on the basis of a two- or three-hour march. Where does it take you?'

'To the area round Lake Maulen.'

'And that, my dear Inspector, is where we shall be con-

ducting our little tour of inspection during the next few
days—for want of anything better to do, you understand.

'I knew that I could bank on your understanding and appreciation of my efforts,' Eugen Eis declared, taking Henriette
Himmler's hand. 'You're one of the happy few who realize
what is at stake in times like these.'

'I'm a very ordinary person,' she said simply.

'No, no,' he insisted, 'you were bred in a very special stable
—it stands out a mile.'

Henriette waved this intended compliment aside with studi-
ous modesty. She liked basking in the reflected glory of
her magic name, but it was hardly necessary to exploit its
advantages in a place like Maulen.

'I regard it as a good omen that I have been privileged to
welcome you, of all people, as the first honoured visitor to
our newly established recreation centre.'

He conducted her through the Gasthaus premises which
had been given over to the scheme. As manager, Schlaguweit
had welcomed them in person at the door, which was decorated
with foliage for the occasion. Beside Eis strutted the inevitable Neuber, also Pillich, the current mayor, their joint
presence intended to stress the official gravity of the under-
taking.

They toured the main club-room, the games room, the small
club-room, the conference-room—all grand new names for
the old public rooms of the Gasthaus. However, the rooms
were no longer 'public', or, as Eis put it, open to any drunken
sod who came along. They had to be booked now, singly, in
groups, or altogether. Eis explained the system to Henriette.

'Servicemen on leave, local garrison troops and girl pioneers
will be treated as guests of the community. They will pay only
for the food and drink they consume, which will be charged at
cost price. Party funds will generously make up the difference.'

Neuber opened his mouth to speak and then shut it again.
Eugen Eis was going to use the funds of the local branch to
finance the running of the Gasthaus—in other words, divert
them into his own pocket, since he was the de facto proprietor.
Mayor Pillich stared at the floor, but Henriette exclaimed en-
thusiastically: 'That's what I call true public spirit!'

Eis could not but agree. 'Times are hard. Men are fighting

and dying, sacrifices are called for and readily made, hardships of every kind are the order of the day . . .'

'Hardships which only we Germans are capable of,'
Schlaguweit interposed proudly.

'And then,' Eis pursued, indicating a plain but durable-
looking guest-room equipped with a double bed, 'Then come
the rare moments of leisure, recreation and relaxation. They
ought not to be spent under degrading circumstances, in barns,
say, or in the woods, or even, as happened recently, in the
church vestry—least of all during cold weather. No, the
valiant defenders of the Fatherland must not and will not
be subjected to such treatment—not here in Maulen.'

'We thought of everything,' Ernst Schlaguweit said zealously.
He fumbled under the bed, pulled out a chamber-pot, and
flourished it above his head.

'That's enough!' snapped Eis. He shot a brief glance at
Henriette, who was staring, fascinated, at the appallingly
capacious white enamel receptacle. To efface Schlaguweit's
blunder, he at once suggested an 'inaugural glass'. This was
served in the games room, where the billiard table had been
laid with plates of sandwiches. Eis hurriedly toasted the
members of the inspection party and told them to make themselves at home. As for Henriette, she was invited to join him
for a brief official conference.

This took place on the first floor in what Eis described as
a private sitting-room. Instead of a bed, the principal piece
of furniture was a roomy sofa upholstered in washable glazed
linen. Hidden in an ice-bucket behind the curtains were two
bottles of Veuve Cliquot. There was also a bottle of Burgundy
—Château Rothschild, not that anyone was struck by the
racial connotations of the name.

'I must apologize for Schlaguweit,' Eis said with dignity.
'That was an embarrassing gaffe he made just now, during
our tour of inspection.'

'Don't give it another thought,' Henriette replied, still
under the spell of the colossal chamber-pot. 'To err is human.'

'How right you are!' Eis produced the ice-bucket and
proceeded to fill their glasses. 'Turk's Blood,' he explained. 'A
recipe given me by a friend who knows Reich Marshal Goering
and has even met the Führer. A nice fellow—my friend, I
mean. Always drinks champagne and red wine, half and half.'

He omitted to mention that he had given orders for the

red wine to be diluted too—with brandy. It was a brev
which no one else in Maulen could take with the possibl
exception of that swine Materna.

'Try some, my dear Henriette.'

'You're a bon viveur,' she murmured, regarding hir
through slightly narrowed eyes as she drank. She flushed, pre
sumably with pleasure.

Eis refilled their glasses, installed himself comfortably o
the sofa, and gestured to her to join him. 'I'm only huma
myself, with all the weaknesses and failings of the breed
I try to control them, though I must confess I find it har
in your presence. Forgive me.'

Henriette laid her hand on his arm in a gesture of under
standing. Her bird-like eyes shone. 'I think I know what yo
mean,' she said softly.

Eis topped the glasses up and edged a little closer. 'Yo
know, Henriette, my job here is no picnic. I've had enemie
and opponents to cope with—quite a few of them. I eithe
eliminated them or spiked their guns. It was hard, sometime
hard but unavoidable. The fur really flew, I can tell you

'You remind me of my uncle, Eugen—intellectually,
mean.'

'Great men like your uncle are a shining example to peopl
like me. Write and tell him that, if you want—he might b
pleased.'

'I'm sure he would,' Henriette replied, holding her glas
out. She was already glowing like a furnace.

Eis edged nearer and slid deeper into the cushions fo
comfort's sake. He put his arm round her and refilled th
glasses yet again with his free hand—an acrobatic feat whicl
he performed with considerable expertise. 'No,' he said
'we don't have an easy time of it, but your presence helps m
to forget a lot of things, Henriette . . .'

'How nice,' she sighed, nestling against him.

Eis continued to dilate on his difficulties. He would neve
surrender to them. On the other hand, willing, enthusiastic an
self-sacrificing though the inhabitants of Maulen were, the
had shown themselves too soft, insufficiently determined, no
fully aware of what was at stake.

He opened the second bottle of champagne and drew th
curtains, allegedly because the sun was dazzling him.

'I'm a successful man,' he declared, both hands busy witl

er now, '—successful as far as my Party career is con-
erned and so on. But as a private individual, Henriette—
h, as a private individual . . .'

'Are you unhappy, Eugen?' she asked, moist lips close to
his ear.

'Not when I'm with you,' he replied, unbuttoning her uni-
orm blouse.

While he did this and other things in the conventional order,
without encountering undue resistance, he told her of his wife:
how she failed to understand him, how she made no contribu-
ion to the war effort, how she refused him out of sheer malice
and consorted indiscriminately with other men. He despised
her, she revolted him and filled him with disgust. . . .'

When it was all over and they were lying side by side,
breathing heavily, Henriette gave a sudden shriek. She
grabbed her blouse and sat bolt upright.

'Oh God!' she moaned. 'What have we done?'

'Not so loud,' Eis chided, caressing her skinny thighs. 'We
love each other.'

'But we shouldn't have done that!'

'Set your mind at rest, Henriette,' he said. 'I'm a gentleman. Even if a child does come along, I shall naturally assume
full responsibility for what has happened between us. After
all, I know what I owe you and your name. Just give me a
little time and I'll arrange everything, I give you my word.'

The next time Peter Bachus visited Materna's farm he rolled
up in a small and decrepit car accompanied by his friend
Konrad Klinger. They made straight for Hannelore and
Sabine in the kitchen.

Alfons Materna was sitting at his desk in his den, where he
could keep the yard gate and approach road under observation.

'It's about time those two regularized the situation by de-
ciding on one girl or the other,' he said to Jablonski. 'After
all, they're grown up now.'

Jablonski scoffed. 'To me, they're still wearing short pants.'

'They're grown up,' Materna repeated. 'We're going to treat
them like men from now on, both of them. Get over to the
dug-out and tell Grienspan who's here. Tell him to come
and greet our new recruits if he thinks he ought to—I do.
Then keep watch outside.'

'All right. I'll be back with him in about half an hour.

Shortly afterwards, the Terrible Twins appeared. Materna gave them a warm welcome.

'Peter has told me everything,' said Konrad Klinger, doctor of law, reserve lieutenant and junior member of Dr Rogatzki's chambers in Allenstein, 'I hope you won't object if I join you. Like Peter, I wouldn't dream of being left out.'

'I took that for granted, Konrad. However, I must draw your attention to one small but not unimportant point. I'm sure Peter has told you all he knows, but he doesn't know a great deal as yet.'

'Just as I suspected. I told Peter there was more to this than met the eye. All right, Herr Materna, let's hear the full story.'

'May I look at my patient first?' asked Peter. 'I'm a bit worried about him, and I don't just mean his condition. The police are making inquiries.'

'Your patient is sleeping quietly for the first time in days. You can look at him later. We'll discuss the question of the police in due course.' Materna shifted in his chair as though to get a firmer purchase. 'I assume you already have some idea of what you may be letting yourself in for?'

'Yes, I've given the matter some thought. I've also found something.'

Materna looked at him inquiringly.

'Well, I was rummaging around in our files the other day when I came across Eis's name. It was in connection with Dog's Meadow. A few months after you presented it to the parish of Maulen he secured power of attorney from Brigitte and tried to get the deed of gift annulled on the grounds that you'd exceeded your proprietorial rights.'

'Yes, I remember. Eis had a lot to learn in those days, but that's all old hat now—just a skeleton in the family cupboard.'

'Precisely, but what about rattling a few bones? Think what it could mean today: Eis versus Maulen, i.e. the Local Group Leader versus the community. It would be a sensation.'

'You're coming on fast, Konrad. I imagine you've explored all the legal angles?'

'You bet. We haven't got much on Eis, but we could make a lot of trouble for him. At least it would be a big laugh.'

Pressed for more details, Konrad told Materna that although the case was as good as forgotten it had not lapsed. Rogatzki's chambers still submitted routine memoranda to the competent legal authorities but were never badgered about them. It was clear that all parties had tacitly agreed to let the matter drop.

'However,' Konrad said, 'we've now got an elderly judge who's very enterprising in some ways. I discussed all the available documents with him, and he's prepared to let the lame old cat out of the bag. It still has claws, in his considered opinion.'

'That could be useful when the time comes,' Materna said thoughtfully. 'It might make a nice little diversionary attack. However, we've got bigger worries at the moment.'

'Let's get down to brass tacks,' Konrad said firmly. 'Tell us what we have to do.'

Materna stared out of the window as though avoiding the young men's gaze. Then he said, almost casually: 'I'm expecting a visitor. You can make your final decision when you've seen him.'

'Who is it?'

Materna glanced at the door. Steps could be heard approaching. Without knowing why, Konrad and Peter rose to their feet.

Then the door opened and Siegfried Grienspan came in.

Materna gave Peter and Konrad time to get over their surprise and joy at the sight of Grienspan and the very fact of his existence.

'You're invited to supper,' he said eventually. 'There'll be plenty of time to pester Siegfried with your questions then. First, though, something else. What was that about police inquiries, Peter?'

'The local station rang me and asked if I'd treated anyone in the past week who might have been suffering from one or more bullet-wounds.'

'Remarkable,' commented Materna, glancing at Grienspan.

'I checked with my colleagues, of course,' Peter went on. 'They all received the same inquiry, so it must be a purely routine matter.'

'All the same,' Grienspan said, 'we can't ignore the fact that the police are interested in the possibility of someone having been wounded. It may not mean that they're launching an all-out investigation, but we ought to find out where we tripped up—if we did.'

Konrad gazed at Materna in triumph. 'I thought it might be you! Somehow, I recognized your signature on all these incidents people have been talking about recently. You're really getting down to business, then?'

'Just helping to bring this madness to an end,' Materna replied quietly, '—making full use of the ways and means still open to us. They aren't very pleasant and we don't find it easy, but we feel it has to be done.'

'We operate in two groups,' Grienspan explained. 'One group works in harness with Polish partisans and includes specialist units, some of which are the relics of our former freight business. The second group is a two-man concern consisting of Alfons and Jacob, occasionally reinforced by us. That was what happened recently, when one of my men was wounded.'

'He'll pull through,' Peter assured him. 'It'll take some time, though, and he'll have to stay put.'

Materna nodded. 'He can stay.'

'We've got enough medical supplies,' Peter went on, 'enough for other cases besides this one. Dr. Gensfleisch has built up quite a stock, so I won't be in trouble if I'm asked to account for our consumption of drugs.'

'Do they make a check on these things?' asked Materna.

'Occasionally. We had one the other day, as it happens. My colleagues and I had to submit a list of all medicaments used during the past three months.'

'And you think it was a coincidence?'

'Of course it wasn't!' Konrad broke in. 'You don't honestly think your firework displays go unnoticed, do you? They've set up a board of inquiry at Allenstein, headed by an S.S. officer. I heard that from a town councillor called Engel who occasionally has a drink with me in the evening.'

'What sort of man is he?'

'Conscientious and unimaginative. That can be a dangerous combination sometimes, but he's also very worried about his job, and that could be useful.'

'Devote a bit of time to him,' Materna recommended. He turned to Grienspan. 'We always reckoned with the possibility of measures of this kind, didn't we?'

Grienspan nodded. The two young men marvelled at his composure. There seemed to be nothing left of his once fidgety and nervous gestures, his diffident manner and slightly querulous voice. He had turned into a hunter, alert, keen-eyed and in full command of himself. He said: 'We've been pretty methodical. Our operations have always been carried out as far from base as possible. The distances there and back are computed with a fair degree of accuracy, and we work a sort of scatter system which distributes our strikes as widely as possible.'

'Excellent,' commented Peter, but Konrad shook his head.

'One moment,' he said, rising uneasily to his feet. 'Do you mean that your operations are based on Maulen and that you spread them evenly—all round the compass?'

'What's the matter with that?'

'Twelve or fifteen miles in each direction—yes? In that case you've drawn a big ring round Maulen with a radius of twelve or fifteen miles.'

'And what does that add up to?'

'A suspicious geometrical pattern, that's what. Somebody could plot that and reconstruct it.'

'You're a bright lad,' Materna said. He pursed his lips and looked at Grienspan. 'What do you think, Siegfried?'

'I just hope the same idea hasn't occurred to anyone else. My compliments, Dr Klinger. I'm doubly happy that you've joined us.'

Further conversation was interrupted by the arrival of supper. The first item on the menu was a broth which accorded with the traditional East Prussian belief that only five pounds of mutton fat could provide one man with a decent bowl of soup. The main course was gammon in sour cream sauce— thick slices of home-cured bacon steeped in milk for two or three hours before cooking. The sour cream was added to the gravy later, producing what passed in Masuria for a light and wholesome dish.

Materna's guests swiftly emptied the vast and brimming platter with a minimum of conversation. They, too, subscribed to the Masurian tradition that food should not be adulterated with talk.

Afterwards, there were oven-fresh marzipan cakes scented with almonds, icing sugar and attar of roses—a long-time favourite with Peter and Konrad, as the girls were well aware.

They left a fair number, their appetite being as big as ever but their staying-power more limited than it had been in their boyhood days.

By coffee-time, they were all huddled round the table again while Jablonski stood guard outside and the girls sang as they washed up in the kitchen.

'About this geometrical pattern, as our boy wonder so aptly called it,' Materna began. 'We must change it. The Maulen area must stop being a blank space on the map, and quickly.'

Peter shrugged. 'The best plan would be to blow up something in Maulen itself.'

'It's a cheeky idea, but that might make it all the more effective,' said Materna. 'There's no harm in considering it, at least. As my grandmother used to say, you can put a skunk to flight with its own stench. All you have to do is to get it to stick its nose up its own arse.'

4

Eugen Eis felt positive that he had entered the crucial phase of his career.

'Well,' Ernst,' he said jovially, 'how's business?'

'Pretty good. The brothel's a roaring success—the recreation centre, I mean. The days are drawing in and the nights are getting colder, and that means an automatic boost in turnover. We're gradually getting a reputation for quality, too. Demand has increased so much, we'll be able to expand soon.'

Schlaguweit was also doing well. Little spenders had been winnowed away and big spenders were making themselves at home on the premises. Customers had lately been coming from as far afield as Lötzen, Lyck and Allenstein—senior Party members, army officers, administrative officials and other similarly well-qualified citizens of the Third Reich. They came to spend a few restful days in attractive surroundings, and they did not come alone.

Eis expressed his approval of Schlaguweit's endeavours and went off to pay a routine call on the mayor, who needed regular doses of encouragement.

'Pillich,' he said, 'I've had one or two complaints about

ou, but you know how I react to these things—I simply urn a deaf ear. I've still got faith in you, so don't let me own. I know at least three people who'd like to step into your 1oes.'

Eis, who always knew at least three men who coveted nother man's job, whetted their appetites with veiled promises hich spurred them on to greater feats of endeavour. 'Every-1ing must be sacrificed in the interests of final victory,' as his usual line. 'Everyone must do his bit.'

Everyone did. Contributions, which were naturally con-igned to him in his capacity as Local Group Leader, in-luded chickens, ducks, geese, sheep, cattle—even a prize ull named Baldur, placed at the disposal of the community y Pracesius, the butcher, who yearned to head the local armers' league.

Self-sacrifice blossomed wherever Eis's imperious gaze urned. The villagers had never greeted him with greater leference than during these months. One old woman—the vidow Beilke—went so far as to fall on her knees before lim, and was rewarded with an extra ration of ten eggs. Even the parson raised his hand vaguely at the sight of him, hough it was uncertain whether this was a form of cursory enediction or a sloppy version of the Hitler salute.

'Unless I'm much mistaken,' the Reverend Albrecht Kamp-nann said cautiously, 'the Russians are gaining more and nore ground. Even so, I hardly imagine that they will ever hreaten our frontiers, do you?'

'Don't count your chickens before they're hatched,' Eis aid reprovingly. 'Keep on praying. You can safely leave every-hing else to the Führer.'

Eis lingered in the village square beside the war memorial, filled with optimism and self-assurance. What could go wrong now that the village belonged to him? Genially, he returned the reverential salutations of passing schoolchildren.

Maulen was still largely a collection of cottages and peat-bogs, pasture-land for cud-chewing cattle and trees for mic-turating mongrels. Very soon, however, immediately after the final victory, everything would miraculously change for the better under his leadership: the school, extended and heightened to form a youth hostel, the fire station a gym-nasium and assembly-place for national festivals, the Gasthaus —his Gasthaus—expanded into a community centre with

a theatre and cinema, bowling alleys, covered terraces, chi
dren's playground, conference chambers, dining-room, ba
and separate W.C.s for men and women. The war memoria
also enlarged, would be furnished with a bust of the Führe
memorial plaques in marble, and an eternal flame. Ther
beyond Horse Hill, Materna's farm—a first-class holida
resort for veterans and war widows. There would be
lido beside the lake, benches beside the forest paths, lawns fo
sun-bathers, sports grounds, a jetty for lake-steamers, and
dominating all else, the swastika banner and Eis himself

'May I have a word with you?' asked Amadeus Neuber.

'Another time,' Eis snapped. He was not in the mood fo
the blatherings of an ambitious lickspittle. Neuber, too, wa
due for the chop at the earliest opportunity.

Eis turned on his heel and walked off, leaving Neuber star
ing after him with profound disquiet. He skirted Party Head
quarters and made for home. Standing beside the elder-hedge
partly sheltered by some birch- and beech-trees, he looked
across at the gravelled terrace in front of the house.

He was pleased by what he saw. His wife was sitting in a
deckchair, apparently gazing into space with a picturesque
air of grief. It was a deceptive picture. Ever a keen observer
Eis perceived that Christine's gaze had a specific object—to
wit, the French prisoner of war Pierre Ambal, who was dig
ging in the garden.

'How are you, my dear?' Eis called cheerfully. Meeting with
a predictable lack of response, he feigned concern. 'It's very
creditable of you to take your father's death so hard—makes
a good impression on the village, too—but there's no need
to keep it up for ever, especially as I'm doing my best to be
kind and considerate.'

For some days now, Eis had been sleeping not at home but
in a private room belonging to Party Headquarters. He did
so not only for the sake of peace but as a demonstration
that he was tactfully giving his beloved wife time to recover
from her recent shock. Last but not least, he did so for
Henriette Himmler's sake. It betokened a sort of transitional
phase necessary to the fulfilment of his solemn pledge.

'Aren't you going to listen?' he asked Christine, who had
got up and was heading for the house. 'I had a couple of things
to tell you.'

He grinned after her. Her malicious unapproachability, as he termed it, seemed to give him as much secret pleasure as the sight of the prisoner of war toiling busily in the garden. He called him over.

'Do you speak German?'

Pierre Ambal nodded. 'My hearing's bad, though,' he said cautiously. 'I've learnt not to listen to other people's conversations, if that's what you're driving at.'

'You're a comedian,' Eis said. 'Luckily for you, I've a soft spot for comedians. We're famous for our sense of humour in Maulen—hadn't you noticed?'

'Not so far.'

The two men exchanged a long look. Each found the other uncongenial but comic, repellent but so utterly alien as to be interesting, rather like the inmates of a zoo. They smiled at one another.

'Have you had a chat with my wife yet?'

'You couldn't call it a chat. Your wife issued me with some instructions and I carried them out. She doesn't seem very talkative.'

'She wasn't always like that.' Eis stared at the elder-bushes in portentous silence for some moments. They had turned brown and lost most of their leaves. 'It's a pity about her. She was such a warm, gay person. Perhaps it'll all come back again some day—I hope so, anyway. She has been through a lot. Nobody but a callous brute could help sympathizing with her.'

Ambal eyed the village potentate with a mixture of surprise and amusement. He pitied his wife.

'I feel sorry for her,' Eis said. 'That's why I sent for you, Ambal, or whatever your name is.'

Baffled and alarmed, Ambal backed off as though to get a better look.

'To avoid any possible misunderstanding, my friend, you're not just here to play gardeners. Look after my poor grief-stricken wife, brighten her day, buck her up, take her out of herself. Have I made myself clear?'

'I think so,' Ambal replied, widening the gap between them a little more.

Eis closed the gap again. For one embarrassing moment, Ambal thought he was going to nudge him confidentially in

the ribs, but this was not so. Eis merely breathed in his fac
—a powerful Masurian blast compounded of beer, tobacc
and stewed mutton.

'Do your stuff,' Eis told him. 'I can't look after every las
little detail, I'm afraid. I'm far too busy. For instance, I'v
got to go off and see my girl pioneers now—they're alway
wanting something. Women are a pernickety lot, but I don'
need to tell you that. You come from France, and that put
you under a certain obligation, what?'

Bonfires were burning in Materna's fields. Children prance
round them, shouting with delight, and dark smoke scudde
across the ground in the cold, damp wind.

'Those little beasts can cram more into their bellies than
a herd of fattened hogs,' Jablonski's tone was commendatory
in the extreme. 'There won't be enough potatoes left in th
ground to go round.'

'Then we'll draw on our stock of seed-potatoes,' said
Materna. 'I can't picture next harvest, but I can still enjoy
the sight of children having fun.'

They were standing on a mound of stones at the edge of the
churned up potato-fields. The village children were romping
over them, children of all ages and both sexes, snotty-nosed
urchins and little girls with long neat plaits, rowdy adolescents
and 'piddle-pants', tiny tots who wore no knickers for prac
tical reasons.

Bright-eyed and ruddy-cheeked, they were all hard at work
collecting potato-tops and throwing them on the flaming
bonfires. They grubbed around in the soil for left-over potatoes
and handed their booty to one or two older boys, who thrust
them into the glowing ashes with sticks.

The children's bonfire party took place in Materna's potato-
fields every autumn. Everyone was invited and almost everyone came because nobody in the village dared to deprive the
boys and girls of Maulen of such an eagerly awaited annual
treat. It not only cost parents nothing but kept the little
pests away from home for hours.

'They'll be getting thirsty,' Materna said. 'We ought to
put out a bucket of fruit juice for them.'

The children's delighted screams suddenly waned in volume.
and two groups near the road switched their activities to the
centre of the field. Jablonski noticed this abrupt withdrawal

t once, also the reason for it. Amadeus Neuber was approach-
ng Materna's potato-fields, a raven-like figure with a slightly
vaddling gait.

'Shall I tell him that we don't allow vermin on our land?'
ablonski demanded.

Materna shook his head. Ignoring Neuber, he walked over
o a small bonfire which was hissing, crackling and putting
ut clouds of blue-black smoke. Here he rolled a pumpkin-
ized stone to one side and sat down on it. Jablonski squatted
n the ground beside him.

'Good day to you!' called Neuber.

'Heil Hitler!' answered Materna. Jablonski emitted a sound
vhich passed for a greeting in Masuria, but not a compli-
nentary one.

Neuber did not take umbrage. He remained standing
atiently beside the two men and bent his smiling gaze on the
young fire-worshippers. The children's unerring instinct told
hem that their headmaster had not come to interrupt their
activities, so they pretended not to notice him.

'You still have an affection for youth,' Neuber observed. 'I
appreciate that.'

Jablonski gave a provocative grin. 'Everyone has his weaknesses, eh? The only difference is, children are just children to
us.'

Neuber was deeply hurt by this malicious insinuation and
found it hard to ignore, but Materna pacified him by inviting
him to sit down on a neighbouring heap of putrescent cabbage-
heads. A covert glance at the sky told Materna that the wind
would soon veer and blow the acrid smoke in Neuber's
direction.

Neuber sat down, drawing up his legs with a faint groan.
'Human beings are sinful creatures,' he said in an ingratiating
tone, 'sinful and subject to all kinds of temptations, urges
and instincts. It takes time to attain a state of mature
knowledge and understanding.'

Jablonski looked as if he was about to comment on these
remarks in his own way, but Materna shot him a warning
glance.

'Fine sentiments, Herr Neuber, but rather late in the day.'

'That's just it!' Neuber said eagerly, shuffling around on
his cabbage-heads. 'It may be late, but it doesn't have to be
too late. That's why I've come to see you.'

'Why me? I'm only a farmer.'

'Yes, and how I envy you!' The wind duly veered, sendin
Neuber into a violent coughing-fit. 'You're the lucky one

'Do you think so? One of my sons was murdered, my wif
left me, the village ostracized me. I can't afford any friend
officially. As for you Neuber, I'm told you impress on you
pupils that people of my sort are a pest.'

Neuber looked disconcerted. 'I'm sure I never called yo
that, and even if I did say something of the sort—which
regret—it must have been long ago. Things have changed
great deal since then.'

Materna, who could picture Jablonski's irrepressible grir
avoided looking at him. Instead, he stared at the bonfires. The
were subsiding into incandescent mounds which threade
the monotonous leaden-grey sky with flying red sparks.

Neuber interpreted Materna's silence as an encouragin
sign.

'The village is in a ferment,' he said. 'Everything is smoul
dering like these bonfires. Not many people have noticed, bu
the signs are quite unmistakable to anyone with half an eye
That old Beilke woman threw herself into the lake las
night because she'd reached the end of her tether. She wa
all alone and starving—demented, in all probability, but th
villagers are saying that the Topich came to fetch her. Th
verger got drunk yesterday and snatched the crucifix off th
altar, meaning to take it to Eis, but he never got there. H
had a heart attack and dropped dead in the village square
Uschkurat has caught the bug too. He used to be norma
enough, but now he sees ghosts. Do you know who h
thought he saw leaning against the churchyard wall the othe
night? Siegfried Grienspan! If that doesn't qualify him for a
strait-jacket, what does?'

Materna laughed until the tears ran down his cheeks. A
last he said: 'All right, but what does it all prove? Simply
that there's still a lot of liquor left in Maulen, and what
could be more reassuring than that? A bottle a day keeps the
doctor away—you know the old saying.' And he burst out
laughing again.

Hard as he found it, Jablonski joined in the laughter.
but his mirthless bark was drowned by the shrill cries of the
children round the bonfires. It was time to share out the
baked potatoes, and everyone wanted as many as possible.

Neuber leant forward in an attitude of prayer, heedless of the glowing embers which turned his face salmon-pink and beaded his brow with sweat.

'You've got a sense of humour,' he said. 'It's a blessing, a sense of humour, because it usually signifies a good conscience, and no one could deny the purity of your conscience, Herr Materna. That's one of the reasons why I came here feeling so optimistic.'

'Optimistic about what?'

'Well, I imagine you credit me with a certain amount of intelligence.' Neuber shifted his bottom again. The rotting cabbage-leaves had soaked the seat of his pants. 'I've been doing a lot of thinking lately—about the general situation, about the country and its present predicament—and I must say, to use a vulgarism, that we're up the creek.'

Jablonski could not restrain himself. 'You're dead right—up shit creek without a paddle.'

'In a manner of speaking,' said Neuber. 'You know it and I know it, but who else does? The village is swarming with idiots—blind, deaf, ambitious, time-serving idiots.'

'Arse-lickers,' Jablonski supplemented helpfully.

'Yes, if you care to put it that way. A man like Eis systematically breeds parasites—murderers, toughs, pimps, extortioners and perjurers. It can't be tolerated any longer, in my opinion—not any longer!'

'Can you prove what you've just said?' Materna asked quietly.

'That and plenty more besides!' Neuber was unmindful of the billowing smoke and scorching heat. The beads of sweat on his face had swelled to the size of cultured pearls, but he did not brush them away. 'I've collected a mass of evidence. It's not only incriminating but absolutely conclusive, and I'm ready to hand it over to you for use in the better days that lie ahead.'

'Herr Neuber,' Materna said, straightening up because the smoke of the bonfire threatened to engulf him too, 'you seem to forget that I'm the father of Hermann Materna, the Regional Commissioner for Agriculture—a son of whom I'm justly proud. I'm also a friend of Baron von der Brocken, who is a friend of Reich Marshal Goering. That being so, I can only describe your recent utterances as provocation of the basest kind.'

Neuber looked bewildered. 'But I confided in you!'

'You made defeatist remarks in the presence of a third party. You not only shed doubt on our prospects of final victory but tried to undermine our faith in a man who has been set in authority over us. All those offences carry the death penalty.'

'You've obviously misunderstood me,' Neuber protested coughing and fidgeting. He got to his feet and shuffled off with his damp trousers flapping forlornly. 'I really didn't mean it like that,' he moaned.

The village children watched him depart with pleasure Having stuffed themselves with fragrant roast potatoes, they were now besieging Hannelore and Sabine for mugs of raspberry-juice. After that, they clustered round Materna and Jablonski and sang them a thank-you song, their clear, shrill voices seeming to pluck at the pale grey clouds on the horizon.

'Why did you send Neuber packing?' asked Jablonski. 'He makes me sick too, but he could be useful.'

'Could be.' Materna nodded his thanks to the children and promised them a series of Christmas parties which would beat anything they had ever known. He shook the grubby hands that were held out to him and patted their owners' predominantly flaxen heads rather like a priest dispensing benedictions. Then he turned to Jablonski.

'I realized what the bastard was after as soon as he mentioned Grienspan. He isn't just taking out insurance. He was planning to join us, and that's a bit more than I can stomach.'

'Yes, but can we afford to give him the brush-off?'

'Him and a lot of other people. Masuria has changed, Jacob. The place has turned into a happy hunting-ground for criminals, so we'll have to play heroes in secret—we've no choice. That's how far we've sunk, my friend.'

Inspector Budzuhn was plagued by the feeling that he was wasting his time. Tantau, who seemed to be taking him on an aimless tour of Masuria, pottered back and forth between Lötzen and Lyck, Sensburg and Hohenstein.

'Just in case you planned to ask me, Budzuhn, I don't know exactly what I'm looking for.' Tantau smiled at the inspector apologetically as he spoke. 'I never do know, exactly

-I just sense it sometimes. That's why I go on rummaging through all the files, lists and documents I can find until I tumble over something that stops me in my tracks. It's like coming to a road junction. However complex it is, every turning leads to the same destination in the end.'

Budzuhn found it hard to translate this into practical terms. He was in favour of solid craftsmanship, of finding leads and following them up, of confrontations at the scene of the crime. He sighed.

'I'm looking for a needle in a haystack,' Tantau went on, '—not that that's unduly difficult. All you need is the right technical aid—a magnet, for instance. In our particular case, it might be a map, a file, or a conversation.'

The little detective was indefatigable. 'We must evaluate all the documents we can lay hands on. I'm also interested in the minutes of Party committees, court proceedings, applications for trial, and so on. In addition, we shall naturally require lists of alleged suspects with brief accounts of why they have incurred suspicion.'

Inspector Budzuhn felt increasingly uncomfortable, and when Tantau intimated his desire for yet another list, this time of the best marksmen in the district, he threatened to go on strike.

'Pardon me, sir, but what procedure do you suggest?'

'Nothing could be easier. According to my information, rifle-shooting has been one of Masuria's staple forms of male recreation for a considerable time. That being so, the best shots in the district are bound to be registered with various clubs of the type in question.'

Tantau seemed to set great store by what he described as 'general information'. He conversed happily with leading figures such as the chairman of the rural district council, the Regional Director, and the latter's regional commissioners. Budzuhn was privileged to attend these interviews. Afterwards, Tantau regularly asked him the following question:

'Well, did anything strike you?'

Budzuhn had almost invariably been struck by a number of things—trifles, as he believed. The Regional Director was a racketeer, for instance. Budzuhn noted five remarks which pointed in that direction. The chairman of the rural district council could be classified as a buck-passer. He had made several attempts to prove that he bore no responsibility for

things which were very much his responsibility. Finally, ther
were several other interviewees of whom Budzuhn could sa
with conviction: 'He's shit scared! I could smell it a mil
off.'

Tantau appeared to do no more than register his p
sleuth's remarks. He almost always opened his conversatior
with officials by asking whether they had any department
problems, and, if so, with whom.

To a man, they not only had problems but enumerate
them with alacrity, first, to show what they had to conten
with, and, secondly, to prove that they contended with
successfully. They were sound fellows, one and all. They cor
verted stones into bread and water into milk, all of them—o
almost all, for Tantau did discover one apparent exceptior

He was a little over thirty, a blond, blue-eyed giant wit
a guileless face which inspired confidence. He supplied th
required particulars simply and without fuss. In his view
there were no problems in his domain. 'We take everythin
as it comes,' was his comment.

This sterling character turned out to be the regional com
missioner for agriculture, fisheries and forestry, a patentl
efficient man who had escaped the buck-passing attention
of the chairman of the rural district council. The Regiona
Director made no reference to him at all, neither favourabl
or adverse. His name was Hermann Materna.

As soon as Tantau had concluded his interview, he aske
Budzuhn the usual question.

'Well, did anything strike you?'

'Yes,' Budzuhn replied promptly. 'He's a man of integrity

'That really would be striking, I agree.'

'Hermann Materna is a model National Socialist, I'
swear to it.'

'Really? I'd prefer to call him a good German.'

'Isn't that the same thing?'

Tantau gave a wry smile as he piloted Budzuhn toward
a bench on the grass verge bordering Allenstein market-place
He brushed away some fallen leaves, sat down, and motione
to Budzuhn to join him.

'Are you a Party member, Budzuhn?' he asked.

'No. I've never got round to making an application.'

'Well, I don't suppose you'll get a chance to make up fo
lost time now. I'm a Party member—or was, between Marcl

and June 'thirty-five. They kicked me out after three months. I brought in two men for committing murder in the furtherance of theft. The only trouble was, the murdered man was a Jew and the murderers belonged to the S.A. The official version was self-defence. The Jew had provoked the Germans, presumably by looking at them, and the stolen wallet had merely been taken for identification purposes.'

Budzuhn frowned. 'Why are you telling me all this?'

'To amuse you, to kill time, to talk for the sake of talking —take your pick.'

'I think I follow you. You're implying that there may be certain differences between a good German and a good National Socialist.'

'One lives and learns.' Tantau picked up a large maple-leaf and examined it. 'Have you ever noticed how utterly different two leaves from the same tree can be? The basic structure is simple, yet you never find two leaves alike. Now think of human beings, each one with a myriad possible variations. How could anyone but a madman or a megalomaniac treat them as State-owned bloodstock?'

Inspector Budzuhn did not reply. He hugged his briefcase to him, wondering if he ought to tell Tantau what he had suddenly remembered. It was a name, a name which figured in two separate lists, though this might be no more than a coincidence.

'He's an exception, but that isn't suspicious in itself.'

'Noteworthy, though, and I'm not harking to my original contention: that acts which are defined as criminal by the penal code may spring from wholly admirable motives—religious conviction, say, or a basic sense of justice.'

'It wasn't Hermann Materna who made you think twice, was it? It was the name Materna itself.'

'Congratulations, Inspector. I see I'm not alone in remembering that we've already come across it several times.'

'Twice, to be exact. In connection with the father of this man, a farmer called Alfons Materna.'

'What files does it appear in?'

'Once in the regional directorate's list—Alfons Materna has made repeated attempts to bring various Party members to trial—and once in the list of expert marksmen.'

'It may not amount to anything,' Tantau said, almost hurriedly. 'It could just be one of those misleading coin-

cidences which afflict everyone in our profession. Even so
I think we ought to explore this line of inquiry a little further.

'It's happened!' cried Henriette.

'Really?' Eugen Eis did not know what had happened
and cared less. Henriette was in a good mood—that was
the main thing.

He had buttonholed her during a P.T. session at the
Labour Service camp, clad in a snow-white sweater and black
slacks with knife-edge creases. The other girl pioneers, who
continued to bounce and skip industriously while Hen
riette stood chatting with him on the edge of the parade
ground, were attired in similar outfits but tended to fill them
to better advantage. Eis resolutely refused to be distracted.

'I've had a letter from Uncle Heini!'

This, Eis had to admit, was indeed a matter of importance.
'Come,' he said, 'let's go to your office.'

She clamped her body against his almost before the door
had closed behind them. Eis returned the embrace vigorously
but retained his sense of priorities.

'All right, show me.'

'Show you what?' she panted in his ear.

'The letter, of course.' Sensing that he might have made
a mistake, he added: 'Business before pleasure.' He slapped
her rump as though he were fondling a horse.

Henriette appreciated this sort of treatment. To her, Eis
was a proper man—the essence of masculinity, rugged as a
primeval oak and Germanically masterful. She used to call
him 'my great big Thor'. Eis not only approved of this comparison with the god of thunder but found it apt.

Opening a briefcase in Movement-brown leather, Henriette
produced a sheet of hand-made deckle-edged paper. In the
top left corner, printed in Gothic lettering, was the august
name of Heinrich Himmler. The paper itself, as she carefully
pointed out, bore a watermark composed of victory-runes and
Aryan sun-symbols—in other words, swastikas.

'Uncle's personal notepaper,' she said.

'Very classy. What does he say?'

She tossed her head coquettishly. 'Have a guess!'

Irritated as he was by this piece of affectation, Eis put
his arm round her shoulders so as to get a better look at

the letter and said: 'Whatever your uncle says is right, I'm sure.'

The matter was not quite as simple as Eis had pictured in his day-dreams. In the first place, Henriette had almost curtly refused to ask her uncle for practical assistance. Eis had envisaged a swift and drastic solution along the following lines: Himmler would go to the Führer and the Führer would decree the annulment of Eis's present marriage, all property rights to be awarded to him. However, Henriette's view was that this could only be done in the last resort. Uncle Heini's motto was: Stand on your own two feet, or, Himmler helps those who help themselves. Henriette assured Eis that she had boundless faith in him. He would sever the Gordian knot all by himself, thereby impressing Uncle Heini beyond measure.

The letter she showed him supported her contention. '*My dear little Henriette*,' it began—a preamble suggestive of tender affection and, where the word 'little' was concerned, of a certain puckish humour. Uncle Heini was a much misjudged man, Eis reflected.

The first section of this intimate but typewritten missive— 'dictated to my personal secretary, Adelheid'—concerned itself with family news and questions of health. For instance, Himmler recommended the wearing of cat fur during the cold nights ahead—a traditional Nordic and Germanic expedient.

Henriette wanted to go into this more fully, but Eis said: 'Later, my dearest, later. First let me read what he says about us.'

The passage in question read as follows: '*As to your choice of spouse and father of your future children, undoubtedly a well-considered choice and one which has, I feel sure, been communicated to me only after mature reflection, I congratulate you, my dear and devoted niece, in the comforting knowledge that, as you yourself have stated, the man of your choice may be numbered among those who still know the meaning of loyalty, decency, integrity—in short, Germanhood, particularly in these hard but glorious times in which we all, each in his allotted place, march with faith and courage towards the final victory of which we can rest assured.*'

The letter concluded: '*And so I send you my kinsman's*

blessing, coupled with a request to keep me informed and to notify me in good time so that I can, when the situation has finally clarified itself, offer my congratulations to the man of your choice, if possible in person.'

There followed the affectionate words, this time written in long-hand: *'Your devoted Uncle Heini.'*

Eis was overwhelmed—nay, dumbstruck. Clasping Henriette in his arms, he staggered to the desk and laid her across it, heedless of her rapidly diminishing protests.

Several files fell to the floor with a thud and a cardboard box slithered off into the wastepaper-basket, where it fell open to reveal a thick wad of blank sheets bearing a symbolic watermark and the name 'Heinrich Himmler' in Gothic lettering.

Henriette gave a stifled squawk which Eis, in his devotion to duty, fortunately and understandably misinterpreted. Having succeeded in dropping her P.T. sweater unobtrusively over the wastepaper-basket, Henriette breathed a sigh of relief and let him have his way with her.

'Bend, stretch! Bend, stretch!' intoned the girl pioneer who was supervising the physical jerks outside.

Konrad Klinger poked his head round the kitchen door. 'Get cracking, girls!' he called cheerfully. 'We want some apple fritters, a large schnapps, and a word with the boss.'

Peter followed him in. The two young men greeted Hannelore and Sabine affectionately and sat down at the kitchen table. They were in high spirits—not quite as hearty as in the old days, but almost as noisy.

'You're cheerful today,' Hannelore said.

'They always are when they've been up to something—you know that,' said Sabine. 'They get that silly look on their faces.'

Peter waved them away. 'You're just trying to get at us again. Look after your pots and pans and get those old lions in here. We've got some rich red meat for them.'

Materna and Jablonski had been visiting Grienspan in the forest dug-out but were expected home within the next half-hour. They had ordered pike stuffed with minced beef in honour of Grienspan, who was planning to make another of his 'trips', and stewed pike did not take kindly to being overcooked. It could therefore be assumed that they would turn up more or less on time.

Jablonski was the first to appear. He reconnoitred the kitchen, muttered something uncomplimentary when he saw who was flirting with the girls, and withdrew. A few minutes later he reappeared with Materna and Grienspan. Removing the bottle of schnapps from the table, he stuffed it in his pocket and went outside again to keep watch.

Back in the kitchen, Konrad reported triumphantly that everything was going according to plan.

'Fine,' said Materna. 'In that case we can eat first.'

They did so for a full hour, the minimum duration of any meal in the Materna household. The stuffed pike were more than adequate, but there was nothing left when they had finished—not even the backbones, which had been removed in advance.

'Right,' said Materna, when the men were alone in his den, 'fire away.'

'Judge Barthels has a sense of humour,' Konrad reported. 'He realizes that we can't make a great deal out of the case, as I told you, but he's determined to have his little bit of fun. I let him win two games of chess running, by the way. That put him in a good mood.'

Materna frowned. 'Come to the point, lad.'

'Well, Barthels has arranged a sort of special hearing for this coming Friday, the day after tomorrow, at 8 p.m. in the mayor's office. Those invited to attend will include Eugen Eis, the ex-mayor, the present mayor, myself, acting for Dr Rogatzki, and you, Herr Materna. I've brought your subpoena with me. The others will be delivered tomorrow morning. I'd like to see Eis's face when he gets his!'

Materna turned to Grienspan, who had been listening in silence. 'What do you think of that, Siegfried?'

'Quick work. Our young friend has obviously got the bit between his teeth.'

'We won't get anywhere unless we act fast,' Konrad said confidently. 'Judge Barthels is an old fox. He's also a sound anti-Nazi. His special hearing may not be a hundred per cent conventional, but it's entirely legal. Evening sessions aren't so exceptional in this day and age. Even the law works overtime in the interests of final victory. Besides, Barthels had taken the precaution of arranging various hearings in the neighbourhood. There aren't any flies on him, I can tell you.'

Materna looked sceptical. 'All right, so he's got a sense of humour and he isn't a Nazi. I suppose he omitted to join the Party and got passed over for promotion—he served as a county court judge here twelve years ago, if my memory serves me correctly. Is that enough, though?'

'He was married to a Jewess,' Konrad said. 'They took her away. He's been living alone for years.'

Silence fell, but not for long. Materna said: 'You've made your point. Go on.'

'Well, you'll be present, Herr Materna, and Jacob will go along too—no one can possibly take exception to that. That gives all three of us an unshakable alibi supported by un-impeachable witnesses. Meanwhile, the balloon goes up. What do you say?'

Materna said nothing at first. He opened a box of imported Dutch cigars—finest pre-war quality—and removed one. He sniffed it, cut it, moistened it, and lit it with deliberation. Then he looked at Grienspan.

'You realize what this young hothead expects you to do, don't you?'

Grienspan nodded. 'Of course. I'm the one who makes sure the balloon goes up—why not?'

'Listen, Konrad,' Materna said, 'your scheme reminds me of the days when you and Peter used to get a lot of fun out of playing practical jokes. You were careless enough then—reckless, I'd prefer to call it—but those days are gone.'

'We've thought it all out very carefully,' Peter interposed. 'Nothing can go wrong if we operate strictly according to plan.'

'You've done more than enough already. Looking after a wounded man is quite sufficient. I don't propose to turn this place into a field hospital.'

'It needn't come to that,' Grienspan said, '—not if we take the proper precautions. If I understand Konrad correctly, the plan is to concentrate all the local dignitaries in one place so as to create a sort of vacuum elsewhere. We shall be able to do our work with little fear of interruption.'

Konrad looked gratified. 'Precisely.'

'Siegfried,' Materna said, wagging his finger, 'you've been bitten by the same bug—you're looking for an evening's entertainment.'

'I admit it. It would amuse me to give a little farewell performance. I'll leave immediately after the fireworks.'

'Say yes, Herr Materna!' chorused the young men.

'No,' he replied, puffing pleasurably at his cigar, 'not unless we really clear the ground first.'

'But what else is there to settle?'

'Well, there's that special board of inquiry in Allenstein, for one thing. If those people possess anything like the intelligence you credit them with, Konrad, I should leave well alone.'

'I must correct myself on that point,' Konrad said. 'They don't know what they're doing—Councillor Engel confided that to me after our third bottle the other night. According to him, the S.S. bigwig spends the whole time yelling at his staff and running them into the ground but they're getting nowhere fast. They've even called in a broken down ex-C.I.D. man called Tantau, but all he does is tour the district at random, twiddling his thumbs and uttering subversive remarks. Engel told me that too. The S.S. chap is foaming at the mouth, apparently.'

'Is that a fact, or just three bottles of wine talking?'

'It's a fact,' Konrad declared firmly. 'I give you my word.'

'I hope I never have to take you up on that.' Materna laid his cigar aside. 'Well, how does the rest of your plan look? What exactly do you want to blow up?'

'Party Headquarters, complete with the results of twelve years' snooping. Dossiers, lists, files—the lot. Eis won't go up with it, I'm afraid. He'll be at the hearing.'

'I'm in favour,' said Grienspan.

'And I stand by my objections,' Materna said. 'However, I'll withdraw them if they're not shared by anyone else. We must get Jacob's agreement too, of course—I insist on that.'

Peter Bachus, who was condemned to take part in the proposed venture only in a medical capacity, went to stand guard in place of Jablonski. Jablonski came in, sat down, and listened in silence, taking an occasional swig from his bottle. No one could tell what he was thinking.

'Well,' Materna asked at length, 'yes or no?'

'No,' Jablonski replied, 'not without Eis. Eis must be there when it goes up.'

Konrad did his best to persuade him. He explained the alibi question and begged him not to expect too much at once.

'No,' Jablonski repeated, 'Eis must go too, or failing him, Schlaguweit.'

'We might be able to arrange that,' Konrad said eventually.

'In that case, I vote yes.'

'I'll cut them to ribbons!' announced Eugen Eis, meaning Judge Barthels and his special hearing. The subpoena requesting his attendance in the matter of Eis versus the parish of Maulen had sent him into a towering rage.

He at once asked for a call to Allenstein and was connected with Barthels's chambers, only to be informed that the judge was out of town. He demanded to speak to Barthels's superior, who listened politely but regretted that he was not competent to intervene.

After that, to cap it all, Eis received a call from Mayor Pillich.

'It must be a misunderstanding,' whimpered Pillich, '—this subpoena, I mean. I don't know what to do about it.'

'Get over here at once!'

Pillich hurried to Party Headquarters and was received in audience by the Local Group Leader.

'First and foremost, keep your trap shut,' Eis commanded him. 'Of course it's a misunderstanding! It's a dirty low-down trick on Materna's part, but I'll pay him back. The main thing is, nothing must get out—not a squeak!'

'It may be too late,' Pillich said plaintively.

'What? You mean you've talked?'

'Not me. I'm discreet, unlike some other people—Uschkurat, for instance. They've subpoenaed him too, but he says he won't turn up. They can play their dirty little games without me—that's what he said. Even the parson heard him. He also said everyone in Maulen could go jump in the lake —the Party included.'

Eis emitted a bellow of rage. 'Get him here!'

This was easier said than done. Schlaguweit was away in Allenstein, making purchases for the Gasthaus, but Pillich managed to dig out one of his deputies. Kurt Stampe, commonly known as 'Cocky Kurt', was not only a keen member of the male voice choir and hog-fattening specialist but an obeyer of orders in the true Party tradition. However, even he failed to find Uschkurat.

'Uschkurat's gone,' he reported.

'What do you mean, gone? People don't just disappear, not in Maulen.'

Eis learned to his boundless amazement that Uschkurat had loaded a cart with bundles of clothing, boxes of food and sacks of flour, as well as hay and fodder for his animals. With two horses harnessed to the front of his cart and two milch-cows trailing behind, he had left Maulen three hours before, proceeding in a westerly direction.

'Get after him!' screamed Eis, amazement yielding to fury. He sounded as if he had just sustained a mortal wound.

Cocky Kurt, not overburdened with intellect but full of Third Reich drive, recognized his chance. Accompanied by two more Brownshirts, he roared after Uschkurat on his official motor-cycle, overhauled him near the village of Luschken, eight miles away, and directed him back to Maulen with a minimal use of force.

Eis met Uschkurat on the steps in front of Party Headquarters, trembling with rage. 'You swine!' he yelled. 'You tried to desert!'

Uschkurat bowed his head. 'I wanted to get away from here. This place is suffocating me.'

'You're a miserable, rotten, stinking defeatist!'

'What's a defeatist?' asked Uschkurat. 'It doesn't matter, anyway. What do you want with me? I was going to visit an old war-time friend in the Rhineland, near Sieburg. He wrote and invited me, so why shouldn't I go? Somebody round here has got to make a start, and I've had a bellyful.'

For the first time in years, Eis was at a loss for words. He opened his mouth but nothing came out. Only the sight of his men staring at him in amazement brought him to life again. He seemed to emerge from a nightmare.

'Never,' he said, squaring his shoulders, 'never would I have thought such a thing possible, least of all in a village like ours.' He no longer deigned to look at Uschkurat. Half in sorrow, half in exhortation, he addressed himself to his men alone. 'That there should be one person in Maulen, one base and cowardly malingerer, devoid of any spark of decency or greatness, destitute of faith in final victory . . . No, my friends, this cannot be tolerated!'

'Don't, Eis!' Uschkurat pleaded, trembling because he was familiar with Eis's techniques and knew what to expect. 'Don't! You don't know what you're saying!' He raised his hands in entreaty and gazed heavenwards. 'We're done for, all of us!' he cried in a quaking voice. 'The Topich has come back, and I saw Grienspan's ghost with my own eyes!'

Eis stared at him in disgust. Then he said: 'Knock some sense into him.'

Kurt Stampe not only issued his men with instructions but set them a good example by lending a hand himself. Together, they seized Uschkurat and dragged him into the building. He dangled limply between them like a bundle of old clothes. One of his horses whinnied as though in protest, but the cows looked on with big, sorrowful, submissive eyes.

Eis lingered on the steps a while, lost in thought. Then, shaking his head sadly, he made his way along the elder-hedge to his house, where he stationed himself behind a tree and peered over the fence.

It was laundry day. The clothes-line was laden with big sheets which billowed slightly in a gentle breeze. The breeze was also responsible for wafting certain words to his ears. He listened to them with mounting satisfaction.

'Grab hold,' said a blithe voice—Christine's.

'Shall I lift you?' asked a man—Pierre Ambal.

'You're tickling me!'

'Don't you like it?'

Of course she liked it! Visibly gratified, Eis gave a corroborative nod. So the lady had found her voice again. She was obviously feeling better—much better.

'There we are, then,' he muttered to himself.

'Thank you, gentlemen, for having the goodness to attend,' said Judge Barthels.

'I object!' Eugen Eis said firmly.

'To what, pray?'

'To these whole proceedings,' retorted Eis, who had taken the precaution of putting on his Party uniform. 'I formally request you to take note of my objection.'

'By all means,' Barthels replied blandly. He was a tall, elderly man with a narrow face. His gestures were well-rounded and his sonorous voice seldom if ever rose in pitch.

'I don't like this business,' Eis pursued. Then, more loudly: 'There's something fishy about it.'

'You think so?' Barthels raised his eyebrows in courteous inquiry. He studied the Local Group Leader as if he were a document, and it was easy to decipher what he saw.

He shook hands with the others: after Eis, Mayor Pillich, a man like a bulging sack of oats, then ex-Mayor Uschkurat, with a bandaged head, sagging shoulders, and a hand which seemed to consist of flabby skin.

'Have you had an accident?' the judge asked solicitously.

'A self-inflicted one,' Eis explained on Uschkurat's behalf.

Konrad Klinger introduced the two remaining invitees, Materna and Jablonski—a pair of old but robust-looking draught-horses, thought Barthels, who had served in the artillery during the First World War.

The judge was a man of the old school, courtesy personified and deliberately ceremonious. It was all very alien to Maulen, alien and a trifle disturbing.

'May I ask you to take your seats, gentlemen?'

Even while the gentlemen were complying, Eis raised his voice again.

'It's a complete waste of time, the whole thing!'

Konrad said: 'These official proceedings owe their existence to inquiries which you yourself initiated, Herr Eis.'

'I wasn't addressing you,' snapped Eis. 'You know what I think of you.'

'That is irrelevant,' said Barthels. He opened his files and began to leaf through them, taking his time. His eyes glinted as he did so, but he showed no other sign of emotion.

Eis snorted. 'To put a stop to the performance which certain parties seem bent on staging here, I make the following declaration: if it really does all stem from inquiries which I am supposed to have instituted, ages ago, I hereby withdraw my application for a hearing.'

Materna glanced at Eis. The man had learnt a great deal over the years. He juggled with words as he had once juggled with hand-grenades, and just as lethally. Mayor Pillich eyed him with an expression of humble admiration, Jablonski growled like a watchdog, Uschkurat sat slumped and motionless in his chair, and Konrad Klinger desperately sought around for counter-arguments. Barthels was the only one who seemed unmoved.

'Herr Eis,' he said, with a faint bow, 'or Local Group Leader—you must tell me which form of address you prefer —permit me to draw your attention to the fact that these proceedings are already under way. They must be brought to a satisfactory conclusion before we may regard them as closed.'

Konrad breathed a sigh of relief as Barthels embarked on an expert account of his juridical responsibilities. Glancing round, he saw that Eis's expression had changed to that of a baffled bull, whereas Materna looked foxy and alert.

'We are here concerned with the erstwhile presentation of Dog's Meadow to the parish of Maulen.'

'Did I make a mistake—a legal mistake, I mean?' Materna asked brightly. 'If so, I apologize. I'm naturally prepared to revoke my deed of gift.'

'That would accord with the terms of Herr Eis's application,' Konrad put in quickly.

'Damn it all!' Eis shouted, pounding the table. 'The case is almost ten years old.'

'But not subject to the statute of limitations,' said Konrad.

'This is sheer mischief-making! After all, I'm Local Group Leader of this place.'

'One of the principal reasons for this hearing,' Barthels said politely, 'is to reassure you that you are being treated with the deference due to your rank.'

'I protest!' Konrad cried in theatrical tones. 'I object to the suggestion that a senior official is entitled to preferential treatment. However great a man's services to the community— and I offer no opinion in this particular case—the basic principle of equality before the law still applies.'

'You must be out of your mind!' thundered Eis. He made a move to rise and hurl himself at Konrad. 'Who the hell do you think you are? You were still shitting your nappies when I was fighting for Greater Germany!'

'Is there much difference?' Konrad murmured.

'What did you say?' roared Eis. 'What was that supposed to mean?'

'Not what you took it to mean, I'm sure.' Judge Barthels

aised his well-tended hands. His voice had an almost gleeful undertone. 'Despite his youth, I credit Dr Klinger with enough sense not to utter potentially defamatory remarks in my presence.' He turned to Eis. 'I also regard Local Group Leader Eis as an avowed champion of justice and integrity.'

'You said it—avowed!' Eis glared menacingly round the room. No one was grinning, not even Jablonski.

Judge Barthels went on: 'I therefore note with satisfaction that Herr Eis has firmly declined to accept preferential treatment in any shape or form. I can only describe his attitude as exemplary in the extreme.'

This saved the evening. Operations already under way in Party Headquarters could pursue an uninterrupted course. Meanwhile, Barthels manipulated his keyboard with bravura and gave a virtuoso demonstration of legal procedure. Before Eis could grasp what was happening to him, he was enmeshed.

Barthels established that Eis—after careful consideration and for the best of motives, no doubt—had opposed Materna's gift to the parish. The present Mayor, who would never have believed such a thing possible, gaped at Eis incredulously. Then, continued Barthels, Eis had changed his mind. After equally careful consideration and for equally sound reasons, he now approved the deed of gift.

'Am I right so far?'

'Yes,' Eis growled uncomfortably, then boomed: 'I'm always guided by my concern for the good of the community.'

'I beg leave to doubt that,' interposed Konrad. 'There is a possibility—indeed, a suspicion—that Herr Eis may have been prompted by motives of a purely personal and financial nature. At the time, when he contested the gift, he was still married to Herr Materna's daughter, through whom he hoped to inherit Dog's Meadow, among other things.'

'That's a vile and malicious slander!' Eis bellowed. 'I won't take that from anyone, let alone a stupid puppy who's still wet behind the ears.'

The judge's voice sounded amiably neutral. 'Permit me to clarify Dr Klinger's remarks slightly. Although uttered in a tone which I deem inappropriate to the occasion, his actual words were in full conformity with court procedure. He doubted but did not dispute. He spoke of a possibility, not a factual assumption. A suspicion is merely conjecture, not a assertion which has to be substantiated by legal argument.'

Eis struggled for words. Materna was clearly enjoying th situation and Jablonski registered amusement. Mayor Pillicl looked dismayed, whereas Uschkurat seemed to have taker on a new lease of life.

'Life is hell,' Uschkurat said. 'We're in it up to our neck and it won't be long before we go under—you mark m words!'

'Shut your trap!' roared Eis.

He looked so distraught that Mayor Pillich was reduced t utter bewilderment. He watched with dismay as Eis's hand knotted themselves into fists, uncurled, then contracted onc more. He felt a sudden and irresistible urge to demonstrat his loyalty.

'Local Group Leader,' stammered Pillich, 'if you think thi gift should be revoked, why not? I'm quite agreeable. Yor must have your reasons—you always do, I know that. You car rely on me to back you to the hilt.'

'Good God!' Eis burst out. 'Am I completely surrounded by idiots? What are you trying to do to me? Has everyone forgotten who I am? I still decide what happens around here.

A violent explosion rent the air. The window-panes shat tered and glass tinkled to the floor. A sudden blast of wind swept the papers off the table. The lights flickered wildly a though in their death-throes and then went out.

'What the hell was that?' demanded Eis.

'A sign from heaven!' moaned Uschkurat.

A dusky red glow pervaded the darkened room. It swiftly grew in intensity, bathing the walls, the table, and the faces round it. The paralysed, expectant hush was brutally shat tered by the dry chatter of a sub-machine-gun.

'We could hardly have foreseen such an interruption,' Judge Barthels said. His voice preserved its immutable courtesy 'I adjourn this hearing sine die.'

Chief Superintendent Tantau arrived in Maulen next morning accompanied by Inspector Budzuhn. Reaching the village square about eleven o'clock, they found that the object of their visit was not far to seek. The still smoking ruins of Party Headquarters stood out like a sore thumb.

Budzuhn surveyed the scene with some astonishment. He aid: 'Reminds me of the war.'

'We are at war, didn't you know?' As though under some nagnetic impulse, Tantau moved nearer.

The senior policeman present, a sergeant, hurried up to `antau and made his report.

'Area cordoned off, sir,' he announced. 'All access barred o members of the public.'

Most of the bystanders were schoolchildren. The men of Maulen seemed to be avoiding the spot, and even the women kept their curiosity within bounds. They watched from a espectful distance, whispering together or staring in fascination at the ruins. The site of the explosion was ringed by three ire brigades. The firemen had unearthed several cases of wine n the cellars and secured them against possible looting. This vas not only customary but an accepted form of perks.

'Who's in charge here?' Budzuhn asked the police sergeant.

'Inspector Kranzler from Sensburg, sir. He was the first o get here. He's in the Gasthaus at the moment.'

Budzuhn knew what Tantau expected of him. Kranzler vas required to report immediately. He also knew what Tantau thought of Kranzler: not a bad policeman but not a good enough detective. But then, was anybody good enough or Tantau?

Perceptibly fortified, Kranzler hurried out of the Gasthaus and delivered himself of the following report, which Budzuhn noted down in a form of private shorthand:

Explosion occurred between 9.30 and 9.35 p.m., followed at once by outbreak of single burst from a sub-machine-gun. No immediate clue to those responsible. Particulars:

1. Explosion. Caused by explosive charge, probably about four pounds of dynamite. Site: Local Group Leader's office-cum-reception-room, brunt of explosion borne by desk of same. Use of normal fuse probable, no signs of automatic ignition.

2. Fire. Outbreak of the same ensured by sprinkling petrol, estimated quantity at least four gallons, i.e. the contents of one normal army jerrycan. Petrol assumed to have been distributed over floor, shelves, and filing cabinet. Fire ignited by explosion.

3. Automatic pistol. Shots fired at heart of conflagration immediately after explosion and outbreak of fire. Seven bullet-

holes found between desk and shelves, three of them in th
body of a man. Seven cartridge cases retrieved from th
vicinity of window, undoubtedly of German army origi

'Always the same basic procedure,' said Budzuhn. 'Th
confirms our theory—I mean, your theory.'

Tantau was now standing in the middle of the ruin
The central room was totally destroyed and two neighbourin
rooms bore traces of severe damage. Such smoke-blackene
sections of wall as remained standing were criss-crosse
with jagged cracks. The roof had fallen in.

Budzuhn poked around excitedly. 'A really professiona
job,' he commented. 'These people are learning fast.'

'You're right,' Tantau replied, rubbing his chin. 'I'd g
further and call this the best job they've done to dat
Remind me to compliment them when the time comes.'

Budzuhn nodded and made a note. Inspector Granzle
eyed his colleague in astonishment, feeling as if he ha
wandered into a lunatic asylum by mistake.

'Where's your sketch-map?' Tantau asked him.

Kranzler looked embarrassed. He had not done one ye
but he promised to make up for lost time. He had been o
the point of starting when summoned from the Gasthaus.

'Who was the dead man?' inquired Tantau.

Kranzler could answer that one. 'Body identified as that o
Ernst Schlaguweit, local S.A. commander, manager of Gas
haus and related enterprises.'

'More of that later,' said Tantau. 'What interests me prim
arily is why the man was there at the crucial moment. Was h
always there at that time? If not, what made him go there?

'I haven't ascertained that yet.'

'Then ascertain it. Furthermore, was anyone else in th
immediate vicinity? Who was usually there at that time:
Did the building contain offices only, or living quarters a
well? I want all these routine questions answered. Yo
have precisely one hour, Inspector.'

Kranzler disappeared, followed by Budzuhn. Tantau sa
down on a neighbouring heap of rubble and lapsed into a sor
of day-dream, rubbing his hands to warm them. The first
snow of winter seemed to hover in the air.

'Can I be of any assistance?' asked an ingratiating voice
Amadeus Neuber was standing beside him.

Tantau looked up, made a brief but accurate assessment of what he saw, and asked: 'Where were you at the time of the explosion?'

'At home.'

'Do you have any witnesses?'

'Witnesses? Why should I need witnesses?' Hurriedly, Neuber added: 'I was reading my little refugee girl a fairytale. I read her one nearly every evening at that time.'

'Perhaps I'd better introduce myself,' Neuber said, drawing himself up. 'I am Deputy Local Group Leader, director of organization, and headmaster of the village school.'

Tantau fumbled in his breast-pocket and withdrew a small slip of paper on which were half a dozen names. After a brief glance at it, he said: 'You must be Herr Neuber, Amadeus Neuber.'

Neuber nodded at this confirmation of his importance. He was gratified to see Tantau get up and introduce himself in turn, though he omitted his rank and simply said: 'I'm temporarily in charge of inquiries here.'

'In that case, Herr Tantau, I wish you the best of success. Please say if there is anything I can do to assist you.'

'Were you an eye-witness? No? Can you give me any positive leads? None? Do you suspect anyone in particular? No one at all? Very well, take me to the Local Group Leader, if you know where to find him.'

Eugen Eis was in the parish hall, which he had commandeered on behalf of the Party. Pillich had been obliged to make two rooms in his own house available for the transaction of mayoral business, and his mood was correspondingly bleak. He had begun to ask himself if Eis really was the guardian angel he had always believed him to be.

'Hunt the rabble down!' Eis adjured Tantau. 'I want to see them strung up! They destroyed our Party Headquarters, but that's only the half of it—we can build a bigger and better one. What matters is that all our files and dossiers have gone up in smoke—information of the utmost importance, irreplaceable documents!' He was temporarily oblivious to Schlaguweit's death.

'Well, at least you're still alive,' said Tantau.

'What do you mean?' Eis asked suspiciously.

'I mean you might easily be dead.' Tantau gave Eis plenty

of time to digest this statement. 'You, instead of that other man. Had that occurred to you?'

'I can't say it had.' Eis slumped into an arm-chair and stared round him as though hemmed in by assassins. 'But of course! It's a repetition of the July twentieth plot against the Führer's life. Unpatriotic, subversive, degenerate elements were at work here too, but I escaped—just like the Führer.'

'It must have been Providence,' said Tantau. Abruptly he asked: 'Where were you when the explosion occurred?'

'No problem there,' Eis assured him. 'I've got an alibi.'

'An alibi?' Tantau said sharply. 'You consider it necessary to have an alibi?'

Eis corrected himself at once, his angry glare clearly conveying that Tantau had better watch his step. 'That's to say I was with several other people at the time—seven in all. We were in conference, here in this room—an official matter. The meeting lasted an hour-and-a-half, up to the moment when those swine . . .'

'Who were the other seven?'

Eis enumerated them: Judge Barthels, his court stenographer, a lawyer by the name of Klinger, Pillich and Uschkurat, Materna and Jablonski.

Tantau jotted the names down with apparent indifference. He only paused once—so fractionally that the hesitation would have been lost on anyone who did not know him well —and that was when Eis came to the name Materna.

'An impressive array,' he said, raising his wrinkled face. 'You have seven witnesses to vouch for you, and everyone who attended this conference can say the same, can't they? That's an unusual feature, if you like.' In a casual tone, he added: 'For instance, Herr Neuber isn't in the same fortunate position. He was reading fairy-tales at the time.'

'What do you propose to do now?'

'Go for a stroll,' replied Tantau, getting up. 'You live in a most attractive part of the world, Herr Eis. I should very much like to take a look round, with your permission. I'm getting more and more of a soft spot for this village and its inhabitants—with a few exceptions, of course.'

Materna's farm dogs barked and rushed to the gate, where they halted, stiff-legged and growling. Their amber eyes were fixed on the motionless figure of a man who was leaning against the cross-bar, emitting a low humming sound.

There was a piercing whistle, and the dogs turned and raced back to Jablonski with their tails wagging. He clapped his hands twice, whereupon they disappeared into the barn like greased lightning.

'Bravo!' said the man at the gate. 'I can see you know a fair bit about dogs.'

'You too,' Jablonski replied, not ungraciously. 'They stopped barking and just growled at you. That's quite an achievement.'

'I stood there without moving and hummed to myself,' said the man. 'It's a sure-fire way of getting dogs to stop and think —it puzzles them, you see. They forget to bark, at least for a short time. All the same, it's impossible to put dogs as well trained as yours off their guard.'

These remarks gratified Jablonski without making him any less wary. 'You didn't come about the dogs, did you?'

'No, I was just taking a stroll.'

Jablonski's suspicions increased. 'A stroll, here in Maulen?'

'I often go for walks,' said the man, surveying the farm. 'I enjoy walking, and as I happened to be passing I thought I'd drop in on Herr Materna. Are you Herr Materna?'

'I only work here,' Jablonski said cautiously. As a farm-hand, he would not be expected to make decisions or supply information. His instinct told him that the man facing him could be dangerous. 'Herr Materna is very busy. What name shall I say?'

'My name is Tantau,' the little man said with a faint smile. 'I'm one of the police officers investigating the explosion down in the village.'

'Is that why you came?'

'Not primarily.'

'I'll go and ask.' Jablonski whistled up the dogs and they returned to their station by the gate, slavering belligerently and keeping a watchful eye on Tantau.

Tantau did not move. He watched Jablonski plod off, then, without turning his head, resumed his inspection of the farm— barn, stables, living quarters. An accurate sketch of the entire premises took shape in his mind.

Then, to his surprise, he saw a man approaching, a man

almost as short as himself, of similar build and gait. Even
the searching eyes were not unlike his own, and the sound
of the man's voice completed the strange resemblance. It was
like his, but somewhat fuller, louder, and more incisive.

'Herr Tantau?' said the man. 'I'm Materna. Please come
in—the gate isn't locked.'

Tantau grasped Materna's outstretched hand. The dogs
not only sat still but, without shifting their position, allowed
Tantau to pat them. Materna smiled at the sight. Jablonski was
right: the man had a way with animals.

'Please consider yourself my guest,' Materna said, gesturing in the direction of the house.

'You have a magnificent farm,' Tantau said, as they walked
across the forecourt. 'It must be wonderful to live here.'

'If you'd visited Maulen five or ten years ago you might
have found it hard to drag yourself away,' said Materna.
'Things are different now. Even the scenery seems to have
changed, and the people have lost their outlines. They've
become pale and shadowy—ghostly, in a manner of speaking.
I sometimes feel as if the whole place had become a battlefield. Does that sound ridiculous?'

'No,' replied Tantau.

Inside the house, he was introduced to two girls—cheerful, friendly creatures who asked what they could offer him in
the way of refreshment. Food and drink were not his principal
vices, he told them, but he would not refuse a glass of some
regional brew or other. If there was a local speciality, he would
be happy to try it.

Materna nodded to the girls and raised his hand with all
five fingers extended, a sign which conveyed that they were
to bring out the best. Then he showed the visitor into his
den and invited him to sit down. After a brief inspection,
Tantau selected Materna's favourite chair. Materna noted
this with a smile and sat down on the sofa, facing Tantau
across the rugged oak table.

'You seem to value your privacy.'

'What makes you think that, Herr Tantau?'

'Among other things, the height of the fence round
your farm buildings and those two splendid dogs of yours.
It's obvious that your household staff are all on very intimate
terms with you. The rest of your employees appear to live

in that building beside the outhouses, about three hundred yards away.'

'You're very observant,' Materna said.

Sabine poured out two glasses of smoky-tasting grain spirit distilled with peat, a choice liquor which Materna only dispensed on special occasions, the last one being Grienspan's reappearance. Tantau sniffed his glass appreciatively and drank. A look of rapture came over his face.

'You're spoiling me,' he said. 'Why?'

'You never know, I may be trying to corrupt you.'

Tantau gave a bleating laugh. He refilled his glass, held the pure, pungent-smelling liquor to his nose, and said: 'I met your son Hermann recently.'

Materna leant forward a little, but there was no hint of tension in his steady voice. 'I wonder what you thought of him. The father-son relationship usually takes some time to mature, and ours is no exception. It isn't easy for an outsider to understand that. Do you have a family?'

'No,' Tantau replied. 'It wasn't only my profession that stood in the way—I'm just not the marrying kind, I suppose. There are moments when I regret it, I must confess, but there are others when I'm glad. For instance, ever since I got to know a little about you, I've been wondering what my attitude would be if one of my sons had eliminated the other with a hand-grenade.'

'You obviously know a great deal about me. Nothing too detrimental, I hope?'

'We live in a suspicious age,' Tantau said, draining his glass. 'We haven't any choice, have we?'

Materna was spared the necessity of replying by the arrival of Hannelore and Sabine. They laid the table expertly and in silence, smiling as they did so. Dish after dish appeared: cold herrings in cream, stewed sausages in beer sauce, slices of smoked ham, sweet-and-sour goose, pickled pork and veal, jellied eel, marzipan, macaroons made with rolled oats, and almond cakes.

'I'm most impressed,' said Tantau. 'You must show me your stocks afterwards—I'd be intererested to see where you keep them. Do you hang your hams in the loft and store your schnapps in the cellar? And what do you put it in—stone jars, carboys, barrels? You must show me everything.'

Materna grinned. 'Have you got a search warrant?'

'Do you think it likely?' Tantau spoke in a mild, almost sorrowful tone. 'Your question, my dear Herr Materna, discloses a remarkable gap in your knowledge of present conditions. You seem to imagine that we still live in a reasonably well-ordered constitutional State. To be honest, I would scarcely have thought you capable of such a misconception. Search warrants have been out of vogue for years. I could comb your premises from cellar to attic if I wanted to.'

'Does that mean you don't want to?'

'Don't tempt me,' said Tantau bending over the dishes on the table. 'I'm magically attracted by your jellied eel.' He tasted some, gently smacking his lips. 'Delicious! Do you have a secret recipe?'

Materna shook his head. Masurian waters, whether lake or river, provided the mud-dwelling eel with a habitat of crystalline, almost chemically refined purity. This was one reason for its unusually delicate flavour, the other being its individual mode of preparation. His own method was to water the eel for another twenty-four hours or so, then simmer it over a low flame for at least two hours, and, lastly, steep it in vinegar to which five different local herbs had been added.

'The final result is sensational, anyway,' Tantau assured him, munching with relish. He then fell silent for nearly a quarter of an hour, by which time the jellied eel had entirely disappeared.

Materna watched his visitor with a half-amused, half-wary expression. He did not speak until Tantau had sat back in his chair, apparently replete.

'Be honest. Why did you really come?'

'Because I wanted to make your acquaintance,' replied Tantau. 'I shouldn't advise you to think otherwise. After all, you're one of the lucky seven with a perfect alibi.'

'Don't you trust it?'

'Trust is a strong word.' Tantau folded his hands on his well-filled stomach. 'Do you judge England by Jack the Ripper or by Shakespeare? When you think of Germany, do you think of Goethe or Hitler? What does America mean to you, Al Capone or Abraham Lincoln? Does France conjure up Voltaire or Robespierre, or something quite different? The world is full of believers who are convinced that their faith can move mountains. Do you know my only firm conviction at this moment, Herr Materna? Your jellied eel was good. What can compare with that kind of certainty?'

'You'll have digested it in a few hours,' Materna said, unimpressed. 'What then?'

'Then I stop being a human being and turn into a detective again—is that what you mean?' Tantau shut his eyes as though the act of eating had exhausted him. 'Quite possible, quite possible. Each of us has moments when he feels like a fallen angel and others when he sees himself for the miserable sinner he is. What's the best way of reconciling the two? There isn't any recipe, as there is for jellied eels. You know that perfectly well, but what do you know about me?'

'He was one of the best!' Eugen Eis declared for at least the ninth time that evening. 'One of the very best. He died in the line of duty.'

He was talking about Ernst Schlaguweit, who had that day been accorded a swift but impressive funeral—a 'home front' burial attended by no one except his immediate friends and associates.

The funeral had taken place during the first heavy snowstorm of the year. Even while the uniformed pall-bearers were still mutely carrying the coffin to its last resting-place, the snow had turned into driving rain. Soaked to the skin, their teeth either chattering or clenched, they had lowered Ernst Schlaguweit into the grave with indecorous haste.

The mourners were now assembled in the so-called banqueting-room of the Gasthaus for a restorative 'Ice-breaker', which consisted of near-boiling red wine laced with arrack, rum, and sugar. It not only banished the effects of cold weather but induced forgetfulness, even of the Russians, who were speedily advancing on East Prussia.

'Yes,' said Eis, 'he was an example to us all.' Schlaguweit's black-draped photograph hung below the swastika banner on the wall behind him, flanked by burning candles. 'Particularly to the younger generation,' he added.

The Local Group Leader scrutinized the thinning ranks of the village élite. The burdens of his office were growing ever more onerous because there were ever fewer people competent to share them. Neuber was a milksop and Mayor

Pillich a brainless nincompoop whose behaviour at the special hearing had been positively dangerous. Pillich, too, would have to be replaced by someone better.

The only trouble was, who? Most of the robust thirty-year-olds were dead or away on active service. The younger generation were willing but green—one of them was already puking his guts up under the table. As for the old guard, they were either worn out or broken reeds. They sat slumped in their chairs, trying to invigorate the atmosphere with song, but it was an unconvincing performance. Were the good old days gone for ever?

No, Eis told himself, a hundred times no! Germany was not finished yet, nor was Maulen. There were still a few citizens with a sense of loyalty—Naujoks, Poreski, Sombray, Bembenneck, Panzer and Perduhn, among others—a trifle limited, perhaps, but fully alive to the requirements of the present situation. Using them, he would revamp the Party leadership and bring the village up to scratch once more.

Finally, there was Stampe, 'Cocky' Kurt Stampe—a promising youngster if ever there was one. Eis raised his glass to him and was gratified to see him respond with alacrity. It was a hopeful sign.

'Go and mix with the younger ones,' Eis told Neuber, effectively banishing him to the lower end of the table. 'Stampe,' he called, 'come here.'

Stampe sat beside him, radiating pride and gratitude. The others continued to bawl, bellow, guffaw, and slap each other on the back. Anyone who had lost the ability to sit upright was shoved under the table.

'No one can say we haven't got a sense of humour,' Eis declared. 'We still know how to be cheerful.'

Cocky Kurt's response was immediate. 'Cheerful—yes, sir!'

'Let's go and have a pee,' Eis suggested.

When they were standing shoulder to shoulder facing the grimy whitewashed wall at the back of the Gasthaus, Eis said confidentially: 'Feel like a good laugh?'

'Any time,' replied Stampe, true to form.

'Come with me, then.' Eis buttoned his flies, glanced at his wrist-watch, and strode off with Stampe trotting doglike at his heels.

They left the Gasthaus, keeping to the edge of the village square, skirted the parish hall and the ruins of Party Headquarters, and made for Eis's house beside the mill. 'Keep right behind me,' Eis whispered. 'Not a sound, mind.'

Shadowed by Stampe, he crept round the house and peered up at the dimly lit windows of the matrimonial bedroom. His calculations appeared to be correct.

It was only just after ten o'clock, and he had assured his wife that he would not be home before midnight—he never was on such occasions. He had also warned Sergeant-Major Fackler that the prisoner of war assigned to him might be required to remain on duty late that night.

Outside the front door, Eis pulled off his shoes and motioned to Stampe to do the same. They crept down the passage to the living-room and ascended the stairs. Reaching the bedroom, Eis applied his ear to the door and listened for some minutes.

Swiftly, he flung open the door and switched on the centre light, which clearly illuminated every detail of the scene he had hoped to see. 'Sorry!' he called, closing the door again. 'I must have come to the wrong address.'

Shaking with suppressed laughter, he shooed Stampe downstairs and out of the front door. Then he sat down on the steps and pulled his shoes on.

'Well, Kurt, did you get a good look?'

'Yes, sir!'

'And what did you see?'

Stampe busied himself with his shoe-laces, wondering if Eis expected sympathy. 'I saw whatever you wanted me to see, Local Group Leader.'

'Good for you,' Eis said, as though bestowing a medal. 'You're a man after my own heart, Stampe.'

They returned to the banqueting-hall, where the party was steadily approaching its climax. The celebrants were engaged in a de-bagging contest. Ranged round the table were a number of glasses, one to every performer save one. Everyone joined hands and marched rhythmically round the table singing an inane version of a nursery song.

As soon as the last note died away, each man grabbed a glass and drained it. The one who failed to secure a glass had to drop his trousers and continue the game in a state of undress, hopping like a kangaroo. If he was unlucky enough to fail again he had to drink three times as much at a single gulp, which generally pole-axed him.

The few who survived the game were entitled to the fruits

of victory. Lurching and hiccupping, they mounted the table, where they poured a triumphal libation down their throats and were treated to the spectacle of the losers dancing round them, trouserless and in waltz-time.

The end of the party was preceded by a recuperative interlude devoted to profound monologues, glazed but happy gazings into space, and quavering renditions of songs with predominantly regional themes. It was also the hour of ultimate intimacy.

Eis fixed Stampe with an adjuring stare. He was comparatively sober, having enhanced his natural capacity for drink—as he usually did before evenings of this kind—by absorbing large quantities of greasy food in advance.

'Stampe,' he said, 'I trust you. Never abuse my trust.'

'Never!' Stampe echoed drunkenly, and, with a blissful grin, slid under the table.

'And now for you, you lump of horse-shit,' Eis said. He stood looking down at Christine, arms akimbo. 'You know what you are? A dirty little tart!'

'If I'm a tart,' she replied, 'you're a pimp.'

'What?' gasped Eis. 'You've got a nerve, I must say!'

He had limbered up in readiness for this conversation. Before leaving the Gasthaus he had doused his head in ice-cold water, ordered a pot of strong black coffee, drunk a cool beer and swallowed three different tablets supplied by the S.A.'s medical orderly: one for heartburn, one for dizziness, and one for headaches.

Now he stood glaring down at his wife as she lay there in bed, alone but brazenly glaring back at him with naked loathing in her catlike eyes and her arms concealed beneath the blanket which she had pulled over her body.

'Aren't you ashamed?' he asked sternly.

'For your sake?' She laughed out loud.

'You'll laugh on the other side of your face by the time I've finished with you.' Without taking his eyes off her, Eis drew up a chair and sat down. 'You don't realize what you've done.'

'You're the last person to preach,' she said contemptuously.

'I forbid you to use that tone with me!' Eis shouted. 'Nobody speaks to me like that!'

He got up, walked over to her, smacked her hard in the face, and resumed his seat.

Christine froze. Her eyes dilated, but she did not move. 'Don't do that again,' she said softly.

'What's that, a threat? That's fine, coming from you!'

'If you do that again,' she said evenly, 'I'll put you out of your misery.'

Eis gave a careless laugh. It was high time to show the crazy bitch that she had reached the end of the line.

'Right,' he said, sitting up straight. 'Let's talk turkey. I'm not the only one who saw what you were up to. I've got an impartial witness.'

'So what?'

'I warn you, don't get fresh with me or I'll work you over. I'm entitled to. I'm still your husband, and I just caught you in bed with someone else, remember?'

'Divorce me, then. I'm quite ready to take all the blame—I love him.'

'Not that too!' Eis laughed again, savouring his immeasurable sense of superiority. 'Rolling around in bed isn't enough for you, eh? You've got to fall in love as well, and I'm supposed to give you my blessing. Well, why not, as long as it pays me—I mean, as long as you accept my conditions.'

'What conditions?'

Eis got up and began to pace the room, swaying slightly. 'Well, I'm prepared to agree to a divorce provided you make over everything you inherited from your father.'

'You filthy swine! You had him murdered so you could get your grubby hands on his property through me.'

'Shut up! You don't know a thing about it. I was the one who made him a rich man, so I'm only collecting my due.'

'All right, you can have the lot. I don't want anything except the Gasthaus. That belongs to my family and always has done. It's part of my life—I helped behind the bar when I was only a child.'

'You're making me weep,' Eis said coldly. 'It's all or nothing—you've no choice.'

'Nothing, then.'

'Suit yourself.' Eis sat down again and crossed his legs to demonstrate how much at ease he felt. 'Either you toe the line and we get everything fixed up legally tomorrow morning, or I prefer a charge.'

w.   Q

'A charge?'

'Two charges,' he amended, 'One against you for having sexual intercourse with a prisoner of war in time of national emergency. They've just upped the sentence to six years' penal servitude and all the trimmings—deprivation of civil rights, among other things. That would leave me in sole control of our joint property.'

'I hate you!' she hissed.

'That's not all, though. Now comes the best part. My second charge would be against the man you say you're in love with, and do you know what that would mean? Under the laws currently in force, the chop! Your lover-boy would be stuck up against a wall, strung up or shot in the back of the neck—something of the kind.'

'You don't deserve to live,' she said in a trembling voice.

Slowly and painfully, as though easing cramped muscles, she withdrew her right hand from under the blanket. It was holding a pistol, and the barrel wavered in Eis's direction.

She pulled the trigger and the gun started to dance and spit flame. Screaming dementedly, Christine shut her eyes and kept depressing the trigger until the magazine was empty.

Eis, who had leapt to his feet, cringed away with a look of incredulity in his eyes, then jack-knifed as though kicked in the stomach and crashed to the floor like a rotten tree-trunk.

Eight shots were fired. Each of the five that hit him inflicted a mortal wound.

5

The Russian armies continued to advance on East Prussia, besieged Warsaw, reoccupied the Baltic territories. At night, Uschkurat thought he could hear the din of battle drawing closer and closer, but he was laughed to scorn just as he had been when he claimed to have seen Grienspan.

'I did see him, too!' he told himself over and over again. He spent whole nights in his stables, wandering back and forth among the animals, talking to them and feeling their flanks. 'What am I going to do with you?' he muttered. 'There isn't enough feed for the whole winter. You're getting weaker and weaker. When it comes to it, you won't be able to travel—not as far as you'll need to. So what do I do with you—slaughter you?'

That would be one way of delivering them, the bony cattle and lean pigs, the bleating sheep and the nervous hens which had almost ceased to lay. He had names for all of them, Biblical ones for the cattle, historical ones for the smaller animals, childish ones for the hens—Goliath, Blücher and Lieschen were typical examples of each category. He also wept over them, and he wept a great deal these days.

During the night when Eugen Eis ceased to be a member of the village community, Masuria was visited by its first heavy snowfall of the winter. It blanketed the countryside like a shroud.

Maulen's Party élite were sleeping it off. Intermittent snores escaped the lips of Naujoks, Poreski, Sombray, Bembenneck, Panzer and Perduhn. The only one who could not sleep was Cocky Kurt Stampe. Swaying drunkenly, he stood in front of a mirror and issued orders to an imaginary detachment of Brownshirts. He seemed unirritated by the pale and foolish face that stared back at him.

Amadeus Neuber was leaning over his refugee girl's bed, bathed in sweat and stinking like a billy-goat. The dear little thing had kicked off her blankets again. Murmuring endearments, he felt her thin legs to see if they were cold, but she was as warm as toast everywhere he touched.

'God alone knows how much I worry about these children,' he groaned, believing every word. 'I can't bear to see them suffer. I want them to be happy, whatever it costs me.'

Alfons Materna and Jacob Jablonski were working in the barn. They had already filled a large chest and two sacks with Molotov cocktails, explosives, fuses, batteries for radio transmitters, and ammunition.

'All these lovely things,' grumbled Jablonski. 'What's the matter, scared?'

'Just careful,' Materna replied. 'The chest must be buried in the woods and the sacks dropped in the lake—tonight, what's more.'

'All because of this man Tantau?'

Materna merely nodded and picked up one of the sacks. Jablonski shouldered the other.

'Tantau reminds me of myself,' Materna said, as they hoisted the chest between them. 'That's a danger signal.'

Tantau was another person who could not sleep in Maulen that night. His bed was in the best available room in the Gasthaus, but the din made by the carousing village élite had kept him awake and the ensuing silence brought him equally little repose.

He flicked through his files, then wandered into Budzuhn's room. The inspector was lying supine with his hands folded on his chest, motionless as a statue. Tantau recognized the condition. It was the sleep of the just, normally reserved for junior members of the force. Budzuhn was recouping his energies for an early-morning start to the day's work. Tantau wondered what results it would yield.

He left the Gasthaus and walked across the village square to the war memorial. The thickly falling snow muffled all sound and curtailed his field of vision, yet he could picture the village spread out in front of him like a map.

Every house was dark save one, whose windows gleamed through the thickening blizzard like owl's eyes. Tantau knew that the house with the lighted windows belonged to Eugen Eis.

'He must have forgotten to draw the black-out curtains,' Tantau said to himself. 'Drunks love light. As long as they can still see, they know they haven't passed out.'

He went back to the Gasthaus and lay down on his bed. He never needed more than a few hours' sleep, and he could easily snatch a couple during his so-called hours of duty.

Christine bent over the corpse at her feet. 'Why are you dead?' she moaned. 'I didn't want you to die. What am I going to do?' A tremor ran through her body. Then she said: 'You deserve to be dead.'

Grunting, trembling and steaming with sweat, she dragged the body to the bed and rammed it underneath with her hands and feet until there was nothing to be seen. Then she mopped up the blood with her nightdress, whimpering to herself.

'You never existed,' she said. 'You were a bad dream.'

She went to the kitchen and came back with a bucket of water. Dipping her nightdress in it, she began to swab the bedroom floor. After that she stood there, stark naked, and surveyed her handiwork with wondering eyes. The floor-

boards shone with cleanliness. It was as though there never
had been any blood at all.

Inspector Budzuhn really did make an early start next morning. He performed twenty-five knees-bends and went into
Tantau's room to report for duty, but Tantau did not stir.
'It's only his due,' muttered Budzuhn, and proceeded to
enjoy his breakfast. For a breakfast served in the sixth year
of the war, this was of truly Masurian dimensions: six eggs
poured into a hot pan with cream, smoked ham, blood- and
liver-sausage, bread warm from the oven, fist-sized nuggets of
golden butter, and lime-blossom honey.

Budzuhn ate with dedication, but not even food could
divert him from the path of duty. He had given orders for an
eight o'clock muster parade of all available auxiliary policemen, all C.I.D. men within call, and as many civilian volunteers as were required to reinforce his column of beaters.

'What's the use, man?' Inspector Kranzler demanded, shaking his head. Kranzler became a different person as soon as
Tantau was out of the way. He grumbled, knew better, could
foresee every snag in advance. 'It's quite pointless combing the
countryside, especially when you haven't got enough trained
men. What do you hope to find?'

'I don't know yet.' Budzuhn's response showed that he
was learning more from Tantau every day. 'Who knows?' he
said pensively. 'We may actually find something after all.'

The commanders of the three columns—uniformed police,
C.I.D. and volunteers—reported to him. 'We'll work in chain
formation,' he told them, 'a yard apart. Begin with Dog's
Meadow, starting from the churchyard and closing on Horse
Hill. Then we'll search the adjoining areas.'

Standing beside him, listening intently, Kranzler felt an
urge to clasp his head. Budzuhn's lack of system offended his
professional pride. If they were really going to comb the area
they ought to start between the mill and the church, where
the few identifiable footprints had petered out. That was the
spot to concentrate on, if anywhere.

'What are we after?' one of the column commanders inquired peevishly. The snow was beginning to thaw, and the
going was wet and heavy. 'What do you want us to look out
for?'

'Anything and everything,' said Budzuhn. 'Anything that

isn't a natural feature of grass-land and fields—spent matches, cigarette-ends, buttons, footprints, threads caught on barbed wire, and so on and so forth. Right, let's go, and keep your eyes open or we could be here for days.'

Kranzler, who had some jobs to do for Tantau, rushed through them and went to look for him in the Gasthaus. He found him sitting beside the window, gazing out into the square.

Tantau already knew most of the meagre particulars and technical findings which Kranzler had to offer. After a while he interrupted him.

'Did you manage to find out why this man Schlaguweit was inside Party Headquarters at the time of the explosion?'

'He was summoned there by telephone.'

'By whom?'

'I couldn't say.' Kranzler hurriedly glossed over this. 'He was in the office at the Gasthaus when the call came. Apparently, he just said "Yes, sir" and went out.'

'When was that?'

'About a quarter of an hour before the explosion, that's to say, somewhere between ten and twenty minutes before.'

Tantau made no comment. He fished out a vast blue handkerchief, unfolded it, scrutinized it for a moment, and blew his nose with deliberation. He still said nothing.

'I questioned everyone I could find, of course,' Kranzler went on. 'I even called on Herr Eis just now, but without success.'

'Eis doesn't come into it,' Tantau said in a tone of gentle reprimand. 'He was at a meeting, and none of the eight people present made a telephone call.' Kranzler hung his head in shame. 'Or did you mean something else when you said "without success"?'

'I meant that I failed to speak to Herr Eis. I only saw his wife. She opened the door a crack and told me he'd gone away.'

'Where to?'

'She didn't say. She was pretty uncommunicative—looked as if she'd been crying, too. Maybe they had a tiff. Anyway, Herr Eis isn't in Maulen. He may be visiting regional headquarters at Allenstein—he often goes there, apparently. That might be worth looking into. Herr Eis is an influential man—he could make trouble for us.'

'Very well,' said Tantau, 'look into it. Consider your duties here at an end.'

'Thank you, sir,' Kranzler said gratefully. 'I'll quickly put the finishing touches to my report and then I'll go. There's nothing more to dig up, anyway. I can hardly believe that Budzuhn's wild goose-chase will produce any results, especially as he's heading in the wrong direction.'

'Is he really?' Tantau asked in an interested tone. 'Please explain yourself more fully.'

Kranzler did so willingly and in detail. He saw Tantau nod, and construed this as a mark of approval. Tantau even chuckled once, grimly rather than with amusement. Convinced that he had made a good impression, Kranzler departed.

Tantau remained sitting at the window. He did not move for two solid hours. The temporary barman, a bombed-out publican from Cologne, circled his strange customer warily and ascertained that he was asleep.

Tantau went on sleeping until Budzuhn woke him. The inspector stood over him, breathing hard as usual. His eyes shone with triumph.

'It paid off,' he said, laying an envelope on the table. It contained a cartridge-case.

Tantau scrutinized the metal cylinder with apparent care. He stuck his pencil into it, held it up to the light and bent over it. Then he said: 'The missing one—it matches the other seven exactly. A stroke of luck, Budzuhn.'

The inspector nodded. 'No doubt about that. It may have slipped through a hole in somebody's pocket or got lodged in his turn-ups and fallen out later. However, the most important thing about this find is the place where it was made. I came across it in Dog's Meadow, near Horse Hill.'

'And what do you deduce from that?'

'Well, the discovery of the cartridge-case is one coincidence and the site of discovery is another, but it points straight to Materna's farm. In my humble opinion, that's one coincidence too many.'

'You must help me,' said Pierre Ambal. 'I've got to disappear at once.'

'Why so eager all of a sudden?' Materna replied, carefully closing the door of his den. 'I thought you'd developed a taste for our countryfied existence.'

'I'm not in the mood for jokes, Herr Materna.'

'I can see that. Well, what have you done?'

Ambal licked his lips nervously. 'Will it make any difference to whether you help me or not?'

'No, but I must know.'

'I'm afraid I did something foolish.'

'What do you mean by foolish, Monsieur Ambal?'

The Frenchman stared imploringly at Jacob Jablonski who was sitting in the background, taciturn as ever. Jablonski said:

'I expect his foolishness had something to do with the wife of our revered Local Group Leader.'

'Has it got around, then?' Ambal asked anxiously.

'The whole village has been buzzing with rumours for days.'

'Well, the village is right—it happened last night.' Ambal paused. 'Eis caught us in the act.'

Materna sat back in his chair—to Jablonski, a sure sign that he was surprised. 'Go on,' he said. 'You aren't marked so he couldn't have used his fists on you. How did he react? He didn't by any chance apologize for the intrusion?'

'More or less,' Ambal replied, looking bemused. His handsome young face was slightly flushed and devoid of its usual serene self-assurance. 'He said something about having come to the wrong address.'

'One of his favourite cracks,' Jablonski explained. 'He's up to something, you can bet on that.'

'What happened then?' asked Materna.

'He went out and shut the door behind him. We were very alarmed, of course. I found Sergeant-Major Fackler waiting for me when I got back to my billet. He asked me a couple of obscene questions and then left me alone—I didn't tell him anything, naturally. This morning, just under an hour ago, I went to Eis's house to report for duty, as Fackler calls it, but Christine—I mean, Frau Eis—wouldn't let me in. She just opened the door a fraction and told me to make a run for it. That's why I came. Will you help me?'

Materna glanced at Jablonski, who said: 'You must be mad, coming up here in broad daylight. How the hell do you expect us to pass you on when half the village saw which way you were headed? It would be sheer suicide.'

Ambal got up, shaking his head slowly. His expression alternated between fear and resentment. He said: 'I wouldn't want to get you into trouble.'

'Of course not,' Materna said firmly. 'That's why you're going to correct your dangerous little mistake, my dear Ambal. You'll continue on your way to Lake Maulen and call on the fisherman. Ask him for some fish—fat carp, Eis likes those best of all. Tell him Frau Eis sent you and he'll hand them over without a murmur. Then you'll carry the fish back through the village to Eis's house, making yourself as conspicuous as possible.'

'What shall I tell Frau Eis?'

'Tell her goodbye.'

'You mean,' Ambal asked excitedly, '—you mean, after that I can disappear?'

Materna sat up in his chair. 'Yes, Ambal, after that you can take off in the direction of Siegwalde, travelling cross-country. Pinch a few clothes on the way if you can—easily identifiable clothes—but don't put them on. Bury them somewhere or drop them in the marsh.'

'I don't understand.'

'No matter,' said Jablonski. 'We've had years of experience at this sort of caper.'

'When you get past Siegwalde,' Materna continued, 'you must go to ground. Make your way eastwards along the edge of the marshes and hole up in the woods until it gets dark. Have you got some thick underclothes? Jablonski will give you some if not. As soon as it's dark, cut through Gross-Grieben Forest in a semicircle and head for the village of Karweinen. That's all.'

'Don't worry,' Jablonski said, 'I'll go over the route with you carefully on the map. There are a number of markers in the forest. It'll take you about four hours—let's say five, so you don't have to rush.'

'All right, but what happens then?'

'Leave the rest to me. You meet me, any time after midnight, just north of Karweinen. There's a barn shaped like a cigar-box a little way from the road—you can't miss it. I'll provide you with some civilian clothes and escort you across the border into Polish territory.'

'You'd really do all that for me?' Ambal exclaimed delightedly.

Jablonski grinned. 'Yes, in gratitude for your achievement in the Eis household. Also because I enjoy these midnight jaunts. I don't want to get out of training.'

Henriette Himmler arrived in the village and asked to speak to the Local Group Leader, ostensibly on official business.

Her first port of call was the mayor's office, now being used as Party Headquarters. Eis's secretary informed her that the Local Group Leader had yet to put in an appearance.

'Do you know where I can find him?'

The secretary, a willing but somewhat feather-brained evacuee from Berlin, was aware that the Labour Service commander bore the magic name Himmler. Respectfully, she said: 'As far as I know, nobody has seen the Local Group Leader today. Perhaps he has gone away.'

'That's out of the question.'

'He doesn't always warn me in advance when he goes away.'

'Not you, perhaps, but he would most certainly have told me.' Henriette left Party Headquarters with a haughty step, as much out of habit as to conceal her emotions. Although she was not seriously worried yet, she could not help feeling a trifle concerned.

Eugen had not devoted much time to her in the last couple of days. Ernst Schlaguweit's funeral was one reason of course, but she had been expecting some sign of life today, if only a telephone call. She planned to gladden his heart, not only with her pent-up devotion, but with a further letter from Reichsführer Himmler. This contained the following passage:

'Please convey my heartfelt greetings to the man of your choice and assure him that I intend to be present on the happy day, always provided that my ever-increasing official commitments do not preclude this, which I sincerely trust they will not, since I look upon your happiness—the which may it please Providence to preserve—as my own . . .'

Next, Henriette called on the mayor, but Pillich pleaded total ignorance of Eis's whereabouts. The Local Group Leader was his own master, he told her. Henriette gave a

:urt nod and transferred her attentions to Kurt Stampe,
he newly appointed S.A. commander.

'I'm busy organizing things,' Stampe told her confidentially,
—orders from the Local Group Leader. He's got enough
>n his hands.' He winked. 'It's his wife—she needs attend-
ng to.'

Henriette determined on the only remaining course open
to her. She strode up to Eis's house, knocked, waited, and
knocked again.

A woman opened the door, evidently Eugen's wife. Henriette could not suppress a mild thrill of triumph at the
sight of her. She was wearing a sort of house-coat, untidy
and not particularly clean, and the face that stared out of
the lank uncombed hair was as pallid as cream cheese.

A slattern, Henriette decided happily, and drew herself
up to her full height. She felt sure that she presented an
impressive picture—clean as a new pin, smartly uniformed,
brisk and vital. 'I'd like to speak to Herr Eis,' she said curtly.

'He can't speak to anyone,' replied the slattern.

'I've come about an important matter,' Henriette persisted.

'What could matter to him now?' Christine muttered. Then,
rapidly, like a mechanical doll, she added: 'He's out. He's not
at home—not to anyone.' So saying, she slammed the door.

Henriette Himmler stood there for some moments. Without
knowing why, she felt a surge of uneasiness. Her legs—the legs
which Eis found so ravishing, if she remembered his phrase-
ology correctly— started to tremble. Drawing a deep breath,
she marched off to the Gasthaus.

Here she drank a glass of water and a brandy in that
order. Two men were sitting at the next table. From what
Eis had told her and what her girl pioneers had managed
to glean, she recognized them as police officers, one an inspector and the other a chief superintendent. Both were
dipping their spoons rhythmically into brimming plates
of pea-soup prepared in the regional manner, with smoked
ham, belly of pork, sausage, and marjoram.

When they had finished their soup they ordered a large
schnapps each. Henriette raised her glass in comradely
fashion and engaged them in conversation. The conversation consisted mainly of questions, put by Budzuhn and
answered readily enough by Henriette. She even asked

if she might join the gentlemen at their table, so interested
was she in their vital work for the good of the community.

'You could call it that,' Tantau agreed, with a smile.

After further conversation about Maulen and everything
to do with Maulen, Henriette said gravely: 'We all have
our worries. I must confess that I'm not altogether happy
about a number of things.'

'That makes two of us,' said Tantau, but Budzuhn asked
point-blank if she had anything specific in mind.

'Well, I'm a little concerned—perhaps unjustifiably so,
perhaps not. Herr Eis has disappeared.'

'Are you concerned about him as a woman or a Party
member?' Tantau inquired gently.

'If you must know, there are certain ties of a very personal nature between us.'

'Must I know that? But of course, if you think so.
What sort of ties, exactly?'

Henriette hesitated, but only for a moment. 'We're engaged,' she said.

'How quaint,' Tantau observed drily. 'So Herr Eis is
married and engaged at the same time—he deserves to be
congratulated.'

'Since when have you been engaged?' asked Budzuhn.

'That is beside the point,' Henriette replied. 'I simply find
it strange that Herr Eis should have disappeared without
warning.'

Budzuhn shrugged. 'These things happen.'

'Not between me and Herr Eis,' Henriette said sharply.
'Kindly take note of that.' A glance from Tantau ensured
that Budzuhn took immediate note of what she had told
them. Satisfied, she went on: 'Herr Eis would have told me if
he had intended to take a trip, I feel quite sure. However,
I feel doubly concerned since I saw his wife. I distrust that
woman instinctively.'

'Instinct,' said Tantau, 'is the personal province of my
colleague Inspector Budzuhn. He will be glad to deal with
the matter.'

Budzuhn fixed the chief superintendent with an owlish
stare. 'Don't you want to take me with you when you call
on Materna?' he asked sadly.

'You have work to do here,' Tantau said, rubbing his

ands. 'I'm placing your services at the disposal of this de-
ghtful lady. Do your best for her.'

antau was sighted long before he reached the farm. Materna
ame to the door in person and flung it wide.

'Come in,' he said cordially.

Tantau entered the house with a show of hesitation. 'Don't
e too welcoming. You can still lock me out, even though
do have any number of blank search warrants. All I have
o do is fill in your name.'

'Why haven't you, then?'

'Let's call it laziness.'

'You're at liberty to look anywhere you like. I'll be glad
o show you round.'

'You're very sure of yourself, aren't you? I warn you
hough, don't take it for granted that you've covered your
racks completely. There are such things as microscopes,
pectrometers, fingerprints, lab tests, and so on.'

'There's always the human element.'

'And human beings aren't infallible, you mean? You're
ight—they do have their shortcomings and emotional weak-
esses. However, human beings are in short supply these
ays.'

'Just as long as you realize it, Herr Tantau. I shall have to
e satisfied with that for the time being.'

Materna led his visitor into the house via the kitchen.
t was a deliberate detour. Hannelore and Sabine greeted
Tantau with perceptible warmth. The girls had recognized
is strange resemblance to Materna, and that was enough to
prejudice them in his favour.

'The green jug,' ordered Materna. Then he showed Tantau
nto his den and waited for the weary-looking little man to
ake a seat. The silence that followed seemed to drag on for
minutes.

'Suppose I really did search these premises,' Tantau
said at length. 'What do you think I'd find?'

'Petrol, probably. I need it for agricultural machinery—
I'm what they call a go-ahead farmer. I also keep guns
and ammunition for hunting purposes. I exterminate pests
and put sick animals out of their misery.'

'I know. You're said to be one of the best shots in
Masuria.'

'There isn't much to that—just a steady hand and a good eye. They're the products of a healthy constitution and almost anyone can have that if he lives the right kind of life.'

'Even so, I see little reason to envy you,' Tantau said mournfully. 'I'm afraid I might find a lot more than petrol and shot-guns—a wounded man, say. Or am I wrong? Believe me, I should be glad to stand corrected on that point.'

'You mean injured, not wounded,' amended Materna, who was prepared for this question. 'One of my foreign workers had a serious accident. Would you like to hear the details?'

'Not yet,' Tantau replied. 'In fact I may not require any details at all, especially as I already know most of them. The doctor in attendance is Doctor Bachus, and you procured the papers for your foreign labourer from the regional commissioner for agriculture, fisheries and forestry.'

'From my son, yes.'

'Valid papers?'

'Absolutely. Would you care to see them? Doctor Bachus will be happy to supply you with any information you require. Date, circumstances, police report—everything is completely in order.'

'I'm glad to hear it, for your sake. I think we ought to drink to that. You're going to need a drink, Herr Materna, in view of what I have to tell you.'

Materna filled the glass. His hand was steady and remained so even when he saw that Tantau was observing his every movement. Although they refrained from drinking to each other, the atmosphere mellowed slightly.

'I've devoted a lot of thought to you,' Tantau confided.

'Have you reached any conclusion?'

'I don't know yet, Herr Materna. That remains to be seen. I can't go on playing cat and mouse any longer. Time is running out, and I've got to produce some results. I think you may be able to help me.'

'By all means. You only have to tell me what you have in mind.'

'I'm offering you two alternatives. The first goes as follows: I arrest you, Jablonski, Doctor Bachus and Doctor Klinger on suspicion. Then I find enough evidence to corroborate my suspicions. I turn your farm upside down, comb it from top to bottom, flush it out like a rabbit warren.' He paused.

Don't look so dubious, Herr Materna—I could do it easily enough.'

'All right. What's your second alternative?'

'Let's stick to the first for the moment. The destruction of Party Headquarters was a stroke of genius. Your alibi was positively classic—unshakable, I grant you, but far too good to be true. The discovery of the seven cartridge-cases meant nothing in itself, and the fact that the eighth was found on your land amounted to little more than a minor flaw. Nevertheless, you did make one crucial mistake, Herr Materna—a mistake which I would never have credited you with.'

'How do you mean?'

'You fell prey to an understandable temptation. I've seen it happen again and again, and in your case I can't help feeling sorry. It was a first-class job in every other respect, my dear Materna—extremely hard to prove, though for me not impossible. I'm not saying that because I'm proud of myself, just stating it as a fact.'

'Well, what's this mistake I'm supposed to have made?'

'Gilding the lily, my dear fellow, trying to kill two birds with one stone. Party Headquarters wasn't enough for you— you had to eliminate Schlaguweit as well. That's what has made this business so hazardous for you and the people behind you. Schlaguweit was summoned by telephone, and that could only have been done by someone familiar with local conditions, not by a group of partisans or saboteurs from outside.'

Deliberately, without even glancing at Tantau, Materna got up and walked over to a cupboard on the other side of the room. Taking out a box of cigars, he proffered it to the chief superintendent. Tantau bent over the box, selected a cigar with care, and lit it. He drew in the smoke appreciatively and exhaled it as though blowing his troubles away.

Materna returned to his chair. 'And the second alternative you mentioned?'

'A simple one,' replied Tantau. 'We work as a team from now on.'

'You've got to help me,' Christine told Sergeant-Major Fackler, who was making his usual vigorous advances.

'Of course I'll help you,' he said, manœuvring her into the

bedroom. 'Later. Afterwards.' He chivvied her towards the bed. 'What's that stench in here?'

'It must be the carp in the kitchen,' she said.

'Never mind.' Fackler shrugged. A fighting man couldn't afford to be fastidious. 'Come on, why so coy all of a sudden?'

'Something's happened.'

'Something else is going to happen, just you wait and see.' He flung her across the bed and started to climb on top of her. She rolled aside, but her house-coat fell open in a way which he could only construe as inviting. 'Come on, girl, stop holding out on me.'

'You will help me afterwards?' she pleaded. 'Promise?'

He promised with alacrity. There was a specially attractive aura about her this time—he couldn't quite define it.

Afterwards, however, disillusionment set in. She had remained as stiff as a board despite his honest endeavours, clenching her teeth and keeping her arms rigid at her sides.

'What's got into you? Annoyed about something?'

She bent over him. 'You will help me now, won't you?'

'Your eyes look funny,' he said in a puzzled tone. 'Are you sick?'

'You've got to help me,' she said quickly. Her voice sounded shrill and cracked. 'You must!'

'Must be buggered!' retorted Fackler, buttoning his uniform with swift and practised fingers. 'What do you want, anyway?'

'It was your pistol that did it.'

'My pistol? I've got several.'

'Yes, but you lent me one a few days ago.'

'You took it, you mean. You said you wanted to get rid of a dog.'

'I did, too!'

'That's all right then.' Fackler was growing restive. The smell of putrid carp seemed to have become even more intense. 'I'm in a hurry.'

'You've got to help me dispose of him. Please!'

'Your dog?' Fackler exclaimed, waxing indignant. 'What do you think I am, a knacker? Find someone else.'

Christine gave a sobbing groan and stretched out her arms to him. 'He's under the bed.'

'Where?'

'Under the bed we've just made love on. You promised to help me, so help me, for God's sake!' Her voice rose to a scream, then sank to an almost inaudible whisper as she added: 'It was your pistol. You gave it to me—for him.'

Fackler stood looking at her with his mouth open. Then he knelt down and looked under the bed. After several seconds of frozen immobility he leapt to his feet like a cork bobbing to the surface.

'I had nothing to do with this!' he gasped. 'Nothing!'

He spun round and rushed out, forgetting his cap and belt. He took the stairs four at a time, tore open the front door, and, leaving it ajar, vanished into the distance.

Christine remained where she was, sitting on the bed which concealed Eis's body. She sat there hunched up with her legs splayed and her unkempt hair straggling over her face. But for the rasp of her breathing, she might have been made of stone.

Minutes passed. Then the sound of rhythmical knocking made her start to her feet. In the open doorway stood a mountainous man whom she had never seen before. A pair of bovine eyes stared down at her patiently.

'Budzuhn's the name,' said the fat man, bowing slightly. 'Please excuse me for barging in like this, but all the doors were open. It isn't wise, not in this weather.'

'Go away!' moaned Christine, sinking down on the bed again.

'I beg your pardon? I've only just come.' Budzuhn approached her warily. He could see at once that there was something wrong with her—something very wrong. He pulled the counterpane off the bed and draped it round her shoulders. She winced at his touch and began to tremble.

'It really is very cold in here. Why did you open the doors? To air the house?'

Budzuhn made the remark without thinking, but now he raised his head and sniffed like a dog taking scent. 'It's true,' he said. 'The air in this room is bad, but why didn't you open the windows?'

'Go away and leave me alone!' Christine said desperately.

But Budzuhn was not listening. It had suddenly dawned on him what the smell in the room was. He recognized the first cloying, gaseous whiff of corruption. His nose, the organ which had been commended so highly by Tantau, began to function like a meter.

'Permit me to offer you another seat, Frau Eis,' he said courteously. 'This chair, perhaps. It is Frau Eis, isn't it?'

He got no response, nor did he meet with any resistance when he gripped her gently by the shoulders, pulled her to her feet and steered her to the chair. She felt like a rag doll 'It's a dog's life, dear lady,' he said sympathetically.

Budzuhn grasped the edge of the bed and tilted it sideways, then let it drop again. He had seen what he expected to see—a spectacle which never failed to shock him in spite of long years of professional experience. This was partly because every corpse looked different—pitifully small, but different. No two people died the same death. Even when they died of the same disease, discoloration, spots and stains formed a wide variety of patterns. The same applied to crimes of violence. No one crime exactly matched another, not even when criminal and weapon were identical.

The victim this time was a fair-haired, jowly, heavily built man about six feet tall. Patches of dried blood with watery yellowish white edges encrusted his chest and abdomen.

It was not hard to identify the man. He was dressed in a pheasant-brown uniform of excellent cut and cloth. Budzuhn recognized him as Eugen Eis, Local Group Leader of Maulen.

'Please get dressed,' he said to Christine. 'I should wear something warm if I were you, and take a coat along as well. The house will have to be locked, so you can't stay here. We shall have to see what happens. For the time being, come with me.'

The news that Eugen Eis's corpse had been discovered under his own bed spread through the village like wildfire. It ran from house to house, instantly becoming a topic of excited female gossip, whispered male conversation, wild and terrifying childish rumour.

It was not clear what had unleashed this avalanche of guesswork, conjecture and suspicion. Budzuhn had merely conveyed the bare bones of the situation to a colleague and sent him off to inform Tantau, but his colleague had stopped off en route. What was more, Sergeant-Major Fackler had stormed into the Gasthaus with a raging thirst and elivered himself of some vague and incoherent remarks, nding with the reiterated assurance that he had nothing to do with it. Most significant of all, however, was the fact that Christine Eis had been locked up in a room in the arty's temporary headquarters under police guard.

Having warned everyone that it was an offence to voice remature and unfounded suspicions, Inspector Budzuhn aited impatiently for Tantau's arrival. Tantau was taking his me, but, as Budzuhn rightly surmised, he had his reasons.

Amadeus Neuber bowed his head at the news of Eis's eath, mainly to conceal his delight. His first words—'What tragic end!' —rang with exalted grief. He waited until he as alone before he vented his true feelings. 'At last!' he ghed, safe in the knowledge that he was now Local Group eader of Maulen.

The vicar decreed a special service at which prayers were aid for the soul of the departed. What could be more mely? After long years of spiritual drought, the elderly arson could at last expect a full house.

'He must have a State funeral!' declared Kurt Stampe. The S.A. will take charge of all arrangements.'

'I'm shocked!' Mayor Pillich announced loudly. Eis's eath had saved him from losing his job, for which he was uly thankful.

'An act of God,' said Ignaz Uschkurat, fondling one of is cows. 'We all have to go sometime, but who would have hought he'd go first and go like that? He was doomed, hough. He shouldn't have laughed when I told him about Grienspan. People who refuse to listen have to take the con-equences—that's life.'

The womenfolk of the village gathered like a flock of crows, luttering, cawing, screeching, putting their heads together, lropping accusations like dung. Eis had done away with imself; his wife had murdered him with the help of Fackler or that prisoner of war—or Materna; he deserved t; he didn't deserve it; it was an accident; it happened by lesign; it was a crime of passion, a political assassination, n act of God. Excitedly, the women fluttered apart again.

Nobody wept for Eugen Eis, not even Henriette Himmler. That would have infringed her built-in code of German liscipline and decorum. Erect she listened to the ghastly letails and erect she remained thereafter, staring into the

far distance. 'He did not die in vain,' was her only comment.
She did not fling herself face downwards on her bed until
much later.

Budzuhn continued to wait for instructions from Tantau.
They came at last, in the form of a message delivered by the
policeman he had sent to Materna's farm. 'Deal with the
case as indicated,' it said.

Budzuhn wondered what Tantau meant.

Tantau took another forkful of jellied eel. 'All in good time,'
he said.

Materna stared at the chief superintendent in surprise.
'It isn't that I begrudge you all that eel, but aren't there
more important things to do?'

'No,' Tantau replied, chewing, 'not for the moment.'

'But Eis is dead.'

'Well, do you regret his death? I'm sure you don't, so
count your blessings. May I have another slice of that
excellent bread?'

'We ought to take some precautions.'

'Far better to fortify ourselves first. Wasn't it Napoleon
who said an army marches on its stomach?' Tantau called
Hannelore and Sabine, who appeared promptly, and ordered
hot apple-and-cottage-cheese purée sprinkled with chocolate.
When the girls had bustled out again, he said casually:

'You mustn't rush things, my friend. Try to forget about
Eis for the moment—concentrate on me instead. I've got
to produce some results. Who can I arrest if I don't arrest
you and Jablonski?'

'You don't expect me to find you a scapegoat?'

'Of course not. I assume that your associates are in a safe
place by now. That ought to make it easier for you to
supply me with a few leads—numbers, weapons, operational
methods and so on. It won't hurt anyone, but it'll be a great
help to me.'

They spent the next half-hour carefully assembling evidence, convincing enough in itself but wholly useless from a
practical point of view.

'Impressive,' Tantau said approvingly, '—most impressive,
even if it doesn't amount to more than a row of beans.'

Materna smiled. 'It'll do, especially as believers in final

ictory aren't as widespread as they used to be. Anyone with
spark of intelligence can see which way the wind is blowing.'
Tantau smiled back at him. 'Are you referring to people
ke me?'

Materna shook his head.

'How do you regard me, then?'

'As a friend.'

'Thanks,' said Tantau. 'In that case, I suppose I can risk
sking for another helping of jellied eel.'

The farm kitchen gradually filled. The first to appear was
acob Jablonski, who paused briefly and then applied himself
1 silence to the array of food on the table. While he was
till eating, Peter Bachus and Konrad Klinger came in.
hey sat down too, but showed a singular lack of appetite.
nstead, they eyed Tantau with a mixture of curiosity and
espect.

Tantau fished out his handkerchief. 'Alfons Materna and
are friends,' he announced, wiping his mouth. 'Just in case
haven't made myself clear, I might also call us partners.'

'So we can speak freely,' Materna said.

'No holds barred?' inquired Jablonski.

Materna shook his head. 'No holds barred. Explanations
an come later, if there's any need for them by then. First
hings first. How's our patient, Peter?'

'He can be transferred to hospital in Lötzen. I've pre-
ared the necessary papers. He's out of danger now—in fact
1e should be up and about in three or four weeks.'

Tantau said: 'Under no circumstances must the date of
he alleged accident fall between the tenth and twentieth of
November.'

'That's all taken care of,' Peter assured him. 'In his present
condition, nobody could prove for certain that it was a
bullet wound. He might just as easily have been jabbed with
a pitchfork. It was a straightforward accident, and there are
several witnesses to prove it.'

'Good,' said Tantau. 'What else?'

'I'm going to act as legal adviser to Christine Eis,' announced Konrad. 'Herr Materna asked me to, and I accepted
with pleasure.'

Tantau nodded. 'Don't overlook Inspector Budzuhn—he
knows his job. However, the busier he is with the Eis case

the less chance he'll have of poking his nose into things that don't concern him.'

'I'll keep him busy,' Konrad promised. 'I've already taken a few precautions. Budzuhn seems to regard it as an open and shut case. In his view, Christine Eis is the only possible suspect, but I've told her to keep mum for the moment— make no statement, answer no questions. She isn't in a condition to make a statement, anyway. The poor thing is completely deranged. I wouldn't have thought it possible—she was such a robust sort of person.'

'It's a sign of the times,' said Materna. 'A lot of people are deranged these days—deranged or demented. Take Uschkurat, who was as strong as an ox, or Mayor Pillich. Pillich could stomach anything once upon a time, and now he's a nervous wreck. Even Neuber must have mixed feelings about taking over from Eis.'

'Anyway,' Konrad said, 'Budzuhn won't be able to prove much if Christine shuts up like a clam.'

'Not good enough,' Tantau interposed firmly. 'Budzuhn isn't to be underestimated. What's more, I have to admit that he's learnt a few tips from me. The best plan would be to dangle a red herring under his nose—Sergeant-Major Fackler will do for a start. He owned the pistol that killed Eis.'

Konrad nodded. 'Thanks for the hint.'

'Your escaped Frenchman is another potential suspect— don't overlook that. The very fact that he can't be traced should enlarge the scope of your defence. Any objections to that line of argument?'

Jablonski shook his head. 'Ambal is safe—I took care of that.'

'Excellent,' Konrad said confidently. 'I ought to be able to spin out the proceedings for quite a while.'

'Yes,' said Tantau, 'but don't forget, some judges deal out sentences with the speed of light these days. Also, Eis's death could be regarded as the assassination of a Party official, not just a domestic drama. There's only one reprieve for that offence, and then only a temporary one. According to a law still in force, execution in the case of a pregnant woman must be deferred until four weeks after the birth of her child.'

'In that case,' said Peter, 'Christine Eis is pregnant—as a doctor, I can certify that. That ought to get her over the hump.'

few more weeks and East Prussia will know what total
ctory feels like—from the losing end.'

'It could be a matter of days,' Materna put in.

Tantau looked round sadly. 'That's why I have to leave
ou at once. I know I'll never eat as well again, but duty calls.
Ve'll keep in touch for as long as possible.'

'It's been good knowing you,' Materna said. 'You've
elped to prolong a number of lives.'

'But for how long, my friend, for how long?'

gnaz Uschkurat appeared at the farm. He was not weeping
or once.

'Alfons,' he said, 'do you believe that I see ghosts?'

Materna shrugged. 'Nothing would surprise me nowadays.'

'Do you believe that I saw Siegfried Grienspan? I did
ee him, you know.' Uschkurat spoke gravely, like a man
aaking a solemn vow. 'He stood facing me in the moonlight,
lain as could be, almost within reach. Do you believe me?'

'Yes,' Materna replied.

'That's all right, then.' Uschkurat straightened up as though
elieved of an intolerable burden. 'If you really mean that, I'm
our man. Tell me what to do—I'll do anything you say.'

Mayor Pillich appeared soon afterwards. He shuffled
ap to Materna with a hangdog air and bowed deeply.

'What ought I to do now, Herr Materna?'

'What you've always done, Pillich—tuck your tail between
our legs and bark whenever someone in authority whistles.'

'I've been misunderstood, Herr Materna. I only wanted to
lo what was right for the village.'

'Everyone has his own ideas about that.'

'Precisely, Herr Materna. I regret our difference of opinion,
incerely I do, and I'm not the only one. Bembenneck, Sombray, Perduhn and a lot of other people in the village feel the
ame—Romeike has for a long time. They all think we ought
o pull together. Couldn't we talk things over with you?'

'I see no point whatsover in discussing anything with a
bunch of spineless hysterics.'

Pillich swallowed this pill without blinking. 'In that case,'
he said, 'please tell us what to do. We're all ready to take
your advice. Just give us some orders and we'll obey them
to the letter.'

Amadeus Neuber was the next to arrive, but he only

got as far as the gate. Materna allowed him to present h
petition in a blinding snow-storm.

'The numerous regrettable misunderstandings between' ι
. . .' Neuber began, shivering with something more than mer
cold.

'Cut it short,' Materna told him. 'It wouldn't break m
heart if you caught pneumonia, but I haven't got much time

'You don't have to tell me that, Herr Materna. Nobody ha
much time—this is the eleventh hour.'

'I know, Neuber. Your beloved Führer has already mad
that abundantly clear.'

'He isn't my beloved Führer!' Neuber cried dramaticall

'Does he know that? I thought you'd taken on the Loca
Group Leader's job.'

'Only to spare our community the worst—only to preve
one of these last-ditch fanatics from taking over. Say wha
you like about me, Herr Materna, but you've got to gran
me one thing: I'm not an idiot. I know what's going on

'Oh, and what's that, in your opinion?'

'I look at newspapers and listen to the radio, but I ca
read between the lines. Besides, I have access to confidentia
Party communiqués. The Russians are just across the Eas
Prussian border, burning, murdering, raping, looting. . .

'Fancy treating their noble German foes like that! An
to think of the chivalrous way we've always fought, sendin
millions of people up in smoke like lumps of coal. . . .'

'I won't argue with you, Herr Materna. My concern is fo
our people, above all the children. We must get them t
safety at all costs.'

'That would conflict with the policy laid down by ou
Supreme Commander. Are you prepared to risk a deat
sentence—now, at the eleventh hour?'

'That's why I came, for the sake of the children. We mus
take the risk, but our only chance of success is to stic
together—all of us, including you, with your influence, you
contacts and connections. I know you won't stand aloof
not when the lives of women and children are at stake. You'r
a true Masurian, Materna.'

'You really think so? In that case I'll behave like one.

Materna bent forward and swiped Neuber across the fac
with lightning speed and tremendous force, first with hi
right hand, then his left.

'So,' he said, 'I feel a bit better after that. Now perhaps we can discuss things in a reasonably adult way.'

The village of Maulen entered its death-throes like a man smitten with fever, trembling and twitching convulsively but not yet ready to die.

Scorched and bloodstained, encrusted with dirt and huddled against the cold—such was Maulen as it neared its end. The villagers' bemused brains were almost incapable of framing any thought save one, namely, how to survive.

People were overwhelmed by the rudimentary problems of existence. They spent sleepless nights discussing them, nights in which the oppressive gaps in conversation were filled by the steadily approaching din of battle. Everyone begged Materna to take over the leadership of the village.

It was Kurt Stampe who clinched matters. Having absorbed vast quantities of Dutch courage, he entered resolutely into the role of S.A. commander and community leader. His first move was to muster the last of the die-hard Party loyalists, of which there were a good dozen, and issue them with arms.

Next, he proclaimed a state of emergency. Without running into open resistance from Neuber, he appointed himself provisional head of local government and assumed the office of mayor. He also assumed command of the local police auxiliaries and mobilized the Hitler Youth and German Girls' League.

Placards, verbal proclamations and provisional mobilization orders summoned the entire population to assemble in the village square at seven o'clock next morning. Rendezvous: the war memorial.

'It is the patriotic duty of all men and women, and all children of eleven or over, to report as instructed. Failure to do so will be treated as sabotage and punished by summary court martial. Each person must come equipped with a spade, shovel, or mattock for the purpose of establishing a line of defence.'

Immediately after this summons had gone out, Materna was visited by a delegation of peasant farmers headed by Romeike, a respected but exceptionally taciturn man. Neuber brought up the rear.

'Now,' said Romeike.

'If we don't do something at once,' Neuber amplified, 'we're finished.'

Materna asked if many people would obey the Party's call. Romeike grunted an affirmative and left it to Neuber to fill in the details.

'Stampe is a violent man,' Neuber explained. 'What's more, he has had quite a bright idea for once. He has announced that the stores in the Gasthaus depot will be distributed among loyal members of the community. That could be a big draw.'

'We'll take that into account,' Materna said firmly, and went on to outline his plan of campaign. Neuber made one last attempt to evade personal involvement, but Romeike glared at him and told him to shut his trap.

Next morning, in predictable obedience to orders, the majority of the villagers congregated in front of the war memorial. Kurt Stampe stood there confidently, casting an occasional glance at his wrist-watch.

Shortly before seven o'clock Amadeus Neuber turned up escorted by Romeike and Jablonski, who were armed with oak cudgels. Wearing his Local Group Leader's uniform for the first and last time, Neuber walked up to Stampe and accosted him.

'I am the senior official here,' he said.

'You're a deadbeat,' Stampe retorted. He felt very sure of himself, but he had reckoned without Jacob Jablonski. Jablonski stepped up to him and dealt him a short sharp blow on the nape of the neck. The S.A. commander fell flat on his face and lay there, dazed and motionless, whereupon Jablonski bent down, picked him up by his collar and the seat of his pants, and carried him through the gaping throng to a waiting cattle-truck. He dumped him into it like a bundle of rags.

'Men and women of Maulen,' called Neuber, who had agreed his little speech with Materna in advance, 'in an emergency such as this, cool heads are what is needed, not bluster and self-importance. I have taken over the leadership of the village, assisted by men who enjoy the confidence of us all. Our first step will be to distribute the stores in the depot. Other measures will follow in due course.'

Universal enthusiasm greeted this announcement. Stampe's

en melted discreetly into the background. It was clear
that their leader had been either deposed or incapacitated, and
they had a deep-seated respect for authority. Besides, Neuber
had made a thoroughly convincing impression. Like the other
inhabitants of Maulen, they sensed that a new and refreshing wind was blowing from the direction of Horse Hill.

Materna now went into action openly. First, he got his
son Hermann, the regional commissioner for agriculture, to
appoint him his local representative. Having done that, he
organized the transfer of livestock to clandestine stables in
the forests and laid down subterranean caches of grain.

Meanwhile Amadeus Neuber had disbanded the girl pioneers' camp on Materna's instructions. He had also, this time
on instructions from Regional Party Headquarters, summoned
the population of Maulen to enlist in the Home Guard.
Reserve Lieutenant Konrad Klinger was appointed Home
Guard commander.

Konrad did not evade the call of duty. His first act as
commander of Maulen's Home Guard was to relieve Sergeant-
Major Fackler's men of further responsibility for guarding
the prisoners of war. Fackler and his detachment were ordered
to the front and the prisoners of war entrusted to Home
Guardsman Jacob Jablonski, who promptly marched them into
the forest and told them to get lost.

Materna's farm was converted into a hostel for invalids
and children. Dr Peter Bachus tended the former, assisted by
Hannelore, while Neuber busied himself with the latter.

Materna organized a premature Christmas party for all
the children in Maulen. Rivers of honey flowed, mountains
of marzipan were devoured, trays of cakes and buckets of
cream emptied themselves into the youthful but capacious
bellies of his guest. Bilious but blissful, the children of
Maulen slept through an entire night and half the next day.
After that they were packed into two hay-wains padded
with straw and taken on what the grown-ups described as
an 'outing'. It was destined to last for more than ten days.

Amadeus Neuber slipped away secretly to join the children.
After him, travelling in carts piled high with their personal
possessions, went Pillich, Naujoks, Poreski, Sombray, Bembenneck, Panzer, Perduhn and Naschinski. Before long the
village was almost bereft of Party supporters. Kurt Stampe,

too, fled westwards, taking three cases of schnapps, two
women, and a swastika banner. Nobody was sorry to see him
go.

Peter Bachus made it his business to see that hospital
trains bound for the interior found room for villagers
who no longer wished to remain in Maulen. Tantau insinuated
over a score of people into a convoy of 'prisoners under
escort', among them Hannelore Welser and Sabine Gäbler.
Materna had insisted on this. 'Who knows?' he said. 'If
all goes well you can always turn round and come back
again.'

Materna never voiced his opinion of future prospects. He
only knew that he wanted to stay in Masuria whatever happened. Uschkurat, Romeike, Mielke and others shared his
resolve, though he made it clear to them that each could do
as he thought fit.

It soon became apparent that Lieutenant Klinger had only
mobilized his Home Guard unit in order to disband it
effectively and in good time. 'The war's over,' he told his
men. 'Chuck your weapons on that pile and we'll drop
them in Lake Maulen. You're dismissed. Make up your own
minds where you want to go.'

Accompanied by Peter Bachus, Konrad went up to the
farm and asked Materna if he had anything more for them
to do.

'Nothing,' Materna replied. 'I take it you're going off to
join Hannelore and Sabine. Look after them, won't you?
And now push off, unless you want to see a grown man
weep.'

The wolves had deserted Maulen. The remnants of the
defeated German armies poured through the village after
them, seizing on anything they could find in the way of food,
drink and women.

Hard on their heels came the Red Army, its approach
heralded by a roaring tempest in which thunder and lightning did not succeed one another but seemed to have
merged. The storm of mortality which was rolling across
Europe engulfed Maulen too, and the air reeked of death.

Alfons Materna went down to the village for the last time.
He left the farm, negotiated Horse Hill and Dog's Meadow,
and made for the village square. He had put on his best
suit, and there was something almost jaunty about his step.

The school-house was a mass of flames and the Gasthaus smoking heap of rubble. Materna halted in front of the ar memorial, which had been shorn off cleanly by a direct t. He picked up a lump of stone from the shattered base. bore his name.

'Alfred Materna,' he read—Alfred, the son who had died long ago. That was how it had all begun, or was it?

He tossed the fragment away. Standing there stiffly, he atched the church disintegrate. It shuddered, heaved, and en dissolved into an all-consuming mushroom of fire.

Materna walked on towards the churchyard, which looked s if it had been trampled by wild beasts.

No one ever saw him again.

H. H. Kirst

Sometimes very funny, often bitingly satirical, Hans Hellmu
Kirst's novels describe Germany and the Germans, from the
Nazi era to the present day. 'Kirst's oblique, deadpan gaze is
deeply revealing, deeply compassionate.' *Sunday Times*

The Revolt of Gunner Asch *35p*

Gunner Asch Goes to War *40p*

Hero in the Tower *40p*

Officer Factory *60p*

The Night of the Generals *40p*

 *Fontana Books*

Famous War Books in Fontana

The Night of Long Knives *Max Gallo 40p (Illus.)*
A blow-by-blow account of one of history's bloodiest week-ends—Hitler's purge of Roehm and the Brown Shirts in 1934.
'A masterly historical and psychological reconstruction.'
Le Monde

The Tunnel *Eric Williams 30p*
The story of the author's two dramatic escapes from prisoner-of-war camps that were unable to hold him. 'The atmosphere of prison-camp life is made more vivid than anything that one has read before. The excitement is maintained to the end.' *Glasgow Herald*

The Last Battle *Cornelius Ryan 60p (Illus.)*
The Third Reich's last stand in the devastated streets of Berlin. 'Thoroughly researched and exciting book.' *Time*. 'Among the best writings of the Second World War.' *The Spectator*. 'Brilliant.' *Daily Telegraph*

El Alamein *Michael Carver 35p (Illus.)*
The battle that turned the tide against the Axis and saved the Suez Canal. This is a detailed—and very readable—account, by one of England's military leaders. 'The definitive history.' *The Spectator*

Skis Against the Atom *Knut Haukelid 30p*
The thrilling story of the Norwegian resistance fighters who sabotaged the Nazis' atomic research plant—and may have prevented Hitler winning the war. 'Pure excitement from start to finish.' *London Illustrated News*

Reach for the Sky *Paul Brickhill 40p (Illus.)*
The unforgettable story of Douglas Bader, legless fighter pilot of World War II. 'This is a handbook of heroism . . . there is no medal yet for courage such as his.' *The People*. 'Moving and enthralling.' *Evening Standard*

 *Fontana Books*

Fontana Books

Fontana is best known as one of the leading paperback publishers of popular fiction and non-fiction. It also includes an outstanding, and expanding, section of books on history, natural history, religion and social sciences.

Most of the fiction authors need no introduction. They include Agatha Christie, Hammond Innes, Alistair MacLean, Catherine Gaskin, Victoria Holt and Lucy Walker. Desmond Bagley and Maureen Peters are among the relative newcomers.

The non-fiction list features a superb collection of animal books by such favourites as Gerald Durrell and Joy Adamson.

All Fontana books are available at your bookshop or newsagent; or can be ordered direct. Just fill in the form below and list the titles you want.

FONTANA BOOKS, Cash Sales Department, G.P.O. Box 29, Douglas, Isle of Man, British Isles. Please send purchase price, plus 6p per book. Customers outside the U.K. send purchase price, plus 7p per book. Cheque, postal or money order. No currency.

NAME (Block letters)
_____

ADDRESS
_____

_____

_____

While every effort is made to keep prices low, it is sometimes necessary to increase prices at short notice. Fontana Books reserve the right to show new retail prices on covers which may differ from those previously advertised in the text or elsewhere.